Long afterward, he was to think of that afternoon, the field of spring flowers, a smell of crushed green, and the two Khir women on horseback, their route a curving *shuh* character, shod hooves throwing clods of dirt and grass aside.

He would remember the veil flying from Princess Ashan Mahara's hat, knocked askew by the wind, and Lady Komor Yala melding with the horse, obviously more skilled than her princess but gracefully restraining her mount just a touch, just enough. It took much talent and practice to lose so neatly and nearly, and when the women rejoined the long snake of the retinue waiting patiently for them, the princess flushed and happy, it was Lady Yala who scolded her gently for giving the Fourth Prince so much trouble.

The princess did not bridle, but took the almost-rebuke with good grace and offered a half-bow of apology, her cheeks flushed and her moonlike beauty turned solar for a brief moment. Makar ventured the opinion that it was only natural to wish to ride upon a spring morning, and of course he was pleased to see such a fine example of horsemanship.

"Next time, *he* shall race with me, and you shall call the route," Lady Komor said, a neat solution, and Makar politely agreed.

It seemed that if the Khir had sent only one lady with their princess, they had chosen the best for the task. She would bear careful watching, this court lady.

He was almost looking forward to it.

THE THRONE OF THE FIVE WINDS

HOSTAGE OF EMPIRE: BOOK ONE

S. C. EMMETT

www.orbitbooks.net

This book is a work of fiction. Names, characters, places, and incidents are the product of the author's imagination or are used fictitiously. Any resemblance to actual events, locales, or persons, living or dead, is coincidental.

Orbit
Hachette Book Group
1290 Avenue of the Americas
New York, NY 10104
orbitbooks.net

First Edition: October 2019

Orbit is an imprint of Hachette Book Group.
The Orbit name and logo are trademarks of Little, Brown Book Group Limited.

Library of Congress Cataloging-in-Publication Data
Names: Emmett, S. C., author.
Title: The throne of the five winds / S.C. Emmett.
Description: First edition. | New York, NY : Orbit, 2019. | Series: Hostage of empire ; book 1
Identifiers: LCCN 2019000764 | ISBN 9780316436946 (trade pbk.) | ISBN 9780316558280 (ebook)
Subjects: GSAFD: Fantasy fiction.
Classification: LCC PS3619.A3984 T48 2019 | DDC 813/.6—dc23
LC record available at https://lccn.loc.gov/2019000764

ISBNs: 978-0-316-43694-6 (trade paperback), 978-0-316-55828-0 (ebook)

Printed in the United States of America

LSC-C

10 9 8 7 6 5 4 3 2 1

For Sarah Guan, who knows why.

And for Miriam Kriss, who does as well.

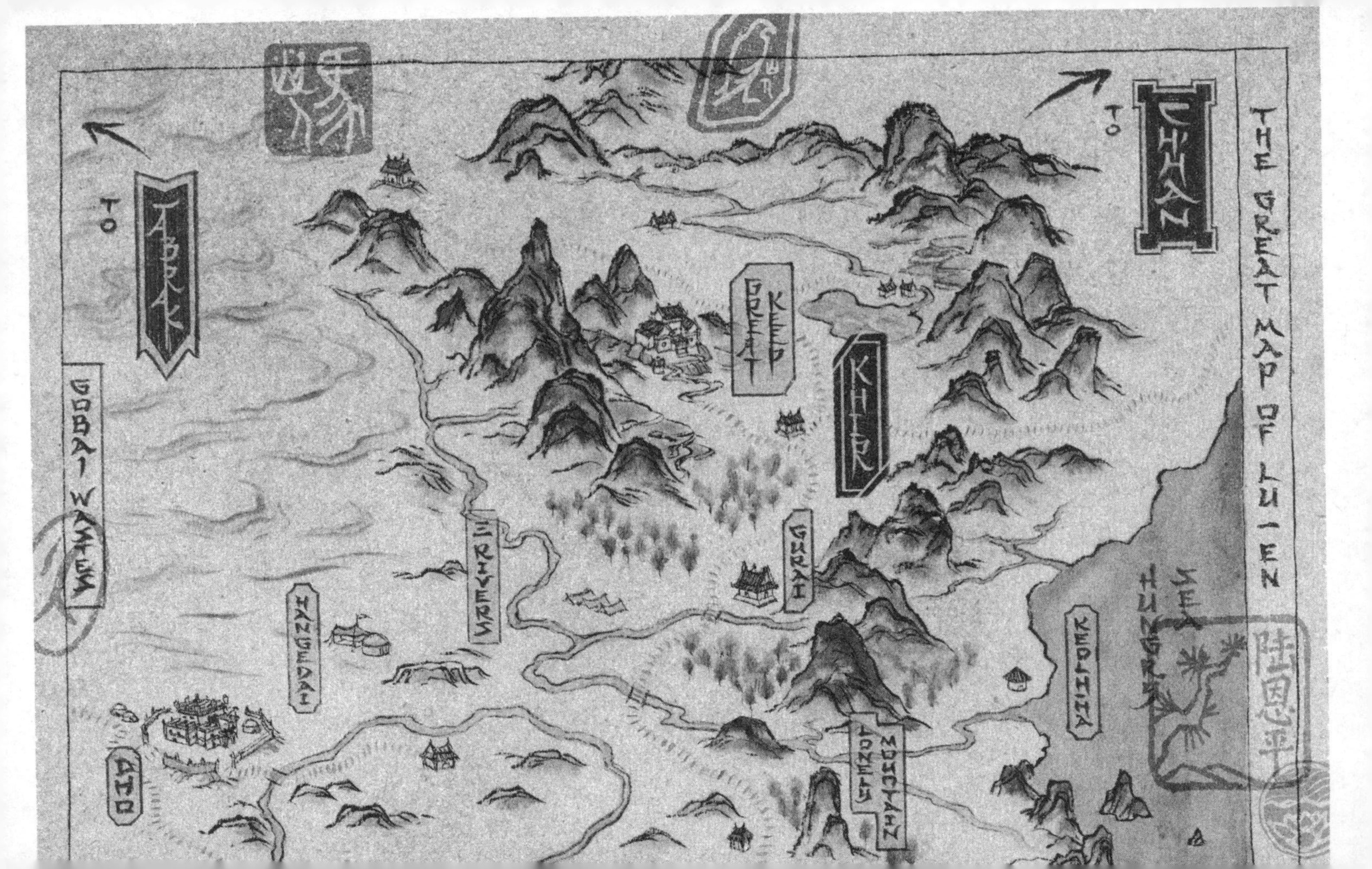
THE GREAT MAP OF LU-EN
TO CH'HAN
TO ABRAK
GOBAI WASTES
GREAT KEED
KHIR
GURAI
3 RIVERS
HANGEDAI
AMO
LONELY MOUNTAIN
KEDLHIHA
HUNGRY SEA
陸恩平

THE THRONE OF THE FIVE WINDS

Tot locis, tot incendis rerum natura terras cremat.

—Pliny the Elder

Translator's Note

Like many languages, Zhaon, Khir, Shansian, Anwai-la, and Tabrakkin have many terms and forms of address with no direct equivalent in English. Every effort has been made to indicate, by note or context, when one is being used. Any errors are, of course, the fault of the translator.

Little Light

Above the Great Keep of Khir and the smoky bowl of its accreted city, tombs rose upon mountainside terraces. Only the royal and Second Families had the right to cut their names into stone here, and this small stone pailai[1] was one of the very oldest. Hard, small pinpoints about to become white or pink blossoms starred the branches of ancient, twisted yeoyans;[2] a young woman in blue, her black hair dressed simply but carefully with a single white-shell comb, stood before the newest marker. Incense smoked as she folded her hands for decorous prayer, a well-bred daughter performing a rare unchaperoned duty.

Below, the melt had begun and thin droplets scattered from tiled roofs both scarlet and slate, from almost-budding branches. Here snow still lingered in corners and upon sheltered stones; winter-blasted grass slept underneath. No drip disturbed the silence of the ancestors.

A booted foot scraped stone. The girl's head, bowed, did not move. There was only one person who would approach while she propitiated her ancestors, and she greeted him politely. "Your Highness." But she did not raise her head.

"None of that, Yala." The young man, his topknot caged and

1. A single family's tombs.

2. A tree similar to a cherry.

pierced with gold, wore ceremonial armor before the dead. His narrow-nosed face had paled, perhaps from the cold, and his gaze—grey as a winter sky, grey as any noble blood-pure Khir's—lingered upon her nape. As usual, he dispensed with pleasantries. "You do not have to go."

Of course he would think so. Her chin dropped a little farther. "If I do not, who will?" Other noble daughters, their fathers not so known for rectitude as the lord of Komori, were escaping the honor in droves.

"Others." A contemptuous little word. "Servants. There is no shortage."

Yala's cloud-grey eyes opened. She said nothing, watching the gravestone as if she expected a shade to rise. Her offerings were made at her mother's tomb already, but here was where she lingered. A simple stone marked the latest addition to the shades of her House—fine carving, but not ostentatious. The newly rich might display like fan-tailed baryo,[3] but not those who had ridden to war with the Three Kings of the First Dynasty. Or so her father thought, though he did not say it.

A single tone, or glance, was enough to teach a lesson.

Ashani Daoyan, Crown Prince of Khir newly legitimized and battlefield-blooded, made a restless movement. Lean but broad-shouldered, with a slight roundness to his cheeks bespeaking his Narikh motherblood, he wore the imperial colors easily; a bastard son, like an unmarried aunt, learned to dress as the weather dictated. Leather creaked slightly, and his breath plumed in the chill. "If your brother were alive—"

"—I would be married to one of his friends, and perhaps widowed as well." *Now* Komor Yala, the only surviving child of General Hai Komori Dasho, moved too, a slight swaying as if she wished to turn and halted just in time. "Please, Daoyan." The habit of long friendship made it not only possible but necessary to address him so informally. "Not before my Elder Brother."

3. Carrion-eating birds with bright plumage, often kept as garbage-eating pets.

"Yala..." Perhaps Dao's half-armor, black chased with yellow, was not adequate for this particular encounter. The boy she had known, full of sparkstick[4] pride and fierce silence when that pride was balked, had ridden to war; this young man returned in his place.

Did he regret being dragged from the field to preserve a dynasty while so many others stood and died honorably? She could not ask, merely suspect, so Yala shook her head. Her own words were white clouds, chosen carefully and given to the frigid morning. "Who will care for my princess, if I do not?"

"You cannot waste your life that way." A slight sound—gauntlets creaking. Daoyan still clenched his fists. She should warn him against so open a display of emotion, but perhaps in a man it did not matter so much.

"And yet." *There is no other option*, her tone replied, plainly. *Not one I am willing to entertain.* "I will take great care with your royal sister, Your Highness."

Of course he could not leave the battlefield thus, a draw achieved but no victory in sight. "I will offer for you."

"You already would have, if you thought your honored father would allow it." She bowed, a graceful supple bending with her skirts brushing fresh-swept stone. "Please, Daoyan." Her palms met, and her head dropped even farther when she straightened, the attitude of a filial daughter from a scroll's illustrations.

Even a prince dared not interrupt prayers begun before a relative's tomb. Daoyan turned, finally, boots ringing through thin snow to pavers she had not attended to with her small broom, and left the pailai with long, swinging strides.

Yala slipped her hands deeper inside her sleeves and regarded the memorial stone. Bai, of course, would have sniffed at the prospect of his little sister marrying a man with an honorless mother, no matter if he had proven himself in war and the Great Rider had legitimized him. Bai would also have forbidden her to accompany

4. A handheld firework.

Mahara. He was not the clan-head, but since he came of age their father had let him take heavier duties and listened to his counsel. Bai's refusal would have carried weight, and Yala could have bowed her head to accept it instead of insisting upon her duty as a noble daughter must before a distinguished parent.

Perhaps that would have been best. Was the cringing, creeping relief she would have felt cowardice? The other noble families were scurrying to keep their daughters from Mahara's retinue, marriages contracted or health problems discovered with unseemly haste. The Great Rider, weakened as he was by the defeat at Three Rivers and the slow strangling of Khir's southron trade, could not force noble daughters to accompany his own, he could only... request.

Other clans and families could treat it as a request, but Komori held to the ancient codes. It was a high honor to attend the princess of Khir, and Yala had done so since childhood. To cease in adversity was unworthy of a Komor daughter.

Burning incense sent lazy curls of scented smoke heavenward. If her brother was watching, he would have been fuming like the sticks themselves. A slow smolder and a hidden fire, that was Hai Komori Baiyan. She could only hope she was the same, and the conquering Zhaon would not smother her *and* her princess.

First things first. You are to pay your respects here, and then to comfort your father.

As if there could be any comfort to a Khir nobleman whose only son was dead. Hai Komori Dasho would be gladdened to be rid of a daughter and the need to find a dowry, that much was certain. Even if he was not, he would act as if he were, because that was the correct way to regard this situation.

The Komori, especially the clan heads, were known for their probity.

Her fingertips worried at her knuckles, and she sighed. "Oh, damoi,[5] my much-blessed Bai," she whispered. It was not quite

5. *Khir. Affectionate.* Elder brother.

meet to pronounce the name of the dead, but she could be forgiven a single use of such a precious item. "How I wish you were here."

She bent before her brother's grave one last time, and her fingers found a sharp-edged, triangular pebble among the flat pavers, blasted grass, and iron-cold dirt. They could not plow quite yet, but the monjok[6] and yeoyan blossoms were out. Spring would come early this year, but she would not see the swallows returning. The care of the pailai would fall to more distant kin from a junior branch of the clan.

Yala tucked the pebble in a sleeve-pocket, carefully. She could wrap it with red silken thread, decorate a hairstick with falling beads, and wear a part of both Bai and her homeland daily. A small piece of grit in the conqueror's court, hopefully accreting nacre instead of dishonor.

There were none left to care for her father in his aging. Perhaps he would marry again. If Bai were still alive...

"Stop," she murmured, and since there were none to see her, Yala's face could contort under a lash of pain, a horse shying at the whip. "He is not."

Khir had ridden to face Zhaon's great general at Three Rivers, and the eldest son of a proud Second Family would not be left behind. The battle had made Daoyan a hero and Bai a corpse, but it was useless to Khir. The conquerors had dictated their terms; war took its measure, reaping a rich harvest, and Zhaon was the scythe.

Khir would rise again, certainly, but not soon enough to save a pair of women. Even a cursory study of history showed that a farm could change hands, and he who reaped yesterday might be fertilizer for the next scythe-swinger. There was little comfort in the observation, even if it was meant to ease the pain of the defeated.

For the last time, Yala bowed before her brother's stone. If she walked slowly upon her return, the evidence of tears would be erased by the time she reached the foot of the pailai's smooth-worn

---

6. A small, slightly acrid fruit.

stairs and the single maidservant waiting, holding her mistress's horse and bundled against the cold as Yala disdained to be.

A noblewoman suffered ice without a murmur. Inside, and out.

Hai Komori's blackened bulk rested within the walls of the Old City. It frowned in the old style, stone walls and sharply pitched slate-tiled roof; its great hall was high and gloomy. The longtable, crowded with retainers at dinners twice every tenday, was a blackened piece of old wood; it stood empty now, with the lord's low chair upon the dais watching its oiled, gleaming surface. Mirrorlight drifted, brought through holes in the roof and bounced between polished discs, crisscrossing the high space.

Dusty cloth rustled overhead, standards and pennons taken in battle. There were many, and their sibilance was the song of a Second Family. The men rode to war, the women to hunt, and between them the whole world was ordered. Or so the classics, both the canonical Hundreds and supplements, said. Strong hunters made strong sons, and Yala had sometimes wondered why her mother, who could whisper a hawk out of the sky, had not given her father more than two. Bai the eldest was ash upon the wind and a name upon a tablet; the second son had not even reached his naming-day.

And Komor Madwha, a daughter of the Jehng family and high in the regard of the Great Rider and her husband as well, died shortly after her only daughter's birth.

Komori Dasho was here instead of in his study. Straight-backed, only a few thin threads of frost woven into his topknot, a vigorous man almost into the status of elder sat upon the dais steps, gazing at the table and the great hearth. When a side door opened and blue silk made its subtle sweet sound, he closed his eyes.

Yala, as ever, bowed properly to her father though he was not looking. "Your daughter greets you, *pai*."

He acknowledged with a nod. She waited, her hands folded in her sleeves again, faintly uneasy. Her father was a tall man, his shoulders still hard from daily practice with saber and spear; his face was pure Khir. Piercing grey eyes, straight black hair top-knotted as a Second Dynasty lord's, a narrow high prow of a nose, a thin mouth, and bladed cheekbones harsh as the sword-mountains themselves. Age settled more firmly upon him with each passing winter, drawing skin tighter and bone-angles sharper. His house robe was spare and dark, subtly patterned but free of excessive ornamentation.

He was, in short, the very picture of a Khir noble—except he was not, as usual, straight as an iron reed upon his low backless chair with the standard of their house—the setting sun and the komor flower[7]—hung behind it.

Finally, he patted the stone step with his left hand. "Come, sit." His intonation was informal, and that was another surprise.

Yala settled herself, carefully. With her dress arranged and her feet tucked to the side, she lowered her eyelids and waited.

Lord Komori did not care for idle chatter.

The great hall was different from this angle. The table was large as it had been when she was a child, and the cavernous fireplace looked ready to swallow an unwary passerby whole. The braziers were blackened spirit-kettles, their warmth barely touching winter's lingering chill. Flagstones, swept and scrubbed even when winter meant the buckets formed ice which needed frequent breaking, stared blankly at the ceiling, polished by many feet. Yala stilled, a habit born of long practice in her father's presence.

The mouse that moves is taken. Another proverb. The classics were stuffed to bursting with them.

As a child she had fidgeted and fluttered, Dowager Eun despairing of ever teaching her discretion. In Yala's twelfth spring the weight of decorum had begun to tell, and she had decided it was easier to flow with that pressure than stagger under it. Even Mahara had been surprised, and she, of all the world, perhaps knew Yala best.

---

7. A native, very hardy Khir plant with seven petals on its small highly fragrant flowers; the root is used for blue dye.

After Bai, that was.

"Yala," her father said, as if reminding himself who she was. *That* was hardly unusual. The sons stayed, the daughters left. An advantageous marriage was her duty to Komori. It was a pity there had been no offers. *I wonder what is wrong with me*, she had murmured to Mahara once.

I do not wish to share you with a husband, Mahara answered, when she could speak for laughing.

"Yes." Simple, and soft, as a noblewoman should speak. She wished she were at her needlework, the satisfaction of a stitch pulled neatly and expertly making up for pricked fingers. Or in the mews, hawk-singing. Writing out one of the many classics once again, her brush held steady. Reading, or deciding once more what to pack and what to leave behind.

She wished, in fact, to be anywhere but here. After a visit to the ancestors, though, her presence at her father's wrist was expected. Brought back to endure scrutiny like a hawk itself, a feather passed over her plumage, so as not to disturb the subtle oils thereupon.

"I have often thought you should have been born male." Komori Dasho sighed, his shoulders dropping. The sudden change was startling, and disturbing. "You would have made a fine son." Even if it was high praise, it still stung. A formulaic reply rose inside her, but he did not give her the chance to utter as much. "But if you were, you would have died upon that bloodfield as well, and I would have opened my veins at the news."

Startled, Yala turned her head to gaze upon his profile. The room was not the only thing that looked different from this angle. The thunder-god of her childhood, straight and proud, sat beside her, staring at the table. And, terrifyingly, hot water had come to Komori Dasho's eyes. It swelled, glittering, and anything she might have said vanished.

"My little light," he continued. "Did you know? I named you thus, after your mother died. Not aloud, but here." His thin, strong right fist, the greenstone seal-ring of a proud and ancient house glinting upon his index finger, struck his chest. "I knew not to say such things, for the gods would be angry and steal you as they took *her*."

Yala's chest tightened. A Lord Komori severe in displeasure or stern with approval she could answer. Who was *this*?

Her father did not give her a chancc to reply. "In the end it does not matter. The Great Rider has requested and we must answer; you will attend the princess in Zhaon."

This much I knew already. The pebble in her sleeve-pocket pressed against her wrist. She realized she was not folding her hands but clutching them, knuckles probably white under smooth fabric. "Yes." There. Was that an acceptable response?

He nodded, slowly. The frost in his hair had spread since news of Three Rivers; she had not noticed before. This was the closest she had been to her father since... she could not remember the last time. She could not remember when he last spoke to her with the informal inflection *or* case, either. Yala searched for something else to say. "I will not shame our family, especially among *them*."

"You—" He paused, straightened. "You have your *yue*?"

Of course I do. "It is the honor of a Khir woman," she replied, as custom demanded. Was this a test? If so, would she pass? Familiar anxiety sharpened inside her ribs. "Does my father wish to examine its edge?" The blade was freshly honed; no speck of rust or whisper of disuse would be found upon its slim greenmetal length.

"Ah. No, of course not." His hands dangled at his knees, lax as they never had been in her memory. "Will you write to your father?"

"Of course." As if she would dare *not* to. The stone under her was a cold, uncomfortable saddle, but she did not dare shift. "Every month."

"Every week." The swelling water in his eyes did not overflow. Yala looked away. It was uncomfortably akin to seeing a man outside the clan drunk, or at his dressing. "Will you?"

"Yes." *If you require it of me.*

"I have kept you close all this time." His fingers curled slightly, as if they wished for a hilt. "There were many marriage offers made for you, Yala. Since your naming-day, you have been sought. I refused them all." He sighed, heavily. "I could not let you go. Now, I am punished for it."

She sat, stunned and silent, until her father, for the first and last time, put a lean-muscled, awkward arm about her shoulders. The embrace was brief and excruciating, and when it ended he rose and left the hall, iron-backed as ever, with his accustomed quiet step.

He is proud of you, she had often told Bai. *He simply does not show it.*

Perhaps it had not been a lie told to soothe her brother's heart. And perhaps, just perhaps, she could believe it for herself.

Concern a Pearl

Vermilion columns marched on either side of the walkway; white stone stairs between two of those silent sentinels descended to a sand-garden. A single chunk of rough black stone stood slightly off-center in the rectangle, pale golden sand raked smoothly in soft wavelike patterns contrasting with the chunk's irregular edges. Morning sun glittered upon the red-tiled slopes of the Kaeje's roof, and Emperor Garan Tamuron of Zhaon, mighty in war and merciless in peace, clasped his hands behind his back, regarding sand, stone, and a single print just past the last step that matched his own slippered foot. His robe, dark crimson starred and threaded with gold, sat easily upon shoulders still broad from long campaigning, though his middle was not as trim as it had once been. His many-times-broken nose was broad, black hair pulled into a sleek, gold-caged topknot, and his dark gaze was just as keen as ever.

To his right, a step back as etiquette dictated, a lean black-haired man in plain leather half-armor regarded the same view, but precious few could have deciphered his expression. General Zakkar Kai was held to have a face of stone, sleepy-eyed, broad-jawed, and chisel-lipped. His own topknot was careless, yet he carried a famous dragon-hilted sword in the Emperor's presence. Muddy irises bespoke some barbarian—or even Khir—in his ancestry, though none would have said as much openly.

Not anymore.

Finally, Emperor Garan Tamuron sighed, his chin settling as he gazed upon a garden meant to encourage contemplation and refinement. The sound usually meant he was seeing old battles—or anticipating a fresh skirmish. "The First Queen visited me this morning."

The general nodded, knowing his warlord would sense the movement. "That must have been pleasant."

A wry smile touched the corners of the Emperor's thin lips. "Oh, exceedingly, my general. Exceedingly." He sobered, his thumb rubbing a sanjai[8]-wood bead meditatively. He had many kombin—beads strung upon silken cord, used as abacus or prayer-marker. This was the one he most favored: simple and stained with use, wrapped about his broad wrist and dipping into his left palm. A gift from a laughing woman long ago, a woman whose shrine was kept ever-lit. "She was full of advice for Takyeo's marriage."

Advice and lamentations, no doubt. If the Crown Prince produced an heir, Queen Gamwone's dreams were that much further from fruition. "The Khir girl." Zakkar Kai, the true architect of victory at Three Rivers, studied the garden's central rock as well. The view was not exactly displeasing, but he'd seen enough of empty sand to last a lifetime. Never mind that he was only seven winters old, give or take, when Tamuron had brought a foundling boy from the edge of the world to the center of civilization. "Ashani's only daughter. A pearl of great price, it is said."

"No doubt the First Queen will be an attentive mother-in-law." The Emperor's mouth was sour. Birds sang close by, in one of the pleasure-gardens full of cool shade and small-feathered life. Most mornings, Tamuron halted here on his way to the Great Hall, sometimes lingering for whatever reason moved the mind of a warlord become royalty. "I take it Takyeo is resigned."

"The Crown Prince longs to please his father. As usual." Kai considered that enough said. Bearing Tamuron's hopes was a heavy task, and Crown Prince Takyeo perhaps longed to lay it aside.

---

8. A fragrant, highly prized wood.

Which made him, in a wise opinion or two, the best choice for the throne. Those same wise opinions, though, were divided upon how long the Crown Prince would survive before climbing to the great seat, with such an honorable longing hobbling him.

The Emperor moved from one trouble to the next. "The Second Queen will wish to outdo the First with marriage-gifts."

"At least hers will not have a sting in the tail." In other words, Kai was well aware, and he had taken steps to ensure the First Queen's gifts would not be true poison.

Just a facsimile.

Tamuron moved down the list of problems. "What of the First Concubine?"

Concubine Luswone was not a simple soul, but she was, in many respects, a largely passive one. Kai knew what would come next on the litany of worries, and moved to answer it. "I believe she is embroidering some silk for the new princess. Her daughter seems resigned, as well."

"Ah." The Emperor nodded. Princess Sabwone was the more ambitious of his two daughters, though her mother did well reining her in. "Never take more than one wife, General. They are trouble."

Kai banished a smile. "And yet the pillars keep the roof secure." It was a fine quatrain, not one of the classics, but close.

"One wonders how the roof feels." Tamuron's pained smile was, at least, better than a scowl.

"We small birds nest beneath the Emperor's grace." A portentous intoning, as his own hands rested behind him. Kai shifted slightly, easing an ache in his left foot. He preferred proper boots to these slippers; the palace floor could bruise even through calluses. At least the Emperor did not list Kanbina among the problems; the Second Concubine was not a dangerous soul.

The Emperor nodded. The set of his shoulders said he was pleased, and his cares had lifted for a moment. "You have been studying your poetry."

A lord of Zhaon should know the classics as well as the blade. "You said I should." So, dutifully though not even close to cheerfully,

Garan Tamuron's head general obeyed. Just as he moved to ease his Emperor's difficulties, or at least draw their teeth.

"Ah." A pause. Tamuron's fingers caressed another kombin-bead. "Is there news of Takshin?"

The largest worry, saved for last. "The Third Prince is on his way to attend the wedding."

A slow nod, gold glittering upon Tamuron's topknot. The Emperor would have his eyes closed now, calling forth a tactical map or perhaps bracing himself for the morning's session with his ministers. "Is Shan pacified, do you think?"

"He would not return, were it not." It was not *quite* a lie, Kai decided, or even a polite fiction. "Their queen was mad, but her son regards Takshin as a brother. Or so it is said." Khir was a Ch'han dagger pointed at the heart of Zhaon, and Shan a shield or a smothering blanket. To pluck the blade and turn the shield outward had been the dream of every petty Zhaon warlord, but it was Tamuron who had performed the feat at last. Three Rivers would have had an entirely different outcome if he had not carefully bled Khir for years, balancing border skirmishes against tariffs. And Shan, sharing language and customs with Zhaon, would seal itself to Zhaon ever more firmly now that the Mad Queen had breathed her last, and when her son was dealt with.

One way, or another.

The Emperor paused. "How does Takshin regard *him*?"

Who knows? Asking what Takshin thought of anything was a fool's game. If he wished you to know, the Third Prince would *tell* you. Kai was in his counsel more often than not, perhaps because he didn't ask, simply waited or guessed. "His letters are careful."

"So he has learned that much, at least." A sigh, supple fingertips moving to the next bead. "I should not have sent him there."

"Of all the princes, he was the one best suited." *And the one you hated least to lose.* Kai hesitated. "Your Majesty?"

"Yes?"

There would never be a better time to ask. "Give me leave to ride the borders. You will have greater peace of mind." *And I will not be in this nest of vipers.*

"No." Kindly, though, the Emperor deigned to give a reason. "I need you here, especially for the marriage and coronation. You are the Crown Prince's ally. Sixth Prince Jin is old enough to take a generalship, should the situation require it."

"He has the gift." And no doubt Jin would prefer soldiery to princely lessons under his mother's roof. "Still, I prefer the camp to the palace, Your Majesty."

"And you think I do not?"

It was not a rebuke, but Zakkar Kai dropped his chin. Instead of the worn stone stairs—this had been a palace since the Second Dynasty, though fallen into disrepair before Tamuron's time—Kai's gaze traced the contours of the footprint in the sand. The lightness in the forefoot bespoke a warrior's training, though the pressure of the heel was that of an aging man. "The Crown Prince has more than one ally. The Fourth and Sixth Princes are particularly close to him, and Court Astrologer Banh as well."

"Makar is a scholar, not a blade, and Jin is an... honorable... warrior. Takyeo needs you, as I do."

"A sword to hand." A commonborn foundling, even one brought to the palace by the Emperor himself, possessed a latitude of action a prince would not. Especially if he was sometimes a little less than choosy about how problems were addressed. Rumor swirled about Zakkar Kai and his habit of winning battles.

High in the Emperor's regard was a precarious perch, especially if the position seemed secure.

"The best kind, my old friend. You will receive a hurai[9] soon."

So. You decided. A prince's seal. That would make the rumors worse. "Your Majesty." A bow to express his gratitude, but not a deep one. "That will cause gossip." The First Queen would be furious, the Second Queen merely mildly irritated. First Concubine

---

9. A royal signet-seal.

Luswonc would ignore it, her cool disdain unchanged. At least there was that.

"It will make the Second Concubine proud, though." Tamuron said it lightly, as if that were the only consideration. His wrist turned, flicking expended beads and gathering new ones. "How does she fare?"

Kai had not yet had time to inspect her new staff, but he had hopes. "Her household should be well-ordered, now." *She has a husband but no husband, and a son but no son.* Kai buried a bright flash of almost-hate swiftly. It served no purpose. Concubine Kanbina, sold to cement a final alliance, and the box of the jelong tea sent to her by First Queen Gamwone... oh, it could not be *proven*, but Kai knew very well.

Very well indeed.

"Good. I worry less for her, with a son such as you."

Adopted son. It was a dismissal, and Kai recognized as much. "She says the same, Your Majesty." It was all the criticism he dared offer. He bowed again, and left the royal presence without waiting for leave.

As usual, Garan Tamuron let him go.

"Kai!" A flutter of rosy silk, a flash of soft hands, and the Second Concubine rose from her playing-couch, her sathron[10] hastily set aside. Its strings resonated with the motion, adding a subtle thrill to afternoon sunlight falling through wide windows with newly repaired shutters. Black hair dressed high in the style of Yanwe[11] gleamed, and her ornament was a simple half-moon of shell, as usual. Too pale and angular for beauty, she was nevertheless agreed to be *arresting*, for those who bothered to comment upon the most reclusive of Garan Takyeo's women. "You've returned!"

He bent to let her kiss his cheek, breathing in her perfume of hala[12] blossom and citron water, and took in her quarters. Much

10. A six-stringed instrument with a triangular soundbox.

11. The rich farmlands of westron Zhaon, many small fiefs under the now-extinct Wurai house.

12. A fragrant yellow flower of a thin-leaved plant; the leaves are often used to scent wine while the flowers are brewed into tea.

better—the draperies were well cleaned and the furniture polished; the windows were open and a balmy breeze floated through. There was no dust or grime upon the floor, and Garan Wurai Kanbina's robes were not mended castoffs but new, and suited her exactly. "I could not stay away from you, adoptive-mother."

"No, no, that won't do." She tugged at one sleeve, then another, settling his under-tunic. "*Mother.* And what is this, wearing armor? Are you going away again?"

Of course, she would worry, and she did not remark upon his sword. So Kai gave her the reassurance she hoped for. "The Emperor has asked me to remain for the wedding. Come, sit, do not let me disturb your practice."

"Nonsense, it is no disturbance." She clapped her hands, once, twice, a lady's summons. "Tea for my son the General. And refreshment. If I know you, you have not eaten, too busy with weighty things."

The close-maids—three of them, engaged by Kai's own steward and new to palace service—hurried to obey, laying aside needlework, grinding, and whatever the third had been doing—ah, preparing brushes. So, she kept them busy, and they set to work with a will. Much better than Gamwone's castoffs, and without them scuttling back to the First Queen with tales and small stolen items, Kanbina's daily life had no doubt eased greatly.

"I had breakfast." His shoulders loosened for the first time since setting foot in the palace this morning. At least, in this one small sphere, he could be certain of a battle's outcome. "Please, do not trouble yourself."

"Breakfast, he says, and it is well into the afternoon." Her dress, patterned with the subtlety of the veining upon jewelwings,[13] made soft, sweet sounds. "You will waste away to nothing. Come, come, sit down. Tell me all the news. What happens outside my walls?"

"Nothing that should concern a pearl." It was a tolerable turn

13. An insect with broad, bright wings.

of phrase, he thought. "War, and unpleasantness. Tell me of your music. How is the new sathron?"

She accepted the compliment with a ducked head and a shy blush, like a maiden again. There was a great deal of grace, but no coquetry, in the lady of lost Wurai. "Beautiful, and very true in tone. You are good to me."

"You were the first person to be kind to me here." He settled upon a cushion, and she set the lacquered sathron in its case, arranging the table for tea with swift grace. Even so, her hands trembled a little. Any excitement caused such tremors.

"It was the Emperor's kindness that brought you here, Kai." *Delicate*, one physician said. *Sensitive*, said another. *A cold fever*, said a third, but it was the fourth Kai had retained, for he fixed Kai with a piercing look and informed him it was a slow-creeping toxin, and to beware any gift. *Especially one from a rich-robed viper.*

Kindness, she said. As if Tamuron saw him as anything other than a tool to be used. "Are you sleeping well? Physician Kihon told me you had a fever two days ago." Kihon Jiao in his shabby coat was worth more than a clutch of Gamwone's prized physicians; Kai had felt little compunction about sending the man from the army to the palace. And with Kai's own steward sent ahead from the field to arrange Kai's quarters and also act for Kanbina, the Second Concubine's living money was no longer stolen, her clothes no longer motheaten, and her Iejo quarters were as pleasant and polished as any in the palace complex.

"It is gone now." She folded her hands, prettily, as the tea was brought. "And you? Tell me, do you still have the same cook? Is he preparing *giaoin* in honey for you?"

"He fusses over me almost as much as you do." Kai paused. "The Emperor has granted me a hurai."

Her mouth opened, her wide dark eyes shining, and Second Concubine Kanbina pressed her palm over her heart. "Oh." Tears welled. "Oh, Kai."

Her joy almost made the thought of the burden bearable. "He thought it would please you."

"I..." She paled alarmingly, and her close-maid—a wide-eyed girl with thick cheeks and a scar near her lower lip—pressed her shoulders gently. "Did he say that?"

"He has no plans to visit you, never fear." Kai nodded to the girl, and waited until Kanbina caught her breath. "He values your serenity."

"I am overcome with gratefulness." Her eyelids dropped, and an uncomfortable pause filled the room before she busied herself with the tea. The thick-cheeked maid hovered, protective of her new mistress, and Kai sipped at his cup. Now that the news had been given, the conversation could turn to other things, and after a short while, a flush returned to Kanbina's thin cheeks. She did not cough quite as much, but still, Zakkar Kai knew it would not be long before she succumbed.

And for that, sooner or later, he would hold First Queen Gamwone personally responsible.

This Is My Pride

Ashan Mahara, her round face delicately drawn and wistful in repose, settled upon embroidered cushions. Her pink-rimmed eyes blinked sleepily; she pulled at the edges of her sleeves, a girlhood habit. "I do not see why we must be trammeled each day." Fretful each evening no matter how many games and diversions were offered, Yala's princess was still as sweet-tempered as possible.

"Perhaps it is how royal ladies travel, among them." Yala peered through swinging beads upon their well-knotted cotton strings, and pulled the shutters close. The diamond-shaped window looked down upon a street, paved—thankfully—instead of a choking mudwallow. This inn was of slightly better quality than the last; the best was offered to a traveling princess as a matter of course, but in war-stripped borderlands, perhaps *best* was a relative term. Yala pushed her shoulders back—she was sore all over from the carriage's bumping motion, and there had been no proper baths since they left the outpost at Gurai, well before the actual border.

Now they were in Zhaon, riding in a box upon wheels instead of a-saddle. The Khir retinue—small, but full of noblemen too old or young for the bloodletting at Three Rivers—had turned back the morning after Gurai with wails and lamentation, and they were in the hands of Zhaon soldiers and eunuchs as well as two sullen maidservants with fine robes and haughty, mushmouth Zhaon accents performing the least possible version of their duties for the comfort of their new—if temporary—mistresses.

Yala held her peace, for now. Travel was always uncomfortable, the classics said. When they drew nearer the capital, no doubt the maidservants' mood would improve. If not, she would find remedies. Before then, though, she would watch and wait to see the slope, as Dowager Tala had always put it.

To know the quarry's ground was half the hunt.

This inn-room was long and low, sleeping-mats behind a partition, the floor of glossy, well-cared-for wood. It was just the same as the rooms on the other side of the invisible border between Zhaon and Khir, except larger. The air did not smell much different here, and the people did not look much different either. The men wore topknots, the women plain loops or hairpins and braids according to their station; kaburei labored in drab clothes and the rich strolled in bright cotton-and-silk edging. Between the two were finer gradations, including scholars in their sober colors and Zhaon civil-scholars in their strange peaked hats showing their supposed impartiality. The buildings were lower, their roofs not as steep once the mountains retreated.

"I hate it here already." Mahara sighed. "Come, the tea will grow cold."

The Zhaons' head eunuch Zan Pao in his eyebird-patterned robe visited every breakfast and dinner, a sneer upon his close-lipped face. A young scholar—Haor Pai, half-Khir from the look of his muddy eyes and sharp nose—translated the eunuch's flowery speeches, leaving out the insults. Yala, listening closely, found herself thankful for the Zhaon lessons her father had insisted upon, since an educated noblewoman needed a knowledge of the Hundreds in translation as well as her native tongue. Zhaon shared a common ancestor with Khir, and the two had borrowed from each other for a very long while.

Still, it was best to keep her facility hidden until needed. Surrounded by the conqueror's language, at least she was not helpless.

She could gauge the feeling against Khir and perhaps send her father observations despite such an act being slightly ill-bred; a scout in a bower might hear things one a-horseback would not.

A Khir noblewoman was not supposed to lower herself to noticing politics, let alone dabbling in them, but Komori Dasho had hinted, at his daughter's last dinner under his roof, that news from Zhaon would be of use to him.

And she did not think it likely that she had misunderstood.

Yala decided the window was unlikely to be peered through by any commoner and crossed the room, wood creaking underfoot. Settling next to Mahara upon the tasseled cushions, she lost herself in pouring fragrant tea, her wrist held correctly, the pot a graceful piece of Gurai slipware. *If it is done at all, it must be done well.* That was Hae Chur, the poet of Anwei's first blossoming, who brought ink-and-brush to Khir.

Holding her sleeve just so, filling her princess's cup, offering it with both hands at the correct angles, was soothing. "Today it is hala blossom."

"Fitting for spring." Mahara accepted the small idir-stone cup—proof against poison, since it would sweat in the presence of any toxins—with both hands, and her tentative smile was a balm. Her fine-feathered eyebrows were no longer drawn together, and the line between them had smoothed. "I'm glad you're here."

Any familiar face would have been welcome, no doubt. Still, they had grown up together, and Khir's court ladies knew that while Mahara was the princess, it was Lady Komor who watched for impropriety and insult. "I am, too. Imagine, Lady Nomar affected to weep when she heard she was not accompanying you."

"Perhaps now she'll be married, since the Yanchen no longer have hopes for me." Mahara sniffed. The Nomar girl held affection for Yancheni Hejo-ai, who had *not* died at Three Rivers; Hejo-ai's aunts and grandmother had pleaded for him not to be sent and the Great Rider had given his assent. He was the last male heir the head House of that clan could count upon, and had paid court to Mahara as a matter of course.

His sister and his girlcousins were kept out of marriage-bonds by their redoubtable grandmother and her phalanx of aunties, careful not to allow any girlchild to steal control of the clan by producing a son for a different house and equally careful not to breed infirmities into their line. Now, of course, with the princess-prize sold to an enemy to buy Khir some peace and time to rebuild, the shape of the game had altered.

A laugh caught Yala by surprise, slipping free of her throat as she poured into her own cup, a rough white porcelain curve. "Can you imagine? Yanchen Uyala would be insufferable after any wedding." The woman considered herself first among the Second Families, though her branch was of the youngest.

Mahara's face twisted. "*What is this, now?*" she said, querulously, a perfect imitation of the spinster Yanchen sister, all sibilants lisped as was fashionable among Khir's court ladies. "*Shocking, simply shocking!*"

Now Yala was not surprised to laugh, and Mahara moved closer upon the cushions. Since girlhood, they had often taken tea hip to hip, and it was a comfort indeed. A faint breath of hala, a touch of silken warmth along the tongue; Yala closed her eyes and savored. Pretending, for a moment, that she and Mahara were in the familiar chambers of Khir's Great Keep hung with draperies against the cold, watched only by the ancient window they peered from, sometimes pretending to be besieged maidens during the Blood Years. The other half of a maiden's day was endless lessons—dancing, hawking, riding, music, the classics, and the brush.

And, for Yala, the other lessons, Dowager Eun and Dowager Tala ruthless and exact. The *yue* did not forgive carelessness, so the dowagers charged with teaching its use had to be twice as sharp as the blade's edge itself.

"Yala?" The princess set her cup down, gently. "I am frightened."

So am I. "There is no need for fear." She took another mannerly sip, letting almost-too-hot liquid lave her tongue. "I am with you, my princess."

Next would come the lightest of suppers, then readying Mahara for bed. Teeth to be cleaned, hair to be combed, sleeping-robe already warming upon its stand over a brazier, all was in readiness. They were not in Khir, but Yala kept as close to the old rituals as possible, knowing it would comfort.

"Why did they only let me bring one lady?"

Could she not guess that the other clans did not wish to lose marriageable daughters to the southron folk? Plain truth was perhaps best, but in this case, Yala had a convenient deflection ready. "Perhaps they think all their princes will wish to marry Khir women, if they saw us." *And we could rise as one upon a wedding night and slay them, as our ancestors did to the Anwae.* The seafarers had been lucky in war for a long while during the Third Dynasty, and had attempted to swallow Khir whole while digesting a frantic, disembodied Zhaon. The women of Khir had saved their husbands and sons as only a woman could, and the night of murder that followed taught conquerors that Khir was not to be trifled with even by a winning draught.

The historians said every child born between nine and eleven full moons after the Blood Weddings had been exposed on the slopes of Mount Khitrai, and the wood that grew there was full of small, soft cries at night, even in this modern age.

Mahara's laughter was a bell. She covered her mouth, her grey eyes sparkling. "*Ai*, you are so bad!"

"Mh." Yala lifted her cup again, seeking to banish a smile that did not wish to be sent forth.

The princess sobered. Her cheeks were so fine, barely needing a brushing with fine-pounded zhu powder to achieve a fashionable matte. "Yala?"

"Yes?" She checked the teapot again. You could not let hala blossom sit; a bitter note came out during longer steeping.

"Will you let me watch you practice, tonight?"

So that was her aim. Yala considered her tea, fragrant amber fluid losing its scorch, bleeding away vital heat. Dropped into the lowlands, you could not drink your tea a-boil, as was proper. "You should practice too."

"Father said I could not bring my *yue*." Mahara made a face, and her chin dropped. "I did not mind."

How very strange. A larger question was why the Great Rider had accepted Yala instead of politely striking the Komori from the families listed in the summons, though perhaps only Hai Komori Dasho would not scruple to sacrifice his daughter with his last remaining son gone. That the Great Rider knew and had counted upon it so he did not have to send his daughter alone was the simplest explanation, but Yala did not think it the *likeliest* one, and that disturbed her sleep even more than travel did. "Well, mine is sharp enough for both of us." *As is my tongue.* Though both had to remain hidden, for now. Mahara made no secret of hating *yue* practice, though she watched Yala's avidly enough.

A soft knock at the door, and they both straightened, arranging their expressions. It was Zan Pao and the scholar, which meant supper was to be brought in. This time, Yala kept the bowls covered until the head eunuch reluctantly withdrew.

There was no need for a person who insulted Mahara to have the honor of a meal shared with a scion of the Great Rider, even if only a girl.

Bend forward, touch the toes. Kick the skirt back, swing the leg up and over, hands on floor light as a jewelwing's touch. Then swing the other leg, the hip joint protesting as tendons and ligaments altered by steady practice from childhood pressed it into artificial motion. A child was clay to be shaped into something most serviceable to clan and family, and doubly so if that child was female.

Suppleness was called for, and jolting in a wheeled box all day did not help. But Komor Yala did not stop.

The *yue* had no hilt. Or, more precisely, the blade and the hilt were one, the end of the too-long dagger or too-short sword merely unsharpened and cross-hatched for gripping. The blade itself was keen enough to part silk with a whisper, and any scar upon a noble Khir girl was referred to as a *yue*'s kiss. Except for the mark of hawk-claws upon a noblewoman; those were often called *hawk's kisses*, and rubbed with astringent ink while still bleeding.

Peasant and kaburei women carried short claw-curved daggers, those of a better class slightly longer ones, meant for carving meat as well as protecting their virtue. The *yue*, however, was only for the Second Families, and its secrets jealously guarded.

Up again, over, foot lightly kissing the floor again as she spun in the low-strike, opening an invisible attacker's femoral artery, twisting against the suction of invisible muscle. Soft, soft as a jewelwing's flutter. Mahara was asleep under coverlets that smelled of home, and the inn was quiet.

In secret, in the dark, Komor Yala's breath came high, light, fast. The blade clove air as she danced. The star-strike, the prayer-strike, the throat-opener, and the parry, flowing through different stances—Hill, River, Hawk, all worn into her bones by long practice.

The maiden's blade was meant for close combat. It was the last resort for a woman whose honor was threatened, or worse, taken. To kill your attacker or open your own throat was the duty of a daughter of Khir menaced in that terrible fashion.

Finally, warmed and loosened, she rested the flat of the *yue*—her Jehng mother's, greenmetal with a dappled blade, the secret of its making long lost with the First Dynasty—against her own pulse, high and frantic in her neck. Warm living skin, throbbing against chill metal.

Each practice ended this way. *You are Khir*, Dowager Tala would say, softly. *This is your duty.*

"I am Komor," Yala whispered. "This is my pride."

Dust shaken free by movement filled her nose. Finally, she lowered the *yue*, inspected it, and slid it into its supple, fine-grained scabbard. Keeping it hidden was merely a matter of sewing your clothes correctly.

Her skin crawled. The closer they drew to the capital, the better the inn-baths would be. She pushed the low table back to its place, slid the partition aside, and watched Mahara sleeping before easing into the bed beside her.

The princess's round face was serene, a moon in a clear sky. Why had the Great Rider told his daughter not to take her *yue*? She was not a married woman yet, her honor not in the keeping of a husband. What would he be like, this Crown Prince Takyeo? A Zhaon, who perhaps would not value her enough to protect what was his.

Even a married woman could use the blade if she had to, or if her husband was truly brutal. But Mahara's nature was obliging enough. She would wish to be a good wife, even to a conqueror's bastard spawn.

Still, it bothered Yala. The Great Rider had to know Komori Dasho's daughter would never dare to leave her *yue* behind.

There were dangers even in the great palace of Khir. Tam Duanam, for one. How long ago had that been—ah, yes, the summer of Yala's thirteenth year. Whispers in the Keep, and the day the tasters took away Mahara's dinner. The princess thought she was to be punished, and wept openly; Yala refused to eat her own dumplings. Some of the other girls had laughed at Mahara's weeping behind their sleeves, but one or two sickened after that meal.

Those who had greedily bitten did not recover well, if at all.

A tenday later, the lord of the Tam family, Duanam, had been broken in the Keep's courtyard for treason and poison. His screams had echoed for a long while. The Tam were dissolved—not a Second Family, so their fate was of little interest to thirteen-year-old Yala.

You do not know how dangerous the world is, little sister. Bai, acting the important big brother, had refused to tell her more and she had poked him in the ribs each time he said it. She had never dared ask directly about the Tam clan.

Now, though, she wondered.

It took a long time, in a tiny Zhaon inn with her princess breathing deeply and regularly beside her, before Komor Yala dropped into an uneasy sleep.

A Weighty Obligation

The melt was well underway, dripping from every eave and corner; early yeoyans in the most sheltered locations had begun to show traces of spring finery. Inside the chill stone bulk of Khir's Great Keep, though, no flowering disturbed tense daily hush, and the cold gardens stood empty. The king's temper was uncertain and the royal women's quarters were shut, the doors sealed with red wax and the royal sigil.

Daoyan's visitor had no doubt attended that ceremony, and worn the same expression he now sported.

"Your Highness," Domari Ulo murmured, folding his hands within his sleeves. He wore no sword, and Daoyan did not motion him to sit in either the comfortable leather chair or the severe, high-backed wooden one. Whatever pretty package of lies or unctuousness the man wished could be delivered standing. "It does me good to enter your presence."

At least when he had been merely a bastard, his so-called betters had not done Narikh'a Daoyan, now Ashani Daoyan, the disservice of thinking him *stupid*. He raised his gaze slowly, taking in the toes of fine, embroidered palace slippers—carried in a perfumed bag when not in service, no doubt—and the severe sumptuous robe of a noble minister with interlocking *shuh* characters stitched upon the cuffs, and finally arrived at Domari Ulo's round face and catlike grey eyes. He took his time with the appraisal; it was perhaps petty, but the Domar clan had never attempted closer relations while Dao's half-brothers were alive.

The *legitimate* brothers.

"Lord Domari. What an auspicious visit." Had he still been the bastard son, Dao might have delivered the line while lounging upon a couch in a darkened room, but now he wore half-armor and received his visitors in a palace study, part of quarters hurriedly shaken free of dust and filled with antique or hastily acquired furniture. The shelves in this study were somewhat embarrassingly bare since his personal books and scrolls were absent, being carefully packed in a banishment-manor on the very edge of the Great Keep's city.

He did not offer the minister tea, either. Domar was of the Second Families, but Ulo was from a junior branch, raised to prominence by the great ill-luck of the clan-head's household. The man did not show offense, but then, a minister with an easily readable face was a minister who fell from favor quickly. "I can only hope it will be, Your Highness." Perhaps the title of First Prince stuck in Ulo's throat.

Daoyan could only hope the obstruction was large, and stayed put. A childhood spent with remote, nose-pinching tutors and iron-backed disapproving aunts was far from the worst training in keeping his own expression neutral and pleasant. "Then please tell me your purpose, minister. I have rather a lot of well-robed people seeking my time these days." His fingers ached with the urge to clench into fists; Komori Baiyan would have snorted and pushed at him with a shoulder like a horse, whistling a snatch of a current popular tune with an applicable chorus. Probably one from the theaters they attended together, sometimes with Yala seated safely between them.

Bai had never treated him as *lesser*. Unless, of course, Dao paid too much attention to his beloved little sister. Who was now wending, step by slow step, into Zhaon, betrayed even by her prig of a father.

And Daoyan, for all his newfound importance, had been unable to help. Thinking upon *that* would make his fists knot themselves despite his self-control, so Daoyan made certain his fingers lay against the veined stone desktop, its chill keeping him likewise ice-clear.

Domari Ulo made a slight *tsk*ing noise. His smile remained the same, and if his own hands tensed, his sleeves hid the fact. "Must we begin in such a fashion? I have never done you wrong, Your Highness."

You have never done me much good, either. Half-armor was uncomfortable while sitting for long periods, but Daoyan wished to make a point of not trusting anything in the Great Keep, even the water. "Khir did Zhaon no wrong. Unless you count the Second Dynasty."

"They are only temporarily strong. Their warlord has too many sons; chaos has already begun, for those who have eyes to see." The head of Domar dipped his chin, affecting to study the desk-top, the rack of brushes, the inkstone and dish of water ready and glistening, the stacks of paper, the blotter and lesser carved seals, the large, shining new seal-box. "I am speaking plainly, to the future Great Rider of Khir. We are weakened, but still dangerous. It is only the southroners who fight on full bellies."

"They strangle our trade with Shan and Anwei, and have for years." Daoyan could have recited the litany of Khir's woes in his sleep. "The Ch'han would like to help, but we are so far away, and it pleases them to have us only strong enough to guard their southron passes, no more."

"You have very good ears, Your Highness." Domari Ulo bowed slightly while delivering a compliment, but those cat-eyes had narrowed. Behind him, hung slightly to the right in order to be seen from the desk no matter who stood before it, a hanging of thick pressed rai-paper held a quotation from Xao Le-ong, a little-known sage with only a fragment of a single work in the Hundreds.

The banked fire burns longest, Komor Yala's brushstrokes read, careful and flowing. She had presented the hanging upon his sixteenth birthday, a somber girl in Komor dark blue with a shy almost-smile offering the wrapped package with both hands, under Bai's watchful glare. Below the characters, a few thick black lines gave the suggestion of wood, and precious crimson ink had been daubed with a thick brush to make coals.

"You flatter me, elder." Daoyan settled his feet more comfortably under the desk. He also wore boots in the palace; slippers were a dangerous luxury. Acrid tanuha incense was burning in the adjoining waiting chamber, to ward off bad air and the ill-luck of disuse. A faint shuffling sounded from that quarter, clients seeking patronage, nobles seeking favors, all jostling to see which way the new prince would turn. "I had tutors. My royal father made certain of that much."

"I do not doubt it." Ulo moved to the reason for his visit with surprising speed. "We were forced to give Zhaon your royal sister." The Domar shook his head, probably pained by the effort of being so direct. "To bring *peace*."

No doubt Ulo fancied he would have fought better in the morass of mud, blood, and shit that was a battle. "An unwelcome event," Daoyan murmured. A sister he had never spoken to lest his mother's dishonor contaminate her, a pretty, moon-faced girl dragging Komor Yala into the abyss. Of course it wouldn't occur to Bai's little sister to go against the Great Rider, much less her father. The study's bright mirrorlight dimmed, clouds veiling the sun as the uneasy border between winter storms and spring rain passed over the Great Keep.

Ulo had apparently decided it was time to be even plainer, surely a sign of great distress. "Your royal father is occupied with grief and rebuilding. It falls to you to ensure Khir's future."

And how do you propose I do so? Daoyan let his hands rest, slack and relaxed despite their burning, upon the desk's ruthlessly organized top. The biggest gilt-chased box held a new royal seal, heavy greenstone carved with a name that should have been his at birth. *Would* have been his, had fate allowed. "A weighty obligation, Lord Domari." In other words, he was disposed to hear more.

"Difficult decisions must be made." Ulo's sleeves did not tremble, but his voice dropped, low and confidential. "Zhaon has occupied us much, of late. But there are other lands, especially to the west."

A thin icy fingertip scratched lightly down Daoyan's back. He'd felt it more than once. A bastard son had to be pleasant, had to display no ambition—and had to place his boots carefully, not to mention tighten his own saddle-girth.

Accidents were common, and there were plenty of nobles who would like to see him blotted from the scroll of the living, his mother's brothers chief among them. A succession crisis in Zhaon was a tiny matter compared to what the so-upright, so-honorable Second Families of Khir would do to each other if the Great Rider died without an heir, however illegitimate.

Or if the last heir met with an ill fate. "Many other lands," Dao agreed. "The wastes keep us from experiencing trouble from that direction." Why bother with sharp-spined Khir at the end of an ocean of sand, if Shan's trade routes and the rich underbelly of Zhaon were available? Even Anwei had learned as much, and merchants acquired their lessons slowly, if at all.

"Oh, true. But others among our neighbors might not be so lucky." Ulo paused.

So that is your game. It was one Daoyan was more than prepared to set a counter or two within. "Where are my manners?" He finally indicated the hard wooden chair, his own private joke. They would assume much from the contrast between cushion and plainness, and those assumptions would tell him just who and what he was facing. "Will you be seated, Lord Domari?"

"You are very kind, Your Highness." The minister bowed and lowered himself onto the seat. "So, Zhaon and Khir are to be married. Zhaon will grow even richer from tariffs and tolls, and that makes them a ripe prize."

"Assuming they breed no more generals like that cursed Zakkar." It had become the practice among the survivors of Three Rivers to spit when that name was mentioned. Daoyan wondered how Ulo would react if a prince did so, here. A rich little tidbit of gossip to carry to his scheming friends, no doubt.

"Their so-called *emperor* grows no younger, and his pet general has mighty enemies at court." The minister made another small sound, expressing either well-bred contempt or slightly less-than-noble satisfaction. Or, more likely, a mixture of both. "Should misfortune befall Zhaon, they will no doubt call upon Khir. Even weakened, we may be enough to tip a balance."

Unless there is a reason not to. The cold fingertip was back, and it was joined by another, raking lightly as a playful courtesan upon a patron's nakedness. "Of course we would ride to the aid of my royal sister, should there be need," Daoyan said carefully.

"Of course." Domari Ulo nodded. "Yes. Of course. If… there is need."

Much now became clear. Idly, Dao wondered what would happen if he rose, strode around the desk, and backhanded this oily, treacherous baryo to the floor. The royal seal was heavy and its box of fine quality. Skull-shattering, even, if properly swung.

But that was only a momentary pleasure, and he had other plans. Many, many other plans, and it seemed this fellow would provide valuable service without even realizing it.

Daoyan's smile broadened, became natural. He touched the gong at his elbow, and called for tea. Domari Ulo's own smile widened as well, and the minister freed one hand to stroke at his chin, a clear sign of satisfaction. His clan's great seal-ring gleamed upon his first left finger.

"It is my belief," Dao said softly, "that the wise men should be listened to when a kingdom is in danger."

Ulo, like the legitimate nobleman he was, assumed he was wise.

And began to speak.

Remember Your Loyalty

"Your Highness!" Zan Pao's forehead met hardwood, his prostration excellent and trembling. He was grease-pale, and his eyebird-bright robes, too fine for his station, would not give up stains easily. Especially since the floor in this tiny inn-room—well off the main road, and unpleasant in more ways than one—had just been mopped.

A prince had specifically requested the cleaning in preparation for this meeting. He had also, politely but specifically, asked it be done with stable water.

Strange were the ways of royalty, indeed.

"It is fortunate our paths met, Honorable Zan Pao." Garan Makar, Fourth Prince of Zhaon, folded his hands and regarded the unfortunate head eunuch. The Scholar Prince was a tall, spare figure, his robe dark but rich. A straight nose and quiet dark eyes added to bladed cheekbones made him a scroll-picture of serenity. It was said he translated the Thousand Pages into common Zhaon when he was eleven, at the same age he killed an assassin in Second Queen Haesara's quarters, defending his mother and younger brother. His sword was more often hung upon a wall-hook than at his belt, though, and the fan tucked neatly in his sleeve was a gift from Daorak Ghen, the famous tutor of the Emperor's youth.

"Very fortunate, yes." At least Zan Pao had sense enough to add nothing else. Behind him, similarly prostrated but upon a prayer-mat of coarse wool, was a scholar—the Haor boy, the one whose careful missives had allowed Makar to catch up.

The Fourth Prince, standing at the latticed window, rubbed his right thumb meditatively over the greenstone ring upon his left middle finger. It bore a fine carving matching that of his hurai, the seal of a royal family member in the high characters of Zhaon. "It is very strange," he mused aloud, "that a princess should be traveling with so few guards." *And two of the First Queen's most junior maids.* No, the Emperor would not like this at *all*. Makar's hair gleamed, his sleek topknot caged not with gold but with stiffened leather. Ostentation was not in his nature.

It made estimating his worth more difficult, at least for the unwary.

"Your Highness..." The full measure of Zan's miscalculation would be crashing in upon him now. Perhaps the First Queen had promised him a minister's post. The greedy were the easiest to bait.

"The honor of escorting the Crown Prince's bride has caused a great deal of excitement." Any enjoyment Makar would take from this would be minimal, yet he still felt a certain measure, carefully reined. "You are relived of the burden, Honorable Zan Pao." He produced the sealed order from his sleeve, handing it to the expressionless royal guard to his right. "Your new posting is Hangedai, where you will remain until recalled." *And the desert will no doubt teach you some manners.* "That is all."

The guard—one of the Golden, in bright-chased armor with Makar's personal sign upon his armband—ferried the order across the room and deposited it in the eunuch's shaking hands. When the mute unfortunate had dragged himself out with many a bow and a large measure of well-disguised and speechless indignation, Makar turned back to the window. The view through the thin wooden screen was unappetizing at best, but at least this town had a paved main avenue instead of a sea of spring mud. The fields surrounding were fragrant with new life, and some of them were even flooded for rai, that king of crops. "Scholar Haor. Please rise. How fares the princess?"

"I tested her food personally." The young man took the invitation with alacrity, brushing at his robe. Wide-faced and broad-shouldered, he was the first son of a lucky peasant family, all the hopes of mother, father, and siblings pinned to his back. Prince Makar, noticing his merit, had smoothed the way, and that small kindness would continue to pay dividends as the Haor boy aged and rose to his level, wherever that happened to be. "Er, she has a lady-in-waiting. Who also did, I'm sure. Khir noblewoman, very quiet."

That cannot be all. "And?" Makar tucked his hands in his sleeves.

"The Khir escort turned back at Gurai, well before the border." The scholar spread his hands, indicating a measure of puzzlement to match the Fourth Prince's. He adjusted his scrollcase, too, and settled his civil-scholar's hat more firmly.

Makar considered this news. "I see." Ashani Zlorih had one bastard son left, and he sent his daughter all but unguarded? It was either an insult, or he did not expect the princess to survive her trip to Garan Tamuron's court. Or, the Fourth Prince reminded himself, there was another reason lurking in his father's royal head to demand the Khir princess come all but naked, not even a dowry train. "Make the princess and her lady comfortable afresh, introduce the new maids; ask them to send word when they are ready for a visitor." He had brought four junior palace-girls not yet attached to a princely retinue with him; the First Queen's two haughty maids would be attended to shortly. Makar rubbed the greenstone band again, the characters' sharp carved edges biting his fingertip, a cat's nibble. Much about this worried him, but as long as he brought his eldest brother's bride to the capital intact, he would be blameless. "And, Scholar Haor?"

"Yes, Your Highness?" The young man was almost pathetically eager to please, his prostration full of the alacrity of the truly meritorious seen at last.

It was almost too easy, Makar reflected, and cautioned himself against overreach once more. "I will remember your loyalty." And no doubt Haor would remember not only his patron's small aid, but more deeply, the care taken to keep his robes from staining.

Details mattered.

He was still young enough to blush, this boy. His last bow was deep and extremely respectful. "Yes, Your Highness."

According to the foreign ladies, winter's bony grip had not relaxed in Khir's mountains and highlands. Here, though, the fields had begun exuberant greening, and the trees were dressing themselves in new festival finery. Enough damp remained to keep the dust of the main road tamped, and the true season of mud had not arrived just yet. Yeoyan blossoms carpeted the roadside, bruised and fading; many of the orchards were alive with fleece. "This is *much* better." The Khir princess, a moon-faced, plump, pleasant girl with a noblewoman's charms, tilted her head back to feel the spring breeze. "Why did they have us in a box, before?"

The cart had been an insult, but thankfully, she did not seem to have recognized it as such. Finding a way to describe this tactfully to the Emperor would be difficult, and Makar would have to understate. To do otherwise would raise a suspicion he was seeking to work against the First Queen. The time was not ripe for open warfare between Queen Gamwone and his own mother—always assuming Second Queen Haesara would condescend to something so ill-bred as *battle.*

That was Makar's responsibility. A son protected his mother. "An oversight, to protect you from prying eyes." Makar bowed slightly, apologetically, in the saddle. At least both of them could ride; the proverbs said when Khir were born, the goddess of horsemanship whispered at least one secret into their still-unformed ears. "Head Eunuch Zan Pao was so excited by the honor of escorting you, his arrangements fell short." And Makar had performed the thankless task of trawling each of Pao's hangers-on, separating the simply stupid from the ambitious and dangerous. The former still attended the Khir princess; the latter were sent with their patron to the northwestron desert, and much good would it do them.

At least, so Makar hoped.

They would reach the main road soon, turning into the heart of Zhaon, and the best inn in each town would be emptied for them. A few aristocratic families along the route would offer accommodation, but the honor of a visit from the Crown Prince's intended might cause unwarranted pride. The nobles were restless enough, under the new taxation and the restriction of the privilege of extracting corvée labor from the kaburei.

"Your Khir is very good." Magnanimous and well-bred, the princess handled her reins very prettily. Her hat, fringed with a cobweb-fine veil, bobbed. Altogether, she made a very pretty scroll-illustration.

"You are too kind." He pronounced the consonants as well as he could, carefully, speaking at a measured walk. The long ribbon of the Zhaon retinue snaked over the hill before them and the one behind, pikes glittering as they marched, horses with proud-arched necks bearing a few squares of the Emperor's personal Golden, the red pennants snap-fluttering to announce this was a guest of the Emperor himself.

Makar was, of course, relieved he had thought to arrange for a proper amount of ceremony. He simply wished the First Queen had not outmaneuvered him at the start—but that could be turned to advantage, at the right moment.

There was always a right moment, and it was rarely *now*.

The one Khir lady-in-waiting, a straight-backed girl in a dark blue, low-waisted Khir dress, measured Makar with pale eyes. It was to her the princess looked when he was introduced, and it was she who inspected the princess's horse and saddle. Her dress could have been an illustration of Khir history, very long sleeves and a graceful high-necked cut; her sober hairpin's shell ornament glittered in a nest of braids whenever she moved. Her hat was not as full, and held no veil.

At least the best of the horses he'd brought—matched black mares, deep-chested and easy-gaited—were fine enough. He had expected several ladies in the retinue. Why only one? Khir had been strangled for years; perhaps this was a signal of their final capitulation.

Zhaon could only hope. In any case, Khir itself was the girl's dowry, and with that dagger at Zhaon's service instead of pressed to the artery of the Ch'han overland trade, everyone could breathe more easily.

"So, you are the Fourth Prince. Your father is blessed." It was the second time Princess Mahara had said it, and she seemed somewhat at a loss for other conversational topics. "How many brothers have you?"

Did she truly not know? He cleared his throat, a little awkwardly, and help arrived from an unexpected quarter.

"There are six princes, my princess." Soft and decorous, the lady-in-waiting spoke, the Khir word for *royal daughter* accented at the front, trailing into a swallowed *iah*. Her family name was *Komori*, a very old noble name if Makar remembered his Cao Zheun correctly. "And two princesses, if I am not mistaken?"

"Yes." It would be the height of rudeness to inquire of the Khir princess's own brothers. They were all dead, except one of Ashani Zlorih's byblows. "They are all eager to make your acquaintance. The Crown Prince is practicing his poetry."

"Oh." The princess blinked, soft confusion very becoming. Her gloves were embroidered with the wheel-like calendar symbol of the Khir royal family at the cuffs, small delicate stitches most likely her own work. "Should I be composing my own?"

"He would be most honored, should you care to." The thought of Takyeo reading a love letter from *anyone* was amusing for any number of reasons, but Makar hoped his expression would be seen as merely a polite smile. "Do you like poetry, then, Princess? The journey is long, we shall seek diversions for you."

"I like riding, and plays." The princess ducked her head, shyly, perhaps aware of her own childishness, and her veil fluttered. "Lady Yala is the scholar, but she rides well too."

"My princess does me much honor." Lady Komor smiled. *Blind-eyed*, they called the Khir, *but sharp-eared, hearing the hawk on the wing.* They had withdrawn into their land during the Second Dynasty, nobility mingling only with their own, and their irises had paled in consequence. The color did not run outside their borders; a Zhaon with less than half noble Khir parentage had muddy eyes, or dark ones. It was disconcerting to see the leaching of a human gaze, and doubly so to see how it vanished within a generation.

"My father kept to the old ways," Lady Yala said. Her gloved hands, innocent of rings just as her wrists were bare of bangles, rested upon the reins with grace just as fine as the princess's. "*To trace the classics, even with a child's hand, is to learn wisdom.*"

Now *that* was surprising, and Makar had just been thinking of that very scholar. "Cao Zheun," he said, studying the lady's profile, too sharp for real beauty but perhaps piquant to a collector of faces. It was now his turn to provide a bit of prose. "*Even a child's brush may show the shape of the world.*"

"Nao Sinlao." She nodded, musingly. "*Unless the land is a flat dish upon a tortoise's back.*"

That particular line was from the Anonymous Fool's Song, ribald and esoteric by turns. Startled, Makar laughed; Lady Komor did not, but she smiled again. Birds rose from the trees upon either side, disturbed by their passage, crying warning to their fellows.

Princess Mahara made a short, aggravated noise. "*Ai,* you two are quoting dusty old books that make my head hurt. Yala! Race me!" The Khir princess touched her heels to her mare's sides; the mare, startled, lunged forward. Makar had a sudden vision of her flung from the saddle or trampled, and his own mount shied, sensing unease.

Lady Yala, though, let out a high piercing cry, and her horse shot forward as well. The princess veered from the road into an untilled field, sticking to her saddle like a burr to rough wool, and Makar began to bark sharp orders for the guards to spread out.

The princess cried aloud, a sharp joyous sound, and Makar's knees clamped home, telling the beast the order of the world had not changed and the human upon its back was still its master.

Long afterward, he was to think of that afternoon, the field of spring flowers, a smell of crushed green, and the two Khir women on horseback, their route a curving *shuh* character, shod hooves throwing clods of dirt and grass aside. He would remember the veil flying from Princess Ashan Mahara's hat, knocked askew by the wind, and Lady Komor Yala melding with the horse, obviously more skilled than her princess but gracefully restraining her mount just a touch, just enough. It took much talent and practice to lose so neatly and nearly, and when the women rejoined the long snake of the retinue waiting patiently for them, the princess flushed and happy, it was Lady Yala who scolded her gently for giving the Fourth Prince so much trouble.

The princess did not bridle, but took the almost-rebuke with good grace and offered a half-bow of apology, her cheeks flushed and her moonlike beauty turned solar for a brief moment. Makar ventured the opinion that it was only natural to wish to ride upon a spring morning, and of course he was pleased to see such a fine example of horsemanship.

"Next time, *he* shall race with me, and you shall call the route," Lady Komor said, a neat solution, and Makar politely agreed.

It seemed that if the Khir had sent only one lady with their princess, they had chosen the best for the task. She would bear careful watching, this court lady.

He was almost looking forward to it.

A Single Blade

For a moment, waking to the faint whisper of metal drawn from a well-greased sheath, Kai thought he was with the Northern Army still and wondered why the fourth watch had not been called. Some part of him was always sleepless, listening for the rhythm of patrol and return, the hiss of torches, the mud and sour smell of leather, metal, and male effort.

Then he was rolling off his low bed, foot flicking to catch the wrapped figure's midriff, Kai's light woolen blanket parting as a blackened blade sliced its top layer. Kai landed with a crunch upon his shoulder, a spike of pain down his neck, continuing the motion to bring himself up into a crouch on the stone floor and kicking a subtly patterned Anwei-woven rug away—he needed good footing, and sliding on a cushion would not help.

The assassin staggered, spun, and dropped into a crouch as well, blade carving a solid semicircle. Kai leaned back, bare toes splaying to grip cold stone, another Anwei rug slipping under his front foot. The breeze of a sharp edge passing just touched his chin, so he took the only possible way out, falling again and rolling aside, shoulders hitting the floor bruising-hard. Then he was up, the laces of his sleeping-tunic torn free, its front ripping. He peeled it loose, wrapping the cloth around his left arm, and the assassin paused, visibly reconsidering, an inquisitive angle to the fully wrapped head.

Kai's knees bent, weight dropping into the answering stance for knifeplay. He was awake now, on his feet, on familiar ground, and the next step was taking the blade from this stupid fellow and questioning him thoroughly.

Thin window-hangings rustled and the scroll depicting two tigers hunting the same fat bronzefish scraped against the wall, pushed by night air and a new, feral current. Kai's pupils, night-wide, drank in every available gleam, and he knew he had been dreaming of war again.

A feint, the short, straight assassin's jadak[14] whispering again as its edge clove resistant air. The assassin's wrist floated to the side, but Kai did not take the bait. Instead, he retreated once more, shuffling, kicking aside the rug again with his back foot. The wall drew closer, and with it a small highly carved table with a thin, highly carved soppah-stone bowl full of water and lilies. Kanbina's gift—*you keep your quarters too spare, my son.*

This slash wasn't a feint; he knew it as soon as the masked man's other hand dropped. The bastard was *quick*, knee bending and the soot-blackened blade serpent-darting. Left arm up, Kai's sleeping-tunic tearing as it deflected the blade a critical fraction, and Kai grabbed the stone bowl, swinging it as his hip hit the table. It hit with a *crack*, but the assassin had moved, so it was a shoulder instead of the man's head taking the force of the blow. Water splashed, lilies falling in a cascade, and Kai was upon him, twisting the knife-hand savagely. Bone creak-snapped, and the man's sour exhalation of gin-hai,[15] garlic, bad teeth, and indifferent bathing folded around him.

"Who sent you?" A soft demand; Kai didn't have the breath for more. Locking the injured wrist, his knee grinding into the floor, using his body weight to immobilize. "Tell me, and you will live."

Frantic bucking. The body under him understood it was trapped, and grew desperate. Again he twisted serpent-supple; the man was skilled in grappling, but a broken wrist and a wary opponent made all the difference. Kai's fingers wormed in; he worked the knife

---

14. A blackened, curved assassin's blade.

15. A pungent aromatic root.

free and bore down upon the wrist again, grating broken edges together and ignoring the man's flopping legs.

"Who?" he demanded again. "*Who?*" Now that he was awake and had the man's measure, he didn't really expect an answer. The assassin worked his unwounded arm free, short broken fingernails digging into Kai's chin, trying to reach his throat to force him away. Another heave, the assassin finally understanding he would not escape, and the confused tangle of motion ended with Kai on his back, a sagging body clasped in his arms and the stink of death filling mouth, nose, ears, and every part of him again. A sweetish exhalation was the poison tooth, bitten to guard the secrets of whoever had sent this unfortunate failure.

One more dealer of death would not be paid his promised balance.

Nerve-death twitched through the corpse, and Kai shoved it aside. Stopped, his ears pricked and the oil-sweat of death's brush painting every inch of him. Nothing, not even the whisper of another's breath, the faint unsound of a living creature waiting to attack while the target was possibly wounded or distracted.

Who would send a single blade to deal with *him*? The wide, wood-shuttered window, worked open with a thin metal tongue to provide access, filled the cup of the room with a soft spring breeze. His palace quarters had been aired thoroughly upon his return, but this close to the floor he could smell the disuse.

Zakkar Kai sat upon smooth stone, his breath coming in silent, heaving gasps, his eyes half-closed. The body's twitches faded, and when he was ready, the general would rise and pace to the door to call for guards. Next would come hurrying feet, shouts, questions, the examination of a body.

But for the moment, he simply stayed where he was, his limbs prickling with the knowledge that once again, he had survived.

Mrong Banh, First Astrologer of the Court of Emperor Garan Tamuron, held a citron-scented cloth over his mouth and nostrils. Awakened roughly, his topknot was a mess; that was, in any case, its usual state. "Only one?" His broad forehead glistened despite the chill in this lower room, and his black hair held early grey at the temples. His scholar's robe was hastily mistied; his shoes did not match. For all that, his glance was bright and keen, and he surveyed the body upon the wooden slab with a great deal of nauseated interest.

"Insulting, isn't it." Kai gestured, and the young, extremely disgusted royal guard on this disagreeable duty peeled back dark cloth over the assassin's face. The body was still pliable, and much could be read upon it if they were careful, and quick to examine before anyone else had a chance to mar fresh ink, so to speak.

Banh clicked his tongue, a habit of deep thought. "Who would only send *one*?"

The back of Kai's neck itched. His shoulders ached, bruises rising like bronzefish slow and sleepy after winter rest. "Exactly." Candles guttered against the dark in this stone rectangle; he lifted his own taper and peered at the assassin's unwrapped face. An older man, cheeks pitted with pinprick burns, teeth blackened by donjba.[16] No wonder he had been alone. There was only one clan of darkwalkers who pricked their cheeks with heated needles after a kill and rubbed ash into the bleeding marks. They were expensive, and one was generally enough for most targets. "Though it salves my pride somewhat to see it is a Son of the Needle."

"A bad omen." The astrologer shook his head, pressing the cloth even more firmly against his nose and mouth. More lanterns were being brought. The windows were mere strips along the tops of the walls; mirrors hung with none of the sun's reflected fire to fill them were shuttered eyes. Come morning, the mirrors would wake and this cave would hold a pitiless glare.

Zakkar Kai's lip curled slightly. "'Tis not an omen, but an assassin, Banh." *I was lucky.* Had he not been accustomed to sleeping lightly, had he not been ill at ease in this familiar warren of stone

---

16. A root with mild analgesic properties, tending to blacken the teeth of those who chew it.

and luxury, had he not been still raw from skirmish and battle both...well.

"A thing may be twain or thrain at once, my student." Another tongue-click, but of the softness that meant Banh was amused while he thought. At least the astrologer was not fussing; he had already examined Kai for wounds.

The young guard turned his head aside, his throat-stone bobbing as he fought bile. Kai let it pass—sooner or later, the boy would see worse. He propped the corpse's mouth open with the hilt of the blackened blade, probing carefully. "Ah. Look, he had *two* poison teeth."

"Really?" Banh leaned close, shouldering the young guard. A ghost of incense clung to the sober dark brown of his scholar's robe. "How interesting."

A shadow in the doorway swelled, and a slippered foot landed soundlessly upon stone. "What is this?" The bright-bleached, sumptuous robe of a successful physician, the tiered hat of the Court, a topknot caged in silver—it was Tian Ha, the First Queen's Head Physician. "A death in the Palace, how unlucky. Are you casting a corpse's horoscope, Mrong?"

The astrologer straightened, the perfumed cloth puffing over his mouth. It would hide the grimace he usually made when Tian deigned to speak to him. "And you, Tian, come to check a corpse's pulse? He cannot pay your fee."

Kai moved about his examination. The body's hands were hardened in the old fashion, calluses made supple with iao oil, feet and calves with the peculiar musculature that came from practicing the lightstep—an assassin without the discipline to learn wall-walking and rooftop dancing did not last long. The dead man was well past his youth, and the marks of childhood deprivation showed around his mouth and nose. Slack in death, his face held all a kaburei's resignation.

No doubt he had been sold to the Sons during a famine, probably in the dead of night when the plump childcatchers went door to door. The Sons did not take children past seven winters high, holding the elders too difficult to train properly, but they paid well for those they did take, and business was brisk in the warring provinces before Tamuron's reunification of Zhaon territory. Where armies moved, hunger often followed, and younger sons were more precious than daughters drowned in their swaddling.

"General Zakkar." Tian flowed down the stairs, his expression unchanging. Oiled hair and swaying prayer-beads, a show of piety and sobriety, and the well-concealed sneer completed the scroll-illustration of a man who had found a high patron and was determined to make the most of it. "I am relieved to find you well."

"I am sorry to disturb your slumber." Kai glanced at the physician, one eyebrow slightly raised. Mrong Banh's own expressive eyes were asking the same question, and the physician well knew it, for his explanation was quick in coming.

"Second Princess Gamnae is awake; I was attending to the making of a tonic to ease her humors." Tian reached the bottom of the stairs, their stone treads worn to deceptively soft curves. "I heard some commotion."

No doubt you came running to gather gossip, like an eggbird after grain. "Merely an assassin." Kai untied the corpse's shirtlaces—fine strong cotton, a padded outer tunic providing some measure of protection and a great deal of mobility.

"Who would dare such a thing?" Tian's shock, performed with round eyes and an open mouth, was perhaps for the benefit of the single guard, who suddenly became very busy studying his boot-toes. They called Physician Tian *the Skull* for his habit of grinning, and the physician perhaps liked the name. A tick, burrowed well under Queen Gamwone's bleached, pampered skin, swelling with putrid happiness. "And in the Palace, no less." His mustache and goatee gleamed in candle and lantern glow, oiled just as expensively as his hair. A seal-ring of carved bone dangling from a thong at his neck, not tucked underneath his robe, was the only marker of his hurry.

"The Emperor's wrath is assured," Mrong Banh murmured, bending to inspect the corpse's nostrils.

"Did the stars tell you that?" Tian Ha approached the body, his long fingers crossed over his lean middle. Only the smallest upon his right hand moved, a twitch now and again. His fingernails, long points dyed with the effluvia of medical tinctures and pastes, gleamed.

"Merely common sense." The corners of Banh's eyes crinkled, as if he smiled pacifically under the perfumed cloth. Either that, or simply baring his teeth as he glanced up. "It is an attack upon a royal family member."

"Ah, yes." Tian's long nose wrinkled. The hem of his robe was dusty—he must have hurried through the gardens. "Congratulations upon your great good fortune, General."

"It is as the Emperor wills." Kai pushed the corpse's tunic aside. A slightly sunken chest, other needle marks down the left side, inked vines clustering the heart. A very proficient darkwalker, indeed, and perhaps that proficiency was why whoever had engaged him had only sent the one. The clothing held nothing of interest, except traces of reddish mud upon the slipper-soles. *Interesting.* That mud was from river; perhaps this fellow had come in through the baths. "As ever."

Tian Ha could not argue with such a formulaic response. No doubt he had hoped to be the first one to examine the body, and perhaps cover traces if there was a chance one of the First Queen's many intrigues had gone too far to halt. Kai was more than happy to disappoint him, and took his time completing the survey. At the end, he glanced at Mrong Banh, whose gaze was level, worried, and entirely too sharp for Kai's comfort. The astrologer would realize, of course, that this was merely a prelude. The conspiracies were rank and ripe, now that Tamuron was older and his sons men instead of boys.

The astrologer would also realize there were precious few clues. Some mud, some needle marks, and pockets empty except for the implements of an assassin's trade—nothing to show who had paid the man, or his guild-mates, for a death.

Kai, however, was occupied with a different question. Who could guess how many assassins had been originally slated for the night's games, and been called off when the news of the hurai gifted to him spread? Killing a general, even a well-regarded one, was nothing compared to attempting upon the life of one given a greenstone seal-ring.

Kai stepped back, beckoning Tian Ha forward with a magnanimous gesture. There was little harm in letting thc ghoul crouch over fresh meat. It might even sweeten the physician's disposition somewhat.

Yes, the thought of how many assassins had perhaps been called off was unpleasant. Even more disturbing, though, was the idea that perhaps it had *not* been news of a prince's seal given to a victorious general that had halted the plans.

Or, worst of all, that this was merely a prelude to the approaching wedding. Kai's loyalty to Crown Prince Garan Takyeo was well known, and Tamuron's first son had many enemies.

Especially in the palace.

Unwelcome Reminder

A beautiful spring sky arched over Zhaon-An, a few creamy clouds serving to accentuate deep, aching blue. The palace, white stone and red-tiled roofs, brooded at the head of the city, safe from the smoke and bustle of the markets, the stink and scurry of the slums. Riding toward the crown of the anthill was never guaranteed to put a man in a good mood.

Not if he had any sense.

Garan Suon-ei Takshin, Third Prince of Zhaon and battle-brother to King Suon Kiron of Shan, drew rein in the stone-walled palace bailey with a clatter and considered spitting. He *also* considered sliding from the Shan gelding's back and drawing his sword. Taking the head of a creature from that familiar but still hateful country would suit his mood perfectly, and it might even send a message that couldn't be ignored through this pile of stone and unrelenting power.

But it was unprincely to strike a dumb beast for no reason other than your own frustration. Especially when one had been considered a dumb beast handy for striking one's whole life.

Banners fluttered from pike-heads, from archer-towers rising squat along the palace's girdling walls. Hung with weighted ends on either side of every entrance large enough to warrant such treatment, painted material pulled taut upon a high, warm spring breeze. Takshin freed one booted foot from the stirrup, slid from the saddle, and landed upon flagstones; behind him, the Zhaon escort thundered to a halt. They had not dared to curb his pace once he crossed the border. Kiron's bloodriders had left them at Haoran, with the traditional bloodcurdling yells the Shan used at every parting from a lord or loved one.

Takshin wasn't sure if he preferred the noise, or the deathly silence he'd left Zhaon-An wrapped in each time he must return to his duties as hostage.

Do not arrive when they expect you. And yet, at the end of this familiar, freshly swept bailey rose a flight of dun-colored softstone steps, and a tall man in a yellow robe stood at their head, his wide gold-worked belt denoting princedom and his square, wisp-scruffed face alight with pleasure. Crown Prince Garan Takyeo leaned forward slippered toes, as if he wished to descend the stairs with a little more speed than such an august personage should display.

Beside him, Garan Kurin the Second Prince stood in bright orange silk, his hand at the Crown Prince's elbow, restraining him. Or seeking to, at least, but Takyeo shook him off and hurried down, his boots landing solidly—he was not in slippers or buskins; perhaps he planned to go riding later. Takyeo's gold-caged topknot was perfectly placed as usual, and Takshin, his own knocked askew by the speed of his passage, set his Shan-style tunic to rights with a few quick yanks, his sword passed from hand to hand with unconscious speed.

"Takshin!" The Crown Prince halted, a polite distance away but still leaning on his toes, a horse ready to race, waiting only for the heel. "You've grown."

Of course, their eldest brother wouldn't mention dust, sweat, road-filth, or the scars, but Takshin felt them all the same. His lip, his cheek leading to the seam running under his hair—reminders, as if he needed them. The lowest of the low, despite his place in the birth order. "Crown Prince." He bowed, just the correct measure of respect. Sweat, road-dust, and grime hung upon his black silk and leather, the costume of his adopted prison.

"No, no." Takyeo finally swept forward, enfolding Takshin in a bear hug. The Crown Prince smelled of mint-water and fragrant hair-oil as well as the faint leathery note of a man past his first youth. "It is good to see you." He pounded Takshin on the back, and a shadow behind him was Kurin, orange silk heavy and fine but only leather caging his topknot. Kurin's expression was set as he surveyed his birth-brother's horse, the winded guards, and the spectacle the Crown Prince was making.

"The servants are watching." Kurin produced an eyebird-painted fan with a snap and waved away an invisible, importunate fly. He had inherited First Queen Gamwone's heavy eyes, and the languid lids had led more than one unwary soul into thinking he was kind.

Or unintelligent.

"Let everyone see how happy I am to greet my brother," the Crown Prince returned, equably, and held Takshin by the shoulders. "Let me look at you, Taktak." The childhood nickname was not meant to sting, at least. "Oh, Father will be pleased, and everyone else, too. Have you eaten? Take his horse, there! Come, come."

A flutter of roseate silk and white brocade arrived at the top of the stairs. Garan Gamnae, birth-sister to Prince Kurin and Prince Takshin, blinked her own depthless, well-lidded eyes. What was indifference and almost unattractive on Kurin was quite fetching on her, and when she was older they would call her *pleasure-eyed*, that languid gaze bespeaking loss of married sleep. "Taktak!" Each syllable ringing against the bailey, that silly name again since Kurin had lisped badly until his ninth winter and refused to address his younger brother properly. Gamnae had called Takshin thus from the start, and no amount of pinching could stop her. "You're early."

"I hurried to see you, sister mine." Takshin barely nodded to Kurin, despite the bow that would be due his elder. A small defiance, one he'd probably hear complaints about later. "How lovely you are."

"Flatterer." Gamnae preened, ear-drops of gold leaf chiming as she turned her head this way and that, conscious of the picture she presented in sunlight. A tense-shouldered palace maid held a rosy sunbell over the Second Princess, and with her hair dressed high,

Gamnae looked very much like the First Queen, except not so plump—or so harsh. "I have had your quarters aired and arranged them just the way you like them."

As if you know anything of what I like. And as if he would sleep in the Kaeje, especially in quarters connected to the First Queen's. The very thought made his skin crawl. "Very thoughtful of you."

"Aren't you forgetting something?" Kurin snapped his fan, a sharp, dry sound. "You cannot bring a weapon into the Palace, brother."

Of course he would be the one to notice, and furthermore to affect surprise. Takshin allowed himself a sour half-smile. "Neither a man of Shan nor a prince of Zhaon should leave his blade behind." *I sound surprisingly steady.* If Kurin decided to play this game and called the guards, Takshin could turn, call for his horse, and be on his way back to Shan in short order.

It might even please him to ride a beast, however innocent, to death.

Kurin's own smile was far less sleepy, and a good deal more satisfied. He had obviously made up his mind to rob Takshin's homecoming of any joy. "The Emperor will not—"

"Oh, it's just Takshin." Gamnae's laugh was clear as a bell, and she took Takshin's sword arm. The scabbard touched her skirts, but she was oblivious. "I'll speak to Father for you," she continued, in a child's confidence-sharing whisper. "He's at the shrine."

Father they said, so easily. It was a wonder the word didn't stick in their throats.

Nothing would ever change. The Emperor was making offerings at the shrine of his warlord wife, the one who had birthed the Crown Prince and died before the overlord of southron Zhaon became conqueror and then *Emperor.* The candles at that shrine were ever-lit, and none were allowed to disturb Garan Tamuron while he prayed there with his kombin, endlessly flipping his hand and reciting whatever moved him.

"Mother wishes to see you," Gamnae continued, and Kurin had no choice but to trail behind. It probably galled his elder brother to no end; Takshin banished a wolfish smile. Now that he had halted his headlong ride, the sun was pleasant, his face no longer whipped by spring chill. Horse-rhythm still beat inside his bones, and he would need a bath or two to shake it free.

"She can wait," he said, shortly. "Crown Prince, my brother, tell me, are you well?"

"I am. And you? How was your ride?" Takyeo did his best to drag Kurin along, but the Second Prince was having none of it and turned away, his fan moving briskly. "Tell me the news. We shall have tea, and you shall eat, or Gamnae will scold us both."

"Will she dare?" Takshin glowered sidelong, and the Second Princess tossed her head and laughed. Her maids, each in the requisite blue-and-white palace garb, scurried to take their places, the one holding the sunbell almost tripping in her haste. Each wore the tiny pink-and-white rosette of Kaeje servants, with the thin yellow ribbon denoting service with a queen's household in their plain, soberly dressed hair.

"I have grown bold while you were away, Elder Brother." Light and winsome, but Gamnae cast a sharp look at the sunbell-maid as a sliver of sunlight managed to slip through its guard and touch her zhu-powdered face. "You shall play hanai[17] with me, for now I never lose."

Probably because you cheat. "A challenge thrown." Takshin let them bear him along, and no more mention was made of his sword. Kurin soon disappeared, no doubt to carry a tale of the Third Prince refusing to give up his slightly curved sword with the Shan ruby winking in its hilt. There would be many a listener, chins wagging and tongues working, to guess at Garan Takshin's intentions.

The game had recommenced.

Bathed, with his black hair oiled and brought to a plain topknot, in a Zhaon-cut robe of dark grey with subtle embroidery at the chest and sleeves and a pair of trousers much looser-legged than the Shan

17. A game of bicolored stones upon a board painted with intersecting circles.

wore, Takshin halted at the end of the hall. His war-trained ears sharpened as he closed his eyes, and the scars were perhaps flushed from the heat of his bath. The thick one across his neck, the cut on the right side of his top lip making a perpetual sneer, the one across his left cheek vanishing on a seam of once-burned flesh under his hair—all of them visible, all of them ugly.

Very well, then. Let the First Queen of the Zhaon, the Beautiful Land of the Five Winds, see what she had wrought.

Queen Gamwone's head lady-in-waiting was still Yona, a dry round pucker-mouthed thing whose dun robe was still spotless, still sharply creased in the appropriate places, and still making the soft, terrifying sound of uncaring authority. Takshin did not miss how the other maids—all but children; his mother must have just requisitioned a new crop, ready to press all life and youth from them at leisure—leaned away from the head lady as she moved among them. Yona's hair held no veiling of grey. Perhaps she stole youth from the terror of those under her as well.

She learned well, from the best of teachers for *that* skill.

Still, Yona's bow to him was utterly correct, and reasonably respectful. "Third Prince Takshin." She slid the door open herself, bent again to motion him inside his mother's informal receiving-room.

Her elbow upon a low table, a fluted glass bottle of sohju[18] set upon a bed of white silk and two small Gurai slipware cups with gold chasing waiting obediently, First Queen Gamwone held a silken-sleeved hand to her mouth, affecting amusement and a well-bred hiding of teeth. Her dress was sun-colored, turning her into a round flame in the belly of a cushioned lamp. Second Prince Kurin, in his orange of a deeper shade patterned with spreading ox-horns, had taken the other side of the table, his elbow resting familiarly as well. It was the picture of a mother and son sharing confidences, and Takshin's empty hands ached for a hilt.

Even a paring knife would do.

18. A drink made of crushed, fermented rai.

He had left his blade behind for this, but not to please her or Kurin. Or anyone else. *A wise man knows himself,* Suon Kiron was fond of intoning, mimicking their ancient, liver-spotted tutor from the days before the Mad Queen's grasp upon reality had completely sundered.

When Takshin was tempted to strike, it was often Kiron's voice he heard. A steady, gauntleted hand upon the leash of a hunting animal—and yet, *brother,* Kiron called him, and even seemed to believe it. Such loyalty was rare in the Mad Queen's court, and Kiron had done what he could to protect the hated, helpless interloper.

That was in the past now. The battlefield before him would not forgive inattention. It irked Takshin to take his knees at the edge of Queen Gamwone's rug, and he hated the low bow a child must give his parent as well. "Mother." The formal inflection. All correct, there was nothing for her to find fault with.

Yet she would.

She poured with a dainty, plump, powdered hand. All of her was round and soft, from her zhu-powdered cheeks to her smooth forehead, the backs of her hands with dimples instead of knuckles, her short legs hidden under high-waisted Zhaon gowns. Even her hair, dressed in fantastical loops and decked with pearls, was round and looked pillowy, though the lacquer keeping it in place would be stiff to the touch. The walls were hung with phoenixes embroidered upon falls of thin silk over wool matting; the window was closed, for she felt chills keenly. As a result, it was stifling, and the heavy rugs deadened every sound unfortunate enough to be uttered here.

Finally, she acknowledged Takshin with a quick, distrustful glance, her gaze doing its best to avoid the scars. "Oh. It's you."

As if you're surprised. "How is your health, Mother?" Again, a correct inquiry, polite and delivered with the proper deference.

Kurin said nothing. Of course, he did not need to, and it was always best not to interfere when the First Queen showed even the slightest hint of displeasure. A childhood spent in Gamwone's presence drove that habit in deep, rubbing dye-ash in whatever small cut it could find, and the marks remained.

"You must not address me so." Her beringed hand waved, a weighted, languid claw. "You were adopted by the Queen of Shan."

A hostage is under no obligation to lie or tell the truth. The thought was just as edged as every other time he'd used it for comfort. "The Mad Queen doused herself with snow-water, *Mother*, and took ill. Her funeral was in the month of heavy ice. Did that news not reach Zhaon-An?"

It was not what she had expected him to say. One of her manicured eyebrows lifted, enough to make a palace maid quake. "And your brother?"

Now was the time for less politeness. "He sits next to you, Mother." The precise tone of bored almost-insolence, well practiced, was both shield and sword now. His back did not prickle with sweat, nor did the hollows under his arms, or so Takshin told himself. "Ask him."

A flush began in the zhu-dusted creases of her neck, her collarbone lost under a pad of wealth. Her little maid-spiders would be scurrying for cover now, and even Yona might pause, stilling with the instinct of a cat sensing a hawk's shadow floating overhead. "Suon Kiron of Shan is your brother." Gamwone enunciated each word clearly. "What of him?"

"Ah." Takshin let his gaze rest upon the sohju cups. A pretty set, even if they did not quite match the bottle. "The Lord of Shan is contemplating marriage, I believe." The couriers upon the road to Shan's borders had fairly flown, once Three Rivers was done and the bleeding of Khir no longer a counterweight to Garan Tamuron's ambitions. "Or the courtiers are contemplating it for him."

"Ah." First Queen Gamwone tapped one bala[19]-lacquered nail against her cup—she did not dye her fingertips as old Zhaon noblewomen were wont to. Instead, she painted the nails with the resin, and the gleam stiffened her claws. She also disdained to wear

19. A heavy-barked, resin-rich tree.

a noblewoman's filigree sheaths upon her smallest fingers to protect their nails, affecting that hers were strong enough not to need the support of a metal cage. "Suon Kiron still lives?"

"That he does." *And he knows what you would have me do about that.*

She abandoned the pretense of calm. The flush had reached her cheeks now, and her kohl-lined eyes narrowed, almost lost in pouches of pampered flesh. "Why?"

"He is young?" What little enjoyment Takshin derived from this conversation lay in his sardonic tone. The phoenixes upon the walls watched this intimate family meeting with secretive grins, their beaks not quite crooked and their eyes imitations of the First Queen's hooded gaze. "And in good health, and takes much exercise? Those habits generally make living easier, I am told." He settled upon his heels. It would have been polite for her to offer tea, or even some of the sohju. It would have been *motherly* of her to greet him properly.

I hatched from a cold egg, he had told Kiron more than once.

Kiron's reply never changed—a peculiar foxlike bark of laughter through a mouthful of bitterness. *Did we not both?*

The First Queen was not accustomed to being openly balked. "Do not play with me." Finally, she could stand it no more and turned to face him, drawing her knees under her with a court lady's practiced movement. "You were to bring me Shan."

Indeed. It was a victory; at least now, he had her notice. Her *attention.* "How could I fit that in my pockets, Mother?" His air of bafflement was completely feigned, and she knew it. The thin wooden soles of his slippers, covered with a pad of cotton, dug into the backs of his thighs.

Kurin, staring at the silk upon the tabletop, looked faintly shamed. It was a lie, of course; he was no doubt enjoying this immensely, for his own reasons. He did not dare reach into his sleeve for his fan, though—she could just as easily turn on him once Takshin was handled.

Especially if Takshin had decided he would not be handled, or dealt with, or vanquished. Had it always been this easy?

No. It had not. He was a man now, not a frightened child.

The stain on First Queen Gamwone's powdered cheeks deepened, each granule of crushed, polished zhu standing out in contrast. "My son must have Shan as a shield when he sits upon the throne!" Every sibilant hissed, but softly, softly.

"Aren't you forgetting something?" He did not bother to whisper. Let anyone who had ears hear it. He also did not shift his weight, regarding his dam with the narrow stare of a hunter used to patience, watching the prey strut stiff-legged as it thought itself safe. "There is a Crown Prince already."

"A bastard—" Her face contorted, and Gamwone drew breath to finish a somewhat treasonous sentence.

It was so easy to provoke her, now. "Be careful what you say, Mother. The Emperor keeps his first wife's shrine lit." Today of all days, the reminder would be most unwelcome. Even the phoenixes looked away, the hangings holding their breath and the stifling, close air suddenly full of sharp heatless anger.

Queen Gamwone stared at her second son, obviously not grateful that he had interrupted an ill-considered statement. "I regret giving birth to you. Even your sister is more useful."

"Thank you, Mother." Takshin's scarred lip curled. His legs tensed. "It was pleasant to see you again, too."

For the first time, Kurin spoke. Nobody outside this room would ever believe he could sound so tentative. "He is weary from his journey, Mother."

"*Useless*," Queen Gamwone hissed, stabbing two fingers at Takshin as if he were a fox-ghoul, or a cannibal ghost. Her vowels had hardened, the accent of a merchant's daughter rubbing through the indolence of noble speech. "Get out of my sight."

With pleasure. Takshin bowed again, rose, and retreated. He passed through the ladies-in-waiting—hastily retaking their place, no doubt after pressing ears to the partition—like a burning wind, and it wasn't until he reached the gloom of dusk outside in a water-garden's dreaming coolness that his eyes filled.

Fool. Did you think she would be happy to see you?

No. He had long since given up that dream.

Still, it stung, a pointless almost-grief mixed with slow dull-crimson fury. His hands burned, begging for a hilt, until he could breathe deeply and dispel the fire. It retreated underground, but it did not abate.

It never did.

Even a Kind One

The noise was unrelenting. They lined the broad stone avenues, a sweltering mass of crafters, traders, merchants, kaburei given or stealing leave for the day, children agog at the spectacle, women selling fruit and cheap fans, mothers lifting babies to see that mythical creature, a princess of Khir.

Mahara, in the heavily embroidered robe and fine linen underthings the Fourth Prince had presented—all red as fresh blood, the color of luck and marriage—stood under a huge crimson canopy. The entire platform moved upon grinding wooden wheels, pulled by sweating horses and pushed by sweating kaburei, lumbering over thrown flowers and scattered slips of red paper, fragrant water splashed in its path. Tiny sparksticks swung in excited hands both young and old; shoving and fistfights bloomed at the edges of the crowd.

Yala lifted a small wooden cup of cooling yeoyan juice to Mahara's dry, carmine-dabbed lips. "Courage," she whispered. "Courage, my princess." The crowd, of course, would not see the sweat or Mahara's fluttering eyelashes, her deadly paleness. They would see the wagons heaped with Zhaon marriage-gifts and the guards in their gold and red livery, the great canopy and the labor expended to carry a lone woman in red and her lady-in-waiting along. Just like a sacrifice bound and dragged to a temple, crashing cymbals, wailing flutes, and the roar of the conqueror's city deafening those brought to be immolated. Before the First Dynasty, such sacrifices were common, or at least the Hundreds hinted as much.

Zhaon-An couldn't possibly be this big. How did the inhabitants *breathe* in this warren of stone, timber, so many people pressed cheek-by-jowl? The Great Keep of Khir and its city-skirts were not half as large.

Yala's head throbbed, not just from the lurching motion or the constant crowd-roaring. She settled watchfully into kneeling, thankfully shielded from view by a hip-high, flimsy wooden partition. She could massage Mahara's legs and provide some little comfort, but the princess had to stand inside the gold-heavy robe, head high with its cargo of twisted, sculpted hair and gold cage-work in two horns, red silk tassels depending from each. The heat was monstrous, crushing, but at least there was shade, and some slight breeze from the contraption's movement.

It had all started before dawn at the massive southron gate of Zhaon-An, with Mahara assuming her place upon the wide platform while horns blared her arrival from the city's newly repaired walls. It was auspicious for the princess to enter from the same direction as the warming spring winds, the Fourth Prince and his advisors had said, but as Yala stole glances at their surroundings, she realized the route was planned to show off Khir's offering to the royalty of Zhaon through as much of their ancient capital as possible. Khir had paid dearly at the Battle of Three Rivers, but so had Zhaon, and this spectacle was to show the common people it had been worth the blood and toil.

No doubt there had also been a triumphal march when their army returned, laden with whatever spoils were wrung out of the borderlands or plundered from the Khir tents at Three Rivers. Heavy tribute was levied from Khir for the next ten years, and Mahara was the first payment. The terms of surrender could even be called *magnanimous,* since there was no military viceroy lording it in the Great Keep and the tolls and tariffs for trade through Zhaon did not increase.

Khir was defeated, its border garrisons withdrawn and tariffs levied upon the goods that passed through from Ch'han far north and the Yaluin's several tribes, not to mention any of Khir's goods traveling through Zhaon to Anwai. Many a petty invader had learned Khir's high wood-clothed mountains and the deep fertile valleys made for stubborn defense, and contented themselves with levying tribute. Zhaon was no different, and furthermore needed their northern neighbor to act as a stopper against the wild tribes of the Yaluin wastes and the designs of far Ch'han.

The sun turned past its zenith. Yala's princess was even paler; her jaw clenched as the contraption wheeled into what Yala later learned was the Yuin, also called the Left Market, cleared over the past few days of stalls and temporary dwellings. Troublemakers, rabble-rousers, and beggars were rounded up and dragged away too, as often happened before a festival. Flakes of dyed paper whirled and scattered; the crowd swirled and pressed against the irregular sides of the stone-floored market-bowl. Heaving forward, foot by foot, the platform passed through another lane, this one between two great theater complexes with their distinctive stacked-angle roofs, their front steps painted scarlet in honor of a royal wedding and acrobats upon them whirling, dancing, doing tricks to delight both princess and crowd. Several corners through the city had held tableaux, or story-sellers with their wooden plaques clacking through painted renditions of ancient scenes, all of marriages. The Moon Maiden and the Warrior, Ha-Wone and the Poet, the Two Wives of Hau Dabeo, and more.

The passage was not over yet. The Yuin was merely a prelude, the smaller market where you could buy the not-quite-legal. The Yaol, or Great Market, had been cleared too, and across its pitiless, burning stone expanse shod hooves clattered, the wheels made heavy noises, and the haulers groaned, their shoes slipping, woven fiber soles walked almost through.

Red and gold, leather creaking and mail jingling, the city garrison spread out, pushing the mass of onlookers back, back. Pikes appeared, the horse of the palace guard in their golden ceremonial finery spokes of a crimson wheel. City and palace, both sending their personal armies to bring one small woman to the gutting-block.

Mahara swayed again, and Yala massaged her princess's trembling thighs, coaxing the muscles to stay to their task.

"Just a little longer," she soothed, though she did not know how much more either of them could endure of this din.

More noise. More golden riders, approaching from the north where a white bulk with red roof-tiles could be seen—the palace, the seat of Tamuron the cursed. Gold-clad riders swept across the stone plain, red plumes waving atop their helmets. Quick hands, belonging to the sword- and pikemen who had marched with their shoulders to the platform's wheels, loosed satin cords. Draperies fluttered, and a bloody shade descended under the canopy as cunningly designed fabric walls were pulled taut. *Now* they had some privacy.

Mahara sagged into Yala's hands; tassels swayed from the crimson horns upon her bowed head. Yala held the wastewater pot, set it aside when the trickle stopped, and chafed at Mahara's legs while hooves thundered outside. Next would come the bridal sedan, and for the rest of the journey Mahara could recline in something close to comfort.

She laved Mahara's hands with cool, crushflower-scented water, pressed a dipped, wrung cloth to the princess's nape. Without the slight forward motion, it was already stuffy inside the tent. Yala's quick fingers neatened the two gold-caged horns of hair, seated the princess's ear-drops hung from thin crimson satin ribbons more firmly, arranged the heavy golden collar studded with gems, helped her princess into the soft embroidered slippers a noble bride should wear. Mahara submitted, her eyes half-closed, her shoulders sagging.

"I will be just outside the palanquin," Yala repeated. "Every step. The Emperor and the Fourth Prince will peer in to see that none else have taken your place. Then the bearers shall take you to the bridal chambers. There will be a proper bath, and dinner." The Fourth Prince Makar had patiently explained it all while Mahara clutched at Yala's hand, whitened knuckles hidden under their paired sleeves. Yala had made him repeat it once, until she was certain of every step and what ceremony was required.

She did not wish her princess to stumble.

"Do not leave me." Mahara's knees buckled. Yala caught her, and both women almost slid to the platform's indifferently cushioned floor. "Do not leave me, Yala."

"You know I will not." Her cheek against her princess's brocaded shoulder, Yala closed her own eyes for a moment. Gold thread scratched at her jaw. She was shorter than her princess, and wished she were not. It would make comfort easier. "The Crown Prince is kind, they say. He will know you are frightened, and will be gentle."

Mahara's reply was a cricket's whisper. "Yala?"

"My princess." Booted feet, outside, the reading of a proclamation. She caught words in Zhaon—the Emperor's name, the Crown Prince's, a list of titles. It would take some little while for the ceremony to reach its agonizing end. "Let us move your legs, my lady. They may stiffen in the palanquin."

"You have your *yue*?" Mahara whispered.

"Of course. You are safe, my princess." Yala's heart thumped along like the hoofbeats outside. The crowd had hushed to listen. Speakers at every corner of the market repeated the words, echoing like ghouls in the mountain passes leading the unwary astray. Mahara's trembling threatened to infect her. This was *not* like a Khir wedding, she decided. Where did they *find* all the flowers they had thrown? What was Zhaon, that it could waste so flagrantly? The magnificence made her uneasy. It was said in Khir that the Zhaon were soft, that they did not have bones-of-the-mountain or the fierceness needed to sustain in adversity.

And yet they had won, and wrested Yala's princess from her home.

"You are safe," she repeated, briskly, as if they were young again in Khir's Great Keep and Mahara awakening from an ill-dreaming. "I will be right beside the palanquin."

The proclamation ended. A massive cheer rose outside, shaking the platform, rippling the cloth screens and curtains. Mahara let out a small, wounded cry, prey caught in the hunter's net, and it took all Yala's waning self-control to remain calm, leading her for a few steps back and forth along the uneven floor so the princess's legs would not fail her. Over and over, she repeated her assurances, and when the three taps of a staff upon the vermilion-painted steps at the head of the wheeled platform resounded, it was time for her to look out between scarlet edges and make certain the temporary passage to the sedan was firmly screened, so no evil gaze or impropriety could descend upon her princess before she was closed in the conveyance.

"It will all be well," she said, softly, as she took Mahara's arm again. Inside her, though, a different drumbeat sounded.

Please, my ancestors, hear me. Please do not let it be a lie.

Even a kind one.

Bears Watching

A toast! A toast to the bridegroom!" Sixth Prince Jin, just past the gifting of his first suit of true armor, raised his lacquered cup with a grin as bright as the golden embroidery upon his belt. His cheeks were still soft and his dark eyes were merry, his topknot held with a short wooden tube and a silver pin.

This banquet-room was familiar, a small private enclosure in the Kaeje's bulk, walled in dark wood and bearing a long, scratched, scarred heavy table suitable for all manner of feast and merriment. The princes had often gathered here, and Zakkar Kai as well once he was old enough. Mrong Banh the astrologer had gone to fetch a jar of what he promised was an exquisite vintage saved for such a wedding, and without that moderating influence the conversation had grown... loud, lapping against wooden screens and pounding at the long, low, heaped-high table.

Second Prince Kurin, grinning foxlike in a fulvous tunic embroidered with long-necked fishbirds, poured another round for every brother. "So, have you seen her? Did you get a peek?"

Takyeo, at the head of the table, was trying to avoid overdrinking, but the brothers kept filling his glass. Candle and lamplight painted his triangular face, and he had laid aside the bridegroom's tufted headpiece for dinner. "Of course not." He reached for his eating-sticks, but Fifth Prince Sensheo with his archer's thumb-ring of heavy, finely carved horn snatched them away to hold hostage. "Makar has, though."

"If you stuff yourself, you will not be able to perform. Drink again." Sensheo's high, whistling laugh punctuated another general shout of merriment. "Makar? Tell us of this Khir girl."

"*Ai*, I cannot say." Makar, relieved of escort duty, scratched at his cheek. He had lost some little weight, organizing the entry of the foreign princess and fending off requests from the aristocratic families along their route. Tonight, he seemed more than ready to drink and forget.

Zakkar Kai, seated upon the least elaborate cushion he could find at the Crown Prince's right hand, downed a cupful of sohju all at once, a soldier's habit. "Come now, Makar. You are the scholar, you must have observed." Directing the conversation into safer channels fell to him, since Mrong Banh was temporarily absent.

Kai did not quite feel up to the task, especially with the amount of sohju flowing. The fare was spicy, to provide the marriage with passion, and it brought about a powerful thirst. Kurin was largely unpredictable and Sensheo wished to be, but you could always count upon the latter to poke and prod.

"Is she ugly?" Kurin leaned aside, his elbow upon a padded bolster. He had wanted the shutters opened to catch the night breeze, he said. Takyeo demurred, not wishing to be on display again so soon. "You can tell us."

"I was too busy arranging inns and processions to notice." Makar made a face, his proud nose wrinkling. Washing away the road-dust had done wonders for his mood, but he was not inclined to give Kurin any leeway. "Ask Father, he saw her more recently."

"You're no fun." Jin lifted his cup again, flushing with excitement and sohju. A fading scrape across his right-hand knuckles was evidence of training, the one thing he seemed to take seriously. "Another toast!"

"Careful." Kai handed the Crown Prince a fresh pair of eating-sticks. "You will fall asleep in the soup, Jin, and wake to find your topknot gone."

"You wouldn't dare!" Jin's eyes sparkled. He had been happy from the cradle, they said, always with a smile and a new plan for mischief. If his elder sister had bothered, she could have had him for an ally instead of an uneasy tribute-payer. Sabwone had little time for a younger brother, unless it was to torment him.

"*I* might not." Kai's grin was unforced, for once, and his cheeks almost hurt with the force of it. "But Sensheo would."

One of the partitions slid open; a shadow fell over the threshold. The Crown Prince lurched to rise, which meant the rest of them had to, and Takyeo greeted Third Prince Takshin with expansively widened, crimson-clad arms. "Taktak! Come in, come in! Now we're complete. You must drink quickly, we're ahead of you."

"Always late." Takshin's scarred lip twisted, and his gaze met Zakkar Kai's for a brief moment. He nodded, and Kai moved to make room between his left and Sensheo, whose full lips tightened with distaste. "My apologies."

"Takshin?" Jin blinked, blearily, and brightened. "But I thought he was in Shan."

"I came back for the wedding." Takshin, in the severe dark costume of a Shan noble, settled himself. "You must have heard as much."

The Crown Prince poured another round. "Now, you must all drink, but not me." Takyeo's shoulders had eased. "If I have much more, I will spend the wedding night sleeping."

"It might be a good thing, if she's ugly." Kurin laughed, a high sharp sound, and picked at a plate of fried haokta. "A blind-eyed Khir witch."

"Elder brother." Makar shook his head, reaching with elegant, sharpened sticks for a slice of pickled taur root. "Your tongue is addled."

Sensheo had decided to be difficult as well. "Don't they say sohju breeds truth?"

"They also say pissing into the rain makes you doubly wet." Zakkar Kai downed his ration, again. At least soldiers did not bait each other this sharply. "Takshin. I've longed to see you. What news from the Land of the Sun?"

"Nothing of interest." Takshin settled himself cross-legged, surveyed the food, and accepted a boneware cup full of colorless liquor. "To you, Eldest Brother. May your marriage be peaceful." Which meant they all had to drink, and for a moment, blessed silence filled the room.

"Is it true she brought but a single lady?" Sensheo's tongue clicked, an imitation of Mrong Banh's favorite thinking-noise. If there was any weakness to be found, he would pick until a fingernail lifted its edge. If it took finding fault with a new bride as a mother-in-law should, he was more than willing. "And no dowry?"

"Khir itself is her dowry," Makar said, quietly, but the words held an edge. He had finally lost patience; no doubt the weariness of travel had not been washed away as easily as the dust. "Must you be uncivilized upon even this occasion?"

"Doesn't their king have a bastard son?" Kurin's cup spun, empty, upon the tabletop, a traditional feat performed for luck. But his sleepy gaze was leveled at Zakkar Kai, who met it calmly enough, a faint smile bringing up the corners of the general's lips. The Fifth Prince had long been fond of holding Kai's parentage against him. No doubt many of the others did too, but Sensheo was usually the only one ill-mannered enough to persist in making it plain.

"Politics at a wedding." Takshin lifted his cup to the Crown Prince again, then bolted it much as Zakkar Kai did his. "How ill-bred, elder brother."

"I thought weddings were nothing *but* politics." But Jin's good humor had fled, and he glanced worriedly from Kurin to Kai, blinking furiously through a screen of sohju, unsure of quite what had happened but aware the mood had changed.

"Can we not have one single dinner without—" Makar began, but another partition slid open and Mrong Banh stepped through, holding a round earthenware jug with a sealed top. He huffed, panting, his small potbelly fighting with the jug for room, and set it upon the table with a clatter, spilling a dish of inksoup. Kurin and Jin both lunged away from the mess, Kurin with a small sound of disgust and Jin with a delighted laugh.

"There!" the astrologer cried. "I've kept it for fourteen years, my princes, and now you shall drink with me."

Kai glanced at Takshin, whose faint, ironclad smile hadn't changed. He was suddenly sure the Third Prince had been aware of Banh's presence behind the partition, waiting for a moment to step in, as well.

He bears watching, Zakkar Kai thought as he often did, and as if Garan Takshin had heard the thought, he met Kai's gaze and raised his cup in a small, mocking salute.

Braided Reeds

The entire compound was full of celebration. Here in the smaller Hanyeo—the Queens' Palaces, attached to the Emperor's Kaeje—it was a quiet, cultured bustle. The Second Queen did not care for loud noises or for display, but the red lanterns were hung upon her steps and bridal presents had been delivered punctually to the chambers in the Jonwa Palace the new princess would take possession of tomorrow. The traditional observances had all been exactly fulfilled, but not a single breath had been taken over their borders. None could accuse her of unfulfilled duties *or* of attempting to overplay the First Queen's presents.

The Hanyeo sheltered behind the chambers of state and the original, now extensively remodeled keep of Zhaon-An, which had given the city its name and now held the Emperor's quarters, the state rooms, and various accretions of etiquette and luxury. As wives sheltered behind their husband, the two halves of the Hanyeo sat side by side, divided only by a single stone wall—and a great deal of icy politeness upon either side.

Second Queen Haesara, a little taller than most of her ladies-in-waiting, dressed simply in burnt orange and with her hair arranged in the high asymmetric style of Hanweo, glanced at her guest. "It is a comfort to me," she murmured, "that you would visit."

First Concubine Luswone, the angular but full-lipped beauty of Daebo, inclined her upper half, gracefully accepting the honor of being thus addressed. "It is ever my intention to ease Your Highness." A small gift—a half-pound of jaewrai,[20] sealed with red wax—lay between them upon the highly carved table, and behind a curtain, one of Haesara's ladies plucked at a sathron. Whoever it was had talent but needed practice, and perhaps it was meant as a mild insult. Or perhaps tonight, Haesara wished for rustic accompaniment instead of artistry.

Tea was brought in exquisite, pale porcelain. Queen and concubine waited for the servants to withdraw from earshot, and gazed through the carved screen at a small pond clustered with broad green leaves. Later in the season, white cupflowers would float upon the broad green pads, pale dreams behind the regimented, geometric wooden slats.

Finally, Haesara touched her white porcelain cup. It was a tiny, refined curve, restrained as everything else she allowed. "I suppose *she* paid you a visit, as well."

The First Concubine's mouth, painted a pale peach, pursed. Her dress was the yellow of a snow-choked sun, and crystalline glitters hung from her hairpins. She allowed very little to crease her face, and patted nia oil into her cheeks nightly to refine already flawless skin. Despite this, fine dry lines had begun at the corners of her eyes and lips. "A visit such as that changes the color of the day," Luswone murmured.

Haesara nodded. The sathron continued, plaintive notes of a Hanweo lament matching the calm of evening, a piquant counterpoint to the sounds of joy and merrymaking elsewhere. Soon there would be fireflowers, great transient blossoms in the sky over the entire palace. It would stink of black powder and metallic dyes until the wind swept from some quarter to cleanse, perhaps carrying rain upon its back. "Was it threats, or blandishment, this time?"

"Some of both." Luswone took a mannerly sip, her smallest finger lifted. The sheath over its long, pointed nail glimmered, very

20. A mixture of spices, herbs, and resins to keep moths and time from stored cloth.

fine silverwork. "She congratulated the Sixth Prince upon his expected generalship."

"And she complimented the Fourth Prince upon his scholarship just yesterday." Haesara turned her attention to her own plump wrist, where a single piece of greenstone had been carved into a bangle, resting delicately against smooth copperbrown skin. "At least we know her targets."

"For now." The concubine gazed into her cup. "My daughter is of age. I wonder if she will be sent to a faraway land."

"It would grieve the Emperor to lose her grace at court." Meaning Haesara had heard nothing of plans to marry First Princess Sabwone off.

At least, not yet. There were rumors, certainly, especially since so many couriers were sent to Shan nowadays. Of course, that could only be diplomacy now that the Mad Queen was safely with her ancestors and Suon Kiron had not succumbed to any stray blade or poison-drop administered by an ambitious noble. The rumors also held that Garan Takshin had something to do with the heir to Shan's survival, which must gall the First Queen to no end.

Haesara found thought of that galling brought a smile to her lips, but dispelled it, since Luswone obviously had a purpose.

Luswone's filigree ear-drops swung, gently, as she shook her head the tiniest fraction. "Is it selfish of me, to wish her kept close?"

"If it is, I am likewise selfish." Haesara considered the concubine, who still stared into her cup. It was unlike Luswone to be so plain with her meanings. The Daebo were eel-slippery; that should have been their house crest instead of the prong-horned, delicate kua-hoof. "I sense you are troubled, Concubine Luswone." There, a politeness in return for the plainness. It was just as well Queen Gamwone was... as she was, or the concubines would have been dangers instead of allies.

Well, the Second Concubine was useless, a suffering mouse in her bower with that parvenu as her adopted son. Still, Zakkar Kai could be useful, with the right inducement. A general, especially a lucky and victorious one, had a latitude of action a queen did not, and even more than a blood-prince.

It was fortunate that Kai seemed one of the few whose loyalty was not at auction. Or perhaps no bidder had been found willing to go high enough.

Luswone had even less latitude than a queen. Her family was aristocratic, even if her position left much to be desired. She had borne two sons and a daughter—not to mention plenty of ill treatment from the First Queen—with grace.

"Our husband, may the stars shine upon him, is not a young man." Luswone's voice dropped even further, allowing Haesara to pretend to ignore the words, if she chose.

The queen studied the concubine's profile, then turned her attention to the screen and its green backdrop. A warlord had married a rich merchant's daughter and used that wealth in his plan to unify Zhaon, and now he was Emperor. He was blessed with many sons, meaning an heir, any heir, was assured.

But no ruler could allow rivals once he ascended a throne. Such ascensions were... delicate, and largely fatal to non-victorious claimants. First Concubine Luswone was right to worry, and her unease matched the Second Queen's own.

"Braided reeds are stronger than solitary ones," Haesara murmured, finally. It was past time for more than a token alliance with the Daebo concubine. "We are mothers, First Concubine. It is our duty to protect our children, and give them good examples."

Luswone nodded. Her relief was palpable, though her face did not change. Instead, her shoulders curved slightly inward, and the sheath protecting her highborn nail tapped the side of her cup, once, a tiny sound lost under the sathron's plucking.

"Your Highness is wise," she said, and, the most serious business concluded, the two women settled themselves to drinking tea and exchanging other, less interesting gossip.

To Want to Live

Mahara's hair, sleek and freshened with sweet oil, was as luxurious as ever. Yala drew the ivory comb down, her thumb rubbing a carved fish-back. She hummed as she worked, a familiar lullaby from Khir. *Hush now, my little one, ugly in your crib, hush now, my little one, a goblin's face, a goblin's face.* One must always dissemble, especially over a cradle. You could not tell when an evil spirit was listening, jealous and ready to strike. To rob a parent of a child, or substitute a dutiful son for a wayward daughter.

Dissembling became a habit. What was her father doing at this moment? It was not a table-day at Hai Komori, so he would be dining frugally and alone, without even a sathron to accompany him. Her father was of the opinion that music was for after a meal, to aid the digestions and to comfort the liver, that seat of all thought and strength.

Yala pushed the thought away, and it went quietly. Windowless, thick-walled, and hung with red, this room glowed with lantern-light. A thick-curtained bed of dark wood sat in its exact center, a small table with two golden cups and a glowing, polished white stone jar of thick sweet kouri[21] in the east quadrant to greet the marriage and the morning with honey. Braziers simmered, taking away evening chill, and Mahara's cheeks were wet. Her sleeping-robe was

21. A mixture of honey and thickened, very strong tea.

unfamiliar and heavily embroidered as well, and she had only picked at the bridal dinner despite the presence of Khir dishes—small birds in dulum sauce, spice-paste, puffs of zhu. Yala's own high-waisted Zhaon dress, the cuffs embroidered with pearls, was a gift from the Crown Prince as well.

The conquerors had dressed their sacrifices well, though the clothes did not fit as well as they could have.

Yala kept combing. There was a certain comfort in the small tasks of readying her princess for bed. When the Crown Prince arrived, Yala would have to leave the room and make her way through labyrinthine corridors, three gardens, and into the Crown Prince's Jonwa palace, where Mahara would be moved in the morning.

Assuming the wedding night went without incident. Or with only such incident as was expected and necessary.

Mahara sniffed, wiped at her cheeks with short, violent movements. Under the heavy sleeping-robe was a thin shift of fine linen, its throat and sleeves gathered close, no doubt to soak up a maiden's tears. "I am sorry, Yala."

"For what, my princess?" She examined the ends of the princess's hair minutely. It would be time for a trim soon, to halt the fraying of travel. Straight and lush, with a sheen of blue instead of the ruddier Zhaon coloring, the mass fell like water down Mahara's back. It was not enough that Mahara had been born royal, she was also beautiful, raised to be a demure wife to a noble Khir house needing defanging or an injection of dowry-gift to rescue its fortunes. Daughters were useless, but a royal daughter could bind a too-strong House to the Great Keep... or raise another House to use as a balance against restive, more fortunate others.

"I... my father would scold me." Mahara shuddered, heavy, stiff embroidery squeaking slightly. "I am weak."

Yala sought soothing words; they came only with difficulty. "Of all the words to describe you, my princess, that is not one I would choose." The Khir had no queens; a royal wife was merely a vessel. In Zhaon, it was perhaps different. Yala would have to discover *how* different, and quickly. Her princess's seclusion as a new wife was to be at least two full moons long, with only short ceremonial visits to break the tedium. Such a seclusion was meant to seal the wife to the husband's side, accustom her to the running of a household different from her own, and also to give her nothing to do but conceive an heir, that most important of duties.

"But I am *crying,*" Khir's only princess whispered, like a shameful secret.

"Well, yes." Yala nodded; though Mahara would not see her she would sense the motion. "You are far from home, and tears are natural on a wedding night. Even were we at home, it would be the same." Except at home, there would be the linked arms, singing, the drinking of makong;[22] the celebration would be reserved for the morning, when a wife was born afresh as salt and earth for her husband's home, an ornament until she was a son's mother.

Mahara absorbed this, still dashing the water from her soft face. "I cannot stop."

"It will halt on its own." What other comfort could she offer? "The Crown Prince is said to be kind, my lady. He will treasure you." *Or I will bury my* yue *in his guts.* She wondered if she truly had the courage to do it.

I suppose I will find out, if I must. Her back was cold with rainflesh, the prickling of unease.

"He is *Zhaon.*" Mahara almost spat the word, but the flare of ill feeling was quickly submerged in a new consideration. "What do they do, upon a wedding night?"

"The same thing Khir men do, perhaps?" There were the illustrations in books and scrolls, of course, and even a Khir noblewoman had seen horses copulating. It was unfamiliar, yes, but no mystery. "Except less well, and less bravely."

That earned a pale laugh. Mahara patted at her cheeks again, forlorn. "Yala, be serious."

"I am, my princess." Now was the time for logic to build a bulwark against uncertainty. "You are a guarantee of peace, and a future

---

22. A traditional drink of fermented milk laced with sohju.

son-mother. They *must* treat you well, or Khir will rise against them." *I wish I believed what I am saying.* Ever since she had known she was accompanying Mahara, belief was in short supply.

"But we are already beaten."

"Defeated, but not *beaten*. Besides, harm or insult done to you would cause even the kaburei to fight, my lady." A pretty sentiment, and one she hoped not to have to test the truth of. Yala set the comb aside and gathered the top third of Mahala's hair for the usual night-braid.

"Leave it down." Mahala's head dropped forward. "Listen."

Yala did, stilling as if her father spoke. "There is no sound," she murmured. It was not time yet. Only the candles spoke in soft whispers, and the brazier creaking out its warmth.

Mahara's breathing came in quiet shudders. "Do you have your *yue*?"

How often will you ask? Perhaps Yala's princess merely wished to see a piece of home. "Of course."

"Let me see it."

Yala rose from the edge of the bed, brushing aside a gossamer drapery on the inner curtain-rod. Her fingers found familiar, warm, cross-hatched metal, and she drew the sharp blade out carefully. This dress was not cut to hide the sheath, and if she sawed at the seams, it could prove embarrassing. "It is here. Does that ease you?"

Mahara slid from the bed, her bare knees meeting the floor of patterned wood with a sound Yala flinched at. She made haste to kneel as well, but the princess threw her arms around Yala's waist and hid her face in her lady-in-waiting's belly.

"Yala..." The word was muffled, and unbearably informal. "Kill me."

She held the *yue* safely away, tried to free herself so she could kneel as well. "What?"

"You must. Quickly." Mahara's face turned up to hers, tear-streaked and deathly pale. "I will die a maid of Khir."

If they come now, I must think quickly. Any faltering explanation she could give would not shield either of them from charges of lying in wait to assassinate a new husband. Yala swallowed, her throat dry as the High Waste buffering Khir from Ch'han's bulk past the protective teeth of the Northern Lid, where only snow and sand-demons roamed. "Is that truly what you wish?"

The candles hissed. The brazier ticked, and Mahara trembled against Yala's legs. "I... should I?"

Why do you ask me? Had Mahara brought her own *yue*, she could have opened her own jugular, instead of commanding another. Still, if the Great Rider Ashani Zlorih had forbidden his daughter her honorable blade... after a long day, the noise, the bustle, and the tension, Yala was not quite certain her head was up to the challenge of sorting such a delicate, thorny thought.

So she set her shoulders, as she had before Bai's tomb, and took a deep breath. "If you truly wish it, if you are *truly* certain, I will, and open my own throat as well." She even knew the correct sequence of moves to do so, including the turning of the wrist to drag the blade free of muscle and the half-step aside to avoid sticky, blinding bloodspray before lifting the flicked-clean metal to her own pulse. Mahara's body shook; Yala expected her to say *yes, do it now*, the verb cut short and imperative.

Then they would have to see if the courage of a daughter of Komor was equal to such a task.

"Then it will be war again, perhaps." Mahara's arms loosened. "Yala, is it cowardly to want to live?"

Relief, hot and acid, boiled in her stomach. "Never." The blade vanished into its secret home, and Yala helped her princess rise. The washbowl behind its partition in the westron quadrant of the room, fish-carved as well to signify abundance, was full. She brought back a small soaked square of cloth, wiped at Mahara's reddened cheeks. "We are not men in battle, my lady."

"It *feels* like a battle." Now Mahara had arrayed herself to receive a charge, her chin set and a familiar gleam in her pale eyes. She often looked thus, when there was a disagreeable event to attend in the Great Keep's high, drafty throne-room, or before a dinner with an ill-tempered father-god. "Do you think my father misses me?"

"I am sure he does. You are his delight." Yala could not tell if *this* was a lie, either, for Ashani Zlorih was given to banging upon the table when his children were at dinner, and shouting if one or two of them had not performed as expected. Her head throbbed, and her shoulders were taut as a fully strung bow. She longed to rest, and such longing was weakness while she could still serve her princess.

"Yala... if there comes a time when it is necessary, you will use your *yue*? Upon... upon me?"

Did all princesses ask their ladies this upon a wedding night? Yala could remember nothing in the Hundreds or other classics to approximate it. Of course, those were written by men, with notable exceptions. Five women had works among the Hundreds, a few flecks of pungent berryspice to give paste-thick arzai[23] some savor. You could not eat berryspice alone. "Mahara... "

"Promise me. *Promise* me."

"I promise," Yala soothed, taking Mahara's hands. They were cold, but so were her own, and her princess's trembling was her own as well. "But do not think upon that now."

For there was commotion in the hall. Gongs, small drums, pipes, footsteps, loud cries.

Mahara's husband was approaching.

---

23. Pounded, stiffened, very bland *rai*.

A Pleasant Occasion

In the recesses of Khir's Great Keep, a small round windowless room with a wide curved hearth held a similarly round table and chairs in the old style, their low arms mimicking saddle-horns. The timbered ceiling was low, age-blackened wood bare of any hangings just like the smooth-carved walls and flagstones with imperceptible seams. The art of making such seams had been lost at the end of the Second Dynasty along with much else, but such floors were a prized reminder of Khir's traditional intransigence.

Daoyan's back prickled afresh as he passed between bowing hall-guards in their dark, sober half-armor; both of them were too young to have been at Three Rivers. He wished he were wearing *his* armor instead of a dinner-robe of heavy komor-blue silk and palace slippers, both embroidered with interlocking long-necked characters, a nod to his mother's personal seal. He could, he supposed, wear the Narikh clan's standard, the graceful cloven-hoof huani sacred to the god of herding and pasturage and as such, not to be hunted. It would fill his mother's remaining kin with fury they dared not show, but the satisfaction of lighting such a fire was not worth the cost of fuel or the risk of burning his hand later.

Yala would have approved of his restraint, even if Baiyan would have considered it beneath a nobleman to even weigh the thought of such a display. But then, Bai was legitimate, and could afford a measure of pride.

Daoyan paused just inside the heavy door. The table was laid, dishes gleaming and the tea ready to be poured.

The royal father was already seated in what must be the habitual royal chair, close enough to the fire to warm not-quite-elderly bones. Ashani Zlorih was possessed of a lean, severe face, his pale eyes piercing and disdainful, the great greenstone Ashani seal-rings chased with silver upon both his first fingers, his marrow-brown robe subtly embroidered with the Great Calendar in slightly contrasting thread, perhaps the work of an absent royal daughter. Zlorih glanced at the door, his mouth pulled into that same disapproving curve it wore whenever child-Dao had glimpsed him from afar.

A Great Rider did not deign to recognize his byblows, though he had visited the sumptuously cold manor still bearing traces of Narikh Arasoe and her dishonor regularly. Each visit had been heralded by scrubbing and tension, Dao drilled endlessly on proper deportment and accomplishments in case the Great Rider decided during that particular visit to lower himself to speak to his bastard son.

This was the first time Dao had been alone in a room with the man who had made him with an honorless mother on a hot summer night. When he was younger, he had longed for such an eating companion. Now he paused just inside the door, studying the table, the chairs, the fireplace with a small pile of unlit wood.

"My son." Ashani Zlorih said, the word cut short and imperative. "Sit. Eat."

A pair of commands, not a greeting. Well, what else had he expected? Certainly nothing of warmth could come from this man, or the Great Keep itself. "Hail to the Great Rider of Khir," Daoyan intoned, bowing deep as a minor courtier. "You honor the humblest of thy servants."

A chill silence scented with damp stone and dulum filled the round room to the brim. There was a dish of small birds in the sweetish, pungent sauce, but the king's bowl was bare and empty. Was he was waiting for a filial son to perform the duty of scooping rai?

Perhaps the shades of Daoyan's elder half-brothers would rise to do so, as in the tale of Ha Buan the Eldest. Dao had a vague memory of a nurse reciting a version of it in rough peasant argot, each hard consonant a click and every sibilant half-swallowed as they did in the highlands away from Zhaon's mushmouth influence.

"Cease the mummery, my son." Zlorih's hands lay upon the table, nails blunt and rough as befitted a warrior. A braid-knotted bracelet of waxed red thread with a tiny greenstone charm peeked from under his left sleeve, perhaps a princess's gift. "I have longed to have you at this table; let us make the occasion a pleasant one."

Of course he wished it to be pleasant for his royal self. Many a powerful man liked to avoid uncomfortable truths or admitting his own cowardice. "Have you truly?" Daoyan straightened, and his tone held nothing but mild inquiry. How often had he dreamed of this—a dinner with a distant father, that all-important childhood god? Lying in his narrow, luxurious bed, staring at a cold stone ceiling, how often had a child hated the trickles of hot water from his own eyes?

Nightly tears had stopped only when Daoyan decided hate was better than longing, and indifference better than either.

Ashani Zlorih studied him. Daoyan tucked his hands into his sleeves and kept his slippers—and the feet inside them—stubbornly still.

"You have her eyes," the Great Rider said. "I've often thought so, over the years."

It was a wonder the Great Rider hadn't ordered them plucked from his byblow's head. Why had Daoyan even been left alive? "Do I?" Again, he spoke mildly, quietly, an impression of a tutor in his adolescence who had been fond of slipping an ink-stained hand into the lap of his almost-royal charge while he recited passages.

What was that man's name again? It bothered Daoyan that he could not recall. Instead, he thought of red blossoms, a burst skull, and a wide spreading splatter. A long open-air gallery with a stone bailey beneath, a weakened wooden railing... oh, it had been easy.

When there were none to defend a boy, he learned to defend himself. Now Narikh'a Daoyan would see if he had been a patient and enduring enough student.

"Will you sit? You must have questions, boy. I am ready for them." The bitterness did not leave the Great Rider's mouth, pulled tight against itself like thread in a loom. "Do you wish to know of your mother? The fever took her when you were but four winters old."

The honorless bitch who whelped me, you mean? Over and over, they had whispered it behind richly embroidered sleeves, tittered into amused ears at the theater while he often sat upon display with the Komori siblings, or even said within earshot at festivals and great dances where he was a half-welcome guest. Royal blood could not be openly sneered at, no matter the admixture, and some among the Second Families no doubt thought themselves clever, hedging their bets by showing a certain bland politeness to Zlorih's mistake.

"I have her *yue*," he said, finally. "It is in the finest box I could commission, and I look upon it frequently, Your Majesty."

Zlorih made an irritated movement. "Will you not call me *father*? I wish to hear a young voice do so again." If the allusion to Narikh Arasoe's honor made any impression upon him, it was impossible to discern.

"I was always told never to use that particular word." Daoyan put on his most winning smile, one practiced even while his teeth ground. "The lesson has become a habit, Your Majesty. Please forgive your servant."

"Stubborn, just like her." Zlorih showed his teeth. "And sharp, too. Eat or leave, Ashani Daoyan."

Daoyan chose his footing with care, crossing the room, and

settled upon the chair he was obviously expected to occupy. "I cannot refuse your invitation." Who in Khir could?

"You must be angry with me." Now it was his cursed father's turn for deceptive mildness.

"The truly filial does not allow anger to enter his heart." Daoyan's smile did not alter. His face had frozen much like the Thread Pass in winter, the sea beyond only a distant murmur.

"Pai Banh, the *Ninth Book of Sorrows*. I see your tutors were worth their pay." The Great Rider indicated the large covered rai-bowl, and as Daoyan lifted the lid he imagined nacre-poison nestling amid the piled grains, io-ia powder in the dulum sauce—what could be slipped into the pickled waxfruit? Perhaps anjba, donjba's toxic little sister, destroyer of the liver and stiffener of muscles.

The very idea soothed him and he piled high his father's bowl, taking only a moderate measure in his own. "My education was thorough, Your Majesty."

"I can imagine." Ashani Zlorih did his bastard son the great honor of carving strips of dulum-drenched meat and placing them in Daoyan's bowl with his own eating-sticks. "A Great Rider must be as stone, Daoyan. Never forget that."

"I listen and obey, Your Majesty." He inclined his upper half, a very proper almost-bow. His hands, occupied with eating-sticks and bowl, could not turn into fists. "Please, speak further, if you will."

The Great Rider of Khir preened under the flattery, but there was a troubling gleam in his pale gaze. He chose a thin slice of meat, chewed with relish, and bent a paternal smile upon some point above Daoyan's head. He had obviously decided to make do with the materials at hand, no matter how shoddy and second-rate he thought them.

Strange, Daoyan mused, as he set himself to be charming or at least inoffensive. He had thought a Great Rider would be different than a merchant or a petty noble, but they were all the same—merely men, grasping and vain.

He had often cursed his own birth, the necessity to pretend a lack of ambition, and the nobles of Khir at once. Perhaps, instead, he should be somewhat relieved his bastardy freed him from having to pretend gratefulness inside his own heart.

The thought amused him, and Daoyan ate with good appetite.

Above Pettiness

"Kurin cannot help himself, he was born feet-first." Fourth Prince Makar, bright-eyed despite the hour, looked up as burning flowers bloomed under the starry hood of night. He straightened his leaf-green robe and his wide, princely belt with quick motions. It was a family truism that he had always hated to be disarranged, even in his swaddling. "*You* should not encourage him."

Sensheo, rubbing meditatively at his horn thumb-ring, blinked owlish in the sudden glare. They had accompanied Takyeo to the wedding chamber; their ceremonial duties ended with that small journey. Jin and Kurin were gone, one to bed and the other to the sinks of the Theater District, Takshin had disappeared again. Zakkar Kai, of course, remained with Mrong Banh, the two of them drinking three more to celebrate, and three more again.

Fifth Prince Sensheo, Makar's younger birth-brother, had other things upon his mind, and a walk to clear the sohju fumes was first on the list. "It pleases me to hear him say what we all think." His topknot was loose, but he did not reach to straighten it. Why bother, when it was so dark?

"And what is this opinion you think the world shares?" As if Makar did not know. With his attire put to rights, the Fourth Prince clasped his hands behind his back and affected the walk of a much older man, unhurried, only slightly swaying from sohju. A line of maids from the palace baths—goldenrod tunics crossed at the waist, long yellow skirts, and the two simple braids marching over their heads—hurried, intent upon some task or another, in the opposite direction, the first and last holding swinging lanterns. They bowed, but neither man acknowledged such lowly creatures.

"Come now, brother dear." Sensheo indicated a familiar flight of stairs, one they had both climbed many times after a celebration. These were new, part of the remodeling, and did not have the softened edges of the smaller, ancient keep Zhaon-An was built around. Time ate all things, even in the blessed Land of the Five Winds. "A hurai, for that commonborn dog?"

"He rendered us great service at Three Rivers, and before." The Fourth Prince kept his pace ever more sedate, despite his longer stride. Their slippers shushed companionably, wooden soles padded with leather outside, silk inside. "Or have you forgotten?"

"You don't give a dog a golden collar for barking." It was a neat turn of phrase, Sensheo thought. Graceful, even. Stinging, and to the point.

He should write it down.

"What do you give a wolf?" Makar shook his head, his cheeks flushed. He was not truly irritated yet, but it was only a matter of time. "You've been attending Saba's little tea parties again, haven't you."

"And why not?" It was not difficult to affect the right note of injury. Sensheo let his step falter a bit. Really, the world was clearer with a little sohju in your belly, and things went easier when people thought you were a wastrel. They said things around drunkards they would never dare voice otherwise. "She's our sister."

"Indeed." Makar's face settled into blurred thoughtfulness. "And every time you and Sabwone play, someone ends up crying."

It wasn't *his* fault if nobody else could take a joke. And at least Makar wasn't making even veiled hints about...other suspicions. "We are not children anymore." Sensheo halted midway up the steps. There was a tiger carving at the top, one First Princess Sabwone had often garlanded with paper flowers and told stories of bringing to life. Baby Jin had ever been terrified of such tales, and *that* was good amusement each time.

"Then do not act as such, Sensheo." Makar's sigh was a direct imitation of Mrong Banh's, right down to the slight whistle at the end. Fireflowers exploded, a transitory gleam, making bright embroidery upon their belts sparkle. "You are a prince, not a courtier. You must be above pettiness."

"And you?" Sensheo put his hands behind his back. "You interfered with the First Queen's travel arrangements, didn't you? And sent one of her eunuchs to the border. How wise was *that*?"

"I did so upon Father's orders. Do you really think he doesn't notice those little games, just because he says nothing?" Makar shook his head. "You do not *think*, Sensheo. Mother worries for you."

"Maki-maki, Father's little lapcat." The pun upon his brother's name was old, and perhaps still had the power to sting.

Or not. Makar simply looked away, across the low stone balustrade and over a small, gemlike dry-garden with three rough stones set in raked sand surrounded by thorny succulents that had to be well-wrapped during winter. "Find a new insult, Younger Brother."

"Why would I need one?" It was distressing, Sensheo admitted, that not much had brought a reaction from his elder brother of late.

Makar *still* did not take offense. "You are drunk."

"Enough to be honest."

"Then I shall give your honesty the weight it merits." Makar's nose didn't wrinkle, but it was close. He stalked away, and Sensheo climbed the rest of the stairs after him, halting again at the tiger. A stone mouth, forever frozen in a scream, dust and other matter collecting between carved teeth. Someone should be commanded to scrub it. Possibly one of the eunuchs, maybe even Queen Gamwone's head physician, the one they called *the Skull. That* would enrage the First Queen, but she couldn't deign to notice if a prince planned the event properly.

Sensheo, his head full of delight at the prospect of arranging such a fine joke, laughed.

The Trouble to Learn

Mrong Banh could not drink as he used to, so Kai gave him to the care of a young golden-armored palace guard to be taken back to his blue-tiled tower full of strange instruments, shelves of scrolls and books, and models of the heavens. With that last duty fulfilled, there was only the walk to his own quarters to worry him, and Zakkar Kai set off through a collection of little-used halls and gardens, a circuitous route meant to avoid any further merriment.

There was much to think upon. The First Queen's attempted interference with the new Crown Princess's journey to the capital, the news from the great merchant city-state of Anwei of spring storms interfering with trade, a few petty intrigues among the eunuchs, and—last but *certainly* not least—how to approach the problem of the last assassin to penetrate the Palace.

It was the last he thought upon most. Mrong Banh had pointed out that so elder and obviously experienced an assassin would not be cheaply bought, and Kai had set his steward to a task or two related to that matter, having little time in the great bustle of wedding preparations and Council sessions.

Tamuron would chide him for not taking a rest where he found it as a soldier should. Or perhaps he would not, comforted by the fact that Kai's brain, ever active, would not stop pawing at certain things lightly, turning them over, shaking them like a child's gourd-toy, waiting to see what fell out.

Sometimes, that ceaseless scrabbling inside his skull was a curse. It took battle or hard drill to force it to slow, let alone halt. Even a courtesan's most intimate attentions did not interrupt it for long.

Even sohju did not, though it filled Kai's head with colorless fumes and he took care to step slowly. Overhead, great flowers of colored flame blossomed, fading at the moment of their birth. The noise was an irritation, especially to those with battle-nerves, so he stopped in a covered gallery, watching the flashes paint a dry-garden with an arched bridge over a river of smooth-polished stones. The moon was near full, quickening as the traditionalists hoped the new princess would soon swell, and between the flashes and the rabbit-face of the night's greatest lamp, shadows leapt and spun. It dizzied him, so he tipped his head back, refusing to bow to brief disorientation.

When it passed, he let his chin drop. For a moment, he thought the alcohol had unveiled ghosts. A woman stood upon the bridge, her own head tilted far back, watching the flame-blossoms. They were reaching their peak now, and would trail away into nothingness after the loudest battle-roar. In the slum quarters, the feasting, tiny burning flowers, and sparksticks would go until dawn.

Black hair, dressed very simply, and a hairpin thrust into the braids, glimmers of red dangling from its proud straightness at a very fetching angle. She rested a mannerly hand upon the bridge's painted-pale wooden rail, her cuffs sewn thickly with pearls. It was a beautiful dress, patterned with swallows stealing grain, other small pearls caught in embroidered beaks. That much he could see, and the arch of her throat as she stared into the moon's face. Another flame-flower bloomed with a thundercrack; she did not flinch.

Instead, she recited. "I cannot, I cannot." In the aftermath, while his dazzled eyes sought to recapture her, she spoke, in careful, heavily accented, very formal Zhaon. "I cannot return."

I know that song. Kai's feet moved without his conscious command, and he was faintly surprised the sohju did not tip him down the stairs and into a stand of wire-warped bonjai evergreens. His voice, sohju-loosened, slipped its bonds as well. "That is Zhe Har the Archer. The next line is the warrior's reply." Which escaped him for a moment, that next line, but he was certain he could hunt it down in a few moments.

Startled, the woman retreated a step, past the crown of the bridge. Pearls, dark hair, and swaying beads of her hairpiece, a pale gleam of eyes—for a moment, he was on the battlefield again, horseback Khir with their strange bleached gazes ranged in serried ranks.

They had refused to flee, those northern highborns. Foolish, and yet he had expected no less, poking and prodding at their borders, out-thinking them, delivering carefully calculated insults to drive them into pitched battle. Once committed, they rode to death or victory.

If a man was measured by his enemies, you could do worse than those proud northern riders.

That pale gaze was a dousing of cold trough-water, shocking a body back into sobriety. *Ah. I think I know who you are.* "The lady-in-waiting," he continued, moving forward step by slow step. "From Khir, yes?" His tongue, unshocked, would not quite obey him, slurring his consonants in Zhaon.

She halted again upon the downward slope, and something in her posture reminded him of weapons practice. A young soldier, but swathed in too much material. Another flash of burning powder and ground-fine dye overhead, showing a sharp-honed face, cat-like eyes blind with the color of Khir nobility, arched cheekbones. She was not pretty—there was no softness to her cheeks, her eyes were too wide and smudged with weariness besides. An inky tendril with a blue undertone had escaped her piled braids and brushed her cheek, evidence of exhaustion as well.

It had been a busy day for any Khir woman in the palace, no doubt.

"Who are you?" She used the most formal of intonations, and the most archaic of grammar. Her accent was not displeasing.

He could have laughed, challenged by this sentry. *And I thought I would be recognized by any in the palace. My pride takes a hit, albeit with weighted wood.* "Zakkar Kai, High General of Zhaon, greets you most humbly."

Her silence lengthened. Somewhere in the palace, a burst of cymbals, singing, and beaten drums reached a brief apogee. He waited for her name, but she did not give it. Instead, she bowed, a hurried but exquisite little movement. "I apologize for disturbing you, then." Her accent, strangely songlike, turned each consonant into the end of a verse. "Enjoy the celebration, *High General.*" She moved as if to turn, the pearl-heavy sleeves swaying under their own weight. She wore the brocade like a soldier in armor, barely noticing the weight.

Wait. "You speak Zhaon well."

"I took the trouble to learn." Again, archaic and formal, but well-accented.

She was *definitely* Khir, and could only be the princess's maid. The silk meant noble-born, so not a servant, and due a formality or two. "What is your name, lady?" The pearls meant she was well bred, at least.

"I am of no importance." Again, in curt, imperative book-Zhaon. She turned, her heavy skirt swaying, obviously meaning to retrace her steps. Like any well-born girl, fleeing a strange man in a foreign garden.

So a Khir could retreat, after all.

Kai's steady movement had brought him within striking distance, a warrior's reflex. He did not quite lunge, but his hand flashed out and caught her sleeve. "Wait." A thin tremor communicated itself through stiffened fabric. A doe of a girl, lost in this stone wilderness. "I won't hurt you," he found himself saying. "You *are* the Khir lady, are you not? The Princess's companion." In Khir, the word was different, the *iah* at the end too clipped for a mouth used to the music of Zhaon.

There was nobody else she could be, and he was soft-headed for even asking. Her response was what he could expect from any demure maiden.

In short, she retreated at high speed, and with surprising strength. "Let go." Material tore, pearls biting his palm. "Or I shall *make* you."

He tried again, but she was quick, pulling up her skirts and achieving shadowed stairs with deerlike speed. Kai was left in the garden with a head full of sohju, holding a scrap of embroidered silk with three pearls sewn securely to their prison. He lifted it as if to examine the stitching, found himself clasping it to his nose like Banh with his folded scraps when faced with something disgusting. A tang of female, a breath of ceduan used to keep moths from fabric—the robe had been a gift, then? No perfume—perhaps there had been no time to anoint herself, caring for her princess upon this auspicious day.

A shattering paroxysm of colored flame burst overhead. It occurred to him that she was *Khir*, and the Zhaon general of Three Rivers would be a hated name to her. Had it been fear, making her shake and retreat so? Disgust?

Both? Of course, being accosted in a strange garden at night would make any woman hesitant.

Kai tipped his head back, looked at the moon again. His own voice startled him once more. "*I cannot return*, the Moon Maiden cried." The next line arrived at last, a guest hurrying through the front door. "*Then I will come to you*, the warrior said."

Pleased at having remembered, he took his bearings again, and set out for his own quarters once more. It took him several steps before he realized he was looking about him, hoping to catch a glimpse of pearls, of dark hair, of embroidered swallows upon heavy silk.

The sohju had made him foolish. He firmed his expression and his step, and strode on.

A Coward After All

Her eyes were full, and Yala told herself it was only the increasing need for sleep wringing salt water free. After wrong turnings, stepping aside into shadow to avoid revelers or guards in their fantastical golden armor, blurred gardens lit by lurid explosions, and the moon's pitiless glare, she finally saw a familiar brightly painted wooden statue of a phoenix rising from a brass censer and behind it, the steps to the Crown Prince's residence, the back half of a palace they called Jonwa. The palace complex was as large as a town in itself, and she could have wandered until morning if not for the habit of watching landmarks while riding the hunt.

Did they hunt here? There was no *room*. Buildings or gardens everywhere, pressing in upon you. Even the mountains above the Great Keep were not this...confining.

She was not challenged at the door, both gold-dipped guards dozing, probably helped along by the thin, fiery, colorless sohju the entire palace was apparently swilling. Once she entered the long low main hall, though, she halted, somewhat at a loss. It was cool, and bare except for a massive stylized carving of a snow-pard lit by thick pillar-candles. The second floor looked down into this space through highly carved stone screens, and the floor was polished pieces of wood laid in godflower patterns, wheeling here and there, enough to make her dizzy.

"My lady?" A soft, hesitant Zhaon voice. "My lady Komori?"

It was a girl in Jonwa garb—white under-tunic, blue over-tunic, with the skirt of a lady's attendant instead of the trousers of the lower servants, not one of the mass of lower palace servants and attendants, with their practical stain-denying goldenrod cloth. Yala blinked at her, searching for a name to go with a halfway-familiar, round, kittenish face. The girl's hair, in two braids over her shoulders, was wrapped with leather upon each side—a kaburei, then.

"It's Anh." The girl spoke very slowly, as if she expected Yala not to understand. Still, she did not raise her voice overmuch as if volume would aid comprehension, as some of the Zhaon did. "Your close-servant, we met before the dinner. I was about to look for you at the Kaeje."

Kaeje. The largest palace, the Emperor's private dwelling; the queens' palaces were part of it, and called by a different name. The ceremony of Mahara's wedding had been planned in minute detail, except for what Yala was supposed to do after leaving her princess to her fate. She had not asked, either, all her concentration upon performing her duties to that point.

"*My* close-servant?" She repeated it slowly, in Zhaon. "Ah. I had not thought I was to be so blessed." Not here, at least. When she spent a week at the Great Keep at Mahara's frequent invitation, the princess's maidservants helped upon the rare occasion calling for much finery. Mahara preferred Yala's attentions to many of the servants', and she was content to have it so.

There was a pride in knowing her place, after all.

The Zhaon girl laughed, cupping her hand over her mouth as they did here to hide honest breath. "You speak Zhaon well, Lady Komori."

"Komor," Yala corrected. "*Komori* is my father, and my house. I am *Komor.*" Merely a woman, an afterthought. She took care to keep her tone from sharpness.

"Oh. Your pardon." She bent in a bow, and those wide dark eyes were full of mischief and awe in equal measure. "Is it done? Is the princess...forgive me, is..."

So someone else did not know quite what to do at this moment, either. It was obliquely comforting. "She is with her husband, in the Kaeje." Yala's shoulders ached as much as her head did. Her back was a bar of iron, and her legs felt heavy, full of wet dirt packed in bags to hold the side of a rai-patch against too much flooding. "May I see my quarters? The day has been long."

High General Zakkar Kai. A name to frighten children with, and she had not cut him with her *yue.* She had fled, a coward after all. She could have struck him down, perhaps, a vengeance in the conqueror's palace.

Except the consequences for Mahara might be...unpleasant. The ones for Yala herself did not bear thinking upon.

"Of course. Come with me." The girl, her red-black braids swinging, bowed her along. Anh was young but capable, and in no time Yala was whisked through a confusing tangle of passages and shown the door to the Crown Prince's quarters, the Crown Princess's antechambers, bowers, and bedroom, Yala's own room as chief lady to the princess with its communicating door meant to be left half-open, in case Mahara needed her at night. Anh's cubicle was across a short passage floored with rush mats, bare and spare, in the event of Yala needing *her* at night. Boxes within boxes; Yala had not needed a personal maid since she came of age and Dowager Eun became senior housekeeper instead of nurse to the Komor daughter.

Lord Komori had not thought his daughter would require one, or he simply had not thought of the detail. Yala had not minded much, except when dressing required another pair of hands.

In short order, the girl freed Yala's hair and slid the heavy overdress from her shoulders. The only difficulty was hiding her *yue* in its plain, supple sheath, but that was easily accomplished when Anh bustled into the chest-closet to bring out a sleeping-shift fragrant with ceduan and fresh air. "It is too big," she fussed. "You are small. Now, your robe…there. Have you eaten? Something small, before sleep? A thimbleful of sohju? No? I've warmed the bed, there now. In you go." Out were drawn the brazier-warmed, satin-soft stones, and Yala sank into unaccustomed softness. "Now, I am a light sleeper. All you must do is call for me. Do you have the night-terrors?"

"No." Was this what Mahara felt at night, bundled into warmth and well-aired bedding? "It smells good," Yala said, taking care with the formal inflection.

"No, no, my lady, do not use the *vu*. I am your maid." The girl pulled the covers up. "I had them wash the bedding twice, and once more for the princess, too. The Crown Prince ordered nothing was to be left undone to make her comfortable."

"His kindness is deep." Yala's tongue was thick, her eyelids heavy. She watched the girl pace the room, snuffing the lamps—so many of them, such luxury. No wonder Khir had been overwhelmed, there was nothing to match this wastefulness. A sea, of sand or water, could wear even the harshest stone bones to smoothness, and swallow them whole.

And yet, there were sharp things to be found under waves too, if the stories were true.

"Oh, yes. It is better than in the First Queen's palace, *shu*! Lady Kue is the housekeeper here, and she does not use the whip, only the sudo.[24] She will be glad of a mistress to care for; she thinks the Crown Prince has waited too long to marry, though the Emperor… I should not say such things."

A chatterbox was useful, if she did not chatter her mistress's secrets about as easily as others. "I shall tell no one." Yala smiled, sleepily. "Is that the proper inflection?"

"It is!" Anh's grin was wide, unfeigned, and cheersome. "You have studied well, my lady. Now sleep."

Finally, alone as she had never been while attending Mahara, Yala turned onto her side.

24. A thin, flexible housekeeper's cane.

Her princess was married to a Zhaon. And she had been within dancing distance of the terrible killer of Khir's sons. Had the general, perhaps, struck her own brother down?

Would he know if he had? A battlefield was a confusing place, the classics said. Songs spoke of the work of untangling the dead after an engagement, crows and human scavengers going from corpse to corpse, bodies locked together in death instead of that other, life-giving congress.

Yala's hand wormed beneath the square pillow, touching the comforting hilt of her *yue.* Small sleight of hand kept her secret safe, and she had a sharp spine to stick in a consuming throat, like the shanshells the Anwei ate in stews. The girls on the quays who shelled them had black-stained fingers from the creatures' bile, like noblewomen with suma or hakua paste, or a physician's tinctured nails.

How strange. I thought I would weep. Before her eyes could fill, sleep claimed her, and Komor Yala spent her first night at the palace of Zhaon-An without dreams.

A Sign of Delicacy

Chill spring dawn rose over the palace of unified Zhaon, greeted by a weeping woman deep in the Kaeje's ancient bulk.

Crown Prince Garan Takyeo, who had faced battle at his father Emperor's side and acquitted himself well, was somewhat at a loss sitting upon a tumbled bed with its curtains drawn half back. Not only that, he was hard put not to sigh with relief when the door slid aside and a half-familiar figure appeared. It was the Khir lady-in-waiting in a low-waisted dark blue dress, her hair braided and coiled high, a simple hairpin with a semicircle of dark shell accentuating the costume's severity. She folded her hands, pale gaze upon the floor, and made a bow in the Khir fashion.

Relieved, he patted his new wife's round, shaking shoulder. Her no-longer-innocent weight in his lap was pleasant, but his legs were starting to tingle with sewing-pins. "See? She is here, your Khir lady." He cast a despairing glance at the other woman, and was relieved when she turned, gesturing others in the door away and closing it firmly. "Do you speak any Zhaon? You do, I think?"

The princess in his lap shook and sobbed, her round cheeks slick and flushed. Her shift, bunched and knotted around her, had ridden up to show lightly muscled legs, a pair of dainty ankles, the soft down of a well-born girl upon calves and under-knee.

"I speak some little Zhaon, yes." Lady Komor turned from the door, regarding them both steadily. Her Zhaon was slow but accurate, and almost unbearably formal. "What is amiss?"

"I know not, she simply..." He kept patting the princess's shoulder, awkward small motions like brushing a tiny dog's fur. A lapful of crying Khir princess was not in any military manual he had studied, nor was there any breath of such a thing in the endless hours of weapons practice or tutoring that were a prince's duty. It had not even been part of his semiformal education in the Floating District's best houses. His own robe was not quite properly laced, but the Khir lady did not seem shocked or even overly concerned. Did her princess weep often? "I hope I did not hurt her. She awoke, and began to weep."

The princess stirred, babbling in Khir with its sharp consonants and rolling rhythm. All he knew of that strange tongue was military—commands for attack, for retreat, a few obscenities.

The lady-in-waiting nodded, made a soft reply, and brushed forward. Her sleeves were far longer than the usual court lady's, almost swallowing her hands, and her slippers were of the soft but point-toe Khir style, modeled upon a stirrup-boot. "Your Highness." Another bow when she reached the distance prescribed by etiquette. "She says you did not harm her, she simply wishes to be sure that is...all. What is required."

"Ah. Well. Yes." A man did not *blush*, Takyeo told himself. His sleep-robe was inadequate armor for this field. "It, uh, yes."

The Khir girl held her bow, a translator's listening upon her severe, high-cheekboned face. "She wishes to know that she is your wife, and you are not displeased."

"Oh. Of course I am not..." He tightened his arms, pulling the shivering, crying woman closer despite the tingling in his legs. "Oh, shhhh. No. I am not displeased at all. Please, tell her so."

More Khir, liquid volleys back and forth with high sharp peaks breaking at musical intervals. The sobbing eased, and after a little while, the Khir lady approached and untangled the princess from him, setting Mahara gently upon her soft bare feet. "She forgot the speaking of Zhaon, in her distress," she said. "Please forgive her, Crown Prince. It was a... trying journey, then everything happened so quickly."

"Of course." Relieved, he could now stretch and take himself to the water-closet. Sohju gave him a sour head, definitely not helped by the thick sweetness of traditional wedding-morning kouri, but Kai had surreptitiously drained Takyeo's cup more than once to help him keep his balance. No doubt the general was feeling worse for wear this morning, and would be at weapons practice in a fine temper.

Takyeo might have even joined him, if there were not so much else to do. At least he did not have to worry about the wedding gifts; that was women's work. Lady Kue would handle what his new wife could not, and he suspected the Khir lady-in-waiting would prove an asset there as well. Why had King Zlorih only sent the one with his precious daughter?

His father would know, but he also might ask, and Takyeo was no closer to a solution upon that front. The possibility of failing one of Garan Tamuron's small tests loomed large any time he was in his father's presence, and he had no desire to endure that prospect today.

More Khir, behind him. In women's throats, it was not quite a barbarous sound.

It had not been that bad at all. He had done what was necessary, without harming her. Or so he hoped. The houses in the Floating District gave a man all the education he needed, but she was not a courtesan or singer trained in such things. The Khir kept their women hobbled in kitchen and keep, unable even to own property as a respectable Zhaon lady did.

The water-closet was close and stuffy, and he stifled a burp laced with sohju fumes and kouri. It was hardly auspicious to begin their married life with tears, but on the other hand, it was traditional enough.

When he returned, several ili[25] lighter and much more sanguine,

---

25. A small measure of liquid, an ounce.

the Khir lady had the princess set mostly to rights, her cheeks dried and the gifted sleeping-robe neatly laced. Lady Komor spoke to her mistress in Zhaon now, slowly and carefully. "There are maids from the Jonwa; we will dress you. Then a palanquin will carry you to the Crown Prince's home. There are many gifts to witness, and this afternoon you will be shown the Great Hall and see the Emperor upon his throne. He will greet you, but you will not speak."

"Oh." Takyeo's new wife smiled tremulously. She was much prettier than her lady-in-waiting, soft-cheeked and perfectly sized, with gentle hands. The only marring was the strangeness of her pale Khir gaze, but that was a small thing indeed. The reddening of tender eyelids and her soft nose were also charming, and wholly his, now. "Forgive me, Crown Prince. I was...afraid."

He was a married man. Head of a real household, instead of a bachelor with a housekeeper. It was the last step into full adulthood, and he had not made any serious mistakes during the ceremonies. "Please, ease yourself." He took his new wife's delicate hands, cradling them like fledglings. The lady-in-waiting retreated discreetly, gliding softly to the door. "You may call me *husband*." He waited for her to repeat the word. "And when we are alone, it is Takyeo. I will call you *wife*, and Princess Mahara."

Now she had regained her child's command of Zhaon. "If my lord is Takyeo, I am simply Mahara." A shy retreat, ducking her head. Her hair, combed and tamed by the other lady's quick attentions, was a fall of ink, with a beautiful blue gleam instead of the ruddy under-glow of his country's women. "I shall remember to address you properly."

"I will help you with your Zhaon." It was far better than he'd hoped. His father would be pleased, too. The Khir were a strange, difficult foe, but this girl seemed...amiable, just like a well-bred, docile young woman of his own country. Some of the books said tears were natural the morning after a wedding. They were even a sign of delicacy and proper upbringing. He had been half afraid he would find a cold, ambitious creature, a princess raised for battle—but the Khir did not like their women so, did they? Even the wife of a Khir king was not addressed as a queen. "We shall see each other before the Emperor, later today. Will you have dinner with me?"

"Yes." She nodded, and Takyeo found himself smiling. His brothers would be full of ribaldry, and his father full of political mutterings now that this one piece of the puzzle had been fitted into its proper place. "It will honor-of-us be."

"My honor." He corrected the phrase in the proper inflection for a wife speaking to her husband, waited until she repeated it, and took his leave.

Each hurdle was higher than the last, and he often wondered what might happen if he ceased to jump, like a tired horse balking before hedge or abatis. The next series of tests were likely to be much fiercer—and much less pleasant—than this, but at least he had not done too badly.

Or so Garan Takyeo hoped.

Even Familiar Cloth

"Now I must give them a son." Sponge-bathed, the sheets examined, the evidence of consummation witnessed upon her person and wiped away, Mahara held her arms out for the under-dress. The Zhaon layers were more complex than Khir clothing, but the two Jonwa maids Yala had brought knew their business and went about it with soft efficiency. Anh did so as well, attending Yala, who day-dressed Mahara's hair herself, fingers moving with the ease of long habit. "Do you think I can?"

"After one night? You are ambitious." Yala tapped her tongue against her teeth as a braid threatened to slip. "A thin pin," she said, in Zhaon, and Anh handed her the one she wanted, nodding because Yala had used the correct, informal inflection, appropriate for servants.

"You are improper, Lady Komor." Mahara's somberness broke into a sunrise-smile, and one maid tapped her cheeks with a puff of zhu powder, a gentle, expert touch leaving a fine crushed coating the princess did not really need. They murmured to each other in Zhaon, and Yala, her ears sharpening, was reassured. They were discussing how dainty the princess was, how fine her skin, and how the Crown Prince seemed well pleased.

So she allowed herself a small smile. "Improper enough to be amusing, I hope." Incense perfume drifted through a crimson overdress, not as heavy as bridal wear but stiff with embroidered snowpards, giving the fabric a ghost of fragrance before it was clasped around Mahara's shoulders and waist. Yala shook her head, touching a maid's hand, her Zhaon coming softly, without too much hesitation. "Not so tight, she cannot breathe... yes, very good."

"They take other wives, do they not?" The princess reflected upon this, stepping into odd Zhaon shoes—too soft, their toes too broad for riding, their soles of thin leather-sleeved wood brushed with stiffening lacquer. "How terrible."

"They must know the Khir do not." Yala chose Mahara's favorite hairpin for this particular braid-style, thrust it home. Chose another, a heavy golden one, a morning-after gift the Crown Prince's housekeeper had presented very properly this morning, and sought a spot for it a little higher. She changed to Zhaon again, choosing the inflection with care. "You must practice your Zhaon," she said, finally. "I am certain these ladies will help, too."

A shocked silence stopped the busy, working hands. "Us?" Anh squeaked.

"I must learn more, too. And quickly," Yala continued. "I have not had much chance to practice my speaking, except with the Fourth Prince."

That broke their reticence. The shorter Jonwa maid, a broad-faced and moon-eyed peasant beauty, tightened a dress-lace. "You met him, my lady?"

"What is he like?" The other maid, a willowy creature with capable, roughened hands, covered her mouth with her palm as she smiled.

"His Khir is serviceable." Yala smiled in return. It would do no harm to let them gossip a bit upon this particular subject. "And he was very kind. Slowly, slowly. There. Now, let us step back." She surveyed Mahara, who, used to this process, submitted with a sigh of relief. Yala walked in a slow circle, tucking, adjusting, straightening, Anh handing her implements when she required them. The kaburei girl was well trained. "We are ready."

It was a bright, sunny spring morning, and Yala walked beside her princess's red-hung palanquin carried by four tall, well-fed kaburei in the Crown Prince's snow-pard livery. Over smooth-raked gravel or stone, hilly bridges in pleasure-gardens both dry and shimmering with water features, past a long portico where a dark, sober-clad line of court eunuchs, in their strange peaked hats, stood to witness the passage of the new Crown Princess. There was much to do—unpacking, listing the gifts so Mahara could write a response to each, learning the full rhythm and the requirements of etiquette while Mahara was in a new bride's traditional seclusion. A Zhaon princess, Yala suspected, did not have the same narrow concerns a Khir one would, and her conversation with the housekeeper Lady Kue this morning had centered upon what precisely was required today—and what was not required but advisable. The Crown Prince's mother was an ancestor now; one of Mahara's first acts should be an offering at the Jonwa's household shrine.

Yala's hem made a subtle sweet sound as she walked at a decorous palanquin-pace. Even familiar cloth sounded different here. She could not pretend she was in Khir, even if she closed her eyes.

Not to mention she might stumble among the enemy, and that could not be allowed.

The walk to the Jonwa was much shorter in daylight, and by the time they reached the Crown Prince's palace, guards and servants had been alerted to their arrival. The bearers set the palanquin carefully upon its resting-legs, and Yala glanced over those assembled upon the stairs before the huge, red-painted doors. There was Lady Kue, in a red-and-brown Shan-style wrapdress and trousers, her hair braided in two loops over her ears and her oval face set. She did not seem unkind, merely reserved, and so far, her explanation of the day's requirements had proved not only correct but also useful. Her questions were all of Mahara's habits and comforts, each query well chosen, bespeaking some forethought.

Hopeful, then, Yala helped her princess out of the palanquin, and, holding her arm, accompanied her into the house she was now mistress of.

Lost in Footwork

Training halted for no event, no matter how disturbed the rest of the palace's flow might be by a new addition to its breathing royalty. "You have not practiced." Zakkar Kai brought the weighted wooden blade down, smacking Second Prince Kurin's round shield with a little more force than necessary. Spring chill had burned away and the sunshine was already brutal in this stone-floored yard. Clatter of wood against wood, the thocks of arrows and cries of *hit* or *miss* bouncing from scrubbed white stone walls—the heat concentrated in spring and summer, just as the cold knifed through in winter. "Come now, Second Prince. You are a warrior, and a son of warriors."

Kurin, the lower part of his face obscured by an orange cloth mask, said nothing. His breath puffed the fabric, then turned it into a dish, and his eyes were narrower than usual, shining with well-banked disdain that probably treaded the edge of outright hatred.

Not that he would let it loose while the Emperor was alive. Leather creaked, both of them in half-armor. Enough to keep a stray shot from being *too* dangerous, but not enough to keep it from stinging.

Makar and Sensheo were at the archery range, good-naturedly keeping score. Or at least, Makar's efforts were good-natured. Sensheo hated to lose at anything, no matter how small. Jin, bundled into his first suit of armor but without his helmet, swept a foot in a semicircle and followed through with the weighted, blunted spear, moving with graceful economy. He took to every new weapon like it was a simple toy; he was one of the war-god's chosen, blessed with great natural talent. He *enjoyed* practice; therefore he danced with little holding back. Kai's only worry was how he would withstand the shock and stink of actual combat.

Or how he would command men, if not inspire them. The right hand and the left, for a general, and if Jin was sent to the borders he would need them both.

Kurin jabbed; Kai turned aside, barely needing the edge of his shield to deflect the artless blow. It would be so *easy*—step in, use his own shield to fling Kurin's wide, a shot to the ribs with lead-weighted wood. At full strength, such a strike could crush bone through half-armor, but he would not do so. He would only bruise ribs and pride.

Would he?

That was a dangerous thought, so he let the moment pass, shuffle-retreating a few paces. "Your heart does not seem in the work today, Rin." The childhood nickname, another jab to bruise a tender pride.

Kurin merely shook his head, the mask still swelling and collapsing with heaving breaths. Sweat greased his forehead, probably stinging his eyes. He darted forward again, and this time he was in earnest. Kai parried, all thought but the next strike and his feet leaving him. Halfway through the song of strike-and-response, his partner lost the thread again and it was not until Kai drove forward, Kurin's gaze flickering over his left shoulder, that he realized the Second Prince's fresh reluctance was due to guests instead of laziness.

As head general of Zhaon he should have administered a stinging lesson in attention, but there was no use. Kurin already disliked him from childhood; open warfare was not advisable. The apple of First Queen Gamwone's eye was a bitter enemy, even if he was intelligent enough to admit Kai was a good weapon for the house of Garan. Kai disengaged, moving out of range in case the Second Prince felt the need to regain a little lost honor, and waited to turn his back until the Second Prince stripped the mask away and slung his shield.

The visitors were august personages indeed. Crown Prince Takyeo, his long tunic a cheerful green with his device—a snowpard, granted to him after his first battle, in the cold throat of Jaion Pass—proudly worked upon the chest, stood attentively next to the Khir princess. Her dress was sunshine-yellow to match the third morning after marriage, her hair piled and braided expertly, and one of the household maids held a yellow sunbell for her. A round soft face, Khir eyes sharp by virtue of their color, and soft, pretty, folded hands completed the picture of a new wife still barred from much of the palace's endless socializing and etiquette. Takyeo was a lenient husband, bringing her into the daylight.

Kai freed his helmet with a practiced motion. The singing of bowstrings had stopped. Behind the princess, with a kaburei maid holding a much smaller sunbell to shield her, was the Khir lady-in-waiting. Her dress was Khir-fashion instead of Zhaon, sleeves swallowing her hands and skirt only short enough for point-toe slippers to peer at him, their tips worked with heavy flowerlike embroidery. Deep, throbbing blue, the color of an autumn evening before winter's breath leached color from land and sky both, suited her, and what was unpretty and sharp in the uncertain light of a night garden was now...something else. Her hairpin was odd, crimson thread wrapped about an irregular head and small red crystalline beads dangling from its jutting instead of matching her dress.

Jin, lost in his footwork, had not even noticed visitors. Makar and Sensheo ambled across the wide, stony space—princes did not *hurry*—while Kurin bowed correctly, a gleam entering his sleepy gaze. "Eldest Brother. And sister-in-law. Good health to you both."

"The Second Prince, Garan Kurin." Takyeo's rounded, triangular face, set in a pacific smile, brightened at the sight of Kai. "And General Zakkar Kai, recently given a prince's seal by our father the Emperor."

The Khir princess inclined in a bow calibrated exactly to greet those of slightly lower standing, and her lady did the same. Kai kept himself a few paces back, and his own bow was more respectful than Kurin's.

"Second Prince." The princess's Zhaon was childish, and very careful, and she kept her gaze low as a new wife's should be. "It is a pleasure to meet you. I am told you are fond of *gyurin*."

"Chess," the lady-in-waiting supplied, softly, and the princess repeated it, nodding thoughtfully.

"Yes, *chess*, that is the right word."

"I am." Kurin, while not preening, was perilously close. His long nose was all but twitching, and the gleam in his sleepy eyes was one Kai had seen before while the prince watched a small struggling thing speared upon a pin. "I hope we have occasion for a game or two, sister-in-law."

She raised a hand to her mouth, a coy gesture. "I am little good at such things. Perhaps we may recite riddles?" She smiled, very winningly, and Kurin thawed a bit.

But only a little. "Alas, I am dismal at riddles." Kurin tucked his mask in his belt, the weighted wooden sword held carefully at his side, as if it were sharp indeed. "You would have better luck with Prince Makar, whom you have met. And this is our brother, Fifth Prince Sensheo."

Etiquette took the conversation through niceties. It was agreed that Makar was a famous scholar, and Sensheo with his constant thumb-ring the best archer, and the Crown Prince a superlative tactician, of course. Kurin complimented all and turned any discussion of his own good qualities adroitly aside, playing at humility. Kai held his peace, while Jin, lost in his dream of attack and retreat, continued merrily unaware.

The lady-in-waiting—Komor Yala, an old, proud name if Kai remembered his Khir—was ever ready to supply the proper Zhaon word to her princess, and did not glance at him. Sensheo attempted to draw her out once or twice, but she effaced herself thoroughly instead of with Kurin's showiness. Which meant Kai could study her in the shade of her sunbell, watching her pale gaze move from one speaker to the next. Several times she glanced at Jin, tensing slightly when he executed a half-turn or otherwise swept his tasseled spear in the general direction of their small group.

Interesting. A soldier might stiffen that way too, raw with combat-nervousness. A woman, though...did she fear they were barbarians? Khir held all outside their borders to be less civilized, but did not every country?

"Perhaps we should move to the shade," Makar said, finally. "Prince Jin seems lost in his practice."

"Another prince?" Princess Mahara viewed him curiously from under long charcoal lashes, her hands folded suitably and her yellow sleeves showing their embroidery in a cascade of claws, bright gold-thread eyes, and spotted flanks.

"Sixth Prince Jin," the Crown Prince supplied. Marriage probably suited him; he was not one for the sinks of the Floating District like Kurin, and now he was a proper head of a household. Perhaps it would give him some relief from Tamuron's constant ox-driving. "He has just received his first set of armor."

"At least he will not be riding north," Kurin added. The obvious addition—*to Khir*—hung unspoken, and Jin's steady movements ceased. He ended with a *hua* that echoed from the stone walls, spear at the correct angle, his topknot loosened, a picture for a scroll-illustration.

An uncomfortable silence bloomed. Sensheo blinked, Makar's mouth tightened, and Takyeo's smile faltered.

"*War may be found in any direction, if a tyrant goes seeking.*" The lady-in-waiting's tone was soft, thoughtful, her Zhaon highly classical as her head turned aside, gazing at the shoulder-high stone wall holding the bowl of the drillyard contained. A simple but effective piece of work, that turning, obviously and pointedly not looking at the prince who had almost-insulted her country. "Or so wrote the sage Dao Lian of Nihua."

A Zhaon sage, at that. Kai's mouth threatened to drop open, and a thin thread of amusement lit in his chest.

Makar recovered his wits first, as usual. "Lady Yala is well acquainted with the Hundreds and other classics. We conversed upon them at length, and so made our journey to Zhaon-An much shorter." He bowed, and Kurin's cheeks suffused momentarily with color that was not, Kai thought, from sun-heat reflecting off stone.

"Jin!" Takyeo called, almost as soon as Makar had finished speaking. "Come, you are rude!" More introductions and tedious pleasantries would no doubt follow, while they all expired of the heat.

Lady Komor did not look at Kurin or pretend to study the walls now. Instead, her pale gaze was finally fixed, steadily, upon Zakkar Kai. He returned the favor as the conversation reached its protracted but inevitable end, and was reminded again of Three Rivers and the serried ranks of Khir nobles before they charged, the hush before death descended to reap the battlefield.

In his pocket, under the leather half-armor he wore for practice, a scrap of cloth with three pearls clinging to silken thread burned.

Much Else to Anticipate

The royal baths nestled against the northern wall of the palace complex were splendid, but the Crown Prince's palace had its own small, exquisite bathing-house, practically unused. The servants trekked to the Small Baths along the northwest wall; the eunuchs and other courtiers made use of bath-houses outside the palace proper. After dinner and readying Mahara for bed it was already dark, but Yala's skin crawled with the need for cleanliness.

Three copper tubs, each set in its own partitioned enclosure with wooden watersheds overhead, waited; Anh scattered dried jaelo blossom in the one Yala indicated and watched her mistress lower herself, slowly, into the silky embrace of hot water. *This* was a luxury Yala could accustom herself to, with no need for a chain of servants to bring a bath bucket by bucket. Instead, scalding water flowed through stone and metal pipes then down the wooden trough when the chain was pulled. She would discover later how it was heated. For now, it was enough that it was, and she could gaze upon a mosaic of butterflies over sun-eye flowers while she soaked.

Yala's hair, unbraided and hanging over the edge of the tub, shimmered in the candlelight. A thin white scar flushed along the outside of her left thigh; there were others on her upper arms. The *yue* did not forgive, but the kisses were butterfly-light; she was a good student. A few inked lines upon her forearms, gifts from the Komori hawks, did not flush.

"My lady." Anh peered at her mistress's arms, settling upon a padded stool with a wooden comb. Quick-fingered and merry, even at this hour, she gathered Yala's hair. "What are those?"

"Hawk-kisses," Yala murmured, the Zhaon words fitting strangely in her mouth. So much to absorb; her head was stuffed full as a festival platter or a Panchwan puppet. She closed her eyes, settling against the back of the tub, and sighed. *Kurin. Makar. Sensheo. Jin.* There was another prince, the Third, returned from Shan and reticent to show himself even to a new sister-in-law.

And the Head General, of course. Zakkar Kai.

Of greater concern were the court ladies. They would have alliances and antipathies of their own, and traditional visits to the two queens, both mothers-in-law now, would eat tomorrow whole. One concubine had retired into private life; she was held to be delicate. The other would be introduced after the fifth day, but her gifts had arrived promptly—exquisite black lacquered jars of cosmetics made by her own hands. That would deserve an appropriate response, but it must be weighed against the queens. The Second Queen's gift, yards of beautiful maroon silk and two fans of costly, beautiful hairpins, was traditional enough.

The First Queen's gift had not arrived. From the looks exchanged by some of the court ladies who met with Yala to prepare the ground for court life—Lady Gonwa and Lady Saru in particular—Yala had gathered the depth of the insult, and let the toes of her right foot drift to the surface of the water. "The Second and Third Princes are the First Queen's sons. Yes?"

"Yes." Anh worked at a small tangle, carefully holding the hair above so it would not tug. "And the Second Princess is her daughter."

Kurin, the Second Prince. *He* was the one who disdained Khir that afternoon. Perhaps her response had been unwise, but it was too late now, and in any case she had studied Zakkar Kai almost insolently after delivering it. It could be said she had addressed the general of Three Rivers instead of the Second Prince, but nobody present was likely to be fooled. Ah, well. "Then there is the Second Queen. Prince Makar and Prince Sensheo are hers, correct?"

"Yes." Anh found another small tangle and worked at it with kitten-tongue flicks.

Yala continued down the list. "The First Concubine." Luswone, what a pretty name, even to Khir ears. "The youngest prince, and another princess? Yes?" Once she met them all, she could begin discovering who was allied, who was not, and who was likely to be difficult. Mahara's own observations would have to be taken into account too. She would see things Yala would not, and together they would map the alliances and small hatreds of this court. It would take quite some time to decide just who Mahara should ally with, but it did not seem that the hills were entirely bare of game for *that* hunt.

It was, in short, just like daily life in Khir's Great Keep, women barred from politics playing petty games of insult and compliment upon each other. There were, however, troubling intimations that Zhaon women not only were allowed to hold property, but also exercised influence in the corridors of male power, something few Khir noblewomen would stoop to.

"Yes. First Princess Sabwone." Anh's steady combing paused for a moment. "She and Queen Gamwone are... very friendly."

I see. "The General Zakkar. He has been raised? He is now a prince?" Tall in utilitarian half-armor, quiet-eyed, his chin somewhat square and his eyebrows heavy, he had looked sardonically amused that morning, probably realizing what Yala was about. At least he knew who Zhe Har the Archer was, though the sohju had probably made him forget the night of the wedding and Yala's brief appearance.

Be careful, Khir mothers had taken to saying over the last seven years, *or Zakkar Kai will come... get... you.*

The entire palace had been head-sore the day after the wedding, except Crown Prince Takyeo. It showed a certain restraint that he had not drunk himself sotted before visiting Mahara. And so far he was proving to be thoughtful, polite, well mannered, and kind enough.

It was a relief. Husbands were unpredictable beasts at best, and a Khir wife was to give no cause for reproach. Here, it seemed, wives were allowed some little leeway, and Mahara was naturally obliging enough. Yala was cautiously hopeful that the peace would endure.

"Some call General Zakkar *the God of War.*" Anh's tone was hushed, respectful. "He is adopted by Concubine Kanbina, and so he receives a hurai. After…well."

"After Three Rivers." *Khir's defeat.* "It is no secret, Anh. You may speak upon it."

"My lady." The kaburei girl gathered a scant palmful of sweet oil, working it into the ends of Yala's hair. "We are all waiting, you see."

There did not seem much else to anticipate. Yala's toes dipped beneath the surface. "For?"

"Is the princess kind? She seems kind, and not likely to use the sudo." Anh paused, then said the rest in a rush. "The Khir are… forgive me, lady. They say the Khir are severe, and very quick to anger."

"Some are." Baiyan would have fixed Second Prince Kurin with an unsettling stare and that slow, paralyzing smile he used upon those who thought Hai Komori too threadbare to be cautious of. Yala's array of options, however, were severely constrained. "Some Zhaon must be as well."

"They…say the Khir are barbarians. Who drink from their enemies' skulls."

"Not since the Second Dynasty." Yala tried not to laugh. "A barbarian is a matter of speech," she added. Delicious, the heat soaking into every ache, loosening every muscle's bowstring. She stretched her left foot, next. Finding a safe place for *yue* practice was another puzzle, one she had little energy for at the moment. "So says *The Book of Insects.*"

"Written upon insects?" Anh sounded as if she did not credit the notion. "Are there such books?"

"That is merely its title, not its paper. It was written by a sage who..." Yala sighed. Lecturing was tiresome. "He was a Zhaon, in the Third Dynasty. What you call the Years of Ash."

"When the Tabrak first came from the westron desert past Shan, and many were the lamentations." Anh half-chanted the phrase. "Are all Khir women so learned?"

"If their noble fathers are wise." Her own father was probably in his study after dinner, with no one to chide him gently into retiring. He rose at or before dawn year-round, and he was not as young as he had been. There was nobody left in the household who could dare to even suggest he care for his health a little more. "Strength in knowledge and strength in hunting make strong sons."

"Ah. That makes some sense." Anh's quiet combing was thoughtful, now. "I hear a Khir man only takes one wife, no matter how rich he may be."

Of course. That is proper. "If he wishes another, the first must die." Yala examined her hands. If you stared long enough, any part of your body could be made alien. Strange. Foreign. Papery jaelo blossoms clung to her forearms, delicate star-shapes. "How many wives must a Zhaon man have?"

"As many as he can feed. Though concubines, 'tis said, eat less."

A small shiver of distaste worked through Yala's entire body. "Are you married, Anh?" It did not seem likely, though she was certainly old enough.

"No, I am a palace girl." She giggled, softly. "Besides, I am kaburei, I cannot marry without leave."

"Would you wish to?" It would fall to Yala to give leave, and also to find a small dowry for a close-servant who wished to marry. Imagine, a close-servant of her very own. The Zhaon were indeed luxurious.

"I do not know." The kaburei girl's tone was thoughtful. "Do you?"

"It seems a troublesome thing." *I doubt I will have a chance, before growing old.* Husbands were bad enough, holding a woman's honor and her chains at once, but to become a dowager auntie...well, that was not something to be desired, even if one could find a comfortable servitude. There was always the chance one's patron would die, consigning a woman to the care, however cold, of the closest male relative. "Two braids, for bed. Loose ones." There was more than enough to think upon before bed, and the heat filled her with lassitude. Sleep would order the world inside her, and she could make sense of the one without after traversing the night-realms.

Anh's bow, sensed instead of seen, was still respectful, and not without its own grace. "Yes, my lady."

Are Both Uses Possible

As usual, the Emperor of Zhaon was not abed though the duskwatch had been set, cried, and passed. Instead, he was at business in the Kaeje's great hall of state, seated upon cushions one broad, low step below the Great Throne's padded bench and sunburst-wall. Daily work took place here; the throne was for high affairs. Columns marching down either side of the hall, carved with dragon, phoenix, tiger, and bear, watched over the minutiae of rule with frozen grimaces. Candles and squarelamps burned since the mirrorlight had died, mellow golden light dripping over gilt fang and shining claw; Garan Tamuron's golden robe seemed heavier than usual tonight. At least, his shoulders bowed a weary fraction, and there was a troubling line between his fierce eyebrows.

Tamuron frowned at the stack of decrees, reports, and various other scrolls or bound items upon the low table filling the other half of the step, the corners of his eyes wrinkling. "If you are bringing me more paper, Banh, I might become displeased."

"May all Heaven save me from such an event." The brown-robed astrologer bowed, his smile wide and genuine, his hurriedly brushed civil-scholar hat and indifferently gathered topknot both slightly askew today. He was not out of breath from hurrying down the long hall, and had not forgotten the third of the bows required when one approached the throne. "Perhaps I should say the current hour is auspicious for rest, Your Majesty."

Kai, wishing he were in armor instead of a court robe, shifted his weight. "You never tell *me* that." Standing for discussion was as tiring as weapons practice, but Tamuron wanted his opinion upon this and that *and* the other, and would not let his favored general free.

Takyeo had already been granted leave to depart, hurrying away for a late dinner with quite an unwonted spring in his step. The marriage, it seemed, had a steady start.

"Because you are too stubborn to listen, Zakkar Kai." Banh folded his hands inside his sleeves. The pitting upon his cheeks from childhood disease looked more marked tonight, and there were shadows under his dark eyes. His beard, recently oiled and brushed flat, held a fleck or two of grey. "I shall hide the wedding horoscope, then, and present it some other time."

"*Ai*, one more scroll." But Tamuron looked pleased, and stroked his own small, neatly trimmed beard. His rings glittered and his cheeks were flushed, but his eyes were bright. A little too bright, almost feverish, and he rubbed at his ribs, callused fingers scratching heavy golden embroidery and grimacing. "Tell me, then. What do the stars say for Takyeo and my new daughter-in-law?"

Mrong Banh clicked his tongue once, a thoughtful sound. His gaze held a twinkle of merriment, and the deeper shine of true interest. People, according to Banh, were all very well, but he preferred to spend his time among the heavenly bodies. Who, after all, would not? "There is harmony in their many houses, Your Majesty, despite some small early obstacles."

"And children?" The Emperor accepted the offered scroll, unrolling it with a practiced motion. He gazed seriously upon arcane symbols in black, red, green, and yellow ink, lines drawn with a steady brush upon thick pressed rai-paper. "What of children?"

Of course an heir from Garan Takyeo and a Khir princess would be useful. It was foolish to put your hopes into a belly, or so the proverb ran, but an Emperor must plan for the best possible outcome as well as the worst *and* the likeliest. Besides, Tamuron was a man with a married son now, and it was only natural to inquire after grandchildren. They would, of course, be the ones tending to his own shrine.

But not yet. Not quite yet.

"None apparent yet." Mrong touched his beard, as if he could not quite believe he had grown one. "But there are signs of increase—the Evening Star is in the third house. It is auspicious."

"Very good, very good." The Emperor surveyed the markings critically, as if he too were an initiate of their secrets. "Your usual fine hand, Mrong Banh. This is a work of art." Dark eyes narrowed slightly, though his tone remained mild. "General, what do you think of the Khir princess?"

Kai glanced at the other end of the hall, where faint movement stirred among a scattering of eunuchs among laze-yawning courtiers. *Ah. That is why he wanted us both here.* "She was raised to be an ornament, not a queen."

"And brought only a single lady." Tamuron's brow wrinkled afresh. "We merely asked Ashani Zlorih to send a *small* retinue; I cannot quite decide if one lady is his insult or his wisdom."

"The Khir guards and other servants turned back at Gurai." Kai studied what he could see of the horoscope. It looked like all the others, an intaglio of mathematics and queer symbols. He denied the heat in his cheeks, sternly, and denied himself also the ease of shifting slightly to soothe his aching feet. "The Khir are thrifty, Your Majesty." *And bled past white.* The latter point would need no stating. Zlorih could very well have read the "small retinue" as an insult in and of itself, which may or may not have been Tamuron's purpose all along.

"And proud." Banh clicked his tongue. The small sound echoed against vermilion columns but would not reach the courtiers at the far end. "To send his daughter without guards, without..."

The Emperor did not speak.

It never did to hurry the astrologer. Mrong Banh chewed thoroughly, and if you bothered to wait for him to swallow, you would more often than not receive wisdom. He scratched under his civil-scholar hat with fingers that looked too blunt for the quality of his brushwork, pushing both hat and topknot further into disrepair. "If it *is* an insult, which is by no means certain, it is one best graciously ignored. Especially since the noble sons of Khir are smoke from the pyre."

Tamuron's topknot-cage, hammered gold, set perfectly and remaining at its post with the same obdurate patience as the man himself, gleamed in the lamplight. "Except the bastard."

"*Acknowledged* bastard," Kai murmured. He had not met that stripling upon the field, or if he had, he did not know it. Rumor and report were all they had on the new Ashani Daoyan. With Ashani Zlorih's two legitimate sons dead—and the second had died much harder than the first, the heavens themselves had witnessed as much—Khir must be restive indeed. The nobles, seeking to consolidate their own power, might have different ideas about Khir's Sixth Dynasty.

Such times were dangerous for any king. The only thing harsher than victory was defeat.

The Emperor rolled the scroll slowly and studied the tabletop before him, his gaze suggesting he was seeing instead the burdens of rule. "How dangerous is that one likely to be?" He did not glance at Kai, but the invisible shift of his attention was plain.

"I do not know." It was best to admit he had not reached any conclusions upon that matter, from either lack of information or conflicting reports. It was always best, when Tamuron looked for counsel, to avoid making any unguarded assumption. "Such an acknowledgment is at least as dangerous to Ashani as to any child from *this* marriage." A Zhaon prince with Ashani blood in his veins might not be able to make a conqueror's meal of that restive land, but the mere *presence* of such a prince—or princess—would be a valuable tool while keeping the dagger of Khir turned from Zhaon's lowland heart. Far Ch'han and Naihon, always hungry, would both like very much to hold Zhaon in chains; Khir would be useful to either giant's grasping claws.

"True." Tamuron shifted uneasily and rubbed at the embroidery over his ribs again. Sometimes, especially when the weather was bad or the battle particularly uncertain, he itched under his skin. *It is like ants*, he had remarked once. *I believe my liver sends them to warn me.*

At the far end of the hall, drowsy Goldens leaned upon their pikes, dark-clad eunuchs fanned themselves and whispered, courtiers dozed upon their richly decorated pillows. To leave before the Emperor had risen was not *quite* a crime, but certainly inadvisable. The more visible to the royal gaze, the closer the throne, the greater the honor—and the quieter but more poisonous the murmurs. Kai longed for the day to be over, and perhaps a cup of tea while he contemplated a garden. "Takshin tells me the Mad Queen's death is little grieved in Shan."

Little grieved was understatement. *Celebrated* was a more accurate term, but even the nobles of that land would realize that to admit their queen's insanity was a double-edged sword. It would be no large matter to unseat Suon Kiron, but the internecine rivalries among the surviving noble houses added to the commoners' restive mutterings that perhaps it was time for Heaven to raise a fresh crop of both nobles *and* royals made that the least appetizing option, no matter how ambitious the Houses might be.

If the new Shan king was moderately lucky and even halfway competent, he would survive. Takshin was not a bad ally for him, even with the Third Prince's temper.

"No doubt." Banh shook his head but did not click his tongue. He had not finished thinking upon Shan, that much was clear. "It is known their new king and Prince Takshin are battle-brothers. Such things are... important, to the Shan."

"Shield or blanket," Tamuron murmured, the old proverb about Shan's smothering or protective borders. Then, more loudly, "I will hear no more business today. Mrong Banh, the horoscope is a fine work, and I wish you to present and interpret it to Prince Takyeo and his new wife as soon as her seclusion permits."

"Your Highness." The astrologer accepted the re-rolled scroll and withdrew with a bow. He would no doubt return from that errand with a greater estimation of the Khir princess's likely value.

Kai, not yet dismissed, took the chance to finally shift his weight to relieve the ache of standing upon stone, that old soldier's trick. It felt good for a few moments, but weariness settled in his knees and thigh-muscles again. He watched Tamuron neaten the scrolls and ledgers upon the tabletop, and when the Emperor glanced up, it was to find his head general regarding him with a thoughtful expression.

"Well, speak." Tamuron's eyebrows drew together, but he did not seem irritated. He was sleeping less, of late, and that patting at his ribs was new. The threads of grey in his beard were not as pronounced as Mrong Banh's, but still visible.

Not until I have something of value to say. "Of what, my Emperor?" Kai made the words bland, unweighted.

"Khir is safe, for now. Shan?"

The Emperor had asked that *twice* now, and Kai had nothing but the same answer to give. "I believe Takshin has the matter well in hand." Parrying the question gave Takshin time to pay the required visit to his father on his own, if he would simply *do* it; Kai sensed that any serious pursuit would only turn the Third Prince into a more stubborn quarry and hence, a more difficult one.

Before Shan, Takshin had been a stubborn but not unreasonable boy. He had even taken the news of his adoption bravely, for Suon Kihar had been king and his queen merely eccentric. At the time, it had been a solid enough strategy. Hostages had been exchanged among Khir, Shan, and Zhaon since the Third Dynasty's troubled coalescence. Who could have guessed, one short year and a hunting accident later, that the Mad Queen—regnant for her son and sole heir—would prove such a deadly, efficient ruler for so long?

"Does he trust Kiron overmuch?" Tamuron's cheeks were faintly flushed tonight. It was not too warm in the hall; spring had only just begun. Still, his robes were heavy. Magnificence was expected of an emperor, but it was not often comfortable.

Why ask me whom he trusts? But Kai knew. He was generally held to be one of the few people who could stand Takshin's company for long, or who could make the Third Prince listen to reason. "I do not think the Third Prince trusts *anyone* overmuch, my lord."

"Then he has grown wise." Tamuron sighed. "Bring him to me tomorrow, Kai. He has been avoiding his duties."

Kai could have remarked he was a general, not a eunuch to run and fetch, but he did not. "Prince Makar may have better luck with that errand, my lord." Takyeo, of course, would have the best of all.

"Perhaps." Tamuron gave a single nod to whatever luck Makar would have. "He does seem to like Makar. But Takshin *respects* you, and I grow weary of his dodging."

If he respects me, it is only so far. Kai's weekly letters to Shan had gone unanswered more than once, and he did not know how many of Takshin's silences were forced upon him. A significant proportion could just be the Third Prince's ill-humor. "At what hour, then?"

"Whenever you may find him." The Emperor paused. Like Mrong Banh, his under-eyes were shadowed. He looked tired more often since the wedding. "I have formally ordered the line of succession."

What was an appropriate response? "Your Majesty is still vigorous."

Tamuron's faint smile was that of a warlord watching his enemy's battle preparations before his own army has been spotted. "Such platitudes have no meaning between us. The First Queen was against this marriage." Anything that put Kurin further down the succession line would gather no help from *that* quarter; it was only to be expected. But then Tamuron, as he hardly ever did, commented further upon Gamwone. "She is, no doubt, preparing to make my new daughter-in-law's life miserable."

Zakkar Kai thought of the Khir lady-in-waiting. Those pale eyes, and her soft, accented tones. Brave of her, or foolhardy, to use the word *tyrant* at Tamuron of Zhaon's court. "She will certainly try." And the Emperor had to turn a blind eye to much of it, especially lately, for the First Queen's clan was still rich, newly powerful, and it was furthermore nearing the beginning of their half-year of primacy at court.

"Do what you can, Kai." Tamuron sighed, a short, weary gust of breath. "Takyeo has need of both shield and sword."

Are both uses possible for one item? "Which do you think the Crown Princess will be?"

"An ornament, Kai. As she was raised." Tamuron moved to rise, and the eunuchs, ever alert, began to rustle. Courtiers and ministers elbowed each other, snapped shut their richly decorated fans, neatened their sleeves. "Let us hope she has the sense to remain so."

Both Due Respect

"My princess has a rather severe headache." Yala fought the urge to massage her own temples. The morning had been… unpleasant, at best, most of it spent in the Jonwa's largest sitting-room between the lateness of round, coldly beautiful Queen Gamwone, and angular, arresting Queen Haesara's chilly formality. Mahara, clasping a pad of silk soaked with fragrant crushflower to her head, was in no mood for company, and Yala could not blame her.

The two queens, the only formal guests allowed to break a new daughter-in-law's seclusion, had conversed at length upon trifles without bothering to acknowledge the princess beyond a single, formulaic greeting. Waiting with eyes downcast and hands folded as a good daughter-in-law should, she had borne it with grace, but when Queen Gamwone rose without even glancing at her and swept out, Mahara's shoulders had tightened. Yala, overlooked upon a small mushroom-shaped stool behind her princess, had composed several stinging lines of poetry inside her head while she listened to the two queens and tried to silently pour support into Mahara's back.

It was Queen Haesara, hair dressed high and held with chohan[26]-figured hairpins to match her robe, who rose more slowly and paused

26. A small bird, brightly colored, whose wings blur as they fly.

next to Mahara's low embroidered chair. *Welcome, to Zhaon-An, child*, she had murmured, her long, scented, delicate fingers brushing Mahara's shoulder like a jewelwing's weightless settling upon a yeoyan branch. *You brighten a room.* Here the Second Queen had paused, and her voice dropped even further. *Be cautious here.*

"It is a warm spring, especially for northerners." Lady Kue, the red-black braids over her ears smoothed and tame, glanced down the receiving-hall. The Shan wore their tunics fastened far to the right instead of down the center, and Lady Kue's sober dark dress-robes and tunics were all made thus. There was nothing lacking in the quality of the cloth, though, no matter how unassuming and bare of embroidery. "The First Queen's wedding gift has arrived."

"Oh?" Yala glanced at the small, exquisitely carved table Lady Kue indicated, part of the Jonwa's spare, deeply polished furnishings. At least the Crown Prince did not follow the Kaeje's overdone, florid luxury; the interiors of this smaller palace were quite restful.

Except for this. A pile of neatly folded, vile-orange cloth sat upon the table, glowering. A greasy sheen shouted its provenance—cheap slurry, the botched leavings of improperly spun and woven thread.

"Cotton." Lady Kue's mouth turned down slightly at the corners. "Orange cotton. The dye seems to be..." She paused, and did not quite look to Yala's face. "Unsteady."

Hakkan dye. The largest component of such cheap color was laborer's piss; the message could not be clearer.

Garan Tamuron is Emperor, it said, *but I am the First Queen, and you are nothing to me.*

Yala swallowed, hard. Silence stretched between her and the housekeeper, each waiting for what the other would say.

Finally, Lady Kue exhaled softly, as if to dispel her own ire. The housekeeper's hands, folded upon the broad ribbed housekeeper's belt at her midriff, had turned white at the knuckles, the ebon ring of her position upon the first left finger glittering balefully.

So this housekeeper feels keenly the insult to her master. "How thoughtful," Yala murmured, when she could speak through the hot rock lodged in her throat. She took care to make the Zhaon plain, neither admitting perfect equality nor denigrating. To look to a housekeeper for direction was not proper, but neither was refusing counsel from an expert of whatever rank. And Lady Kue would be an expert upon the palace's web of female alliances, if Yala could gain her trust or cooperation. Both would be best, but one or the other would do. "To show her opinion so plainly."

"Indeed." Lady Kue nodded. Did she look relieved Yala was not likely to scream with rage? A susurration down the hall—maids going back and forth, fetching, carrying, cleaning. And gossiping, no doubt. How many had seen this? Enforcing silence would be impossible; this would run through the palace like wildfire.

The reaction of the Khir princess's only lady-in-waiting would run alongside. A few prickles of sweat touched Yala's lower back, collected under her arms.

"Is this…traditional?" She strove to speak in a normal tone; touched the cloth with a fingertip. Yes, the dye was unsteady; that was the kindest way to put it. She rubbed the contamination against her thumb, failing to quell a moue of distaste. "I ask because I am imperfectly acquainted with the customs of Zhaon."

"It is an insult." Lady Kue was past hint or intimation, apparently. Her toes, side by side in slippers embroidered subtly with thread only a shade different than their fabric, poked from beneath her long wide trouser-cuffs. "The First Queen is known for them."

I have guessed as much. Still, that the housekeeper would speak plainly was a good sign. "And it is an insult to the Crown Prince as well as my—*our* princess?"

"One he cannot answer." Two patches of dull color bloomed high upon the Shan woman's cheeks.

So, would the Crown Prince's wife be called upon to answer for him? Was that Lady Kue's message? Yala did not think much of the move, however initially satisfying it might be, so she sought a gentle refusal. "And we might not either." *Not at this moment, at least.* "What do you suggest?" Her hands longed to turn into fists.

Thankfully, this dark blue dress embroidered with komor flowers in a lighter blue was of Khir make, so her sleeves covered evidence of ill temper. Still, she forced her fingers to uncurl, her breath to come evenly; ill temper said ill breeding. "I am a stranger here, Lady Kue, and eager to be of help to my lady's lord."

"I suggest we leave it in a damp storeroom to molder." Lady Kue smoothed her tunic-skirt with both hands, a quick graceful movement. The ring of keys upon her belt made a soft, melodious sound, chimes under a gentle breeze, and her sudo's filigreed knob-handle depending from the same loop glistened in soft mirrorlight. "Will you tell the princess?"

And make me the carrier of ill news. Well, it is hardly the first time I have had to tell Mahara something unpleasant. Yala folded her hands inside her sleeves, touching the handle of a fan with one fingertip. Warm lacquered wood reminded her that a noblewoman did not stoop to pettiness—at least, not yet. "Yes, certainly. But not just this moment."

"That is wise." Lady Kue clasped her hands again, a quiet, demure movement. She wore no ear-drops, and her hairpin was a straight, unadorned stick. "I have served the prince since his mother died, Lady Komor. The First Queen wishes her own son as Crown Prince." Another bald statement, as if daring her to disagree. "I would be... cautious, of her. In every way."

"I shall be. And so shall my princess." One truth deserved another, so Yala chose the one that would serve best. "My princess's husband is my lord now, too. I would not do aught to cause him difficulty." *At least he is gentle with her, and seems kind enough.*

The lady's tension eased somewhat, the ring of keys and implements at her belt clicking again as she shifted. "I would be quite heartened to have you as a friend, Lady Komor. Zhaon-An is dangerous for the unwary—is the palace of Khir so too?"

So, she had passed Lady Kue's tests. At least the housekeeper was not jealous of her prince's esteem, as some might be. Yala found a proverb to match the occasion, and forcing herself to think in Zhaon and find the proper inflection for its ending verb calmed her nerves somewhat. "Every great house is dangerous, Lady Kue." The urge to kick the table, no matter how innocent and finely carved, was overpowering and useless at once. "I hope to be worthy of your friendship, and to return it tenfold."

Lady Kue's dark Shan gaze glittered. She had the deeply folded eyes and generous mouth of that land; how had she arrived here? "Then we understand each other."

I certainly hope we do. "It seems so. The cotton may go in a storeroom, the dampest one possible." And there it would hopefully rot. There would be no making dresses from *this* wedding gift, and if the First Queen affected anger at her "gift" gone unused, Mahara could blame her lady-in-waiting for the lapse. "I shall inform the princess personally, both of the gift and its use."

In other words, Yala was prepared to take the blame. It was an elegant solution—the First Queen could not be seen to be feuding with a lowly lady-in-waiting, but if she decided she *could* indeed be seen so, a flagrant and too-ornate apology would be a most satisfying response. It could even be delivered in writing.

"I am most grateful." Lady Kue bowed, and Yala accepted the gesture with a nod and a slight inclination of her upper body.

All the same, Yala somewhat dreaded carrying this tale through the spare, paneled halls into Mahara's darkened bedroom. "I believe I shall explore the gardens for a short while this morning, to restore my temper."

"Take a sunbell." The housekeeper's palpable relief was, at least, one pleasant thing amid a sea of irritations. "The sky is unkind today." It sounded like a proverb, and Yala occupied herself with thinking upon how to place it upon a scroll as she walked away, taking care to keep her expression remote and neutral.

It was better than brooding, but not by much.

Yala wandered, opening and closing the cheerful yellow sunbell as she moved from shade to glare and back again. This Zhaon spring was indeed too warm, without the mountains to bring the five winds from Heaven. At home the nights would still bear frost except in the valleys, and the farmers would be singing as they planted upon terraces or the rich valley floors. The melt would be well under way, cistern and reservoir filling, terraces bearing traceries of green as frost-hardy weeds resurrected from black earth recently iron-hard.

A colonnade of white stone upon one side and a stone wall pierced with occasional arches upon the other invited lingering. Upon the colonnade side, a yellow-and-blue garden drowsed, bees bumbling and a yellow jewelwing cavorting over flower, leaf, and other insects. Farther away, a small pond scaled with green pads held itself still, brilliant dragonwings[27] zipping and darting. Yala halted just beside one of the arches, her sunbell closed and lowered, and watched the dance. It was worthy of a poem, and she shuffled through quite a few before deciding Soguen Muor, the Mad Monk, was most appropriate. He had wandered far from Faejo-that-was-now-Shan, unable to return, and found himself among thieves and bandits who, enchanted by his songs, often fed and sheltered him.

Later, she would often wonder what would have happened had she found the correct poem a moment sooner, for her mouth opened and she inhaled to recite a passage.

Before she could, another voice intruded.

"You are worthless." The last word was a tongue-throttled hiss, and Yala froze. The woman's voice was familiar, soft mushy Zhaon with a slight, affected lisp. Many in the palace spoke that way, as if sibilants were ill-bred.

A man replied, each Zhaon word polished-sharp and the inflection chillingly respectful. "So you keep telling me, Mother."

Yala shrank against the wall. Grey stone, chill-damp despite the sun filtering through the wooden lattice-roof overgrown with jaelo vines. When they flowered, a canopy of scented stars would make the air heady, almost too thick to breathe. It was too early in the season for them to hold such a profusion of swelling buds; she tried to think whether retracing her steps was wise or folly. If she could

27. A large insect with paired wings, closely resembling a dragonfly.

hear *them*, they would certainly hear her, no matter how much care she took.

The dreadfully familiar female voice spoke again. "You are to return to Shan, and take care of that—"

He did not give her the opportunity to say what he should attend to past Zhaon's southwestron border. "I do not intend to return. At least, not yet."

"You *dare*?" She did not quite shriek like a tradeswoman shaking her fist from a stall, but her tone was not well bred at all. Yala found her eyelids dropping and her head tilting, the very picture of an eavesdropper, and hot shame mixed with cold almost-fear. It could not be. The woman could not be who Yala thought it was.

"What else would a worthless child dare, given the chance?" A soft, mocking little laugh finished the sentence. "You bore me, Mother dear."

A thin, stinging sound—a slap. Yala shrank further into the vines, her lungs burning. She let out her breath, softly, inhaled just as silently. It *was* the First Queen, of that she was sure. Who else? Prince Kurin? No, it did not sound like him; this voice was slightly deeper, with an accent almost like Lady Kue's soft Shan drawl. Yala's fingers wrapped tightly about the sunbell's stem, thin resilient babu[28] threatening to creak or snap if she clutched too hard.

"I regret giving birth to you," Queen Gamwone said, soft and bitter as khep poison. So it was not Kurin; the palace rumors held him to be her favorite. There was another son, Yala was certain, but at the moment she could not think of his name.

"You've already said that. Several times."

Silk, moving low-heavy and sweet. Skirts, of course. A woman's footsteps, quick and mincing, passing behind Yala—and, thankfully, behind the wall as well.

Yala's free hand touched cold stone, her knees weakening, but the queen did not enter the covered passageway. Tension drained, and she closed her eyes fully. To be caught would be embarrassing,

28. A segmented, fast-growing, almost-wood.

to say the least. Had the man left? She could not tell through the pounding in her ears.

Finally, she opened her eyes again to examine her sunbell. How long should she wait before moving?

She was not given the chance. A hand closed around her other wrist, fingers digging in, and he almost yanked her off her feet.

"Ah, that's what I smelled." The man, in expensive black cloth, his topknot uncaged, twisted her wrist. A soldier's boots, but of high quality, and a sharp oval face, his eyes narrowed even further than their folds dictated. "A Khir spy."

For a moment, Yala's voice failed her. She could only gape. To draw her *yue* would necessitate dropping her sunbell, but her fingers would not work. Her heart leapt into her head and threatened to explode at the same moment.

Perhaps he did not mean to sneer, but the vertical scar bisecting the left half of his mouth made it seem so. Another long-healed scar across his left cheek vanished into his hair, altering the pattern of red-black strands. A third, thicker than the other two but just as well healed, clutched at his throat. Arrogance and a dull banked fury fought for primacy in his expression, both claiming equal shares.

Thankfully, her wits recovered quickly. Yala tugged against his hold, her arm stiff between them like a rope for playing heave-the-plow. "Let *go*." Her sunbell slid in her sweating palm.

Unarmed, his hand still bore calluses speaking of soldier's practice. His tunic buttoned far to the right, a Shan cut like Lady Kue's; that faint trace of an accent in his Zhaon was like hers as well. It could only be the First Queen's second son, the one sent to Shan as hostage, and he did not seem overly concerned with manners. "Do you know the penalty for spying in the Palace?" The left side of his mouth, bearing the scar, twitched upward. "Hot lead run into both ears and eyes. After, of course, the rack."

"I am no *spy*." Yala twisted her wrist toward his thumb with a decided motion, breaking free. "I came for a walk in the pleasure-gardens, nothing more." Her sunbell hit the stone flags with a small, shattering sound. "It is only ill-luck that I have happened across *you*, whoever you are." There was only one person he could possibly be, but they had not been introduced. Should she address him by his name, it would be confirmation indeed that she had been listening.

Besides, Yala could not quite remember the name. It was on the tip of her tongue, but it needed a few moments before it would jolt loose, time she did not have.

"And who are *you*?" He surveyed her from top to toe, unhurried.

Would every stranger here demand her name? "I am Lady Komor Yala, companion to Princess Ashan Mahara of Khir." Her cheeks were afire. She had not been this close to a man since her father's short, excruciating embrace in Komori's great hall. "*You* are a barbarian."

One corner of his mouth curled up. It was not quite a smile, but bitter amusement lurked in his dark, narrowed eyes. "You would name me thus?"

She retreated a step and cradled her wrist. It did not hurt, but his grasp had not been gentle in the slightest. "In the absence of anything better, yes." A faint warm breeze entered the passageway, ruffling the green vines, mouthing her skirt. "You have not given your name, barbarian."

"Such a sharp tongue for a Khir girl. Are not your kind trained to be silent?" He folded his arms, weight balanced just-so, and something in it reminded her of her brother.

The memory was a needle to her pounding heart, so she stepped back another pace, two. The distance helped. "Does *your* kind treat guests in this manner?"

"You are a court lady, not a guest." Yes, Bai had stood just like this, especially when he was sharply amused and ready to cause mischief. This man was as tall as her brother, and possibly just as infuriating.

"Both are due some respect, and an introduction." Yala's temper, frayed already, mounted in her chest, an almost physical pain sharpened by the consciousness of being, however unwittingly, in the wrong. Eavesdropping, no matter how necessary, was not well-bred at all. Slim bars of sunshine pierced carved stone, speckling both of them. "Even in Zhaon."

His eyebrows rose, sharply. "Indeed." He bowed, a graceful movement even if perfunctory. "Then accept a prince's apology, Lady Komor."

"Ah, a prince, no less." There was only one she had not seen, and thankfully, his name danced onto her tongue without further ado. "I have met your brothers, so you would be Third Prince Garan Takshin."

"I would be, yes." His face closed with an almost audible snap, his weight shifting to his heels for a brief moment as if she had swung at him with a weapon. "If I cared enough to claim the honor."

Footsteps echoed behind her, boots ringing upon stone. Yala whirled, her blue skirts whispering as they swayed, and was faced with yet another extremely unpalatable occurrence in a day full of them.

General Zakkar Kai, a dark green tunic moving with vine-tinted dapples of sun and shade, bore down upon them with a measured step. He carried a sword; the prince did not, and Yala was not certain if she should feel comforted by that fact. He halted, bowed a trifle lower than absolutely necessary, and she was forced to return the honor, somewhat stiffly. When she straightened, he did not.

Instead, he bent farther, to scoop up her fallen sunbell. "Lady Komor, what a pleasant surprise. I take it you have met Third Prince Takshin?"

Her cheeks were probably as red as tirifruit. How on *earth* could she explain this? "We somewhat surprised each other, General Zakkar."

"The Third Prince has often surprised me, as well." Zakkar Kai straightened, and his gaze focused past her. "I come from your father the Emperor, Prince Takshin. He requests your presence."

"Does he." A slow, disdainful word. Prince Takshin's hands had dropped to his sides. There were more scars across his knuckles, thin white ones Yala recognized. A short, sharp blade would bite its bearer during practice; this prince had held a knife or two. "Then I suppose I must answer, since he sent you to drag me."

"A fool's errand, I know." General Zakkar offered Yala her sunbell with both hands, decorously enough. "Will you excuse us, Lady Komor? The Emperor does not like to wait."

At least *he* had some manners. "I am certain he does not." *Help from an unexpected quarter*—that was the Mad Monk as well, a quatrain on being caught in a rainstorm and finding a hidden cave in the Wailing Cliffs near the Hungry Sea. She forced herself to incline her top half to the prince, a stiff and not very mannerly bow. "My apologies, Prince Takshin. I did not mean to startle you."

"Had you meant to, the morning would have turned out differently indeed." With that, the Third Prince turned upon his heel and strode away, a black blot upon an otherwise sunny afternoon. The grace of a swordsman, with a slight stiffness in the shoulders, as if in pain.

If his mother treated him thus, perhaps he was. The First Queen seemed to sour everyone she came across. It was a pity, for she was so beautiful. There were beauties that could sicken in every corner of the world, though, from fragrant *anjba* to the exhalations of a marshy lake.

"He is not known for polished manners." Zakkar Kai let go of her sunbell's slender length. "Do not let it trouble you."

"Thank you, General. I will not." Yala fought the urge to bow again. *He* did, though, and very respectfully before setting off after the Third Prince with a stride unhurried but long enough to catch up. The green of his long tunic melded with the shade, and turned him into a retreating forest spirit.

Except *those* did not carry swords. The wild *tengrahu* did, but they were clad in sharp black feathers. A pair of spirits in a palace garden, and her an unwilling audience in more ways than one.

Yala sagged, clutching her sunbell and exhaling sharply once they were out of sight. Did the prince suspect what exactly she had heard? Even if he did, there was little *proof*; she could keep the entire incident stored behind a stopper. She was certain there would be several more occurrences of that type in the near future, and her own shoulders ached. It was time to return to the Crown Prince's palace and give the news of the First Queen's gift to Mahara.

Still, as she hurried away, it troubled her. *I regret giving birth to you.*

What mother could say such a thing?

Stitchery

Clad in a bright silk working-robe, Second Queen Haesara slid the outer rim of the circular babu frame over the inner, stretching gossamer-fine blue fabric at just the required tautness. Hair-thin needles stood ready, carried step by step by traders from the great bowl of Anwei that collected trade from all over the world, their points pushed firmly into a pom of silk over horsehair to keep corrosion at bay. She considered the fabric for a long moment, her long eyes pond-still.

This Kaeje room, small and dainty, windowless and private, was swathed with tapestry. Fantastical beasts mostly worked stitch after stitch by her own hands hung upon polished wooden racks and softened the walls. The pillows, embroidered by her ladies and maids, were changed every year at the great lunar festival, the old ones given to those among the merchant families who had earned her favor. This early in the year every pillow was plump, and every color vibrant. A thin-walled, glowing white cup of cooling fan-yehan tea sat upon a small cow-carved table at her right.

Her second son, his elbow braced upon a fat bolster covered in swirling peacocks, rubbed at his horn thumb-ring. For once, he looked ill at ease, his topknot caged in carved bone painted with red lacquer. Finally, he spoke. "I hate him. I always have. You know as much."

"He is your brother." The queen's face did not change. One

corner of her mouth perhaps tightened slightly, that was all. Her ear-drops, feather-flutters with tiny rubies, dripped to her shoulders, and her crimson dress whispered as she reached for a basket of thread. Her sewing-robes were always red, so the luck and vitality would pass through her needle and into the creatures she created, piercing by tiny piercing. "Your *eldest* brother."

"So they say." Sensheo's nose wrinkled. He had never liked being caught out, and sulked at even the gentlest of scolding. "And Makar is a coward."

"You owe the Crown Prince your obedience." Makar had already visited that morning, and brought unwelcome news. The Second Queen took a firmer hold upon her temper than ever, and kept her tone soft, reasonable. "And Makar is your elder too, the son of Zhaon's Emperor just as you are."

"So *you* say."

Queen Haesara's steady motion, searching through the basket, paused. Then she held up two rolls of blue thread, comparing them critically. "Will you treat your mother in this manner?" Her throat pinkened slightly, or perhaps it was a reflection of her dress. "You have always been my favorite sewing companion. Must that change?"

He subsided, pouting as prettily as the boy he had just recently been, but only for a moment. "Why do you let them—*all* of them—insult us?"

"We have our place beneath the sun." She selected another roll, this time of gold. "It is no insult to stay within its warmth." Very soon, now, she would have to tell him she knew, and that if Makar knew, the High General of Zhaon could only be a step or two behind.

"Mother—"

She laid all thread aside, folded her hands in her lap, and regarded him. "You are ambitious, Sensheo. Despite my best efforts, I might add. Can you not simply take your seat?"

"Why must I? I am a prince!"

"Do you think any of your schemes, even if they bear fruit, will save you from your father's wrath?" Heat mounted her throat, touched her zhu-powdered cheeks. "You think you are cunning, Sensheo. You are a *child*, and Makar has saved you more than once from folly. Including this latest attempt upon that parvenu."

Sensheo stilled. The small, furtive gleam in his eyes spoke volumes. Not that she had doubted her eldest son at all, especially when he brought ill news.

"Yes, your elder brother has saved you. The middleman you used to engage a Son of the Needle will never be questioned." The Second Queen rarely raised her voice, but she did so now, and if the tapestries could have, they perhaps would have shifted uncomfortably. "I have spoken to Makar, though, and he will not save you again."

"Mother—"

"*Now* you call me Mother? If your brother had not covered your tracks, Zakkar Kai and that astrologer would have found out who commissioned that blade. And you thought to economize by only sending one and using a Left Market agent, like a parsimonious *merchant*?" Her contempt was withering. "The penalty for the murder of a prince is the Hell of the Red-Hot Tongs, my son, and do you think I could have saved you? No, your brother and I would have been forced to watch."

"I was not the only one." Sensheo stretched, a picture of languor. "I know for a fact that First Queen—"

"Any others had the sense to recall their blades when the Emperor announced the granting of a hurai. You are hasty *and* stupid." Queen Haesara's eyes glowed, coals well past their first fanning, while the heat is fierce but the surface is still dark. "What possessed you to do this?"

"It was *supposed* to be at the army camp; I didn't know Father would—"

Even her ears flushed now. "I cannot decide which is worse, that you failed or that you might have succeeded before Three Rivers."

"You cannot recall a Son of the Needle once you have paid him." Sensheo waved an airy hand, as if imparting great wisdom to a silly woman. "Besides, Kai is an *orphan*, Mother. A commonborn—"

"I do not care if he is the son of the lowest whore in the Theater District, he saved the house of Garan and has been granted a hurai." Could he imagine the implications had Zhaon's general been murdered before victory over Khir? Haesara searched her son's sullen face for a sign, *any* sign, that he understood what had almost happened. None was apparent. "Next time, Makar will not save you from yourself, and neither will I."

"Mother—"

She lifted one hand, her fingertips dipped in and stained with *suma*, the mark of a Hanweo princess. Her House was ancient, rulers of their land too small to be a country and too large to be a province since the Second Dynasty's bloodbaths. "Go. I weary of your games." A small wave of dismissal, familiar—for she waved away merchants in such a manner—and hurtful, for she had never used it upon her son.

Sensheo rose, an ugly flush staining his cheeks as well, not nearly as attractive as suma. Even his fists were clenched, as if he were three winters old again and missing a toy from the nursery. "Had I succeeded—"

"You would have been the first one suspected, and that astrologer would have caught you." Did he not *see*? "Must I tell you again? *Go.*"

He did, closing the sliding door with far too much force. The queen stared at thin blue cloth, stretched taut, and exhaled, sharply. It took some few breaths before she could find the tranquility so necessary to the needle. He worried her, this second son. In one of Makar's intelligence, such ambition would have been welcome, pruned and nurtured like a tiny enclosed garden in an exquisite second house, one built for aesthetics instead of defense.

But Sensheo was far too hurried and saw only the bauble before him, not the larger prize in the storerooms. Or even, as her elder son did, a prize invisible at the moment.

"I wish my children to live," she murmured, and set aside the frame. Delicate work, too easily ruined. She had been looking forward to losing herself in tiny stitches, in a world bounded by a frame where things behaved as they should. It was just as well Sensheo was only attempting to rid himself of a childhood enemy, instead of setting himself to a larger prize.

The Crown Prince gave every indication of being a just, wise heir. Unfortunately, he gave no indication at all of being a ruthless one. Which meant the throne, while it might pass into his keeping, would in all likelihood not stay there. The First Queen's prideful first spawn would rise to eat what he could; none of Tamuron's other sons would be safe, unless they were judged to be no threat.

And Sensheo, her darling second son, who had been such a winning, charming child, would not see the blade until it was already between his ribs. Makar had room to maneuver, and the wisdom to do so. Her hopes should rest upon him, but she did not wish to lose another baby she had suckled, a son she had raised, a prop in her old age, and a support for the Hanweo interests during the half of the year that the First Queen's clan instead of her own was primary at court.

It was no use. Tranquility was nowhere to be found. She turned her attention to sorting thread, her nostrils flaring slightly. If she left her sewing so soon after her son burst out of the room with a thundercloud over his face, notice might be taken.

Trapped by appearances, Queen Haesara simmered, and thought. Sooner or later, a decision would have to be made. There appeared no way out of the tangle but the one most unpalatable.

It was best to conserve what one could, if a... defective... thread snapped and ruined every neighboring stitch. For a short while Haesara studied the tapestries hanging upon the walls, and a sudden longing to tear each of them down and order them burned in one of the gardens seized her.

She could not, so she returned to her sorting, her mouth set.

A Careful Study

A few days later, on a bright clear afternoon, Fourth Prince Garan Makar settled upon a soldier's thin square cushion and accepted a cup of pao tea full of whipped butter, served tepid in the old style. His robe was somber burnt sienna and his belt the absolute thinnest acceptable for a prince's costume; his topknot was uncaged today and his expression was that of a man preparing to enjoy himself immensely, lips slightly curved under his long nose and fine dark eyes. Zakkar Kai's closemouthed steward Anlon, a military stick-insect well past his prime and no doubt ready for a pension, bowed and retreated after ushering the tea-servants away, closing the door with soft authority.

The talent of inspiring loyalty was one Zhaon's head general had in good measure, and Makar thought it very likely it was part and parcel of whatever the god of war had whispered in the orphan's ear after birth. You could whip a soldier into the ranks, but you could not make him fight even in bitter defeat. Not that Kai had been defeated yet; anything that was not a clear victory had been part of a larger strategy.

Of course, the same could be said of any general until ill-luck struck him down. Had not even the great Khao Cao been brought low by a pair of strategists and a woman pouring tea?

Kai's palace quarters were spare almost to the point of uninhabitable, but the wooden floors were well-washed and waxed, the few cushions were comfortable, and there was a martial neatness to stone and wooden walls painted pale and hung with a scroll or two to break the monotony. Even the garden his rooms looked onto was minimalist, a sand-bottomed pool under rough but very aesthetic clumps of very green, very tender babu set against two rough, hip-high volcanic stones.

The chessboard stood where it had at the end of last week's session, on a low, polished wooden table with chunky square legs. General, minister, firemouth, horse, chariot, oliphant, soldier, all carved of heavy cool white stone or glassy black xindai,[29] all entirely obedient whether upon the battlefield or retired to the sides. Neither combatant appeared to hold much of an advantage, but this was a game of patience.

If Makar were to be absolutely honest, he enjoyed the sessions too much to wish for an end to them. He and Kai would simply start another match at Makar's house outside the palace complex when this board had been fought to a draw. He breathed easier there, but a weekly trip to Zakkar Kai's quarters in their forgotten corner of the Iejo gave him an excuse to gather information he might not otherwise gain.

Besides, worthy opponents were difficult to find. Makar took a sip of pao and enjoyed its silken texture, caught between warmth and coolness. At the very end, the tea made of strong, fermented leaves made itself known, swiping the tongue clean. "And did Takshin bow his head meekly? I can answer my own question: No indeed."

"His refusal was polite, in its own fashion." Zakkar Kai, his deep-set eyes half-lidded, tested his own pao and apparently found it acceptable. The teapot and cups, of rustic brown Anwei clay, nevertheless held thin hammered gold rims and subtle fingermarks frozen into their sides, marks of a master potter. "All the same, I was rather surprised he chose *now* to dig his heels in."

---

29. Glassy black volcanic stone.

"The Mad Queen," Makar murmured. There was no need to say more. A royal death liberated more than one soul. "Whose turn is it?" As if he did not know, but to ask was etiquette, and their tradition besides.

They had been at chess ever since Kai arrived, a fierce half-civilized boy from the deserts with the goodwill of only a few to shield him. Those few were mighty, though—Garan Tamuron and his eldest son chief among them—and Makar had seen immediately it would be no good to protest at the inclusion of a filthy common brat upon palace life as Kurin did.

Besides, Kai was better company than the Second Prince from the beginning. He was not a bully, and he could not run crying to his mother when balked, for he had none. All other considerations aside, Makar quite liked Zakkar Kai, and as long as the general made it possible to be friendly, the Fourth Prince was quite willing to do so.

"Yours." Kai in house-tunic and trousers was a different beast than the general in armor or even half-armor. Catlike, he relaxed the grim hold upon his expression necessary for any who wished to survive political life—what was war but politics continued, he had remarked wryly to the Fourth Prince once—and even sometimes sat with one knee up, hugging it like an adolescent while he contemplated the board.

"Hm. The pao is quite good." Often, the tea did not cut the butter at the end, and it was easy for an inattentive preparer to mistake *tepid* for *cold*.

Kai nodded. "I cannot take any compliment upon that account. It was a gift, and Anlon makes it."

"Even better." With the amenities summarily disposed of, they could turn their attention to the game, and Makar let himself savor the event. Long silences interspersed with soft observations, the pouring of more silky-smooth pao with its lingering astringency, halting every so often to look out at the rough darkness of stone balanced against shimmer-flat water and rustling babu—all quite restful. Serene. "It has quieted some little of late."

Kai glanced briefly at him, back at the board. His gaze was

smooth too, unruffled, and he did not tap his fingers or fidget as he had so long ago. All that restless energy had been contained and channeled now. "The wedding is past, after all."

"Yes." Makar touched a firemouth with a fingertip. Let his hand rest there, balanced like an acrobat upon one leg. "How goes your investigation?"

Kai did not glance up. His nose was buried in his teacup; he took a mannerly sip. "Banh made a careful study of the markings." He paused, perhaps warning Makar that the proposed movement was a dangerous one.

Makar's hand moved; he selected a soldier instead. "This poor fellow," he said. "Trudging hither and yon."

"Such is a soldier's lot." Kai's mouth curved slightly, a smile belonging on a scroll-illustration of a general in repose. "I went into the Yuin last night."

Makar already knew as much. The only person likely to escape notice leaving the palace complex was Jin, with his habit of going over walls. The boy was part longtail and all mischief. "Searching for plucked flowers?" The euphemism for prostitutes who did not ply their trade inside a brothel's rooms was not terribly polite, but it had a certain fittingness.

"The kind that bite your fingers off." The phrase could mean teeth closing, or a serrated knife.

Makar watched Kai return his attention to the board, contemplating each option. Such a marvelous contradiction—a blade in service to the house of Garan, and apparently no ambition to turn the edge inward. Certainly, after Three Rivers, Makar had thought they would find the measure of the man. A victorious general, after all, was how Garan Tamuron had ascended to the ancient throne left empty since the middle of the Warring Days, when the only thing worse than invading hordes was the petty warlords strangling each other upon the battlefield for victories barely deserving the name.

He wondered, not for the first time, exactly what loyalty *was*. It did not reside in the liver with a man's thoughts, nor in his loins.

A man's head-meat was occupied with advantage and survival, not fidelity. The scholars and poets did not know where the beast made its lair either, and it exercised them roundly.

For a long while they played in silence, stopping only when Kai's steward appeared to bring more tea—plain and hot this time—and a platter of pounded rai baked into amusing shapes both savory and sweet. The general's cook was a master; Heaven alone knew where the Second Concubine had found such treasure without leaving her bower, and why she did not keep it. But then, did not every woman without sons wish for one? Would they not pay almost anything for such a gift?

It was upon the second cup of plain tea, stinging-hot and satisfying, that Kai evidently decided the time had come. "The assassin was not a Son of the Needle."

"Yet he had the markings?" Makar studied the babu, moving gently on an afternoon breeze. "How very interesting."

"Oh, it was a riddle indeed." Kai selected a bit of pounded, baked rai shaped like a horse, considered its beautiful crisp edges. "Care to guess?"

There was only one solution, since the Sons did not take kindly to assassins not in their guild bearing their marks. The usual remedy was to flay the offender—alive. "Dishonored."

"He had a wife." Kai clicked his tongue, very much like Mrong Banh. "Poor fellow."

The children of the Needle did not mind marriage—babies born into their training grew into double deadliness. The "poor fellow" had married outside the guild, thought his brethren would not uncover the transgression, and had taken to selling his services through a Yuin market middleman. Had Kai not taken his life, his brothers would eventually. The women of the Needle, chewing poison roots to proof themselves against toxins and training those desperate enough to seek entrance to their particular Shadowed Path, would have pronounced him traitor and forsworn, and nowhere within Zhaon would be safe.

"So it could not be an *official* contract." Makar nodded. The

Sons of the Needle had a nasty habit of sending more to finish what one of their kind could not. "You must be relieved."

"Hardly." Kai bit the horse's head free and chewed, enjoying whatever it was stuffed with. A small, satisfied smile touched his lips. "There is still the little matter of who paid him. But then again, *A balked river finds another path, from one stone to the next.*"

"Xao Xheung." Not quite of the Hundreds but still an essayist a cultured man should know. The particular quotation was from his Book of the Garden, written while under house arrest after the Affair of the Five Deaths. The ruler of northern Zhaon at that time was the half-Khir called Hundiao in the old histories for his habit of mounting enemies—real or imagined—upon stakes while they still breathed.

Hundiao had an exorcist's luck, for the Five Deaths had been intended for him and miscarried at the last moment. The conspiracy had died not quite in its cradle nor yet grown, for its component parts had not merely been in league against him but against each other as well, each of them seeking the high seat.

"You have been studying," Makar added. "Father will be pleased."

"Let us hope so. I dislike his displeasure." Kai finished the small horse and washed it down with tea. His manners were unpolished but by no means rough; he enjoyed playing the bluff general with little time for niceties.

Suitably fortified, they returned to the board. Fourth Prince Makar settled himself to play well and also to enjoy the tea. Kai did not skimp when a guest arrived; you had the best of his tent or household.

It was one more thing to admire about him, however grudgingly.

When the visit was done, the Fourth Prince would have to call upon his mother, as always when he set foot within the palace complex. He would have to tell her Zakkar Kai knew of Sensheo's... indiscretion, but was not inclined to bring the matter to the Emperor for his own reasons.

At least, not yet.

Perhaps Regret

"Seclusion" in Zhaon did not mean what it did in Khir. The Crown Princess, though barred from banquet and any male company without her husband present for another two full moons, could nevertheless take chaperoned tea during the first new moon of her marriage with her younger nieces-in-law. Perhaps it was intended as a gentle introduction to court life.

Yala settled upon her heels, her hands arranging her skirts with no direction from the rest of her, quick habitual movements. Mahara smiled, tentatively, and Second Princess Gamnae, her hair fantastically curled and piled until it seemed ready to slide off her head, smiled back. Chief Court Lady Gonwa, iron-backed and round-hipped in a lily-orange cotton dress patterned with indigo dragon-wings and edged in viridian silk, bowed *most* correctly and indicated the tea-table. "All is in readiness," she said, eschewing the slight lisp of those who attended the First Queen. "Allow me the honor of pouring, Crown Princess Mahara."

"It is *our* honor to have you do so." Mahara's Zhaon was improving steadily. A very simple dress of forest green patterned with the segmented characters for *babu* at sleeve, belt, and hem was a fine choice, saved from severity by a deep purple silken under-robe just visible at neckline and cuffs. Her hairpins were both wedding gifts from the Second Queen, and wearing them upon this first semi-public occasion was a mark of respect in that direction. "Princess Gamnae, is this a tea you prefer?"

"It is steeped with jaelo." Second Princess Gamnae's ear-drops shivered and chimed, along with the small yellow beads dropping from her three hairpins like rain. A shade somewhere between green and yellow, her dress suited her, but only because she was so young. It was also cut too low, the twin swells of nascent breasts plainly visible, straining against a linen band meant to keep her from overstepping the bounds of decency. "When in this particular style, we call it *heaven tea*. I like how Lady Gonwa prepares it; it always tastes sweeter."

Court Lady Gonwa accepted the compliment with a slight, gracious bow. Yala studied the other princess—Sabwone, the First Concubine's daughter. Straight-nosed and gem-eyed in heavy, rich dark silk patterned with subtle geometrics, she was visibly conscious of her greater age and supposedly greater seriousness. She fanned herself, a trifle ostentatiously, and leaned slightly aside to whisper to Lady Kanhar, an acknowledged beauty in viridian cotton trimmed with only the slimmest band of black silk as befitted her station.

Court ladies gathered in strictly defined ranks along the sides of the North Pavilion. When the weather was fine, the female half of Court life gathered in this wide wooden porch nestled in the angle between the wall of the Emperor's quarters and the jutting of the Second Queen's apartments. The effect was supposed to be one of harmony, women drinking tea or embroidering, feeding small pets or reading, sometimes aloud, from approved scrolls. Eunuchs hurrying by upon court business often paused; courtiers also took the time to stop and glance, no doubt appreciating the picture. In reality, the jostling for position was eternal, and those who affected to read were more than likely planning a cutting remark. Gossip flared from one end of the pavilion to the other, and Yala already had some idea of its main sources. Anh was invaluable, chattering on while dressing her mistress, but of course that was a double-edged sword.

Yala had toyed with the idea of dropping an item or two into

Anh's well, to see if the ripples spread outside the Jonwa walls. Such an operation required subtlety, and she had not quite decided which stones to toss. Today would no doubt give her some ideas.

There was Lady Huan, whose daughter—a thin, tall, wan girl with a fine mouth—had a rich dowry. Lady Huan was rumored to have her bowl set for Prince Makar, but her daughter was held to be averse to the notion despite the advantages of such a match. Lady Jae the Elder was a great favorite with the First Queen, but not so great among the ladies, and her small coterie did a great deal of laughing behind their sleeves as they surveyed the rest of the Pavilion. Lady Jae the Younger, a cousin from the provinces, had attached herself to Lady Gonwa's faction, nominally favorites of Concubine Luswone. Queen Haesara rarely appeared in the Pavilion, but when she did, it was the group around Lady Aoan Mau who received her patronage, with their embroidery and habit of singing unaccompanied. They dyed their fingertips with suma as the Second Queen did, and took many opportunities to show their graceful wrists and long sienna nails. Some even wore small glittering shields over the nails of their smallest left fingers, flaunting the delicacy of court life and pausing just at the edge of the sumptuary laws.

Some few played instruments. The sathron was held in high regard in Zhaon, and one or two ladies plucked desultorily at theirs while they eyed the newcomer and her attendant.

"I am told Khir ladies ride well, Crown Princess." Gamnae raised the back of her fingers to her mouth as her nose wrinkled, suppressing what might have been a sneeze with well-practiced politeness. Every lady present paused, looking away for a fraction of a moment, but the Second Princess was more than a match for a nose-tickle. "And that they play a game upon horses, with sticks?"

"You must mean *kaibok*." Mahara brightened visibly to match her under-dress. Amber beads depended from one hairpin, both thrust at the required angle, and her hair was simply but most becomingly dressed. A hot breeze whispered catfoot through the Pavilion, ruffling hair and dresses. It was like standing before an oven. How did the Zhaon ladies bear being wrapped in such material, under this heat? And it was only spring. "It is a good game. The sticks have...oh, a stiffened net." Her hands shaped the air, and Yala leaned slightly forward, ready to supply any word she might need. "You ride, and seek to take the ball—it is *this* large, and heavy—from your opponent. Yala and I have played many times."

"Isn't it dangerous?" The Second Princess's eyes widened. She had a soft, blurred beauty; if it sharpened as she grew, she might become a coquette. Thin gilt bangles chimed upon her wrists. She wore enough adornment to double her weight, and Yala wondered at the display. Did her mother not chide her, and was the Emperor not a strict father? Gamnae's honor was, after all, in her father's keeping until she married.

"Oh, a little." Mahara accepted a fine, almost paper-thin cup made of Shan bonefire clay, cupping her right wrist with her left hand and dropping her chin slightly to thank Lady Gonwa. The secret of Shan bonefire was jealously guarded, and perhaps this was Gamnae's showing-off as well, a gift from her recently returned brother? Or perhaps the tea service was Sabwone's? "But Yala never falls. She played with her brother, too." Mahara paused, probably aware that mentioning Bai was not quite polite but also knowing Yala would forgive her.

"A brother?" Gamnae laughed. "They are a trial. Lady Yala, tell me of your brother. I have two."

Yala gathered herself, deliberately not looking into her blue-clad lap. She would not give any Zhaon the satisfaction of seeing her abashed or grieving. Bai would have looked at this girl with a curled lip and scarcely concealed impatience. Kaibok with him was exhilarating; all her strength and skill stretched to the limit, their horses neck to neck and lathered. "There is not much to tell," she said, carefully. "But I agree, they are trying."

"Pulling your hair, poking you with brushes, breaking your toys—Sabwone has a brother too. Sixth Prince Jin is not so bad, though."

"I disagree." First Princess Sabwone deigned to take notice of the conversation. Her ear-drops were simple, her hairpin holding a string of three modest golden beads, stamped with good-luck characters. "A younger brother is a pest and an annoyance." Her pronouncement was delivered gravely, with a single arch of her well-manicured left eyebrow.

"And elders are two generals with one army." Gamnae looked pleased to have drawn her elder sister out. "Which is yours, Lady Yala?"

"Elder," Yala managed. "He was firstborn." The Zhaon even sounded natural, instead of strained.

"Ah, those are the most insufferable! Kurin used to pinch me, when we were children. Takshin would make him stop, but then *he* was sent to Shan." Gamnae sobered. "Did yours pinch you?"

"Princess Mahara has brothers, too." Sabwone's lips stretched, a cat-satisfied smile. She had finally seen her opening. "Two. And a half, I hear."

Mahara's expression did not falter. "My brothers are riding the Great Fields now," she said, softly. Of course she would not speak of Daoyan in the same breath. It was ill-luck, and the king's acknowledgment did not mean her half-brother had been presented to her before she left the Great Keep, or that she could speak upon him with more than embarrassment.

"Crown Princess." Lady Gonwa visibly decided this had gone far enough. "Tell us more of Khir. It is very cold there, no?"

Yala leaned aside slightly, her left foot sliding from under her hip. It brought her shoulder closer to Mahara's. Not enough to touch, but enough to feel the heat from her clothes, different from the oven-breath of Zhaon's spring. It was all the comfort she could offer. The thought of pouring ink into Sabwone's tea was entertaining, but not as satisfying as it would have been in Khir.

Bai would have distracted the group so Yala could accomplish mischief; he would only need a glance to understand what she intended. He would have also taken the blame, should anyone else notice. A sewing-needle had stuck itself in Yala's heart, and would not dislodge.

"Yes." Mahara took the subject change gracefully. "There, it would not be warm yet, as it is here. The *yeoyan* blossoms have perhaps all fallen, but the *paiyan* should be in bloom."

It was a lovely image, very poetically delivered, and Court Lady Gonwa gave a small, encouraging nod of appreciation, her round zhu-powdered face starred with faint perspiration at her hairline.

So she felt the heat as well.

First Princess Sabwone lowered her own white cup. A single ring, of smooth greenstone, clasped her left middle finger. It looked akin to the rings the princes wore, except theirs were carved with characters. Hers was blank, but Yala thought the echo of her brothers' adornments was intentional.

Zakkar Kai wore a greenstone character-ring, too; his had carving upon its curve. It must have something to do with his recent change in status. She filed away the observation for later.

"Riding the Great Fields?" Sabwone tapped the ring against the side of her cup, a small, bony click. Her pale-peach mouth pursed. "Prettily put, but what does that Khir aphorism *mean*?"

A scalding went through Yala, followed by a crackle of winter ice. When the great Lioa River running along the Teeth at the eastron edge of Khir froze from dangerous crunching floes to a solid sheet, it made the same noise. Later, it surprised her to think no one else had heard. "It means they have met death as noblemen," she said, in sharp, clear Zhaon. "Cowards who flee battle go into darkness. One who stands fast to greet the end goes to the Great Fields, and rides eternal."

Silence greeted her statement. The Khir nobles had refused to retreat at Three Rivers; many of the Zhaon conscripts had broken before their charges. Zakkar Kai had won, certainly.

But any Khir able to ride a horse had not fled when the battle turned, choosing instead to stand and die.

Mahara turned her head. She could not, of course, look directly at Yala, but could take her in with peripheral vision. Her princess's mouth had the slight, pleased, startled curve it wore while she watched Yala at *yue* practice.

Verbal fencing was not so different, after all.

"How very interesting." Second Princess Gamnae recovered first, and with far more diplomacy than her costume suggested she possessed. "I have heard there is a cave in Khir where a sage goes each winter to meditate, and the entrance freezes shut. Is there such a thing?"

"There is a legend of a man who lived in such a cave," Mahara began, choosing each word with care. The tale was a simple one, and she should have no trouble telling it, even in Zhaon.

Yala sipped at her tea. It was still hot, and the scent of jaelo was overpowering as a bath. Her gaze locked with First Princess Sabwone's, and the Zhaon princess's zhu-dusted cheeks had flushed slightly. No doubt from heat; it did not look as if that proud girl had it in her to be embarrassed.

When the fury inside Yala died, perhaps she would regret her words. At the moment, however, she did not.

Let Me Win

The Old Tower, clothed in blue tile and looming over the Artisans' Home, was full of cluttered, comfortable coolness once the weather turned warm. Each room had seen several years of princes, running feet, and impatient questions as Mrong Banh explained science and stars to Garan Tamuron's sons, but the round room most crowded with memories was this one in the middle of the cylinder, its sliding door opening onto a walkway-hall two floors above the ground. A long heavy wooden table stood in the exact center, and a small arrow-chamber off its interior side, curtained away, was where the astrologer often prepared tea for his guests. Shelves and scroll-racks marched in orderly, curved ranks in every direction, crammed with paper and scroll cases of wood, hide, ribbons of jointed bone. Some of the shelves held astrologer's implements or other scientific junk, and good-luck charms hung from them next to babu and paper models of fantastical machines or structures. The high wooden ceiling was studded with hooks, and sometimes Banh had hung particular models or constellation-shapes from them to teach princes the movements of the Five Winds—or other forces—upon the night sky.

"Kai!" Sixth Prince Jin, his topknot askew, yanked the partition aside. Even his belt was pulled off-center, and a tendril of red-black hair had come free, pushed behind his ear. "You have to come see—oh."

Mrong Banh, in the act of pouring tea at a low table while scratching at one mildly stubbled cheek, blinked like a sleepy owl. Kai, a rough, square black pottery cup halfway to his lips, tilted his head. On the other side, Third Prince Takshin, in his customary black Shan cloth, lowered his own cup, his left hand twitching as if it sought a hilt.

"Jin." Kai beckoned, somewhat airily. He was in half-armor today, which meant he had not been called to Council, and that accounted for his cheeriness. "Come in, we are discussing theater."

"We are *not*," Takshin said, but not very loudly. He, too, looked uncommonly at ease, and set his cup down, flicking his left-hand fingers as if to rid them of water droplets.

Jin hopped from one foot to the other, alive and alight, bursting with news. One end of his belt had come untucked, and danced with him. Spring sunshine outlined him from head to foot, catching stray hairs escaped from his topknot in a floating halo. "The Khir! The Khir girls! They're—"

"They are *what*?" Mrong Banh shook his head, clicking his tongue. The shadows under his eyes said he had been up late again, studying the paths of Heaven. "Look, I've spilled." He reached for a rag amid scrollcases, scattered notes, empty teacups, and stacked plates in varying stages of cleanliness, and couldn't find one. "You are very rude, Prince Jin."

"They are playing a game, the Khir princess and her lady! With horses, and a ball, and—"

"*Kaibok*," Kai said. *Interesting.* Of course, noble girls would play. It was almost the only freedom a Khir girl could lay claim to, even while in a bride's formal seclusion. "That will make the court ladies gasp."

"A game? Women? On horses?" Takshin frowned. Shan was not a country where noblewomen rode other than upon light palfreys for pleasure. Wearing that expression, he looked very much like his father. "This sounds... unconventional."

"It's true!" Jin's cheeks were reddened from running, and his robe was pulled almost sideways. He'd almost worn through his slippers, wooden soles peeking through leather sheathing. "They have sticks, and a heavy ball, and they are both masked. Riding back and forth on the big cavalry practice ground! Hitting with the sticks!" His eyes danced. "Come *on*!"

"I've read of *kaibok*," Mrong Banh said. "But...women playing it?"

"Noblewomen," Kai supplied. "They ride to hunt, and to play. The Khir believe it grants them strong sons." Otherwise, a Khir woman's place was in bower or kitchen. Even in the market they had to be shepherded, for a Khir husband was a jealous one, or so the proverb went.

"The Crown Princess is playing?" Mrong Banh set the square red-lacquered teapot—his favorite, a gift from Garan Tamuron before the Second Battle of Wurei—down and abandoned his hunt for a rag. The spilled tea would simply dry where it was and leave a ring to match the others blooming upon the tabletop. "With her lady-in-waiting?"

"All the court ladies are watching." Jin, hopping from foot to foot, visibly decided telling them more was a worthless task, spun-slid on his heel, and almost put his hip through the edge of the partition, avoiding it by a mere hairsbreadth. He vanished into the dark hallway, and Kai was already rising.

"Kai?" Takshin scrambled to his feet. So did the astrologer, bumping the table. The teacups chatter-danced, and a spill of scrap paper floated from the far end of the table.

Kai was already out the door, following the Sixth Prince's retreating back.

The horses were a fine pair of matched bays, slight figures wrapped in spring blue upon their backs. They cantered down the cavalry training-rectangle, hooves bell-chiming, and one of the riders was almost out of the saddle, leaning drunkenly aside, a long stick in gloved hands flaring into a cup near the ground. The heavy leather-wrapped ball bumbled and rolled, shoved along, and the rider, masked, a long tail of braided black hair whipping in the wind, neatly turned her wrist, knocking away the other rider's stick-cup. Her opponent did not lean so dangerously, perhaps too cautious—or too wise.

That caution appeared to be rewarded as the ball shot forward and the first rider, knee hard-tucked against the high saddle-front, slipped even farther. Her bay, sensing something amiss, lunged, and the second rider let out a high piercing cry of incipient victory.

It was close, very close, to a Khir battle-yell.

Kai's heart leapt into his throat. He halted at the edge of the high stone gallery along the east side of the ground, where a cavalry commander and his honored guests would stand to watch maneuvers performed. Bright plumage gathered at the other end, the court ladies whispering among themselves, none so ill-bred as to point but visibly longing to do so. Crown Prince Takyeo was a tall green-clad figure upon the stairs, his topknot slightly disarranged, and had clasped his hands behind him and was staring with an expression halfway between mystification and pride—of course, he had to be present. Beside him, Makar, his eyebrows nesting in his hairline, frankly stared, openmouthed, the edges of his sumptuous brown scholar's robe fluttering. Second Princess Gamnae, in a bright-patterned orange and blue dress, her arm through her brother Kurin's, halted at the near end of the ground, on the path from the gardens clustering the Kaeje.

The first rider caught a fistful of mane and almost slithered from the saddle. A collective gasp echoed from the court ladies, and Takshin appeared at Kai's elbow. Behind him, Mrong Banh skidded to a stop, out of breath.

The bay, sensing what the first rider wanted, did not slow. The stick-cup touched the ground, a splintering jolt used to propel the first rider *up*, thigh tensing, gaining the saddle again with natural grace. She dropped into the bay's rhythm like a potter's thumb into spinning clay, and the other rider—slightly taller and rounder, Kai thought it the princess—overshot the ball as it turned upon a stray buckled paver and bounded to the left.

"Born in the saddle," Kai murmured, unaware of speaking.

Takshin glanced at him. "Which one's which?"

"I think that's the princess?" He cupped his hand, indicating the slightly taller figure, but remembered his manners just in time. His hand fell back to his side.

Lady Komor—it *had* to be her, visibly smaller than her opponent—touched her heels to her mount's sides, and her bay shot forward again. This time she leaned to the right, the fractured cup at the bottom of her playing-stick catching the ball. Another turn of her wrist, the horse obeying the pressure of her knee-shifting and curving aside, and the ball bounded off the cavalry ground, almost shattering a carved stone torch-holder. It whistled as it flew, and Kai let out a sharp breath. Hopefully, there was nobody in the tangle-garden beyond to attempt catching it.

She regained the saddle with another swift movement, straightened, and threw her head back. Behind the blue cloth mask, another cry lifted. He'd heard its like before, fighting the Khir, but not so high-pure or shrill. The princess brought her mount around with skill, but Komor Yala had the gift of their horse-goddess.

"*Ahi-a!*" the princess called, stripping her mask from her face. Her knees clamped home as her bay slowed, and she rode with easy grace, only one hand upon the reins. "Yala! I thought I had you!"

Komor Yala let her bay slow to a trot, then to a walk. The horse tossed its fine head as she stripped her own mask, and the court ladies whisper-giggled, their dresses fluttering at the edges. Kai found himself upon the stairs, his heels landing hard, and lengthened his stride. Behind him, Crown Prince Takyeo hurried down another flight, his dark wooden topknot-cage gleaming. Kai was barely aware of Takshin at his shoulder and Mrong Banh's puffing in their wake.

It was Jin who reached the women first, though. "Marvelous!" he crowed. "Do all Khir ride like that? Can you teach me? What is the ball made of? How did you—"

Lady Komor's grey eyes burned, a high flush in her sharp-curved cheeks. She shook her head, but her smile was broad and breathless, stray blue-black strands sticking to her forehead and cheeks.

The spring-blue costumes were Khir riding habits, wrapped close to allow freedom of movement while blurring a woman's outline. She finished unwrapping her head with one hand, the other draping her reins with a quick habitual twist. "Easy there, long-legged one," she crooned in Khir, leaning forward, looking down the bay's right front leg. "Easy."

"What does she say?" Jin blinked at Princess Mahara, who pulled her own mask free.

The princess's soft, round face was alight too, and it suited her. "Husband!" She straightened in the saddle, her light eyes dancing with glee. "Did you see? Yala won, again."

"I do not *always* win," Komor Yala said, leaning to the left now, checking the front leg on that side. Her Zhaon, sharp-accented, was not quite as musical as usual.

"This is the only game she does not let me win." Mahara slid from the saddle, landing light as a leaf. Even the boots were blue, and supple—probably a gift, plovers stamped and embroidered around their cuffs. "What ails your horse, *aenbak*?" The Khir word for *sister*, with an affectionate lilt—a high honor, indeed. At least Ashani Zlorih had sent a lady his daughter liked, even if he meant her lonely self to be an insult to the Zhaon who had required a small retinue.

"I never *let* you win." Lady Komor shook her head, her long braid swaying. "I do not know. His weight is off."

"You *do* let me win, but not at kaibok." Mahara patted her mount's neck. "Did you see? You cannot let someone else take the ball." Kittenish now, she peered up at Takyeo, who looked frankly poleaxed, beaming soporifically. The Crown Prince reached for his wife's gloved hands, and took the reins from her with courtly grace.

"We must walk him," he said, in soft, clear Zhaon. "What is that, in Khir?"

The princess told him, and he repeated the words. She laughed, correcting him, and a strange relief mixed with unease filled Kai's throat. The marriage was indeed upon steady footing, and he should have been glad of it—but to show affection so openly, did Takyeo not have any *sense*?

Lady Komor slid from her saddle. She resumed her soft singing to her own mount, who flicked his ears in her direction, his sides heaving. The bay gelding looked, as far as Kai could tell, extremely satisfied with himself, but the lady's expression had clouded.

"Lady Komor." Jin was still full of questions, towering over her by a good head and a half even before he finished the last of his growing. "Can you teach me how to play?"

"Perhaps." She glanced at the knot of onlookers, a quick calculating look. "Sixth Prince Jin, it is? Do you like horses?"

"He cannot stand them," Takshin said, a little too loudly, and slowly, his Zhaon exaggerated at every edge. "He is afraid."

"I am *not*!" Jin rounded upon him, as if they were much younger; Takshin simply folded his arms, his stare not quite as cold as usual but nowhere near warmth, either.

Lady Komor ducked under the bay's head, clicking her tongue much like Mrong Banh. The astrologer scuttled cautiously backward as the bay sidestepped, though it was nowhere near him. The Khir girl led the horse away, a big lathered beast docile as a trained pig. By the time Jin and Takshin realized she had left, she was already taking the bay down the narrow, close-walled slope leading to the stable complex.

For a Khir, care of a four-footed cousin would come first.

Zakkar Kai watched Takyeo and Princess Mahara amble after her, deep in conversation. Mrong Banh halted at his side. "The whole palace will hear of this," the astrologer said, quietly. "And the Emperor, too."

"It may amuse him." Kai lost sight of her. He glanced at the older man, while Jin let out an ebullient whoop and ran in pursuit of his latest amusement.

Prince Takshin stood, looking after the small group as well, his scarred lip twitching once.

They Weigh upon Me

Anh gently pressed the water from Yala's hair with a long thirsty cloth while her mistress, seated at a low writing-desk in a round pool of mirrorlight, broke the thick red seal. Letters spilled out of heavy oiled-canvas wrapping. Most bore her father's familiar brushwork upon the outside, his name written boldly but without pretension, the simplest character for each syllable or word chosen and practiced for long years. She remembered the smell of inkstone, her father's fingers gentle upon her wrist as he guided her through the symbols.

Ko. Mo. Ri. It was the only time she had been allowed to sit upon his lap, while she was practicing her brushwork. For her own name, *ko-mo-or*, but her father and brother had the honor of the *ri*, with its proudly lifted stallion-tail.

There were three letters in another hand. She frowned slightly, examining them. The ink was sepia and the strokes delicate, though the horizontals were a little too thick.

The mystery was solved when she opened one and scanned the first line. It was the second of three letters from Narikh'a Daoyan, once a royal byblow, now Ashani Daoyan, Crown Prince of Khir.

She set them aside, arranged her father's missives in the proper order according to the small, exquisitely brushed date on the back of each, and began to read.

Her father wrote of spring spreading through the two house gardens, and that he had visited Bai's stone and found her arrangements for it, not to mention the upkeep she had performed, very filial. He wrote of the household, much quieter now since he had no need of servants for his son and daughter, and of the bronzefish in the south garden's pond. They had survived the winter, of course, wise enough to sleep beneath the ice instead of wasting their energy upon fruitless struggle against the seasons.

As did the komor flower, with its tiny blossoms.

"So many characters," Anh said wonderingly, chafing Yala's hair. "Can you read them all?"

Of course. But the girl was merely curious, not sarcastic, so Yala did not mind questions upon the border of impertinence. "Yes."

"Are they Khir, or Zhaon?"

Of course, plenty of kaburei did not read. Their traditional name in the Hundreds was *shua-rei*, the Voiceless. Yet times had changed some little—and slowly—since the canonical texts had been immured by the great Huan sage whose name was so auspicious it could only be referred to with the first and last characters of its flow, *k'oh* and *oung*. "We use the same characters," Yala answered, patiently. "Many Khir kaburei are literate; you are not?"

"I know only my name. *Ah, Na.*" The girl laughed, tossing aside scholarship and reading with a quick jerk of her chin. It was a motion she performed often, shaking away anything she had decided to leave to wiser heads. "Braids?"

"Just one, unless I am called for dinner." It was not likely. Yala moved her shoulders slightly, her back taking its accustomed straightness. It was permissible to relax in the bath, but not here.

Not where anyone, even a kaburei, could see.

"Not tonight, Lady Kue said the Crown Prince and Princess are at dinner together. Love-birds." Anh sobered when Yala did not laugh or otherwise respond to the sally. "I shall be quiet, lady."

"Mh." Yala kept still as the comb drew through her hair. She opened another letter, scanned it, another. Closer reading could wait for the second or third time, and she could also search between the characters for other meanings.

House Komori did not lower itself to much politicking, but she would be a fool not to send her father what information she could glean of Zhaon's intentions, even though a mere woman was not supposed to worry over or notice such things. Her father was *no* fool, and would no doubt keep her apprised of anything that might impact her princess, too.

Her father wrote of the flowering trees, of household matters, of the price of sohju, salt, and rai, of fine silk in the market that he would send her if she wished for it. The dresses she had left behind were kept safe in the ceduan clothespress, and if she wished, he would send them as well. Perhaps she would find a use for them, even in the south.

All the letters were full of such mundane things, and Yala's eyes prickled with heat.

The last letter broke off halfway, then continued after a long, curving line meant to denote time had passed.

I received a packet of your letters, written every week. You are very faithful. The South is a warm place, but a dangerous one. Take care with the princess, but more importantly, care for yourself. Keep your honor close and your sight unclouded. I keep you in my thoughts, daughter.

The character for *thoughts* was close to the one for *heart*, especially with the small added fillip on the last upstroke. Now she wondered if her own letters, full of careful distance—how long they had traveled, what they had eaten, the strangeness of the Zhaon houses with their roofs that would not shed snow so easily—had not pleased him. Or had they perhaps... wounded him, in some oblique way?

She sighed, folding the last letter carefully, returning it to its folded sleeve. Perhaps it was possible to say things with a brush that you could not, otherwise. She would have to speak less generally and more distinctly in future missives.

She opened Daoyan's letters, arranged them, and paused for a moment as Anh began a loose braid. "Anh. Some tea, perhaps, before you commence."

The kaburei girl paused. "What kind?"

"Something soothing." Dinner would be brought soon, and kaibok gave one an appetite. Still, she wished to read whatever Daoyan had to say without someone breathing behind her.

Even a kaburei.

Anh retreated to the door, bowed, and pulled the partition closed. Her soft footsteps, hurrying away, were the release of familiar bonds, and Yala's shoulders dropped a trifle, then a little more.

Komor Yala, greetings. You have been gone two days, and they weigh upon me. Dao also spoke of spring, but not as her father did. Instead, he spoke of the planting, and that he waited for news of Zhaon, and hoped her journey was smooth and her health did not suffer. He wished for her to write, if she could find the time.

Komor Yala, greetings. You have been gone twenty days, and they weigh upon me.

She shifted, her legs aching. A game of kaibok after not riding for a few weeks jarred muscle and bone. A hot bath instead of a tepid one was called for, but it would make her sleepy, and the letters required thought and attention.

She did not wish to be sleepy. Not now.

Komor Yala, greetings. You have been gone thirty-two days, and they weigh upon me.

Oh, she recognized the quotation, of course. It was from Kao Yanbin's letters to Princess Shurimake in the Third Dynasty. Kan's play about the lovers had been wildly popular the winter before Three Rivers, when Zhaon was just a slow-boiling menace ravaging borderlands and choking the Anwei trade-roads. She had gone with Bai and Dao to see it, at the theater in the royal quarter. Seated between chaperoning brother and friend, her fan fluttering, nothing worse on the horizon than Mahara's pestering—Khir's princess could not attend a play, even chaperoned, and was forced to find amusement when the Great Rider summoned a theater troupe to the palace—for every detail of the staging, how the lines were delivered, recitals of the most passionate moments...

Each day, I ask the Great Rider if there is news of the princess. Perhaps he suspects I have thoughts above my station. There are rumors that the marriage has indeed taken place. I think of you alone in the palace of our enemies, and my blood boils within me. I know such a statement is unwelcome, but I cannot stop myself. Forgive me.

She touched the brush-lines of his signature. He signed himself in the old way, without any pretensions. *Dao*, the character for *a shield*, not a small buckler but a heavy round shelter.

Perhaps she should have stayed. But any offer he made for her would have foundered upon the king's need to keep his only remaining heir—unless he had other mistresses likely to carry fruit—available until the political situation settled. And her brother's shade might well have risen to throttle her, should she have entertained Daoyan's ideas.

What would her father have said?

I denied them all, I kept you close.

"My lady?" Anh pushed the partition aside, brought the tea-tray through, and knelt to close the door again. "I brought you ao-sai, it is powerfully calming. There is honey, too, and flatcake. It is almost dinnertime."

Yala set the letter aside and smiled, her face a stiff mask. She could not think upon what might have been. "Very good."

No, there was no use in *what might have*. Instead, she had to think of *what is*. It was well enough for Daoyan to write such things, safe in Khir as he was. Nothing but jealous nobles and poison to avoid, and the king's favor to court closely instead of at a distance as he had done all his life. It was still a dance he was well accustomed to, and well practiced in.

The problem of how to reply to her once-friend, she decided, could wait until morning. After dinner she would write her father, again, and perhaps, just perhaps, find a way to tell him...what? That she was well, and the princess was well, and that he should not worry. She busied herself with arranging her sleeves as Anh settled and poured the tea, offering a fragrant blue-painted cup with both hands.

And that he must take another wife, she reminded herself. *A junior branch must not take Hai Komori.* A daughter's duty to family and clan, even over the many leagues separating them, was not done.

It would *never* be done.

Who Is Common

In the antechamber to the Crown Prince's bedroom, the table was laid and servants retreated. On other occasions they would not withdraw, especially when there were guests at the table in the great dining-room, but for now, dinner was often at this small, intimate board. It was a pleasant enough room, with a sliding door to a porch overlooking the Jonwa's largest water-garden, full of small stone pagoda-fountains and their tinkling music restarted now that any danger of ice was past.

The antechamber was sparely furnished and full of the smell of dusk as the day's heat leached away, a note of brassiness from the water, a breath of sweet-panil vine blooming early upon trellises at the garden's far end. Two scrolls hung upon the plain wooden walls, both bearing quotations from Cao Lung's *Book of Rule.* Round and draped with restful black fabric, the table had room for four. Only the most honored of guests would share this intimacy, but that was for later.

After she had given them an heir.

Mahara set her carved eating-sticks down carefully, tips resting upon the fish-shaped holder like during a festival. "It is very good," she said, diplomatically. "I am merely unaccustomed to Zhaon cuisine. Forgive me."

Her new husband was not so bad, even though his eyes were… troubling. In a noble Khir gaze you could see the thoughts moving;

a black gaze was a kaburei's slyness, they said. Waiting to betray, opaque because they lacked trustworthiness.

"There is nothing to forgive. I should tell you, Lady Kue has found a new cook, one adept at northern dishes." His eyebrows drew together, a worried look she began to suspect was habitual. He was handsome, yes, especially his wide forehead and growing beard—the very illustration of a scholar-warrior, with wide shoulders and leonine grace. She had not seen him ride yet, but surely he would not be *bad* at it. He did not seem bad at anything a prince should do.

It was better than she had hoped, really. Except the food. Mahara studied polished rai, pearls jumbled in a crimson porcelain bowl. The meat was bland and there was no curd. "That is very kind of her." A drink of tea, then, to calm her stomach. She lifted her cup, other hand holding her sleeve just so, and studied him afresh.

A pleasant, triangular face, and those shoulders. There was a deceptive softness to his cheeks, but his middle was lean and his legs long. His topknot was caged in leather, but the cage was finely wrought, and the stick holding it fast was threaded with hammered gold. He did not shout, or strike the table like her father did in private when momentarily displeased, even when she dared to pour his tea without asking. Of course, it was early in the marriage; he could change at any moment.

Even honorably secluded in a princess's bower, she knew *that* much of men.

Her husband selected a few strips of meat and indicated a plate of spear-shaped green vegetables in lacy breading. "Do you like these? Have you had them?"

She had to shake her head, hoping he would not be insulted by her lack of knowledge. "I have not. What are they?"

He also did not look pained or nose-high when she made mistakes in her Zhaon. Mahara was very conscious that she was not a scholar, and that she perhaps should have spent more care and time learning the southron language. It had all happened so *quickly*. First the rumbles of war intruding even into her bower, then the certainty that nothing could defeat the fine Khir army... then Three Rivers, and now she was a married woman, without a friend except for Yala.

And she had cried, in the safety of her maiden's bed, after her father had informed her that *only* the young Lady Komor had stepped forward to accompany her; the rest of the noble girls who attended her at court had hastily found reasons not to and a Great Rider defeated in battle could not force them. She was to go almost alone into the southron dragon's jaws. When the tears passed, she had decided she was lucky, for Yala was clever and loyal, and never looked nose-high either.

At least, not at her princess. More than once another Khir noblewoman had earned a scathing glance or two, and Mahara had sometimes dreaded being the recipient of one of those quiet, bone-slicing looks. Some girls were born decorous and demure, and others less fortunate had to live in fear of never filling even that small measure.

Takyeo laid three of the long, spearlike green vegetables atop the bed of rai in her bowl. He did it gracefully, too, his sleeve held away and his fingers dexterous with his own smooth wooden sticks and their gold sheathing. "Try them. They're very good." Patiently, without any indication of irritation.

She picked one up, and nibbled at its end. Took another bite, suddenly very interested. A new taste, and not a bad one. "It's good." She sounded surprised, even to herself.

"Only married women can eat them." A shy smile. "Because of the shape. They are called *mother's soldiers*."

"Ah." Her cheeks turned hot. But *she* was married now, and surely there could be nothing wrong or embarrassing if her husband said such things, could there? "Do *you* like them?"

"They were my mother's favorite."

A painting of his mother hung in the Jonwa's ancestor-shrine—a woman with a long pale blue robe, a high forehead, and a rather sweet, sad smile. The painting seemed very likable, with a gentleness lurking in its brushwork, and Mahara's offerings of incense were in the Zhaon style. Yala had quietly told her what was expected, and was never wrong. "Then I shall like them. She was very beautiful, your mother."

That made the worry-line between his eyebrows deepen. "The First Queen would say she was common. She married my father before he was Emperor."

It was also Yala who had told her the gossip—that Garan Tamuron's first queen had been a merchant's youngest child, with only a faint claim to nobility through her own mother, a daughter of an impoverished house sold off like so much mutton. A woman's lot, to be handed to another when circumstances dictate. "It is the First Queen who is common." The words burst out. Mahara stole a glance at his face, and continued, emboldened by his expression. "I dislike her."

Her husband nodded thoughtfully. "So do I, wife. But we must be careful. She is very powerful."

"But she is merely a woman, and you are *Crown Prince*." She mispronounced it, but he did not look pained.

"Yes, well, her family is powerful, and I often wish I were not." His gaze sharpened, measuring her.

Mahara nibbled at the spear-vegetable. Another new thing, one she considered at length before nodding. There were some who would crave the power, and affecting humility did not disguise that craving. A Khir princess was to avoid meddling with men's concerns, but the Zhaon women did not seem to share that stricture.

Yala would be able to find a couplet or a winning line from the books stuffed in her head, but the princess was alone here. She was not doing too badly, either, Mahara decided. "Yes," she said, finally. "It must be a great burden. I will be a help to you."

Now he smiled without a shadow of worry, and she had to admit, it gave him much more handsomeness. Though his eyes were dark, they were appealing enough. "I am sure you will. Have you tried this? It is similar to Khir curd, I am told. Tomorrow there will be Northern dishes; the new cook will be pleased to offer them."

Perhaps this would not be so bad. She could play kaibok here, and if she was careful, he might stay calm. Their food was bland, but that was to be expected. So far, there had been nothing she could not face.

The princess picked up her bowl again, with the pretty, habitual curve to her wrist. Polished rai was a royal food, at least. "You are very kind, husband."

"I wish to be," he said, and when he smiled again, something in Mahara's chest bloomed like a panil flower.

Wary and Prepared

Bai would have pretended unwillingness, but he would have gone with her. Or, if it were a moonless night, he would have shaken her awake to share the night's pathways. He loved mischief, but what he loved more was training his little sister to ghost through the halls of Komori, even out onto the tiled roof, dodging guards and achieving whatever objective they had agreed upon. Their father's library, or the Great Hall, or a particular attic-room full of dusty, shrouded, ancient furniture—the game was to reach it silently, with all others unaware of their presence. And, of course, to return to their chambers with none the wiser, especially Yala's talon-sharp chaperones, ever watching their charge's deportment to keep her honor unstained.

It is not enough to be quiet, little sister.

Yala whispered past the nodding guard, a shadow in shadow, musky southron night-breath filling her lungs. Bai's careful tutelage echoed in her heartbeat, filled her arms and legs with a clear sparkling excitement better than sohju.

Step so, and spread your weight thus... little idiot, do you wish to be caught? Do it again, and better.

Like much else, it was relatively easy if you watched, and waited, and smiled. The guards eventually looked the other way, rubbed their eyes, caught a few moments of sleep leaning against pikes or posts. If a girl was quick, practiced at muffling the rustle of betraying skirts, the darkness was a friend. She was a silent fish in a nighttime pool, a bronze darter below winter ice, slipping into a Jonwa gallery leading to a dry-garden full of spines and succulents. This pleasure-walk had no bridge, but there were flat rocks arranged in a winding path. Here, in her long-sleeved night-robe but safe from prying eyes, she amused herself by hopping from one rock to the next, holding herself in absolute stillness on each as soon as she landed in one of the Four Stances of the *yue*. Hill, Valley, River, and Hawk, each the base from which the blade would flash, arm, leg, and will intent upon a single purpose.

Ten stones, not enough to repeat the stances thrice. This irked her a little, but she decided to hop back to the center of the garden and finish there. It could not be helped, the world was imperfect even when harmonious, as Yian Kayuo had often said in his *Book of Four Earrings*—

What was that?

She froze, head tilted, her indigo night-robe swaying. Replayed the noise inside the secret chambers of her ears. What was it? Scraping, something drawn across stiffened leather? A muffled clatter?

It was a man's small miscalculation that saved her. That, and hours of practice under the eagle eyes of two iron-backed noblewomen, one a maiden aunt and the other an impoverished cousin, dedicated to service of the house sheltering them both. An unmarried woman had little to look forward to, especially among the noble families, but Lord Komori was only severe, not cruel.

A shadow heavier and taller than Yala landed in the sea of pebbles surrounding the large stepping-stones, her sudden halt throwing off his balance. The grinding of small stones brought her around, her night-robe's skirt flaring, and her hand, with the ease of long habit, blurred for her *yue*. Her teachers had often tossed tiny objects while she practiced her stances, making it a game—when she heard the object in the air, or even the slight creak of weight transferred from foot to other foot against whatever flooring there was as the throw commenced, she was to draw and strike. Best of all was to bat the thread-spool or the blunted dart aside with the flat of her blade without losing flow or altering breath.

A game, indeed. Now in deadly earnest, she did not pause.

Knee bending, the *yue* tearing stitches as it whipped free of her low-belted Khir robe, and a musical clash-slither broke night-quiet as a curved, darkened blade met hers. Bending backward, then, for a slight breeze was the whisper of his second knife, striking for her throat. Her foot flicked, glancing off a leather-clad knee that turned a fraction but was unable to fully dodge the blow. Her *yue* flipped, wrist moving in the floating-of-the-lure motion, fading into the swallow-tail to bite both flesh and cloth at the end of its arc.

The man in night-dyed cloth and leather, his head wrapped and the only betraying gleam that of his eye-whites, did not retreat. Instead, he spun, both blades flickering out, meaning to strike at her middle.

But the *yue* was prepared for just such an attempt. The Dancer's Pose pushed her waist aside, weight dropping into her left hip even as her knee bent, and her left hand rose gracefully as her right, freighted with the slim blade, whispered down blinding-fast. Both the man's knives—harshly claw-curved and shorter than a *yue*, their flats blacked with something—passed within a hair of the wide, stiffened band of silk drawing the robe against her navel. The *yue* bit again, a glancing, stinging slice across his forearm.

Sweat gathered in her armpits, at the hollow of her lower back, along the sides of her naked throat. It happened so *quickly*, there was no time to think. Her knee straightened, the *yue* performing a half-moon with its edge still outward, and the River Stance pushed her in the opposite direction, bending again as the man swiveled and struck once more, perhaps angry that the woman in a low-belted, long-sleeved Khir night-robe over a thin linen shift was not dead yet.

Assassin. The consciousness of danger crashed upon her, but the *yue* knew no fear. It was a needle, and she the thread following.

Another crunch and splatter of stones was a second man's feet landing in the dry-garden. Two-against-one changed the stance she must use; she pitched forward, shifting from River to Hawk, from the gentle curving of defense to the speed of wings, talons, and razor beak striking from a clear mountain sky. The *yue* buried itself in the first man's throat; she wrenched it free and pitched *back*, leaping, her forefoot grinding in small stones as a solid meat-carving *thunk* echoed against the colonnade and a dripping point burst from the murderous shadow's swathed chest.

She gained another stepping-stone, her heels bruising against its surface as she shifted to Hill Stance. She was wary now, and prepared. Let them come, she would show them how a noblewoman met... death?

I do not wish to die. Surprising, to realize it so clearly.

The muffled attacker dropped like a string-cut puppet. The sword was wrenched free of his back with another awful, tearing sound. Blood spattered from his cut throat, though the fabric wound around stopped the spray from reaching her. Yala, her *yue* held diagonally and her grip firm despite palm-sweat greasing bare, cross-hatched metal, fought to contain her breath. Her ribs sought to heave, her pupils swelling, shadow and dim light full of skittering movement.

"Shh," the new arrival hissed. "Do not fear, princess. He is dead."

Princess? She blinked, unwillingly—a single moment of blindness might leave her open to another strike. Her heart thundered, and the sweat all over her was grease-cold. Small stones click-shifted under a pair of boots.

"General?" she whispered. "General Zakkar?"

"Yes." His Khir was tolerable, but only that. He was not muffled, but in leather half-armor, and it was *his* sword that had struck the assassin from behind. "Ah. You are not the princess. Easy, Komor Yala. The battle is over."

He must have seen the shape of her dress, and thought she was Mahara. Yala did not drop her guard. A sudden sharp stink rose. For a moment she thought she had soiled herself with fear before she realized she was clean, and it was merely the... the corpse.

And Zakkar Kai, his sword a long bar of moongleam, stabbed the body again to make certain life had fled.

This Is Not Well

Kai exhaled sharply. There were no other assassins, which was welcome news. However, now he was presented with quite a different problem. Small stones crunched underfoot as he stepped onto a larger one, instinctively seeking firmer ground. "You carry a blade. In the *palace*."

"So do you." Komor Yala, her nighttime braids disarranged and the low belt of her Khir night-robe askew, stared at him, ghost-pale, her strange eyes wide. Thus disheveled, she looked far smaller than her iron-backed daytime self. When she spoke, her Zhaon was halting. "It is *yue*. Every Khir noblewoman—"

"You are neither prince nor guard, my lady." His pulse had yet to return to its usual even rhythm. What was she doing here, in a robe, her hair down? "You could be flogged or tortured for bearing a blade, here."

She lowered the weapon in question, slowly. Not quite battle-mad, but from the look of her she had only narrowly decided he was not a threat. "For defending my princess, or my own honor? I would open my own throat before I allowed such a thing."

"How very Khir of you." He bent to clean his own blade on the assassin's clothing. The dragon-headed sword had claimed yet another soul. It was an old blade, and sometimes he wondered if it hungered. "If I were to raise the alarm, they would wonder what I was doing here." In the Jonwa, after dark, with a half-dressed woman and a fresh body at his feet? The scandal would be unpleasant at best.

"*I* wonder that, General Zakkar." Her Zhaon had become more natural. At least she was not screaming.

"I saw him climb the wall, and followed." *I thought him a lover, or intent on mischief.* Now they were faced with this. It was a headache, as sharp as the thorny succulents just recently unwrapped from their winter finery. "Be quiet for a moment."

She approached, stepping carefully over the sea of small stones, her weight hardly disarranging them. Bent like a panil flower's stem, wiping her own blade upon the dead man's clothing. When it was clean, she examined its gleam critically in the dimness, and cast a quick glance over her shoulder at a rustle in a nest of thornback. She stiffened, preparatory to a defensive stance, and he realized she was... unused... to this manner of event.

Which was a great comfort, but still. Kai had to throttle a thread of uncharacteristic crimson rage. *The battle is past*, he repeated to himself. "It is merely a night-rat." The bumbling masked creatures cleaned every crevice and corner better than a kaburei's scrubbing, and their clever little hands also thieved valuables not locked away, an event much celebrated in amusing illustrations.

"Rats. In a *palace*." Her shudder spoke for itself, though she could not have been unaware rats, masked or otherwise, were just as desirous of luxury as men. Was she in the habit of wandering unattended at night? Had she done such things at home? It did not seem likely, given what he knew of the Khir and their trammeled women.

"Listen." Kai moved to offer his hand, but she stepped hurriedly back. The *yue* moved, a slim wicked blade ideal for close quarters. Did she carry it everywhere? She was certainly skilled with its use. *Every Khir noblewoman*, she had said. "Does the princess have one of those?"

"She... my father kept to the old ways, General Zakkar." Her breathing was still ragged, and she brushed at her face with her free hand, pushing at stray hairs. Her braids had loosened with the exercise, and the contrast with her daylight self was...arresting. "Some modern fathers may not see the need for *yue* practice, perhaps."

In other words, perhaps not, but she was not willing to trust *him* with the information. Was she an assassin? He did not think the Khir would let a noble lady...and yet, Ashani Zlorih had only sent the one attendant with his daughter, ostensibly in response to Zhaon's request for a retinue not overlarge.

Kai had several thoughts upon why the crafty old fox had done so, and none of them were comforting. "Well enough. Keep yours hidden well, Lady Komor. I will deal with this."

"How, exactly? A...a corpse is heavy." The blade vanished, he did not see quite how. So she had a sheath for it, perhaps sewn even into her night-robe? No doubt the assassin had seen her silhouette, and thought her the princess out for an insomniac walk. Or a sleep-journey; there were some who went abroad while unconscious, the body slipping the chain of conscious will.

"I shall find a way," he said, grimly. The problem of *moving* a corpse was simple. Where to let it land was not quite so, and deserved a few moments of careful thought he was ill-disposed to spend just now, with that strange anger filling his belly. Where did it come from? It was of another type than the irritation of knowing yet another shadowed blade had been sent after Takyeo.

Assassins were, after all, a danger common to princes.

Lady Yala brushed afresh at her hair with trembling hands, rearranged her robe, and straightened her sleeves. Kai took another step, between her and the body. She closed her pale Khir eyes and swayed, and when she turned aside to retch he caught her waist, keeping her upright. The slim heat of her burned through her shift, her robe, his half-armor; her shaking infected him.

Would an assassin, even a young one, do so after such an event? She was a noblewoman; they did not often take the Shadowed Road. When they did, they were to be feared, for they were swift and deadly, and often intent upon vengeance for a family's dishonor.

Or so the tales said. Even in the Hundreds there were mentions of vengeful noble daughters striking enemies and falling into a maiden's grave.

Lady Yala did not vomit, but it was close. When the retching had finished, he pulled her closer, his left hand threading through her hair to cup the back of her head, his right flat against her back. It was a measure of her shock and disbelief that she did not struggle.

"Shhh," he soothed. She smelled of jaelo blossom, the acrid tang of fear and effort a sharp counterpoint. His chest-armor would be uncomfortable, pressing against her cheek. "All is well, my lady."

"This is not well," she whispered, in Khir. "It is *not*."

"It is well enough," he replied, haltingly, though handling the sharp consonants tolerably well. Or so he hoped. "Go to bed. Think no more upon this." He did not rest his chin atop her head; that seemed too intimate even for *this* situation. His half-armor did not creak, supple and well used, but he was heavy enough to wring betraying noises out of stone or roof-tile. Carrying a corpse, he would have to stay upon the most solid of roads. It was not a pleasant prospect.

"How can I..." She did not move, stiff slender iron instead of pliable flesh.

Was this your first? Of course it was; at least he could take this as proof she was not a face-dancing shadow intent upon killing Garan royalty. Perhaps she was merely a defender. It was a neat solution to the question of why Ashani Zlorih had sent only the one lady, but not, he suspected, the *entire* answer. "Listen to me." *Do not stand in their way next time. They will think nothing of killing a lady-in-waiting.* And why, in the name of the gods, did such a thought turn the crimson thread into a flood of colorless, acidic sohju rage?

She stilled. Her ear was pressed to his chest, and his traitorous heart was still pounding. Did it think he was still in combat? The muffled blade was dead, he had made certain. Why was he still nervous?

"Listen," he repeated. "Are you listening, my lady?" As if she knew and trusted him. It did no good to imagine, and yet.

"Yes." Slightly muffled. She did not draw away, but she did not soften, either.

What should I tell her? Mercifully, he found good advice in the soup his thinking liver threatened to become. "Return to your chambers. Do not let yourself be seen. Do not think upon this, and do not fear."

"I am not afraid," she whispered in Zhaon, and they both knew it for a lie.

"Good." He decided to let her keep the fiction. "There is no need for fear, my lady." *Now that I am involved, that is.* Had he not been returning from a late council session with Tamuron and some few ministers, all would have turned out much differently. "Now go."

His arms loosened, but for a moment, she paused. Then she took a single step, leaving the circle of his arms, casting one more glance at the slump-shrouded body. The back of her left hand rose to her mouth; she hurried away with her robe whispering and her slippers noiseless upon large stepping-stones.

It lasted no longer than a breath, her pause, but while it did, Zakkar Kai wondered at the sudden sweetness of a night containing murder.

Then he, too, looked at the body, and took a deep breath, settling his shoulders under their armor and grateful the man's wrappings would keep the effluvia of death from making the task before him even more disagreeable.

A Blade of Higher Quality

First Princess Garan Sabwone wrinkled her straight nose, her largest fan moving gently. It was a beautiful morning, and she liked to spend those upon this particular porch with her breakfast waiting upon a covered tray, her hair not yet dressed and her favorite deep yellow morning-robe, patterned with embroidered dragonwings, loosened. The green-garden was at its best on late-spring mornings, with dew still sparkling and the light sharp and clear. "Disturbing," she murmured.

"Isn't it, though?" Second Prince Kurin closed his own fan, set it aside. He had already breakfasted at his mother's palace; the servants were scurrying to bring him tea. The First Concubine's household rustled and ran with morning activity. A sathron was plucked—the mistress was at her daily practice with that noblest of instruments. A flute slowly followed the notes, Prince Jin resentful of any demand that took him from training but an obedient son nonetheless.

A prince must learn such things, even if he had no taste for them.

Well-regulated, Concubine Luswone's part of the Iejo did not admit of gossip or excitement. Still, some of the servants whispered, and Prince Kurin, bearing the news, found Sabwone already knew.

"The body was savaged," he said softly, lingering over each word. "The fingers were hacked off."

"Disgusting." Sabwone's nose wrinkled again. Her fan flicked, brushing away the unsavory details, and snapped closed with a flick of her own, very pretty fingers. "Perhaps I shall lose my appetite, Kurin."

He did not think it likely, but he also did not provide further specifics, settling his orange sleeves with a decided twitch. "The guards saw nothing; they must have been asleep. My mother is beside herself."

"No doubt." The First Princess stroked her jaw with her closed fan, an indication of deep thought. "Perhaps your family has a secret protector?" The corollary—*or someone else does*—lay between them, invisible under a cool breeze full of a scented morning.

Such a question could mean she was innocent, or that she knew very well who the target had been. A search of the assassin's body had provided thought-provoking instruments—grip-sole shoes full of roof-tile dust, wicked curved knives with blackened flats, small twine-wrapped glass bottles of venom or unidentifiable substances, and the like. From the position of the corpse, it appeared it had been thrown from the roof of the First Queen's part of the Kaeje.

"Makar suggested as much." The Fourth Prince *and* Kurin's younger brother Takshin had also examined the corpse minutely where it lay, before nodding at those sent to carry it off. There would be a ritual to cleanse the front steps of any corpse-pollution, and the Emperor would no doubt visit his first queen afterward.

That should be amusing, if Kurin cared to attend. Perhaps even his little brother would be there. If Gamnae was, she would seek to smooth the folds; at least the barbs his mother threw and his father returned would largely pass over her head.

His little sister was not, alas, very bright. At all. Marrying her off would be a relief, yet Kurin had not decided where it would be most advantageous yet. His mother had her ideas, but *he* would withhold consent for a while yet.

It would do the First Queen good to understand her son was no longer a child, and must be consulted upon such matters.

Sabwone lifted the tray cover and peeked beneath, holding her smallest finger elevated in order not to disturb the resin-lacquered nail upon it. Her loosened robe moved aside, showing a fascinating slice of gentle swelling, the beginning of her right breast. "Sweet rai again. I should refuse."

He could have said *sweets for a sweet* or something similar, or needled her with a simple *to sweeten your disposition*. As charming as she was when prodded, Kurin found he liked her far better otherwise, especially lately. "Send it to Jin." Kurin almost laughed at the thought. "*He* is still a child."

That earned him a sideways glance, her bright, very fine eyes half closing. This particular look of hers always pleased Kurin—she looked thus when she could not decide whether his last words were a compliment or a roundabout needling. "He is," she answered, finally. "But even the old like honey, now and then."

Oh, she never disappointed, this beautiful, clawing sister of his. Kurin's cheeks bunched as his smile turned genuine, and her laughter had a familiar edge. His tea arrived, and the girl who poured it was his spy in the First Concubine's household, a little slip of a thing whose peasant family had fallen into debt and consequently sold her at a low price—a small initial investment for a prince, reaping large rewards later. They were always his preferred ears, loyal out of fear or gratitude.

It did not matter which.

He settled upon his padded cushion, sipping at roasted-rai tea—his favorite, and held to be a great cleanser. You could not be too careful with your health.

Sabwone lifted the cover again, set it aside. She chose the clear broth accompanying the sweet rai, and sipped with her hands held just so, wrist cradled in opposite palm and smallest digit lifted the requisite few fingerwidths again. Kitten-small mouthfuls, and when she had finished, she set the pink slipware cup, painted with yeoyan blossoms, down with a tiny click. "I wonder..."

Kurin waited, but she did not continue. "What do you wonder, pretty sister?"

"Someone seems to be sending single assassins." She selected a slice of white, crunchy-pungent walanir, laid it upon her delicate pink tongue. "Are they are thrifty, or merely unintelligent?"

Kurin's good mood evaporated. "Perhaps both," he murmured. "Or perhaps a new enemy sent a blade of higher quality, but only one, to avoid suspicion."

"Possibly." Another slice of walanir, plucked from its bed of peppery greens. "Are you certain you will not have something to eat, Elder Brother?"

He refused, just as politely. The conversation turned to other, less exciting court gossip, and when the servants came to clear her breakfast and hasten her to the dressing-room, Kurin took his leave. They would meet later, in a garden or elsewhere. He had to ration the enjoyment of seeing the First Princess. A pleasure that could wound was one to ration.

All in all, the morning was quite satisfactory. Even if the money paid for a high-quality service was lost, which made it all the sweeter—except for the fact that he did not know quite who had lost it.

He did not even have a guess, and that was, for Second Prince Garan Kurin, very unusual indeed.

A Delicate Balance

Mrong Banh folded his hands inside his sleeves, his round face somber. For once his topknot was not askew but drawn painfully high and tight, held securely by a bone pin and leather cage. "Tossed from the roof." Perhaps his hands were not quite steady, for he kept them tucked as if he were cold. "The assassin's fingers were... missing. Removed after death, I should say. But not long after." That was the most puzzling thing in the entire affair, and the astrologer had the deep and maddening sense that if he could just answer that question, the rest of the riddle would fall into place.

Physician Tian Ha, his court-hat laid aside and his topknot also firmly in place, remained upon his knees. Deprived of his usual skull-grin, he looked very much like a puffbird, snub-nosed and round, ringed eyes opened wide in perpetual surprise. "The First Queen is abed, my lord Emperor. The shock was too much for her delicate nerves."

"Delicate as caltrops," the Emperor muttered. His gaze was piercing and distant though his eyes were somewhat glassy, and the threads of grey in his beard might not have thickened overnight—but it was perhaps a near thing. A fine misting of sweat stood upon his forehead, though it was no more than spring-warm in the gardens or the great court hall.

Mrong Banh coughed, casting the Emperor an apologetic glance; it would not do to let the head physician carry poison to Queen Gamwone's ears. Not that it mattered—what he could not carry, he would invent. Still, the astrologer did what he could to smooth the folds in that fabric. "I beg your pardon, Your Majesty. The dust is thick outside."

Tian Ha busied himself with flagrant knee-bowing yet again, the customary attitude of a courtier giving bad or even moderately unpleasant news. When he straightened, he tugged at his court-hat, keeping it near his knees. "There has been a thorough search of both queens' households. Nobody is missing, nothing seems amiss."

"And no hero has stepped forward to claim this deed?" The Emperor stroked his beard with his fingertips. "How very strange."

"Perhaps it was a quarrel among assassins?" Tian's thin lips drew against themselves. That was the surest indication *he* knew very little; he did not generally look so sour when he had at least a suspicion. "If the body was brought from outside, Your Majesty, it is an insult to—"

"Let us not be hasty." It was perhaps rude to interrupt, but Mrong Banh was almost at the end of his considerable patience. It was an insult or threat to the First Queen whether the body was brought in or made in the palace, so to speak, and *that* lady was not above manufacturing such things to serve her own ends.

Such a thing, of course, could not be said, and Mrong Banh did not wish to give Gamwone's creature any leeway. If the physician was planning an accusation for his patron's ends, he could do it without an astrologer's or emperor's help.

A long, swaying shadow appeared at the end of the hall and resolved into Zan Fein, the Head Court Eunuch. Dark robes flagrantly bare of any ostentation but still sumptuous enough to whisper, his elongated beardless face a rising moon, he minced along on high jatajata[30] sandals. The wooden bars upon their soles click-clacked when he wished others to know of his presence, but were catspaw when he did not. As usual, a draft of umu-blossom—expensive, and cloying—followed him, an invisible veil ready to seine unwary fish. He took his time, pausing at each courtier's station for the usual bow when entering the Emperor's presence, giving both onlookers and the Emperor a few moments to consider the situation.

By the time he arrived before the Throne of Five Winds, Tamuron's expression had turned to granite; Mrong Banh had taken advantage of the pause to breathe deeply and unclench his hands inside wide sleeves.

"May Heaven smile upon the Emperor." Zan Fein settled upon his knees at Tian Ha's side. The physician leaned away slightly, a draft bringing the umu to his face like a soaked rag. "The corpse has been examined."

"So Mrong Banh was telling me." Garan Tamuron turned slightly, gazing at the astrologer standing at his side. The Emperor was also more flushed than usual today, and his under-eyes bore the smudges of sleeplessness.

Banh cleared his throat. "Yes. His fingers were removed, shortly after death—a very traditional punishment for a thief, to be sure, but applied a little late."

If the Emperor was annoyed at this re-treading of ground, he did not show it. "You suspect he was simply a thief?"

"Not at all." Mrong Banh folded his hands outside his sleeves, sedately. The work could now begin, and with both Banh and Zan Fein to maneuver, the First Queen's pet physician would find it significantly more difficult to further his patroness's ends. "There are a few other interesting things. Honorable Zan Fein noted the man's origins."

Tian Ha settled on his heels, perhaps realizing he should have

30. Named for the sound made while the wearer walks.

been with the body instead of tending the First Queen's so-delicate nerves. A few prickles of sweat showed upon his forehead, too. "No doubt there are some signs visible even to untrained eyes," he murmured.

"We guess the man was from Keolh-ha originally, by the wrappings of his blades." Zan Fein's slight smile did not alter, but then, it rarely did. A somber Head Eunuch was a dangerous sign, and a grinning one had never been seen—at least, not publicly. "It is strange, I did not think assassins sent their trainees so far afield, but he was definitely from the northwest, and definitely a walker of the Shadowed Path."

"Not a thief at all." Mrong Banh repeated what he had said this morning, examining the body. "And twice now, an assassin brings unanswered questions."

So too did Zan Fein repeat the chain of logic from the morning's discoveries, for the Emperor's benefit. "Or perhaps he was pursuing a target local assassins had decided against? He, unlike the most recent unpleasant individual to make an attempt within the palace, had only one poison tooth. Intact, too." The eunuch spread his own surprisingly strong, elongated fingers. His palms were soft, delicate as a highborn woman's.

Strangler's hands, Zakkar Kai had called them once, and Banh had been forced to agree.

"And the General?" Tamuron's gaze was piercing. He did not wear a ceremonial hat; his topknot was wrapped in gold beaten thin to be malleable, and carefully pinned. Mrong Banh thought it very likely a shy palace girl from the baths had been selected for the honor of dressing Tamuron's hair this morning, one with quick hands and the habit of glancing at the ground before she spoke in the accent of Tsueruei—Tamuron's own birthplace.

And what of it? When a man grew in age, the things of youth—his own, or another's—became precious. The Emperor had not visited either of his queens or the First Concubine in quite a while, perhaps unwilling to give any of them the appearance of being in favor.

"General Zakkar was not disturbed last night," Mrong Banh replied. It was a lucky thing, for Kai needed all the rest he could gather lately. The Emperor used his favorites ruthlessly, and Zakkar Kai was among the highest regarded. "He wished to examine the body too."

"This fellow is very popular in death." Tamuron's wry tone did not approach true amusement. He gazed down the great ceremonial hall, the bear-carved pillar returning his look with interest. "The First Queen..."

Physician Tian Ha hurried to supply a few words. "Beside herself, my lord."

"Women." Zan Fein's mouth curled. His topknot, silky black, was caged with delicate beadwork, fragrant polished ceduan held by spider-thin silk thread. "Honorable Mrong Banh noticed something quite strange about the body, too."

Tamuron's eyebrows rose slightly. He tucked his hands inside his sleeves, and his full attention settled on the head eunuch. "Oh?"

"There appear to be two different styles of wounding." Zan Fein inclined slightly, giving the honor of that discovery to the astrologer though it could have been shared. "A sword, relatively broad, applied from the back, then very deftly to the chest, between ribs. The man's throat was opened by a sharper, shorter blade."

The Emperor nodded, his gaze sharpening. His broad gold-embroidered belt creaked slightly as he shifted upon the padded bench of the Throne. "So which killed him?"

"They appear to share the honor." Then, Banh thought, the fingers had been sliced free—for what purpose?

"Other assassins? A silent hero in the palace?" Tamuron freed his seal-hand and stroked his beard, the great greenstone-and-silver ring clasping his first finger glittering dully. "This is a riddle." Finally, the Emperor nodded, the short, sharp movement that said he had reached a decision. "Physician Tian. Thank you for your care of the First Queen. You may return to her now, and tell her there is no danger. Her guard will be doubled for a few weeks, as well."

Of course the physician did not wish to be dismissed. "Your Majesty..."

Tamuron, unmoved, simply looked at the man. Tian Ha endured that cool, remote gaze for a few moments, then prostrated himself again and backed from the august presence. He hurried away, his court-hat bobbing, and Mrong Banh's nose twitched with a suppressed sneeze. It was probably the umu perfume.

Zan Fein's eyelashes, thick as a woman's, swept down and fluttered up. "Such strange occurrences lately." His bloodless lips curved like half a cat's smile. "I have a theory."

"Not another one." Mrong Banh almost rolled his eyes. Zan Fein liked theories, and his skull was said to contain a multitude of them. But the eunuch had granted Banh the honor of noticing the wound-styles, so the astrologer must grant Zan Fein the honor of advancing the most likely explanation for the morning's discovery.

"We shall hear it." Tamuron settled himself upon his cushion. If he enjoyed the not-quite-friendly rivalry between two of his counselors, none could tell; he did not bother to add fuel or damp the flames. "If you care to grant it to us, Zan Fein."

"I would not deny such an august request, however little use my poor skills may be." Catlike again, the eunuch's eyes half-closed, attention turned inward. "I believe this particular assassin was intercepted, and flung from the roof to send a message." The eunuch's chin dipped in a nod. "Indeed, I would be willing to bet a silver tal[31] or two upon it."

Tamuron nodded. "And why do you think thus?"

"Consider what has changed in the palace of late, Divine One." Zan Fein settled on his haunches. "And how such change disturbs a delicate balance."

"Was there such a balance?" Mrong Banh folded his hands inside his broad brown sleeves edged with dark blue cotton again,

31. Half an ingot of precious metal.

but in a far more relaxed manner. He did not *like* the head eunuch, but at least Zan Fein was not stupid. There was much to be said for a colleague—if not an enemy or precisely a friend—worthy of some respect.

The numberless heavens knew there were few people worth any measure of *that* precious resource.

"Of a sort." Zan Fein allowed himself a larger smile, now the expression of a cat basking in strong sunshine. "Now there is a new prince, and the prospect of an heir for the Crown Prince. Even the happiest of families may suffer a small amount of tension when additions are made."

"Mh." The Emperor nodded. He removed a square of thirsty fabric from his sleeve and dabbed at his forehead. Thankfully, there were few courtiers or eunuchs even at the end of the hall to note the movement, for this session was early indeed. "Are we to be awash in assassins, then?"

"More than usual?" Mrong Banh could not help sounding sardonic. "Honorable Zan Fein believes this will be the last for some short while." The devotees of the Shadowed Path were, like most merchants, creatures of profit. There was little to be gained when their victims were wary and prepared.

Tamuron looked to the far end of the hall, but his gaze did not see the pillars or the few courtiers yawning into their sleeves. This was, instead, the expression he wore during the start of a campaign when his foe had been alerted to his intentions and required some manner of ruse to be drawn to defeat. "And?"

"And I concur." It irked the astrologer to agree so unreservedly, and the Emperor must have known as much.

"Then we may leave the matter for a moment." Tamuron returned his hands to the royal sleeves. Today the brocade was heavy; perhaps that explained the sweat. "There are larger issues. The delegation from Anwei has arrived." He gestured, and Zan Fein rose with murmured thanks at the mark of high esteem. To be on your feet before the Emperor was a noble thing indeed, even if it turned your legs into solid bars of pain after several hours of bearing the honor.

"I see." The eunuch produced a fan from his sleeve; when opened, calligraphy was visible upon its rai-paper-and-cotton fabric. A line from Cao Zheun—*in winter, a butterfly is slow.* Morbid, but completely in keeping with his aesthetic. His long eyes blinked quickly, now a lizard's tongue-flick. "Honorable Mrong Banh, perhaps, has suspicions of their message?"

The Emperor had no patience for protocol upon this particular question. "Tabrak." He almost spat the word. The Pale Horde, sweeping from their high northwest almost-desert, descending as locusts upon the richer lands, were not a plague to be taken lightly or turned aside without cost.

"It has been over thirty winters." The astrologer nodded. "Enough time for them to replenish their ranks."

"*As the rains come, so do the white ghosts.*" Zan Fein's fan began small, regular motions, indicative of his full attention upon a particular problem. "And Shan?"

Everyone wished to know the astrologer's opinion upon Shan, from the Emperor to Prince Makar. It was the question of the hour. "I believe Prince Takshin has that matter well in hand." Another draft of umu reached Mrong Banh. The Anwei used thick tar-smoke in naval battles to confuse and choke their opponents.

Zan Fein was a close reader of tactics. "At least the Mad Queen is no longer a concern." A delicate flick of the fan. "The Third Prince is no doubt grieving for his . . . adoptive-mother."

What a way to phrase the question. "As is Suon Kiron, no doubt." Mrong Banh's mouth pulled down at the corners. He had always been against sending a prince as hostage, but his opposition had weighed but little those many years ago. At least the Mad Queen's son was not quite an unknown quantity. "Prince Takshin tells me the coronation ceremony was the occasion of much relief upon the part of noble and commoner alike."

"So. Shan is more certain, but Anwei is worried." The Emperor brought them back to the matter at hand. "And Khir is married to us."

"It may be time to send an ambassador to the Tabrak." Zan Fein's fan did not pause. "Simply to be certain." His expression suggested he did not care for the idea, and after he finished the sentence his fan flicked once, dismissing the prospect even as voiced.

"An ambassador might be mistaken for tribute," Mrong Banh pointed out, knowing very well the eunuch agreed. When he played the snake-eater, Zan Fein played the snake, and vice versa. Between them, the possibilities were explored, and Garan Tamuron could choose the path Heaven willed Zhaon to take.

The common people had begun to place small figures at their family shrines, the Emperor's name painted in whatever crimson could be found upon the small terra-cotta figures. Prayers offered before the evening meal included his name. Such was the effect of victory—and ceremony. When there was an Emperor, Zhaon was strong. They longed for a ruler to keep them safely enclosed just as dogs longed for masters to feed and train them.

"Who among the ministers is likely to suggest we send one?" Tamuron finally asked.

Ah, so that was what the Emperor wished. Mrong Banh shifted his weight, easing his left foot. It ached dreadfully, and his robe made a soft sound. "Hanweo, certainly." The Second Queen's uncle, Minister of the Eye, was not quite craven, but Hanweo lay astride the traditional path of the Pale Horde's invasion, and such things were bad for noble coffers. "And Nahjin." The Minister of the Left Foot was ever nervous.

"Tansin might protest, but he will follow Hanweo." The eunuch shook his head, slightly. His thin, beardless cheeks sucked in. "In opposition... the First Concubine's eldest brother, perhaps. And General Zakkar will not think much of such a gesture."

"His opinion carries much weight," Tamuron murmured. "The Crown Prince must be in attendance this afternoon." He would provide a counterweight to those seeking to swim against his father's current, as well.

"Yes, Your Majesty." Mrong Banh inclined his upper body slightly, acknowledging the command.

"Newly married men are peacemakers," Zan Fein added. But not very loudly, for Tamuron's gaze settled upon him, and the royal visage, reddened with a rise of fiery humors, was also stern.

"He will do as his father bids him," the Emperor said, and they moved to other matters.

Attempt to Render More

A bright, hot midmorning brought much of the court to the Artisans' Home. It was a short walk from the Jonwa, and since Mahara had decided to spend the morning taking a Zhaon lesson from Lady Kue, Yala was free to follow a streamlet of brightly clad court ladies, fluttering ribbons and mincing steps, to the great low-timbered complex full of tiny apartments and stalls. Its tiled roof was not red, for no royalty resided within, merely artists, apothecaries, and eunuchs waiting the seasons until called to attend the Emperor and his flock. At its westron corner, the Old Tower loomed, ancient stonework, blue tile, and a five-pointed roof over its bulbous top. Yala had heard that the court astrologer spent much time there, an artificial hill to watch the night sky from. For special occasions, there was a greater tower along the north wall.

At home in Khir, artisans would have been allowed into the Great Keep for performance, or if summoned to show their wares. But this—a whole palace quarter of court-supported makers of fine things, or teachers of skills princes and court ladies would desire—was something new, and she wandered among the painted, much-partitioned passages and small houses for a long while, halting when a particular display caught her attention. Weavers, distillers, gold- and silversmiths, binders, musicians, dressmakers, tea blenders, perfumiers, and more kept tiny apartments here with the most appealing wares. The artisan families allowed to nestle under the Emperor's eaves could display a special symbol in the Great Market beyond the walls, but if delicacy or etiquette forbade a court lady from sallying outside the walls, she would find plenty to tempt her within.

Water-gardens threaded through and around the Home, full of dew that had not yet burned off and alive with flickering dragon-wings. Yala kept to the shade and found a cunningly carved stone arbor near one of the smaller ponds, a clear eye unscaled by green pads. Starvine looped and rioted over the support, spreading along a low balustrade, about to unloose its pendulous, yellow, waxen flowers in cascading handfuls. This particular pond was regularly dredged; its bottom raked, pale sand shimmering under a clear weight. Reeds fringing the edges glowed green. The effect was of a lidless mirrorlight, laid to reflect the sun into the sky's vault.

So much trouble and effort to keep sand clean and water clear, and nobody to witness the brilliant lapping but a Khir lady-in-waiting in a green and blue hajo[32]-patterned dress, her hairpin holding a common, angular stone and red beads. There was bound to be a poem for disquiet in the face of this luxury. She leaned against one of the arbor's supports, contemplating the question, and heard light, firm footsteps.

General Zakkar Kai, in a sober dark tunic but his topknot wrapped with a crimson silk band, halted beside her. He turned his back to the pond, watching the downhill path to this shaded place.

Yala's mouth turned salt-dry. Her palms ached, and it took a few deep breaths before she could loosen her fists. Driving her nails into her own flesh would not change anything, or provide relief.

The general dispensed with pleasantries, but still did not look at her. "Are you injured? At all?"

She had to cough, softly, to clear the way for her voice. "No, my lord." Her thighs ached, and her right wrist felt bruised. Using the

---

32. A pattern of rushing babu leaves.

yue against an attacker was not the same as practice, but she had not done badly. Although the... honor of the kill had gone to the General.

Was it an honor, to him?

"Please, address me as Kai." From the side, his nose was proud, his deep-set eyes not so shadowed, and his lips not quite so overlarge. "Surely we have moved past formality."

I am not so certain. What was the etiquette for this situation? She settled herself to be polite, as if he had not put his arms around her in the dark. And, useless to deny it, as if she had not let him do so. "I did not thank you for your aid."

"There is no need." He made a slight, dismissive movement. Of course, he was general to the Crown Prince's family. He was merely protecting Garan Takyeo, and she a mere corollary.

At least he was not attempting... familiarity. "Nevertheless." She still felt the leather of his half-armor under her cheek. It was different than Bai's rough affection, certainly, and different from Dao's attentions just over the border of formality. The Khir said the Zhaon all stank, but they seemed to bathe just as much as anyone else, and Zakkar Kai had not reeked.

Quite the opposite. A slight, hot breeze touched starvine, ruffled the water's clarity.

"It must pain you, to thank one such as me." He shifted his weight slightly, his left hand twitching before it subsided. Did he mean to touch her, or did he think her about to strike him? "Therefore, avoid it."

"*Pain is inescapable, until one reaches Heaven.*" Zhe Har the Archer said as much, and Yala felt a weary surprise that in the presence of this man, after last night, poetry was still applicable.

"I do not wish to be its cause." He paused, his back just brushing the carved stone of the arbor's fence. "Not to you."

At least he had some manners. She could hardly do less than be somewhat kind in return. "What a pleasant thing to say." Her palms were too damp, and underneath her dress, the silken band below her breasts was dampening rapidly too. It was not the heat.

Her body now knew what it was to strike flesh with the *yue* in earnest. It would not soon forget.

They stood for a short while, almost shoulder to shoulder, the silence alive with soft watersound, the murmur of voices uphill, the whisper or buzz of dragonwings. She was alone with a man in Zhaon, and the thought filled her with a variety of unsteady panic.

Finally, the general spoke again, half-turning his shoulders in her direction. "I would ask your opinion of something, Lady Komor." He dug, two-fingered, in a pocket, and brought out a small dark object. "Tell me, do you know what this is?"

She turned her head, studied his cupped palm. Upon his warrior's calluses lay a ring with a queer metallic glitter that was not metal. It was sin-stone, that eater of ill-luck, highly prized among those in unclean occupations. A sinuous curve, the ring bore stylized swollen wings that would grip the wearer's finger.

Yala's jaw threatened to drop. *"Shinkesai."*[33] She extended one trembling fingertip to almost touch its mellow gleam, then snatched her hand away. "I never thought to see one here." Her throat was too dry to speak properly, and her knees had become soaked babu instead of bone, liable to bend when she did not wish them to.

"So it *is* Khir. I wondered." Zakkar Kai looked merely thoughtful, as if holding a ring to eat the terrifying ill-luck caused by harvesting souls were a mundane, everyday occurrence. "What does this signify? A flightless serpent, but with wings?"

"It is not Khir. It is a *kesaicha*. They live on the edges of the Yaluin and the West Mountains where the Yellow Tribes congregate. No few of the Yellow Tribes worship them." Yala folded her hands inside her sleeves, hoping the ring had not sensed her attempt to touch it. "The wings are poison sacs. The rings are worn by... by..."

"Assassins." He saved her the trouble of saying it and closed his hand, hiding the awful thing from sight. "The Yellow Tribes? That is a long way to send a walker of the Shadowed Path."

"Is that what they are called here?" Her pulse beat thinly in her

33. Literally, "death eater."

throat, her wrists, even her ankles. "Where did you... no. It was not upon *him* last night, was it?"

"Khe Ganwon said Zhaon-An is the navel of the world." Zakkar Kai made a fist and dropped his hand, turned to face the path again. "It is not so strange that one from even the Yaluin would come this far to sell his services. Yet it worries me somewhat."

"Only somewhat?" Yala's voice was a cricket whisper. She had to cough again to clear her throat, but Zakkar Kai's expression did not change.

"Of course, Khe is not part of the Hundreds." He shook his head, a slow, thoughtful movement. The crimson on his topknot-cage gleamed—the most fortunate color, and a prince's right. "You are partial to Zhe Har, I take it."

"Should I not be?" She watched his profile. Why would he show her the ring, and why did he have his back to the water? He stared at the path as if he expected reinforcements. "Are you meeting someone here, General?" *A Zhaon lady, perhaps? Or a contingent of palace guards?*

"Hm?" He glanced at her, returned his attention to the path. "No. I saw you entering the Artisans' Home and followed in the hope of exchanging a quiet word. To caution you not to speak of last night."

"I am not *stupid*, General Zakkar." Tartly, and she wished she had brought something to occupy her hands. They ached to move. Her right palm bore a slim red mark from the *yue*'s handle, but no one had remarked upon it. She could blame a tightened ribbon, perhaps.

"I do not think you stupid at all, Lady Komor. Are you carrying your *yue*?" His Zhaon laid a different weight upon the single syllable, softening until it lost every edge.

"A noblewoman always has her honor." A faint attempt, not at levity but dissimulation. Her right hand, covered by a long Khir sleeve, tensed a little. She shook her left hand free, rested her fingertips upon the carved stone balustrade. To put his body in the pool... how often was it dredged? And how could she escape detection, were it necessary?

She had not much appetite for her breakfast, and now she was glad. A *shinkesai* was no laughing matter, and the thought of another... another *corpse* was unpleasant in the extreme.

Did men ever feel this revulsion? Bai and her father had never spoken of it.

"Do not be troubled." Zakkar Kai's boots were hard-soled, not the glove-shoes of the palace men, as if he would ride to war at any moment. His tone was, all things considered, rather gentle. "But be careful. A man carrying a weapon inside the Palace without leave would be put to death. You they will simply flog. That will leave your princess in an awkward position."

Flogging was for traitors, and kaburei. A noblewoman would not suffer such a thing. Yala's temples began to ache. "Do you threaten me, General?"

"Of course not." A slight shake of his head, as if he considered the idea ridiculous.

"Then what?" Should she face him? What would that look like, if anyone happened along? So she simply leaned to her right a fraction at a time, sinking her weight. Her own shoes were soft, meant for palace halls or small decorous steps upon paved garden paths. She had not brought a sunbell—perhaps she should not leave Jonwa without one; they could be usefully jabbed at a foe to give her time to draw.

And strike.

A small, pained sigh escaped him. "I would like to be your friend, Lady Komor."

"Friend to a Khir?" She did not have to try to sound baffled. *One such as me*, he said. At least he understood his very name was cursed in her country. "You show me a *shinkesai* and say you wish to be my friend?"

"I wanted to know what it was, and now you may put it from your mind, Lady Komor. And your princess has need of all the friendship she can muster here; therefore, so do you. Am I not a worthy ally?"

Oh, the general tells me I may put it from my mind. Yala could not help herself; she quoted Zhe Har again. "What is the price of alliance?" The poet's song of rivals for Princess Sakyewone's hand was not quite a well-bred choice, but she had already stabbed a man in full view of Zakkar Kai. In her night-robe, even, with her hair loose, and now she was exchanging unchaperoned words with the architect of Khir's defeat.

Did he think her honor available, or was this somehow a threat? She could not decide, especially since he had dealt with the corpse last night. And stripped it of the ring he now carried in a pocket, as if he did not care what contagion would leach from it into his clothing, his skin, his *self.*

General Zakkar's Zhaon changed, became the high-accented formality of quotation. "*A few moments of your time, no more.*"

Zhe Har. Again. The warrior's first address to the Moon Maiden. "You have had as much." Yala's cheeks began to burn. The Maiden's reply was *I am late, let me go; My sleeve is caught.* "I am grateful for the aid you rendered me, General." Formally, and in Khir, he would understand the dismissal. In Zhaon, however, it lacked sting.

Or he chose to misunderstand. "Then I shall attempt to render more, Lady Komor."

"Crown Prince Takyeo will appreciate it, I am certain." Yala suspected taking refuge behind Mahara's husband would become a depressingly familiar occurrence. She badly needed a few moments to gather her thoughts, and further suspected she would not be granted them for some short while.

"I will not be serving *him* in this matter, Lady Komor. I take my leave, and wish you a pleasant day." Zakkar Kai left as suddenly as he had appeared; she listened as his footsteps—very light, and deliberate—retreated up the path.

If it was a warning, it was a strange one. Whom did he serve in this matter, then? More importantly, even if Zakkar Kai did not know what a *shinkesai* was, was the appearance of one here truly of so little concern?

Yala waited in the arbor's shade for the fire in her cheeks and the trembling all through her limbs to recede. When it did, she found her stomach had settled somewhat. Now she had a puzzle to work upon and thinking to do.

If she could regain the Jonwa without being waylaid, she could send Anh for tea and busy herself with writing a letter to her father. It was not yet the day of the week she had appointed for that duty and she could not breathe a word of this just yet, but brushwork might bring her some clarity.

Of course the most disturbing realization only appeared after the General was gone, much as a crushing retort to one's rival did not show itself until well after said rival had swept away victorious.

Zakkar Kai had mistaken her for Mahara, in the darkness. Had an assassin bearing a mark of Khir's westron borders done the same?

Last Fading Flower

Spring's first pale green strengthened, deepened, and spread in every garden around the Great Keep of Khir; the rai was sprouting well. The Low Belly festival was still far away and it was never wise to celebrate so early in the season, but if the summer was kind there would likely be another good harvest in terrace and valley.

In his high, spare great hall, Hai Komori Dasho settled in his seat, iron-backed and thin-lipped. He touched his seal-ring with a thumb-tip, then rested his hands upon his thighs. "I am an old man," he said, finally. "I have little time for idleness or games. State your business, Crown Prince."

Grey-eyed, broad-faced Ashani Daoyan, standing as if he were a supplicant instead of the Crown Prince of Khir, visibly reminded himself not to scowl. Court life had not blurred his outline, and reports did not have him among the sinks or amusing himself with theater flowers. Instead, he paid attendance to Zlorih's court and the Second Families, listening much and speaking little. On the practice square or at the hunt he was disdainful of danger and skilled with bow, javelin, and sword; he had not lost a hawk at hunting.

All good signs. And yet.

"I find myself in a dilemma, Lord Komori." Daoyan folded his hands, the statue of a warrior at rest. When he was merely a byblow and not the last flowering of Ashani's tree, he had been the friend of Komori's son, and often Dasho thought he sensed interest toward Yala in this princeling's glances.

It was kept well reined, if it existed. Yet Yala's letters sometimes spoke of receiving news from Khir her father had not sent.

And what letters! Careful, cautious, decorous. Still, she had begun to express such things as preferences, and assured her father more than once that she was well, the princess was well, and Zhaon not as bad as she had feared. She had even begun to send him news, after a fashion, testing delicately to see if her father would chide her for speaking of politics as a Khir woman never should.

A dear child, his only light in the world, now carried far afield. Dasho throttled the cough that had settled in his chest with spring's damp. The dry days would be here soon enough, and the unaccustomed shortness of breath and weakness of limb would retreat.

He highly doubted he would see another flowering of the yeoyan trees, and there was much to be done before that came to pass. A clan-head anticipated both the best and worst, not to mention everything between, and did not leave those under his care adrift. "And you believe I hold a solution? Or advice?"

"Either would be welcome. The Great Rider has spoken, but I do not agree." At least the boy had a clear honest gaze, bright Khir eyes. His mother, the Narikh widow, had been a highly accomplished lady, even if honorless.

What could a woman do, when a Great Rider pursued her? Perhaps Lady Narikh had set her *yue* aside, since her pursuer was of such high station.

Komori Dasho considered every answer he might give to the boy's extraordinary statement, and settled for the barest honesty. "That sounds like treason, Crown Prince."

"Yes." The boy's pale gaze met his unflinchingly. "And yet I come to you, Lord Komori, most upright of men, whose honor is famous."

Pretty words. Komori Dasho did not tense, but his gaze cooled perceptibly. So did his tone. "If treason be your aim, I will hear no more."

"Even if it concerns Komor Yala?"

Komori Dasho's chest became hot, but no sign of anger could be shown. Instead, he made certain his shoulders were a motionless rod, capable of carrying any weight. "My daughter is no betrayer."

"No, your daughter is far too loyal." Ashani Daoyan hurried to dispel the insult. "I did everything I could to stop her going to Zhaon, but now she is there, and in danger."

Now *that* was interesting. Yala's careful hints, twice in the well-guarded cipher of their clan, took on a new and troubling cast. Dasho did not let his hands, resting against his thighs, tense. Not even a finger-flicker was allowed to betray his mood. "What could we do, *Ashani* Daoyan? Our princess was demanded, to bring peace."

"Oh, demanded, certainly." The boy's expression showed plainly what he thought of such ill-bred things as *demands*. "But Hai Ashani Zlorih, my most-honored royal father, is not so certain peace is ideal. Neither are many of his councilors."

Komori Dasho finally moved. He leaned forward slightly, now resting his elbows upon his chair-arms, and steepled his fingers before his chest, an attitude indicative of attention and thoughtfulness. "Be clearer, *Ashani* Daoyan."

The boy, for all his faults, could speak crisply and to the point when needful. He did so now, and each year of Komori Dasho's life weighed more heavily upon his thinning bones, his congested chest, his failing eyesight. He could no longer see the hawks circling the mountain meadows on clear days, or the tombs cut into the high slopes. Only meaningless smears, as if age sought to bring his attention to what was close instead of far away.

So quiet, his household now. No children in its halls, no sense of breathing life in the women's quarters, though the maiden aunts and widows thrust upon the grace of the clan still lingered in those corridors. He allowed them because they reminded him of Yala, and some of them had trained and taught her well. If she had missed a mother's care, she had not shown it.

There was much she had not shown, and he had only himself to blame for that blankness and the sharp loneliness in his chest every evening as he sat alone before the fire in his study. No son, no grandchildren, and his daughter sent into a wolf-den with only a single metal tooth to guard her.

"I see," he said, finally. "And you come to me, Prince, because you wish to avert this?"

"I wish to see Komor Yala safely returned to Khir, my lord Komori." Daoyan shrugged, spreading his own hands. His sword rode his back; he had given a good accounting of himself at Three Rivers, the witnesses said, and had to be knocked unconscious and dragged from the field at Zlorih's express order. "And it appears to me you are the only man among the Second Families I may express this to as well as my only means of obtaining sound counsel. And perhaps help."

"You wish me to commit some form of treason to save my daughter." He should rise, Komori Dasho knew, and refuse to hear more. Or even stride for a weapon and slay this princeling for treason, accepting the inevitable consequences.

He knew what would follow such a course. Ashani Zlorih could not afford to execute his own bastard-born son for treason; his grasp on power was precarious enough. Should Komori Dasho strike down a Crown Prince, his lands would be forfeit and his clan dissolved, and those who relied upon him for protection and shelter most likely executed in their turn. His name would be blackened, and Yala…

"Yes, Lord Komori. I am determined upon treasonous acts." At least the upstart did not deny it, or seek to coat the bitter paste with sweetened, pounded rai. "We cannot save Ashan Mahara. Yala, though… it might be possible."

At least his liver and head had not gone soft or brittle with age, Dasho mused. The consciousness of danger sharpened even an old man. "You speak as if this is already afoot."

The boy shrugged. He did not value his elders as he should, but perhaps a bastard would not feel overly filial. "Why do you think I am here?"

The decision was simple, and already made. Dasho did not struggle with the inevitable, though he should have. Honor and rectitude demanded such effort, no matter the cost.

Yala. His throat had dried. "What would you have of me?"

"You have business which goes to Zhaon-An." Daoyan had obviously spent some thought upon practical steps, and Komori Dasho wondered if he should be insulted by the lad's certainty. "I ask only a place upon a southbound caravan, and a seal from your hand so your daughter will know to trust me."

"Does she not already?" One eyebrow raised, and Dasho would never know how much likeness to his daughter that one small motion called forth in his features. It would not have comforted him if he *had* known.

Such is the faint mercy of Heaven granted to old men.

"She would deny *me*, Komori Dasho." Daoyan's tone was slightly bitter. Yes, he had cast his gaze upon Yala more than once, it was obvious. "But her father? Never."

Dasho listened to the quiet of his empty halls. He felt again the slight weight of a child in his lap, and a chubby child's fist closed awkwardly around a brush under his fingers as he taught brushwork. *Ko. Mo. Ri.* Characters unreeling from a brush's bristles, paper and ink his only tenuous link with a somber young woman in severe dark blue.

"I am dying," he said, finally. "Hai Komori dies with me, no matter the success of junior twigs. She is the last flower upon a fading branch." *My little light.* He straightened, forestalling whatever the young prince planned to say with one raised, iron-slim hand, upon which the great seal of Komori glinted. "But when she falls, I would have it be upon fair soil, at least. Come closer, princeling, and bring a chair." His smile was all bitterness, and Yala would not have recognized the fierce glitter in his pale Khir gaze, for she had never seen her father ride to skirmish or war. "We have much to discuss."

Serve a Paragon

Physician Tian Ha, in sober brown and high-peaked scholar's hat instead of an embroidered court cap, bowed as he backed from the room. The passageway outside the First Queen's examination chamber was dark and somewhat drafty, pale maids hurrying back and forth in shushing skirts. All very young, they were of the type Gamwone preferred—cow-eyed, thin-cheeked, and creeping. It was the custom to settle a dowry upon them if they left service, even kaburei, but there were ways to evade such an expense. Very few of the First Queen's qujei—the word for baby spiders—lasted more than two years, and those who did were crafty, sly, and had a certain droop-eyelid look, a bitter cast to their mouths, and premature weathering. Their matriarch Yona was a dry stick, of the type used for beating rugs.

This hall always lent itself to such thoughts. It was perhaps treasonous to think the next occupant of the First Queen's small palace, enclosed within the same massive red-roofed building housing the Emperor's private and public rooms as well as several chambers of state, might actually open the windows or allow some mirrorlight into this dim drafty passageway.

Or it could be merely wise to consider such an eventuality. Nothing was eternal, as any physician knew.

When he emerged into the mirrorlight brightness of the receiving-hall hung with the First Queen's sansho-flower device upon scroll and tapestry, he halted to blink away dazzlement, slow as that cursed lizard-eyed eunuch Zan Fein. Tian Ha's clearing vision settled upon Prince Kurin's sky-blue robe patterned with stitched, stylized huar blossoms in orange, a fashionable if slightly effeminate choice. The prince's hands were folded and his topknot caged with a brass ring; Tian Ha hurried into a bow. "My apologies, Prince Kurin. The inner hall is very dark today, and your presence is blinding."

"A lovely piece of flattery." Kurin's habitual half-smile was no more indicative of pleasure than anger. His was a hooded gaze as well; perhaps that was why the First Queen favored such things in her qujei. "What of my mother, physician?"

"She is much improved," Tian Ha hurried to reassure, and did not dare to straighten. "It will ease her mind when the exorcist arrives, and—"

"Oh, that." The Second Prince's expression did not change, but he turned away, clasping his hands within his sleeves as was his wont. "Women, spending silver on theatrics."

"Your mother is very devout." Tian Ha's mouth had dried alarmingly. Now he could rise, but he paused, according the prince more honor than his due.

It was safest that way.

Kurin stroked meditatively at his *hurin* with his opposite fingers, his sleeve rippling as he did so. "Come, physician. Walk with me."

Tian Ha braced himself. *Between two fires,* Zhue Can the Younger had written, *one must keep one's robe precisely arranged.* "It would be my pleasure."

That particular passage had been in Tian Ha's final examination, and he took it as an omen.

Once the shoe-servants were waved away and with the prince's attendants following at a safe distance, Tian Ha followed the Second Prince down the wide steps. A slight discoloration halfway down, ringed with impassive golden-coated guards, showed where the body had landed that morning. The exorcist, a slight man in a dusty robe, surveyed the scene, casting an incurious glance at sauntering, rich-robed royalty. Masked and hooded even in this heat, the man bore a long crook-topped staff, its arched snake-head wrapped with flutters of waxed paper daubed with blood-ink charms. A certain amount of theater was necessary for his calling, Tian Ha supposed, but he did not restrain a sniff at the ragged appearance.

The physician hung back until the prince, with a sharp gesture, beckoned him to walk alongside. "Give me the benefit of your observations upon this morning's events, physician."

"With pleasure," Tian Ha repeated, and decided to start with the most bizarre point. "The man's fingers were removed shortly after death."

"How very…traditional. And yet, not." Amusement colored the prince's voice. He eschewed a sunbell, since a man should not care for his skin as a woman did, and he did not seem to feel the heat as lesser beings. Perhaps it was the fine-ground zhu pressed onto his forehead with a pad. It was rumored his attendants ground salt into that courtesan's mix, and dabbed it upon him with trembling hands.

"And yet, strange." Tian Ha matched his steps to the prince's, slightly too long; the prince probably liked making him hurry, seeing if he could force the elder man out of breath. "A walker of the Shadowed Path is not a common thief."

"Assassins steal lives." Thoughtfully, as if the prince had devoted some thought to the matter. "Perhaps this was a warning that one particular life is well guarded."

So Tian Ha had thought, and it was gratifying to hear it from another's lips. "You have a poet's tongue, Prince Kurin."

"Save your flattery for my mother, physician." The prince frowned, but did not direct the expression at him.

Which was a mercy. It had been a most unsatisfying morning, Tian Ha decided he might as well say something truthful. "If she did not enjoy it so much, I might dispense with it altogether."

"Now that is interesting." Kurin paused and glanced at the physician, the corners of his long mouth tilting up. His thin, well-brushed beard lay obediently against his chin and upper lip. "That is the first hint of a spine you've shown in many months, Tian Ha."

Even the most well-hidden, well-reined irritation could make a man incautious. There was a difference, though, in sending a message one had brooded upon for a long while. "Perhaps not the last."

"You are ambitious." As if a Second Prince, with his disdain and his courtier's habits, were not.

Tian Ha quelled the urge to fold his own hands inside his sleeves. He kept them visible—another message sent, that he did not fear scrutiny. His were honest hands, innocent of the rings of high station, their fingertips stained from decoctions as a good physician's should be. He had not done badly for a peasant's son sent to take the civil examinations twice while the rest of his family starved, and he sent money to his aged mother each new moon, well wrapped in a hank of silk to show her he was not doing badly. "I prefer to serve where ambition is a virtue."

"What of gratitude?"

"The ambitious are also gracious." Tian Ha remembered when Garan Tamuron was merely a warlord. A successful one, but no divine being. When power came late to a man, he was mistrustful and sometimes forgot his friends. Not like those nourished upon rule's very essence. "If they are wise."

Prince Kurin indicated the entrance to a small, shimmering everbloom garden, its gate threaded with twining creepwood vines. "Ambition, graciousness, wisdom—you would serve a paragon, then."

The conversation was treading in dangerous waters. Creepwood was poisonous to horses and humans alike, but only if treated differently in each preparation. "Our Emperor is a paragon. He has a god of war at his beck and call, and many vigorous sons." Common weeds could be as dangerous as pampered flowers, too. The medicinal could so easily become its own reverse.

All it took was care, and a little thought. A single twist of the wrist while stirring, a pinch of the wrong powder—innocently, of course. Always innocently. Always with a certain vague regret as one looked into the distance, letting the hands do what the eye must not see and the thinking liver not quite rest upon.

"Precisely." Kurin's sleeves fell back as he halted at a carved stone balustrade and looked over masses of jaelo, thin stalkvines woven into lattices. The flowers would not reach their full potency until summer nights closed sticky-hot upon the city. They were best gathered while dew-heavy for tea, but dry in afternoon's full sun for the bath. The prince rubbed at his greenstone hurai with a well-manicured first finger, thoughtfully. "Heaven has granted my royal father good fortune."

"Heaven favored him in battle many times," Tian Ha murmured. "Yes."

"And now my eldest brother is married. Has Mother sent many gifts to my new sister-in-law?"

"I do not know." The physician shook his head, stroked at his own wispy beard. Perhaps he should shave it off; a clean face was an honest face, was it not? "She did not mention it, nor consult me upon any medicines to be sent."

"I am told tea is a splendid gesture." The Second Prince gazed at a small pond, its surface choked with broad bluegreen huan. The flowers, creamy cups shading into pink at the edges, would appear in fall. On the far end of the garden, the winter-blooming spinuan with its prickle-green, curled leaves hunched, waiting for snow before its clusters of slow-ripening cones would turn crimson. "Especially from Hanweo."

Ah. Tian Ha's stomach turned sour, and there was a most uncomfortable scratching sensation behind his heart. If his conscience had not been so clear, perhaps he would have classified the latter as something close to panic. "Tea is always a gift, the Hundreds say. Hanweo is justly famous for its leaves." And for certain tinctures of herbs grown in swamp-rank patches at the edges of rai ponds, blooming waxen-white. The thick roots of one such plant, when treated with a maximum of care and mixed with fragrant *hrebao*, would vanish into most tea blends and was quite virulent in its abortifacient effect. Too much, and there was permanent damage not only to the womb but to other bodily systems.

It was also well-nigh untraceable, and consequently very expensive.

"Gifts are such a difficult business," Kurin continued, lightly. "Why, festivals are approaching, and I have no idea what to give our newest prince, either. And his adoptive-mother."

"The Second Concubine is reclusive. Such women are difficult to bring gifts to." Tian Ha rested his own hand upon the balustrade. His palms were damp. Had Queen Gamwone told her cherished firstborn of the use of a certain Hanweo weed-root? What was this prince's purpose?

Did it matter? *I know what you have done, you and my mother*, Prince Kurin was saying. Whether it was a warning or a subtle appreciation, only time would tell. And of course, the First Queen was safe from most repercussions.

Her physician, however, would not be, unless he had another powerful patron to ensure his...indiscretions...committed at a certain behest never came to light.

"Still, I should like to be polite." Kurin turned to gaze at the physician. He was slightly taller than the elder man, and gazed down his nose to prove it. "We must have harmony in the many palaces, must we not?" His smile stretched, a cat's satisfied humming at a scuttling creature under its paw. "Tian Ha, you must do me a favor. If my mother wishes to send...a gift, you will tell me? I would not wish to duplicate her efforts. That might be misunderstood."

"Indeed." Fresh unease filled Tian Ha's throat, was sharply checked. It was never wise to relax *or* panic until the conversation was well and truly finished. If Kurin knew about Tian Ha's... indiscretion, what *else* did he know? "Rest assured, Second Prince, you shall know everything I know."

"That is well, then." Kurin inclined his head, and beckoned his attendants forward. "I must give more thought to the matter of gifts. Especially for...faithful...servants." He gestured, a languid waving of fingers.

Dismissed, his heart pounding and his mouth dry, Physician Tian Ha hurried away, for once not seeing the gardens and performing only the most perfunctory of bows to passing, rich-robed courtiers. Queen Gamwone was a powerful patron, to be sure.

Her eldest son was a truly dangerous one. Tian Ha would have to be very, very careful. They were rich, and royal, but he was a *physician*, a learned man in his own right. What one queen had ordered done, another might be willing to do in turn.

The trick would be knowing the exact moment his skills were required elsewhere.

He hoped it would come soon.

Predictable Storm

Kai shifted upon the embroidered cushion. Half his hind end was numb, and the other half wishing it were. This was just like any other battlefield, except the dangers were honeyed words instead of shrieking steel. A certain amount of physical discomfort was to be expected.

He could not decide whether he preferred the stink and screaming of an actual battle to this. Much better was to be alone, in a small but comfortable house, perhaps with the sea breathing at the door. Or the desert, either the grudging, rasping sand he had been born in or the cold reaches of the Naibei.

But not, he thought, the Yaluin Desert. Lady Komor had gone alarmingly pale at the sight of the ring, and he had put it away as soon as possible to save her distress. It did not seem likely another one would show itself, but if it did, he would be ready.

Thinking upon that was a distraction he could ill afford at the moment, but he returned to it over and over. The wondering would not go away. Nor would the soft, subtle breath of jaelo. She must bathe with the dried flowers, that was the only way to achieve such delicacy of aroma.

"An envoy should be sent." The Minister of the Right Eye Hanweo

Hailung Jedao, head of Hanweo and uncle to the Second Queen, did not stroke his closely trimmed beard, a sure sign he did not expect his advice to be taken. He must have a bottom half of iron, to judge by his apparent comfort during long court sessions. "If only to gauge their mood."

"Their mood is to be troublesome." The Crown Prince did not shift in discomfort, but his gaze and tone were both unwontedly sharp. "We do not need to send a calf-sacrifice to them to discern as much."

Perhaps Takyeo was overcompensating for his newly married state and its traditional drawbacks in war-councils. It would be unlike him. Far more likely was that the Emperor had given his eldest son the part he must play, and the young man, as always, was ready to do his best.

"It would not be an offering. Merely an envoy." Nahjin, Minister of the Left Foot, *did* move upon his cushion. He was lean and full of nervous energy, much as a sharp-horned guasa upon the great shelf of the Yaluin steppe. His robes were utterly traditional, in somber scholar-colors, but the rumors said he barely passed his examinations. Certainly he was not the intellectual, say, Fourth Prince Makar was.

Very few were.

The Feet were occupied with finance, the Hands with enforcement and daily counsel. Eyes, Ears, Feathers, left and right, all had their places and duties. The queens were held to be ministers to the Emperor's heart, the concubines to... other areas, to judge by bawdy songs around the markets and in the theatrical districts.

"It will be seen as anxiety." The First Concubine's elder brother Daebo Luashuo Tualih was tall but round, his oily sheen bespeaking a love of rich meals. Under that corpulence, though, was hard muscle, and he rode daily. Kai pitied the horse that had to lug that frame about; even the large palace greys would have trouble with such a burden. "They will scent weakness as hunting dogs do, and begin to bell."

The Emperor, stolid and silent upon his dais, listened with half-lidded eyes. Sweat gleamed upon his brow, and his cheeks were reddened again. No minister would be foolish enough to think him inattentive, though. All remembered the fate of one or two who thought his silence meant lack of notice—the lord of Duogei Province, for one. There were one or two songs about the destruction wreaked upon *that* particular noble's castle and private holdings, but since Tamuron had only been a petty warlord then, those ballads were not sung in reputable theaters or near imperial buildings.

"Or they will see it as outright fear." Lord Tansin, Minister of the Right Feather, held a fan carved of whisper-thin, fragrant ceduan. It flicked lazily, as if its owner saw a fly but was too halfhearted to truly chase it. His dark gaze was quick where his hands were languid, though, and Kai was interested to see which route he would signal support for. Most likely he would follow Hanweo, but he had not leapt to do as much at the beginning, which was... unusual. "Is it wise to let the Pale Horde think us apprehensive?"

Silence fell. Ideally, each man would be mulling the matter at hand, but it was more likely Hanweo was gauging support and Takyeo waiting for his father's signal. The Left Eye was downcast, the Left Ear leaning against a low table in an attitude of deep thought but more likely calculating which faction would pay more for his support, the elderly Minister of the Right Ear bolt-upright upon his cushion and disdaining any decision until he could go home and pore through scrolls for something profound-sounding but ultimately meaningless.

The Right Ear was thought of, in some quarters, as partly senile. Zakkar Kai was not quite certain it was so, but it served Tamuron's purposes to keep such an enigma on hand to counterbalance some of the more ambitious of his ministers.

These, then, were the innermost courtiers. There were other ministers, black-robed and working busily in state chambers, stamping, sealing, making smaller decisions according to the policies decided here. Kai was no minister, but overall command of Zhao's armies—not just the Northern—now rested upon his shoulders.

He wished he were seeing to *that* instead of witnessing this group of old men jostling for each sliver of influence or tax skimmings. The dispatches would be a mountain by the time he returned to his quarters.

"General Zakkar." Luashuo Tualih leaned forward slightly, and Kai almost heard the man's overstuffed cushion creak. "Can our armies stand against Tabrak, should it come to as much?"

Another silence, shocked, as if cold water had been dashed upon unsuspecting nakedness. It would no doubt gratify some of them to hang whatever ill occurred upon his door, whether Tabrak attacked soon or late. Still, Kai gave the question due consideration, allowing his left-hand fingers to tap at his knee. "We have before," he said, finally. "At great cost."

Hailung Jedao finally shifted upon his cushion, a short, irritated movement. "Can we do so again, with the armies in their current state?" No doubt the head of Hanweo did not mean the question to sound so . . . sharp, or insulting.

No doubt.

"*To see the mountain and valley as they are is the heart of strategy,*" Kai quoted.

Lord Tansin's fan paused. "Tuan He," he murmured. One of the Hundreds, and the quotation was from his *Book of War*. It was better to arrange the battlefield so the enemy was lost before he began. The passage went on to speak sharply of those who wasted men's lives upon the field by improperly choosing their ground—or not anticipating their opponent correctly. "Our general is thrifty with his sons' lives."

For, as Tuan He said elsewhere, a general was a father, and every soldier his son. "I do not wish to squander what may earn us victory," Kai corrected, mildly enough. Another quotation, and curse him, Tamuron was likely to be smiling internally, hearing Kai use forced study to advantage. "The Horde will see an envoy as tribute, and if he does not bring salt and earth with him, they are apt to send his head back and come riding sooner." For he did not view it as a question of *if*, only of *when*, but to say so openly would not be politic.

"They are led by a stripling." Hailung Jedao dismissed the entire problem with a wave of one elegant, beringed hand. As a queen's uncle, he often winked at the sumptuary laws...but none of his rings were greenstone.

Winking was one thing; giving Garan Tamuron a reason to remove your insolent fingers quite another.

Kai doubted he could educate the Second Queen's noble uncle upon that point, but as the Emperor's general, he must attempt it. And thinking of fingers was... disconcerting, just at this moment. The ring in one of his many pockets was oddly heavy, and Lady Komor's reaction had told him much. It was, at least, not *hers*.

He returned his attention to the present matter. "A young viper's poison is often more potent." The Horde's current *hetman* was merely a cousin of the great Aro Ba Wistis, but to have survived *and* risen to the head of that collection of blood-mad, dust-choked savages was a considerable achievement indeed.

"A young snake is easily crushed under a strong heel." Lord Hailung permitted himself a small smile, his gaze aiming at some misty point between Kai and Crown Prince Takyeo.

The Emperor's chin dropped fractionally. He studied his second queen's uncle for a long, uncomfortable pause full of Lord Tansin's fan-flicks. "If you are possessed of a plan for doing so, Minister of the Right Eye, let us hear of it."

"Is it not the Head General's duty to frame such plans?" No doubt the noble who held Hanweo now as a gift from the warlord who had married his niece thought that a neat bit of misdirection.

Kai's jaw ached. He forced his teeth to unclench.

"Ah." Tamuron nodded, and there was a familiar gleam in his dark gaze. Anyone who had seen him upon the battlefield might well have leaned forward, anticipating a decisive stroke. "His is the duty, and yours is the estimation of it. I see." It could have been a rebuke, or the Emperor simply noting the weather.

Kai examined his own left index finger, bearing heavy carved greenstone. Rings troubled him today, and, he suspected, would for some while.

"The Horde will come." Prince Takyeo produced his own fan, its arc decorated with a summerfat bronzefish, the brushwork sedate but very fine. He may have even done it himself. "Perhaps visiting them with an army instead of an envoy might satisfy a few among us."

Ah. Now Kai saw the battle. The Crown Prince was the swift hound and Kai the slow; between them, Hailung Jedao would have no room to clap his wings and announce someone incompetent.

"A Horde of our own," he said, as if mulling the notion. "Much forage and fodder will be needed. Levies, of course. And no exemptions from service for the rich or noble."

Lord Tansin had gone pale. "Even the First Dynasty merely stopped at Tabrak's borders." Of course, he was blessed with two sons, and daughters to find dowries for. Levies stood a chance of denuding him of both sons and dowries; no doubt the Emperor had taken that into account.

"Do you think my father less than Zhaon Lao?" When Takyeo sobered and his gaze grew piercing, one could see Tamuron in his features, the rock under the riverbed.

Comparing Garan Tamuron to the one who had first unified Zhaon's disparate parts and drew tribute from his neighbors would also undercut Lord Hailung's influence, and draw attention to the fact that every minister in this room was a tick hanging upon the flank of a phoenix. Whip or spur, both made a beast listen, and the horse of state was no exception.

The trick was in not maddening your mount. And thinking of horses pulled his thoughts quite naturally again to the Khir princess and her lady. Or more precisely, to Komor Yala standing slim and tense in leaf-patterned blue. Had she expected him to strike her?

What is the price of alliance? A deeper question than she suspected, that. "The Emperor has unified Zhaon," Kai found himself saying, somewhat soothingly. "We are at peace and prosperous now, and likely to remain so for a short while. I would not have us show weakness by hurrying to answer a question Tabrak has not directly asked."

"The Tabrak will do as they please," Nahjin the Left Foot said, startling everyone. "Like the Fifth Wind. We must hold ourselves in readiness, but not provoke."

"An envoy would certainly provoke," the Emperor said. "We shall not make any move, but if Tabrak comes riding, I wish for all present to remember this conversation."

The council moved to other matters, but Hailung Jedao studied Zakkar Kai closely, and said little for a very long while.

If the Tabrak were a large storm, the Second Queen's uncle was a small one—of an exceedingly predictable variety, too.

After the Council meeting, Kai did not linger; nor did the Second Queen's uncle. Still, Kai made a point not to hurry down the long hall for the gardens, and allowed the man to catch up. The pillared passage was painted with scenes from every dynasty, from Zhaon Lao to the ill-fated Zhe Danwei, a puppet with his strings held by eunuchs. The last Emperor of the Third Dynasty had a short, uncomfortable life, and battles of ink and scholarship were waged over whether he was poisoned or drank yongbeoh[34] to rob the Horde of Tabrak of the honor of killing him.

Hailung Jedao smiled as he drew close upon slippered feet, a soft, paternal beaming. His topknot-cage held a chip of greenstone, the greatest sliver allowed in sumptuary laws for a man of close kin to a royal wife. "Yap, yap. The master points, and the dog flushes the bird."

"A strange turn of phrase." Kai decided it was better to pretend stupidity, as usual. A peasant's obdurate strategy, but still a fine

34. A quick, excruciating poison made and used by peasants when they wish to commit suicide during famines.

one deployed in its own season. "The start of a new poem, Lord Hanweo?"

"They call you the God of War." The long-eyed man's smile widened as he matched his stride to Kai's, sparing not a glance for the carved columns or the painted walls. "Poems are not your concern."

The inference, of course, was that Kai was a mannerless parvenu who might be planning to unseat the unifier of Zhaon, and using his temporary popularity to do so. What was made in war could be undone by it, and Hanweo had played kingmaker before in Zhaon's history.

King-maker, but not *Emperor*-maker. Hanweo, for all its airs, had never given Zhaon a son strong enough to meld the land into one. No doubt Hailung felt he would be the one to do so, if conditions were right.

The hallway rustled at both ends, servants and courtiers about their business. They would note the head of Hanweo conferring with the Head General, but only the unintelligent would think the two of them allies, no matter how temporary.

Kai let himself use a broad, cheery grin, another peasant's tactic. "So I think, but the Emperor makes me study. It is enough to make a man reach for his sword." There. Let him take that as he willed.

"Some say you are half Khir."

"Do they." *If I were, perhaps I'd've known what that cursed ring was without having to ask.* It only occurred to him now that Komor Yala might think he suspected her of congress with assassins. No wonder she had politely turned aside.

The Second Queen's uncle tried again, lengthening his stride to keep pace. "Others say you are half Tabrak."

"Are they fighting over the butcher's cuts, or laying bets?" He would not lose his temper, Kai decided. But he also would not lower his banners.

A flush crept up Hailung Jedao's throat, touched the collar of his courtier's robe. No hurai, but a thick golden ring upon the traditional finger, marking him as noble and perhaps in unconscious imitation of his royal niece. He traveled with bodyguards to keep that elegant finger from being severed; Hanweo was not poor, but restless bandits plagued the byways. The tax farmers were rapacious in those rich lands. *If only the Emperor knew*, the farmers said to each other.

Garan Tamuron knew. Moving against the house of his Second Queen's kin was not worth the trouble, though. Not yet, and perhaps not ever.

"Even I cannot tell." Hailung Jedao eyed him afresh. "Peace would benefit Zhaon most, General Zakkar. More dead upon the fields mean less taxes, less taxes means—"

"I'm aware that peace is more profitable for merchants, Lord Hanweo. But I am a soldier, and we know peace is not of infinite duration when the pale ghosts come riding." A condescending history lesson and an additional insult, likening a noble to a merchant, all delivered in rough Zhaon. It was surprisingly enjoyable. "Like all carrion, Tabrak has a nose for weakness."

"Stray dogs and carrion." The flush mounted higher. "You think a hurai makes you noble, *Zakkar*?"

As if he should be ashamed of the name Garan Tamuron had given him. "Not any more than a roll of goatskin, Hailung." Impolitic, to insult the man's genealogical scrolls. Gossip held some to be good forgeries—not all, by any means, but any noble house was tender upon that point, even the most unimpeachable.

Between the First Queen's merchant clan and the noble grasping of Hanwei, even an emperor had to step cautiously. So, too, did Kai...but too much caution was worse than none at all, and he had reached his limit for the day.

Hailung's step faltered, the even swaying of his courtier's robe arrested, fabric moving uncertainly. "You are a mannerless dog, *General*." He hissed the title, though his pleasant expression did not falter. "I long to see you collared."

"Careful, *Lord*. I am not quite tame." Kai lifted his left hand, the hurai gleaming mellow-greenstone, and strode away toward the clustered shoe-servants.

If they continued calling him a dog, he might decide to bite. But not today.

Red Time

Filtered mirrorlight softened every edge in the small stone room, fell through dancing dust motes upon the far wall. Mahara sighed fretfully, laid her head upon Yala's bare shoulder. "Will they be angry?"

"I think not. Your honor is known double now." Yala shifted on the padded bench. Always, at the red time, her lower back ached. During her flow, a noblewoman did not practice with the *yue*. Instead, she stretched, working out the stiffness of a day spent abed or upon a slatted, padded bloodcatcher. Even thrice-daily baths did not help the low spine-grinding.

"They seem not to concern themselves with it much here. The princesses act very strangely."

If by *strangely* Mahara meant that one was an empty-headed bird and the other a nose-high cat, Yala agreed. "They are daughters of the house." In other words, their behavior was not scrutinized as a new wife's would be.

"Mh. They are old." Mahara loosed her wrap, folding it at her waist, and dabbed at the tops of her breasts with a citron-soaked rag. Her nipples, larger and paler than Yala's, moved gently with the motion. "Will they marry?"

"There is no gossip yet." Yala loosened her own rectangular wrap as well, damp heat from the braziers collecting in every corner and wringing sweat from her underarms. "The Emperor may not wish to let his daughters go."

"But if he waits too long, nobody will want them." The princess's cheeks flushed, but not with embarrassment. "Especially Sabwone."

"She is a sour fruit, indeed." *And a poisonous one, unless I miss my guess.* In Khir, the play upon Sabwone's name was delightful.

Mahara giggled. They lapsed into silence. Often, their red times overlapped, and had ever since menarche. The bloodroom in this palace was much warmer than the ones in Khir and full of soft mirrorlight, maids occasionally moving behind the partition near the door. There was a bell to call for attendants; kaburei upon their red time in Zhaon wore cotton clouts and went about their duties.

Yala almost thought them luckier. If she could ride, perhaps the aching would ease. On a hunt, a woman upon her red time was held to call better prey—wolves, boars, fiercer birds. It was worth a stained saddle to have such quarry, the old masters said.

She had thought travel would save her the inconvenience of Red Woman's gift, but it seemed to have jarred the flood loose instead. Changes in food, in bedding, in temperature or harvest—all were things that could halt the red times and disturb the delicate balance necessary for the generation of life, or have a reverse effect. If she was lucky, and ate sparely, she might return to her normal courses.

Of course, even when Yala's red time was merely a thin trickle Mahara sometimes had a full flow, and must be attended in a familiar bloodroom. The one at the Great Keep, with its stone floor worn to satin by many generations of soft-slippered feet, was small, the tapestries to wrap the walls threadbare. The room at Komori was even smaller, and sometimes Yala had attended to her flow alone, books filched from forbidden shelves in her father's library consumed whole by mirrorlight cast through thin crimson weavings.

Even her dreams were red, then.

Mahara's head was heavy upon her shoulder. A simmering iron tang reached Yala's nose, as familiar as her own sweat or hair-oil.

This was the heaviest day, and when the mystery receded they could bathe thrice and go about the Jonwa again.

It was well enough. She did not wish to be alone just now.

"Yala?"

"Hm." She stirred slightly, to show she attended. At least here she and Mahara were safe from prying gazes, and could speak somewhat freely.

"It is not so bad here."

Yala's thighs stuck to the padding. She enforced stillness again, her body a mount requiring firmness. "No." Not if what they had expected was dishonor, or worse.

"I like it better than home." A whisper, caught guiltily behind a soft, cupped hand.

I do not. Did her princess think Yala likely to be angered by such a confession? *Angered* was not precisely the word. Slightly surprised, perhaps. Yala's hair was a heavy damp weight against her back, an unwelcome shawl. "Do you really?"

"There are fields in a part of Zhaon that belong to me. There is my name upon paper, and a seal."

Yala had seen the latter, a finely crafted greenstone weight, Mahara's name and title in Zhaon carved into its end. A heavy, substantial mark of her rank and station, setting her name in a holy stone. "Fields?"

"The income from the fields is mine. For spending, or saving." The princess did not quite credit the notion, it was plain. "The fields belong to me, and the kaburei too. They grow flax, *mhung*, and rai."

All good crops, and the beans could follow the rai to keep the fields from exhaustion. "The land..." Yala thought about this. "It says the land *belongs* to you?"

"Yes." Mahara repeated it in Zhaon, *belongs to me.* "That is exactly what was said."

"So different," Yala murmured. In Khir, a woman owned nothing. A daughter passed to a husband, a widow to a brother or uncle of her husband, or back to her father's home. An unmarried woman was the clan's burden, even the fabric of her robes technically the clan's possession. "You have the papers? I may examine them?"

"Of course." Mahara shifted, as if to say that was a silly question. "I must hire a steward, no?"

Which meant Yala must delicately find a way of broaching the subject with someone, most probably Lady Kue, since Mahara must not concern herself directly with grubby merchant tasks. "Yes. I shall take care of it." There were arrangements to be made, and now Yala was glad her father had let her listen to the balancing of household accounts with his own steward Haelon Nujin as soon as she could add and subtract.

"And we must have dresses, Yala." Mahara sounded pleased indeed at the prospect. "Of new cloth."

"Mh." Many of the wedding gifts had included silk. There was also the artist's quarter inside the walls, and that without. Anh would no doubt be full of information about the latter, and while it was not quite proper in Khir, no doubt in Zhaon Yala could leave the palace upon her princess's errands with a close-servant in tow as a nod to propriety. "That means measuring and sewing. We must ride regularly, too. You must strengthen yourself."

"Yes." Mahara shivered, though she was far from cold. "I must give them a son. And soon."

"Not tonight, though." Yala smiled at Mahara's soft laughter. She reached for a round silvery tray upon a low-crouching table, and poured a measure of crushed fruit from a sweating clay jug. Apparently Zhaon women ate unpolished rai and drank soups during their red times. "I am glad you do not hate your husband. Even if he is Zhaon."

"He is kind, Yala. He does not yell or pound the table. He is even gentle, at night."

Yala considered this, as well. "I suppose you wish to tell me exactly how—"

"Yala!" Scandalized, Mahara bumped her with a rounded elbow. "I must find you a husband."

"A Zhaon?" *I would rather open my own throat.* The thought was reflexive, and Yala's back chilled, pinflesh walking in rivers along either side of her spine. How long ago had she thought quite clearly that she wanted to live, and dragged her *yue* across a man's throat instead of her own?

And the shinkesai. It was, she supposed, just barely possible that it was a coincidence. The Yellow Tribes were not homefast, and perhaps there was an enclave of their kind in Zhaon-An's great seething heap. Among that enclave, no doubt there was a death-bringer or two, working as a laborer or a guildfree artisan and waiting for their other talents to be called upon.

"Perhaps one can be found for you." Mahara's tone was light, laughing, but practical. "A rich one, and old, so he may die soon and—"

"Mahara!" It was her turn to sound shocked, and their paired laughter was bright plumage ruffling. Shadows moved behind the partitions, but for once, Yala did not hush her princess or herself.

She had not told Mahara of the assassin. The secret lay behind her breastbone, a cold stone, and it would not shrink when shared. Let her princess worry upon other matters, for this blade had probably been meant for her husband instead. This was Yala's burden to carry.

Her mother's *yue* had tasted blood in defense of Ashan Mahara, and Yala suspected it would do so again, sooner or later.

Insufferable Today

On a small, crooked street with no name close to the palace walls sat a ramshackle inn, its bottom half full of tables and partitions upstairs to provide a patron privacy—if he paid enough.

"More." Takshin gestured at the bowls, and the wide-eyed kaburei hastened to comply, pouring somewhat sloppily into unglazed earthenware. No doubt they would charge him for overflow as well as for anything that vanished down his princely gullet.

Let them charge. There was no shortage of alloy chips, iron, or silver to pay his bill. There was a distinct lack of company, however, which was just as well. The faraway sound of clinking and conversation from under the floorboards or past other flimsy partitions was a low irritant. There were other inns more suited to a prince, with gardens and pretty flowers playing sathrons—and eyes in the walls eating you alive, as well as tiny tapping feet ready to carry tales.

The small, quick-fingered kaburei flinched when Takshin raised his bowl. Any serving-boy would hesitate, pouring for a man with a sword. The scars probably gave Takshin away, as well as his clothing.

Let his mother hear he drank in flea-bitten holes. Let *anyone* hear it.

Yes, he was in a fine mood, but at least it did not blacken when the partition slid aside and Zakkar Kai appeared, a dark mantle over his half-armor despite rising spring heat. *He* did not surrender his sword inside the palace, either. Then again, Kai was probably the son the Emperor wished he had, instead of the rest of them. Except Takyeo.

What would it be like, to know yourself wanted instead of unfinished, unformed, a failure?

"We missed you at Council." Kai settled easily upon an ancient much-mended cushion and accepted the bowl the kaburei poured. He waved, his hurai glinting, and the leather-braided boy scuttled from the room with more alacrity than was perhaps quite seemly.

"I'm sure you did." Takshin tossed the sohju far back. It burned, but it was not even close to strong enough. The mirrorlight here was dim, beams losing their vigor as they passed through screens, even the lamplight low and guttering.

Kai came directly to business, as a nobleman would never condescend to. "Your father wishes to speak to you again."

No, the sohju was *definitely* not strong enough. He should change to atai[35] and take refuge in complete drunkenness, except for the risk of being caught unawares by an enemy real or imagined. "Will he send his golden guards to drag me this time, or just you?"

"I came here to drink, Takshin." Kai's mouth turned down. He knew better than to take offense. It was one of his most winning qualities.

"Council leave a bad taste in your mouth?" Takshin blinked. His gaze was beginning to unfocus, softening just a trifle. The welcome blur did not soothe him, but it made living inside his own skin a little more bearable.

"Yes." Kai filled the prince's bowl, and filled his own as well. He was the elder, but it had always been thus—just one of the small unspoken things added up since Garan Tamuron returned from

35. A very strong, clear liquor that, in its unwatered form, can render one blind after drinking.

the deserts with an orphan clinging to his saddle and announced his intention of adopting the brat.

Kurin and Sabwone had done their best to make the castaway learn his place, Sensheo delighted in tormenting anything helpless, and Makar was only interested in scrolls and bound books. It had fallen to Takshin and Takyeo, already hemmed in by expectation and iron parental fencing, to scrape together what welcome they could for a newcomer.

The Third Prince of Zhaon hated thinking about the past with a passion. He hated everything at the moment, except for perhaps the man drinking across the spill-crusted thinwood table. "You look tired, Kai." Sometimes Takshin wondered if even Takyeo preferred Kai to him.

Probably. Who wouldn't? It was almost inevitable.

The general's grin was startling, an echo of his younger self. "Shall we go to the practice ground, and you may see if my edge is blunted?"

"Why drink sugared soh[36] when the real thing is so readily available?" But Takshin's mouth curled up at one corner, almost unwillingly. "Your letters were...quite welcome." The general had not missed a week, even during the war in the North.

And oh, how that curdled, knowing he was immured in Shan while Zhaon rode to war. It also rankled that he was not present to guard Kai's back.

Assassins and soldiers Zakkar Kai could manage. It was his adoptive-brothers Takshin had to guard a foundling against, if for no other reason than it pleased him to rub a stone into Kurin's heel.

Kai poured them both more. His armor did not creak, put to hard use and softened to fit its wearer almost perfectly. "Yours were brief, but ever welcome as well."

"You sound like a mother. *Write more often.*" Now that they were together, the hum of faraway conversation was not an irritant. Instead, it was almost soothing. Even the dingy, patched partitions

---

36. Watered and sugared sohju given medicinally to cranky children.

held a certain charm, and the dim lighting was suitable for exchanging confidences.

"Hm." Kai did not take the bait. His eyes were a little puffier than usual, whether with irritation or exhaustion was difficult to guess. "Having none, I cannot tell."

"Is not Father your father and mother?" Takshin's lip twitched. Sometimes, when exhaustion set in, the left side of his face took to shivering.

"Careful." Mildly, but Kai's eyelids lowered a fraction. "Your tongue will cut your teeth out, Takshin."

"Sharp as a pin." The pun on his name was not bitter, but it was unpleasant. "Like a certain lady-in-waiting." He hadn't seen her again... but then, did he want to?

"The Khir girl?" Of course Kai would remember Takshin paying any attention to a court lady, at all.

At least he could ask a few questions without being mocked. "What's her name?"

"Komor. Komor Yala." Kai shook his head, and poured yet another measure. They were both drinking too quickly to be prudent. "She handles Zhaon like a blade. I do not envy her position."

"I hear our new sister-in-law is a winsome creature." Calling to pay his respects to his newly married brother was another duty, one that seemed almost pleasant.

And yet he had not, yet. Maybe Takyeo would even be hurt by the refusal. Or, it was more likely he would understand, which was his eldest brother's curse.

No, it was not the understanding. It was the compassion that followed that forced Takyeo's hand. Weary disgust married to comprehension was Takshin's particular lot, and it would have served his eldest brother better than it did a rejected royal cub.

"Takyeo seems happy." At least Kai did not call him *the Crown Prince*. The general lifted the jug, tested its burden with a single shaking slosh. "Drink more, until you mellow."

"I like not the idea of blunting *any* edge, Kai. Unless it is aimed at me."

"Difficult to strike a shadow."

"Is *he* that desperate to speak to me again, then?" Takshin well remembered the screaming when news of his father's impending second marriage reached Garan Gamwone's ears, despite his youth during that chain of events. It was burned into his hide, his mother's anguished cries and his father's cold reply.

You are frightening the children, Gamwone.

She had given him two sons and was bellied with a daughter, and yet the warlord of westron Zhaon took another wife. Takshin, a second son surviving his naming-day, had been meant to cement his mother's position, yet he had somehow failed. The genesis of all his later failures lay in that.

Each time Garan Suon-ei Takshin was in Gamwone's presence, the First Queen was no doubt reminded of her own failure, too. Who knew what the Emperor was reminded of, seeing his scarred, worthless son?

Perhaps you should alter the playing board, Shin-he, Kiron would say. He had an easier temperament, despite his own mother's madness. Takshin sometimes dreamed of the well, the close cold rankness, and Kiron's sudden appearance. *Hist, brother*, the Prince of Shan had whispered. *I am here.*

No matter which way the tangle of memory turned, there was a blade ready to slice.

Kai appeared to consider the sohju in his bowl closely, as if searching for a solution to a riddle. Which meant he was ready to speak of what truly ailed him. "Of all his sons, I think he understands you least."

"Understands? Or likes?" Takshin bolted his own bowl. Suddenly he was nowhere near as drunk as he wanted to be, and the fish-leaping of memory inside his skull yet another irritant. "Since I am the one he threw away."

"That was your mother's doing." Kai bolted another bowlful of sohju, to wash the taste of an unpleasant truth from his mouth. Gamwone had not expected Garan Tamuron to call her bluff when it came to suggesting her own son as the Shan hostage.

She should have, she was married to the man. Of course he would not have waited until his second wife's children reached their naming-day to send a hostage to Shan; the First Queen's theatrics had only served to hasten the inevitable. She had miscalculated both her position *and* her husband badly, and how that must have rankled her indeed.

In any case, Takshin had mentioned mothers first; he was now roundly served by it. "Or so you are told."

"Will you tell me what is truly pulling your tail, Tak?" Kai did not quite sigh like an aggrieved auntie, but it was probably close. "Or will you continue to chew old leather?"

There was no way to explain. So Takshin chose a believable lie. "Tabrak."

"Ah." The general nodded, refilling both bowls though Takshin's hardly needed it. "You definitely should have been in Council."

"Hailung Jedao would love that." The Second Queen's uncle was a grasping goatskin roll, and Takshin generally lost no chance to puncture or madden him.

"You would have enjoyed seeing him caught between two millstones." But Zakkar Kai's mournful aspect did not change. The man was thinking of something else, too.

Takshin gave a soft, unprincely half-snort. "He would have enjoyed seeing the dog of Shan sitting and barking."

"You are truly insufferable today." Now Kai *did* sigh. He was perilously close to aggrieved, that sound said.

"Every day. Not just today." Takshin decided to be curious about something else. "Tell me of the body, Zakkar Kai."

"Which one?" Kai spread his right hand, indicating the drinking-room as if it were stacked with corpses. "There have been a few, of late."

"Well, I am here now." The Third Prince turned the cup a quarter, then another to make a half. Good luck, a blessing to a new venture. Sohju left ring-marks upon the table. Drunken hurai, soaking into cheap wood, staining everything in their orbit. "Either I shall split the hunters or watch your back."

"They are not after me now." Kai sounded very certain.

Oh, Takshin suspected as much. Had there been other attempts while he was immured in Shan? More than likely, though the letters from Takyeo or Kai himself had not even hinted as much. "Takyeo, I'd wager." A newly married Crown Prince could produce an heir, and move his brothers further down the line of succession.

Kai drank, and grimaced. "Or his new bride."

"Unlikely." Rumor had the Khir princess as pretty and docile; the Khir expected their highborn women to merely sew and provide heirs, not influence their husbands. Why would Kai think *her* a target? Takshin's callused fingertips touched his swordhilt, and the sohju was heating him. The scars would flush soon. "An attempt upon her would upset things, would it not? Another war with Khir would be unwelcome."

Kai's expression changed slightly, eyelids contracting and his left thumb rubbing at the hurai much as Makar touched his while thinking deeply. "Perhaps the buyer of the latest services thinks that far ahead."

Now that was interesting. Services, plural. Takshin set that aside for later thought. "Not Kurin, then." A good man, he reflected, would not say the name of his elder brother in such a manner.

"Unless he saw a chance." Kai did not say that Kurin's attempt upon Kai would have been a great deal better planned *and* better financed, but then again, that went without saying. "What we have now is a body on the First Queen's steps and a needle-son with two poison teeth a short while ago as well."

Takshin had heard of that, too. Rumor of an attack on the Head General, beloved of Zhaon and the Emperor, flew upon wings, especially in the low quarters where a man with a high dark hood could drink in peace—and listen his fill—during long curfew-watches. "And Mrong Banh?"

"He is troubled."

Well, when was the astrologer *not* troubled? Even in Takshin's childhood, the man had been a tongue-clicking old maid, possessed of a mind far too fine for a commoner and a loyalty too complete to be safe. "As well he should be. So. What does Takyeo think?"

"He is resigned to it."

There was the entire theme of Takyeo's life. Takshin suppressed an acrid sohju-burning belch. "Now he has a wife to protect." Foolish of Eldest Brother, to agree to a marriage that was only enough to paint him brightly for the hunters. But then, the Crown Prince always longed to make Father proud.

Takshin had decided not so long ago to settle for resisting the Emperor's demands. It was surprisingly simple once he aimed his prow in that direction. Freedom was bitter, but better than eating shit. "I will do what I can."

"That would please your father." Kai found the jug was empty and banged it upon the table twice, summoning a refill. Hurrying feet in the passage said his wish had been heard and would be granted by whatever spirits lurked in passageways of fourth-rate taverns.

"I will not be doing it for *him*." Takshin glowered into his half-full cup.

It was Takyeo who had protected young Takshin from Kurin, as much as possible. It was also Takyeo who had sent letters as Zakkar Kai had, once a month instead of weekly but still welcome. Some were admonishments, some were simple recitations of passing events, several were passages or quotations a man of Zhaon education should know. Between each brushstroke was a simple message, all the more powerful for its quiet.

First Prince Takyeo, not yet Crown Prince, had also abased himself before the Emperor many years ago, asking that Takshin not be sent to Shan. A child's plea, of course.

And yet.

"Takyeo is a good man." Zakkar Kai poured them both another measure. "An honorable one."

Takshin nodded. Therein lay the problem. "I will not be returning to Shan."

"The Emperor will be disappointed." Kai picked up his bowl. "I, on the other hand, will be relieved."

Something in Takshin's chest eased. How did Kai do it, relieve that awful pressure? It was a mystery, and one Takshin was no closer to solving than he had been before he left for Shan, the Mad Queen's grasp, and his scars.

He tilted his bowl, and smiled his wolf-smile. "Then let us drink to that."

A Woman's Battle

A clear morning with the promise of heat later swallowed the palace, and while the dew was still fresh was the best time for walking. Anh and another servant—Nawo, not kaburei but beholden to Lady Kue in some fashion, moon-eyed and plump with dexterous fingers—followed at a respectable distance, keeping to the shade as much as possible. The first few gardens the princess and Yala peered into held brightly colored blots—palace ladies, but none Mahara wished to speak to even though the end of her formal seclusion drew near. So it was that they kept to the broad colonnaded passages at the edges, working their way north and slightly turning the corner to drift vaguely westward.

Riding would have been better exercise, but Mahara had not asked the Crown Prince's permission to leave the palace complex and the cavalry square was taken up with guards at their morning practice. No kaibok today, and Yala's back still contained an ache or two from the red time.

A slight headache from the rising heat-haze was *also* teasing at Yala's patience. How did the southroners move, with this oven-blast hovering over them? And it was only spring. Modesty demanded linen even beneath the under-robe, but she was beginning to see why the Zhaon dresses dispensed with yet another layer of material, no matter how gossamer.

"I do not see why I should." Mahara's lower lip pushed out as she walked, peach silk moving softly in time and her veil pushed slightly aside to give her room to breathe. The pout was not enough to truly spoil her looks, but certainly too petulant for the Crown Princess of Zhaon. "She sent *cotton*."

Yala nodded, her hairpin beads swinging. The First Queen's insult was a dire one, but it must be met carefully to be turned aside. "Consider the advantage, though. If you respond with grace, it shames her much further, and for a longer time." *How can you not see this?* Her own dress, new and high-waisted in the Zhaon fashion, still had long Khir sleeves, and she longed to retreat to the Jonwa and take it off. Spending the day lounging in an under-robe, or better, in a tepid bath, sounded incredibly enticing.

Mahara's lip could not push out more. "We could put something in her tea. Ink. *Chuokon*."

Their skirts brushed together, a companionable sound, and Mahara's arm was steady in Yala's. The paving, swept and sprinkled, dried in bony patches. "I doubt a laxative will teach her any lasting lesson." The idea was extremely humorous, though, and Yala could not help but swallow a laugh.

Which made Mahara ready to plan mischief, if not to attempt it. Tiny prickles of sweat gleamed upon her forehead, gems to match her bright ruby ear-drops. "If I invite her to dinner—"

"—and she takes ill, what do you think the gossip will be?" Yala did not mean to sound so sharp, but the sunshine was too bright, and the sunbell, while perfectly adequate for herself, was a little less for both of them. Still, Mahara wished her to hold it, so hold it Yala did. There was no reason for a kaburei to hear them speaking so, even in Khir. "I asked Lady Kue. The cook would prepare the dishes, all you must do is write the invitation and endure some little time with her."

"Would you be there?" The ear-drops were a gift from the Crown Prince, bearing much luck in their red glitter and swaying. The princess's dress, high-waisted and wide-sleeved in the Zhaon fashion, was of beautiful peach silk embroidered with black thread to suggest the fluid shapes of snow-pards, and a likewise gift.

Yala suppressed an uncharacteristic rasp of irritation. "I doubt such a grand lady wishes to dine with *me*. But I can be behind the partitions, and you may pretend ignorance of anything bad-tempered she says."

"I do not like it." There went the jutting lower lip, again. This time it held a quiver.

"I know." Yala did not like it either, but they must bend with the wind or be beaten down by its force. *That* was a Khir proverb, and the only reason it had escaped inclusion in the Hundreds was probably the shape of the character for *wind*. "But it is best."

Mahara's face smoothed. Heat, a new marriage, and being far from home would have an effect on the sunniest disposition, but at least she tried. She brushed at her veil, a little irritably. "You always know what is best."

Now was not the time to admit any doubt. "No. But in this case—"

"You *do*, Yala. You always have." Mahara sighed, fretfully. "Sometimes I think you should have been born Ashan, and I Komor."

"I would not wish the burden of royalty." The thought of her father's iron gaze bent upon her princess was amusing and terrifying in equal measure, if only for Mahara's sake. And the thought of having to eat dinner with the Great Rider and his habit of smashing his fist upon the table in private was unappetizing. At least Komori Dasho never struck his daughter.

He did not have to. A single look of displeasure was enough.

Mahara swung her right hand softly, describing a thoughtful arc, watching how her sleeve belled. "Still, to invite a guest... perhaps we should ask my husband?"

If Mahara was seeking to avoid the responsibility of refusal, well, there was the best way to do so. It was an inspired suggestion. "Certainly. He is, after all, the prince."

"Crown Prince. Like Daoyan, now."

That was a warning. Mahara had never spoken of Dao before. A bastard scion was beneath her notice, even if Yala's brother had sought his company. "Mh." And now, Yala wondered if perhaps her father had hinted to Bai that cultivating a royal byblow was perhaps wise?

"Father even liked *him* more than me." Mahara sighed, a soft, lonely sound.

What did she expect? Even a bastard son was better than none, and both better than the daughters who would leave the family, married into another line and producing heirs elsewhere. "Fathers love their sons, my princess."

And yet, her father, upon the dais steps with his arm awkwardly about her. *Little light, I called you.* His letters were punctual, too, and full of that odd... un-distance.

Mahara sighed, her steps slowing yet again. The sun was a brazen coin beating down upon paving stones and glittering steps. At this rate they would not return to the Crown Prince's palace before becoming soaked with salt-sweat. "I shall give the prince a son soon."

Hopefully, yes. Yala was choosing the proper quotation for such a wish when a low liquid sound, light and rippling, reached them.

"What is that?" Mahara heard it too. "It's from there."

They both halted, and the breeze picked up as if delighted to hear such skillful plucking and sliding. The player had a great deal of practice to add to natural artistry, that much was clear, and Mahara closed her eyes, tilting her head to listen.

Yala turned her chin and beckoned; Anh hurried to approach and bow. "My lady?"

"Who is likely to be playing such wonderful music?" Zhaon was harsh in her mouth after so much Khir, so Yala took care to smooth every syllable.

"This is the Iejo. It's probably the Second Concubine." Anh looked sober, and perspiring. "She is a great artist, and sometimes plays all day."

"Hm. She is the Head General's adoptive-mother now, and a recluse." Yala glanced at Mahara, who opened her eyes halfway and nodded, answering the unspoken question. The Second

Concubine's wedding gift had been a sathron of beautiful blackened wood, and now Yala guessed why. It was permissible, at this stage of seclusion, to pay a visit to a mother-in-law, and Mahara was not averse. "Go to her door and ask if we may listen more closely to her playing."

Anh hurried away, the importance of the mission bouncing her leather-wrapped braids rhythmically against her shoulders.

"Maybe she will be kind," Mahara said, wistfully.

"If she is not," Yala replied, "we may withdraw." Even in Khir there was no shame for a woman in fleeing such a battle.

A high-ceilinged sitting-room, hung with lovely, plain, light fabrics and full of a cool breeze, accepted them as a garden pond accepts poured-in bronzefish.

"Come in, come in." The Second Concubine was a thin, nervous woman with a gentle face, her eyes slow and deep, her eyebrows well-plucked and darkened with a brushing of kohl. Her hair was thinning but still lustrous, piled atop her head with great simplicity and a plum-lacquered pin. She lifted her likewise plum-colored sleeve to her mouth and coughed, slightly, hectic color blooming in pale cheeks. "You honor me, indeed."

"The honor is ours. We heard your music." Mahara's Zhaon, slow and accented, was still proper in every respect, and her half-bow, Crown Princess to elder and royal concubine, was impeccably correct. "Forgive our intrusion onto your solitude."

"We were drawn by the beauty," Yala murmured.

"No intrusion at all." The woman's smile was wide, and quite lovely. "Music brings a great deal of solace, especially to shy maidens."

It was a lovely turn of phrase, and Yala could not help but smile in return.

"I am Garan Wurei Kanbina," the Second Concubine continued, "and you must call me Auntie. May I offer you refreshment?"

"Oh, no, we could not impose. We were simply passing by and heard you playing; we longed to hear more of your sathron." Mahara fluttered, expressing graceful distress at the thought of putting her hostess to any trouble. Fortunately, Khir manners were much stricter than Zhaon in this respect, so it was impossible for her to overstep.

"Indeed? I love to play, and should very much like to have an audience today. You have a kind face, Crown Princess Mahara. Did I say that correctly?" More anxiety deadened the color in the Second Concubine's cheeks, but her maids were well trained and moved to forestall any disaster. Palace gossip whispered of dark reasons for her reclusiveness, and Anh had hinted of some unhappiness in her past. Perhaps it was only ill health. A new bride should be careful of that, but still, Mahara had the rubies to shield her from any ill-luck.

Crushed fruit was brought, tea produced, and small new-moon cakes of pounded rai with sweetened paste filling their plump crescent shapes. Lady Wurei Kanbina slowly forgot her shyness, Mahara hers in turn, and after a short interval the older woman beckoned them into a jewel of a water-garden. White lattices rose full of green vines, shaded walks ambled, and in the center of a clear pond a small white pavilion held pillows, braided fans, and a short wooden lap-brace for a sathron.

Her instrument was indeed beautiful, a restrained curve of ironwood with only the faintest of inlay in contrasting varnished yeojhan wood, its strings well tuned. Lady Kanbina played for them, and for a few moments Mahara rested her head upon Yala's shoulder as if they were girls in Khir again, safe in a bower. Yala was glad of the chance to sit and listen, for it gave her time to turn inward and mull the unpleasant appearance of a ring carved from sin-stone resting in the palm of a Zhaon general.

There was no help for it. She was going to have to use the cipher, and tell her father something. Just what she could not decide, and it occupied her so much she did not enjoy the music as she should have.

It was cool and lovely here, and the Second Concubine, when she halted her afternoon playing, had more tea brought and said quite firmly over and over that they must visit her anon.

"For I am a little lonely, and since you are new to Zhaon, perhaps you are lonely too." She hid her mouth with her sleeve again, and coughed delicately.

"It seems a very lonely place," Mahara replied, "even if one is not new to Zhaon."

"Well said." Garan Kanbina's glance was not sharp, but it was intelligent, and kind.

The Second Concubine was too fragile to be an ally, Yala decided that evening as she lay in her bath, but perhaps, just perhaps, Kanbina's part of the palace complex could be a refuge.

Brushstrokes

Late-spring storms gathered every afternoon, dark masses sweeping furiously across farm, village, town, and finally the city before galloping south or southeast over more clustered habitations until its force was swallowed by the great grain-bowl. There were tales of sages who knew the correct words, forcing a storm to halt while it was still small so they could climb into a dragon's damp, brocaded saddle, looking down upon Zhaon as rain and thunder galloped through.

Normally, such stories ended with the sage set down in Anwei, where he provided the populace of that city-state with many tales of his experience before saddling a winter storm to take him home. Occasionally, though, Heaven decided to punish such a man for impertinence, dropping him into river or rock. The red smears that rose upon certain iron-rich hills after winter rains were often called *scholar-blooms* as a result.

Kai pushed his shoulders back, the music of joints crack-popping reminding him of morning's training on the practice ground. Stormlight pressed close against the shutters, a deep sickly yellow-green, and the heat was just about to crest. It was perhaps unsoldierly to be grateful he was safe under a roof instead of fighting under a canopy of sky-bruise.

He dipped the brush, smoothed it over the inkstone, and set to work again. Curse Tamuron for demanding this of him—his fingers were simply not dexterous enough. Now that he had a judgment of line and twist, he found his own lacking. Just as he could admire Prince Jin's talent for weapon-play, and know he would never cut the fine figure that lean lithe youth would.

"Hard at work, I see." Fifth Prince Sensheo brushed away a bowing hall-servant, settling the sleeves of his ceduan-green robe with quick habitual motions. His topknot was caged in ivory today, with a filigree-chased wooden pin. "A credit to the Emperor's grace."

"Fifth Prince." Kai concentrated upon the character—line, space, line, the dot placed just so and held for a bare moment so the ink could spread in fine tendrils, but not *too* long, which would produce a sodden mess. "An unexpected pleasure."

"Your steward said you were not to be disturbed, but I said a loving brother would no doubt be welcome."

He would be, if I had one. Kai set the rough practice sheet aside. In lean years kaburei ate rai-paper scraps, even the red-dyed twists hung from ancestors' tablets. There was a whole clutch of tales about the consequences of such a repast, too. He glanced up, taking in Sensheo's long stride, the flutter of his orange robe an early sunset, probably worn in imitation of Second Prince Kurin. "No doubt. What troubles you, Fifth Prince?"

"Trouble?" Sensheo halted, smiling winsomely, his head tilted in a parody of puzzlement and one finger stroking his archer's thumb-ring. "What could possibly trouble me? I simply came to see you."

Oh, and if Kai believed that, no doubt there were storytellers and gullcatchers in the Great Market who would relieve him of any coin, sliver, triangular, or round. Still, he laid his brush aside. "Come, sit. They will bring wine for such an august guest."

Now it was mock astonishment, gap-mouthed and eyes rolling, one of Sensheo's favorite childhood faces. "Drinking before the storm?"

Kai restrained the urge to shrug. "What better time?" His back straightened; it was just like the Fifth Prince to interrupt a pleasant afternoon. To think, Kai had just been enjoying himself.

Clearly such an event could not be borne. "Indeed." Sensheo's face returned to a rueful normality, and he dropped both his hands. He was beginning to soften at shoulder and middle, too much rich living and not enough drill-practice. "You sound like Takshin."

"A high compliment." It was probably not meant to be one, but Kai could take it so and remove any sting.

"I went to see him." Sensheo stood, perhaps very conscious of his green princely silk moving slightly. So he was wary of his welcome here.

Good.

And you could not find him, so decided to seek another victim? "And?" Kai affected curiosity, neatening paper, brushes, touching the inkstone holder to move it forward a fraction.

"He was not at home." Sensheo managed to sound both baffled and relieved by the event.

Where could *home* be, for the Third Prince? No doubt Takshin would treat the very word with contempt, and change the subject. "Deep and shadowed are his ways."

"Gao Lan." Next, Sensheo tried a careless smile, but he still did not move. "You've become quite the scholar."

"Not necessarily." *How many other knives have you sent, Sensheo?* It was not difficult to face the Fifth Prince alone, Kai found. In childhood he had been a terror; now he was simply another palace danger, no more, no less. "I simply practice what the Emperor sets me."

"You could call him *Father*, you know." Even when he attempted to look kindly, Sensheo only managed a smirk. Or perhaps it was only because Kai knew what manner of creature lurked below his adoptive-brother's silk and leather.

"Could I?" Oh, Hailung Jedao and the First Queen would both have a merry time with *that*, if it ever crossed Kai's lips. "Well, the Emperor is father to us all, in Zhaon. In any case he is my lord, and I am very content for it to remain so." *Chew upon that gristle, Fifth Prince. Do you like the taste?*

For a moment Kai toyed with the idea of hinting. Proof was another matter entirely, but Kai *knew*, and letting Sensheo sense as much might even shame him a fraction. Kai suspected his own name had merely been upon a list of potential victims, and the disgraced assassin perhaps had thought him easy prey because he slept relatively alone in the palace complex where servant, kaburei, and attendant clustered each personage of any rank at all.

"Well spoken indeed." Sensheo waited until the servants scurried in with warmed wine, pillows, a low table to match Kai's, practice-paper, inkstone, and brushes. "Ah! Does every guest practice when you do?"

"Only the most esteemed." Kai fought back a smile. His steward Anlon—an old soldier, and a sardonic one—was no doubt commenting upon the ill-mannered man breaking his master's privacy. "Come, Fifth Prince. Tell me what ails you."

The Fifth Prince settled gracefully. If he found the soldier's cushion not soft enough, he made no sign of it, arranging his ceduan-patterned robe and deep green belt, stretching his long fingers. "Nothing *ails* me, unless it is my conscience."

I was not aware you possessed one. "I would have thought yours to be untroubled."

Sensheo affected a small bow at the compliment. "We have not always been kind to each other, General Zakkar."

A serving of truth, with an undertone of poison. As usual. It would be difficult to be "kind" to an elder prince who had always, without fail, spared no effort to remind Kai of his own muddy bloodline and capped off his efforts by sending a cut-rate blade to press the point home.

"Have we not?" A mild inquiry, as if Kai could not remember, while he scrutinized his brushes.

Sensheo's reply was equally, deceptively mild. "Children can be cruel."

"Yes." Kai laid another practice sheet down, settled the weights to keep it from moving, selected a brush. The ritual had a certain calming power, like sharpening each blade before a battle. "They certainly can."

"That was in the past, and I would not have the past rule us."

Kai knew the allusion; he had written similar quotations several times just two days ago. "Sao Shen." And a play upon Garan Sensheo's own name, to boot. Even when making allusions, the Fifth Prince could not fathom a single line that did not have something directly to do with his own position.

"Your studies have borne fruit." Sensheo's smile was quite winning if you didn't know him, or if you had never seen him torment a small animal to death while still in a boy's laced trousers. He cast a critical eye over the brush-rack before selecting one.

Kai studied the blank page. "How could they not, under your august father's direction?"

"Under his direction, yes." Sensheo tapped at his lips with the wooden end of the brush. "I shall write a passage, then."

"Please do." *And then get out*, Kai added silently. He suddenly knew what he would write. "I look forward to admiring your brushwork."

"You are too kind." The storm-dark deepened; Sensheo had probably timed his visit for just such effect. The dry-garden outside this particular room rustled uneasily under a hot, flirting, unsteady breeze. A brief rattle-spatter of drops hit the stones, but Kai was thinking of quite a different garden, and the thunder of flameflowers over a spring evening.

He had not seen Lady Komor for a week, and now, as he practiced a long sinuous stroke that was the backbone of the famous Zhe Har poem about a snake in a hawk's claws, he realized that was a dissatisfaction he could remedy, if he wished to.

Did he?

Sensheo wrote with much swaying, his wrist held at an angle and his sleeve pulled back between two fingers. It took him very little time to finish whatever he wished to accomplish, but Kai kept his gaze upon his own work. Each time the brush lifted, the small tipstroke looked like the curve of a woman's skirts; each time it dove, it was the flashing of a slim, sharp blade.

Finally, the last character was drawn, and Kai rinsed his brush with fussy precision, set it delicately upon the rack, and spent a moment observing whether it would drip into the shallow rectangular catcher.

"Well." Sensheo lifted his sheet fingertip-carefully. "Not my best work." He laid it upon the hinged teacher's board and lifted it to face Kai.

"Sao Shan again." Kai nodded, but did not move. Now Sensheo's purposes—or at least, one of them—became clear. "*Does not the wolf wish for freedom, when the Moon rises?* But you have used the character for *a clouded Sun*, instead." Was it an invitation for Kai to vanish into the distance like a restless warrior at the end of a sad tale, or did he honestly think Tamuron's head general spent more than a passing thought on what a warlord could win?

The Fifth Prince's smile had hardened somewhat. "There must be some wolves who hunt by day."

"In the far North, no doubt, or in the dust beyond Shan." *Be plainer in your meaning, Sensheo.* It was not that Kai didn't suspect, but there was no reason to admit as much. Forcing your opponent to be plain while remaining subtle was a general's art.

"And you have been to the border of their northern home."

Was it Khir Sensheo wished to discuss now? Kai longed to be free of this intrusion, but if Sensheo was seeking to gather support or—more likely—start upon a clumsy new intrigue, it was better to know than to suspect. "I saw no wolves. No doubt the Khir have hunted even the day-walking ones."

"No doubt. Let us see yours, if you've a mind to show it."

Kai did not, but he lifted the practice-paper carefully, fingertip calluses rough against its nap. Heaven sounded its gongs overhead, perhaps celebrating a marriage in its own crystalline halls. Now *there* would be a subject worthy of a poem, if Kai had any skill with such things.

He lifted his own teacher's board, and Sensheo glanced at the paper without seeing its contents. "Interesting." He was back to stroking his thumb-ring. "Uncle came to visit Mother, you know."

"I would have thought that a very regular occurrence." Kai lowered the board, somewhat relieved by Sensheo's inattention.

"He said some very uncomplimentary things about you, Kai." A lowered tone, a play at speaking in confidence. In this light, Sensheo's face looked much younger, round cheeks and a slow, rather sweet smile.

"Did he." This was the point of Sensheo's visit, then.

"Shall I tell you Mother's response?"

Kai laid out a fresh sheet. The insult was coming, he was certain. The only surprise would be the shape it would take. "If you must."

The Fifth Prince forged ahead. He no doubt thought he was being terribly subtle. "She said mistaking a wolf for a dog never ends well."

That particular proverb was not part of the Hundreds. Hailung Jedao might have uttered his favorite insult to others, having failed to wound Kai personally; it was just barely possible he would do so in his niece's presence. What beggared belief was the Second Queen lowering herself to comment upon the matter, or Kai himself.

Kai selected another brush, said nothing. Let Sensheo think his darts would strike.

"When treated kindly, such a creature is loyal, is it not?" *Tap-tap*, his manicured finger upon the horn thumb-ring; Sensheo's eyes were sleepier than usual in the storm-dimness.

Kai's steward was no doubt readying lamps against the momentary night, and would bring them in with some haste. "Wolves have long memories." Kai allowed himself a slight smile, testing the inkstone and examining bristles, as if the brush needed trimming. "Or so I have been told." *There. Take that as you will.* It was also vanishingly unlikely Hailung Jedao had gone scurrying to the Second Queen merely to speak ill of Kai. If he had visited his niece at all, it was only for the business of House Hanweo. Queen Haesara affected to hold herself separate from her clan in the granting of favors or begging the Emperor's attention, but she was merely far more subtle than the First Queen. How she had birthed a son with Sensheo's brashness was a mystery, unless Garan Tamuron's young disdain for his own safety had been distilled and passed through fine material that sieved out some of the Emperor's intelligence.

If Sensheo had received a full measure of *that*, he would be dangerous indeed.

"So I understand." The Fifth Prince lapsed into uneasy silence. Kai's brevity could be a refusal, or a hint, or something else. More spatters of rain fell upon thirsty, dusty stones. If the downpour was long enough, one or two of the thorn-skinned succulents might flower early. "I would like to be a friend to you, Kai. We are both princes now."

Is that the measure of your friendship? A hurai and a blade in the dark? "I have always been well-disposed toward you, Sensheo." And he had. It had taken years of slights and ill treatment before that disposition had changed.

Whatever reply the Fifth Prince might have made was lost in a flash and a crashing of thunder. More rain began, skittering in earnest across dust, gravel, roof-tile, and thatch. Perhaps Sensheo would have lingered, but the lightning began to stab close, thunder following on its heels, and he took his leave in just as much of a hurry as his arrival.

He had not gained what he wanted, after all.

When he was gone, Kai settled upon his cushion and stared long at the doorway, while Anlon moved about with a padded stride, arranging lamps. The steward did not speak at all, sensing his master's mood.

Yes, Sensheo might well have realized, of late, that assassins were nothing to play with. He might further have realized his uncle's sneering and poking might be a handicap when aimed at a victorious general.

On the other hand...yes, treated kindly, almost any creature was loyal.

Except for a scorpion. Or a prince.

Etiquette of Visiting

Mother had been livid, of course. *Who does that barbarian bitch think I am? I am the First Queen of Zhaon!* Gamnae had nodded and made soothing sounds, waiting for the rage to blow itself out. Kurin stared into the garden, visibly bored, until he finally lost patience and told Mother the servants were listening and it was unbecoming of a queen to rave. The silence that fell afterward turned Gamnae's stomach into a black pit like in the novel of Lady Beohyan's Passions, the one she had stolen from Sabwone's room last year. Saba probably knew she'd taken it, but she couldn't do anything about the fact, and that was a nice change.

In the end, it was decided that Second Princess Gamnae would attend the dinner in Queen Gamwone's stead, and it wasn't until afterward that Gamnae realized Mother must have sent a nasty wedding gift like she threatened to but then promised Kurin she wouldn't.

Kurin probably knew she had, too. Which meant they would fight again, and the pit in her stomach would grow teeth.

So it was Gamnae, heart beating thinly in her throat and her ear-drops chiming softly upon their ribbons, who was loaded into the palanquin and carried along a familiar route. Answering a formal invitation from her elder brother, she couldn't very well *walk*, though she would have much preferred it to settle her nerves. Perhaps the new princess—Mahara, a strange name but not entirely unpleasing—would be angry at Mother and revenge herself in some way upon Gamnae?

A court lady could be kind one day and icy the next, like Mother herself. There was no certainty, *everyone* changed, except Takyeo. And maybe Makar, but he had no time for the younglings. Gamnae touched her hair, settled her cuffs, and blinked, hard. The Crown Princess seemed nice, but she was *Khir*, and they stole Zhaon babies to eat. That was just a tale to keep children from misbehaving, true, but... what if?

Kurin would have told her she was being ridiculous, if he noticed her distress at all. There was no telling what Takshin would do either, ever. And of course the new Crown Princess had a right to be angry, even if Mother was First Queen. She might decide Gamnae was an easy target.

They will all try to take your place, Mother often said. *You must not let them.*

But it was so hard. It was the palace, Gamnae had decided. It made people cruel, like houses built in defiance of ancestors. Father had chosen this place because it was the oldest, the First Emperor's home, and surely the wisest man in all Zhaon wouldn't have gone against the ancestors.

It was too big a question for her, so Gamnae tugged at her sleeves again and hoped she'd chosen the right dress, plain dark green silk with segmented yellow babu-shoots upon the cuffs. Sabwone always knew what to wear; she had been *born* knowing. She would cut her gaze at Gamnae's dress and her eyebrows would rise, and Kurin would laugh. Sensheo only told Gamnae she was a child before he hurried away upon whatever errand he had set himself, and Makar was always reading one book or another.

It was far better to steal away with Jin, though all he ever wanted to play was warriors. Swinging blunted blades was stupid, and he always won, but at least he didn't laugh at her. And sometimes they could walk along the riverbank and talk.

He never called her stupid, at least. She didn't even sense he thought it; everyone else did, though. Including Father, who petted and praised her, but never for anything she had *done.*

The palanquin stopped, and the etiquette of visiting took over. A runner sent to the door to announce her presence, a hurrying of the Crown Prince's guards to make a hedge of honor, a swaying of skirts as Gamnae was freed from the palanquin's interior, rising gracefully as her hair decorations and ear-drops chimed. Music followed a princess wherever she stepped, especially in novels.

Lady Kue, tall and severe in her dark Shan dress, and the Khir lady-in-waiting stood on the steps. Lady Kue did not smile, but Lady Komor did, gently, her sharp, unattractive face starred with those strange, ghostly eyes. Her dress was a sober dark blue, again, low-waisted and long-sleeved despite spring heat. Yesterday's storm had opened the floodgates, and the weather had grown torrid-wet. Another storm would arrive, probably during tea.

Lady Kue bowed deeply; Lady Komor a shade less so. "Second Princess Gamnae." At least the Khir woman had tolerable Zhaon. "We are quite honored to receive you."

Which was exactly what she *should* say. Gamnae could have sniffed, like Mother no doubt would have. "It is my honor to visit my esteemed Eldest Brother and his new wife," she said instead. Her voice trembled, but maybe they did not notice. "Lady Komor, is it?"

"Yes, Second Princess." The Khir woman straightened; Gamnae minced past, her high, formal jatajatas click-clacking upon worn stone. Her ankle almost turned as she climbed the second step, but Lady Komor's hand cupped her elbow and steadied her, a movement so neat and graceful it was all but invisible. "Pardon my clumsiness," the Khir woman murmured, her hand vanishing back into her sleeve.

"It's quite all right." A rushing filled Gamnae's ears. She could never do *anything* right, but at least the Khir woman hadn't let her fall. Would it be all over the palace tomorrow, how she'd almost gone sprawling?

"I'm glad you've come," Lady Komor continued, as the doors opened before them. "My princess is eager to receive you."

Lady Kue would stay upon the steps for some short while, giving directions to arrange the palanquin for Gamnae's return, dismissing the quartet of the First Queen's household guards, and arranging whatever presents would be sent back in Gamnae's wake.

Maybe that was where the insult would be.

Takyeo's entry hall looked just the same as it ever had—high, dark, and spare, with that strange air of warm refinement so different from Mother's well-padded quarters. There was Takyeo himself, a genuine grin creasing his usually somber face. Princess Mahara trailed him by three steps, in the fashion of Khir wives, and she did *not* dart Gamnae a piercing look. Instead, she beamed too, a pacific smile Gamnae could find no hint of anger or reproach lingering in.

"Gamnae!" Takyeo did not halt and expect her to bow. Instead, he swept her into a bear hug, as he had when they were young. "What a pleasure! I am sorry the First Queen is ill."

"H-her nerves." Gamnae's voice firmed, became natural. Takyeo wouldn't let anyone insult her, at least not openly. "It has been rather trying for her, lately."

"So I understand." Takyeo pretended he didn't know what Mother said about him. He always had. "Please, come in. You have met Mahara, I know, but may I present her again? Wife, this is my favorite sister."

Was that true? Of course, Takyeo had always protected Jin and Kai from Sensheo and Kurin; Sabwone had lost interest once Gamnae was able to stop crying.

Give her nothing to see, and even the most vengeful cat went looking elsewhere.

So Gamnae put on her prettiest smile and clasped the Khir princess's warm, soft hands.

"I shall call you *sister*," Mahara said, and there seemed no anger in her fingers either. "If you will let me."

Gamnae could find no reason to disagree. "So shall I call you," she replied, and hoped it was not a misstep.

Generous

She is not so bad." Anh drew the comb through Yala's hair. "She and the First Princess were very friendly when they were children. Then, the First Princess put away her dolls, and for a short while the Second Princess was her doll."

"Hm." Yala drew a small damp cloth down her arm. The bath was tepid, unscented, just the thing to end a hot day upon. Another afternoon storm hung over the city, not quite breaking, oppression lingering in every corner.

Dinner was well underway. The Second Princess was losing her hunted-fawn look, the Crown Prince was no doubt relieved the First Queen had not deigned to appear, and Mahara doubly so. They were at tea, so Yala could withdraw. Lady Kue had the arrangements well in hand, and the gifts for the First Queen were tasteful, appropriate, and a high contrast to the wedding cotton.

All in all, the dinner was a success.

"*I* think they would still be very friendly, if the Second Princess were still a doll." Anh clicked her tongue, a soft thoughtful sound as she arranged the light dinner-robe's sleeves. "But little girls grow up." It had all the quality of a Zhaon proverb.

"They do." Yala passed the wet cloth down her other arm as Anh finished combing and moved away, knowing her mistress preferred fine-combing after her bath instead of during. Water lapped against the tub sides, and if she could only stay in water until the summer was past, it might be bearable. "Sometimes I wish I had not."

"I *like* it." The kaburei girl brushed at Yala's dinner-robe, settling it upon the stand and turning to the fine, folded linen shift, shaking it open and searching for anything amiss. At least she did not poke and pry too badly; the *yue* was safely hidden. "I was always afraid, as a child."

A childhood knowing you could be sold away did sound somewhat frightening. A kaburei girl did not even have the faint comfort of marriage as her asking-price. "And now?"

"Only sometimes." Anh decided the shift was in acceptable condition and refolded it. "If I work well, I may be manumit. If not, I go into the Weavers' House outside the west wall when I am old, to drink tea and scold everyone else."

"And weave?" Yala could not help but smile. The girl was a slice of bright mirrorlight, always cheerful.

"Well, yes." Anh settled at the cosmetic table and passed a practiced gaze over the jars, the two combs, the hairpins on a pad of folded cotton. "Old women are best at the looms, and at packing donjba."

"So they say." Yala lifted her right toes from the water, examined them. She would turn into a dried fruit if she stayed here much longer. "Is it often this . . . sticky, in summer?"

"'Tis still spring." Anh set about organizing, though the table did not need it. "The real heat hasn't come yet."

"It gets worse?" Of course it did. Zhaon was a land of deepening worseness. She longed for home, for a clean wind from the mountains and a good hunt or two, a hawk at her wrist, and a light-hooved horse. For Hai Komori's dark ceilings and chill-damp corners, even for the Great Keep's frowning bulk.

"Oh yes. There is the Dry Time at the end of summer, too, no rains to break the heat."

That sounded utterly unpleasant. "How do you bear it?"

"There are the baths, it's not so bad." Anh checked the zhu-powder container. It was still half full; Yala used but little. "But you are northern. The heat will make you wilt."

Too late. I am already wilted. "I certainly hope not."

"We must water you. Many baths, like a rai field." The kaburei's chatter was amusing, and just on the edge of familiarity.

Yala was disposed to be generous, but not familiar. Or perhaps she was fretful in the heat, a horse denied a chance to dust-roll and work burrs from its coat. "Flowers fade," she murmured in Khir. "Only the blade survives." *And even that may tarnish.* She could manage a translation into Zhaon, and not a bad one, but lacking some polish. She should spend some time upon it, perhaps her father... but no, he would worry over the implied meaning.

And he would find plenty else in her planned letter to worry over, already.

"My lady?" Anh's busy hands halted.

"Nothing." It was annoying, to have to speak in Zhaon. "A phrase I must translate, perhaps. Two braids for dinner today."

"Yes, my lady." If she bridled at the implicit rebuke, at least she did not do so openly. Instead, she brought both combs back, her quick fingers going to work.

And since the kaburei was graceful and cheersome, Yala was prepared to offer her a treat in exchange. "After dinner you may retire, and do as you please." Besides, she longed to practice. Stiffness had settled in, and Yala was uneasy.

There was much to be uneasy about, and the discipline of the *yue* helped her think.

"Are you certain?" Anh pressed at her hair with a thirsty cloth and set to work. "You may wish for something cooling, before bed."

"I will be well enough. Perhaps there is someone you would wish to visit, in a little spare time?"

"I could go to the baths." Shyly. "I would like that."

Yala nodded, careful not to disturb the girl's work. "Then you may." The palace baths were a social occasion as well as a cleanly one, especially for servants.

"Many thanks, my lady." Anh's fingers, quick and gentle, braided expertly. When Yala rose, dripping and cool for a few moments, there was the pad to blot her dry, and Anh lingered upon arms and thighs. "What are these? Some punishment?"

"Hawk's kisses," Yala murmured, again in Khir. "The marks of a noblewoman," she added in Zhaon. "Here, along the arm, is where the talons may slice, and if you earn such a mark, ink is often rubbed in to show it proudly."

"Does the princess..." Anh caught herself, bowing her head. "Ah, forgive me, my lady."

"She is royal, Anh." *And you are* too *familiar.* There was no need for a lady-in-waiting's servant, even a close-servant, to comment upon the body of a princess. "My robe."

Loosely belted in gossamer linen and thin evening silk already sticking to damp skin, Yala settled at her own tiny round table with covered dishes—a much smaller repast than the one served to Mahara tonight. At least Second Princess Gamwone was not likely to be actively harmful, except for the tales she would carry to her mother.

More than a morsel of pickled urjo,[37] that purveyor of vigor, polished rai, curd very much in the style of Khir, greens that were tender and no doubt from palace gardens. Beef in the Zhaon charcoal-cooked fashion, with a piquant sauce—needing some little spice, but a rare treat nonetheless. She did not quite hurry her meal, but did not take her time either. It would be beneath her to linger when she had promised the girl a few moments of her own, even if Anh was kaburei.

A nobleman is measured by his kindness in victory, Cao Shan said, though Yala had read enough of the histories to know such a kindness was very rare indeed.

The mirrorlight in her chamber dimmed as Anh set about lighting a lamp or two. Yala's second piece of beef was accompanied by a crack of thunder, its violence muffled by the Jonwa's bulk, and Yala

37. A thin-skinned root vegetable held to be very healthful, since its flesh is red.

was startled into a watchful glance directed at the ceiling, as if she would find the clouds gathering there.

If the storm continued past dark, she could practice without fear of being overheard.

Finally smiling, a wry, wistful expression, Yala continued her dinner.

Delicate Condition

It was not a perfect day for riding, but, as Komori Baiyan had often said, if they waited for a perfect day they would die before setting foot in stirrup. So Mahara essayed permission from her husband, and was surprised to be told that as a married woman past the first full moon of her seclusion she could go where she willed in the palace complex, and go riding outside at her will too as long as she took Yala and a brace of golden-armored palace guards.

"Does he not fear for my honor?" she asked Yala worriedly, but her lady-in-waiting shook her head firmly.

"No, of course he does not. It is Zhaon, they do such things here."

So it was hats, gloves, veils, long tunics, and wide-legged Zhaon riding trousers for both of them, and two kaburei hurrying after them with closed sunbells. There was only a suggestion of a breeze if one stayed near the water-gardens. It was there, along the bank of a tamed creek with clipped green edges, that the Crown Princess saw brightly colored motion in the near distance and stiffened, her arm through Yala's. "Should we turn aside?"

"Nowhere to go," Yala answered, her lips barely moving. They had to pass this way to reach the royal stables. "Besides, they have seen us."

Mahara's heart sank at the prospect of halting to exchange pleasantries. "Bad luck."

“Fear not, Ha Jin. Our swords are sharp.” Yala’s voice dropped into an imitation of a man’s, with a broad nasal accent, painfully refined.

Laughter rose in Mahara’s chest, was swiftly repressed. How long ago had Yala seen that play, coming back to report faithfully on every aspect, even wrapping herself in half a curtain to declaim as the sage Ha San, that perpetually drunken but very wise master of fate? And Ha Jin—no relation—his ever luckless and drunken companion, too.

“And we can outdrink them,” Mahara whispered the next line in return.

Yala had to cough to hide her amusement, hiding her mouth with a bound sleeve. The party farther along the bank turned out to be the two queens of Zhaon, their retinues waiting behind ornamented palanquins, and a pair of Garan princes to boot.

Greetings were exchanged in Zhaon. Queen Gamwone, round and soft, held her lacquered head high, the pins thrust through her hair’s fantastical architecture shivering with tiny gems set in bright wire bees. She accepted Mahara’s polite inquiry after her health with a sniff, but Queen Haesara, her own hair in a high, asymmetrical pile with a cascade of pearl-laced braids on the left, took both Mahara’s hands and kissed her cheeks. The tall woman, her robe the plain sumptuous blue of a summer sky in late afternoon, was an elongated Second Dynasty statue next to Gamwone’s plump, bejeweled glitter.

“And how is *your* health, Crown Princess?” Queen Haesara inquired in her well-bred swallow’s-tone, lilting the Zhaon almost as if singing. “It is much warmer here than in Khir.”

“Yes, and the storms are somewhat different too. I am well enough, and honored at your asking.” Mahara’s Zhaon was still careful, but it was easier now. She found a smile for Fourth Prince Makar, too. “Good morning, Prince Makar. I trust you are well?”

“Well, and missing my conversations with Lady Komor.” Makar’s bow was slight, but his dark eyes kindled. “We still have not resolved our argument over Tang Shun’s last words.”

"Argument?" Mahara's brow creased. Had something happened? Impossible, Yala would have told her—but the prince was smiling, the corners of his eyes crinkling, and she gathered *argument* was not the word it was in Khir.

"A small disagreement at most." Yala did not move from her place at Mahara's shoulder, and indicated the scarred man. "My lady, this is Third Prince Takshin."

So they had been introduced, at least, and Yala had not thought him worth speaking upon.

"Crown Princess." The ill-favored one's bow was perfunctory at best. Oh, his cloth was fine, black Shan silk and dark leather, and his topknot was graceful enough. He even had warrior's scars. But the Third Prince's gaze was cold as a cave-mouth in winter, pupil and iris almost the same shade, and he seemed ill at ease. Mahara strained to remember what present he had sent, and if it warranted a mention.

"He has returned from Shan," Makar added helpfully, "and the manners there are somewhat different."

Yala's stillness was unusual. The Third Prince looked past Mahara, all but staring at her friend. Yala would have told her princess of any danger from this quarter, would she not?

The Third Prince barely glanced at his younger brother. "I lack the polish of those who have not ridden to war." Tossed like a challenge, the syllables sharp and cruel. His lip twisted as he finished, and the scar sliding under his hair would no doubt flush when he grew angry.

"A warrior's manners are no stranger to the Khir," Yala replied, deft and certain. Mahara hid a smile—it was like watching her with the *yue*, every fluid motion accompanied by a bright sharp glitter. Yala was more than capable of handling this prince, so Mahara could simply let her.

Which was a relief.

"He has been rude since birth." Queen Gamwone tossed her head, and her piled hair did not move. Even her hairpin decorations simply gave a muted clicking, as if afraid to call attention to their swaying. "Come, Crown Princess. Take a small walk with us."

Mahara would have preferred to go directly to riding, but there was no way to avoid it. Yala, of course, had to trail at a distance, her gaze upon her princess's back, a comforting warmth and support. A murmur of conversation—the princes, or at least Makar, making well-bred allusions, which of course Yala would match in her accented but quite proper Zhaon.

"Tell me." Queen Gamwone produced a jeon-wood fan from her sleeve, and began to move it in quick, sharp arcs. "How do you like married life, Crown Princess?" She used Zhaon's informal address, and said the title as if it were a slightly obscene word.

"My husband is kind." Mahara's stomach turned into a fist. If Takyeo's mother were alive, would she be this disdainful? Mothers-in-law were supposed to be unpleasant, or at least severe. "And Zhaon is mighty." Surely there could be no argument with that statement, even for a queen.

"Yes, the Khir like war, do they not?" Still informal, each word overenunciated, as if she spoke to a child. Queen Gamwone's scent was a mixture of umu-blossom and an attar of crushflowers, perhaps very expensive. "It is good to be with the winners."

As if she did not know that Khir's borders were still inviolate, and Mahara's marriage was to bring peace for Zhaon as well as her own country. "Have you found it so?" Mahara strove for an artless tone. If the First Queen thought her stupid, she might escape some needling.

Queen Haesara laughed, low and melodious. "The First Queen is always a victor."

"First among rivals." Queen Gamwone stared straight ahead, swaying upon high-boned jatajatas as if she feared the loss of her vital energies into the earth. "I must ask, child, where are you going, dressed like that?"

Mahara strangled a sharp bite of irritation. "Lady Komor and I are riding today."

"Surely that is not advisable?" The First Queen's zhu-powdered face turned into a mask of concern, her eyes glittering like an angry doll's and her crimson-dabbed mouth turning into a round O of surprise. She shook her head again, with that same muffled clicking. "What if you were in a... delicate condition?"

"A delicate condition?" The words were strange, and she could not glance at Yala for aid.

"She means, you must protect the Crown Prince's heir," Queen Haesara supplied. She took Mahara's other arm, and for a moment Mahara thought the two were about to halt and commence pulling, one on either side, children at a rope or dogs with a choice pile of offal. "A Zhaon conqueror needs many sons."

Your Emperor certainly does. Mahara's veil swayed. Hopefully neither woman could read her expression behind its fine weave. "A strong rider makes strong sons."

"How quaint!" Queen Gamwone let loose a high, tittering sound of amusement. "But think of it. All that jostling cannot be good for your insides. Did your mother ride?"

My mother is dead. Mahara's lips curved just a little, the armored smile necessary for long formal dinners at her father's table. A Khir noblewoman must never speak upon politics, nor when a man was speaking, but she could listen, and Mahara had.

Listened, and learned as much as she was able. "My mother rides the Great Fields."

"Does she?" A shade of bafflement crossed over Gamwone's round, zhu-pale face. The First Queen had expected some other answer, obviously, but Mahara thought it just as well that she gain only this one.

"What does that mean?" Queen Haesara wanted to know.

"It means she died in battle." The childbed was a battlefield too, and Ashani Zlorih's wife had met the enemy and conquered twice before winning her last battle bringing Mahara into the world. That she died afterward and only brought out a daughter did not detract from earlier victories.

Queen Gamwone raised her free hand, laying a thoughtful, claw-nailed finger alongside her reddened mouth. "I thought Khir women were all chained in the house, used only for rutting and cooking."

Queen Haesara halted, which meant Mahara had to as well. "We are keeping you from your riding," she said, softly. "You must be about it, or the day's heat will be bad for your mount. My son!" She beckoned, and Prince Makar hurried forward, his blue robe just a few shades lighter than hers.

"I suppose if you *must* ride, we must let you." Gamwone's small, satisfied smirk was a cat's. "I shall send you herbs to strengthen you, Crown Princess."

"Your generosity is extreme," Mahara parried. In other words, she was well aware of the insulting wedding gift, and looked forward to more of the same.

"Careful," Queen Haesara remarked, apparently to empty air. The pearls in her hair glowed. "A true artist does not sing the same song twice."

That made the First Queen drop Mahara's arm as if it burned her, and she darted a venomous glance across bright morning air. "You are so interesting, Crown Princess," she cooed. "I hope you will invite me to dinner again."

"Certainly, if you agree to bring Princess Gamnae. She is a most gracious guest." Mahara half-turned, finding Yala approaching as well. Her friend's veil was held aside with a bentpin, and her cheeks were damp as well as unwonted pale. "Come, we are for the stables."

"Yes, my princess." Yala's farewell bow to the princes was respectful enough; the kaburei behind her had to trot to catch up. "Thank you, Fourth Prince. We shall have to continue another time."

"I look forward to it." From the gleam in his fine dark eyes, it might even be true, and Mahara wondered if he felt an affection for Yala.

It would be nice, she thought, to have her lady marry a prince as well.

"Takshin!" Gamwone turned, the bee ornaments glitter-swinging and refusing to make more than a soft clicking.

Third Prince Takshin, however, was nowhere in sight. Mahara, reprieved, did not hurry away but dawdled while they were still in sight of the palanquins.

When she was certain they could not be witnessed she pushed aside her own veil and gasped in a deep breath. "That woman is a plague," she muttered, in Khir.

Yala did not disagree.

Feasible

His mother kept the slatted window upon the right of her palanquin open, so Makar drifted along at the pace of the kaburei carrying her, his hands clasped behind his back and his soft palace shoes finding every stray pebble. Keeping his expression while he bruised his feet was good practice. Spring sun showed every crack and divot in the paving, poured gold over Zhaon-An, and beat unmercifully upon the shoulders of prince and peasant alike.

"What did you speak of, with her lady-in-waiting?" Queen Haesara looked thoughtful, but Makar noticed the tension in her decorously clasped hands.

Did she worry he was likely to amuse himself with a foreign woman? He felt a curl of not-quite-irritation at the thought. "We disagree upon the matter of a sage's last words. In Khir they are given differently."

"And?" She did not move, and her tension did not abate.

He could have pretended to misunderstand. His own irritation at Queen Gamwone stationing herself on his mother's return route from the apothecaries of the Artisans' Home was, however, quite considerable. A beautiful spring morning spoiled, and all for that round, venomous nincompoop's pettiness. "Lady Komor is one to watch."

That earned him a single sideways glance. "In what fashion, son of mine?"

"A worthy ally, Mother." Others would think Komor Yala simply plain and retiring, a blank page at the side of the Crown Princess. Behind that blank page lurked a very agile mind indeed, one steeped in the Hundreds. She was adept at hiding her feelings, too, and he wondered just what her role had been at home in Khir.

"Hm." Another sharp sideways glance, and his mother's pearled braids swung. "I detect admiration, Maki." An affectionate nickname, and from her it did not irritate.

"Your senses are ever sharp."

"And your brother?"

"What has he done now?" His brother's brain, while agile, was not quite deep enough to remain unruffled; his fingers were not skilled enough to stay still, like a bad sathron player's. Also, if his mother had discovered one or two more of Sensheo's small intrigues, she might be peeved again.

He had not told her Zakkar Kai almost certainly knew whom to blame for the most recent assassin, despite Makar's own best efforts. It would only worry her more; let her have some peace, his decorous dam.

"What does he think of Lady Komor?"

In other words, was Sensheo likely to commit some foolishness in that quarter? "She does not seem his preferred prey." Makar pressed his sweating fingers together. Both Khir women were overdressed for riding, and Lady Komor's cheeks held a sheen of sweat. If she were softer, rounder, and a little taller, she would be accounted arresting, but would never be a beauty. Provincial, of course.

It was the Crown Princess who possessed beauty to spare, and that was fortunate. Takyeo would not have *complained* of an ugly wife, but he had few enough joys as it was.

"One worry less, then." But Makar's mother could always find a fresh concern. To have children was to have disquiet, all the sages agreed. Even the most filial of offspring were hostages to Fate. "Has he been drinking in the city again?"

More like plotting with a shred of drink to oil the hinges. "A few times near the Left Market. He has been visiting fortune-tellers, of late." Makar's foot rolled over a small, sharp stone; he quelled a wince. Not all battle-practice required weaponry.

"Seeking answers from Heaven?" The Second Queen did not sound as if the prospect soothed her, and well it should not. The fortune-tellers Sensheo visited were not known for accuracy, choosing instead to pass word of paying clients to other artisans in much darker guilds.

"Or other quarters." There was no reason to add to his mother's disquiet, Makar told himself again. The palanquin moved slowly through a slice of shade, a projecting roof blocking the sun's fury for a few blessed moments.

"It worries me, my eldest."

He searched for the right tone, found it. Calm and steady, to tell her he had the matter well in hand and she could turn her attention to other matters. "And me, my mother."

"What of the Third Prince?"

"He merely left as soon as was feasible, Mother." Takshin did not like the First Queen any more than Makar did. If Gamwone showed him any affection that might change, but such a thing did not seem in her nature. Even her eldest, favorite son received his share of ill treatment from that woman.

Well, what could one expect from a merchant family? They might have bought power and influence, and their coffers paid for a warlord's road to the Throne of Five Winds, but greasy palms and purchased goatskin genealogies would show through any aping of nobility.

"Will he return to Shan?" Queen Haesara sounded curious, and thoughtful. Her fingers relaxed a fraction, then a fraction more.

"I do not think it is his intention." Which was putting it mildly. Takshin would probably rather peel his own scarred skin free than return to that land.

"That must please *her*."

It was a mistake to think Gamwone would be satisfied by anything. "Very little seems to do so, Mother."

Her small laugh was a reward all its own. "Hm." She wished to make another comment, but doing so within earshot of straining kaburei was not prudent. "Will you have tea with me, Makar?"

"The very thought fills me with joy." She was ever calm, his dam, and beautiful in the style of Hanweo. Her cleverness was much deeper than Sensheo's, but still... Makar saw even her small, subtle intrigues, and moved to forestall those with the potential to cause her embarrassment. Like the copper bracelets affair, or her repeated snubs of Mrong Banh.

A son cared for his mother, and an eldest brother reined his siblings. Sensheo was mostly harmless, as long as Makar kept him leashed. It was growing more difficult lately, and Mother was at the end of her considerable patience.

If only Takyeo possessed Second Prince Kurin's ruthlessness, the throne would be assured and Sensheo's little indiscretions could be allowed to reach their natural conclusion without help or hindrance from Makar's quarter. As it was, he was uneasy, and he suspected his mother had further complaints about Sensheo to voice over cold hurang tea.

Queen Haesara closed the small sliding window, and Makar quickened his pace. The kaburei, bare callus-horned feet shushing upon pavers, stared straight ahead. Shade and sun were all the same to *them*.

He knew one of the bearers was Sensheo's creature. One was his own, as were two of his mother's maids. Takyeo's staff were loyal, but Makar would have felt better if he could have—oh, very quietly, of course—inserted a pair of eyes close to the Crown Prince.

In the absence of such a thing, perhaps a pair near the Crown Princess might do as well. As long as Lady Komor was unaware.

Or... helpful.

Therein lay the problem, and the neatest solution would be, of course, applying some care to the lady herself, alone and adrift in a foreign court. It would require no little patience, if he were to attempt it.

Fortunately, Fourth Prince Garan Makar possessed that quality in abundance. Even if his little brother was straining its outer borders.

Of Service

It was spring, and the big greys—royal and guard mounts, petted and preened—were restive. Like soldiers, they required action to drain away fear and exhaust them into docility. Kai's left shoulder ached from the strike of a weighted practice sword taken on the drillground, Jin's enthusiasm providing an opening where skill alone would not. Now he had the prospect of riding for the rest of the morning and retiring before the heat of the day crested and the usual afternoon storm made the beasts restive, and he was not enchanted with the notion at all.

He'd ridden under worse conditions, and not for pleasure. It was good practice, and it would keep him out of the palace for council meetings. If he was a-horseback, it would be more difficult for Tamuron to call him back. Even a hawk did not rise every time.

It took a few moments for the buzz at one end of the stable complex to register, and when it did he halted. He was somewhat sweat-stained and his topknot was awry, but the discomfort vanished in an instant as he gently pushed aside Khaneng's muzzle and peered over the half-door to the grey's stall.

"It is well enough," Lady Komor was saying, in Khir. She was dressed for riding, albeit a bit heavily. But the Khir were modest, and she did not seem one to loosen a belt, so to speak.

Not unless attacked by an assassin.

Kai hurried out of Khaneng's stall. He did not tug at his long tunic or straighten his topknot, but his hands itched to do so.

"I wished for us to ride a matched set." The Crown Princess's wide, pretty smile robbed her tone of any petulance. She was overdressed too, but looked very fine. "Come, let us be gone."

"A moment." Lady Komor tested the girth again, and clucked at the chestnut mare she'd chosen. "I do not like this bridle, but I suppose the others are worse."

Crown Princess Mahara laughed, a winsome, trilling sound. "Will you blame the bridle if you lose a race?"

"Too hot for a race, my princess." Lilting and affectionate, the phrase dropped into hay-scented, dust-ridden air. She shifted to informal Khir, addressing the bay. "Come then, my fine lady. Let us see."

"General Zakkar." The Crown Princess peered around her own mare, a fine-chested black eager to be out and away from the stable. "Are you today for riding?" She winced very prettily, realizing her Zhaon was mixed with Khir. "Ah, no, forgive my lapse in manners. Are you about to ride?"

"I could, if you would not mind a slow and clumsy companion." He swept her a bow, hopefully fine enough to overcome his dishevelment. "I am no Khir, to ride like the goddess upon her endless hunt."

That earned him a smile, and the Crown Princess loosened her veil, letting it fall across her face. "Excellent! My husband says we require a guard to go riding."

Ah. "The Crown Prince is cautious, and prizes you greatly. A moment to bring my own mount to the bailey?"

"We shall wait, but not long. Yala, look! The General himself will accompany us." If it irked Princess Mahara to have the enemy of her people dogging her steps, she did not show it.

"Hm? Ah. Zakkar Kai." Lady Komor brushed irritably at her veil. "Seeking to be of service?" Khir accent rubbed through her Zhaon, sharpening each consonant.

"If you'll have me." *A fortunate meeting*, he could have quoted, but she did not seem in the mood for poetry now.

Flushed along her high cheekbones, her mouth pursed, she nodded and dismissed him from her attention, turning back to the horse. "Come along, cousin fourfoot. We shall find shade somewhere."

No sooner had he turned away than he was hailed from the other end of the stable. "Kai! Eh, Kai!" It was Prince Takshin, his Shan trousers stuffed carelessly into boot-tops and a quite uncharacteristic gleam in his eyes. "Care for a gallop?"

"My services as Head General are engaged." Kai did not miss the other man's glance over his shoulder. His voice dropped. "Did Takyeo send you?"

"I sent myself," was Takshin's reply. "And we'd best be gone before my mother comes looking for me again. She wants blood this morning."

Perhaps she thinks it will keep her young. The night-demons who sucked youth and vital fluids from the ancestorless and hence unprotected poor were plump-faced, too. Kai grinned. "I take it you want to ride the Tooth."

"He remembers me." Takshin's smile, marred only by the scar upon his lip, was not bitter for once. "They're saddling him now."

Small Pain

The Tooth did indeed remember Takshin. Cob-headed and high-blooded, the mottled grey was possessed of uncanny intelligence and stubbornness, and that endeared him to the Third Prince more than any fine lines or great pedigree could. Besides, Takyeo had taken the foal into his own stable-quarter when Takshin had indirectly expressed a kinship with the beast upon his second-to-last visit home, so riding him in attendance to the Crown Prince's wife had a certain symmetry.

The stink, clamor, and dust of the High Road cleared before them, kaburei and peasant, artisan and scholar scattering before the sound of hooves and the sight of the two large greys accompanying slighter, veiled female riders. Those mounted on less-thoroughbred mounts moved aside as well, and it only took the sight of Zakkar Kai at the North Gate for them to be waved through the smaller throat of the postern. Kai took the lead, choosing the Qulon Road where the pleasure-woods spread beyond a few large nobles' clan-farms. At least that had not changed while he was enduring a deranged queen, Takshin thought, and his smile was too grim for the pleasure riding was supposed to bring a prince.

The Khir women held their mounts to a canter for a short while, perhaps thinking the large Guard-bred greys would tire attempting a gallop. When it was time to cool, they pushed their veils aside, and liquid scarves of Khir flowed back and forth. Eventually, a wide sun-dappled meadow opened upon the left, and the Khir women amused themselves with horse-games before leading the mares to a clear stream almost buried in sedge.

Takshin found himself next to Lady Yala, and decided it would be easy to fret her again. "Have you forgiven me yet, spyling?"

"For what?" Her grey gaze, much lighter than a Guard mount's coat, did not move from her feet, placed carefully upon two mostly dry hummocks. Her mare shouldered forward a step, two, and bent gracefully to drink. The Tooth, also slaking his thirst, blew bubbles in the stream and lifted his dripping mouth.

"For catching you out at eavesdropping."

Her mouth turned down for a brief moment as she smoothed her mare's neck with gloved fingers. Her profile was severe, a carver's attempt to turn stone into flesh. "Since I was not, Third Prince, there is nothing to forgive."

"Well, since I heard no gossip about our meeting, I am forced to conclude you may keep a secret as well." Throw a handful of rai, see what rose to the surface. Just like feeding bronzefish in a garden pond.

She still did not look at him. Why wear so much heavy cloth to go riding? "Or I could simply be indisposed to gossip itself."

"You are a *woman*." They talked, and talked; it was what they *did*. Even the Mad Queen had been fond of monologues, delivered in her sweet, clear, utterly reasonless voice.

The Khir woman did not rise to the lure. "So I am told." A soft rustling spring breeze combed the banks, whispering in its own tongue.

Oh, she was amusing. "Or you could have decided the tale was unworthy to tell, being about the ugliest prince of Zhaon."

"Do you hold that distinction, then?" Mild interest, no more. She did not seem offended, or even flustered. Perhaps only a little bored.

That stung him more than open disdain or fear could. "Do you want to know how?"

"How what, Third Prince?" Her glance only rose to his chest before being returned, with well-bred reticence, to her feet.

"The scars."

That brought her chin up, and she regarded him for a long moment. Would she affect pity, or be disgusted? Either were not to be borne.

"If it pleases you to speak upon it." She left her feet precisely where they were, but her weight shifted a fraction. Strands of blue-black hair clung to her damp forehead, one curving on her cheek. It was too warm for a veil, and for those heavy riding trousers. Even wrapped in several layers, she was slight, with sharp shoulders. "Some warriors speak of their wounds, others do not."

"It was not a battle." He would not tell her the story of the one upon his left cheek, vanishing under his hair. But his lip, perhaps. That was enough of a story. "I was seven winters high. The Mad Queen of Shan ordered me thrown into a dry well, for calling her *Mother*." As he had been commanded to do by Her Serene Majesty the preceding day, of course. The rules changed at whim, a terrifying inconsistency he had found oddly familiar even as a child. "That night her son climbed down too, while I lay bleeding."

"Kiron?" Her lips shaped the name strangely. "That is his name, correct? The Suon prince of Shan?"

"Yes. He tied me to his back and carried me forth." *What was I to do?* was all Kiron would say of the matter. *I missed my playmate.* "I lay near death for three days."

Her chin dipped, an approximation of a nod. "And those are… the marks?"

"Some of them." He was lucky his ribs had not been staved in, merely battered. The scar upon his jaw was another tale, the gift of a bandit with a knife while he and Kiron escaped the castle to ride in the woods.

That nameless bandit bore the distinction of being Takshin's first kill, and he had told no one, not even Kiron. Of course, the High Prince of Shan could guess.

Now Kiron was king, and Takshin was home. Or at least, the Third Prince of Zhaon was where he chose to be. *Home* was merely a word, holding no meaning in Zhaon or in the Shan dialects.

With her veil tucked aside, Lady Komor looked like a nun or exorcist, a fantastical headdress robbing an onlooker of the sight of a woman's hair, that crowning glory. "You have ridden to the Great Fields."

"What?" Takshin's smile was less sour now, and unfamiliar. The phrase sounded important, from the stress she laid upon the last two words.

She glanced at the mare again, who flicked a lazy ear, finishing her drink. "Among the Khir, when a warrior has been sent away from death we say he has returned from the Great Fields, where all must ride one day."

"Ah." It had a certain ring to it. "Great Fields." He tested the words, found them strangely pleasing.

Lady Komor nodded, and the corners of her lips curved slightly upward. Did she mean to smile? "When he is recovered, his ear is pierced as a sign—and so the Fields do not call so loudly."

"Ear pierced? Eardrum, or...?" He thought again as she shook her head. What a strange custom. "Like a noblewoman? A court lady, or like a courtesan?"

"No, with a hoop." Her gloved left hand rose slightly as if to sketch a shape in the air, but dropped back to her side. With her head covered and veiled, you could not see *her* ears. "None who have not lain as you did, near the Fields, may wear it."

An exclusionary mark. Fitting. "Ah. I see."

Lady Komor hesitated. Takshin braced himself. Now would come the mockery.

Instead, she regarded him calmly, if a trifle earnestly. Those strange clear eyes held no hint of pity or mockery, or even amusement. "You have ridden to the Great Fields, and come back. If you like, I shall pierce your ear. It is a Khir custom, and may not be welcome to you, but—"

"No." The word was unnaturally loud. "It would please me, I think." The instant he said it, he knew regret. *Now* she would mock him.

Her expression did not change. "There is some small pain."

"I am accustomed to *pain*, Lady Komor." Did she think him a rai-paper prince, a bluffing, empty tiger?

"None of us may live without it." Now she looked away, across the streamlet, the clean line of her throat showing between the collar-edges of her riding tunic. She even wore cotton *and* linen underneath, two pale fabrics showing neatly seamed edges.

"So the sages say." He searched her profile for any hint of disgust, no matter how well camouflaged. None was evident, unless she was a face-dancer. His boots squelched, his right heel sinking into mud. "Do you offer this service to all, then?"

"Of course not." *Now* she was irritated, and moved away, stepping with care to keep her boots dry. It was akin to a warrior's precision, and that was interesting as well. She was a dancer, this Khir girl, with both tongue and footwork. "You would be the first, and I almost regret offering."

Oh. Of course, he had treated her badly. He treated everyone badly; she was no different. "I do not need pity."

"Then I shall give none," she replied, each consonant an acerbic spike, and led her horse away.

The Tooth made another burbling noise in the streamlet, as if laughing. Takshin cursed at him, in an undertone, but the beast was unmoved.

Letters

The Zhaon celebrated when the rai in wet fields reached knee-height, and such an occasion meant the entire palace complex throbbed with febrile activity. A court banquet was planned, which meant choosing fabric and sewing as well as decorous small steps along the paths to visit the Artisans' Home. Not only that, but Yala must also brave a market or two outside the walls with only the chaperonage of Anh and a single one of Crown Prince Takyeo's household guards, a thing unheard of in Khir. And to get there, she must climb into a palanquin instead of riding.

The din, the stink, and the bustle was overwhelming, but at least she could open the slatted palanquin windows when the bearers halted at the edge of the nobles' district to mop their brows and change position. Bumping and swaying past the gates to the large clan-houses, each one with their device worked into lintel and wall, Yala sought to make connections with the faces she had seen so far.

Mahara, now in semiseclusion instead of formal seclusion, had yet to accumulate a faction around herself as the two queens and the First Concubine possessed. Had more noble daughters of Khir come with their princess, they could have begun the work already, but it was no use to bemoan fate. Yala would begin sorting through Zhaon's noble daughters for her princess after the festival, when the seclusion was fully lifted. It was always a ticklish task, and here among the Zhaon, a misstep had consequences it would not at home.

Home. The word had lost much of its meaning. She was trapped here; she might as well pretend she could find somewhat to like about it.

Near the walls of the palace complex, the houses became even larger, greening boughs touching the tops of enclosures, the lintels bearing the names with the characters *Ga-Ra-n'* before them—the abodes of adult princes, for when they did not choose to sleep within the Emperor's home. The Second Prince had a fine one with crimson-rubbed wood lintels, the Fourth Prince's gate was a restrained curve and looked more like a scholar's. There was also one overgrown and obviously in disrepair, its lintels scratched clear.

She thought it likely that house had been intended for Third Prince Takshin.

Had she really offered him a *kyeogra*? A momentary impulse, a kindness offered to one whose warrior scars and ill-ease were evident, and it had met with the disdain she expected.

I was seven winters high. He had said it flatly, as if daring her to pity him, and the reminder of Bai was so strong it had all but clouded her eyes with hot salt water. *I lay near death for three days.*

Not all his scars could be from that cruelty. A dry well—how terrifying, to be thrust into the throat of earth like that. But there was the mark of a blade along his jawline, and Anh's stories of the Third Prince were of his ill-luck in being sent far from civilization into the barbaric pierced dish of Shan, and the perpetual small battles with nomads and bandits on that land's far edge.

The palanquin swayed, and at least she had time to think while it passed estates clinging to the palace's walls like small eggfowl huddling against a larger feathered rump. Before the shallow rise to the Small Gate, she had to close the windows again and sit in the simmering of the small ovenlike box, breathing ceduan, the light enha[38] scent she had commissioned from the royal perfumier, and her own sweat.

---

38. A scentwood perfume base.

At least Anh could walk in the free air and chatter to the guard—a slim, tall youth with a downy chin and a serious gaze, mostly silent lest his speaking betray what Anh called a provincial accent.

It was likely the kaburei girl found him amusing, or attractive.

Between the Great Market and the Left Market was the theater quarter, and Yala had in mind to inquire if court ladies ever attended performances. There were players and jugglers at the Emperor's meals, she had heard, and the once-weekly Open Court banquet, but Mahara as a new bride did not attend *those* until a full moon after seclusion was lifted.

When she did, Yala would no doubt be required to go along for at least a few. She could not even feel pleased at the notion, trapped in this box as she was. It was lucky for a new bride to attend the Knee-High Festival, but against decorum for her to appear so soon at her father-in-law's table otherwise.

A dance of rules, hemming both princess and lady-in-waiting. At least they knew their roles, and had not stumbled yet.

Yala closed her eyes, deepened her breathing. A thread-thin slice upon her left arm stung under salt-sweat, the *yue* punishing her for inattention. Or perhaps she had flinched last night, Heaven striking gongs while demons or criminals were executed in purgatorial swamps and the *yue* warning her to keep her honor unstained so she did not fear the weighing of her life or liver in beaten-silver celestial scales.

Finally, she let herself wonder about the strangest thing of all. A letter had appeared that morning, borne from the front door by careful hands. It was not the day missives from Khir normally arrived; the letter, upon thick paper, bore a seal she had not seen before. The brushstrokes of her name and title were well-placed and gracefully executed.

She had left it, unopened, upon her writing-desk in a small woven basket. Anh, no doubt bursting with questions, had glanced at it but said nothing, and Yala was certain the fact that she did not break the seal immediately would be noted if the kaburei gossiped.

What, after all, could Zakkar Kai have to say to *her*?

* * *

"I wish you could come along," Mahara whispered, forlornly, picking at the embroidery at her cuff before remembering herself and putting her hands decorously away. Crown Prince Takyeo waved away his close-servant, a sleepy-eyed Zhaon youth with quick, narrow fingers and a scanty topknot. The prince was not quite irritated, but the set of his mouth, usually serene, was much tighter than usual.

"You will have your husband with you," Yala whispered back, guiltily glad she was not required to attend this event. "All will be well."

"I must walk at his side, instead of behind." Thin golden discs hanging from the princess's single hairpin shivered as she did, soft music. "Zhaon women are like men."

"Apparently not, since they bear sons." Yala took one more last, critical look at Mahara's sunset-colored dress, the heavy embroidery at cuffs and collar worked in subtle catlike characters for luck and hunting, the sash very broad and tiny edges of whisper-thin orange linen under-wrapping showing just enough to draw attention to the richness of the fabric and the traditional Zhaon lines. Lady Kue's seamstress-maids were wonderfully adept, and the dame had petitioned for them to be given a double pot of sohju to celebrate their skill in dressing the Crown Princess for tonight's ceremonies. The house weavers would be content with their single pot, and all within the Crown Prince's palace would no doubt sleep well tonight.

The princess giggled, hiding her mouth behind a sleeve that brushed perilously near the ground when her arms were down. Yala fussed over her other sleeve, the fan and three thin, scented cloths tucked into well-sewn pockets, a bahto[39] thrust through the many-folded sash and dangling a tiny greenstone snow-pard. A similarly tiny lai-blossom bag holding other small, exquisitely crafted essentials was tucked into her other sleeve, its crimson string about her wrist.

There was a soft commotion in the hallway. A messenger had

39. A decorative belt-pin.

arrived, and the Crown Prince leaned down briefly as his steward—round oily Keh Tanh, whose heavy iron manumit ring lay upon his sober brown chest, proudly dangling from a leather thong—muttered in his ear.

For a moment, Prince Takyeo's face turned to granite, and the likeness to his father was marked. Yala had only seen the Emperor once during the welcoming ceremony, but the portraits and statues all shared the same remote, unyielding expression, the small beard, the long nose and thoughtful eyes.

"Husband?" Mahara, tentatively. "Are we leave-going-yes?"

Yala did not murmur the correct Zhaon, but placed her hand upon Mahara's sleeve. If he was angered by sudden ill news as the Great Rider Ashani Zlorih often was, a moment of feigned clumsiness would distract and hopefully avert any wrath.

But the Crown Prince did not snap a disdainful word or raise his voice. "Leaving soon," he said, mildly enough. His face did not ease. "Steward, does the messenger wait for a reply?"

Keh Tanh's gleaming round-moon face did not alter one whit. A burn scar across his left knuckles meant that hand was perpetually somewhat clawed, but it was well healed and he was visibly proud of his station. "He does."

Prince Takyeo folded his hands. "Inform him that we have already left."

"Crown Prince..." Keh's lips pursed. He shone like a dumpling just taken from the steam basket, but it did not seem to be fear-sweat. Instead, he was merely one of those men whose skin produced its own coating. "It may not be wise."

An idea sparked in Takyeo's dark gaze. He turned his chin slightly and regarded his wife and her lady-in-waiting, narrowly. "Lady Komor?"

She bowed, gracefully. It was only a matter of time before she was called upon in this fashion. "My lord Crown Prince?"

"There is a messenger from the First Queen, bearing a letter. The Crown Princess and I have already left for the festival. Will you accept receipt of the letter?"

Ah. A neat solution to a possible problem. Whatever Queen Gamwone wished delivered just before a festival was likely to be borderline unpleasant; choosing not to receive it could be seen as an insult—and used to embarrass both crown prince and princess if not handled carefully. Yala's status was just imprecise enough to avoid open insult if she, possibly ignorant of etiquette, received the messenger and subtracted the letter from his grasp. Lady Kue could be reprimanded if *she* did so, and the steward, though manumit, would no doubt be eager to both shield his lord and avoid unpleasant repercussions for himself.

"Yala? But why?" Mahara's forehead creased. "A letter?"

Yala turned her hand on the princess's sleeve to a soft brushing, as if settling the nap of the fabric. "I would be honored, Crown Prince. Steward, please show the messenger to my receiving-room. Anh, bring tea." Yala glanced at the steward, whose gaze had turned worried. "I shall write a pretty apology for my forwardness in accepting such an august missive, and tender my regrets that so important a piece of paper arrived while its intended is unavailable."

The steward's jaw turned slightly loose, and he glanced at his prince, who smiled like the snow-cat he had chosen for a device.

"No doubt it is sealed." Takyeo's dark Zhaon gaze held a question.

But however far Yala was prepared to bend a polite truth, she did not think it wise to be *overly* useful in this small matter. "No doubt it is." In other words, *I will not find a reason to break the seal, and thus be blamed.*

If he pressed... but he surprised her, for he did not. "Yes. Well." The Crown Prince settled his unembroidered saffron sleeves with an air of relieved regret. "Go, Steward Keh." The round man backed away, bowing before he left the room; Anh vanished and the other kaburei scattered. "You are quick, Lady Komor."

And sharp. "You compliment me, Crown Prince." She changed to Khir, murmuring to Mahara. "My princess, a letter from the First Queen is bound to carry nothing good."

"Yes, she does not seem the sort to send pleasant tidings." Mahara suppressed a shiver. Each move made those thin golden discs sway and glitter. "What now?"

Takyeo smiled, and all resemblance to the Emperor of Zhaon was lost. "Now, you take your husband's arm. The best part of the festival is the fireflowers, but those are not until after dinner."

Yala bowed as they swept into the cleared hallway beyond, folding her hands thoughtfully as she straightened, for a moment the sole possessor of the receiving-room. The Crown Prince was not unintelligent, but asking Yala *openly* if she would break the seal upon a royal letter?

He must trust his household deeply. Which was the measure of a kindly lord, but not of a Crown Prince. Daoyan, though simply a byblow, would never have broached such a subject with kaburei present. Nor would Mahara's elder brothers, or even Komori Baiyan.

It troubled her.

He had not sharpened his tongue upon Mahara, or even upon the steward. It boded well for Mahara's marriage that her husband was not one to shift ill news onto a lower back.

And yet...it did not bode as well for a man whose own younger brothers might wish to do him some harm. And if Yala—a stranger—could see as much, who else could?

Protecting Mahara was one thing. Seeking to protect a Zhaon crown prince from his own good nature was something else, and a task Yala suspected beyond her capabilities.

It did not change what she was called upon to do at the moment, however. Yala raised her chin, smoothed her skirt, touched her eardrops hanging from their thin ribbons, and set off to do her duty to her princess's lord.

Life's Study

There had been a time, Garan Yulehi Gamwone reflected, when the Knee-High was her favorite festival. When the rai reached the knees of its tenders spring was assured, and the world would not slide backward into winter's bony grip.

To have reached a handhold, a brief moment of rest before clawing onward, was to be celebrated. And of course there were the fireflowers, the feasting, and when she was the eldest daughter of the Yulehi—not merely a merchant family, but one in whose veins flowed the blood of the Third Dynasty according to goatskin rolls that were *not* purchased despite what gossips said—there had been dancing after the groaning tables were cleared. A whirl of color, sensation, suitors begging for her hand, compliments and small gifts, her smile like the sun and her future bright.

Garan Tamuron settled upon a low blue-cushioned seat, barely glancing at the table of appetizers and tiny Shan bonefire cups of last year's sohju. "You look lovely."

"Thank you." For a moment, she could pretend this was what her marriage was. A husband grateful for the effort of inducing kaburei and lazy maids to produce a prettily dressed table in a room draped with tapestries, a wife assured of affection, at least, for doing her duty and producing heirs.

Two fine sons she'd given him, but he was greedy. Being blessed in war and having two fine sons—three if she counted the brat from his dead sword-wife—was not enough for him. No, he wanted all of Zhaon, the Land of Five Winds in its ancient incarnation before the dynasties began their endless warring. Now one held the rai-bowl, now another, endlessly chasing themselves around a wheel.

Garan Tamuron wished to own the wheel, and she had liked the idea before she knew what its cost would be.

"How do you feel?" Tamuron's shoulders were still broad and his topknot was still luxuriant. There were lines in the corners of his eyes that had not been there before, and bracketing his mouth under the small beard. His cheeks were ruddy, and the skin along his neck looked slightly irritated, as if his robes chafed. "I heard you were ill."

"Of course I was a trifle unwell." *She* was still unwrinkled, and firm. She took care, and massaged oils into her face and body every day to make herself pleasing. Even though the red lanterns never hung from her door at night, there was small comfort to be found in the fact that they did not hang elsewhere, either. "A corpse was dropped upon the front steps of my home." A *mutilated* corpse. Distasteful, though the exorcist assured her there was no lingering contamination.

Perhaps she should hire another. The first, with his ragged clothing and haughty gaze, had been expensive enough, but certainty occasionally required more.

The Emperor, lord of all he surveyed, regarded her over a round table meant to bring luck and new growth into the summer. "Yes." There it was, the distance. The hint of suspicion.

Injured innocence filled her. After everything she had done to prop up this warlord and make him Emperor—filled his coffers, filled his bed, filled her own belly with sons, and he treated her so coolly. Disagreeable things had to be done sometimes, and a good wife did them so her husband did not have to. She had more than once, and well besides. "The investigation into the occurrence…" Her tone lilted upward, a question.

"Is complete." Did he look uncomfortable? One should not mention death at the Knee-High table. "There is no further evidence."

She would have chosen a different robe for him, Gamwone decided. And a different topknot-cage. An Emperor should exercise restraint, certainly, but not at festival time. The lower orders did not respect a king who gave them nothing to marvel at. "And your newest son? What of him?" Mentioning that parvenu was distasteful as well. The Second Concubine was a meek little mouse, and Zakkar Kai was very crafty indeed, insinuating himself into her favor.

The general won battles, certainly. But he did not know his *place*.

"What of him?" Tamuron made a restless movement, as if he longed to rise.

Surely she could be forgiven for thinking it a trifle cowardly of him. "He was attacked as well."

"You were not attacked, Gamwone." Tamuron settled his gaze over her right shoulder, a sure sign she was losing his interest.

Did he think her a weak, foolish woman? Perhaps once she had been, but not now. "I have many enemies." As if he did not know. They whispered and elbowed each other, especially that Hanweo bitch. The concubines were all very well—a stallion sired what he could, where he could—but to take a second queen was a deadly insult to Yulehi's eldest daughter.

Even if it had been necessary.

"Do you?" he inquired, mildly, pretending to examine an expensive hanging of brightly patterned silk. Did he begrudge her every scrap she used to keep her position, to make this nest comfortable? To show the world that she knew and understood the duty of royalty?

"You could protect me, if you wished to." If only her father were still alive. He could shame a warlord who insulted his daughter.

But he had fallen in the Battle of Yu-lenei, consigning his coffers and his daughter to the care of a petty warlord who needed prodding and poking to do anything worthwhile. Now Tamuron was Emperor, her maternal uncle was immured in the provinces for half the year caring for the clan, and Gamwone was insulted daily even when that august clan-head returned for his duty to the court.

"You imply I do not?" Garan Tamuron lifted one hand to rub wearily at his eyes.

The conversation was a well-worn rut. She could not change its course, even if she longed to. "Tamuron." Her prerogative, to use his name. "I gave you sons." Even if Takshin was worthless, with his cat-eyes and his ungrateful pride.

Sooner or later he would bend. A son was meant to care for his mother, especially when a husband did not.

"Heaven has blessed me, indeed." In other words, *I have many sons.*

Perhaps she should try conciliation, since appealing to his duty would not work. "Your throne is assured, Tamuron. It has been assured for years."

Again, he gave only the blandest of replies. "So it seems."

Her hands, lying decorously in her lap, tightened. She denied the urge to make fists. Stretching skin over a woman's knuckles was unsightly. "Then why do you continue this farce?"

"What farce is that, First Queen of Zhaon?"

"*First* queen." The bitterness could curdle the small dishes of sweet things, the traditional sticky buns, the very rai itself. She was bringing ill-luck into spring—no, *he* was, because he was provoking her.

"Yes. First in Zhaon, first in my heart." A slight, mocking smile. That was part of the songs sung in the marketplace. They admired him, this upstart, the common people longing for a familiar hand to hold the whip poised over their backs.

If they only knew what she did about his dealings. Or how he cried on their wedding night, moaning the name of his commoner sword-wife, dead in childbirth in the ruins of a gutted town, squeezing out that pup called the Crown Prince who lorded it over his proper sons.

His *true* son. "Do you *have* a heart?" she hissed. "Do you?"

"Gamwone." A warning. *Be patient*, he had said, when she confronted him after the Battle of Red Clay, when that ill-starred slut Haesara's family sent their poisoned proposal. *This is something I must do.*

Well, now he was Emperor, and his true sons were adult. One was Shan's creature, true, and it was ill-luck that the Mad Queen had not killed the already-marred brat who refused to do his duty. Sending him abroad had been necessary, both to give the Shan a hostage and to place at least one of her sons beyond the reach of Zhaon mischief-makers and assassins. She could see that now, even if she'd raged against the necessity when it occurred. "You could send Luswone back to her sheepherding kin, she wouldn't mind a bit. And that prig Haesara can be settled in Do-yen, she'd be comfortable there." Her family was powerful, true, but he was *Emperor*, and she had married him before it was obvious that he would do what he aimed to and unify Zhaon. "You can keep the boys here, that is only right. That Second ninny won't last long anyway; you can keep her walled in her hole like a mouse." It was so simple, why would he not simply agree?

For the second time, he issued a warning. "Gamwone." Pennons lowered and raised, a salute before the battle.

She knew his strategies. How could she not, having made Garan Tamuron her life's study? "What? *Just wait*, you said. *Be patient*, you said. I *have* been! You have your precious firstborn, you have two other sons in adulthood, why do you make me suffer this? Other wives, other *concubines*." A wife had to please her husband, but he was incapable of being pleased at all.

Greedy. Just like every other man, except her darling eldest son. She had seen to it *he* was raised properly, at least. And Takshin—oh, if only she had been less willing to believe his father's lies, she could have found the strength to finish what she had started instead of letting the knife be pried from her hands when she heard of her husband's proposed second marriage.

He was the one who had placed her second son in danger, maneuvering her into those terrible words—*oh, why not send Takshin, since you will have more sons soon?*

Garan Tamuron sat across the Knee-High table from her, and had the effrontery to look pained but not shamed.

Not shamed at all.

"I cannot send the Second Queen and the First Concubine to their kin. It will be taken as a disgrace, no matter how rich their trains." Tamuron recited it like a scholar with a dim-witted pupil. "They have done nothing to deserve such treatment, Gamwone, even from you." Terse, like a battle-bulletin, each syllable a character with slashing diagonals. "They gave me sons too. The political situation—"

"Oh, *politics*." As if he did not have the stranglehold upon Zhaon he had so long desired. "The same song as ever." She was glad she had armored for this skirmish—her most beautiful greenstone ear-drops, the heavy cuffs of gold meshwork, the stiff embroidered robe catching her body heat and bringing out sweat-prickles along her lower back, behind her knees, behind her ears. "How much more will you insult me? I could have left well enough alone, yes, but then you add to my pain by adopting that *dog* of a foundling."

"He has been of more use than you, with your endless scheming." Now the cavalry was let loose, and the archers raising their tips. "Do you think I did not know, Yulehi-a?"

Gamwone bristled at her clan's proud name in his lying mouth. "Every *scheme*, as you put it, is to keep you upon the throne and—"

"Every scheme of yours is to keep your own position safe, against illusory enemies. I weary of this." He moved as if to rise, and obviously remembered that the ceremonies demanded he stay with his first wife for at least a token interval. Tonight he visited each of his wives in turn, then passed each concubine's door as they stood and waved small green handfuls of rai torn from its liquid home and afterward planted near their water-gardens to bring festival-luck into their homes.

Then came the feast in the greatest hall of Zhaon. And afterward the dancing, but of course Gamwone would be on the dais, unable to step into the measured patterns of flowers, the gentle swaying of branches, the imitation of prowling beasts as the night wore on and the music quickened as the rai, the fruit trees, the gardens, the bellies of animals and women were encouraged to do.

"Come. Let us not have this argument again." He extended one brown, callused hand over the table. "You are still my first queen. Let it be enough, Gamwone." Ruling had not robbed his palm and fingertips of roughness. There was a time when she had thrilled to imagine that scraping touch of a warrior's hand upon her own soft yielding, as a woman should.

Now she was cold. A fallow field, left unplowed even though the soil was still rich. He could have had more sons from her, but instead, he had taken that cold Hanweo bitch because her family had a drop or two of exhausted nobility in their veins and saved him a little trouble upon the battlefield.

Gamwone regarded him. She finally consented to lay her own soft, scented hand in his, and smiled prettily. Her throat was full of an iron taste, the inside of her cheek bitten until it bled. "Very well, husband."

Oh, she knew he would not consent to send them away. Would it have caused him any harm to pretend he *wanted* to? No, he was not even willing to grant her that silly little fiction. It might have even satisfied her.

But she would never know if it *truly* would, since he would not even grant her that tiny, necessary comfort.

Oh, she had known he was greedy when she married him. Yulehi Gamwone had thought it good, for it matched the burning in her. Together, she had thought, they would divide the world.

But he had what he wanted, and consigned her to one of four quarters instead of sharing what she had brought him, what her "scheming" made possible.

The heart of strategy was to see into your opponent's mind and overturn him without needing battle. Or, if that failed, to meet your enemy where he least expected you and throw his plans into confusion. She set herself to amuse him, and that night's victory was that he stayed longer than he had perhaps intended to. Tongues would wag, and there would be a comparison of the time spent with each of his queens. Gamwone would win. She *had* to win.

Nothing else would soothe the hollow ache inside her where more sons would have been, if only he had loved her.

Second Father

"This is like being peeled alive," Takshin muttered, motioning for more sohju.

The greatest banquet hall in Zhaon was built with immense timbers from the Lonely Mountain's shadowed slopes, festooned with the black of fresh-turned earth and the green of new rai, and hung with sheets bearing characters of *increase*, *luck*, and *happiness* written with brushes the size of brooms.

"And you would know?" Mrong Banh, his topknot only slightly off-center and his dark, somewhat sumptuous robes—new for the occasion, and he had been embarrassed to receive them from the Emperor's messenger that afternoon—too heavy for the stuffy Great Hall, poured the Third Prince the last measure of the jug. It was just like Takshin to bring the astrologer to his table.

Perhaps he thought the older man needed a chaperone, or he disliked pouring his own drinks.

"More than you'd think." Takshin tapped his eating-sticks upon the side of his bowl for luck and glanced mistrustfully at the server bending to set more sweating clay jugs of sohju amid the platters, dishes, and cups. Unglazed or only half-glazed ware was traditional at the Knee-High, "rustic" as the lords of Zhaon played at country living.

None of Tamuron's sons had ever gone hungry, except perhaps

Zakkar Kai. Sometimes, lately, Mrong Banh had found himself thinking perhaps it would have been better if they had.

Kurin, for example, leaning upon an embroidered bolster while Court Lady Hanak—the eldest of that clutch of daughters, a tender offshoot of war-ravaged House Hurekano—poured him another measure of sohju and gave a perhaps slightly forced smile. She was a round-faced, round-hipped beauty, promised to Lord Sahei's middle son; if they produced heirs, the two Houses might merge. And yet the Second Prince had issued her an invitation to his table for the Knee-High, as if he had designs upon her. Hurekano could not afford to anger a prince by refusing the invitation, but it was unlikely Kurin had anything in mind other than vengeance for some petty slight the eldest Sahei boy might have given him.

Hunger might have taught Kurin some kindness, or Sensheo some restraint. The Fifth Prince, having both his sisters at his table, was sulking, no doubt from something the elder girl had said. He tapped his fine horn thumb-ring against the table to irritate First Princess Sabwone. The girl had her hair piled high and asymmetric to please her mother, and next to plump, beringed, beribboned Gamnae she appeared certainly older, slightly more serious—but not more beautiful. She lacked Gamnae's shining good nature—and Concubine Luswone's serenity.

Mrong Banh thought it quite likely Luswone, from a threadbare house used to marrying money to stay alive every time they spawned a profligate, had known enough hunger to learn circumspection. It was a pity she had not passed the lesson on to her daughter.

And Gamnae? Well, the youngest of Garan Tamuron's brood was spoiled, and so was Prince Jin. Though they had different mothers, the two were akin, a sweetness in their temperaments that might have been given some edge by a day or two without a meal.

"Kai's lucky," Takshin continued. "He gets to avoid this."

The astrologer refilled their cups. On the high dais, the Emperor sat flanked by his wives. The smaller dais to his right held Concubine Luswone's table, full of bright fluttering court ladies with sienna-stained fingertips and asymmetrical hairstyles, all dressed in deep purple to accentuate their patroness's pale rosy silk like the heart of a fruit. No doubt the First Queen was writhing with jealousy.

The Second Concubine, of course, was absent.

"Your father required my presence." Mrong Banh knew he was drinking too quickly, and if he continued, he eventually might not care about the discomfort of his new robes *or* the pace of his imbibing. "And yours." But not the General's. Zakkar Kai was free tonight, and had intimated that he had plans for special company during the festival.

"He wants another horoscope." Takshin's mouth twisted, a crooked but genuine smile.

Oh dear. Banh gulped, though there was no sohju in his mouth. "Does he?"

"I don't know." Takshin waved the subject aside. "Probably not, Banh. Don't fret, it will spoil your looks."

Mrong Banh snorted, and hid a smile behind his sleeve.

Then there was Fourth Prince Makar, who had already been approached thrice by favor-seekers. He allowed each to sit at his table with the invited scholars, listening to their requests with a soft, bemused expression that almost hid the quick intelligence in his dark eyes. Quietly building a network of gratitude, if it could be called that. Perhaps Makar would have learned that a show of sobriety and modesty could be hubris as well, if he had been an ordinary scholar's son studying to take the civil examinations. Prince Jin would have a table next year, but for tonight he was at Makar's, sitting bolt-upright and looking miserable among the dark robes and peaked caps.

No doubt the conversation, entirely lacking military subjects or the rough jokes of those who practiced the warlike arts, was not to his taste.

A few days of hunger would do Jin nothing but good, and use his excess vigor for more than mischief. The boy was over the palace walls at the slightest opportunity, and his "friends" among the

Golden were of the quality that enjoyed a free drink but might not hesitate to leave their patron in a sink or two. Banh clicked his tongue, and Takshin's low, knife-edged laugh was a warning.

"You are more than fretting." The Third Prince lifted his bowl, unpolished rai and strips of pickled turo—a peasant dish, and good luck besides—decorated with a slice of boiled fantail egg. "You are outright *brooding*. What ails you, Second Father?"

Of course Takshin would be the one to call him that. Banh wrinkled his nose and made a shushing motion. His own scholar's cap lay upon the table; he didn't want to wear it with such luminaries as To Kheon and Harung Bei in the room. He was only an astrologer, not a sailor of the classical sea, and lately the stars had been... unkind, hiding their meanings behind layers of anxiety. "It is unwise to call me that," he said, finally. "I was thinking upon hunger, Takshin." Precious few could address the Third Prince thus, and each time he did, Mrong Banh wondered if it would be the time Takshin would take offense.

This time, however, the young man simply gave him a piercing, sideways glance. "A subject you know much about?"

"I was not always astrologer to the Emperor." Banh was not nearly drunk enough to think about his early years. Sometimes, he heard the dishes clanking in his dreams, and felt the shame spread hot over every part of him... but that was in the past, and little good came of thinking upon it.

Takshin aped surprise. He had a very mobile face, when he was not sneering. The boy he had been before Shan sometimes peeked through the mask of this scarred, spiked man, and was always a welcome sight. "Were you not?"

Banh poured himself another measure. If the dreams were coming again tonight, he would have to swallow much sohju to fend them off. "Did you think me eternal?"

"*Him*, once." It was clear who Takshin meant. At least he did not thrust his chin in his august father's direction. "You? Maybe. When I was very young."

On the smaller dais directly below the Emperor's, the Crown Prince sat in state with his new Khir wife and her pale eyes. She had dressed beautifully simply as well, and that was perhaps another reason for the First Queen to dislike her. Not that Gamwone needed reason to hate; it seemed to be her preferred state.

Outside the semicircle of princely tables, the Court proper made another horseshoe, and the temporary stage at the mouth of the bottle was a bustle of activity. Acrobats with long poles took their places, and the Court applauded—some politely, like the head of Hanweo, others loudly like Lord Daebo Tualih, both already flushed with sohju and merriment.

"The dance of the flowered rai!" a leather-lunged steward called, and the acrobats—masked, their bodies swathed in green cotton—began their contortions. Poles thudded against wood, and the musicians in the screened balconies set up a long, quavering melody.

"Perhaps you could let the past fade a bit." The astrologer picked up his own bowl. Unpolished rai packed a man's bowels closer than the slum theaters upon farce nights, but it was tradition. Some of the old women said it was even good for you.

Takshin stiffened and set his eating-sticks down. His hand crept for the sohju jug, and Banh hurried to finish his mouthful and pour more. The prince's cup didn't need it; it was full, and sohju splashed.

"I am clumsy, my lord." The traditional words of a servant's apology escaped Mrong Banh, a reminder of patrons in a common inn and a much younger Banh shuffling between tables with his head full of stars and his back sore from blows.

Takshin said nothing. His hand closed about his wet cup instead of the jug, and his eyebrows drew together slightly. Prince Kurin leaned closer to Court Lady Hanak, and if his fingertips settled upon the back of her wrist none remarked except Banh and perhaps the Emperor, whose smile had faded a whit.

The music intensified, poles providing rhythm as they pounded, performers braced between their spines or balancing against smooth shafts, sweat beginning to darken green cloth at the armpits. To be wrapped in fabric, unable to breathe freely, to wear a mask while sweating—Heaven was indeed kind, in that it had not made Mrong Banh an acrobat.

"Prince Takshin?" Banh downed his own brimming cup of sohju. Why bother to remain even close to sober? If the Emperor called upon him, it would no doubt be for amusement. He could always say the stars required a clear head, and that his was not. It was far less worrisome than the truth. "Come, drink and be wise. It is the Knee-High, after all."

Tchuk. One acrobat twisted upon a pole, his grip slipping, and the Court gasped. A scrape of wood, a knee hooked around the pole's slim stalk, a twist of a cloth-wrapped wrist, and there was a gleam atop the pole that should not have been there.

The acrobat landed upon slippered feet, bending knee and twisting, the pole breaking neatly along a sawed split. Takshin erupted into motion, his boots smashing plates and cups as he leapt atop the table and flung himself into the missile's path. His right hand whipped forward, sohju splattering and deflecting the acrobat's aim for a critical moment, and the flung spear flashed through space, landing with another solid sound between the Crown Prince and his new wife. It stood almost upright, quivering, for a long moment before falling. The Crown Prince grabbed the spear, wrenching himself upright, and his wife's hands were at her mouth, perhaps catching a small cry.

Shouts. Screaming. Prince Jin's battle-cry, his young voice breaking in the middle. It was Prince Takshin who reached the stage first, going over tables with the unconscious grace of a long-legged Tabrak racing hound, scattering unpolished rai, vegetables, sohju, platters of roasted fowl, and other hearty fare in every direction. He unfolded into another leap and landed upon the temporary stage, slapping aside the remainder of the assassin-acrobat's pole with a contemptuous motion.

"*Takshin!*" the Crown Prince yelled. "*Takshin!*"

Some thought the eldest of Garan Tamuron's sons had cried out his brother's name to stop the Third Prince from killing the assassin. Others whispered perhaps it was an accusation, a suspicion that the Third Prince and his foreign ways from Shan had brought ill-luck—or worse, malice—to the festival.

But Mrong Banh knew Takyeo's cry was fear for his younger brother, and fury that the Crown Prince had not been the one to see the danger in time.

Enticing Invitation

"It was kind of you to come." Second Concubine Kanbina clasped Yala's hands. Her fingers were cold but her cheeks were rosy with excitement, and her dress was stitched with tiny fanbird tails in crimson thread against deep yellow silk. "I did not think you would."

"How could I not?" Yala's shoulders eased. This sky-blue dress was new, low-waisted in the Khir fashion but with shorter Zhaon sleeves that did not cover her fingertips, only her knuckles. Though not yet embroidered since she had not found thread to match or contrast, its cut and fineness made it equal to the occasion. "I long to hear you play the sathron again."

Lady Kanbina's flush deepened and her dark eyes sparkled. "Oh, *shuh*, such compliments will inflate my chest and I shall become a box-bird. This is your first Knee-High?"

"In Khir it is held when the rai reaches the oxen's knees, and we call it *the Low Belly* since it comes before foaling." It came after the Green-Yeoyan festival, the lowlands rejoicing and their lords in the spine-mountains above accepting the last draft of winter-storehouse grain to clear the way for new.

"Here we eat unpolished rai and drink, though I have never liked sohju. And there? What do they drink in Khir?" As full of questions as a child, and no guile in any of them.

Or at least, none apparent.

"They drink *kharis* in Khir, Mother." Zakkar Kai appeared in the rounded doorway at the end of the hall, his own festival robe brown silk and cotton with fine thread at the cuffs shaping ceduan combs, belted with wide leather. His bow lacked nothing in respect or polish, and his topknot was caged in carved wood with a dull silver pin. "Lady Komor. It is kind of you to come."

"Your invitation was enticing." Yala could not help but smile; Kanbina beamed fondly at the man. "Sometimes we drink *konha* in Khir, too. And yes, eat unpolished rai." The peasant's staple filled the belly, true, but Yala did not like its texture, or its effect upon her digestion.

"I am glad my brushwork passes inspection." He stepped forward to offer Kanbina his arm, and the Second Concubine leaned upon it just as any mother with an adoring son. "It means the Emperor will not scold me."

"Your brushwork is very handsome." Yala touched her sleeves; her under-robe was not quite settled correctly. Dressing in a hurry never ended well; she should not have put off opening Zakkar Kai's missive. She had also dawdled over her reply to the First Queen's letter as if writing pained her, taking care to touch the brush-handle to her lips once or twice to denote some difficulty with Zhaon. The messenger, a stolid, nervous man with the Second Prince's crush-flower and honorific character worked onto the shoulder of his robe in pale thread, had shifted from foot to foot, obviously willing her to hurry, and she had only grown more obdurate. Now she produced a small weight from her left sleeve, its wrapping of raw burlap set off by a knot of crimson silk to match the theme of rustic luxury. "I brought a small token of—"

"Keep it." Zakkar Kai smiled, though the word was imperative, cut short. "It is ill-luck to give anything but rai at this festival."

"Oh." At least Yala had not already offered it with both hands.

She tucked the lump back into her sleeve, and half-bowed to express her regret. "It will give me a reason to return, then."

"Do not be a general to my guest, Kai." Kanbina clicked her tongue and hurried them along, her robe's hem just barely touching freshly washed wood. "Come, the table is set. We shall have dinner, and watch the early fireflowers from my garden. It is long since I have had guests for the festival. My health..." A cough caught at her throat; she lifted her sleeve to trap it. Her heavily padded house-slippers with their rounded tips faltered.

"The Emperor allows my mother to dine privately." Zakkar Kai finished, smoothly, folding his free hand over hers, a steadying motion. "A custom of long standing."

"I do not like banquets either." Yala decided it was an acceptable untruth and glanced away, admiring a scroll upon the wall to give her hostess time to recover. A long-legged bird with rough black feathers regarded her sideways from the scroll's surface, its long curved beak a single fluid stroke. Fine work, though unsigned. "The noise, the confusion... I am glad the Crown Princess did not require my attendance. So, there is to be no sathron playing tonight, Second Concubine?"

"Please. Call me Auntie." Kanbina, her cheeks scarlet, indicated a small kidney-shaped table draped with raw cotton cloth. Half-glazed ware, each piece slightly but charmingly flawed, gathered like eggfowl with their chicks. "The Emperor sent dishes tonight, the same as his own table. He is very kind."

Yala did not know enough to measure Garan Tamuron's kindness. Still, he did not force Kanbina to appear at banquet. In Khir she would have been compared to a skittish horse, one requiring head-wrapping before it could work and useless for hunting unless its bloodline, strength, or speed was exceptional and likely to breed true.

"Who could not be kind to you, Auntie?" she murmured. It was meant to be a compliment, but Zakkar Kai's eyelids dropped a fraction and his mouth firmed.

Kanbina, however, spread her free hand and laughed, a thin but merry sound. "Oh, my dear, here at the heart of Zhaon, there is unkindness aplenty. But we need not brood upon it. Come, sit."

Yala arranged herself upon the square gold-and-blue cushion pointed out to her, and found to her relief that she was to face Zakkar Kai instead of sitting next to him. Kanbina clapped her hands, the servants hurried in from doors on either side, and for Komor Yala, the Knee-High Festival began.

An Attentive Son

A great display of flame-flowers still throbbed and trembled in the sky, stars hiding behind acrid smoke and transient light-blossoms. Two kaburei in the sunny midsummer yellow of Kanbina's house held beehive lamps of waxed paper upon long sticks, careful not to let them sway too roughly.

"She was kind to me from the beginning." Zakkar Kai clasped his hands behind his back. He had taken only enough sohju to render him warm, but not enough to dull him. Or at least, so he hoped. "One of the few."

He had not thought Lady Komor would appear, but she had. And now, at Kanbina's request, he walked her to the Crown Prince's palace. *There are drunken men about tonight*, his adoptive-mother said, quelling Komor Yala's protest.

He did not know whether to be grateful or blushing, like the young man in the Swallow's Song. Kanbina saw more than most, even through her protective walls.

The Khir woman watched the graveled path before them, choosing her steps with care. A string of beads from her hairpin swung in time; she did not hurry. "I am told you were very young, and the Emperor...?"

"Bandits razed a northwestron village, a long time ago. Garan

Tamuron's scouts saw the smoke, and found me." He took care to make each syllable precise. Why speak to her of the reek of the dead, the sick-sweet of roasted human flesh, the sand and scorching in a child's throat? Or the confusion of being found and bracing himself, a broken spear clutched in his small hands, determined to sell his life dear if it was the bandits returning.

"How old were you?" Was it merely curiosity? She did not look at him, but that could be etiquette. He could expound upon the subject or turn them to another without fear of rudeness.

"I don't recall." He recalled nothing but the night spent wandering between flaming huts and the cold dawn that followed, bringing with it more thunder of horse-hooves. "Five or six winters, or so they told me."

She nodded. Her hairpin's beads depended from a small, irregular stone, wrapped with silken crimson thread as if precious. If it gleamed, the fireflowers did not show it. "And the Emperor adopted you?"

"Not until recently. I began as an archer's carrier." Bundles of arrows too heavy for his thin arms, but he hauled them nonetheless, ox-stubborn. And at least with the Garan warlord there was all the food child-Kai could eat, and his potential was remarked upon by a young astrologer Tamuron had invited along after a stop in a Yulehi tavern. "But Garan Tamuron said a boy who could survive a night of ashes was meant for great things."

"I see." That seemed to amuse her. Or rather, she smiled, and a drench of red from the fireflowers cast shadows under her pale Khir eyes. The plainness of her gown did not detract from its heavy sumptuousness. She was noble enough to wear silk to match the princess, which made her, in Khir, very noble indeed. "And are you meant for great things?"

"I cannot tell." Would she like it better if he lied, pretended a surety? Khir valued strength; those who did not fight were merely fodder. "My adoptive-mother is a gentle soul. She likes you."

"I am fond of gentle souls." Lady Komor's smile had lost its defensive quality. She clasped her hands inside her sleeves, settling the cuffs with an entirely feminine motion. Her profile, as she tilted her head up to view another burst of thundering light, was sharp as a statue's. "Do you remember your parents? In the village?"

"No." His own fingers tightened against each other at the small of his back, and he watched the walk before them. There was nothing in their way and the servants would sweep aside detritus, but he did not wish Komor Yala to stumble. "Only fire." Even his name was not his own. *Kai* was the only part he remembered when questioned, and Tamuron had chosen *Zakkar* because the characters looked attractive next to each other, and made a phrase of good luck. *Wolf-I-found*, it could mean, or *fang-on-the-ground*, depending upon how you wrote it.

"Born in fire." Lady Komor's pace slowed further. "They call you *the God of War*." The kaburei holding the lamps were no doubt eager to return to Kanbina's house and the remains of the feast, but neither of them dared an attempt to hurry the Head General and his companion.

Kai almost winced. Winning a few battles was as dangerous as losing one, or so Zhe Har the Archer said. "He may hear, and take offense."

He had been reading the Archer much, of late. Especially a certain tale concerning a moon maiden's torn sleeve, with a sad but fitting end.

"Would that trouble you?" Softly, as if she were curious.

"When Heaven takes offense . . . "

" . . . *the wise man trembles.* Zhe Har." She accented the name a little strangely; Khir shaped the *ar* differently than Zhaon. "Are you shaking, Zakkar Kai?" Lady Komor raised her sleeve a little, as if to catch a laugh. Her smile widened, teeth glinting, and it was pleasant to see.

So he *did* amuse her. Well enough. "Are you offended?" And did she have that slim, sharp blade sewn into this blue dress?

It was enjoyable, to know something of her that none other suspected. Except perhaps the Crown Princess.

Yala halted. Her skirts swung, and she faced him. The smile

retreated into her habitual somberness, and the lamps swayed as the kaburei halted as well. "What is it you wish of me, General Zakkar?"

Did she think he had an unpleasant answer to such a question? He had written the invitation thrice, crumpling and burning the first two and sealing the third before he could lose his nerve. A cousin of the gut-clenching feeling before a battle accompanied the messenger, though that man was probably unaware of the hope riding upon such a thin piece of paper. "A little of your time, Lady Komor."

Now she was on her guard, that clear Khir gaze level as one of her country's soldiers. "For what purpose?"

"Must there be one?" And what would she consider an acceptable reason? The crackle of sparksticks echoed, and children's laughter with it; many servants had young ones, and they were having a fine time of it tonight.

Komor Yala considered him closely for a long while; he suffered it. When she spoke, it was soft, reflective. "My brother joined our ancestors at Three Rivers."

Ah. Did she think he was personally responsible? Garan Tamuron said *fight*, and Zakkar Kai fought. The leash was slipped and the pit-dog leapt. That was truth, and likely to be cold comfort to a grieving sister. "I shall offer incense to his shade, then." Dead soldiers held no grudges, the classics said, being occupied with their living descendants, if they had any.

Still, he wondered. Did the shades of dead soldiers follow him, held back only by incense and prayers, or by the lamp kindled in every human liver by the goddess of fate?

A spate of blue fireflowers turned Komor Yala pale, brought out the depths of her silk, and glinted in her hair. "I do not think he would approve."

"Of what?" He was not, after all, *courting* her. Was he?

It was a good thing he had his hands occupied with clutching each other. Otherwise, the slight weight in his left sleeve—pearls, and a scrap of silk—might have drawn his touch like a needle brushed with a dragonstone found north.

Komor Yala made a small, restless movement, instantly controlled. “I ask you to be plain. What do you want?” If the blade was in *her* sleeve, was she touching the hilt?

What would it be like, to spar with a woman? He would have to hold back, but the thought had a certain charm. Fighting was close to dancing, and both were close to other acts performed with a willing partner. “What do you think I want?” An opponent would often give you the advantage just for asking.

“To watch my princess, to see if we are treacherous women.” Her chin set and her shoulders settled, taking on a burden far too heavy for their slimness. “To see if there may be an advantage in befriending a foreigner in a conqueror’s court. To amuse yourself.”

“That is a heavy list.” He was almost relieved she did not add more charges. The servants would see the general and the lady-in-waiting deep in conversation, facing each other and lit by heavenly explosions. Gossip might spread.

He found he did not mind.

“Is it untrue? Any of it?”

“Your suspicions are natural. But yes, untrue.” He was well within range, should she decide to strike. When did she practice the blade’s use? Perhaps at night, though not in the gardens now. Or so he could hope. “I wish to be your friend, Lady Komor. What shall I do to prove it?”

She glanced at the patiently waiting kaburei, and her voice lowered further. “You have already disposed of a corpse, and since I was not questioned you obviously did not mention my involvement.”

Not only that, but she was certain to have heard of his method of disposal. Kai had surmised the ring would provide a clue, and he could not very well leave a finger with an indentation *or* merely chop off one digit. He had also meant the mutilation to send a message, and perhaps she was uncertain of its meaning since it had not been aimed in her direction. He contented himself with a single word. “Obviously.”

“Which means you will not, or you are waiting to use the information to your advantage.”

If he told her the assassin's fingers were in a garden pond, feeding fat bronzefish and slow, bottom-sucking cahuan with their bristled mouths, would she be comforted? "You are an adept fencer, Lady Komor, but you are striking an enemy who does not exist. You need allies, I am one—if for no other reason than your kindness to Second Concubine Kanbina. She has had no easy time of it, and you will not either."

"That, at least, we may agree upon." More fireflowers, this time yellow as Kanbina's livery, drenched the palace complex in jaundice.

Zakkar Kai pointed. "The Crown Prince's door is there. I shall not approach, if you do not wish me to."

"You might as well, or Auntie will be cross." Her smile had returned, welcome as the rai itself, and her shoulders had eased somewhat. "I would like an ally, General."

So would I. Kai swallowed. The sohju left his throat dry as the sands. His hands did not know quite what to do without a hilt or a bow to fill them, but he could not keep them clutched behind him. His belt was too tight, as well. "All you must do is call, and I shall answer."

They reached the Crown Prince's steps. Lights hurried to and fro in the hallway, and there was a buzz of activity. Lady Komor halted upon the lowest step, perhaps wishing for higher ground to face him from. "Thank you for your invitation, General."

If I send another, will you answer? There was a better way to ask that particular question, though, to receive the answer he wanted. Much of a victory was choosing the battleground to your liking. "When may we see you again, my mother and I?"

"Second Concubine Kanbina may see me any time she likes; if she writes, I shall make time to visit." Yala hesitated. "And if you are there, Zakkar Kai, I will not ignore you."

Zakkar Kai's chest filled with a fireflower of its own, and the sensation was not as transitory as the sky-blossoms. It lingered, and he hoped he was not smiling too broadly. "Then I shall be an attentive son." He watched her sway gently up the steps and through the great door, slightly ajar to welcome the good luck of spring. Waiting until she was lost to sight, simply so he could be certain of her safety as Kanbina had charged.

Or at least, so he told himself.

It was upon his return to the Second Concubine's palace that the Emperor's messenger found him and gasped out news of an assassin.

Tongues

It was ill-luck to spend the Knee-High in a dungeon, but duty respected no festival. Zan Fein's toes curled and released in turn as he eased down the rough-cut stairs into a long, malodorous stone rectangle lit with rufuous lamp-flickers. His slat-sandals were difficult, yes, and his back ached when a day involved more than casual movement, but they reminded him with each step of his position and his pride.

In the eunuchs' quarters, the festival was proceeding apace with khansa—the Children of Two-Face drank no sohju, only the weaker frothing their patron had invented—and trays of sweet paste-pastries after the platters of roasted fowl and rosettes of pickled, preserved, and early spring vegetables.

But Zan Fein, like any good father, was called away upon business and went without complaint. It was strange to think of himself as such and he prayed Two-Face would forgive him, but there was no use in arguing with the heart. Man, woman, or eunuch, a human could control their breath, their manners, their behavior.

But the heart? That organ did what it willed inside its fortress of ribs. What one prayed for was forgiveness, and the strength to keep the walls intact. So they feasted and were merry, the only children he would ever have, in their long black robes, while Zan Fein edged into a version of Hell.

He was not the last to arrive, for when he was halfway down the stairs the door swung wide and Zakkar Kai was admitted, dressed in festival finery and a thunderous scowl.

A palace Golden with a lean, very dark face hurried to turn the lamps up. Crown Prince Takyeo's nose did not wrinkle, but his expression was set. And there was Third Prince Takshin, disdainful as always, who folded his arms and watched as the acrobat-assassin, still wrapped in green cotton, was laid with tender care upon a thick wooden slab.

You wanted them whole before they were broken, Zan Fein reflected. Just like horses, and children called to Two-Face's service. "Crown Prince, Third Prince, greetings," he murmured, and bowed.

Mrong Banh was in the shadows, flushed and smelling of sohju. He had little stomach for this work; his inclination was the dry fields of Heaven where the stars rode their strange wavering chariots. Still, he was quick, and he did not make the mistake of thinking Zan Fein had lost his liver and brain along with his twinfruits. For that, he had Zan Fein's respect, if not quite his liking.

Then again, it did not matter. They were both in the service of the Emperor, and specialized tools were needed by any artist. "Crown Prince," Zan Fein said, urbanely. "Are you injured?"

"No, Honorable Zan Fein." Takyeo dropped his chin slightly, acknowledging his bow and the inquiry.

"And your wife?" There would be much disorder if the Crown Princess was struck. And at a festival, too.

"Unharmed as well." The Crown Prince's expression changed slightly. If he looked thus more often, the rumors of his soft heart might well find little purchase. "I sent her home."

"A woman's place." Zan Fein studied the quivering body upon the slab. "Unwrap the head. Let us see what we have."

The Golden with the dark face—there was, no doubt, some very faraway blood in his lineage—finished locking manacles about the acrobat's ankles, and hurried to the head. Green cloth parted, starred with bright welling crimson.

Prince Takshin had not been gentle. Zan Fein could see no

other wounds, but he was certain they existed. The boy who had been sent to Shan had returned with a temper to match that barbarous land. His ruthlessness was far more suited to the heirdom than Prince Takyeo's kindness, but the considerations of an Emperor were deeper than a mere eunuch's understanding, were they not?

Zhaon was served well by Garan Tamuron, and Zan Fein was content. Perhaps what was necessary to keep the realm a father had conquered was not more conquering. Time would tell.

"What happened?" Zakkar Kai asked, in an undertone. It was Takshin who gave him a more complete understanding in a few clipped sentences, while Zan Fein busied himself with the long roll of heavy felted cloth he had carried step by step from his own quarters.

When unrolled, it revealed bright metal, lovingly polished, leather guarding whisper-keen edges. Tongs of various sizes, bentpins and crookpins, fine hair-thin needles and thicker ones in many lengths. Other curious shapes lay under cunningly sewn flaps, waiting to be revealed at the proper moment. The lamps brightened, a soft hiss of approval drowned by other noise.

Listening to the subtle as well as the spoken was the heart of much art, and his was no different.

"Has he spoken?" Zakkar Kai surveyed the unwrapping, and his jaw was iron. He eschewed the silk he now had rights to, preferring to dress plainly, but there was unwonted care taken with his topknot today.

Interesting.

"Not yet." Takyeo was not pale, but his gaze held a quite unwonted gleam. By all accounts, he was quite enamored of his new foreign wife. Had the Khir girl been ugly, no doubt it would have been a different tale, but a young man's heart followed his eyes, and his liver, that seat of courage, was not far behind. Perhaps a threat to the winsome new wife would prove the sharpening the Crown Prince needed.

"He will," Takshin said, softly. Almost caressingly. "You should return to the feast."

"In a short while." The Crown Prince dropped his hands. "I should also thank you, Taktak." An affectionate diminutive, and Zan Fein expected the Third Prince to bridle at it.

He did not, though. Instead, the scarred young man regarded the unwrapped face, his lips slightly curved, and leaned over the table, causing the stupefied thing to flinch. "Thank me when this piece of offal is on the heap where it belongs."

The acrobat was male, which was a good sign. The habit of childbirth gave women greater resistance to the Art of the Tongue, no matter that many treatises called them intrinsically weak.

"Give it some water." Zan Fein smiled kindly into the dazed, uncomprehending glare of a stunned child. The acrobat's gaze was muddy, and its lips crack-dried. "Are you certain you wish to stay, Crown Prince? You may leave this to me, I shall take great care with it."

"Perhaps he will save himself some pain, and tell us who sent him." Mrong Banh had turned decidedly greenish. He did not enjoy watching Zan Fein work.

It was a shame. Someday, perhaps someone would appreciate the Art of the Tongue, and he would teach all his secrets with care. Only Fifth Prince Sensheo seemed interested at all, but he was not an aesthete. Too much undiluted cruelty lurked in the Fifth Prince's manicured hands.

The Tongue had to be administered with coolness, not malice.

First came the revealing. Zan Fein attended to it personally, cutting layers of green cloth free. Was it a mute? It said nothing, even with the cold scrape of the blunt backs of paired blades against the skin underneath. The musculature revealed was quite fine, and the Golden—now Zan Fein remembered his name, Uyek—brought the lamps closer without being told.

"Was there only one?" Zakkar Kai examined the acrobat's head. "And did you maze his wits, Takshin?"

"The others are being questioned." Mrong Banh coughed slightly. "They swear he is not one of their number, though he knew their act."

Acrobats were raised and trained together—but one who walked the Shadowed Path would have the endurance necessary to perform an approximation of their act. And once they were shrouded for their spectacle, who could tell the difference? The eye passed over hill and valley, seeing only what it expected. True attention was difficult and exhausting.

"I did not hit him hard enough to remove his speech." Takshin shifted his weight, hitching a hip upon another empty table, this one with semicircles cut in its top to facilitate certain positions. "Is his tongue taken out, then?"

Zan Fein probed delicately in a mouth possessing a few fine teeth, none of them cored and stoppered with a lid to keep poison beneath. A faint sweetish odor rose; the saliva was slippery, and fine sugary flakes had collected between the top lip and the gums. "Ah. It has chewed hansong,[40] the naughty thing." He clicked his tongue, and peered at its eyes. The pupils swelled and shrank with no rhyme or reason. "To make it flexible, no doubt, and to guard against unwary speaking."

Mrong Banh shifted uncomfortably. "They cannot all have chewed the dreaming leaf. I sent the Golden to the acrobats' quarters, too."

"To see if there is a body stuffed in a basket?" Zakkar Kai nodded. It was possible—even probable—that this fellow had taken the place of another, and that theft was best performed when the original item was smashed beyond repair. "If he is a dreamer, there is nothing to be done. He may die before speaking."

It was not like the general to be so pessimistic. Zan Fein did not bother to disillusion him.

"A street acrobat, given hansong and a task? Or an assassin dedicated enough to mimic a performer?" Takyeo smoothed his mustache with a fingertip, looking away as Zan Fein produced a handful of needles. "Either way, a well-planned attempt."

---

40. A narcotic that grants much physical endurance and flexibility but robs its user of speech. Withdrawal is particularly painful and often fatal.

"The Emperor will be wrathful." Mrong Banh produced a plain, folded cloth from his sleeve and pressed it to his nose. His discomfort was no doubt acute, and his forehead shone with sweat. "Crown Prince, you must rejoin the festival, or rumors will fly."

"So must his wife," Takshin pointed out, pitilessly.

"And you?" The astrologer refolded the cloth, pressed it to his nose again. He could not screen the smell of this place, though. Even Zan Fein's umu scent could not.

That was not why he wore the blossom, though.

Takshin's lip lifted slightly. "No one cares what *I* do."

"There should not be another reason for tongues to wag at Takyeo's expense, Takshin. We shall examine the acrobats' housing." Zakkar Kai, a peacemaker for once, took one last look at the naked body upon the table.

"Fear not." Zan Fein chose a gossamer needle; he traced along the sparsely haired chest with a fingertip, searching for the proper point. The subtle body touched the physical at several points, and applying the smallest amount of pressure could twist much from even a dreamer eaten by the leaf. "If there is anything to wring from it, we shall gather the droplets assiduously. I shall attend to the others personally, until I am satisfied there is no treachery or information lurking."

Now even the Crown Prince looked greenish. It was a pity he was a kind master, the type whose kaburei and vassals would cheat unmercifully. Hopefully he would temper once the fire of rule had found him. Heaven protected its own, and the Five Winds reshaped the world at will. There was steel in Garan Tamuron's first son, it had merely not been struck yet; Zan Fein devoutly hoped the spark would show soon.

"Come." Zakkar Kai took Takyeo's arm. "Leave this matter to Honorable Zan Fein, Yeo. And leave the rest to us." There were few who would shorten the Crown Prince's name thus, but the affection in each syllable made the address respectful enough.

Mrong Banh kept the cloth clapped to his nose and bowed as the princes left. Takshin gave Zan Fein—and the beginnings of his artistry, already beginning to moan weakly as the needles worked their science—a long considering look from the top of the stairs.

If Fifth Prince Sensheo had the desire to learn but not the coolness, Third Prince Takshin had the coolness and the will, but not the desire. It was a pity, indeed.

"During a festival," Zan Fein murmured, once the door had closed with a heavy, hopeless sound. His hands were cold and he would rest them against the stone if they warmed. He sensed more when the fire had withdrawn from his wrists. "Quite disturbing. Say what you wish to, Honorable Mrong Banh."

The astrologer did not dissemble. "Does it seem, Honorable Zan Fein, that the target may not have been the Crown Prince?"

"And what has led you to this question?" Oh, he did not *like* the astrologer very much. But it was so good to have a sharp mind to strike a spark from one's own; such minds were in short supply. Zan Fein selected another needle, and pushed it in.

"His legs." Mrong Banh lowered the cloth over his mouth, forgetting his disgust for a bare few moments. He was steadiest when occupied by a riddle or discovery.

Ah, was that it? "Strangely developed for an acrobat."

"Slightly bowed."

They bore all the marks of youthful malnutrition and heavy riding, young bones like clay pressed into shape that older ones remembered. "Yes."

"Perhaps he does not speak, this one, because he does not possess a tongue."

"His mouth is unmarred, except for the hansong's kiss." Zan Fein dispelled a smile. This was serious work. "But I suspect your meaning is poetic rather than physical."

"It is, Honorable Zan Fein. It strikes me that this false acrobat—for they will certainly find a body in the acrobats' quarters, of one *this* fellow took the place of—is one who has traveled far."

The eunuch set aside his needles. His long, spidery fingers caressed the hilts of one or two implements before he selected a fine, thin blade, very flexible, with a spurred point. "I am inclined to agree, astrologer. I would go so far as to guess this naughty thing rode from the North."

"I was afraid you would say that." Mrong Banh refolded the cloth and tucked it into his sleeve, obviously determined to master his stomach and his unease at once. For all his sohju flush, he did not seem drunk now.

This room, Zan Fein mused, had a sobering effect.

He bent to his work in earnest.

Do Not Be Obtuse

A breathless afternoon made even the most shaded water-garden oppressive, wet yellow sunlight blanketing arching boughs, beating against gazebo roofs, and flattening even kaburei who did not hurry. Guards in their golden glitter-armor edged for slices of shade, and even the small drab jumyo[41] birds were hiding instead of dust-bathing.

Outside the palace walls, on the long verandah of Fourth Prince Makar's severe, old-fashioned home, Second Prince Kurin settled onto richly padded cushions brought out for a guest, yawning as his fan flicked.

Long-nosed Makar, in his usual somber scholar's robe, nodded at the servant pouring tea. The girl quietly withdrew, her leather-wrapped braids swinging, and for some short while the silence was only broken by the click-thump of a carved water-clock at the other end of the sand-garden.

Finally, though, the Fourth Prince spoke. "That was ill done." Makar lifted his cup but did not drink. The tea merely touched his top lip, a scorch-caress.

A line had appeared between his elder brother's eyebrows. "What was?"

"Marring a festival, here in the heart of Zhaon." He could not

41. Brown birds often nesting in small bushes, said to never drink water.

be plainer. Someone had gone too far, *much* too far. There were rules even to the game of succession, and they were best observed. Otherwise, the entire board became a mess, and that Makar did not like.

Anything done shoddily displeased him.

Kurin's fan continued its work. "Perhaps the rai will rot in the fields? I had no idea you were so superstitious, Brother Scholar."

"Do not be obtuse, Elder Brother." Makar finally took a sip, closing his eyes for a moment to untangle heat, aroma, and flavor. The sand-garden needed a fresh raking, especially around the two large, rough rocks set at the most pleasing angles from his accustomed viewing-place. A carefully pruned batus tree arching at the end near the water-clock's trickle and thumping had scattered fallen blossoms, and he had given orders to leave them be—a reminder that artifice was often interrupted by nature, and the wise man kept a light touch upon both to achieve his ends. "First Zakkar Kai is troubled with a Son of the Needle, then a corpse is thrown upon your mother's steps, and now this. Father must be displeased."

"Do you think *he* sent the assassins, then?" Kurin's fan described a lazy half-circle, and he laughed as if the suggestion delighted him.

It probably did. He was disposed to be difficult today, it seemed.

"Obtuse again." Makar set his green Anwei rakka-fire cup down. His housekeeper had no doubt guessed this would be unpleasant, and had chosen one of his favorite tea sets to ameliorate. Servants knew, and only the unwise did not give them just enough to gossip about. The morning spent writing business letters had been pleasant enough, but the fact of this visit had hung over it like a cloud of cheap scent. "And an insult to our father as well."

"Don't tell me you haven't considered the notion." Kurin took a small sip of tea with air, pretending to enjoy the bouquet.

Oh, Makar had—every permutation of the possible should be considered—but was it wise to admit such a thing? "If only to set it aside as preposterous."

"Is it, though? I am only asking, Makar." Kurin's orange robe held a yellow tone that did not suit him very well, but to choose a color that did might have been unmasculine, since the cuffs were heavily figured with the character for *a crushflower's thorns.* "I am aware you are the one who knows Father best."

If it was an appeal to his vanity, it went wide of the mark. Kurin was usually a much better archer. "I cannot lay claim to that." Makar paused. It was time to be plainer. For all that he did not *like* Kurin very much, they were still brothers. "Your ambition is princely, but it will bring you grief."

"I have no ambition. Unless it is to aid Zhaon." Kurin lifted his cup again. "You really think I bought the acrobat-assassin?"

It was the most likely possibility. Now, however, he was not so sure. There was something about the entire affair that bothered him even more than the unmannerly deploying of an assassin during a festival. Makar studied the sand-garden. He let the question rest between them for a long moment. "I think you wish to prove yourself to Father. As do we all." It was only filial, was it not?

The line between the Second Prince's eyebrows deepened. "He is ever disappointed."

"He loves his sons."

Kurin's mouth drew down in a bitter curve. It was unlike him to show such feeling so plainly. "Oh, no doubt. One or two of us, though, he loves *best.*"

"Are you so certain?" It was the way of the world. Even the Hundreds were full of unfair affection. The trick was, Makar mused, not to let such an evanescent thing as someone else's *affection* dictate one's course.

"Aren't you? Did you invite me here merely to accuse, or to lecture me?" Kurin made a slight movement with his cup, swirling fragrant, steaming liquid. His topknot-cage, an eyebird tail dipped in filigree and bent into a cone, held a similar filigree pin. Both gleamed even in the porch's shade, venomous glitters. "Both are unbecoming, and unwelcome."

"Neither, Kurin." Makar suppressed a sigh, settling more firmly upon his cushion. "I invited you because we have not spoken in some time, and because I am worried."

"Ah." Kurin studied the sand, the rocks, the batus at the end. Aesthetic appreciation was not his strong suit, and he was probably thinking the gardeners should be punished for not clearing the spent blossoms. "What worries you, Younger Brother?"

"My own younger brother." *Among other things.* Kurin seemed genuinely innocent—unless he had grown far better at dissembling even with someone who had known his many lies since childhood—so they could move to other matters.

Kurin took a small sip, raised his eyebrows as if just tasting the tea for the first time. "Since Jin is in fine fettle, I conclude you mean Sensheo."

"I do."

"Is his archery going badly, then?" An artless inquiry. Blossom-heavy branches moved upon a hot breeze, and a few more flowers flutter-fell.

Makar watched them settle among their dead siblings. "He aims at things he should not."

"As do we all." Kurin acknowledged the repetition with a slight, sour smile. He set his cup down and set his fan to work again. The day was warm, and he apparently did not believe in hot tea creating cooling humors. "Again."

"I believe he may cause some small distress." None of his brothers were scientists, Makar thought as he had more than once, and he sighed internally.

That perked the Second Prince's ears. "To whom?"

"Oh, everyone." Makar decided that was enough leading. His elder brother was not stupid, but he sometimes played at it in order to draw an opponent out.

Did he consider Makar an opponent? It would denote a certain lack of imagination, but then, Kurin often preferred certainties to artistic risk.

"He does love to make mischief." Kurin's fan, figured with undulating storm-dragons, settled into a lazy rhythm. "Rather like our eldest sister."

Mischief was not the word for some of Sabwone's intrigues. Or for Sensheo's. The two of them were cats with a single mouse, and woe to the rag of fur and bone caught between them. The worst was the affair with Lady Aouhuro and her Golden paramour. "Cruelty is unbecoming," Makar said, severely.

"Sometimes necessary."

Oh, certainly, but driving a court lady to suicide and arranging for a Golden to be flogged to death hardly fell under the rubric of *necessary*. The entire affair left a bad taste, and Sabwone merely laughed when any reference to the unfortunates were made. Sensheo did not laugh, he merely looked satisfied, and *that* was disconcerting.

It was also ancient history. Both of them had become more subtle since that intrigue, and consequently, more malignant when piqued. Makar chose his next words carefully. "It pains me to see any of my brothers commit an error which could be avoided."

"Does it? How remarkable." Kurin's thumb caressed his hurai. He kept his fan moving but rinsed his mouth with tea, swallowing with a slight grimace. "Be honest, Makar. Do you not sometimes think, even for a moment, of what it would be like?"

Did he think Makar would admit to such thoughts? "You have confused me, Elder Brother."

"Come now." Kurin set cup and fan down, tucked his hands in his sleeves, and turned his entire attention to his brother, a faint sheen of sweat gleaming on his brow through carefully applied zhu powder. "What would you do, were you Emperor? You must know it is a possibility."

Makar paused long enough to make it clear he wished his words to be attended closely. "For such a thing to happen, much sadness must occur."

"Perhaps you are correct." Kurin still studied him, hands hidden and his nose slightly lifted. "In any case, we are brothers, and should help each other."

An invitation to intrigue, or a meaningless pleasantry? No matter, Makar had already achieved his purpose. "You may be assured I will do everything I can for you, Elder Brother."

Kurin's smile was very like his mother's, lacking only a hard lacquer patina. "That is pleasant to hear. You should come to dinner, in a ten-day or so."

"A fine invitation."

The talk turned to other matters—the racing season about to begin, the difficulty of finding properly trained servants, the strange behavior of spring storms. When Kurin left the Fourth Prince's house, it was with a light step and a small, satisfied smile.

Prince Makar, however, sat upon his verandah for a long while, watching heat shimmer over the sand-garden, and his brow was troubled. Of course Kurin would not be so foolish as to send an assassin after Takyeo in so public a setting, if for no other reason than suspicions—including Makar's—would fall upon him as the one with most to gain from misfortune befalling the Crown Prince. It was doubly unlike Kurin to engage in such a dangerous affair to blind his opponents, seeking safety in apparent idiocy.

A nagging sense of the solution to the puzzle hanging just out of reach troubled Fourth Prince Makar deeply.

The blossoms, uncaring, continued to fall.

Slow-Rising Bird

Dropping into the northern rim of Zhaon's rich heartland, each town on the caravan's route was larger than the last. When the dust-eating snake of oxen, wagons, outriders, and hangers-on halted outside Zhaon-An's North Gate in a wide beaten area reserved for such things, one of the outriders—a strange, lean young Khir nobleman—vanished with his very fine horse, a trick gone unnoticed by the caravan master or anyone else. The outrider had proved his worth several times, especially in the ravaged borderlands teeming with bandit groups taking advantage of recent chaos, but former soldiers were in large supply these days, and the trade-road to Shan much easier than its northern sister.

Those entering Zhaon-An were traditionally required to give their name, occupation, and business to the wall-magistrate of their particular gate-quarter, but a few triangular silver slivers into the palm of a liveried postern guard dispensed with that annoyance.

Of greater concern was the sheer *size* of the place. It dwarfed Khir's Great Keep and outlying city; the crowding throbbed like an infected tooth and stole the breath from a man. He had only a scrap of rai-paper with a sketched map upon it to guide his course; consequently, the outrider spent the usual spring-afternoon storm sheltering in one of the taverns, shaking out his cloak since he would not go inside until his horse was safely stabled.

When the rumbling and downpour had ceased, the young outrider spent yet more time wandering to the very edge of the King's Retreat before sighting a fellow Khir, a muddy-eyed acrobat performing on a street corner. Another silver sliver tossed in his countryman's bowl gained him better directions in his own tongue instead of Zhaon mushmouth.

So it was that as deep blue evening stole breathless and humid into the streets where Khir congregated in Zhaon-An, the nobleman found himself before yet another inn, this one with a leaping, long-legged horse painted in the northern fashion upon its large sign matching the one upon his rudimentary map, and perhaps felt more relief than was strictly acceptable. A few words passed with the portly, also muddy-eyed innkeeper gained him one of the better rooms but not the finest, and finally Ashani Daoyan was able to strip half-armor, quilted padding, and his topknot, scraping road-dust free with bone implements and sliding into the relief of a tepid inn-bath.

Of course, the bathhouse was where gossip lingered, and he listened as the attack upon Zhaon's Crown Prince during the Knee-High was embellished, embroidered, passed from mouth to mouth, and the Crown Princess mentioned only in passing. The heir to Khir's throne retreated to his room with much to think upon, but his work was not done yet.

Finally, wrapped in a comfortable, sober cotton merchant's robe, his grey eyes ringed with exhaustion and reddened from dust, Daoyan descended into the common-room with his sword and passed a few more words with the innkeep, who finally indicated a small table in a darkened corner, holding an indistinct figure also in brown. There was no teapot or jug upon the slightly slanted table yet, for the fellow Dao had come south to meet had just arrived.

Daoyan made his way between other tables crowded with patrons calling for dishes, servants pouring tea and calling orders to the chief steward who passed them into the kitchen's smoky rollicking, sohju and kouriss jugs thumping down, merriment rising as dinners commenced. Even the servants were all male, a blessed relief from Zhaon taverns and their sly-eyed southron slatterns. Finally, he halted at a respectful distance, and said the words Domari Ulo had given him. "Blessed is the wind." It was a relief to fill his mouth with the purity of Khir again, and to hear it spoken only lightly salted with a few Zhaon terms at the other tables.

The man in brown had a long narrow nose, dark kaburei eyes, and the other half of the pass-phrase in archaic Khir. "It brings ash upon its back." He indicated the only other seat at this table, a chunky graceless thing without a cushion, its flat wooden bed polished by many a cloth-clad buttock.

Daoyan settled with only a token hesitation. It put his back to the rest of the room, never a comfortable position. He ached all over, and would have been glad of any bed without fleas, no matter how small. "Have you eaten?" The polite, traditional inquiry for a guest or stranger was, he decided, the most appropriate here.

"Not yet." The man's head-wrappings were in the fashion of the Yellow Tribes, but he had none of the heavy-jawed insolence of those nomads. He gestured for an inn-servant's attention; both his hands were bare of rings but not of scars and calluses. "What news from the North?"

In other words, had the plans changed? This fellow was not well-bred at all, to engage in business so swiftly. "Not so much," Daoyan said. "I am of the nature of reinforcements."

"Ah." The fellow scratched under his head-wrapping, pushing aside two layers of dun material. "A prick for a slow-rising bird."

So this fellow had a hawk's temper, or liked to play at one. He certainly had the beak for it. Daoyan shook his head, and decided his sword was best kept across his knees instead of hung upon a chair-back. "No, my friend—if I may call you thus?"

"That depends upon your House." For a moment, the false tribesman's mouth turned down as if he tasted something bitter, a man unwilling to acknowledge his "betters" since they often proved nothing of the sort.

How often had Dao felt that, and had his expression ever been that transparent?

An inn-servant, a heavy-lidded lad with a mobile mouth and bruised fingertips, splashed a brimming jug of sohju and two clean-ish wooden cups upon the table, spat a query, and was answered with a single nod before disappearing at high speed in the steward's direction. The man in brown must eat here often, to be assured of such service.

"I'd rather not say." If Dao had to give a name, he would use the one he had ridden south under. There might even be a certain satisfaction to the borrowing. "We are both safer that way, no?"

"Then you may call me *friend*, for I'd rather not as well." In other words, they knew enough about each other as it was. The man reached for the jug, pouring both of them a healthy measure, and toasted Daoyan with a single, economical motion. "I suppose you have heard the news."

The cup was likely to be dirty, but Daoyan swallowed the sohju anyway. So far, all he had seen of Zhaon was filth, luxury, and wastage; no wonder they had overwhelmed Khir's noble sons. He set his empty cup down. "An acrobat at a feast. Rather showy." Sohju exploded behind his ribs, a welcome warmth like fireflowers.

"One works with what one has." The man in brown refilled both again, but his wary examination of Dao didn't change. "I didn't expect that fellow to succeed."

Why bother, then? But Dao merely nodded; despite his robe he was no merchant to find fault with an artisan confined to lower-quality materials through no fault of his own. "I suspected it was an opening gambit."

"Well." That brought a shadow of a pleased smile to the man in brown's weather-darkened face. "What did you bring, if not news?"

"Ingots and slivers," Daoyan said, and watched that smile-shadow widen. "I have only one small matter to add to your orders."

The impresario—for so one who found, paid, and orchestrated

assassins was called in Khir, like a theater master—laid a finger upon his lips. "Let us have dinner, and you may tell me afterward, friend. The cups are badly turned here, but the cook is Northern, and his curd is well-made."

"I look forward to sampling it," Daoyan murmured, and toasted the impresario in turn.

End Is Always Assured

The innermost heart of the Kaeje was draped with tapestries and hangings to ward off the chill from sweating, ancient stone walls. A small shrine in one corner held a closed portrait-case, candles burning before carved, fine-grained ceduan. There was no pleasant verandah leading to a garden; this room was a sanctuary and defense. Still, its occupant liked it more and more, if only for the fact that he could leave his attendants in the outer chamber.

Garan Tamuron, Emperor of Zhaon, sat upon a mildly uncomfortable—but very expensive—cushion embroidered by the First Queen and exhaled dutifully as a physician in slightly ragged robes probed for his pulse with dry fingers. "Ah, Mrong Banh. Good of you to come." As if a summons could be disobeyed.

Still, if there was one man in the world he would forgive open disobedience from, it was probably the perpetually disheveled astrologer, who performed the ritual bow at the door with an air of distraction that had fooled many a lesser man into thinking him unintelligent.

"How could I not? I thought there a prospect of sweet buns, but instead I see you are engaged with medicine." Banh's wide, genuine smile was the same as it had been those many years ago, when he ran to fetch tea and preserved headfruit for tavern drinkers—and told their fortunes with a shy gleam to his dark eyes and an air of utter earnestness. His topknot was held by a simple wooden pin, no cage to denote high rank or attention to aesthetics. He had probably put the new robes away with a sigh of relief, too.

The physician did not look at the curtained door. "Your Majesty's servant must examine the royal chest." He was rumpled too, dressed in dark sober cotton, but he had arrived with Zakkar Kai's seal upon his recommendation and set to with the alacrity of a small merchant.

"Why, it's Honorable Kihon Jiao." Banh straightened, and his smile widened with genuine pleasure. Mirrorlight showed the tender flesh under his eyes, marked with the perpetual sleeplessness of one who followed the stars. "You are in expert hands, Your Majesty."

"You know this man?" Tamuron tried not to sound amused as he unlaced the side-placket of his sitting-robe. There was the small council this afternoon, and he did not look forward to it. Hailung Jedao had taken to sniping at Kai lately, and Tamuron could not be seen to be overly partial to the general until the waters had settled. Takyeo would have been a welcome balance against such behavior, but the Crown Prince was no doubt soothing the nerves of his foreign wife.

Or using that excuse to avoid something likely to be disagreeable. Tamuron could not precisely blame him—the boy was a dutiful son in all ways, and it was best to give him what rest was possible now, while he was merely heir and not Emperor.

Later, there would be no rest to be found. Would his eldest son find this room first a refuge, then a prison, as Tamuron had?

"A fine physician. I have read two treatises of his, both highly original." Mrong Banh settled himself at his usual scribe's desk, his scrollcase clattering against polished wood. The front of the desk held beautiful, restrained carving, the god of archery on his endless hunt with a leaping stag before him and his high-peaked cap a reminder of foreign invasions. "Forgive my clumsiness, Your Majesty."

The physician regarded Banh for a long moment, head tilted

like a stilt-bird's seeing fish in the water. "Ah. Astrologer. Honorable Qurong, is it not?"

Banh shook his head. His family name—or its mispronunciation—was often a source of much merriment, yet he refused to change it to something less amusing. "Mrong."

"My apologies." A slight, very correct bow. Kihon was a peasant name, but this fellow lacked nothing in politeness.

Tamuron suppressed a chuckle. "I am pleased to find you know each other. It shall make conversation easier."

"Conversation?" The physician's eyebrows rose, as shaggy as his head; he wore no topknot, but did not have the curving side-locks of one who had cut his from grief. "I must listen to the royal liver, Your Majesty. Please be silent."

Banh lifted one sleeved hand to his mouth, unsuccessfully attempting to hide a chuckle. Tamuron's lips pulled down, but he let the man do as he wished.

Kihon Jiao fitted the cold metal bell of an ear-cup to Tamuron's chest; though it was padded with brushed-on bendtree gum, it still caused a ripple of shiverflesh. Kihon bent, and the Emperor discovered that while he looked shaggy, the physician in fact smelled of citron soap and a faint note of fresh air. Without a tang of leather, though, it was not a soldier's aroma.

Tamuron missed that. Sweat, weapon oil, stiffened or glove-soft hide, the smoke of night-powder and the grassy pungency of horse…sometimes, when he retired in search of sleep's inverted country, he told himself to dream of an army camp. Of the tents in regimented rows, of the ordered bustle and the anticipation of hard marching. A soldier never found it difficult to drop over the border into rest.

An Emperor, however, often did. And dreams did not obey even one Heaven had smiled upon.

"Hrm," the physician said. He was not one of the court physicians, which was all to the good—the First Queen's creature led that pack of medicinal hounds, and Tamuron did not want them carrying tales of his worsening ailment. Not yet, not until there was at least the prospect of an heir for his eldest son. "The sweat, it rises at night?"

"Yes." When was the last time he had felt truly well? Tamuron could not remember, and it bothered him. The rashes had come before, usually just after battles or tricksome negotiations, but now they came monthly like a woman's red times and his joints were swollen-tender.

The physician selected a small ivory pointer from his tools and touched a few spots upon Tamuron's chest. Each one was tender, and Tamuron nodded. Under sparse, greying chest hair, the rashlike marks had faded somewhat, not quite glaring angrily but still looking askance. "And here?" The physician glanced up to see another nod. "Ah."

Tamuron suppressed a measure of irritation. "Well?"

"I have not completed my examination, Your Majesty." Kihon set the pointer aside and selected a small jar from his heavy leather satchel. "When I do, I shall speak upon my findings."

Mrong Banh looked down at the scroll he was unrolling, but not quickly enough.

"You are worried," Tamuron said.

The astrologer did not bother to argue, or pretend confusion. "Should I not be?"

At least this physician's discretion could be trusted, if Kai and Banh both agreed on him. So Tamuron's shoulders dropped, and he glanced at the door. There could be an ear listening, quick to carry tidings to another tapestry-shrouded room. "I am not yet certain," Tamuron said. What remained to a man, once the summit of his ambitions had been reached?

Only leaving something fine for his sons, and this he would do.

"Your Majesty has a suspicion," the physician said, somewhat sourly. "You are seeking confirmation instead of diagnosis, which is unwise."

"An Emperor must always be suspicious." Mrong Banh made a short jabbing motion with his inkstone-case, very much like Ha Jiau, the current darling of the Theater District.

The physician sniffed like a farmer testing the quality of fertilizer. "And yet we must *discover*, not *confirm*."

Tamuron tried not to sigh. "If the learned men are finished?"

The physician bent to his work again, smearing a small amount of a pleasant-smelling paste upon one of the rashes. He sniffed Tamuron's armpits, examined his ankles, the hollows behind the knees, his nape, all with that same ivory pointer. He peered into Tamuron's nose and ears with a small silver mirror polished to a high gloss, examined his teeth, smelled his saliva, and asked several low questions about his appetite and bowels. The royal stomach was palpated, and the royal fundament and its crevasse subjected to some inspection. Finally, he scraped the dried paste away from the rash gently with another ivory tool, sniffed the paste, and studied the rash.

When the poking and prodding was finished, Kihon Jiao bowed low and retreated some few paces to another small scribe-table, this one with a flat cotton-sheathed cushion he had brought himself.

Tamuron resettled his clothing and turned his attention to Mrong Banh. "You have the scrolls?"

"Yes." Banh hesitated, though. "My lord..."

My lord. Not *Your Majesty*, or even *Emperor*. It was somewhat of a relief to hear the familiar syllables, to remember a time inside a general's tent, the taste of copper in his mouth and his forces ready for the morning's action.

During the smokescreaming chaos of battle there was no time to think, and afterward there were the wounded and dead, the smell and the grief. But *before*, anticipating his opponent's moves and drinking one last swallow of sohju to sharpen the senses and warm the belly, ah! That was the finest thing in the world.

He sometimes envied Zakkar Kai, who would feel that sharp anticipation again. He had even, inside the secret halls of his heart, taken to envying the youth of his sons. "Tell me, Banh. Who attacked my son?"

The astrologer did not glance at the physician, which was an encouraging sign. On the other hand, his mouth turned down, and a weight rounded his shoulders. "The assassin died without speaking."

"No doubt Zan Fein was dismayed." Tamuron watched the physician, who appeared to take no notice of this conversation.

Wise of him.

Mrong Banh, with another anxious glance, continued in a low, confidential tone. "He turned his attention to the other acrobats. The body of their true fellow was found stuffed in a wicker basket for their poles; the assassin was an imposter who had often watched their practices and joined the crew already costumed just before the performance. They know nothing."

It had a certain neatness, and yet. "Is Zan Fein convinced of that last assertion, my friend?"

"Reluctantly." Banh's grimace spoke for itself.

Of course the acrobats could not ever be allowed to leave the dungeons, even if innocent. The best they could hope for was a draught of sleepflower[42] to ease their passing. And of course there would be no order, simply a hint given to the head eunuch after Council.

Zan Fein would serve Takyeo with the same quiet diligence. Faint comfort, but what other kind was there? Tamuron began to tie his robe-laces. His fingers were slightly clumsy, instead of Dho Anha's slim, capable attentions. He must settle something upon the bath-girl, a poor recompense for the ease she brought him. It did a man good to speak to a woman who was not seeking favor or ingot. "And there is nothing else to add to your report?"

Banh spread his hands, a helpless movement. So there was more, but even a discreet physician should not be privy to it.

"Your Majesty." Kihon bowed over his table. "If it would please you to hear my conclusions?"

"It would. Approach, both of you." Tamuron gave the short, sharp motion of a general beckoning scouts in to hear their reports.

---

42. A powerful narcotic, capable of sedating or pleasantly relaxing a subject, but lethal in higher doses as the heart, lungs, and liver shut down under its weight.

"Physician, whatever you have to say, Mrong Banh may hear. Hold nothing back."

They settled themselves before his cushion, finishing the movement with identical bows. Kihon Jiao spoke clearly, simply, and to the point. "It is not infectious, but it *is* only a matter of time," he finished. "We may slow it, Your Majesty, but the end is assured."

At least he did not coat the bitter paste with pounded rai to make it easier to swallow.

"The end is always assured," Tamuron murmured. It was a classical allusion; perhaps Makar or Kai would have recognized it. His throat was dry and his hands were already cold, lying in his silk-clad lap. He had begun to lose his sword-calluses. Each day was so damnably short now, and paradoxically an endless waste to be trudged through. "Kihon Jiao, you are now our personal physician. You will be housed in the Kaeje and attend us daily."

The man took the news with barely a flicker of eyelash. He simply nodded, and settled his hands upon his thighs. "I beg leave to attend my other royal patient as well, Your Majesty."

"Certainly." Poor Kanbina. Did she resent him now? There did not seem room for it in her gentle nature, and yet a corner devoted to that purpose could be found in any human soul. Hadn't he thought Gamwone reasonable enough, in the early years? "How is the Second Concubine's health?"

"Precarious. But then, such is often the case with poison."

Banh winced visibly. Knowing was one thing, knowing something rumor was occasionally correct about was another, and hearing the rumor confirmed with disarming candor was yet another.

Tamuron stroked at his beard. "You would not happen to be able to discern *which* poison, would you?"

"Not at this point. And if I did, would it be healthy to possess such knowledge, Your Majesty?"

This fellow was certainly a sharp one. The Emperor made certain his shoulders were set correctly, and bent his gaze—royal and impartial now—upon Kihon Jiao's face. "A physician concerned with his own health?"

The man looked singularly unmoved. "I cannot aid others if I am unwell, Your Majesty."

Or dead. Which he would be, if Gamwone knew her crime could be proven instead of simply suspected. Tamuron nodded. "Indeed. Banh, draw up a commission for the physician. He may take it to the Under-Steward Narung Hei and begin court attendance immediately."

"Yes, Your Majesty," they chorused, and for once, Tamuron found the ritual response soothing.

Yet Banh's intimation of information gleaned from an unspeaking assassin was troubling. Tamuron half-lidded his eyes, his fingers searching for the beaded kombin in his pocket as the two men withdrew to Banh's scribe-table and made small conversation while the commission was brushed and sealed.

By the time Mrong Banh approached for the great seal to affix to the commission, Garan Tamuron had arrived at his answer, helped by satiny wooden beads slipping through his fingers, and he did not like it at all. It was simple, really. He had assumed Takyeo was the assassin's target.

But that might not be the case.

Sudden Hurry

The needle went in easily and Mahara hissed, swallowing the sound almost as soon as it was born. She took care to set the silk down before snatching her hand away and examining her fingertip.

"Let me see." Yala was already reaching for a small jeweled box with a hinged lid.

"Third time today." The princess sighed. "I wish we were playing kaibok instead." Takyeo had not outright denied permission, but she thought it unwise to ask.

In any case, she did not feel like riding, or like swathing herself in the habit necessary to such an endeavor. Here, on a shaded porch, listening to small birds hiding in a tiny jewel of the Jonwa's private central garden, she was safe. Even if she kept stabbing herself with the sliver-needles for fine work.

"Yes." Yala took her hand, blowing upon the wounded fingertip to push away ill-luck. Deft and certain, with her head bent and a string of silver beads falling from her hairpin, she was the embodiment of a noble Khir girl attending to her lady. A dab of stinging, jellied jau to cleanse the wound, more soft breath to push the pain away in trembling drops, then a small felted pad to stopper the hole and convince Mahara's blood it was more congenial inside than out, as well as to bar the passage of any lurking evil spirit. "We could, if you like."

"No." Mahara shifted slightly, the saffron silk of her skirt making a slight pleasing sound. Her tenderest parts were not quite raw, but certainly unaccustomed to such use. Her husband was somewhat enthusiastic in performing his duty, and she longed to be obedient, but...how could she tell him *not tonight, my lord*? What did a Zhaon woman say, and would he be angered? "Yala?"

"Hm?" Yala peeled the felt away, delicately, clicked her tongue and replaced it. "A little longer. Yes, my princess?"

"We must find you a husband."

Yala laughed, her hair-ornament swinging with merriment. "What, here?" She sobered quickly after glancing at Mahara's expression and reading seriousness instead of jest. "Do you think so, then?"

"Perhaps I shall write to my father?" Mahara's monthly letters, formal and restrained, were also excruciating. She would welcome a change of subject; it would give her something real to put into brushstrokes instead of empty formality and wishes for his continued good health. He had even added a note to his own last brief missive, telling her not to bother him with frivolous southron gossip. A Khir woman did not speak of politics. "A good Khir noble, one who can come to this place and...or should I ask *my* husband first?"

Yala considered the question, but she apparently arrived at no answer, for she changed the subject. "Whence comes this sudden hurry?"

"You must marry too, so we may speak of our husbands." Or could she—*should* she—speak freely of the night-habits of men? It was, after all, *Yala*.

"Is there aught you wish to speak upon?" Yala's smile returned, familiar and reassuring. "And I thought you did not wish to share me."

"But you will still be here. I merely wish to see you settled." Mahara bit her lip. "It is my responsibility."

"There are more weighty matters at hand." Yala's gaze was clear but troubled. A faint misting of sweat showed along one side of her neck, and her dress today was of Zhaon cut, cut low enough to see a faint dewing upon the top slopes of her small breasts. In

Khir it would have been scandalous, but here it was too hot to wear a proper neckline. "Such as your *yue*." She glanced at the garden, a quick sideways motion, though they were more at risk of being heard from the hallway.

"Father said I would not need it." In fact, he had demanded it of her before she left, and Mahara, a dutiful daughter, had expected it to be merely a test.

But he had kept the thin, ancient, hateful piece of sharp metal, and she had been glad.

"And yet." Yala's fingers were gentle. She held Mahara's hand, a soft, warm touch that comforted even though both of them were sweating. "My princess, I cannot be with you at every banquet."

"Perhaps if you were married, you could?" It was a silly idea, but she was not quite ready to admit defeat just yet. A hot breeze skipped over the garden walls, touched the surface of a pond, and rustled secretively among flowers and leaves. The birds paused before continuing their small chirping and twittering. They were drab little things, but they sounded cheerful indeed.

"Only to a prince, and which one would sacrifice his chances for a Khir lady-in-waiting?" Yala suppressed a laugh at the thought and shook her head, her hairpin's beads swinging again. "There is another solution. My princess, perhaps *yue* practice might provide you with some safety."

"I..." Mahara's voice dropped. "I am afraid of it," she finally whispered, bending over her hand as well, as if it pained her. An onlooker would only see two well-born women conferring. "The scars." She had seen them upon her friend many times, and the thought filled her with unsteadiness, like sohju trembling in a jostled cup.

"Then we practice with a blunted blade at first." Of course, the solution was obvious, and Yala would see as much. "It is not so difficult, my princess."

Sometimes it was annoying to have such a practical lady-in-waiting. What Mahara really wanted was a solution that did not require swinging one of those nasty, sharp slivers. "How will we steal away for practice, then?"

"Let us not rush." Yala's expression turned to deep thoughtfulness, which softened her sharp face considerably. "First, I must acquire a *yue* for you. I cannot do so in the Artisans' Home; it will require their Great Market. I dare not go to the smaller one, even with a chaperone. I gather it is not wholesome, even as the Zhaon account such things." Yala took the pad away. "There. Where is your thimble?"

"I do not like it for this fine work. The silk is beautiful." It had arrived with a small note from the Second Queen, perhaps an apology for the First Queen's insults before the festival. Mahara had already embroidered four handkerchiefs with Queen Haesara's personal device; she had only to finish the fifth and send them to express her thanks.

"The Second Queen is not so bad." Yala tucked the bloody felt into her sleeve. Disposing of something so precious would have to wait until she found a brazier.

The thought of more heat on this awful day made Mahara's sweat prickle even worse. "No. But her daughter, *shuh*."

Yala's laughter, now free to rise, was the same as it had always been, and it cheered Mahara roundly. They bent over their work again, small expert stitches and tiny knots, color and meaning made steadfast in cloth. Perhaps even the winter would be warm here, and that was a blessed thought.

They sewed in companionable silence. In a little while, tea would be brought, and they would compare progress. "Would you really go to the Market?" Mahara finally asked. *Alone*, she meant to add, but of course Yala would.

She was fearless.

"The only question is when," Yala replied, softly, as if she had already thought the matter through.

It was good, Mahara thought, to have a lady you could trust.

A Tranquil Heart

The Crown Prince's palace had an attic, furniture, and other items standing shroud-silent sentinel. Dust lay thick in forgotten corners, but Lady Kue's housekeeping discipline was seen in the tidiness of every pile and the arrangement of winter linens in ceduan-packed crates, as well as the marks of recent sweeping.

Yala bent, fingers tucked under her toes, and exhaled. Her braid slithered forward, landed upon the floor. Mahara was in the Crown Prince's bedroom; on evenings when he was called away or his ardor cooled, they could begin practice. It was, Yala thought, somewhat similar to a lover waiting for a lady in the classics, though there was no longing in her impatience.

Only fear.

Yala flattened her palms upon grit-dusty floorboards, exhaled, and pitched forward. Toes leaving the ground, her shoulders creaking, knees tucked on the outside of elbows, her face growing scarlet with effort. Sweat began, and she held her position for five breaths. Seven.

Her strength had faded. Stealing enough time to continue her own practice was difficult here.

That is not an excuse, her father's voice said, softly, in the halls of memory.

Nine breaths. Yala's slippered feet hit the floor with a thump; she froze and exhaled, listening.

When she was certain, she unfolded, breathing through the momentary dizziness as her humors rebalanced. She flowed into the stretches—the archer's pose, the hawk in flight, the startled lizard, the lesser and greater wheel poses. Finally, warmed and loosened, she reached for her left thigh, and her *yue* whispered from its sheath.

A blunt, weighted practice *yue* was given to a noble girl upon her fifth winter, when the threat of demons carrying off a child was greatly reduced and her name added to the clan register. Yala was fairly certain she could find something similar in the Great Market. It was the question of finding an actual blade that occupied her most, and she moved through her practice at half-speed, stances blurring into each other instead of crisp and distinct.

Now, of course, so much more made sense. The particular way of holding the wrist, the twist at the end of certain movements to free the blade from the suction of muscle, the bracing of certain small jabs with the other hand... all intended to prick an attacker like a festival bladder and let his blood out into open air.

Two assassins already. More would certainly come. The Zhaon apparently loved to kill in darkness instead of honorably. It mattered little who sent them; Yala's only concern was halting the blades before damage was done.

Should she speak to Mahara's husband of the blade she herself carried? Or to Lady Kue? Zakkar Kai already knew. *Keep it secret*, he counseled. And *I wish to be an ally.*

He had disposed of the corpse, and even cut the man's fingers off. If he did not know what the *shinkesai* was, why had he done such a thing? Put that way, the answer was blinding-obvious: He had not known, he had only thought it might be important or personally identifiable, and Yala, by her knowledge, may have made herself suspect.

And yet, he had said nothing. He appeared that rarity, a man who could keep news within his own ears instead of spilling it from the mouth at the slightest provocation.

She flowed into the Dancer's Pose, and began working through very simple, short movements.

The First Queen's eldest son was next in the line of succession; perhaps Zakkar Kai would not comment until he could prove the provenance of the assassin. Or maybe his silence was merely meant to confuse. Asking would do no good; it was enough that the man did not spill Yala's secrets.

Thinking upon that particular matter brought her no closer to a solution to the problem of finding Mahara a *yue*. A court lady in a smithy would be a spur to gossip, and she could not send Anh. Lady Kue would be bound to report Yala sending a kaburei upon such an errand to the Crown Prince.

And would Zakkar Kai? She should not trust *him* with such a thing. He was far too trusted already.

"*Shuh*," she hissed, and closed her eyes, falling into Mountain Pose. The *yue* quivered. It was thirsty tonight, and she was distracted.

She imagined the spires of Khir's Great Keep and its bowl-city seen from the mountainside tombs, smoke rising from chimneys, the palace roof glittering scarlet with red tiles repainted every third summer, and Komori itself lost among other dark roofs and quiet, noble houses. Her father's face, and his last letter.

The king's heir visits often. He mentions he has written you. A worried question behind the brushstrokes, Komori Dasho writing in his study while spring's full spate reached the highlands at last. What was Daoyan's purpose?

We must find you a husband, Mahara said. Did she think it so easy? What was Yala's duty—to marry for her clan, or to protect her princess?

If she kept swinging her *yue* in this state she would mark herself badly. She stilled, listening to the creaks and mutters of a timbered hall at night. Dust tickled her nose; sweat prickled under her loose-belted sleeping-robe.

Slowly, the fretting inside her bones calmed. She imagined Bai crouching next to her, peering over the edge of a rooftop. *The shortest road to the goal may not be the quickest, little one.*

The answer was laughably simple. Of course she could not commission a blade for Mahara.

But nothing stopped her from obtaining a gift for an ally. Or for Mahara's husband.

Yala smiled in the darkness. She touched her lips to the *yue*'s cold flat, her weight shifted, and she began to practice with a tranquil heart.

The *yue* did not sting her that night, and when she slipped past a sleeping kaburei's door to seek her own bed, dreams did not trouble her.

Such Ideas

A princess hurried along darkened halls, slippers shush-shushing and hairpin's beads tucked into a twisted braid so their swaying would not clink and betray her. A veil touched her nose, irritant and comfort all at once, and surely this dark silk was unremarkable enough. She could be any court lady upon her way to an assignation, or even a rich commoner come to seine coin from a palace notable's pocket.

There was much activity in the palace complex at night. Rule did not rest, reign did not sleep, and intrigue kept its glowing eyes open in every corner of day or night. A sleek fish in dark waters, she avoided the torchlit passages and hurried through a spring night luxurious with blossom and the heavy smell of incense from wayside shrines, sweetening the air and keeping night-riding spirits at bay.

She was not quite late. *He* was, and First Princess Sabwone spent a short while in an overgrown garden they had often played barbarians within, her brothers hiding from Mrong Banh and tutors' endless lessons in history, brushwork, poetry, Sabwone hiding from the governesses her mother insisted upon saddling her with.

Gamnae never played here. The little idiot cried if you pushed her, and went running to the First Queen. A creeping, nasty, spiteful little child, just like her mother.

But she was Father's favorite daughter now, so Sabwone simply smiled. At least she'd make a good marriage first, and rule her *own* household. She drew into the shadow of a hau[43] tree, its unpruned branches fountaining down. A shaded, scented bower, like in the songs of the Moon Maiden.

She watched the garden entrance but still almost missed him, a flicker in the deeper darkness, his step light and his robe as dark as her own. Sabwone smiled.

Of all her brothers, she liked him best.

He halted, cocking his head, and glided straight for her hiding place. She made no noise, but still, something had given her away.

"Well?" he said, quietly, just outside the hau-bower.

"Won't you come inside, Fourth Prince? You are expected." She used the same tone as some of the court ladies—soft, a suggestion of the First Queen's affected lisp, but not enough to make the words unclear. Mother would be livid, of course; she did not *quite* say they spoke like the flowers of the Theater District, but it was close.

"Of course not, Sabwone. I have other business, and you should be at rest." Garan Makar stood just out of whisper-range, clasping his hands behind his back. He'd started doing that when he was twelve, solemn-faced and tall for his age, and it had been funny at first. Now she wondered what he could not keep his hands from that he must hold them so. "What is so important?"

Could he see her pout? Unbecoming, but it was dark. "I wanted to talk."

"You could have visited."

He didn't have to wear a veil at night, or tell his mother where he was going whenever he wished to step outside. He could simply stand and go. Even Jin could move without Mother's heavy hand upon him, and he was a baby. "Oh, I know I'm supposed to be locked in the Kaeje. Mother is cross with me."

"Did you pinch Gamnae again?" Makar's head tilted slightly, his listening look. "Or perhaps put something in Jin's soup?"

"Don't be silly, Makar." Childhood pranks were all very well, but she was a woman now. And to prove it, she was out after dark

---

43. A water-loving tree with long, flowing, flexible branches and thin leaves.

with a veil, her bedding rolled and rumpled to suggest a sleep-shape if her mother or a servant should glance in. "She just doesn't like Kurin visiting me."

His chin lifted a little. "I would not either, were I her."

Was he jealous? That was a good sign. "What's wrong with him visiting his sister?"

"I did not come here to discuss the Second Prince."

"I did not, either." But she preened a little, hopeless to deny it, at the thought that he did not like Kurin's attentions to her. Hope was a weed, the novels said. And wouldn't Mother be furious if she found Sabwone reading some of them? They were exciting, and forbidden, probably because they were *true*. Not historical, and not practical, certainly, but the feelings contained in them were more honest than court life allowed. "Come now, Makar. Let us be friends. We always were, before. How is your mother?"

"A social call in the dead of night, Sabwone?" He did not fidget, but there was a sense of contained irritation spreading from him. "Out with it, or I shall leave you here and return to more appropriate pursuits."

And what, exactly, were those at this hour? Dusty scrolls? He did not visit the Theater District like Sensheo did. Sabwone parted the hau's hanging branches and peered at him. "You are not amusing anymore."

"Have I ever been?" He waved the question away with a short, sharp motion, his sleeve fluttering. "What do you *want*?"

His impatience was delightful. Sabwone decided to reward him. "Merely to tell you that your little brother visited me again, and was very clumsy. He wanted to know about herbs."

"Perhaps he means to study medicine. Or culinary refinement." Now Makar had grown still, his eyes gleaming above his handsome nose. Not a hair out of place, ever. Takyeo might have been the eldest, but Makar looked the part of prince ever so much better.

"Oh, no doubt, no doubt." She played with the hau stem-branches, twisting them in her supple fingers. "But he mentioned that physician again."

"Which one? There are so many." But by the sound of it, Makar already suspected what she was about to say.

"That ghoul who attends the First Queen." She raised her sleeve as if to hide a smile, or a grimace of distaste. Branches caressed her shoulders. She was a court lady in a novel, hiding in the darkness, whispering to a lover. Her imagination, as usual, lingered upon the image. "You know what they say of *him*." An open secret, and Father had allowed the mousy Second Concubine to adopt Zakkar Kai.

Giving her a son after all, even an upstart, solidified her position. The First Queen was probably furious, as usual. Delicious to think of that painted merchant's daughter striding through her palace halls, ripping things from the walls like Lady Ohku in the last installment of *Heart-Gems in Twilight*. She wasn't noble like Mother was. Why, her clan had *bought* its genealogy rolls.

But Sabwone had other business tonight. The next step, of course, would be visiting Sensheo, or arranging to make their paths cross. If Makar did not behave as she wished, Sensheo certainly would. The prospect of inconveniencing the elder brother with the younger was satisfying indeed.

Makar kept his stillness. It was a new quality of his, freezing in place like a thinleg bird or a cat intent on prey. Like everything else, it only made him more handsome. "And you tell me this because...?"

"You know how Sensheo is." She found a thin, pliable green branch and wove it between her right fingers. Tighter, tighter. "He gets ideas in his head, and then he cries when they don't go well."

"Who puts such ideas in his head, Sabwone?" Makar did not fold his arms, or move away from the hau. He was worried, that much was plain.

Which meant Sensheo had been very naughty lately. "I'm sure I don't know." It was just too easy, really. "I admire my elder brothers, and I'd hate to see one do something... rash."

"I'm certain you would." No warmth in the words.

Now she aimed for her true objective. She'd warned him, so he would be grateful. "Will you take me to the Blossom Festival?"

Perhaps, like a woman, he could not agree right away. "Why not ask Sensheo?"

"Because I want to go with *you*." He had never been this dense before. Was he deliberately misunderstanding her?

"No doubt Kurin would accompany you, then."

"I don't want to go with him, either." Now was the time to apply pressure. "I could tell Father what I know of Sensheo and silver."

"And what is that?" He already suspected, his tone said as much.

"Just that I'd seen him with a company of acrobats before the Knee-High. And that Sensheo asked me for silver."

Of course it was true. Or, well, *mostly* true. Sensheo had come to her for money, since she was thrifty with her allowance and he had begun the yearly gambling early. She had made certain the household steward knew she was giving her brother a few slices of silver ingot, but not what it was for.

The part about the acrobats... she could very well come up with plausible details. It would be up to Sensheo to think quickly then, just like skip-whip in the hallways, dodging guards and chaperones, accomplishing mischief that could be blamed upon another. She did not have to hide her smile in the darkness, and the dark enjoyment filling her was better than the thimbles of sohju Mother would let her taste.

Makar was silent for a long moment. "This is not a game, Sabwone."

"Take me to the Blossom, and I won't say a word." She hoped he'd be reasonable. After all, when he was twelve he had kissed her cheek and promised her he would always care for her.

"No." Makar turned. "Do as you please, Sabwone. You will anyway." He set off for the garden entrance, and Sabwone's mouth fell open a little.

Had he forgotten, or did he not care what happened to Sensheo? "You'll be sorry," she said, loudly enough to carry, and drew back into the branches. When he halted, her heart leapt. Had he reconsidered?

"Or perhaps," he said, not even turning to look, "you will be the sorry one. Ask Kurin which suitor Father's chosen for you, little sister."

It was ridiculous. "Father won't marry me off just yet," she managed, but her cheeks were hot and her pulse had decided it did not like her ribs. Instead, it gathered in her throat, a dry, feverish weight.

Makar did not reply. He simply glided out of the garden, vanishing into the dark at its mouth. Sabwone grabbed a fistful of tree-limbs, green and sap-full in the dark. She closed her eyes, uselessly. After a few moments, though, a series of new ideas struck her.

Makar already suspected Sensheo of something naughty, which meant Father did. Hard not to; he'd always been a bumbler, lagging behind even Gamnae, who at least could strike without warning if she was prodded hard enough. All Sabwone had to do was wait for an opportune moment, and tell Father. She could even summon tears, be pale and somber, and then *both* the Second Queen's sons would learn it was better not to ignore a concubine's daughter.

It was a pity about Makar. But he was only the Fourth Prince, anyway. There were plenty of other possibilities for Garan Tamuron's firstborn princess. All the same, her cheeks were slick and her eyesight blurred. Nothing had been satisfying lately, and she would have to find new amusement.

And someone, *anyone* else to take her to the Blossom Festival.

Sign as It Pleases

A clack-clatter of weighted wood hitting weighted wood under a hammerblow of spring sunshine, sweat stinging his eyes and his leg all but numb from a lucky shot—Takshin leaned aside, boots scraping on stone, and unleashed a flurry of blows that ended with his sparring partner sprawled upon dusty sun-hot pavers, helmet slightly askew and his knees bent, a turtle upon its back.

"Well done." Takshin pushed aside the face-guard on his own padded helmet and offered a hand.

The man—a spare, wide-shouldered Golden whose silent ferocity cared nothing for his opponent's rank—had a firm friendly grip, and when he was set upon his feet again he stripped his own helmet free and shook his sweat-damp topknot. "My thanks," he said, pleasantly. "It is a pleasure to dance with you, Third Prince."

"Likewise, Jolong." An unaccustomed smile stretched Takshin's mouth, and the other man didn't look at his scars. Jolong simply bowed and turned with military precision, setting off for the edge of the drillyard with his splinter-edged practice-blade.

Most of the Guards avoided sparring with him, Jin was at his brushwork, and Kai was at Great Council with the Emperor, no doubt wishing he were here. Sun and sweat were preferable to sitting upon cushions and mouthing platitudes and politics.

You simply dislike speaking, Kai had said once, and Takshin had shaken his head.

I dislike empty words, when a sword will do. And there they had left it. It was not quite true—a sword was a tool with only limited applications—but it was close enough.

The heat would soon become unbearable and there was no prospect of another reasonable opponent, so Takshin placed his own splintered practice-blade in the pile for sanding and stripped his practice armor, consigning it to the care of a kaburei too old for pink cheeks and a stammer. The man *did* stare at Takshin's scars, and perhaps that accounted for the Third Prince's savage mood as he strode along a long colonnaded walkway. It was almost forgotten, this avenue, but it passed close to the Crown Prince's palace.

Of course Takshin found himself using it almost every day. At different times, and of course only to judge whether Takyeo's palace was watched.

Of course.

Today, of all days, while he dripped with sweat and his leg threatened to drag, he saw a swaying shape passing between bars of light and shadow, silk the green of new yeoyan leaves embroidered with soft curving yellow at the sleeves. Her hairpin dangled a single amber bead, catching fire when she passed into sunshine and dying as she moved into the shade of a column, and she held a well-oiled rainbell carefully away from her skirts with her left hand.

If she recognized him, she made no sign, moving at the same unhurried pace. Takshin would remember it long afterward, the heat, the slight breeze ruffling the edge of her skirts before mouthing sweat drying upon his skin and pushing dust in lazy golden whirls inside glowing bars. A prison of shine and shade, holding a small guttering flame.

He stopped at a reasonable distance and let her draw closer. Her course did not waver, her gaze fixed at a moving point some body-lengths ahead, pale Khir eyes tracing a route among stone flags.

"Lady Spyling," he said, and cursed himself for not making her speak first. "Peering between columns again?"

Her chin rose. She halted at a decorous distance, in shadow, the edge of her green skirt flirting with sunshine. "Third Prince." A bow, correct in every degree, a bending of a supple stem. The amber bead kindled, was snuffed. "Your manners are ever the same."

What could he say? He had learned to treat all with equal indifference. A crackle-glaze of sweat all over him itched. "Are you well?"

"Well enough, thank you. The weather is very warm." She was a wary fencer, her gaze not quite meeting his.

Takshin's throat swelled with a few inconsequentials. He was trying to decide among them when she straightened, and took the first thrust.

"I am glad to see you. There is something I would speak upon." Careful Zhaon with strange edges to the consonants, not blurred as it was in the Shan dialects.

"Then speak away." Takshin winced inwardly. He did not mean to sound harsh, did he? It was merely a habit.

She did not seem to mind overmuch. "You were at the banquet for the Knee-High Festival."

"Yes." He regarded her warily. His leg throbbed, not yet accustomed to its work again. Was she asking for gossip, or after information?

"I would thank you." *Now* she looked at him directly, pale eyes thickly fringed with charcoal lashes. "For my princess's life."

Oh. Was that it? He had moved to protect Takyeo, without thought or intention. "The Crown Prince is my eldest brother." A reflexive parry, dismissive and stinging at once. "It was my duty."

"He is very kind to my princess, and so to me." She studied him, cool and remote, her skirt moving a little. The wind was uneasy today. "I will thank you for both lives, then."

So she thought Takyeo kind. Who would not? "It is nothing," Takshin managed. It had been a long time since anyone, especially a woman, offered more than perfunctory politeness. "Anyone would have done the same."

"In any case, Third Prince, I am most grateful, and give you my thanks. I shall trouble you no further." She stepped aside, slippered feet testing the walkway toe-first before committing her weight, moving with the assurance of a cat or a body acquainted with swordplay. Or it could simply be a dancer's grace. She moved as if to sway past him, but Takshin took two gliding sideways steps of his own, blocking her path. The edge of her skirt, brushed forward by that soft stray breeze, almost touched the top of his boot. Her right hand dropped close to her side and her steady, mistrustful gaze rose to his face again.

"I have something to speak upon as well." The words even came naturally. Now he had a course, he might as well commit himself. "You mentioned, a few weeks ago, something about an earring."

"A *kyeogra*." She nodded, and her rainbell was no longer quite so ready to rise in her defense. Did she expect to be caught in an afternoon storm? Where was she going? "I recall you did not like the idea."

"That is not my memory." What did a man say, in this situation? He thought it quite likely she might poke him with the closed rainbell if he fretted her again. "I would be honored, Lady Spyling. If you are still amenable."

"You wish me to pierce your ear?" Wary in turn, and very soft. Khir women seemed incapable of raising their voices.

His throat was dry, and blocked. He had to cough to clear it, but to do so in a court lady's face was unprincely indeed. So he croaked an affirmative, like a stone frog in a child's tale. "Yes." Salt and dust itched all over him, and his leg, while glad of the rest, was also full of the deep ache that meant a bruise was rising for the skin-surface.

She studied him for a few more moments; that pale gaze held the shadows of thought moving swift as bronzefish in a bright spring stream. "Very well, then. It will take me some short while to find the implements in the markets."

"Have you...I shall ask...do you require an escort then, Lady Spyling?" At least his scars and a glower would keep market thieves from accosting her. He could be useful to a court lady; there were a few who had found as much before they inevitably moved to less difficult prey.

A slight shake of her head, that amber bead almost touching sunshine before hastily retreating. "There are many kaburei and guards in the Crown Prince's household to accompany me. In any case, I am not bound there now."

"Where are you bound, then?" The question slipped forth before he could halt it, and if she showed disdain now, he would fling whatever cutting words he had into the breach of his walls.

"To the Second Concubine's palace, to practice the sathron since my princess and her husband are viewing the gardens." So she knew the Second Concubine, and by the softening of her expression, liked her too.

Which meant she had fine taste, this Khir girl. "Auntie Kanbina? You know she adopted Zakkar Kai, yes?"

"Yes." A small smile, working wonders on her sharp, solemn face. Was it affectionate? Polite? Amused, disgusted?

He couldn't decide, and his discomfort grew by the moment. "Well, then. When shall we meet again?"

"I shall send you word when I have found the implements, Third Prince?"

A familiar scowl took refuge upon his face. "My name is Takshin."

"Third Prince Garan Takshin." A mischievous twinkle in those pale eyes. She might have bowed, except he was far too close. "Where shall I send my messenger, to find you?"

"The Old Tower. I stay there, with Mrong Banh." He was abruptly conscious of his topknot in its leather cage askew, his black Shan costume rumpled and stiff with dust, the sweat and grime in every crease. His scars would grow livid if he flushed. "Or send word to Zakkar Kai. He will find me."

"Will he?" A bright spark of interest in her gaze now. What would a Khir lady like about the God of War? Of course, Kai was unscarred.

"He always does." He did not mean it to sound so grim. "When we were young... but that would bore you. Go, Lady Spyling." The right half of his mouth pulled up, an unwilling almost-smile, and he stepped aside with a bow. "If I may not accompany you, I shall await your letter."

"Will you know who it is from, if I sign it?" She did not return the bow, simply regarded him sidelong, and he realized, with a measure of shock, that she was *teasing* him.

There was no hint of ill-humor in it, or of Sabwone's languid waiting to pounce. Instead, she looked a little like Jin when he was about mischief, or Gamnae when she was very young and attempting to fret one of her many elder brothers into paying attention to her. Except with her eyebrows slightly up, and that catlike curve playing at the edges of her lips, she was not a child.

"Only if you sign it *little spying nuisance*." It was a tolerable pun, he decided, since the last two syllables could rhyme with *Komor*.

"I shall sign as it pleases me, Third Prince Garan Takshin." A slight, deliberate mispronunciation, turning his name into a high, inaccessible cliff, distant and forbidding. She did not bow as she stepped away, and he did not follow.

He watched her float upon her path, a yeoyan branch laden with green, its blossoms spent but still fragrant in a drift about the tree's roots. Something beautiful, and fragile, waiting to be stripped by a spring storm or a sudden icy wind.

He was cold, Takshin realized, just before a scalding went through him, topknot to toes. Sweat crackled on the side of his neck when he scratched, and the warm satin of his greenstone hurai reminded him of status, of power, and of things he disdained.

"Third Prince," he murmured. Even sent to Shan and adopted by the Mad Queen, he had his hurai. And his pride. Neither would be very attractive to a court lady from Khir, now would they?

It mattered little. Still, when she vanished at the far end of the colonnade, he turned sharp right and stretched his legs, going up stairs and into a timbered half-hall that would eventually spill him in the direction of the Old Tower. He could bathe, and change, and if he hurried, perhaps Auntie Kanbina would be glad to see another boy she had fed plums and gently scolded long ago.

Unhappily, Mrong Banh caught him as he was unlacing his armor, and the astrologer bore a message.

The Emperor wished a word with his most disappointing son.

An Unwitting Jug

The royal baths along the north wall of the palace complex were usually busy with courtiers and court ladies. Much gossip was exchanged in the partitioned rooms, and many an intrigue was accompanied by hot or tepid water—the character for *graft*, after all, was two ministers in the same tub. The attendants moved through mist in winter and steam in summer, their fingers perpetually wrinkled, and more than one had found a helpful hand among Zhaon's elite.

The price for that help was not often immediately visible, but there were no shortage of hands to clasp.

A bath-girl stood in the curtained doorway, her hands clasped prettily before her, and trembled. Divided skirts and long laced tunic of plain dun cloth showed she was of the most junior of those artists of cleanliness. But the girl's black braids, wrapped around her head, held a long ironwood pin with a single mellow golden bead, a gift from a patron of high status.

Mirrorlight glowed through steam, gleamed upon oiled wooden walls sealed against the daily moisture. Second Prince Kurin settled in hot water in a satin-smooth stone tub reserved for royalty, hissing a long, pleased exhale. "Don't be so shy," he said, quietly. "Come forward. Anha, is it?" Almost a kaburei's name, saved by an extra syllable.

"Yes, Your Highness. Dho Anha." An oval face, eyebrows fine as thin brushstrokes, a pale but budding mouth. Her hands looked small but capable, but were clasped hard enough to whiten the knuckles. "Your servant."

"*Anha.*" The characters for it could not be noble, but there were at least a plethora of pleasing options. "What a pretty word, for a pretty girl." He beckoned again, his hurai glinting. "Do come closer."

"Do you wish some citrus for your bath, Your Highness?" She was quite alarmingly pale, too. "Perhaps some sweet oil—"

"When I wish for such things, I will tell you. Come here."

She did, unwilling step by unwilling step. Bare feet upon white and dark tiles, toes straight but somewhat overlarge. Altogether she was a nonentity. What did his father see in this particular bath-girl? Or was she simply inoffensive enough to be soothing, a blank face to paint whatever character he wished upon?

"That's a good girl." Kurin relaxed against the back of the stone-carved tub, lazily moving his own princely toes. The nails were a little too long, but that was work for a close-servant, not a bath attendant. "Now, Dho Anha, you are a very good servant, are you not? Especially to my father."

Her reply was almost too soft to be audible. "I try to be, Second Prince." That golden bead upon her hairpin glittered in mirror-light; steam rose in lazy curls. Outside, summer heat was choking, in here, healthful essences were spread upon water or rubbed into skin, and ministers sat in damp rooms with eunuchs, discussing the races, the theater, the policies, Zhaon itself.

"I am told he often takes solace in your company." Kurin examined her again from top to foot, searching for whatever his father found so attractive in this creature.

"I am merely a bath-girl, Your Highness." Her trembling intensified. The girl looked ready to faint, and he hadn't even truly started questioning her yet.

Irritated, Kurin shook his head, and rested it in a convenient hollow. "Wash my hair."

"Yes, Your Highness." Of course, what else could she say? Scurrying movement filled the hall outside this private room reserved for royalty, whispers flooding the corners along with oil scraped from limbs with bone implements and spent water.

If her position was difficult with one royal patron, two would simply make it that more acute. She had quick fingers, and worked at his wet scalp gingerly.

"Harder," Kurin said. Soaking was pleasant no matter the weather, and a pour-over of tepid liquid would provide contrast and freshness to the afternoon once he left. "How long have you been attending my father, Anha?"

"I've been at the baths for two winters, Your Highness." She poured cold water over the long red-black strands, shielding his eyes with one soft, wrinkled palm.

"That is not what I asked, bath-girl."

"I…well, I attend whoever asks for me, or anyone when I am Second or Third Attendant. So, perhaps…I do not know. Your servant does not recall, Your Highness."

A cagey little thing. His mother would, no doubt, have already been at belittling the girl if she did not prefer bathing in the privacy of the Kaeje.

But Kurin had other methods. "You do not recall the first time you were called to attend the Emperor of all Zhaon?" He sounded baffled, and extremely mild.

"Oh, I do. It was in the first summer, and I was so nervous I dropped a jar of su-zhin clay. I expected a scolding but His Majesty said…"

"What did His Majesty say?" Was she really just a creeping, cringing mouse? The First Queen called the Second Concubine that, though it took some doing for that woman to cling to life as Gamwone's opponent, however slight the rivalry.

What his mother called this little bath-girl did not bear repeating.

"He was very kind, and said that the damp makes a grip uncertain." She paused, then rushed onward, as if defending herself from accusation. "Sometimes he calls me to attend his dressing, for my hands are often cool in summer."

"An imbalance in your humors." Kurin's chin tipped up as she rinsed his hair again. Cold water there, heat all along his body, his bathing-clout floating...it was a fine sensation, to have your head doused. "Perhaps a physician should be consulted."

"I will try, Your Highness." Almost pathetically eager to please, forgetting to be afraid.

"My father seems to find solace in your company," Kurin prodded again, gently enough.

"I do not know, Your Highness Second Prince."

Irritation rasped at his nerves. Either she was so skilled at dissimulation she put Makar—and Kurin himself—to shame, or she was simply cloudfur[44]-stupid. A small fragile ornament, and not even much of one at that. Looking at that pinched, frightened face was enough to destroy a man's appetite.

At least she did not pull his hair while wringing it dry. She knew her trade after two winters. "And how did you come to be a bath attendant, Dho Anha?"

"My aunt was one, Your Highness. When she died, Mother offered me to take her place, and the Head of Baths agreed."

Simple enough. "Is it good work? Do you like it?"

"Yes, very much." She wrung the ends of his hair, and again did not pull. There was nothing to fault in her attentions, rare enough in any servant.

So he was disposed to be kind, at least for the moment. Kurin watched the ceiling, water gathering on heavy-resined beams and sucking-plaster that would not rot under the assault of moisture. "Your family, Dho? Yes, Dho. Where do they live?"

"Beyond the city walls, Your Highness. In Suyon, along the West Road."

---

44. A wool-coated animal, grazed upon high stony ground.

Ah. Petty traders, then, possibly with an inn. He could find out later. Kurin relaxed as she chafed at his hair with a drycloth.

"Shall I comb, Your Highness?" the girl asked, meekly.

"Yes." He restrained yet more impatience. Cloudfur-stupid, indeed. Was Father simply amusing himself, or did he actually enjoy conversation with an empty-headed, cringing trader's daughter? His queens were highly cultured, and even his concubines were of noble blood.

There were those who liked female terror, thinking it added spice to brothel-games. Courtesans trained in imitation of noble girls' shocked modesty were much in demand. Or perhaps the Emperor only wished for rustic fare, like at the Knee-High or the Last Flower festivals.

Which reminded him, the Blossom Festival was soon, but he had no intention of attending Sabwone during it. Whispers had reached his ears, very disturbing ones. His beautiful sister, sold like a prize animal. In the end, however beautiful and clawing, Sabwone was helpless against political necessity.

For a few moments, Kurin allowed himself to think upon his plans—which ones could be set in motion, which reserved forces could be marshaled. There was simply no way of making an attempt at rescue Sabwone could be grateful for. Not yet.

If Heaven was kind and the Crown Prince as foolish as he usually was, they would see. It would be quite useful to have Sabwone well-disposed to her brother Kurin, if his suspicions proved correct.

The bath-girl drew a horn comb through his hair, the tines scraping his scalp just enough to send a pleasurable shiver down his spine. He could decide later how to handle *her*. Other whispers had reached him concerning his royal father, and this colorless little thing was only one avenue of verifying their truth.

Still, it would not do to abandon his groundwork halfway. So Kurin half-floated, enjoying his bath, and took care to speak as pleasantly as possible to Dho Anha as she brought citrus and kon-leaf infusion. He would ask for her to attend him again, and soon. After that, he would make much of her, very subtly. The Emperor might not even notice, if Kurin was careful.

But this little trader's brat would notice. Much could be drained from an unwitting jug.

The turn of phrase delighted him, and he smiled, resolving to write it down, as the bath-girl finished combing long black strands and asked, very shyly, if he wished for a temporary topknot to hold it free of his soaking.

To Promote Friendship

A white stone gazebo, familiar now, provided welcome shade. Trained vines threaded through waist-high lattices and ran thin juicy fingers up the roof supports, tiny buds swelling where maha flowers would bloom, pale and waxen, as summer deepened. "Lift your wrist, so." Second Concubine Kanbina stroked sathron strings, producing a liquid rill. "Gently, gently, my dear."

"My playing is barely passable," Yala said, as she had so many times before. Each time, the embarrassment was just as acute. "I despair of it."

"The sathron is jealous. It wants all your time." Kanbina's hair was loosely braided today, and there were shadows under her liquid eyes. Her starflower-patterned robes were loose, an invalid's dishevelment. *If you do not mind my disarray, I would very much like to see you today*, her invitation had read, thin careful brushstrokes full of frailty. "Of course, I used to stay up all night playing, when I was younger. It was a comfort."

Yala nodded. No doubt this woman had learned to take comfort where she found it—a very classical lesson indeed. "Sometimes I play for my princess, though not often. She is much better at it. The music does not speak to me."

Kanbina's wan smile lit her thin face like a candle in a darkened room. "Is that what they say in Khir? Here we say *the music is its own master.*"

"What a lovely sentiment." Especially when one thought of the characters that could be used to express it. Perhaps she should write it upon a scroll and make it a gift to the Second Concubine. The idea was as pleasing as this new dress, and her hairpin's amber bead.

Kanbina laid her thin hand flat over resonating strings, and breeze-sound replaced instrument-breath. Bright interest showed in her dark gaze, and she pushed a few stray strands of red-black hair away, tucking them behind her ear. "Do you think it untrue?"

Yala gazed across the garden. Somewhere, a water-clock of babu *thunk-click*ed, a comforting sound. Kanbina was silent, waiting upon her answer.

So few people listened instead of filling their heads with whatever they wished to say next. It was one more thing to like about the woman. When the water-clock spoke again, Yala followed suit. "So few can claim to be their own master."

"Only the Emperor is free, and we are not?" Kanbina, thoughtful, stretched her fingers one by one, a musician's habitual movements.

Yala followed suit. Her hands would ache before long. "Is ruling freedom?"

Kanbina considered the question, her fingers dropping to the instrument and plucking an endless note from the sathron's deepest string. The drone became a rhythm, and when it halted, she smiled slightly. Color had returned to her cheeks, now that she was settled and resting. "Long ago, I would have said yes. Now, though, I know better."

"A difficult lesson." Yala's neck had loosened, and her back likewise. Last night's practice had done her good. It was also very pleasant among this green and flowing water, the gazebo's shade a mercy. The afternoon heat was circling, about to settle like a fowl over nesting eggs. "Zho Zhuon the Yellow Sage says true freedom lies in accepting one's lot."

The elder woman's mouth tightened, and she dropped her gaze to the sathron's face. "Do you agree?"

"I have bent before the current all my life." Yala plucked a series of jagged notes, ugly and clashing.

Kanbina's wrist lifted, her fingers drummed, and the discordancies were resolved into harmony, a long phrase of exquisite music. Dragonwings, their bright carapaces flashing, zipped over placid water, and somewhere in the garden's recesses a bird took flight, clapping wings a startled heartbeat broken in half by the water-clock's *thunk-click*. Yala smiled and plucked an extremely simple counterpoint, one almost impossible to fumble. The music dipped, rose, flew—but she was content to keep her part small.

Easier to avoid a mistake.

Kanbina's eyes half-lidded; the music soaked through her and into the sathron, only needing the lightest of touches to set it free. It rose like the immortal whitebirds in Anwei's great harbor, with their distinctive bowed wings and habit of sleeping upon the waves; it flowed like the Golden River in the fabled land of Qin far past Ch'han's great girdling deserts; it cried out in anguish sharp as the Moon Maiden's when she realized her lover was wounded by the poison blade. Sometimes Kanbina's eyes closed entirely, and Yala had the chance to admire a true artist lost in creation.

It would not be so bad to be immured in a small gemlike palace, able to spend her time as she wished. Sewing, riding—but Kanbina did not ride. Perhaps she should; it would bring strength to her frame. In the meantime, Yala continued her soft rhythmic accompaniment, taking no chances, letting the other player set the direction.

Like all restful moments, it was over too soon. There was a well-regulated bustle behind the verandah; another guest had arrived. Kanbina's music wound to a languid, melancholy finish just as Zakkar Kai, in dark subtle silk embroidered with blue, appeared. He halted in the gloom, looking toward the gazebo, and Yala was suddenly aware of her fingers aching.

The sathron bit those who touched it casually, or those who did not respect it enough to practice in increments.

"Kai!" Kanbina rose hurriedly; her step turned as light and quick as a young girl's.

He met her halfway on the raised path to the gazebo, clasping her hands. "I heard beautiful music, like Shi Hanh before the Battle of Sonon. Come, back into the shade with you, Mother."

"*Shuh*, now look at you, Head General, ordering me about like one of your soldiers."

"A disobedient one, no doubt. Physician Kihon tells me your sleep was troubled." He cupped her elbow with his palm, steadying her upon the gazebo step. Dragonwings dove and whirled behind him; even though he was robed, he had likely arrived in soldier's boots, since his house-slippers were those Yala had seen him wear before in these halls.

"Carrying tales. I shall scold him." Kanbina clicked her tongue and settled upon her cushion again. Kaburei and servants appeared, bearing a small table and a cushion for the new guest; she directed them with languid movements. "And your sleep, my son?"

"Untroubled, except by rain." He quoted the proverb with a smile, and bowed to Yala. "Lady Komor."

"General Zakkar." She kneaded her fingertips. "I fear my sathron practice has suffered."

"You should see my hands." Kanbina spread them. "The calluses sometimes rip free, when I am unable to sleep. I play, and play."

"Like Shih Ao's Milk-White Sister." Yala stretched her own fingers again. No more playing for her today, if she could avoid it. "Playing a horse into life, to run with the wind."

"Or a white boar, to lead hunters astray." Zakkar Kai examined the gazebo carefully as a battleground before lowering himself to the offered cushion. Judging by its slightly tattered orange and black stripes, it was perhaps made for him many years ago. "Have you ever hunted boar, Lady Komor?"

"That would not be seemly. I have ridden to deer, and with

hawk. Once or twice to wolf, as part of a *kha-iyu*.[45] Princess Mahara did not often hunt, but my brother did." Bai hunted only to ride, really—he did not care much for the joy of the kill, but the freedom of a gallop enchanted him much as it did Yala herself.

"Your brother?" Kanbina indicated the precise spot where she wished the tea-table set. Her close-maid, red-faced except for the white scar along her jawline, hovered at her shoulder, ready to aid her frail lady.

Yala did not mind so much when there was no malice in the question. "He rides the Great Fields."

"May the wind carry him," Kai said, softly, in Khir.

She dropped her hands into her lap. Her sathron made a faint breathing noise as the breeze touched its strings. What would Bai think of this man?

You respected your enemies, of course. To do otherwise was to court disaster. "Eternally to the Sun," she replied, blinking back a suspicious saltwater fullness.

"What does she say?" Kanbina asked, somewhat anxiously.

"Her brother has ascended to the ancestors." Zakkar Kai accepted a cup from a heavyset kaburei in the Second Concubine's livery and blew across the top to cool its cargo.

"Ah." Kanbina's worried gaze bent upon Yala next, and there was no reason to make the older woman uncomfortable.

So Yala smiled encouragingly and settled her borrowed sathron in its case. "What is this tea, may I ask?"

"It is yohaelo, scented with roasted rai." On safer ground, Kanbina relaxed. "Since we are past the Knee-High, I thought it correct."

"Quite right," Yala agreed, inhaling the scent from her own cup. "We do not roast the rai for tea in Khir. It smells delicious, like a meal in itself."

"It is held to be cleansing for the blood, and to promote friendship." Kanbina covered her own sathron with reverent movements,

45. A ceremonial group hunt allowed only to the Second Families of Khir.

closed the case, and let her touch linger upon the clasp. "I would like us all to be friends."

"Yes." Yala held the bone-clay cup, her left-hand fingers just below its lovely ridged belly, and toasted her hostess with a slight bow. "General Zakkar Kai and I are allies, Lady Kanbina. And it would please me immensely to call you a friend."

"Friends are difficult in a palace." Kanbina lifted her own cup; thc round, attentive close-maid behind her cast Yala what was no doubt a grateful glance. Interesting. "But we shall persevere."

"Indeed," Yala murmured, and took a single, scorching sip.

A Mighty Ally

Courtiers crowded the great hall with its frozen animals caught in vermilion pillars, but the Emperor had waved them back. Mrong Banh stood in his usual spot at Tamuron's side, though he had paused at Takshin's shoulder before ascending to attend the throne as if he wished to offer support.

That was useless, but at least the Crown Prince was next to Takshin, giving his younger brother a single indecipherable glance. It wasn't like the Emperor to make his prize son sit upon his knees like the lowlier ones, but today the royal brow was clouded and there was a slight, unfamiliar flush creeping up the royal throat.

Takshin performed his bow, and waited.

"Third Prince Garan Suon-ei Takshin." The Emperor raised a finger trapped in one of the great twin hurai, stroked at his beard. "How is your health?"

"Tolerable, Your Majesty." *Except for the fact that I am in this particular room, which gives me a stomachache.* For a moment he toyed with the idea of saying as much, but laid it aside. "And yours?"

It was not quite rude to inquire instead of uttering the formulaic *May the Emperor live ten thousand years*, but it was close. Takshin settled himself for the skirmish. Of course his father would want to pack him off to Shan again. That was the plan, both to give the shield-country a hostage and to rid the First Queen of half her sons.

While Takshin did not mind the latter so much anymore, the former consideration was past its time.

"Well enough. I am touched by your solicitude." The Emperor's dry tone was almost as mocking as Takshin's own. His forehead glistened. It was not overly hot in the Great Hall today, but perhaps his robes were too heavy. "I have made a decision, my son."

"And what decision is that?" He ignored Mrong Banh's agonized look. The astrologer was ever seeking to smooth the folds, but in this case, Takshin was determined to be a wrinkle in any way possible.

"You have a sister, Takshin."

How observant of you, Father. "Your Majesty be praised; I have two."

Takyeo's mouth twitched. The Crown Prince said nothing, but he did shift upon his cushion the slightest fraction. His eldest brother would see the humor in the situation, surely. Bleak humor, but a man took what amusement he could in the face of pitiless authority.

The Emperor continued. "Princess Sabwone is of marrying age."

Surely you don't plan to have her marry me. But Takshin saw the game clearly, now. "Is she? It is, no doubt, as Your Majesty says."

"You are brother to Suon Kiron of Shan, my son." The Emperor's flush mounted another notch, and his fingers twitched. His robe was indeed heavy, phoenixes worked with gold thread on a background of spiral-patterned black silk, somber and ceremonial.

For a moment, Takshin thought he might be unable to speak. A curtain of red passed over his vision, and he knew his face had hardened. "I was sent to the Mad Queen of Shan many years ago, yes."

Let the Emperor test *that* fact beneath his strong white teeth.

Garan Tamuron regarded him narrowly, and *still* did not take offense. "First Princess Sabwone will be married to King Suon Kiron of Shan. You will accompany her to—"

"I will not return to Shan." There. It was said. Takshin raised his gaze to meet his father's, prepared for the blow.

A muscle in the Emperor's cheek twitched. He let the statement sit in its own echo for a few moments. "Do you disobey your father, Third Prince Garan Takshin?"

"Did you not send me to Shan to be rid of me?" Takshin did not bother to keep his tone reasonable, or his voice low. Let the courtiers hear, let the eunuchs rustle—and let those who would take gossip to his mother. Perhaps it would even disturb her. "Unfortunately the Mad Queen was not quite up to the task. Perhaps you should have planned more thoroughly."

Takyeo cleared his throat, folding his hands inside his wide saffron robe-sleeves. "Father," he began, diplomatically enough, "Takshin has just returned, and no doubt wishes some time to rest. He was in Shan for many long years, with only infrequent—"

"I was." Takshin again did not bother to lower his voice. "Shall I tell you the tale of the Mad Queen's hospitality, Your Majesty? You have never inquired of it."

Garan Tamuron eyed him as if he were a new creature, neither meat nor insect, as the saying went. "I should have thought the marks were visible." His gaze flickered past Takshin to the courtiers at the far end of the hall, no doubt straining to hear what passed between a recalcitrant son and his royal father.

Cold red rage threatened to return. Takshin smiled, his cheeks bunching and his eyes burning. Soon his lip would begin to twitch. "Indeed."

Takyeo's shoulder bumped his as the Crown Prince leaned closer. "Are you *trying* to provoke him?" A fierce whisper, uttered through motionless lips.

Ah, his eldest brother *cared*. How touching.

"Let him speak, Crown Prince." Garan Tamuron folded his hands in his lap. The dark-robed eunuchs and brightly clad courtiers at their scribe-tables among the pillars leaned forward to catch the august words dropping like rain from Heaven. "We have long missed the sound of his voice in these halls."

And whose fault is that? Still, this was different than the empty formalities exchanged when he first came home, or the passionless recital of evidence after the attempt on Takyeo's life.

The Emperor wanted something, and he wanted Takshin to give him a reason to get it.

Takshin forced his breathing to slow, willed his pulse to turn deep and hidden as the rank sludge in bandit-infested marshes. There was time enough to consider anything if you simply slowed the world outside enough.

A fly hung in the air over the Emperor's head, caught between wingbeats. Tapestries and character scrolls draped midripple in drafts rising from braziers. A eunuch—one of Zan Fein's lean little favorites, with an ill cast to his left eye and a beardless chin—was in the middle of a stifled cough.

Ah. Takshin found what he wanted in mental storehouses, and the world resumed its natural pace. "I shall be happy to be a prisoner within the Crown Prince's palace," he announced to both Emperor *and* the Court. "That is what you were about to suggest, O Great Emperor of Zhaon?" The words reverberated, the most august title of the Land of the Five Winds turned into a festival jest.

Mrong Banh's expression went through several small changes in a single moment, and Takshin could have laughed. The Emperor's eyes narrowed slightly, but that was all.

"Ah." Takyeo folded his hands inside his sleeves. Of course, now he had to play along. "Indeed. I would be honored, Younger Brother. My duties have grown somewhat oppressive, of late."

Father thought to play the magnanimous patriarch, allowing you to seemingly save me from a return to Shan or a spell in the dungeons. Not that it would matter. If Takshin did not wish to be held, he would *not* be. One way—or another. "And the sudden swarm of assassins is no doubt a factor in this invitation."

"Takshin..." The Crown Prince sighed, and brought his hands forth to spread them in a peacemaker's weary brushing movement. "I told Father you would not return to Shan. Is being my guest so unpleasant?"

"The blood-brother to the King of Shan is a mighty ally," Mrong Banh weighed in. His topknot was very tight today, and only a few critical fractions off-center.

Takshin's mouth twitched, whether with amusement or distaste he could not quite tell. The Emperor regarded his sons mildly enough, but there was a balked gleam in his gaze. It must irk him, that Takshin had seen the trap.

If he stayed here, it had to be of his own will. On the other hand, where was there to go?

"Of course I'll stay, Takyeo. I'll guard you like a wolf guards his lair." Takshin inhaled, and knee-bowed to the floor, playing at great humility. When he straightened, he delivered the final blow. "After all, you are the only one happy to see me home safely."

With that he rose, but he did not back from the Emperor's presence as protocol demanded. He also did not pause as he strode through the crowd jammed at the far end of the hall. They had come like wasps to rotting fruit, eager to witness his humiliation and carry tales of it far and wide, perhaps even to his mother's heavily hung rooms.

Not today, though. They, like his cursed dam, would have to wait.

I Suggest Before Lunch

Maybe it was because he whistled a theater aria on the way home to his mother's palace, and that was a certain way to bring the spirits of ill-luck to your door. Or maybe he had offended Heaven in some fashion during the night's furtive drinking in the city. In any case, Jin, youngest prince of Zhaon, had an otherwise marvelous morning, and doom did not strike until he reached the familiar steps and heard a quite uncharacteristic amount of noise.

First Concubine Luswone was not as elegantly restrained as Second Queen Haesara, but it was unheard of for there to be raised voices in her household. Of course her two children sometimes stormed at each other, but such displays were quickly put to rest by a mother's intervention—or by the threat of sending the stormer in question to the Kaeje's Great Hall to answer to the Emperor.

Even favorite daughters quailed before that prospect. And Sabwone was probably *very* sure she was the favorite, though Jin thought Gamnae had a better chance at that title. She was definitely more pleasant to spend time with.

Jin peered through the wide double front doors, ajar because today was a visiting day. Yes, there was actual *yelling*. It sounded like Sabwone, and his mouth hung open slightly as he sought to remember if he'd done anything mischievous before leaving for practice.

Nothing really sprang to mind, but just to be safe, he decided he should sneak over the garden wall to reach his quarters. He might have made it, too, had not his old tutor Zan Kanh spied him.

"Prince Jin!" Kanh hurried forward in his dark eunuch's robe, his high-peaked cap bobbing. Rheumy eyes blinking furiously, liver-spotted hands trembling, and his breath sweetish from khansu,[46] the elder shuffled out of the dimness of the pillared hall and beckoned him through the door into the cool gloom of the receiving-hall. "Oh, thank goodness, thank Heaven and the Fifth Wind you have come!"

"Honorable Kanh. Is that Mother I hear?" His heart in his boots, Jin dragged both heart and feet across the fresh-cleaned wooden floor. A statue of two longneck stilt-birds, their beaks dipping gracefully, stood in a pool of mirrorlight. Sometimes, when he was young, he had thought they would come to life, their carved feathers rustling. "And Elder Sister?"

"Indeed, indeed. Come in, come in." Kanh wrung his limp hands. Thankfully, he didn't pat at Jin's shoulder, fussing with soft paws.

Jin hated that.

"Well, what are they arguing about?" He peered into the hall's depths and saw hurrying kaburei at the far end, servants bustling on a thousand errands, hoping that motion would keep them anonymous and also afford them overheard gossip to spread.

"*I won't do it!*" Sabwone screamed from the depths of the house, and there was a shattering noise. She'd thrown something. "*I won't!*"

"Oh, it's terrible, terrible, Prince Jin!" Kanh's eyes rolled. He was obviously enjoying himself immensely. "Such a display, such, *such* a display!"

"I can *hear* that, Kanh. What seems to be the, er, the difficulty?"

---

46. A milder addictive herb than djonba, with slight analgesic properties.

He was the man of the house, Jin reminded himself, and not a boy anymore. Well, Father was the man, but in this household, it was Jin who should keep the peace.

Not that Sabwone was likely to cooperate.

"It's simply terrible!" Kanh abandoned himself to theatrical weeping, continuing to wring his old hands. "It's First Princess Sabwone!"

I can hear that, too. Jin swallowed his impatience. Kai said a real man did not lose his temper, and a strategist—which was, as far as Jin could tell, a step above that—was calm at all times besides.

"She is to leave us, leave us!" Kanh reached for the front of Jin's robe, and the young prince deftly avoided that moist clutching, stepping aside and plunging past him into cool high-ceilinged space beyond, full of shafts of mirrorlight and a sticky, not entirely unappetizing breeze full of the scent of meatbuns.

His mother must have decided he needed stuffing again, like a prize longneck eggbird. She thought Jin's leanness dangerous, as if he were still a child at risk of wasting away when a bad spirit caught wind of a concubine's quiet pride.

He reached the cross-hall just as kaburei and servants scattered like raindrops upon a greased dish; Sabwone, her hair unbound and her embroidered morning-robe flying, burst among them. His disdainful older sister, usually straight-backed with glittering hairpins in her high-piled hair, was now mottle-faced with weeping and wrapped her slim hands in his practice-tunic the way Kanh had failed to accomplish.

"You can't!" she yelled, and her breath smelled like honey-citrus in tuang tea.

Jin realized, with a start, that he was now a head taller than her. He'd grown again. Now he looked down, his mouth slightly ajar and his sword-scabbard dangling from his left hand. The blade, lean as himself and marvelously balanced, was a gift from Kai, and he carried it everywhere he could.

"Tell her she can't," Sabwone raged, attempting to shake him. "Tell her! You tell her, Ji-ha! *Tell* her!"

He caught her left wrist, but she pounded at him with her other hand, her fist striking the same point upon his tunic, a bird's ineffectual fluttering.

You cannot strike a girl, Kurin used to say. *Unless it's a kaburei.* And then the Second Prince would smile in that peculiar catlike way. You could never be sure if he was joking, or not.

The older he got, the more Jin thought Kurin pretended to joke, just to see what those around him would agree to from a prince. Kai said a true man did not strike a woman, and Jin thought the general was probably right about almost everything.

"Be about your work," First Concubine Luswone said, resolving out of the hall to the women's quarters. Shimmering peach silk hung from her shoulders, and her long eyes were wide and snapping with a fire Jin had rarely seen. "All of you. *Now.*" Her golden leaf ear-drops swung, and her hairpin, thrust hurriedly through a simple twist, glittered sharply in a shaft of mirrorlight.

"She can't," Sabwone sobbed, hanging on to Jin's tunic. "She can't if you don't let her, don't let her, I won't do it, I *won't*."

"You are making a scene," Mother hissed, and Jin swallowed, hard.

"Sa-bi, shhh now." He put his left arm around his sister. "What's all this, hm? What is it? I can't help if you don't calm down and—"

"We have received blessed news." Mother halted and touched her cheeks, reminding herself to smooth her features. *Laughter and grief cause lines*, she had often told Jin as he watched her rub attars and oils in with small fingertip circles. *A noblewoman must float above such things.* It didn't matter so much for a prince, and he always watched, fascinated by the many steps his mother had to take to achieve that grace. Like the lightstep, it took practice and infinite patience. "This is a most auspicious day, which your sister will recognize once she regains her senses."

"Mother?" Jin cleared his throat, tentatively. Sabwone sobbed into his chest, obviously deciding it was up to Jin to smooth this fold for her. "Uh, hello. You are lovely this morning."

The slightest of curves visited Mother's pretty lips. "Thank you, my son." Her approval, a warm bath on a cool day, was a sweet breeze on feverish skin. "Bring your sister, let us have some tea."

"To the Infinite Hells with your *tea*!" Sabwone reared back and shouted at the ceiling, chin tipped up and throat working. "I *won't do it*! You can't make me!"

"Uh, Sa-bi..." Jin gathered himself. "You won't do what?"

"Your sister is to be a queen," Mother said quietly. "She is behaving ungratefully, and if this continues, your father the Emperor shall hear of it."

Even that threat didn't stopper his sister's mouth. "Oh, he'll hear of it! I'll go to Father, and *he'll* tell you not to send me away."

"You're...getting married?" Jin blinked. *But who would want to marry you?* Oh, she was his sister, and you were supposed to take care of mother, sister, and aunt as a dutiful man, but...marry Sabwone?

Who under Heaven's wide vault would be so foolish?

"Yes." Mother stretched her hands with a sigh, her chin rising a fraction. "Your sister, the First Princess of Zhaon, is to be Queen of Shan."

Really? Jin swallowed disbelieving laughter. Mother did not play pranks, it was beneath her; her infrequent jokes were subtle, like her perfume. For a moment he thought she meant Sabwone was to marry Takshin, before he remembered Shan had a young king.

Some of the rumors said Queen Gamwone had intended her own younger son to take Kiron of Shan's place, but just how the First Queen thought *that* was going to happen was beyond Jin too. He had never worked up the courage to ask Takshin if it was true, either. "Oh. That's..." He searched for an appropriate word.

"I'll hang myself," Sabwone hissed, her head tipped back, her throat working. "I'll hang myself and haunt this wretched place!"

"Good." A shocked silence followed Mother's single, clipped word. "If you must, do it quickly. I suggest before lunch."

Sabwone dropped her hands and whirled. Jin flinched, but Mother's face was deadly pale, her eyes blazing, and the sight halted whatever either of them might have said.

"I have the silk," Mother continued, "and I will tie the noose, I will even help you climb onto the railing. But I will not have any more of this disgusting, disgraceful *display*. You will either hang yourself, or you will attend to your dressing, visit the Emperor, and express how thankful you are that he has made such a glorious match for such an undeserving, spiteful child." First Concubine Luswone turned upon her slippered heel, pulling at her peach robe to right its lines with her soft, manicured fingers. "Jin. Come along, our tea is waiting."

"Don't leave me," Sabwone whispered, and Jin put his head down.

"Come, Sa-bi." His throat was dry. "Some tea, and we may find a way—"

"Garan Jin." Mother halted, her chin almost touching her left shoulder. "You will leave that girl to make her decision." *That girl,* dismissive, the word for a misbehaving servant-child. "The Emperor has sealed his decree, the marriage is contracted; an emissary of Shan is coming to take her to her husband. It is done, and wailing will not undo it. Come along."

Sabwone pinched him, hard, high up on his left arm. Her face was dead pale as well, eyes bruised from weeping, and her glare promised trouble if he didn't do what she wanted.

But... Father had spoken. An emissary was coming. It was done. She was going to go to Shan.

"I'll try," he whispered, and hurried after Mother, his head down and his neck aching.

He was, he supposed, not a very good brother. Because what he felt, instead of righteous anger on Sabwone's behalf, was...

Well, *relief.* He had never dreamed he would be free of his beautiful sister's poking, prodding, pinching, and ill-tempered games.

No, Sixth Prince Garan Jin thought, miserably, he was not a very good brother at all. But at least he could hurry and be a good son.

First Session, Ladies' Court

Seclusion was lifted, the North Pavilion was cool with garden-breezes this early in the morning, and Mahara's first formal appearance since she had made her informal debut with the princesses was going extremely well. A small coterie formed, Lady Aoan Mau sending a kaburei to inquire if the Crown Princess would honor her by hearing a sathron-song, and Mahara's genuine smile in response had thawed one or two faces. The Second Queen's favored faction closed around Yala and her princess, and a few other court ladies—including Lady Huan, wan and tall in dragonwing-patterned silk and cotton—gracefully drifted closer, bowing like supple stems to those higher in rank before sinking onto cushions plumped and placed by servants. Maids and kaburei ran to fetch pomade, scented bags, small birds in cunning cages to be fed one grain at a time, sewing baskets, all the little things needed for a moment's diversion.

"Did you hear?" Court Lady Gonwa poured a steady stream of amber tea, her thin wrist still held at the correct angle. She did not bend in the middle, but moved her entire torso as a unit. Mahara wondered if she wore armor under her sunshine-yellow robe—vertical ribs in stiffened leather, like those for the back-injured. "It is the season for weddings."

Mahara nodded. Takyeo had told her, warning her of gossip, and even thought to include the most becoming phrases etiquette demanded. "Most felicitous news."

Lady Aoan Mau coaxed a soft ripple from her sathron. "Now only the Second Princess remains to be settled."

"She is young yet." Lady Huan coughed delicately into her sleeve, and motioned for a handkerchief. Her youngest niece, a sloe-eyed girl in wide pants, round-cheeked with a sober mien, a single braid down the back of her child's tunic, hurried forth to produce one from the basket over her arm, bowed in Mahara's direction, bowed in Lady Gonwa's, and froze, clearly unable to recall what came next.

Yala caught her eye, tipping her head at Mahara again and smiling when the girl performed her prescribed second obeisance and settled with a cheeky, grateful little wink.

"Ah, youth." Lady Gonwa's expression was rather set. "Sometimes children do not know what is best for them."

"And sometimes it is the elders who mourn." Lady Aoan Mau's fingers danced, producing a discordant mutter from the strings. "There is bound to be lamentation in the First Concubine's house, losing a beloved daughter." News of Sabwone's display had raced through the complex like fire among rai-paper slum houses, and very few seemed overly inclined to pity the First Princess.

"And relief, for a good marriage made." Lady Huan produced a fan and flicked it open, her faint smile intensifying. The relief, her tone intimated, was widespread.

"Would that all mothers had such news." Lady Gonwa poured Mahara a measure of tea. "Crown Princess, perhaps you could offer some words of comfort to Princess Sabwone."

"My Zhaon is still so clumsy." Mahara accepted the tea with both hands and a gracious nod. Her crimson-wrapped hairpins glittered, and Yala busied herself with arranging the sewing basket upon her own green-silk lap. "What could I say?"

"Perhaps there is an expression in Khir?" Lady Gonwa's expression was bright, and somewhat hard. It was likely one or two of the

First Princess's ill-natured intrigues had inconvenienced those she cared for.

Mahara looked into her tea, so Yala leaned forward slightly. "*Losing a daughter means gaining sons,*" she said in Khir, then repeated it in Zhaon. "Among the Khir, a wife to bring strong sons into a family is a celebration."

It was true enough, though the proverb held an overtone of disdain. You could not trust that a new wife would produce strong heirs immediately, and the food she ate before bringing her first son into her husband's clan was referred to as a gambling debt if a father-in-law was in an uncharitable mood.

Many were.

"Is that so?" This was young Lady Eon-ha, of Lady Aoan Mu's coterie. She wore her hair low, her pin thrust through the braids at the back and its fall of thin silver threads a glitter when she turned her head to glance aside, which she did infrequently but perhaps more than *strictly* necessary. "Perhaps we should draw it as a poem—should we send for paper?"

"Oh, no." Yala let herself smile and lift her sleeve, as if to hide a blush. "My lady princess will no doubt have a much better suggestion. There is Hai Lung, of course, who wrote maxims for girls upon marriage in *The Book of Water*, and there is Ne Shao's *Correct Poems*, though he never married so is held to be somewhat less than an expert."

"A scholar!" Lady Gonwa set the teapot down, and Lady Huan poured for her. "Are all Khir women so learned?"

"Yala's father is a very upright nobleman." Mahara turned her head slightly, taking in Yala's stance with her peripheral vision. She looked pleased. "And very traditional. He made certain she had the three graces."

"And what are those?" Lady Huan inquired.

"Riding, reading, and *re-shuan*." Yala found the fabric and the hoops she required, and drew both free.

Lady Aoan Mu's fingers stilled upon the strings. "*Re-shuan?*"

Her accent was tolerable, and she lowered her chin slightly to express modest dismay at her lack of knowledge.

"Silence," Yala and Mahara chorused in Zhaon, and the ladies all laughed. Lady Gonwa hid her mouth behind her sleeve, but Lady Aoan Mau threw her head back, her bare brown throat gleaming, and her sathron chuckled too. Lady Huan's youngest niece, perhaps not understanding the joke, still giggled, a bright unaffected note sharing adult merriment.

Lady Gonwa dabbed at her eyes with a folded cotton cloth and lifted her cup, which meant the teapot could be passed to other high-ranking ladies. Yala's own teapot, full of fragrant siao,[47] meant that her rank had not yet been fully decided, so she set out the traditional three empty cups upon the tray before pouring her own.

"Is that siao?" Lady Gonwa leaned forward slightly. "Please, Lady Komor, do me the honor of allowing a taste?"

"It would please me like nothing else," Yala answered, "as long as I may have some of your heaven tea soon. Princess Gamnae is correct, it is sweetest when you prepare it."

So, her rank as the Crown Princess's first court lady was above Lady Gonwa's, or at least it pleased the matron to have it seem so. Very well. Now that seclusion was lifted, the delicate process of sifting through the noble daughters to build Mahara's faction could begin.

Mahara smiled, sipping at her own cup and watching a pair of eunuchs clip-clopping along on their slatted jatajatas, perhaps called to the Great Court to trace edicts or fetch seals. Their swaying was not a woman's, and the shoes were either to keep their vital essence from draining into the earth, according to Cao Lung, or to stop them from contaminating a proper woman's footsteps, according to Zhe Har. There were no eunuchs in Khir unless they were kaburei taken as booty in border raids or bought at the Sunken Market. In their dark robes and strange, careful, mincing walk was the character for *longleg bird*, and the character for *two-faces*

---

47. A tea from the south of Zhaon, light and fragrant.

as well. The Zhaon held there was a god for them, a father who gathered those not quite male or female into his household. In both Khir and Zhaon the gods of battle, of course, held those men who shortened a clan's bloodline by spending themselves upon male companions, and there were two goddesses of hearth and one of harvest who did the same by holding female companions closest.

Conversation turned from Princess Sabwone's impending marriage to the state of the palace in general, the next state banquet, and the First Queen's latest attempt to set a fashion for a pad-shouldered dress. It was generally agreed that Zhaon's first lady felt the cold easily, so of course she would not mind the extra weight in spring, but in summer it would be intolerable and perhaps the court ladies would find them overly stifling. Too much warmth, and the balance of vital energies inside a woman—naturally cold, often expressed as the character for *a deep layer of chill water felt while swimming*—could be upset.

A few girls were brought forward. A plump cousin of Lady Gonwa's with a slight, charming gap between her front teeth and a shy fetching blush when addressed directly by any elder, another of Lady Huan's nieces in a cotton dress embroidered with spread mockbird wings, and young Lady Su Junha, kinless at court but of a highly noble family. The last was in a faded, plain silk-and-cotton dress that had been prettily reworked at least once, and her slightly guilty glances and reddened palm—not chapped, but only because it had been soaked in some forgiving oil, and the bridge underneath the finger-bases losing a callus of manual work—spoke volumes. However noble her pedigree, her family was no doubt desperately poor, and this was the first test of Mahara's graciousness.

By the end of morning tea-time, Yala had selected both Su Junha and Lady Gonwa's cousin Gonwa Eulin, but kept Lady Huan's nieces at a slight distance. Another girl, with a pleasing smile and quick dark eyes, was lost in a book until Yala called her forth to answer a small, very easy question about the division of the Hundreds in Zhaon, which she answered with alacrity that showed a quick mind, even if her modest stammer betrayed nervousness.

They would do to begin with, and Lady Gonwa signaled her approval of Yala's choices by sending Eulin to fetch a basket of her freshly mixed heaven tea to be taken to the Jonwa, where the inner court-lady chamber had been aired and freshened in preparation for new arrivals. Su Junha, of course, would accompany Mahara and Yala on their walk back to the Jonwa; her belongings, no doubt scanty, would be sent for. The mockbird-dress girl, Lady Huan's niece, was invited to embroider at the Jonwa tomorrow, as was Lady Aoan Mau's lone suggestion, a thin coltish noble girl distantly related to the house of Hanweo, who Yala suspected would be an eye for the Second Queen.

The book-girl, Hansei Liyue, was of a junior branch of the First Concubine's clan, one with no claim upon the main family but still noble enough to be sent to Zhaon-An with a collection of dresses and a small stipend augmented by Luswone's charity. To take responsibility for her and Su Junha was a pair of gracious acts, and well within the household budget; Gonwa Eulin would be a strong link to the acknowledged chief court lady, and later Lady Huan's niece and the coltish girl an indirect one to Second Queen Haesara if they did not pall upon closer acquaintance.

The First Queen's ladies at the other end of the Pavilion did not approach even to take a sip of tea, borrow a book, or compliment the group around Lady Aoan Mau and their soft sathron-accompanied singing. But Yala took her time studying those shapes in the middle distance, marking their faces in memory, and she also marked who among those clustering Mahara this first day did not possess the ease of long acquaintance or warmth. There would be missteps, certainly, those she did not at first know were eyes for another, but all in all, the first session of the ladies' court—much less straightforward than the men and clerks clustering the Emperor's daily sessions, positions inferred or implied instead of worn upon their shoulders with embroidered marks of rank—had not gone badly at all.

A Natural Betrothal

The edge of Summer's thick green robe brought a rare cloudless afternoon, filling the palace to the brim with thick golden sun-heat and hurrying excitement. The kitchens were flame-hells and the deep cellars, cool and weeping, gave up casks and crocks. Beggars crowded the palace posterns and a few enterprising ones even shook their bowls outside the Alwan and the baths sloping away from the great curve of the complex's northern wall—shared with the rest of Zhaon-An's ancient borders—into royal hunt-woods. Both large markets, as well as the smaller ones, were full of sparksticks and sweetbuns, red thread and cheap pink paper lanterns.

The delegation from Shan had finally arrived, and the Emperor sat in state that long afternoon while the gifts were brought and piled high. Behind a thin dragon-figured screen, a semitriangular shape in heavily embroidered crimson silk was the First Princess, the jewel of Zhaon, sitting demurely as a maiden should.

Fans moved in soft eunuchs' hands, and the courtiers applauded politely with fingertips against the back of the left hand. The Emperor smiled, a proud benign father, as lean dark men from Shan stacked precious ingots, bolts of costly bright fabrics, ivory and lacquered ceduan chits denoting so many head of cattle, so many fine horses, so many bushels of rai and flax, so many kaburei and embroidered robes—Shan, the shield of Zhaon, showed his wealth like an eyebird spreading its vast tail.

The Mad Queen had been vicious and erratic, but her household accounts had ever been in order. It was to be hoped no latent streak of cruelty ran in her son, but even so, this was a fine showing.

No royal maiden could hope for more.

Third Prince Takshin, placed next to General Zakkar Kai upon the third dais of the Great Hall, simply wore a very slight smile through the entire affair and often accepted bows from some of the higher-ranking Shan emissaries, greeting each obeisance with a nod. He wore dark Shan-style half-armor as well, and his topknot was held with leather and silvered bone, a cage that matched one Kiron of Shan was rumored to wear often.

A varnished portrait of the groom Suon Kiron, King of Shan, was brought and ceremoniously unveiled, the Shan bowing before the painted gaze of a tall, narrow-hipped man in somber armor holding the reins of a galloping black warhorse. Many gazes turned to Third Prince Takshin upon a square cushion, seeking to judge by his reaction whether the rendering was a true one.

Takshin's expression did not change.

The princess behind the screen did not lean forward, yearning for the sight of her intended. Of course a maiden would be reluctant to show any eagerness, or to leave her parents' house. It was only natural.

Second Prince Kurin was impassive, his own fan flicking lazily; Fourth Prince Sensheo smiled broadly and leaned aside often, commenting upon the proceedings to his elder brother Makar, who wore bright summer blue and held his favorite fan. The Crown Prince and his new wife upon the second dais sat very close together, the picture of fresh matrimonial harmony, though some thought it a trifle inauspicious that a bride sent as conqueror's tribute watched the gifts being piled. However, the Crown Princess, pleasingly plump and placid, her hands folded over a middle that had not thickened yet—it was too early, though—lowered her eyelids modestly whenever the Crown Prince spoke softly to her, no doubt explaining the finer points of the ceremony in simple Zhaon.

On a smaller cushion placed near the throne, First Concubine Luswone sat elegant and smiling as a mother of a bride should be, in the high-necked peach silk she preferred. Sixth Prince Jin was at her side in sober rich brown, often glancing at the screen and its motionless crimson blur. Of course the young prince was concerned for his sister.

The final gift was set ceremoniously upon a pedestal of fragrant dark cheo-wood, and unveiled in degrees.

A high-peaked birdcage of very fine ironwork appeared as rich red watercloth was drawn aside, two noble Shan girls in fantastically embroidered riding-dress delicately spidering their fingers to make sure no thread was caught and no thin ornament snapped free.

Inside the cage, something glittered, and a ripple went through the assembled Court.

The taller Shan girl turned a key, and the glitter whirled into life. It was a clockwork taufo bird, its beak opening, the carven curve of its throat swelling as strings inside the cage's base were plucked and a winsome melody fell upon the astonished silence.

When it finished, the applause was deep and far more genuine. The Crown Princess clasped her soft, plump hands, and all remarked that her surprised delight made her even more agreeably pretty. First Concubine Luswone's cheeks relaxed and she looked wonderingly upon the cage; even the Emperor tapped his flat right hand into the cup of his left several times, denoting deep approval.

The highest-ranking lord of the delegation, Haon Suron, completed the ceremony with a deep bow to the Emperor and a mercifully brief though extremely learned speech of well-wishes for the health of the august Emperor and his family as well as the devout wish that under Heaven, Shan and Zhaon would prosper together. More applause swelled, cymbals and gongs brought by the delegation crashed, and all agreed it was a very fine occasion worthy of the banquet that followed.

Behind the screen, First Princess Sabwone did not move.

Late that night, the markets ran with torchlight and much custom in aphrodisiacs, paper lanterns, and celebratory sweetbuns while outside the palace gates, the scraps and leavings of the feast filled many a beggar's bowl and belly.

Everyone, it seemed, was well pleased.

Find Other Amusement

His letter to Lady Komor—not *spyling* as he had threatened, though the characters for her name could be taken as a somewhat winning rhyme if he were more than an indifferent poet—left the blue-tiled Old Tower the day after the betrothal ceremony, and Takshin might have been impatient for a reply had he not been called upon to attend archery contests, state dinners, and negotiations. How Kiron must have smiled when he wrote the orders for his emissaries to include his battle-brother; he would know how Takshin loathed each moment. His slender stock of diplomacy and patience was exhausted each day, and even retreating to the Old Tower brought no relief, for one of Kiron's bloodriders might take a fancy to slumming in the sinks and of course it was Takshin's duty as host to see they were not soaked with cheap sohju, relieved of their stipend slivers, or knifed in a malodorous alley. Suron especially had a mind to sample everything Zhaon-An had to offer, since the Mad Queen had been fond of torching brothels with the customers inside whenever the dark god inside her royal skull whispered too loudly.

Like all newly liberated warriors, especially those relieved and not quite believing their own survival, the Shan delegation was drunk with relief.

Some of it wasn't unpleasant, like the familiar drinking games, lean hawk-nosed Suron and round knife-scarred Taonjo Kahi spinning their cups and roaring with laughter while Lord Buwon sang a filthy ditty in the dialect of Shan kaburei. Takshin could even believe he was in the sinks of pierce-towered Sho the capital of Shan, the only missing piece Kiron at his shoulder with that lynx-like smile and rough affection.

I missed my playmate. Kiron's hand-carried letters, their seals breaking with a satisfying snap like a bone between teeth, were full of incident and amusement. Takshin almost felt guilty for not writing as often as Kiron made time to.

It was upon the seventh night, on the edge of the Yuin and the Theater District, that a short sharp fistbrawl between three gamblers and Lord Buwon's retainer Ohjosi unfolded, and Takshin, his knuckles bloodied and his throat sore from a battlefield yell, did not move when Lord Buwon clapped him upon the shoulder.

"Ah, there is the prince we remember!" Buwon trumpeted, and pounded on his shoulder again—but not very hard.

Ohjosi smeared the blood upon his mouth with the back of his hand. He was a long, thin man with a mournful face, not often given to such displays of temper, but an accusation of cheating was nothing a lord of Shan—or his retainer—could brook. "My lord," he said in his precise, accented Zhaon, his nose still seeping crimson, "have you been touched?"

Takshin realized the man was asking *him*, and shook his head. "Only by enjoyment." He replied in the highborn Shan dialect, the cursed tongue that invaded even his dreams. It was like, and unlike, Zhaon, the words full of doubled sounds Zhaon would never allow to touch each other. "Where did Ku Wuoru go?"

"Over here," the round, smiling lord of Toakmisho called from a smashed table in a dark corner. The gambling den had cleared quickly once the first strike landed; the proprietor was no doubt waiting at a safe distance for the victorious to retreat so he could be about carrying the vanquished out, picking their pockets clean. "He fell upon me, the bastard."

"Why did they draw no steel?" Suron wanted to know, still keen-eyed despite the quantity of sohju he'd taken down at their first to fourth stops that night.

"Against nobles? In Zhaon, such a thing is not done." Takshin stepped through the ruins of the gaming platform, scattered counters, one of the dice-maidens' torn overwraps. The women had vanished as soon as the accusations had begun, and their retreat had been a spur to men denied the sohju-soaked pleasure of looking at low necklines and bare ankles, not to mention well-modeled arms. "Besides, they are gamblers, armed only with wood. Or knives, if they are serious, but a knife planted in the back of a prince's companion means the loss of a right hand."

"How...oh, your ring." Suron righted a halu lamp, still flickering because the wick-cover had been improperly latched. It was a miracle the entire wooden structure hadn't caught. Burning down half of White Feather Street would be a disappointing end to the embassy, if not the betrothal. "There is blood upon it."

"No doubt." Princedom was a brutal business. Takshin grasped the edge of the splintered tabletop and heaved; the bare-legged, semiconscious Zhaon gambler atop it moaned. "Come forth, Wuoru. The battle is done."

"I didn't *ask* him to fall upon me." Ku Wuoru rolled free, gaining his feet with a spearman's lunge. "Excellent! Now we collect our winnings."

"Only ours?" Suron laughed, bending to pick up a clinking, silken purse. "We shall ride home with bulging saddlebags."

"Though still much lighter than when we came. Unless we carry the princess's ladies back upon our saddles!" Lord Buwon glanced at Takshin and sobered.

I might pay to see that. Still, Sabwone was his sister. A wolfish grin lingered on his mouth, and he did not bother banishing it. "Come, we must find other amusement. Or are we done for the night, my friends?" The Night Guard, though dedicated to their work, would not come hastily to the site of such a small battle.

"We have had drinking and fighting." Ku Wuoru shook his

head, tapping above his right ear to settle his thoughts. "Women are next."

"*Ai*, Wuoru, do you intend to leave byblows in every brothel?" Buwon cleared his throat, stretching his limbs one by one. "I am bound for the palace."

Which meant the rest of them had to at least accompany their elder, unless Takshin dissented. He did not. By the time they arrived, no doubt even Wuoru would be ready for sleep instead of sport.

The Old Tower's quiet would be a marked improvement, and Mrong Banh would have any letters that had arrived. She probably would not reply until the delegation left with Sabwone in a scented palanquin.

An entire cortege of ladies were being readied. Not like the Crown Princess, bringing a single one. Khir might be bled white, subtly insulting, or simply restrained, but Zhaon would send his daughter with a prodigious procession.

Takshin frowned as he made certain another lamp was righted and found his own winnings under the arm of a groaning, spindle-legged combatant. At least they could be certain the gamblers were still alive by the amount of noise they were making. All in all, this small group of Shan lords had been extremely restrained.

The Street of White Feathers—only Heaven knew what had given it that name, since neither a feather nor anything death-colored was to be found along its length—ran with light from torches and lamps as well as calls from the doorways of other gambling dens and a few brothels Takshin had recommended they stay clear of. Retainers like Ohjosi brought the horses forward, worried for their masters but ordered in no uncertain terms to keep the valuable beasts from being led away or worse. The Tooth, his grey bulk looming like a storm-cloud, made his displeasure at being out late known by doing his best to soak his rider's boots with a mighty stream of piss, but Takshin was quickly in the saddle and safe from the spray.

"To the palace!" he called, and commoners scattered. He set a quick but not bruising pace, suddenly eager to be... well, if not *home*, then at least in the comfortable clutter of Banh's quarters. His move to the Jonwa had to wait for an auspicious time, and Banh mumbled that the stars were being difficult. Besides, the Crown Princess had only just left her honorable seclusion as a new bride. Moving another prince into the house would have been slightly indecent.

Takshin chose the shortest route, through a patchwork slum-jumble at the edge of the Theater District before bursting through a slim malodorous alley onto the Street of Mirrors, more lamps swaying and blue-varnished windows open to usher in any coolness that could be found in darkness after stone and dirt had lost the day's heat, as well as to let men and women lean out like long-necked stilt-birds, singing their enticement songs. The theaters were full of higher-stakes gambling, actors pouring sohju and other refreshments for their patrons, and the crowd contained other mounts as well, most with their riders swathe-cloaked and masked.

It would not do for some to be seen in the Theater District after dark. Others rode proudly, barefaced, and heads turned as the Shan passed with Takshin before them like the hunters of the fire-god coursing valleys in dry autumn.

The palace was ablaze with lights and shouts, and running feet. For a short while Takshin thought news of a brawl had reached someone, though it would have had to wing like a jaheo[48] bird, before the news was shouted up at him and he understood there had been an assassin caught in the Crown Prince's household.

And Takshin wondered, grimly, why the news caused his heart to lodge so firmly within his throat.

48. A round but very quick-flying bird, sometimes trained to carry messages.

Warrior Wife

It was almost too hot to sleep, but Mahara had just managed relaxation when sudden movement from the other side of the bed roused her. A soft noise of complaint was all she had time for before the clash-slither clangor brought her, sweating, into terrified wakefulness.

Two shadows with glittering, metal-crashing eyes crunched into the screen—a familiar bulky shape, now shuddering like a winter ghost come to strangle a couple in their bed—across the room. Mahara screamed, and Takyeo later told her the cry was quick thinking to alert guards, servants, and others of the danger.

But that was later. The princess rolled from the bed and landed with a thump upon unforgiving wooden flooring, and now she wished she had brought her *yue*, even though she disliked her practice and had felt only relief when Father told her not to take it.

You will be a woman of Zhaon in all things, and give them no cause for complaint.

"Yala!" she screamed in the close, hot darkness, her voice breaking upon a high note of anguish. "*Yala!*" But Yala would be rooms away, in her own quarters.

More clanging, and a sudden short, sharp cry from the other side of the room. *Assassin*, she realized, and with the thought, her witless thrashing stopped.

There was a small table at some distance from this side of the bed, holding fruit, small knives for paring, and an unlit lamp—traditional, in case a newly married couple hungered at midnight, or sleep was hard to find. In Mahara's own room, of course, Yala would be across the hall, and already alerted.

Mahara lunged for the table, her knees striking the floor hard enough to jar her teeth. The taste of metal warred with night-breath upon her tongue, and she almost ran into her goal, sensing more than seeing it. The dark was a bandage against her eyes—of course, the assassin would have quenched the lowlamp by the door, preparing to do murderous work.

She clutched the wooden edge and heard faraway commotion. Heaving herself up, a crash of pottery breaking as her elbow hit the table-edge too, her hands skidding frantically across the surface.

Yala would already have the knife, or she would have her *yue* ready. Mahara's fingertips skated across a familiar wooden shape and she snatched the paring knife up, hoping the lamp was not broken too. A sweet citron tang-scent was the bowl full of early murueh,[49] its bowl broken and the yellow-skinned fruit easily crushed before it developed its summertime rind.

The table bumped and skidded, and a wet crunching noise of terrible finality cut through her gasping. There was not enough air in this hole of a room, her thin night-shift—damp from her own sweat and from her husband's attentions trickling free as she sought to find a cooler place to lie—flapped about her knees. Some Zhaon slept naked when the heat rose, but the only concession a princess of Khir was prepared to make was hemming her shift at the knees instead of the ankles.

The door burst open, torch and lamplight flickering ruddy, and Crown Prince Takyeo rose from the ruins of the screen near the water-closet. He was naked, hard planes and angles of muscle gleaming with sweat, and his hair was a wild glory. Blood decked his left hip, and Mahara gasped, the paring knife clutched in nerveless fingers.

---

49. A melon, sweet when young, musky when it develops its late-summer rind.

Takyeo's sword, clasped in a likewise bloody fist, twisted in an indigo-clad body at his feet. The screen was broken beyond repair, and as Mahara watched, her husband ripped the blade free and stabbed the assassin again.

Voices. Guards with likewise naked, shining blades. Cries in the hallway, and Takyeo glanced at the bed. His gaze found Mahara, and relief passed over his whitened face, followed by a flicker of something—was it admiration?

Perhaps. Mahara straightened under the weight of his gaze, aware of dishevelment and of her own idiocy. A paring knife? Ridiculous.

By the time Yala appeared, in a hastily belted robe with her hair a river down her back to match Mahara's own, the Crown Prince was being attended by Guard Liu, who had some physician's skill. At least, the somber guard had enough to assure them all the blade was not poisoned.

"Princess!" Yala, winded, reached her at last. She smelled of sleep-sweat, ceduan, and jaelo blossom, and flung her arms around Mahara. Behind her, Anh the kaburei wiped at night-crusted eyes, and Lady Kue—similarly disheveled and sleep-lidded—began to give crisp orders for fresh linens to be brought, warm water for bathing and cool crushed fruit for drinking. "Mahara, my Mahara, are you harmed?"

"No, I..." She realized she was still clutching the silly knife, the blade turned away from her friend. "I..." Words would not come, in Zhaon or in Khir. Her throat was a desert, dry as the season of cracking ice that filled your hair with restless popping and turned every beast fractious.

Yala's familiar pale eyes swam with tears. "Thank Heaven and all the gods," she whispered. "Oh, thank the Heavens, each one of them thrice and thrice again."

"A knife," the Crown Prince said, as quick serving-hands tied a light sleeping-robe at his bandaged hip. "Truly you are a Khir warrior, my wife. I would not have thought of that."

Yala dabbed at her eyes and released Mahara, only to touch her shoulders, her hips, patting at her. Mahara almost pushed her hands away, but realized she was only seeking to prove her princess was undamaged. "Your knees," the Komor girl said, and Mahara looked down.

Her knees were bloody from the mad scramble across the floor, and Mahara longed to ask if Yala had her *yue*. But of course she did. "Yala," she whispered, her lips almost dry enough to crack. "Husband."

"The Crown Princess is not harmed, except for her knees," Guard Liu said. "Our lord required I examine her first before tending his own wounds."

"Many thanks," Yala said, correctly, and slid her own robe free of her shoulders, bundling Mahara in its long flow. Yala's nightshift brushed her ankles, and was sodden under the arms and at the curve of her lower back. Her small breasts pressed against thin, damp fabric, but she seemed not to care as long as Mahara was covered. "Anh, fetch another robe, and the case with yellow crushflowers painted upon it. Go."

The kaburei scurried away, her leather-wrapped braids marred from toss-turning. Lady Kue clapped her hands, and in a few moments, full order was restored.

"I am well enough, Liu. Lady Komor, how fares my warrior wife?" Takyeo was still grimly pale, but he bent a warm smile in Mahara's direction.

She buried her face in Yala's shoulder, a river of shaking seizing her by the shoulders.

"Well enough, Crown Prince." Yala's Zhaon was sharper than usual. "The battle is done, so she shakes."

Don't tell him that. Mahara winced.

"Braver than most," her husband said. "Send for General Kai and Mrong Banh, and also send a runner to the Kaeje. My father must be told."

"All is well," Yala said, in Khir. "All is well, my princess. It is natural, to feel this after a skirmish." She used the word for a victory dearly bought, a near-run race.

Later, it would occur to Mahara to wonder how Yala knew. At the moment, though, she took deep breaths against Yala's sweating shoulder, and tried to control her shivering.

Still... a soft, secret thread of pleasure remained at the bottom of fear's dark well. A "*warrior wife, braver than most.*"

Did Takyeo really think so?

Good Faith

Rumor raced through Zhaon-An, fluttering under eaves, mantling invisible over dinner tables, winging from girdling wall through noble quarters to merchant houses, seething in the slums. Another assassination attempt upon the Crown Prince, it seemed, had been foiled, this time by the prince himself. Or by his wife, who was of course a fierce Khir barbarian. Some, especially in the Theater District, said a kaburei had taken the blade meant for the prince and died in his arms, but *that* was a tale no reasonable citizen believed, though they would flock to the stage later that month to see a play loosely based upon it—complete with two songs, both laments, enjoying a transitory popularity among loaders and weavers.

"Sisters," the man named Huo said bleakly, shifting uncomfortably upon his wooden bench and resting his elbows upon the table. "It's difficult, you know. My favorite one, she needs a dowry."

"Even the thriftiest of brothers might find that a burden." The impresario, his head still wrapped like a tribesman, affected the smooth cadence of a merchant born in the northern borderlands. He had the singer's gift; his Khir was good enough for a nobleman's and his Zhaon could take many different dialect-shades. His guest at this tavern-table wore a heavy coat despite the heat, but fine rich yellow cloth peeked from under the raveled collar. "Along with sending much of his pay home."

"*Ahi-a*, yes." Huo barely glanced at the rest of the tavern; even at this early hour there were many laborers and the like drowning the heat in sohju, chewing khansu, or clattering dice upon a table despite the prohibition upon gambling in taverns. There was no mirrorlight, only a few guttering lamps, for this was a place many of the lower classes came to in order to find work to augment slender incomes—and some of the employers did not wish their faces seen. It reeked of spilled sohju, strong tea, and sweat. "But that isn't why I'll do it."

"Zhaon deserves better," the impresario agreed. This fellow was a fine catch, even if not overly bright. "At least the Emperor's wives are not barbarians."

"I was in the Northern Army." Huo scowled into his cup. "I saw what those Khir bastards did to the dead."

"Barbarians." The impresario, his dark eyes gleaming, poured another round. "But are you certain, Honorable Huo? I thought you might find us merely a pair of eyes." Fortune favored those who leapt to grasp, but it also favored those who allowed the prey to approach; the "accidental" meeting of a Golden Guard looking to gain extra pay and a merchant who wished to know details of the palace's newest addition partook a little of both.

"I'll do more than that." The man's jaw set, and his own dark eyes were burning coals. "You've got your man, Honorable. You may have to wait a bit, though."

Of course, there were many factors involved, and Huo was not the only pair of eyes he was soliciting. "Patience brings a man all he needs." The impresario's smile only lifted half his thin mouth, but he placed a small leather bag upon the table, pushing it with a fingertip until it crossed the invisible border into his drinking companion's slice of the table. Then he returned his fingers to his own cup; it was impolite to actually *hand* the money over. "They say that in Wurei. Consider this a sign of good faith."

"That where you're from?" Huo regarded the bag but did not reach to take it. It was better than it being passed under the table; an onlooker might know they both had something to hide rather than just suspecting it.

"No, I'm from the borderlands." The almost-lie unreeled smoothly, and he managed to inject just the right amount of coolness, mimicking Huo's banked fury. "That's why, if you're wondering. I saw what those barbarians did, too." It was best to stay close to the truth in all things, and he did not say just *who* were the barbarians.

War made a bandit of every man, even he who merely fought to survive.

"Then we are brothers." Huo raised his cup; the impresario did the same. They drank to brotherhood, and when the palace guard left to return to his shield-square and his duties, he took the small bag, tucked safely in a trouser-pocket.

Eventually, the impresario gestured for tea instead of sohju, and a tavern-servant bore his half-full jug away. No doubt he would steal an importunate gulp or two before he returned it to the cask-room, but the impresario did not judge him harshly.

In this life, you took what you could.

At least the nobleman sent to hold his leash understood the need for caution. He was probably related to one of the princess's ladies, with the care he took to stipulate that only the royal bitch be... touched. He also brought ingots, welcome indeed to a man in the impresario's position.

The impresario wondered idly if the nobleman would hold the knife himself. It would be interesting either way, and afterward relieving the pale-eyed lord of the remaining funds and disappearing must be accomplished.

Tea arrived, the impresario leaned against the wall behind his chair and watched the tavern-room. None approached his table, but he had time before evening and his return to the nobleman to report progress. He could use that interval most profitably by thinking, motionless as an adder under a rock.

It was always best to have more than one plan.

Spur to a Tired Horse

Tamuron's skin twitched, an invisible seamstress pulling at fabric over muscle to right its folds. The invisible insects come recently to plague him were excited today, perhaps sensing summer's advent. Even mint oil worked into the rashes did not help, and water-tree bark in boiling water barely alleviated the worst discomfort. His dressing-chamber was particularly close today, the walls bearing the entire weight of unified Zhaon and pressing inward.

Zakkar Kai, wearing a look of peculiar concentration, settled heavy crimson-dyed leather, adjusting the weight the way he knew Tamuron liked to wear his breastplates. Purely ceremonial half-armor with little to no battlefield utility, it was still important. "Normal, I suppose," the younger man said, and threaded the catch. When he concentrated upon a task in this manner, you could glimpse a shadow of his youth, and it was both a comfort and a needle to the heart.

"She won't eat." Tamuron's hair was loose. The topknot came later, and one of the round-faced bathhouse girls, pale and tense with the importance of her task, stood ready to dress the royal hair. It was not Dho Anha, whose gentle hands he preferred, but the girl had other duties at the moment. She did not complain that his preference made things more difficult, but he sensed as much. "Luswone is worried, I know she is."

Anha did not share his bed, though Tamuron supposed he could insist if he didn't mind losing her steady quiet companionship. A man weary of his wives could wish for a completely uncomplicated female to spend a few moments with, even if the time did not include bedsport. He had earned a few moments of respite, had he not? The Land of the Five Winds was a harsh weight upon shoulders swiftly tiring.

The illness, now sensing Tamuron's flagging vigor, was gathering speed.

Kai exhaled, a short sound not quite a whistle, familiar from many years of attending to his lord's armor. "I am told it is natural for a young maiden to be apprehensive." He did not point out Sabwone would be a queen, which should suit her roundly, but he was probably thinking it. "Does the First Concubine protest, my lord?"

"Of course not. She would never." At least, not openly. Another thing that need not be said. The air was crowded with them, lately.

Kai tightened the left shoulder-cup. Tamuron was favoring that side more and more, the long terrible scar along his ribs paining him even when late-spring storms did not sweep over the city.

All the old injuries had settled hard upon his bones lately. Old friends, but not particularly pleasant ones.

"Still, she loves her daughter." Kai's gaze was bent upon the buckles, straps, lacings.

"As does Sabwone's father." Tamuron glared balefully at him, a high flush under his beard. He loved them all, and it pained him to see petty rivalries and suspect any one of them of... improper deeds. Why could they not simply trust he knew best, as they had when younger? He had worked unceasingly to provide them a patrimony they could be proud of, a broad shield against ill-luck, and they were too busy squabbling over the shadow to think of the sun. "What is your meaning, Zakkar Kai?"

"I am merely making conversation, my lord." A mild glance, but Kai's chin was stubborn-set. Even *he* was treating Tamuron cautiously, as if the Emperor were merely a querulous old man.

"Don't." The Emperor's brow was damp, too. That was new; he used to rarely sweat, even during the zanpai eating contests where the tiny, hideously curled peppers nestled in every bite and burned afresh when sohju was swilled. "Your talents lie in the sword, not the tongue." Tamuron's eyes half-lidded, the spearing pain from bright light new as well.

He had lost weight. Just this morning, he had performed the daily unarmed exercises he was accustomed to, and had to stop before the last sequence.

"Yes, my lord Garan Tamuron." *My lord*, not *Your Majesty*. The general did not have a body failing under him; he was flush with health and strength.

The Emperor shifted irritably, mastered himself. "Ah, Kai. Forgive me, my own tongue is too sharp."

Kai finished the buckling, tested the strap. Finally, he glanced at Tamuron's face. "The pain is worse." It was not a question.

"A small annoyance." At least Dho Anha never treated him like a petulant elder. "Like a stone in the shoe."

"Puts one in a bad temper." Kai did not take offense, or if he did, it did not show. It rarely had, even when such a show was his right.

Tamuron sought calm, and restrained the urge to scratch at his ribs. "Or lames one."

"Only if one is a horse." Kai's lopsided grin was natural, and a relief. He beckoned the girl forward with her tray of implements, glancing at the selection of cages and pins. Most were of filigree, two of highly tooled leather. The girl set the tray down and bowed to the Emperor's back upon a drift of clean citron-blossom scent before gathering his hair and working through the greying mane with a wide wooden comb. Strands came free against her skin; she wrapped them deftly around her fingers and deposited the resultant thread-nest upon a golden salver.

Kihon Jiao would examine the contents of the salver after the dressing. The physician was performing this duty with a worried air more often these days, though never when a minister was present. At least he understood discretion, even if he did not care for it personally.

He never treated the Emperor as a peevish grandfather, either, and it was refreshing.

Kai's worried gaze settled upon the salver. Tamuron sighed. "Yes, I know. More and more of it falls out. Dho Anha wishes to pad my head with horsehair, but I will not. Let them chatter."

"The Second Queen is worried." Kai's tone was perhaps not quite neutral. His own half-armor, freshly polished, was supple from use, and if *his* old injuries were speaking, he made no sign. "She sent her physician to confer with Kihon."

Tamuron dispelled a wince. Of course she would. "And what did Honorable Kihon Jiao tell him?"

"A reply you agreed upon, the good physician said." Kai folded his arms, his brow slightly wrinkled as if studying dispositions on a sand-table or pieces upon a chessboard.

"Good. It would not do for Haesara to worry." Perhaps she and Luswone would make an alliance. It would do them both good, and provide a counterweight to Gamwone.

"She has enough to worry her, indeed." Kai paused. "It is perhaps time to take Prince Makar drinking, if the man can be pried from his scrolls."

"An excellent idea." It was a shame the general was not truly Tamuron's son. Of them all, he was perhaps most suited for the throne—except he showed little interest in the damn thing, content to simply aid Takyeo. Which was another sign of his fittingness—a man who *wished* for power was a dangerous animal indeed.

As if the thought had summoned him, the Crown Prince was announced outside the curtained door; the Emperor gave assent for his approach. Takyeo, in somber yellow court robes instead of half-armor, had a most unwonted spring in his step, but when he saw his father he almost halted.

Yes, the damage must be visible today. He would need all Kihon Jiao's arts to provide a false bloom of health until Sabwone was safely past her new husband's lintel.

"Father." Takyeo turned the pause into a polite, very proper bow. His eyes were not Shiera's, but his mouth bore a startling resemblance when he was not wearing a frown. "All is in readiness."

Tamuron affected not to notice the hesitation. His eyes half-lidded, and he winced slightly as the bath-girl began work with the finer comb, smoothing greying strands. Time was breathing upon his head more heavily of late. "How is Sabwone?"

"Furious, I should think." The Crown Prince glanced at Kai. More to the tale than either would tell, but he had not raised both of them for nothing. You learned to read your children, and the habit held even when they had spouses of their own.

"Oh?" Tamuron kept his tone mild, a distracted inquiry.

"She hates travel." Takyeo glanced at Kai again, uncertain if his father's inattention was feigned or not. "And she would prefer anger to fear. She is, after all, your daughter."

"Ah, yes." It was a pity she had not gained Luswone's serenity. "But marriage is not a battle."

"I have not found it so." But Takyeo's mouth turned down at the edges. The latest assassin's poison tooth had broken, either deliberately or when Takyeo had fought the man off; both face and body had contorted so badly it was almost impossible to tell whence the blade had come from. The skin, ghastly discolored from said poison, bore no markings, but the Sons of the Needle were not the only walkers of the Shadowed Path.

Far from.

"Khir women are fierce," Kai murmured.

"And how would you know?" Tamuron grinned, slapping his knee to hide the grimness of his thoughts. The girl combing his hair into a topknot pulled a little sharply, and sucked in a gasp as if she expected him to stab her. "Ah, the Crown Princess has a lady-in-waiting, who often visits the Second Concubine. Does Kanbina like her?"

"My adoptive-mother likes everyone, my lord." Kai's tone softened when he spoke of Kanbina; it suited him. If he was not a born son, he would, at least, make a filial one.

The indiscretion of liking—or even trusting—everyone had, really, been Kanbina's only flaw. Tamuron knew he had not been kind to her; he had not seen the danger from Gamwone until too late. He had thought, after a second wife and another concubine, that his First Queen's viciousness was spent.

The woman seemed to have a limitless supply. She should have been born a man, and put that and her deviousness to good use.

And probably been hanged for it, which would ease everyone around her considerably.

Kanbina's tortured breathing, and the blood on the sheets... so much of it, and her stumbling apologies through the miscarriage, as if she thought he would blame *her*.

Was he truly so terrible? Harshness was needed in battle, and to keep what one had fought for. But he had never unleashed it upon the undeserving.

Had he?

"Lady Komor is eminently likable." Takyeo's smile turned genuine. He had nothing but soft words for the Khir princess, and nothing but compliments for her lady-in-waiting. Regardless, the Crown Princess's food and drink was tested thrice before it passed her lips, and it was quite possible the Khir servant girl tested it again to be certain. "Lady Kue has quickly grown to depend upon her, and my household is quite harmonious."

"Perhaps Ashani Zlorih sent his best to accompany his daughter, and considered the rest superfluous." Tamuron did not quite scowl, though he longed to. "Be careful, Takyeo. Spies make themselves agreeable."

"Assassins do not." Takyeo watched the wrapping of the topknot.

"That one." Tamuron indicated the cage he wished used. "You should have left some of him to question, my son."

"I was somewhat hasty, true." Takyeo's patience was truly deep and wide, but being shaken from sleep as a hired blade came to kill your wife—who would restrain himself? The poison tooth's breaking was unfortunate indeed.

Tamuron had killed his share of treacherous men in darkness.

Sometimes he thought he should have arranged for Gamwone to meet a fate worthy of her deeds, but after all, she was only a woman.

The bath-girl in her dun, high-collared overdress held a bronze mirror for the Emperor to consider, his eyebrows—still black, and somewhat lush—slightly raised. At least those had not failed yet. Tamuron's hollowing cheeks bunched as he attempted a pained smile at his reflection. He nodded; the girl bowed and retreated with her tray and implements at an almost unseemly pace.

"I am become an evil spirit to frighten children," he murmured, and glanced at Kai. "I hear Sabwone will not speak to her mother. She mutters only the most formal of responses to me."

"Shan must be bound to us." Takyeo massaged his hands together as if they hurt. He did not have to add that without Sabwone's urging Sensheo would lose a great deal of his venom, and Jin might find some joy that did not involve weapons practice. "And she is old enough."

"It is a father's duty and happiness to see his daughter married." Tamuron uncrossed his ankles, and Kai hurried forward to check the lacings on his boots.

"Lao Lung," the general said, and accomplished his task with the same swift exactitude as ever. Not too tight, or they would pain the Emperor, not too loose or they would irritate him.

The Emperor nodded. "You have studied."

"Of course, my lord. You required it of me." A quick grimace, another tug upon the boot-lacings, and Kai glanced up.

"The joy of scholarship should be its own reward." The Emperor did a fair imitation of Mrong Banh, when he had a mind to, and both his eldest sons laughed.

"Makar says the same." Kai's wry half-smile said exactly what he thought of scroll-diving.

Tamuron coughed another laugh, moved his knees. The pain was a spur to a tired horse, driving deep into each joint. Perhaps a tepid bath tonight, and Dho Anha pouring him sohju, though that would inflame the rash more. When she forgot her reticence and spoke openly, she was full of quick observations and witty descriptions of her home village, and both were a relief from affairs of state. "You are good sons," he said, quietly, and rose from the padded bench. "Both of you."

Takyeo's startled smile was Shiera's. *Do not be sad without me*, she had whispered, blood slipping from her mouth. *Marry again, give my son a mother.*

In the dead of night, guards drowsing at his door and courtiers sleeping in the next chamber ever ready to be called, Tamuron sometimes held the simple bone-handled dagger that was her wedding gift to him, and the longing to see her again was enough to make him consider opening his veins.

But he was Zhaon now. The Five Winds coursed over a united land, north, south, east, and west.

He had served the last wind, that of Heaven, and until it saw fit to take him, he would not risk his chance of seeing his most beloved wife once more by defying the Fifth Wind's will.

A Prize Mare

The procession wound through Zhaon-An, gold-armored imperial guards followed by musicians of every kind playing wedding-chants from Daebo province, then the Shan honor guard upon their blooded chestnuts, their manes—man and horse alike—knotted into stiffened spines with red ribbon. A third of the household retinue came next, young court ladies in their wheeled palanquins, a steward upon horseback, two eunuchs, and Lady Daebo Nijera upon horseback, straight-backed. The good lady, a distant cousin, had a reputation for rectitude, and would no doubt chaperone the First Princess well. The First Concubine had been heard to remark as much, at least.

Women pressing to the forefront of the crowd wailed, keening along with the professional mourners marching at intervals along the column and stopping every now and again to sob-scream as was traditional when a beloved daughter left a noble home, beating at the chests of their torn dresses. Small alloy bits—the tiniest triangular denomination, one-thirtieth of a square copper—were thrown into the baskets they carried and shook; the money-changers in the Left Market would reap a percentage from that largesse. The mourners would also eat well that night, unmarried or widowed women feasting in honor of a marriage and the promise of new life it carried.

First the wailing, then the feast; such was the proper way to send off a Zhaon princess.

In the place of honor, a large wheeled palanquin glittered, pulled and pushed by seven hefty kaburei with high-peaked leather helmets. Gilt and crimson threw back the sun in hurtful darts; the dragon of Garan and the broken-horned bull of Daebo worked along the surfaces of the box, a pretty package carrying an asphyxiating girl toward doom. A prince of Zhaon rode on either side, safeguarding their royal sister.

Behind the palanquin, the rest of the retinue and the Shan delegation rode, the lords appropriately somber though one or two no doubt had reddened eyes from a last soak in the sinks of the great city. Afterward came servants, oxen pulling carts high-piled with the gifts of a kindly Emperor to a king. The greatest gift was in the red-and-gold palanquin shell, a nutmeat to be pried free. More Golden Guards came afterward, and then the street-cleaners.

Dung was valuable.

Sabwone shut her eyes as the palanquin jostled and joggled. Books and scrolls in a small rack, a basket of light snacks, stoppered flasks of crushed fruit. No tea, but should she require it at any stop, kaburei and the ladies would flutter around her. She had refused to choose any companions, so her mother had taken care of the invitations. They would find high-ranking husbands in Shan, or be sent home after a few years full of reflected honor from their royal mistress and find marriage in Zhaon-An.

On either side of her gilded cage, a brother—Kurin on her left, straight in the saddle and helmed with a high crimson plume. On her right, the place of honor, was Jin upon a restive Guard grey head-wrapped to keep the dumb beast from plunging into the crowd.

Where is Takshin? Sabwone had hissed at Kurin. *Find him. Make him come along.*

But he had not. Outside the city gates Kurin and Jin would bid her farewell, consigning her to the care of servants, guards, and foreigners.

Barbarians.

Each step took her farther and farther away from civilization, there was no crunchy walanir for her breakfast, and Takshin had flat-out refused to accompany her. *I will not return to Shan just yet*, he had said, and it was one more thing for Sabwone to fume over, confined as she was.

There was a basket of sewing supplies, as was customary. No doubt there was a hank of silk large enough to knot around her throat if she wanted to take her mother's advice. She could bite through her tongue and bleed to death, too. The paring-tool for the fruit among her snacks would do as well, if she had the strength to plunge it into her own neck.

Luswone had dared to *cry* this morning, as she stood upon her steps outside the Iejo. The Concubine's Palace, every nook and cranny familiar, was an enemy now, because her mother lived there.

I have the silk, and I will tie the noose. I will even help you climb onto the railing.

Jin had not saved her. *Maybe it won't be so bad*, he'd offered meekly, and Sabwone longed to slap him. Her palms tingled at the thought.

Then there was Kurin. She could open the slats on her left and peer out, but he wouldn't look at her. *Sister dear, my hands are bound.*

He could have helped. Gone to Father, who had clasped Sabwone's hands and said, *My dearest daughter, it will be difficult, but he will treat you well.*

It mattered little how her prospective husband treated her. She would be among *barbarians*, and all her storming had availed her nothing. It was the first time she had been truly balked, and Garan Daebo Sabwone did not like the experience.

Worst of all was Makar's smirking all through the ceremonies and feasts, the speeches and the drinking, the piling on of gifts and everyone pretending she hadn't been sold off like a prize mare. How long had he known? It burned, the thought that he had sat upon the knowledge like a qurra on its nest, satisfied and sleek.

And useless, useless Kurin. *It will not be so bad. You will be a queen.*

No more stolen moments with him, no more compliments, no more pretty gifts. The Shan were uncivilized brutes, and even that clockwork bird—oh, how she longed to go into the royal storerooms and smash that useless, insulting thing—could not change that. Why, they hadn't even started drinking tea until the Third Dynasty. They weren't like Khir, old and at least respected. They were jumped-up peasants, a merchant family from Anwei gone north and buying their way into a semblance of nobility, and their last queen was *mad.*

A madwoman for a mother-in-law. At least *she* was dead.

Sabwone pressed the back of her hand to her mouth. She had not eaten for five days now, but nobody cared. Not Father, not Mother, not Jin, not even Kurin.

She was alone.

Yes, there was the silk in the basket. There was the paring knife. There was biting through her own tongue rather than letting a filthy merchant barbarian touch her. A heroine in Lady Surimaki's stories—not part of the Hundreds, and not *scholarly*, but read avidly over and over all her life—would not hesitate.

The absolutely unforgivable thing, though, was that Sabwone... doubted. An Emperor's daughter should be brave and proud. An Emperor's daughter should suffer no dishonor.

The First Princess of Zhaon ground her teeth, light-headed and nauseous, trapped in a rolling cube, simmering in her own sweat under bright ceremonial robes.

She had long suspected she was weak, and the thought filled her with fury. Her reticence to take her own silly, useless life was proof.

Sabwone shut her eyes. Her hand crept for her sewing basket, then traitorously, stopped again. It occurred to her, finally, that if she killed herself in Zhaon it would not be seen as a protest. No, they would whisper that perhaps Garan Tamuron's eldest daughter had a dishonorable reason for such an act.

The Shan capital was far away. She had time.

The First Princess, almost a queen, ground her teeth and waited.

Do as You Will

Two days after Princess Sabwone left amid crashing cymbals and the shrieks of hired mourners to be married in far-off Shan, Lady Komor's reply reached him upon thick cloth-paper, the seal a setting sun and a triple-lobed flower mimicking a character for *duty*. She invited him to one of the Jonwa's small gardens for the discussed matter—unless, of course, the Third Prince had changed his mind.

He could not tell whether that was an indirect invitation to do so, and he did not care to. He sent a reply setting a time the next day, and her acceptance was conveyed with exquisite brushwork upon the back of that missive.

The weather had broken somewhat, an eastron wind bringing cooling breath to a small blue-glazed gazebo set amid a thicket of virulent green vertical poles of segmented babu. A small folding table held appurtenances—a flask of acrid jau, sometimes consumed when a drunk had no other option despite the risk of blindness; a small, unlit, enclosed hau lamp; two thick needles; a heavy golden hoop; two metal thimbles; puffs of unwoven cotton in a small jar with an openwork lid; all nestled in a pad of raw silk upon a lacquered tray. He examined them with care, his hands clasped behind his back, and when Lady Komor appeared, stepping down from a small porch ideal for breakfasting or moongazing, he kept her progress in his peripheral vision. She was in dark blue again today, Khir cloth but a dress of Zhaon cut, almost severe except for the pale lunar curves embroidered at the cuffs. It was too high-necked, but other than that, pleasing.

Very pleasing indeed. His own Shan black would set her to advantage. Perhaps that would please her, in turn—did not several court ladies bemoan pampered, pretty men stealing their female prerogative?

"Third Prince Garan Takshin." She bowed, very prettily, before setting a slippered foot upon the gazebo steps. Her hairpin dangled three indigo beads, glowing-mellow in sunlight and black in the shade. "You brighten the day."

He searched for any sign of mockery in her expression, and found none. "I have never been accused of that, Lady Komor Yala." What he wanted to say was, *So do you, Lady Spyling.* But no, he was to be conciliatory, and circumspect. "Are you well?"

"Well enough." She acknowledged his politeness very pleasingly, too. "The South is very warm, especially at night."

"Difficult, too, when your sleep is interrupted by rude visitors?" In other words, had she suffered during the attack on the Jonwa? Kai had verified it was merely a single assassin, and his expression had been thunderous indeed.

Takshin had amused himself guessing who would be so stupid as to send a blade during the Shan delegation, but the entire affair made him…uneasy. And he did not like that he had been trammeled in the Old Tower, unable to move into Takyeo's home until after the Shan left, as well.

"There was much excitement in the household that night, yes." She climbed the stairs, that same dancer's grace, waiting to commit her weight until she was certain. "But it is your health that should be inquired after, since we are about to inflict a small wound."

That managed to nettle him. "Do you think me likely to turn coward and retreat?"

Lady Komor examined him gravely, a faint flush upon her thin cheeks. Did she find Zhaon food unsatisfactory? Her princess was much more pleasingly round. "I think it is more likely you would refuse retreat at all costs."

"Then you know me better than most, Lady Komor." He restrained the urge to grant her a mocking bow.

She indicated the table with one partly cupped hand, too well bred to point. "Shall I explain? The jau cools the implements and the skin, the needle is chosen and passed through, then the hoop is fastened. I commissioned it from the Artisans' Home, which was the delay in responding to your letter."

"Ah." As if he had not cared one way or the other, or waited for the reply. "I had thought it was the festivities."

"You did seem rather busy." Her acknowledgment was grave, but amusement lingered in her pale gaze. "There were friends of yours among the Shan, no doubt."

"No doubt." He settled upon the tri-legged stool, conscious of her slightness and of still looming over her.

Lady Komor studied him for a few long moments. If she was irked or fearful at his closeness, she made no sign. Her skirts moved gently under the breeze, and her slipper-tips were pointed in the Khir fashion. "Perhaps a cushion upon the floor instead, if it does not incommode you? I do not wish to pass the needle at an angle. It must be level."

Was that the real reason for her set expression? Takshin nodded. "I shall do as pleases you, Lady Komor Yala."

A thoughtful soul, she had two pillows as well, both with Khir embroidery upon their faces, probably brought step by step from the cold North. Did she miss her home? Could he ask? He settled upon the one she indicated, and she brought the tray of implements from the table with swift grace.

When she was settled upon her knees as well, she laid the tray between them. "Normally, a sister does this for her brother."

He tried to imagine Gamnae this careful or prepared, and failed utterly. "What if a man does not have a sister?"

"His mother, or his wife." She paused. The beads from her hairpin were smooth and round, and their color suited the dress exactly. "But we are in Zhaon, so a friend will do."

"Ah." Did she call herself his friend? He stilled, considering the notion, but she spoke again and he found he wished to attend, and closely. "As you like."

"The hoop is important. We call it *kyeogra*, a stopper—it must be endless, to catch the voices calling you and keep them chained." She struck a flame for the lamp and the tiny box used for such a purpose vanished back into her sleeve. What else did she keep in there? A cloth or two, certainly. A needle for mending? A paper horse, like the Great Sage Mhong, to be brought out and restored to flesh by a muttered incantation?

Takshin sought further conversation. "I should learn more Khir."

"There are teachers." No opening in her response, the absolute minimum required for politeness. Still, she was here, and had sought him out, to whatever degree.

"Perhaps you may teach me." Takshin aimed for a light tone, as if he were Jin bedeviling Gamnae. Who was the man using his voice for this? He sounded ridiculous.

But Lady Komor smiled, passing the needles through flame again. "My duties to Princess Mahara may not permit it."

"Mahara." A pretty word, but nonsensical in Zhaon. "What does that mean?"

"Crown Princess Mahara is named for the wind that comes from the south in summer, and brings warmth." Yala dipped the larger needle into acrid jau again. "The Great Rider was joyful when she was born."

"I thought Khir hated their daughters." He could have cursed his tongue out of his mouth, for a shadow fell across her expression.

She looked away at green segmented pillars, lush every summer and harvested at the first snow. Dipped the needle again.

"A daughter is not a son, but some daughters may delight their fathers." A polite proverb, a closed door.

He liked her better when she was fretted, and he could not imagine a father being anything less than delighted with one such as her. "And your own father?"

"I am his only daughter, too." A small shift of her weight upon her knees and haunches, as if she meant to leave. Or as if the memory was painful. Her strange, pale eyes darkened as well.

Keep her here. "What does your name mean?"

"*Yala* is a small bird, very gentle, very soft. They are used as lures for the hawks; they freeze when the shadow drifts over them." Her long sleeves, folded back, exposed slim coppery wrists marked with thread-thin, inked lines; a faint misting of sweat showed at her temples.

All of it suited her, and he remembered her clutching a sunbell, cautious but unafraid. *Both are due some respect.* "I cannot imagine you thus, Lady Komor."

A small smile was his reward. She passed the needle through the enclosed flame one final time, and her expression lightened. "In my clan, the Komori, it is a little different. I am named for one of my ancestors during the First Dynasty, who was able to make a hawk rise and return without a lure."

"First Dynasty." Of course, she would have her pride. She wore silk like the Crown Princess, which made her noble indeed. "When Khir ruled."

"When Khir ruled Zhaon, and Shan, and as far as Anwei." The beads of her hairpin made a sweet sound as they touched each other, and a breeze from the pond, fragrant with latai blossom, made the babu rustle secretively. "Those days are gone now, are they not, Prince Takshin." It was not a question. Rather, a soft, sad finality.

Did she suspect him of seeking to entrap her in a treasonous wish for Khir's primacy? He searched for something else to say as she brushed his hair back, a bentpin holding the black strands free of his ear. "I am named for a warlord who never lost a battle. His chamberlain poisoned him."

She was so close, he could smell the faint smokiness of ceduan in silk. Did she wear this dress often? The color was strange but lovely, and she seemed to favor it. "A sad story." She dabbed at his ear with jau-soaked cotton, a cold touch sending rainflesh down his back.

"He trusted someone."

A nod, her hairpin beads swinging; all her attention was bent upon her task. "Dangerous to do so."

"Is it?" He did not mean to sound disingenuous, but her consciousness of such danger was interesting.

"Here? Of course." She bent her head, busying herself with the pin, the bowl of solution, the small shielded flame, the hoop. "At least in Khir, I knew who my enemies were."

"Do you have enemies?" *Tell me. I will bring them to you bound and gagged.* What did women like, if not that? He should ask Makar. Better yet, Takyeo. A married man should have some idea.

What, precisely, was Takshin thinking? Behaving in this manner was certain only to bring him grief, and yet he was unable to stop.

She glanced at him, those strange eyes fathomless. "It is impossible to live without them, the poets say."

"Here, you should know your friends too." Was that too plain? Was she laughing at him, inwardly?

"Another difficulty." She paused, and regarded him levelly. "Are you certain you wish your ear pierced, Third Prince Garan Takshin of Zhaon?"

"Address me informally, Lady Komor Yala." His eyes half-lidded. He was committed to this course. Let her mock if she willed, he would teach her not to if she did. Others had learned. "I place myself in your hands."

"Very well." Another pause. "This will sting."

His hand flashed out, caught her wrist. "Little lure." Slim, much smaller than a man's, and soft-skinned. He could squeeze, grind the bones together. How could you touch something so fragile without the urge to break, and the contradictory imperative to cradle tenderly at the same time? "You should run away while you can."

"I am here, in the palace of Zhaon, many miles from my home." Was that bitterness in her tone? He did not know her well enough to tell.

Yet.

And she misunderstood him, this time. Of course. "It is too late," he informed her, knowing she would *still* misunderstand. His fingers loosened, one by one. There was a luxurious sense of release in going too far to halt. "Do as you will."

It was not painful at all. A pinch, a stinging, and the unfamiliar weight in his ear was a dull throbbing when she laved it again with jau. The hoop was small but felt much heavier than it should, and as she took the dabbing cloth away the faint sheen resting upon her forehead had intensified. When she held the burnished bronze mirror, he did not see the scar upon his throat or his lip, or the seam under his hair. A gleam winked from his left earlobe. Mellow gold, brushed along a flaw to seal it shut.

Instead of a broken jar, he was a decorated blade. A transformation, a passing god or sage performing a feat of illusion-made-truth.

"There," she said, softly. "Now you are marked as one who has ridden to the Great Fields, and your ancestors will not call you before your time. Do you like it?" She settled onto her cushion, and there was no pity or disgust in her strange, pale Khir gaze. Merely interest, and the faint consciousness of a task well done.

I do not care. "Do you?"

She examined him critically, a faint line between winged black eyebrows. Finally, Lady Yala nodded. Blue gleams showed in her black braids. "It suits you, Your Highness."

"I told you to address me informally." He sounded irritated, could not help himself.

"Then you would address me so." She lowered the mirror. "And that is not correct." Lady Komor Yala rose, gracefully, putting the table between them, tidying the implements. Retreating.

His course decided and the tension of indecision vanished, Takshin allowed it.

For now.

An Exciting Morning

Summer lay over the Great Market, but underneath its bell-dome the work of commerce went on unabated and Zakkar Kai, sweating in his half-armor, was on the hunt for something that could not be found at the Artisans' Home. The Left Market was also out of the question, for it held nothing a woman might want unless she was swelling unexpectedly or looking to rid herself of another impediment.

No, he wanted something small, and subtle, and glorious, and so it was the Great Market's vast clamor he quartered that breathless afternoon. The year had turned into the stretching of the rai and the deepgrass brushing mares' bellies, the rich lands of Zhaon bursting with food not yet ready for harvest, a promise of abundance at every step and upon every fingertip, every eyelash.

The promise, burgeoning, was painful to a man. So was uncertainty. Some affected to like it, valuing the chase more than the possession, but Zakkar Kai was not of their number. The work of victory was better than the prospect of defeat, even if bought with bowel-cut and blood.

Still, this battlefield was a gentler one, and hence he was uncertain.

Lady Komor visited the Second Concubine often, bearing small gifts and playing the sathron. Her skill with the instrument was only middling, but he saw the fluidity in her wrists and the way she did not commit her weight until the step was sure, and it reminded him of the darkened garden and an assassin's gurgling death.

Which was nothing a woman should have been party to, and yet Kai found himself thinking of it often, always with the same sick thump in his stomach. What if he had not been passing by, catching the flicker of motion where none should be near the top of a wall? What if he had not been curious? Most distressing of all, what if she had not been trained in the use of that sharp, slender blade?

Such things were not spoken of in the Hundreds, he thought sourly, as he pushed between a pair of arguing silk merchants and halted to contemplate a wall of osier cages, the birds inside lamenting their loss of freedom and waiting for a larger confinement with a lady's hand to scatter grain and fill the water-dish.

Or for a poor girl to keep them in a hovel, and eat them in a lean year. Songs did not fill a hungry belly.

Sometimes Kai wondered what he would be if Garan Tamuron had not plucked him from the ashes. What was a fire without fuel? He probably would have starved to death, a witless, wandering child.

The Emperor's rash had spread, turning into suppuration. Kihon Jiao was able, with a salve made of bellyroot and crimsonpod the cousin of sleepflower, to ameliorate the irritation, but the Emperor was short-tempered these days and Council sessions stormy. Just that morning, Takyeo had openly disagreed with his father upon the question of the salt tax, and Hailung Jedao was full of dire prognostications about the imperial purse if the smallholders and peasants were not burdened afresh. The salt flats were a Daebo concern, but the Second Concubine's family was still in the custom-mandated half-mourning for the loss of a highborn daughter before she passed her new husband's doorway, and Luashao Tualih was thin-lipped and uncommunicative.

Apparently First Princess Sabwone had sent her uncle a letter from the road to Shan full of allusions to certain passages in a lady's novel, and there was much concern. Kai frowned, laying a hand to his own purse as he spotted a gang of pickpocket children sizing up the crowd in front of a puppet show. The story of a princess married to Shan and becoming queen was popular now, scraps of red cloth wrapped around a female stick with high-painted eyebrows, the groom shown as a fearsome triangle with a high-peaked Shan hat and stamping boots. He bleated and gobbled in an approximation of a strange language, and a dragon popped into being overhead, showering the puppets—and no few onlookers—with cheap confetti. Exclamations of delight rose, and the pickpockets went to work.

The children would pay a portion of their gleanings to the puppeteers, no doubt, and would take the rest to their thief-hive. The quickest and most canny among them might even survive to adulthood and create their own hives, or hire themselves for darker work.

Kai walked on. His half-armor and the sword at his back earned him some small measure of room among the crowd's buffeting. Another wall of birdcages, and vats of bronzefish in tepid water, flicking their tails and waiting to be scooped out for travel in buckets to rai patches or small garden ponds, and other tiny pets—crickets, a clutch of ornamental goats, live eggbirds flapping and squawking as they were examined by prospective buyers—added to the noise. He turned aside, passing another puppet show—they were in fashion now; festivals and feasts always made for great interest. Those with a few alloy bits to spare went to the theater, but all you needed for watching puppetry was a set of eyes.

A pair of acrobats cavorted upon a faded blanket set in the sun, sweat greasing bare coppery limbs and close-cropped hair. Kai halted again to watch. How long had he been here in the dust and the noise, and had not found a single suitable gift? A hairpin was a lover's token; other jewelry was improper upon their acquaintance; she already had a borrowed sathron, but perhaps he should commission another?

He knew what would please six princes and two princesses, a

gift that would please the Emperor of Zhaon himself, and others that would delight his adoptive-mother. Why was a simple token for a court lady giving him such trouble?

Excited babble rose, sharp voices arguing. Kai craned his head and set off for the source of the hubbub. It was perhaps time to return to the palace, scrape the dust away, take a tepid bath. No doubt the next Great Council session would be fractious too. It was a day of inconveniences and frustration.

Or so he thought, before he saw a familiar shape, a long flow of deep blue—she favored that color, it seemed, and someone in Khir had sent her silk for a dress or two. This one was new, cut in the Zhaon fashion, and her hairpin held a single thread of silver glitter ending in a winking topaz eye. Her sunbell, a red flower, bobbed as she half-turned, and the shadow beside Lady Komor was Third Prince Garan Takshin, glowering in black with his wrap-hilted sword in his left hand, held carefully away from his companion but still ready, in the manner of a Shan warrior.

Lady Komor pulled at his sleeve with two fingers, her sunbell dipping and bobbing even more. A small bag hung from a strap on her right wrist, brushing her skirt as she sought to draw the Third Prince away, and as Kai forced himself between two burly bare-chested layabouts in loosened laborer's pants obviously on their way to a tavern for a midday refresher, he saw the danger.

It was a mixed show—puppets much larger than usual and masked actors as well. One of the large puppets balanced upon sticks and chortled, holding a vile-green bar dripping streamers of the same color. It was in black and had the same triangular figure as a Shan puppet, but it had a Zhaon topknot and a dried-puddle crackquilting of red threads cruelly cut its fabric face. It screeched something and a plague-dragon appeared, waving over the heads of the live actors—slim youths in ragatag mockery of court dress cowering before a stiff wooden replica of a padded throne-bench. Upon the bench, a puppet in imperial robes clutched at his heart, while a red-clad female puppet was bundled into a palanquin and drawn away.

The throne-bound puppet declaimed, in a bass voice, a list of symptoms, and the plague-dragon bubbled overhead, twisting sinuously on long sticks. The puppeteers were masters of their craft, indeed.

Kai's skin flushed, but his insides turned to ice. So, news of the Emperor's illness was common. It had been only a matter of time, certainly, and yet he had hoped for more room to maneuver. So had Tamuron.

"*Plague in the East!*" the dragon shrieked, and the Shan-clad puppet with the scarred face did a jumping dance of glee. "*Plague in the West!*"

Lady Komor's mouth moved. No doubt she was remonstrating with Takshin, who wore a remote, icy expression Kai knew all too well.

Zakkar Kai strode forward. The audience scattered as his own dragon-hilted sword left the sheath, a high ringing note of metal drawn, and he barked a battle-cry as his feet found the makeshift, waist-high wooden stage. It flexed and trembled underneath him, not meant for a warrior's moving, armored weight, and his bright blade cleaved the plague-dragon's supple length.

It even gave him a grim manner of joy to do so.

Shrieks and curses rose behind the curtain, and the stage thudded underfoot. The sudden application of his weight forced a splintering groan from thin wastewood. Live actors scattered, their painted, sweating faces now pictures of real consternation. Kai plunged past the billowing curtain at the back, following the lines of the black-clad Shan puppet, and found a portly stickmaster in a clout, sweating oily-profuse and screeching as Kai grabbed his topknot and tore him past cloth into unforgiving daylight, tossing him upon the stage. Which, with its own sense of the dramatic, decided it had endured enough and splintered around the crashing impact.

Kai leapt free of the rubble, and such was his furious look that the crowd scattered, actors vanishing, puppets falling. The Emperor-puppet swayed drunkenly on its sticks, clutched by one of the child-actors in a tattered version of a eunuch's robe.

Zan Fein would not find that amusing, Kai thought, and a grim smile touched his mouth. "Who is responsible for this?" he barked, this time at the pudgy, splinter-striped man moaning amid the stage's wreckage. Whistles sounded in the distance—the Market Guard was on its way.

Good.

A blot of crimson in Kai's peripheral vision was Lady Komor's sunbell. She hurried toward him, a thin thread of jaelo scent bright amid the dust, reeking sweat, fear, and smoky fury. "General," she said, somewhat more loudly than necessary. "General Zakkar, my friend, please, calm yourself."

Takshin trailed in her wake, two bright spots of red high upon his cheeks. Gold glittered at his ear, and Kai recognized the jewelry. Several Khir at Three Rivers had sported the same thing—a closed loop, so their ancestors would not call them to the afterlife too quickly.

So. Kai set himself, stiffly, and gazed down at the pudgy stickmaster. "Well?" he demanded, once more. "Who is responsible for this?"

"General Zakkar, *please*." Lady Komor's sunbell dipped and wove. Takshin, catching up, steadied it, but she did not glance gratefully at him, and his motion was impersonal, a quick instinctive movement.

"Kai." Takshin's topknot gleamed under fierce sunshine. "Kai, my brother, enough."

More whistles, shouts, the crowd pressing close. Explanations would be necessary. Takshin gave one passionless glance at the blubbering stickmaster, who visibly realized just who had torn him from his hiding place and exposed him to scrutiny.

Kai lifted his left hand, spread his fingers, and the light caught his hurai. Greenstone glittered, and onlookers took in a collective breath. "Hello, Takshin. I did not know you were a-marketing today."

"Takyeo asked me to accompany Lady Komor." A shrug, spreading his free hand too, a subtle indication of his own status. Takshin surveyed the wreckage of the stage. "And you?"

"Looking for a certain article. But what I find is treason."

"Is it?" Takshin sounded merely interested, but that glint in his dark eyes promised trouble. Oddly, the stickmaster did not seem nearly as frightened of the sword-point at his throat as of the black shadow at Lady Komor's side. "An actor may not portray royalty, so, puppets."

"Insulting any member of the royal household carries a penalty." It was a new sensation, to be the one restrained from temper. It held a certain freedom, but was not quite comfortable. "Your father, may he live long, will hear of this."

Lady Komor's pale eyes were wide, and her mouth turned down. "Perhaps it would be better to ignore this particular puppet show," she suggested in an undertone. "My lord general, perhaps it would be wise—"

"You are the soul of decorum, Lady Komor. Takshin, perhaps the lady should be returned to the palace. It is very warm, and this is an unpleasant sight." Kai leaned forward—not much, just a fraction, and the sword-point pricked a little harder.

The Market Guard appeared, green plumes on their brown leather helmets, and a moment of confusion ensued before they realized they were dealing with two princes and a collection of street artists who had clearly overstepped their bounds.

It was Takshin who graciously insisted they be freed, though Kai refused any idea of reparation for their broken stage. Lady Komor, a fan produced from her sleeve, drew back into shade and watched, a lone spectator upon a suddenly deserted slice of Yaol Street. The Guard took the pot of alloy bits and a few triangular coins, leaving the actors and the head of the troupe—the cowering, crafty-eyed stickmaster—only a handful and a strict warning to choose better subjects for their foolery next time.

Since the alternative was a stint in the local guardroom before being hauled before a magistrate, the stickmaster bobbed and bowed. Kai finally consented to letting the man slither away, and Takshin tossed the head guard a pierced silver for his pains—a princely show of generosity, indeed, and one the man would have to share with his fellows, since it was given him in their sight. The remaining actors and sticktossers hurried to pack up whatever of their gewgaws and props had not been broken, and fled after their master.

It was unlikely any of them would be with him come morning. Skilled workers liked to avoid ill-luck.

Which left Kai and Takshin in attendance upon a very pale Lady Komor, her brow glittering damply and her fan fluttering. "Quite an exciting morning," she said, in her light, lilting Zhaon spiked with Khir consonants. "The news will no doubt reach the palace before we do."

"There is no need for you to worry." Kai settled his sword-strap more firmly, rolling his shoulders to make his half-armor settle. "It is known that I am the Third Prince's friend, and better for me to cause a scene than him to appear to take offense."

"I was not about to take *offense*," Takshin said, somewhat grimly. His lip was not twitching, which was a very good sign. "I might have pointed out the scars were in the wrong place, if anything."

Lady Komor cast him a single, almost nervous glance. "Was that intended to be you, then? And . . . the Emperor?"

"Plague from the East, plague from the West." Kai shook his head. "Come, my lady, you are wilting. Let us find a more congenial climate for you."

"There is illness in Zhaon, as there is every summer. It is the season of heat and bad air." Takshin's knuckles were white upon his scabbard. No, he perhaps was not about to take offense, but had he drawn, there might have been corpses instead of a tale spread of Zakkar Kai's umbrage and the Third Prince's magnanimity. "The Emperor should hear of this."

"Did you know?" Kai glanced at the market-aisle, just beginning to liven again. As soon as the trio of nobles left, ragpickers and other carrion would descend upon the shattered puppet-stage, stripping it of anything even slightly valuable. They were probably impatient to begin their work. "That he is . . . ill?"

"Everyone knows," Komor Yala said, flatly, and closed her fan with a snap. "Though none say it directly. Yes, General Zakkar, we should leave here. Will you and Third Prince Garan Takshin accompany me to the palace gates, at least? After that, no doubt you will have men's business to attend to."

"We shall see you to the Jonwa itself." Takshin offered his arm. "I think it would be wise to speak to the Crown Prince first."

"Indeed." Kai's hands itched. It took an effort not to let them curl into fists. Takshin had never shown this much attention to a court lady before. The Third Prince was also uncharacteristically polite, in her presence.

It was maddening. But as much as Kai's insides writhed, he was only glad he had not made a fool of himself. After all, Takshin was a prince, and Kai merely a lowborn general who had slaughtered many Khir.

"Very well." Lady Komor took Takshin's arm. To do so, though, she handed her sunbell to Zakkar Kai, so he must keep close to her side through the Market, and her skirts brushed his knee more than once.

And Kai, uselessly, angrily, could not help but hope the walk would be slow.

Two Small Pearls

Stretch, my princess." Yala, in loose-legged linen trousers, leaned forward, her legs spread into the straight bar of a *li* character. Then she bent, almost touching her forehead to the floor. Mahara followed suit, though her hips ached and she could not lower herself as far. Yala exhaled, and her body turned to water. "Zakkar Kai was there. He drew upon the stickmaster."

"Really?" Mahara thought this over. It was strange to not be in a skirt or shift; the undergarments for their kaibok wraps allowed far more freedom of movement. The attic space was stuffy and close, umbrous with dying mirrorlight, but her husband had left to confer with his father, Lady Kue had gone to the baths, maids and court ladies were absent on assorted errands, and they had a short while to practice before dressing for a dinner taken in the cool of the evening, perhaps on the long porch near the water-garden. Bloodflies would be thick; coursers and brown nightbirds would be swooping through to sup upon the ghoulish bloodsuckers though the smoke of taik lanterns would keep the worst unpleasantness away. Besides, it was too hot to eat much. "So. The peasants know the Emperor is unwell." She had to use the Zhaon word for *emperor*, since Khir had no equivalent. The king was the Great Rider, tall in the saddle, instead.

"And they blame Shan for it." Yala's voice was muffled by the floor. "Or at least, some of them do."

Peasants blamed anything new or strange for their ill-luck, it was in their nature. "No wonder there is plague, it is so hot here." Mahara sighed, trying to relax as bonelessly as Yala was able to. "And the Third Prince?"

"He restrained General Zakkar." Yala's toes pointed, flexed. She moved her shoulders slightly, too, settling her long flexible spine.

"That is strange." The scarred, dark man did not seem the type to *restrain*. "He gives me the shivers."

"Why is that?" Yala did not move, but her attention sharpened. Mahara could feel it.

"Always so cold, and never with a nice word." A shudder raced through her, settling in her aching thighs. Her lower back ached too, and her breasts were overly tender. Her red time was late, too. "Why did you give him a kyeogra?"

"He asked." As if it were the simplest thing in the world. "And he has lain near the Great Fields not just once, though he only told me about the well."

"Imagine. Throwing a boychild down a well." Dust and heat tickled her nose. It was all very well to drown useless girl mouths during a famine—sad, of course, but the stories were full of such things. But a *boy*? A prince, even if adopted? "This Mad Queen sounds truly mad."

"I gather she was indeed." Yala sighed once more and straightened, pointing her toes again. "Now to the left, my princess."

"Did you find a metalsmith?" It was a dilemma—she hated the idea of another *yue*, but upon the other hand, having something better than a paring knife if another shadow intruded upon her husband's bedroom was a powerfully comforting prospect.

"A few. I commissioned a blunted copy from one the Third Prince recommended, as a test. We shall see." Yala reached up with her right hand, bent leftward, and became a *hua* character. "He did not seem to find my search strange, and thought the proposed gift a fine one."

Mahara did her best to emulate. Childhood stretching had not been this onerous. "My husband says Third Prince Takshin is trustworthy."

Her lady-in-waiting exhaled, a long sigh, and her stretch deepened. The sharp curve of her ribs sloping into her waist was a master's decided brushstroke. "That is good to know."

Well, it was his brother, of course her husband would think so. Mahara was more interested in Yala's estimation of the scarred, cold Third Prince. "Do you agree?"

"Perhaps. He reminds me of my Elder Brother." Yala's eyes closed, her face become a still, somber mask.

She did not often speak of Bai. Not since Three Rivers, and the news from the south, and Father's ashen face in the great hall of the Keep, before the giant stone calendar-wheel that filled Mahara's dreams with uneasiness. *My daughter*, he had said. *You must save us now.*

Strange, that after the men's battles it was a girlchild's duty to save the whole of Khir. What if *she* had been thrown in a well?

It was a troubling thought, and one Mahara did not much like. "What do you think of the Su girl?" Yala had been quietly building a retinue for Mahara, and so far her choices were very good. Decorous, perhaps a little quiet, but at least none of them seemed haughty or likely to run about carrying tales to other households.

"I think her clan wishes for her to make a good marriage." Yala flowed upright again, stretched her left arm overhead, and bent to the right to make another *hua*. Mahara copied her. "I also think she is very glad not to be at home."

In that, Mahara suspected, they were akin. "If you could go home, would you?"

"My place is with you, my princess." Yala's smile, though strained as she stretched, was a contented curve. Her ankles swelled as she flexed both feet. Around them, shrouded shapes kept sentinel. "*Ai*, I am stiff. We must ride more often, and not just pleasure-jaunts."

"But would you go home? If I were to send you?" After all, Lord Komori was fearsome—but not loud. He did not yell and bang upon the table.

The idea seemed to give Yala pause, and her lips skinned back from her teeth briefly as she encountered a knot of tension somewhere. "Have I displeased you, my princess?"

"Of course not." The very idea was absurd; what would she do without her lady's steady attentions? "I just..." Mahara sucked in a long breath, her ribs spreading, the insides of her thighs burning, her arm shaking as she held the proper curve. "I wish to know your feelings, that is all. If you *could*, Yala, would you prefer to?"

"I am not certain." Yala's eyes half-lidded. A comforting, honest gaze, focused just past Mahara's shoulder. "It is too warm here, the food is bland, I dislike this stone warren, and the darkness is full of sharp things and bad dreams. And yet."

Put that way, only a madwoman would remain. "And yet?"

"The land your husband gave you is good." Yala's arm trembled too. So even she found stretching difficult sometimes. "The income will be *very* good, and Steward Ur Kahn is most diligent." Lady Kue had indeed recommended a fine steward, not overly round but not painfully thin, with plain but clear handwriting. "And it is *yours*, as the Zhaon do things. It cannot be taken away."

That was indeed a consideration. "True."

"Would *you* return to Khir, given the chance?" Yala sounded only mildly curious.

Mahara took the chance to sit upright. She had hated practicing at home, but now it was a comfort to have something from childhood within her breath and bone. It was also comforting to think of another *yue* close at hand, sharp and ready to do service. If she mastered her fear of the sharp tooth, she would truly be a warrior wife. "I like it here," she said, softly. "Even though it is too hot, and dangerous. The other night..." Could she admit to fear? Would Yala understand? Her voice dropped even further. "I do not wish to return to Khir. Unless my husband should cast me off."

"Well, if he does, we may retire to your Zhaon land." Yala straightened, too; her cheeks had flushed with effort. "There is a manor there, it could be made ready. We will worry over crops and taxes, and the steward will argue with laborers. We will hold festivals for the kaburei and name their children."

Said thus, it did not sound so bad. "I know nothing of farming."

"Nor do I, but there are treatises. We may learn." Yala nodded, a single sharp motion putting all worries in their proper baskets. "Now, come, up we get. Do you remember your stances, my princess?"

Mahara almost groaned. But she gathered herself and flowed obediently upright. "I am glad you came with me, and no other."

"I am glad to be here as well." Yala pushed her simple braid over her shoulder. "Now, we will begin with Mountain Pose. Your knees, my princess, remember your knees. Good. The hand comes up—see, you remember this. It is easy."

"Not so easy," Mahara grumbled, but as long as she had Yala to follow, she did indeed remember it well. "Yala?"

"Hm? No, turn your wrist like so... good. Yes?"

"You are my best friend."

"And you are my princess." Yala smiled, almost achieving a wistful beauty though her face was not nearly round enough. She would never be likened to the Moon Maiden or to Fair Ta Chei. "We shall survive here, two small pearls inside our own shell. The sea of Zhaon is large, but we may live very happily in our own tiny corner. Now, lift your hand—no, that movement comes later, running ahead, my princess? There, very good. Follow me."

She was a much gentler teacher than the mistress tutors of the Great Keep, that was for certain. They could not perform all the movements, for time was short, but Mahara was warmed and loosened when they hurried to slip back into their bathing-robes and steal out of the attic and down a cramped, dusty back staircase while dusk robbed the mirrorlights of their shine. And Yala, her hand warm and certain and sure, was there to lead Mahara without a misstep through the gloom.

Less Decorative

Mrong Banh peered up from a table littered with scrolls and flat-bound books, alembics, flat metal instruments for measuring star-angles, and all the minutiae of his vocation, scratching luxuriously at his loose topknot. "Who on earth—ah. Kho-ador, is it? Khir lady to the Crown Princess?"

"Komor," the girl said, flowing into a slight bow he hastened to answer more deeply. "I am Komor Yala, Honorable Mrong Banh." She mispronounced his name, but then again, even his own countrymen did so at the slightest provocation, and he had butchered hers. Her hairpin, thrust into a nest of sober braids with a gilt dragonwing at its head, glittered. "I apologize for disturbing you; there was no steward below in the entry hall."

"I have no need of one, I am not a great man. Come, come, sit. Do you care for tea? I have some very fine eong,[50] I was just about to put the water on." It was a lie, but one must be civil even when interrupted in the blue-tiled Old Tower.

"I would not put you to any trouble, Honorable." She was cat-faced and pale-eyed, this lady, in deep green low-waisted in the Khir fashion but Zhaon-cut at the neck and sleeves. She laid her bright crimson sunbell aside near the door and straightened her sleeves—embroidered with tiny pale jaelo flowers—as she inspected

---

50. A smoke-cured tea from Daebo.

the scroll-racks and bookcases, smiling faintly. It could be an appreciative expression, Mrong Banh decided. She was supposed to be somewhat of a scholar.

"It is no trouble at all. What may a humble astrologer help a lady with today?" It was faintly rude to ask so directly, but he was no lord, and anyway, a noblewoman would not deign to take offense at him any more than at a merchant inquiring when she planned to pay a bill. Such offense was for stewards and servants to deploy.

"I come bearing a message from Crown Prince Garan Takyeo, and am in search of Third Prince Garan Takshin to deliver it unto." Her smile widened as she approached the bookcases, and perhaps her eyes were sparkling. "I was not told you stored treasure in this tower, though, so I may seek to charm you so I may return to admire afresh."

What a pretty turn of phrase, though wasted upon one of his rank. "Treasure?" He spread his arms, his brown sleeves flapping slightly. "Only dusty scrolls and unscholarly flatbooks full of strange things. Nothing to tempt a lady." She would not find certain of the, er, *racier* texts; those were well hidden where prying young princes could not get at them without approval. Except Jin—the boy had a longtail's cunning, and had dropped a certain treatise in a fountain just last week.

"So, you are of the opinion that a woman should not read?" Her hairpin darkened as she moved out of a bar of mirrorlight. "Some among my countrymen are, though my father was not."

Oh, dear. Mrong Banh shook his head, clicking his tongue dolefully. At least she looked amused. "Oh, no, Lady Komor. Merely that my poor library may hold nothing of interest for someone so gently born. It is, however, entirely at your service, and so am I. Takshin is upstairs searching for something or another, I shall put the water on and fetch him." He brushed his hands against his robe-front, realizing too late he had ink upon his fingers.

"I would not like to disturb your work," she began, but Banh clicked his tongue again.

"None of that, my lady. I should warn you, though, the Third Prince is in a fine temper today."

Her smile widened still further and crinkled the corners of her strange eyes. Her Zhaon was remarkably good, though almost painfully formal. "Is he not in a fine temper every day?"

"Ah, you have some experience of his company, then." Curiosity warred with manners—she was an unknown quantity, but on the other hand, where would *she* gossip? To Takyeo? The Crown Prince already knew Takshin's temper, such as it was. Light, familiar steps on the stairs reached Banh's ears. "*Ai*, here he comes. Perhaps he knows we have a visitor."

"Banh, I can't find a single shred of—" Takshin, in dark Shan cloth with his topknot caged in leather, pushed the door-hanging aside and caught sight of Lady Komor. "Ah, little lure. Come to taunt the wolf in his den?"

"I came to deliver a letter, Third Prince." Her equanimity was staggering, in the face of Takshin's glower. "But now that I have been granted a sight of this library, I shall stay to read as long as I may. There is also an offer of tea; the Honorable Mrong Banh is an excellent host."

"So he tells me." Takshin actually smiled, a lopsided grin that made his lip-scar crinkle as well. Banh's jaw threatened to drop. "What does Takyeo want that cannot wait for me to call at the Jonwa?"

Lady Komor produced a letter from her sleeve, its thick waxen seal bearing the snow-pard of the Crown Prince. "I do not know. I was merely asked to bring this, since he thought you might ignore a lowly messenger."

"Even the lowliest of *his* messengers is worthy of respect," Mrong Banh said, severely, and earned himself a glower from Takshin. At least *that* was usual.

Takshin skirted the table and bore down upon Lady Komor, but did not snatch the letter with a snarl. Instead, he held out both hands and executed a very proper, very slight bow as she placed it gently in his palms. "My thanks, little lure."

"It is merely my duty, Third Prince." The Khir woman did not retreat hastily, though he loomed over her.

Takshin did not move away, either. "Will you stay for tea?"

Mrong Banh's jaw did not merely *threaten* to drop; it hung almost to his chest. He stepped outside, onto the small floating-porch holding the charcoal stove, and strained his ears.

"I have been invited to." Lady Komor's tone did not change at all. Polite, restrained—but with a thread of mischief, lilting at formal Zhaon.

Takshin was equally mischievous, which was no surprise. The startlement lay only in his matching politeness. "But does that mean you will?"

"Would it disturb you if I did?"

"Not overly." Who was the man using Takshin's voice? He sounded very amused.

"Then perhaps I shall." Laughter ran underneath the lady's syllables. "The books are very attractive."

"You are a scholar, Lady Yala." Was Takshin glowering at her while he slouched through polite conversation? Or was he—it beggared belief—actually being *polite*?

"Merely a reader, Third Prince."

"You do yourself too little credit."

Banh shook his head, examining his ink-stained robe. He was lucky he hadn't rubbed at his face; he would be striped like the gounha of Qin in faraway Ch'han were rumored to be.

"It is kind of you to say so." Did Komor Yala bow, accepting the compliment? He could not see.

The creaking kettle was brought to a boil with little fuss. Mrong Banh almost resented it, both for the slight noise and for the time spent attending its humors. Was Third Prince Garan Takshin actually attempting to make pleasant conversation with a court lady? The stars had given no notice of this amazing occurrence, or perhaps Banh had not looked closely enough.

When he re-entered, carefully carrying a hot, steeping iron pot of eong upon a padded tray, Lady Komor was examining a collection of turquoise-titled flatbooks while Takshin, at the other window, had broken the seal of the Crown Prince's letter and was reading, his forehead furrowed and his mouth drawing down. His new earring—a small gold hoop, not a courtesan's dangle or a nobleman's heavy stud—glinted, somehow very fitting against black hair, copper skin, and his dark Shan longshirt buttoned at the side. At least there were three matching cups, small rough-glazed Raema ware. Two of them were even clean, and Mrong Banh poured for the noblewoman and the prince, reserving the cup that held a half-ili of sohju from last night's late session with the stars for his own use. It would taste terrible with strong, smoky eong, but that was his own fault for not accepting a servant to wash his cups. "Come, the tea is ready."

The lady turned from the bookcase, her hairpin glimmering. "You have much of interest here, Honorable Mrong Banh." Mispronouncing his name again, as she approached the table.

Still, he was charmed by her effort. "You are familiar with Su Rhon?" he asked, offering one of the clean cups and its cargo of tea.

She accepted with pretty grace. "Only as referenced in the Hundreds."

"It is farming itself that interests you, then?" A strange idea, a noblewoman interested in rai growing and pig-breeding. Khir nobles left such things strictly to the lower classes.

"My lady princess was gifted an estate by the Crown Prince." She inhaled the eong's fragrance, her strange eyes half-lidding with appreciation. "The steward is most diligent, but it does not hurt to accustom oneself with a matter one has entrusted to a servant's care."

Wise of her, and the Crown Princess, to recognize as much. "Quite right. Takshin, come, there is tea."

"Hrm." Takshin refolded the letter and tucked it into his sleeve. "Do you know what my saintly eldest brother wants, Banh?"

He clucked his tongue sharply. "I am sure I cannot guess."

"It is the *formal* invitation, now that the Shan are gone with Sabwone, for me to move into his household and stop bothering you." Takshin glanced at Lady Komor, who studied the implements upon the table with a great deal of interest that might even be genuine.

Etiquette had demanded the Third Prince observe his distance until the Crown Princess's wedding seclusion had at least run most of its course, and further demanded he be available for the high-ranking among the delegation. Now that Sabwone had left the city in the care of her bridegroom's guards, perhaps the palace complex would settle, a sleeper turning and dozing after a disturbance.

It was not likely, but Banh could still hope. And he was willing to wager there was more in Takyeo's letter—but if Komor Yala *was* disposed to gossip, she would know only the invitation. "You are never a bother, Third Prince."

"Liar." Takshin accepted his own cup with quite uncharacteristic etiquette. "Since when do you drink eong?"

"It was a gift."

Bright interest bloomed in Takshin's gaze as he settled in his usual chair. He had waited until Komor Yala chose her own seat, and that was different, too. "From whom?" He had not looked this much at ease since... oh, Banh could not remember.

"A certain lady." A very upright one, too, worried over the prospects of an adoptive-daughter's marriage. Banh had been able to set her mind at ease and it had not taken art to do so, merely common sense. "Do not ask more, for I cannot say."

Normally, Takshin would tease him mercilessly until he gave a name. But now, the Third Prince studied Lady Komor over the cluttered table. "And what do you think, little lure?"

If it was an insult, she bore it with grace; if it was a nickname, it was a strange one. The lady inhaled the fragrance of eong again, soft satisfaction blooming upon her features. "Of what, Third Prince Garan Takshin?" She lilted the honorifics, and Banh realized he was hearing a woman—a court lady—tease Garan Takshin.

Well. Perhaps the stars were just as shocked by this event as Banh himself.

Takshin's smile held no trace of wolfish ill-humor at all. He did not put his boots upon the table, either. "Would it please you to have me in the Jonwa?"

"It is my lord the Crown Prince's house." She lowered her eyelids, apparently considering that the end of the matter, completely unmoved by Takshin's sudden glare. "Honorable Mrong, is it possible that I might study some of your fine books upon farming? Perhaps I might bring you some tea, too, since you seem a man of fine tastes."

"He eats bodong,"[51] Takshin muttered, and Mrong Banh had to try very hard not to smile.

"Lady Komor, you are welcome to borrow any of my humble scrolls or manuscripts at will. I am sure the clutter of my home is painful to a lady of refinement, but you are a most honored guest at any hour you choose to visit." He inclined the top half of his body, and her slight almost-bow in return was finely graded, conscious of the difference in their station but also quite kind, without any severity.

"He's never this nice to me," Takshin muttered, a little louder.

"Perhaps because you are less decorative, and more..." Lady Komor raised her eyebrows. "...princely?" It was delivered so sweetly, and with such grace, that Mrong Banh lost the battle with himself, dropping into his own chair and choking back a braying laugh.

Amazingly, Third Prince Takshin's mouth twitched, and he shook his head. "Your tongue is sharp, little lure. Tell my brother I shall accept his offer with all haste."

Lady Komor studied him for a moment, her head cocked slightly and her hairpin aglitter. "Should you not write him a reply, since he has written to ask?"

"I prefer to have it carried in your pretty head." Takshin took a gulp of tea, and Mrong Banh almost winced. It could not have

---

51. A bland, cheap peasant dish of organ meat and unpolished rai.

been comfortable, fresh-brewed and still hot as it was, but the Third Prince showed no sign of scorching. "What else would he have of me, this eldest brother of mine?"

"I was simply to deliver the letter, my lord."

"Ah. We've grown a little more informal. It will be *Takshin* before long, as Banh here addresses me."

"I am sure the Honorable Mrong Banh is allowed such familiarity with the princes of Zhaon." She took a decorous sip. "I am a mere lady-in-waiting, and cannot dream of such things."

Banh choked, merry tears streaming down his cheeks. Takshin granted him an irritated glance. "You are enjoying this, astrologer?"

"Not at all," he spluttered. "Not at all, Taktak."

Now it was Lady Komor's turn to smile without reserve, and a wistful almost-beauty bloomed over her odd face and strange pale eyes. One legend said the Khir used to stare into the sun during the Golden Times, that bountiful age of miracles, to honor their horse-goddess who walked the Land of the Five Winds among the humans she and her fellows had created. The sun had bleached Khir irises and given them a hunger for conquest as all fires craved fuel.

It could even be true.

Lady Komor turned the conversation to astrology, asking small questions about the stars that showed she had at least read Cao Hu Shuzien upon the motion of heavenly bodies and Zho Zhaong's lone treatise on constellations. Takshin settled with his tea and listened, eventually leaning back in his chair and tapping at his knee with strong, scarred fingers. When the cups were dry and Lady Komor had twice refused more, she rose, and both men hurried to their feet.

She made her good-byes quietly, formally, and took her sunbell and the two-part *Treatise upon the Lower Rivers*, a fine overview of farming methods during the Third Dynasty. When she had gone Takshin's expression clouded, and the prince retreated upstairs with his letter—and without a single further word to Mrong Banh.

Who smiled, shaking his head, and began clearing the table, his hands working independently of his mind, which raced with several very intriguing thoughts. The Lady Komor did not seem so much *decorative* as clever, restrained, and miraculously capable of moderating Garan Takshin's black temper.

Wonders were still alive in the Land of Five Winds.

Girl-Ring, Sinuous Snake

Great towering black clouds threatened a return of the afternoon storms, moving over Zhaon-An like a slow eyelid winking. If they had held any concomitant promise of coolness, Yala would have been overjoyed. As it was, she opened her sunbell with a snap in the bruised afternoon light and almost pitied poor Anh, struggling with the oiled cloaks the kaburei insisted they bring along in case of rain. "We must hurry, to return in time for the dressing."

"My first formal banquet." Behind her veil, Mahara might have grimaced. "Inconvenient, but one must."

Yala managed a faint smile behind her own. It was too stifling under another layer of cloth, no matter how fine. "You already sound like a lady of Zhaon."

Flanked by a quartet of golden-armored guards was not the most discreet way to pierce the Great Market's bustle and noise, but it was more comfortable than Yala's other expeditions. With Anh alone, she was buffeted and had to be mindful of her reticule and sleeves; with Third Prince Takshin a certain amount of space was accorded but his fierce glare and scarred countenance caused inevitable comment. With Anh fussing at the guards and directing them at the top of her lungs while she maneuvered the cloaks—Mahara's deep scarlet, a wedding gift, and Yala's a drab brown but sturdy and well-made—there was little to do but amuse Mahara and keep a sharp eye upon the eddy and flow of the crowd.

"That was what Father told me," Mahara said, somewhat darkly. "*You must become a lady of Zhaon.*"

Yala nodded. Her veil, a necessary irritation since she was abroad with her princess's honor to keep unstained as well as her own, did nothing to blur the cacophony of sellersongs and cries, animals bleating—pets and small livestock, both a sign of abundance since famine would thin their ranks to almost nothing—and fierce bargaining. "We seem to have both succeeded in that."

Mahara slowed, eyeing a trio of acrobats in knotted clouts, sweat greasing bronzed skin twitching with long straps of muscle. One was a woman, her shallow breasts all but nonexistent, bent into a backward hoop. She clasped her thin ankles, and the other two lifted her to make the character for *house*, a circle over walls. Horn-callused feet slipped against grit-dusty stone paving, and Yala gasped as one acrobat's hand slipped...

...but the girl-ring became a sinuous snake, and Mahara clasped her hands to her chin like a child as the female acrobat, her hair a short-shaven crop like her brothers', landed lightly upon her own blunt-toed, flexible feet. Yala lifted a hand to her veiled mouth to catch a sound of surprised wonder as well. The three bowed, Mahara gestured, and their third Golden Guard, his sleeve knotted with a scrap of cloth bearing a snow-pard's print to show which prince he guarded today, tossed a handful of small alloy bits in the general direction of their set-out basket.

The acrobats descended upon the slivers, picking them from the dust, and knee-bowed even more deeply.

"Generous," Yala commented, and nodded to the guard. His flat dark gaze gave no sign of caring, passing over the flow of market traffic in smooth arcs.

"They made you laugh." Mahara's tone was amused, now, and they swept on.

Yala wondered if accompanying the prince's foreign wife was a duty the Golden relished. Certainly it was a prestigious one, and now she knew the names of the two guards Anh was fussing over in front of them, if only because the kaburei girl addressed them familiarly. Another court lady would have been welcome to rein Anh and flank Mahara's other side, but they were all three busy with the last-minute details of tonight's banquet robes.

She almost wished they were at the Jonwa in the princess's quarters, stifling warm but at least shaded and with small feathers to dip in earthen jars of cool water and draw across the arms or the tops of breasts, as well as fans to give an illusion of coolness with moving air. But the metalsmith had sent word the blunted preliminary blade was done, and having Mahara handle it, in the guise of approving a present for her husband, was necessary at this point.

Besides, the princess was fretful, full of strange aches, seeking new amusement, and her last red time had been scanty indeed. It was difficult to tell if she was a-swell with new life, but Yala hoped.

"*Ai!* Crown Princess, *ai*!" The shout pierced market noise and Yala's head snapped up, chin held high, shoulders tensing.

It was Sixth Prince Jin, his topknot in a cheerful yellow leather band and his walking-robes echoing the sunshine. The guards recognized him and drew aside as he bowed deeply to Mahara, accepting Yala's bow with a smile and a half-incline of his torso. They drew aside into uncertain shade under a striped awning, a restaurant fronting the Market's bustle suddenly alive with faces peering through grillwork windows as august personages were noticed. "I thought it was you," he said cheerfully, by way of greeting. "Out shopping for the banquet?"

"We are to a metalsmith's, for a princely present," Yala answered smoothly. "And yourself, Sixth Prince?"

"I like to watch the sword-dancers. There are some very fine ones upon the northern end, and in the south they work with foreign weapons."

"You are quite the warrior." Mahara did not push her veil aside—she could not—but her warm tone more than made up for it. "My husband says you must only touch a weapon to know all its secrets."

The youngest prince swept her another bow to thank her for

the compliment. "*Ai*, if only that were true. Zakkar Kai says it's only because I practice, having nothing else to occupy me, being the youngest." He dabbed at his smooth brow with a folded cotton square, yellow as his topknot-cage. "May I accompany you, and escort you to the palace afterward? Or perhaps engage a teahouse room, and pass some time?"

Mahara's delight was visible even through the veil. "We must return for the dressing, for tonight's banquet. But your company is most welcome, should you choose to share it."

"Excellent!" He offered Mahara his arm, and Yala trailed them, somewhat relieved at not having to make more conversation in the terrible, oppressive heat.

Mahara chattered away, her Zhaon remarkably fluid—of course, the Sixth Prince had such an easy manner, and was so cheerful, it was hard not to relax and smile fondly. Yala concentrated upon her feet, and told the lightness in her head to cease. It was only heat, and soon they would return to the Jonwa. If she pleaded a headache, she could perhaps nap before the dressing. The banquet itself was likely to be entirely tedious, despite the prospect of entertainment.

"Have you heard from the First Princess?" Mahara inquired, solicitously.

"She writes a letter at every stop." Prince Jin's mouth turned down at the corners. Yala suppressed a twinge of ill temper—*he* could go abroad without a veil, and without being swathed in several layers. "She's…oh, I don't know how to say it."

Yala thought it quite likely the Sixth Prince knew *exactly* how to describe his sister, but what good brother could use such terms?

"It is difficult to leave your home to marry," Mahara said, diplomatically.

"Well, yes." Jin glanced down at Mahara. He had a pleasant face, broad and open, and held his arm solicitously at the angle most likely to support Mahara's smaller stature. "Was it difficult for you?"

"Very. But I have Yala. And my husband is kind." Mahara's gloved hand lay lightly upon his arm. "What manner of man is King Suon Kiron, do you know?"

"Well, Takshin says he's good. But Taktak has his own pins for measuring; that could mean anything."

Taktak. A child's nickname, one the astrologer had used as well. Had the Third Prince ever been a child? It seemed unlikely, and yet he must have.

Yala almost flinched as a deep, nasty rumble echoed overhead; the market crowd began to scatter. Hot, stinging drops danced in the dust, a brief spatter-prelude. Yala's sunbell dipped—it was not meant for storms, and its thin taut fabric might well fray under a serious assault. She should have brought her rainbell, instead.

"Come, it's not far," Anh cried, and even the guards hurried, loath to risk a soaking of their gleaming armor. It must be like an oven inside such a burnished casing, Yala thought, and her skirts threatened to tangle her ankles. At least she was not wearing jata-jatas, though if mud rose in the unpaved alleys she might well wish for their height.

At first she thought the crashing noise was another peal from Heaven, spears shivered in celestial battle. But it was the guard behind her, the one who had thrown the bits to the acrobats. He went down hard, metal plates sewn onto leather chiming and his helmet spinning away, its cheekpiece breaking with a small sweet lost sound, and a bright blue feather at his throat was the fletching of an arrow buried in flesh.

The world halted for a moment, shock greying the edges of Yala's vision, before the consciousness of danger filled her with crimson-copper fear.

"*Run!*" she shrieked in Khir, and a bright fork of lightning flashed over Zhaon-An's Great Market.

Bait, Sweetened

He didn't think it would be like *this.* The two rearguards were down, arrows blooming upon their corpses, and Jin ducked uselessly as another arrow split the air by his cheek, burying itself in the back of the guard before him. The kaburei girl, shocked into silence, had halted with her arms full of cloak and Heaven alone knew what else, but Lady Komor's cry forced her into dream-slow motion. The princess, her waist-length veil spotted with raindrops and golden dust, made a queer gulping sound, and Jin thought perhaps she had been hit before the last guard spun aside, putting his shoulder to a splintering door. Lady Komor hit Jin's back, and that forced him into motion too.

The biggest surprise was how he seemed to have all the time in the world to think, but no time at all to *act.* He blundered after the remaining guard's broad back, yellowish instead of gold in the strange stormlight, and carried the kaburei girl before him.

Screams and shouts spread in a rippling ring from the sudden advent of death, and more thunder crackle-boomed. Jin gulped at air gone hard and stale, and Lady Komor shoved her veil aside. "At least two upon the roof," she snapped, in heavily accented Zhaon. "Princess, my princess, are you injured?"

"No, I..." Princess Mahara gasped. "No, I think I am quite—"

The guard threw his helmet into the corner. The clatter was the only warning Jin received, but it was enough for one who had spent countless hours under Zakkar Kai's tutelage on the drillfield or over padded mats in the practice-room. Jin's body moved without his conscious direction, his hand flashing down onto the hilt to smash the guard's sword back into its scabbard. He leaned aside, the guard exhaling sourness into his face, and a moment of confusion filled him—he did not recognize the fellow at all, and it smelled like he had a rotten tooth.

Then the consciousness of battle took over, and his free hand batted away a strike aimed for his own face, helping the gauntleted fist upon its path. *Do not meet force with force if you can help it*, Kai had said more than once. *Rather, let your enemy expend uselessly, then strike.*

Footwork was half the battle, and the guard's boots were better than Jin's softer market-walkers with their thin leather soles. Still, speed was a princely edge and he used it, his hip dropping and the room—a dim, fusty warehouse stacked with goods under sheeting or locked in crates—spinning around them both. The small splintered door leading to the Yaol's tangle had been left unlocked, and was not shattered.

Treachery? More than likely, but he had enough to occupy him at the moment without wondering about such prospects.

The bigger man went down face-first, his commitment to battle carrying him as a river carried small waxed-paper boats. Jin skipped neatly over one leg, stopped, and drove the point of his toe deep into the man's now exposed nethers where the armored back-skirt, split for riding, flipped up. He caught a patch of deeper resistance, and hoped he'd managed to find the bastard's twinfruits.

"Anh. The cloaks." Lady Komor could give Kai snapping lessons; her tone was brisk and no-nonsense. "Sixth Prince Jin, are you harmed? *Are* you?"

"No. No indeed." His ribs heaved. Why was he sweating? It took a few moments for the full realization to douse him, a tepid ducking after a very hot bath. The man on the floor began to curse, breathless. Was he really a guard? Wouldn't the other three know him, though, since he was of their square? Jin bent to grab the man's topknot, fingers slipping in sweat and oiled hair, and wrenched his head aside. *Get his sword. Once you are armed, everything will be better.*

A faint silvery drumming was rain outside. The clouds had burst and would wash market, palace, and field all together. "Listen," Lady Komor said. "*Listen* to me. Take my cloak. You and Anh run as if you are afraid; do not take off your veil. Do not *stop* running until you are at the palace. Raise your arms... there. Yes. Prince Jin? Sixth Prince Jin. They will have others along soon."

"What will..." Princess Mahara sobbed in a deep, distracted breath. Dust tickled Jin's nose as he worked at the man's body. If he could just get the sword—"What will you do? Yala, oh, Yala, *no*."

"I shall distract them." Lady Komor, her thin face pale under its torn veil, shrugged into the oiled crimson cloak. "The only question is how to keep Prince Jin—"

"No," Jin said, sucked in a breath. Said it louder. "No. I will not be *safe* when a lady is risking herself. If you are to be bait, Lady Komor, it shall be sweetened."

She shook her head. "The cloak shall make it sweet enough. Hist, Anh, the door! Where are they?" Lady Komor's grey eyes glittered feverishly. Her hair had been knocked askew; she thrust her hairpin into Princess Mahara's braids and took the princess's own. "Forgive me, my princess."

Mahara's hands were soft round fists. "Yala... *no*..."

Lady Komor pushed at her princess's shoulders. "Do *not* take your veil off."

A scraping clatter above them ran ice through Jin's veins. "Above us. Of course, for the arrows. And this fellow—" He finally managed to tug the sword free.

"Go!" Yala hissed, pushing the other two women for the door. "Anh, protect my princess. With your life, do you understand?"

"Yes." The kaburei girl swallowed, her throat moving, her eyes huge, one of her leather-wrapped braids coming loose. "Yes, my lady Komor. With my life."

"Go."

Princess Mahara let out a sob. Lady Komor bore down upon Jin, and he almost quailed at the approach. His body reacting to training was one thing, but this was quite another. "Sixth Prince Jin," she said, quietly, "give me the sword. And follow the princess. They are descending from the roof; they will not see you if you slip out."

"I cannot," he began, but she stepped close and laid her hand over his mouth. Her palm was chilly and damp, and those grey eyes blazed.

"Princess Mahara *must* reach the palace safely," she whispered, fiercely. "Forgive my impertinence, but they will see us in a few moments. You must reach Crown Prince Takyeo and tell him everything. What happens to me does not matter. Go. Please. I beg of you, go, follow my princess, and deliver her safely."

Bile crept into Jin's throat. He glanced at the man upon the floor, and Lady Komor reached for the sword.

"No," he said, softly, and put the point between two platelets. "I can do this much, at least." It was not right for a court lady to do *this* thing when a prince was available. He leaned forward, and there was more resistance than a training-dummy. The man began to thrash, but Jin knew his work, and blood spread in a sticky pool.

Lady Komor plucked at his shoulder. "Away," she whispered as the clattering overhead resolved into shouts. At least four men, perhaps more. "Please, care for my princess, I beg it of you."

The storm had broken and rain drummed blindly upon cloaked forms, smudging in the downpour. Whistles blew, but the Market Guard would have a fine time sorting this mess in any time, let alone a reasonable one.

Jin ran, choking on bile.

To Strike a Prince

"No, no, no," the kaburei girl whispered, clutching Mahara's sodden arm. Breathing was torture, but at least they had stopped running. This alley was full of malodorous refuse and only half-paved; the mud was beginning to rise. "We must not be seen, we must not."

Mahara struggled to *think*. Yala had sounded so certain. The rain was cold and came in curtains, as if all Heaven's sluices had opened at once to drown the land of Zhaon like a rai-patch. The veil tried to seal itself to her nose and lips, her soft-shod feet were bruised from running, her sunbell was gone, and Yala, poor Yala... what would they do to her?

"We must not be seen," Anh repeated. "I know a way, princess, great lady, *please*."

"Yes." Now that she had a moment to catch her breath, she understood. "Yes, a way in without being seen. It would cause talk if we..." *Oh, Yala. My brave Yala.* The world was roaring too quickly upon its axis, and Mahara's breath could not catch up. "What will they do to her?"

"Nothing good," the kaburei said, practically, and pulled Mahara into yet another crooked alley. The middle of the street was a river;

temporary stall awnings had collapsed, horses moving nervously as more thunder roll-roiled the tiled roofs. *Archers, and a single treacherous guard.* If not for Prince Jin, what might have happened?

It was obvious, they wanted Mahara alive. Either that, or... oh, there was no point in trying to decide their motives now. She had to reach the palace and her husband.

Takyeo would do something. He *had* to. Mahara would cast herself to her knees, if she must, and plead. *Yala. What are they doing to you?*

A shadow loomed next to her; Mahara's thin cry of surprise was a bright copper sliver. Anh's shriek was lost in the thunder, but it was Prince Jin, his topknot draggled and his sodden robes no longer cheerful but the terrible deathly color of a plagued invalid's face. He slapped aside Anh's ineffectual windmilling blow, and the kaburei girl went deathly pale to match him.

She had attempted to strike a *prince.*

"'Tis me!" he called, over the roar of the rain. "'Tis me, come *on*!"

"We must reach the Jonwa without being seen," Mahara stuttered, and cursed her recalcitrant tongue as well as the silly Zhaon language. Why couldn't they just be reasonable and speak solid Khir?

"I *know.*" Sixth Prince Jin rolled his eyes just as her eldest brother used to, long ago in the bright time before councilors began their worried whispering and Father's face grew grimmer each day.

Then, her only worry was displeasing Ashani Zlorih, the god of her childhood.

Sixth Prince Jin, wet clear through and with a high hectic flush upon his downy cheeks, made hurrying motions with both hands. "If word gets out... in any case, I know we have to get there quietly. Come on, I know a way."

Mahara shoved her veil aside. The relief of being able to *breathe* was deep and instant. "What will they do to her?"

Jin shook his head, as if he could not hear her—or did not wish to answer. He pulled Mahara along, slipping and sliding over pavers awash with rain and a tide of less savory things from the Yaol's floor, and Anh took Mahara's other arm. They reeled and slid in mud like drunkards returning home after a festival, and Crown Princess Mahara, future Queen of Zhaon, wept at her own helplessness.

Leave It to Me

The rain took a deep breath, gathering itself for a damp night. Small comfort to those wishing to sleep, but after the banquet no doubt several would be too deep in sohju's approximation of slumber to care. The bulk of the Jonwa closed away much of the storm's fury, but thunder would not be denied. It penetrated stone, wood, bookshelves, and flesh, crouching in bone and breath. The cabinet against the southron wall rattled slightly, everything in its drawers uneasy at the sky's wrath.

"Quick thinking," Takshin murmured, his fingers steepled before his face. He had not moved from this seat, his boots propped on Takyeo's ruthlessly organized desk in defiance of good manners. Even the news had failed to jar him from this lounging insouciance, and Takyeo was too distracted to take him to task.

Besides, it was best not to let his most difficult brother know he had irritated you, or he would do it again, mercilessly, no matter the emergency they faced. "The kaburei girl will tell whoever asks that Lady Komor returned with a headache, and will not attend the banquet."

"The guard," Takshin said, and his eyelids dropped another fraction. "The one who was not shot, Jin."

Sixth Prince Jin, wet clear through and sadly bedraggled in a soaked yellow robe bearing scallops of deeper sunshine embroidered upon the cuffs, almost hopped from foot to foot with impatience. "I do not know him, Taktak. I saw them in the Yaol and offered to accompany them, then...we must go fetch her, Takyeo. We *must.* She's all alone, and when they find out she's not the princess, they'll—"

"Shhh." Takshin lifted a finger to his mouth, staring very hard at a space somewhere to Takyeo's left, perhaps at the scroll of Hao Fong's dragon eating the demon of famine. "Let me think."

"There will be a scandal. Father will be wroth, again." Takyeo lifted his spread hands, almost wishing he could slam them upon the desk. Such a display was not princely *or* manly. "We may find some story—Lady Komor taken ill, or—"

"I said to be quiet." Takshin, very low. He did not move, but his expression had darkened, his scarred lip twitching once. "Let me *think*, Eldest Brother."

"What is there to think about?" Jin exploded, shaking water from his hair-ends and robe-hem. "She's a *lady.* She kept the princess's cloak to delay them; she needs rescuing."

"This is not a novel, Jin." Takyeo massaged at his temples. His own banquet robes were waiting. His wife, pale and tear-stained, was at the bath with a solicitous Anh, and both women apparently understood very well the need for hiding what had occurred.

"But it's not *right*!" Jin's market-shoes squished as he stamped one foot. It was his perennial cry when Sabwone or Sensheo were tormenting someone and he had failed to halt their games.

"Will both of you stopper your mouths for a single moment so I may *think*?" Takshin's tone was ice, but he still did not move. "You are irritating me with your fretting."

Takyeo rounded upon him. "What are you thinking, Takshin? If you have a solution—"

"Eldest Brother, you are the Emperor's favorite and I admire you, but if you do not shut *up* for a few moments I shall be forced to strike you." Takshin delivered the threat in a monotone; an ugly flush had begun upon his scarred neck, creeping toward jaw and cheekbones.

Takyeo turned away. There were no ears at the door, but all the same, raised voices would not be prudent.

For this was not an assassination attempt. Had it been, arrows from rooftops were efficacious enough and the attackers could have been gone before the screaming crowd trampled each other to paste in confusion. Lady Komor must have realized as much, and perhaps the kaburei had too, who knew? Something would have to be done to ensure the servant's continuing trustworthiness.

Or her complete, permanent silence. Did Father ever feel this sickened, contemplating such things?

Someone had known of Mahara's plans made just that morning. *I am gone to the market, husband, if you will give leave. It is a surprise.*

Well, this certainly was. The Khir women had intended to arrange a fine market-gift for him, Mahara admitted, and looked so pale from her ordeal he had not inquired further.

There is a traitor in my household. First hot, then cold, the waves passed through him.

Only the Great Emperor of Heaven, sitting upon his greenstone throne and listening to the seashell whispers of every human heart, could have known how Takyeo hated this. Was it so much to ask that someone, anyone be trustworthy? That some of them—oh, maybe not Sensheo, but perhaps Kurin—would realize that "*Father's favorite*" did not have so many luxuries they took for granted? Other children could fall and skin their knees, but not Garan Takyeo. He had to be better, faster, princely in all ways, and a prince kept a well-ordered household.

Lady Komor was too good to be wasted upon an assassin's blade, or worse, outraged in some fashion. Honor would demand he avenge such a thing, for she was of his household, a noblewoman, and...yes, his wife's friend. It was Lady Komor who selected Mahara's companions, who helped Lady Kue with the daily business of the household, whose steadying presence eased Mahara's transition into Crown Princess and smoothed over small difficulties in translation whenever they arose. She was the only piece of his wife's homeland, and poor Mahara should not be robbed of her.

Yet they were all robbed of anything that mattered here in the palace, and the sooner the Crown Princess grew accustomed to the fact, the easier it would be for her. And for Takyeo, though it was unprincely of him to think such things.

"It will cause a scandal," he murmured, and found he was twisting his hurai. He had dreams where he took the heavy thing off and his feet left the floor, his robes turning thin and transparent along with his skin.

They ended with him awake, gasping and sweating, as they had since childhood.

"No," Takshin said, and swung his boots from the desk. "It will not, Eldest Brother. Leave it to me."

"What do you plan to do?" He sounded like a querulous maiden aunt, demanding to be soothed. Takyeo's hands ached, and his belly was full of sourness.

"Do you really want to ask me that, Ah-Yeo?" The old childish nickname rolled upon his brother's tongue as Takshin rose, black as a thundercloud in both cloth and expression. "Go to the banquet. Let comment arise about my absence. Oh, and make some sort of excuse for Zakkar Kai." Takshin's smile turned wolfish. "I'll need him."

"What do I do?" Jin hopped from foot to sodden foot, glassy-eyed and fever-cheeked, a restive horse stamping in anticipation of a task.

"You? Get to the baths without anyone seeing and dress yourself properly. Go to the banquet and amuse the Crown Princess. Keep her from weeping, if she's prone to such things." Takshin set off for the door, a long swinging stride. "Your steward has the guard roster, Takyeo?"

"Of course, but—" The relief at someone else attempting to salvage the situation was unprincely as well, especially since Takyeo should be the one with a plan. *He* should be the one attending to this matter, not delegating it to Takshin. The books on the shelves—annals, treatises, classics—watched in disapproving silence.

"Wait, I want to come with—" Jin reached for Takshin's sleeve, but the Third Prince stepped aside with a warning look.

Jin's hand fell back to his side and he gulped, audibly.

"Do as I tell you, and stop worrying. All will be well." Takshin's smile intensified, and it was not a pleasant one. "Between us, Kai and I shall set things right."

"Thank you," Takyeo began, but Takshin waved it away, his broad back bisected by that cruel wrap-hilted sword.

"Don't, Eldest Brother. I'll ask a price for this someday, you know."

And with that, Third Prince Takshin was gone.

A Matter for Hope

I need you, Takshin said, bluntly, and Zakkar Kai reached for his dragon-hilted sword.

It was good to know that of a man, and even better when the man asked no questions until they were in one of the long, high-ceilinged Golden barracks, upending a possibly traitorous guard's basket of personal possessions onto his narrow cot. The barracks were mostly deserted, but their presence would cause some small amount of comment.

Takshin was almost past caring. Na Duanh, the head of the traitor's shield-square—the five men who trained together, ate together, and took their guard oath at the same time—was pale and uncomfortable, sensing trouble for one of his responsibilities. Shit flowed upriver instead of down in this case; the head of a square was held to account for his underlings as a minister was for his, but without money or influence to cushion the blow.

"His name is Huo Banh; we fought together in the Northern Army, General. He sometimes stays near the Left Market; we all pay for a room there for nights off. So we have a place to take girls, or..." Na Duanh, lean, nervous, and only half in his gleaming armor, bowed when Zakkar Kai glanced at him, a reflexive bobbing like a duck upon troubled water. He had been at a late luncheon with two others of his square; the fourth man was on duty at the fringe of the royal baths and mercifully oblivious. "He stayed there last night, though he shouldn't have. We had to stuff his bed for roll-call."

"A square looks after its own." Zakkar Kai nodded, shortly. He did not judge, that nod said, and his tone—curt but not uncompromising—was no doubt calculated to calm the fellow.

The sergeant looked relieved. "Is he in trouble? He took Mu Dailao's place at the Jonwa this morning; they were joking about it. Dai's in love with a girl who works at the baths; that's why he gets every chance he can to stand there."

Takshin saw no need to tell the poor fellow one of his square was a traitor. "There was a small altercation in the Yaol." He finished shaking the basket, and something heavy fell out.

It was a half-ingot, copper, wrapped in a sheet of rai-paper. Careful brushwork upon the inside—a letter, written with the standardized, impersonal brushwork of a public scribe.

"He has a sister," the head continued, seeing it. "He was always sending scribe's letters home."

Takshin read the address. "Huo Liha? His sister?"

"Yes, that's her name." The head smoothed his scanty mustache with a nervous fingertip. "A half-ingot. Well, he saves his wages, does Huo Banh."

Takshin scanned the letter. *By the time this reaches you, I will probably be gone. Po will be kind to you, I approve of your marriage. But do not spend this or tell Po, or Mother, or anyone of it. Keep it secret, and think of your brother sometimes.*

"What does it say?" Great clear drops of sweat stood out on the square-leader's forehead. Of course, it boded ill when superiors came to rifle a shield-brother's belongings.

"See that this gets to his sister, Sergeant Na Duanh." Zakkar Kai tossed him the half-ingot. "Along with the message that her brother wishes her to keep it secret and approves of her marriage, for I shall be taking the letter. Where is this room you share? The Yuin, what street?"

In short order they had clear directions, the letter was in Kai's pocket, and Takshin, boiling with restrained impatience, lengthened his stride. The rain showed no sign of slacking, but stopping for a cloak was a waste of time. They would get just as wet, oiled cloth or no. "Two horses," he snapped to the palace runner at the barracks door, who took off for the stables at a gallop, ducking against a curtain of cold falling water. The princes would take the drier route, and by the time they reached the stables, Kai was just as deadly pale as Takshin.

He had reason, Takshin supposed. This was ill news.

"Lady Komor?" Kai repeated.

"Changed cloaks with her princess. Swift thinking." Oh, she was sharp as the pin she had put through his earlobe, the little lure.

"Yes, she is prone to that." Kai's jaw hardened, a look familiar from the drillyard when soldiers were not attending to their practice-duties thoroughly enough. "And this guard, Huo, Jin killed him?"

"Is it his first? He did not seem overly marked by the experience." Takshin's boots all but struck sparks from the stone paving. Gardens bent and blurred under the assault, blossoms beaten free of branches. "Jin was certain the man is dead."

"So they may not know they do not have the princess."

Little lure. Takshin's fury mounted another notch. "All the more reason to move swiftly, before they discover their error."

"Yes." Though slightly taller, Kai still had to stretch his legs to keep up. "What were they doing in the Yaol?"

"A gift for Takyeo, Princess Mahara said. Four guards and a kaburei with them; the arrows did not touch Huo or the women."

"Ah. So yes, they wanted the princess."

Ridiculous, to state the obvious. Takshin made an irritated noise. "I do not care *what* they wanted. They took Lady Komor, and we shall have her returned."

"Let us hope." Kai's expression was thunderous. Of course, he had reason to be grateful to their Eldest Brother, too. Takyeo was refuge and intercession when the Emperor decided a youth had gone too far, when Kurin and Sabwone decided to play one of their little games, or when Sensheo, when much younger, had done his best to poke and prod another child into tears.

"It is not a matter for hope." Takshin touched his swordhilt. *Soon*, he promised. *They will die for taking her, and if they have harmed her, they will die badly.*

A little lure indeed, and he was a hawk winging for prey. Takshin put his head down and broke into a run, and after a moment, Zakkar Kai did, too.

Filthy Little Corner

'M jest sayin' I doan' like it," the thick-legged man repeated. Perhaps he had wrapped his lower half against the damp, like an old rheumatic farmer. "She stabs Huo, and we ent stabbin' her?"

"You're an idiot." The thinner man, the one in charge, wore a filthy scrap of cotton over the lower half of his face and tried to stamp mud from his hempen sandals. "We stab her, there's no reward."

"We ent no kaburei to drag packages." This from the bowman, squatted against a pile of wooden boxes and carefully checking the fletching upon each of his arrows. "An' who was t'other on the roof, with a bow? Not one of *us*."

Yala huddled upon dirty straw, hugging her knees, her back pressed into the small room's stone corner. Her bound wrists ached, and her head rang. She should have drawn her *yue* and made certain the stinking, traitorous guard on the floor was gone, but she would have to trust Prince Jin's handiwork and in any case, she had been occupied with keeping just ahead of her pursuers until a basket of drowning, flapping, screaming eggfowl washed down a crooked Great Market alleyway had swept her legs from under her. Now, half-drowned herself and stripped of Mahara's cloak, she shivered and pressed her forehead against her knees, listening intently.

"We ent no idiots to kill our singing pig, either. An' the other arrowflinger ent none of our business. Prolly there to make sure we didna foul it." The masked man's tone clearly said *that's that.* "Get a fire g'n, I'm half-dead."

Other arrowflinger? Had there been another archer?

It mattered little in her present situation. At least they had not molested her, not yet. The thick-legged one with hairy moles on his neck had cuffed her almost absently while pulling her from the streamlet; the masked man had hissed at him to stop. In a trice, she'd been thrown over a broad laborer's shoulder, and now here she was in the basement corner of a hovel somewhere in the teeming of Zhaon-An, and these men were discussing what to do with her.

They still thought she was Mahara. So far, she had gleaned that they thought their situation a fine one, since they had escaped detection and had their prize, and the reward—offered by a gentleman they did not name—would not be split with the hapless, traitorous guard Prince Jin had stabbed.

She supposed she should not feel anything for the man who had betrayed his fellows and his prince, but the way the stunned body had moved when Prince Jin's sword slid in...

Bile rose to the back of her throat. She longed for tea, for a brazier to warm her numb hands. Her ankles were bound too. She could perhaps get to her *yue,* though. It would require some thought and planning, and her head seemed full of uncombed cotton. Her nose was full, but wiping it upon her skirt was not permissible.

None of this was *permissible.* And yet, it had happened.

Had Mahara reached the palace? She had to. Anh was clever enough, and Prince Jin would no doubt have some ideas about slipping into the Jonwa undetected. Palaces were meant to be strongboxes, but instead, their walls were as porous as pierced, unglazed Trong ware with its beautiful scallops and gradations of earthy color.

After all, assassins could slide even into the Crown Prince's room at night.

Yala took stock. Wrists bound cruelly tight, ankles bound less so since her shoes interfered with the rough cord. Mahara's hairpin dug into her scalp, her dress was sodden clear through, and no attempt had been made to search her or take her reticule. Her *yue*-hilt dug into her thigh, the careful stitching around its sheath perhaps a trifle loosened. She raised her face, peering at sudden garish shadows cascading over daubed walls as they nursed a small, smoky fire into being.

Her captors, perhaps thinking her witless, went on with their tasks.

"When the Big Man comin'?"

"He'll be along, don't you worry."

"I ent easy about Huo."

"Me either. But he did what he did."

"You figger she did for him?"

"Figger the boy did, then scooted. Wif'out waitin' for her."

"Ent that always the way?"

They thought Mahara's attendants had abandoned her from sheer cravenness. Yala's throat ached with the pointless urge to scream. A waist-high pile of wooden boxes mostly sheltered her from view, but also blocked any warmth the new fire spread in her direction. Dirty straw and dead rushes underfoot, a floor of packed earth, no windows—of course not, this was a cellar. The smoke caressed a low ceiling blackened from previous fires and rose for a doorway at the top of shallow stone steps, their centers worn down by many passing feet. Did it lead to the street, or one of the small, hideously crooked alleys?

The *yue* was to defend her honor. Could she perhaps use it to saw through her bonds and creep stealthily to the end of the boxes? From there... three men to run past, or to use the stinging, slicing blade upon. It was different than a sudden attack in a darkened garden. This would require coldly, calmly using the *yue* to tear at their throats.

And what if she was overpowered? What might they do then?

That is not the question, Yala. The question is, who would want your princess taken in such a manner? Were there those in Zhaon who wished further war with Khir? Was this simply to embarrass the Crown Prince by staining his foreign wife? A noble Zhaon family who thought one of its daughters was a better match for the Crown Prince? An attempt at extortion? Each possibility made her aching head spin more than the last.

Most troubling of all, of course, was how they had known where to set their trap. Had her visits to the Yaol been watched? Or had one of the Crown Prince's household let drop an inadvisable word—or, worse, a treasonous one?

Shivers gripped her in waves. Perhaps she would expire of chill in this filthy little corner. Once Mahara appeared at the banquet, whoever had planned this would likely realize their error, and Yala would become expendable.

No, a frontal attack was not the best use of her *yue*. Yala lifted her head a little more and began shifting cautiously upon the straw, edging further into shadow.

A bubbling noise, a sudden aroma. Her captors were making tea.

"Mebbe she wants some."

"Mebbe you should shut your face."

"She ent pretty. I heard the girl was pretty."

"You ent pretty either after a dip in the street."

"Some rain, eh? Bad omen."

"Good omen, for us. Means we got away."

"G'on now."

"I ent no priest, but I can tell a bad sign."

Hideous, misshapen laughter. Yala squeezed her eyes shut, shifting some more. Stealthy, silent movement, an increment at a time.

The *yue* was meant for confined spaces, and for defense. She could draw it carefully from its sheath if she could move a few layers of silk, then saw through the bindings at her wrists and ankles. When they came for her, she would be prepared, a viper lying in wait for an unwary, bare ankle.

If they overpowered her, well, there was a remedy to keep her honor. Heaven seemed determined to grant her a chance to find out if she was worthy enough of the Komor name to open her own throat.

The heavy, nasty drumming of rain began to recede and her stomach growled. She told it to be quiet, braced her knee against the stone wall to her left, and strained.

Her fingers slid through silk, searching, and finally the tip of her right second finger touched warm metal against her left thigh. She let out a silent sob of relief, her mouth contorting. Sweat dripped stinging into her eyes, yet the shivers would not stop. Her teeth clenched so they did not chatter, and she listened to smacking lips and desultory talk, three men deciding how they would spend the silver they would earn from handing her to a shadowy Big Man.

Slowly, with infinite care in the odorous darkness, Yala kept at her work.

Trapped at a Feast

It was a great success. The great banquet hall was hung with brushwork characters upon flowing fabric, each as tall as a man, *joy* and *home* and *Heaven* in reddish-brown ink. The Emperor's table groaned under delicacies, mounds of snowy polished rai and small finger-bowls with crushflower petals floating to dip the fingers between each course. Each pair of eating-sticks was carved with the name and rank of its user, and Mahara's were rubbed with crimson. Each toast lifted had its ending-sting dedicated to her, and she had to smile and duck her head shyly each time, letting the gold beads from her hairpin chime sweetly in decorous thanksgiving.

She had to perch upon a soft pillow, her knees numb and her throat dry, and take a mannerly, infinitesimal sip of sohju whenever the Emperor or one of the queens raised their own cups—mellow burnished silver, in the Emperor's case, or fine polished gold thimbles in the queens'—in her direction. Second Queen Haesara did so thrice, smiling each time; First Queen Gamwone, perfunctorily, once.

The Emperor showed special favor to his first daughter-in-law, raising his cup thrice as well. A shout went through the banquet each time, implements and fists tapping the tables, and the Emperor was heard to remark that soon, Heaven willing, he should be a grandfather.

Wonders were dragged from the steaming hells of the kitchen, the Head Cook bellowing at his flushed, almost-naked underlings. Small disasters were covered up, sauces saved at the last moment, inauspicious bits trimmed away, platters arranged; kaburei chopped and sliced, feeding the fires, scrubbing cooking-surfaces free of splatter and crust, plunging dishes into water and scrubbing with handbrooms and wrinkled, aching fingers.

"Do not be afraid," Takyeo kept saying, leaning close as the court beamed at this example of a solicitous young husband, perhaps tempting his new bride to taste an unfamiliar dish. He laid strips of basted tahnu[52] from his own bowl upon her polished rai. "Takshin will do what is necessary."

If he believed it, she could not tell. She was trapped at a feast, her stomach a mass of writhing and her throat too dry to accept much of what she put in her mouth. She chewed each bite thoroughly, dutifully, bland Zhaon food without the heat of home.

Would she lose her taste for spiced su-hua, or high mountain tea? They did not have mu-erh here, the milk thickened by days in a gut-bag attached to a saddle. Nor did they have the long thin peppers each house scraped the seeds from all winter to plant in a kitchen garden's rich furrows, the most sheltered, sunny corner gathering heat all through torrid summer to explode with flavor in the bleak months.

Yala should have been at Mahara's side, refilling her glass and making small observations that tormented both of their faces with the effort to keep from laughing. She should have helped Mahara dress, fussing over the waistband, tucking the undersleeves correctly, clicking her tongue at the kaburei. Instead, Su Junha filled Mahara's cup too much each time and did not know how Mahara liked her fingercloth folded, or that she did not care for their shudua sweetmeats. Gonwa Eulin did her best behind Mahara, gesturing to the hurrying servants when lady or lord required or wished for aught.

The hollows under Mahara's arms were full of rank dampness.

---

52. Tender dark meat from a male eggfowl.

The banquet dragged on, and on. The small of her back was sodden. Su Junha had a fan, and fluttered ineffectually with it until Mahara was struck with the sudden vicious urge to slap her.

Yala would not have irritated her so.

But Yala was…who knew? Was she wandering the giant city, lost and at the mercy of passing men? Had those who wished to capture a princess been furious upon discovering their error? Or had they merely wanted to draw close enough to kill her without possibility of an arrow flying wide?

She did not know, and her head hurt. She accepted a toast from Second Prince Kurin, whose lips moved with something that made the Emperor's faint benevolent smile turn hard at the corners.

Takyeo affected not to notice, turning aside as if he had dropped a fingercloth or wished to arrange a fold of his banquet robes. Mahara blinked, staring into her rai-bowl. Beautiful whisper-thin Aulon ware, made by monks famous for their devotion to the goddess of the river cutting through the clay banks they used for their bowls, cups, and tiny statues of the Great Consort whose throne of silver-chased greenstone stood in the innermost chambers of Heaven itself. Her handmaidens came forth with the Great Edicts, those immutable laws that even the Emperor of Heaven could not alter, subtle and carved into time itself.

The Aulon river-goddess was held to be an emanation of the Consort, but some said she was instead an emanation of the Huntress, sister of the thunder-god, and sometimes their respective monks came to blows during arguments. The nuns, immured in their temples, were silent upon the matter.

Or if they were not, who would listen?

Yala would make an allusion to that. Yala would know what Mahara was thinking upon, and smile. The heat in the banquet hall, an oven-breeze fluttering the character-hangings but cooling no brow, turned the bright robes and laughing faces, the chewing jaws and the gleaming jewelry, into a scroll held under calm water, ink blurring and lifting from paper.

Oh, she understood very well they could not acknowledge the

attempt on her life or worse, her honor. Third Prince Takshin's absence caused little comment, but a few people remarked upon Zakkar Kai's. The Emperor seemingly took no notice, flushed and benevolent, gazing at his heir and the decorous foreign wife bought with bloodshed.

Who had to sit and chew like a cow, nodding and smiling with bovine good temper, while her stomach boiled and her throat was a scorching pinhole, while tears she could not allow to drop blurred the entire banquet hall. Su Junha exchanged nervous looks with Prince Takyeo, but neither remonstrated with her.

There was no need. Mahara understood, very well, that Yala was most likely dead or worse, and not all the glittering hairpins, greenstone hurai, mounds of food, or costly fabrics would bring her friend back.

Her *only* friend.

"Are you well?" Takyeo whispered, hiding the words with his sleeve and indicating a platter of roasted ruddy-breast birds, their skins crisp and golden with cooked honey and their tiny heads dipped in chu powder.

No. But she had to lie.

So Mahara lifted her chin and smiled, nodding a little. The banqueters beamed and cheered at her modesty.

Speaks a Strategist

The closet near the Left Market shared by Huo Banh and his shield-square was cleaner than Kai expected. He opened a cabinet affixed to the wall with thin laths and began searching, a clay lamp purchased from a weary street hawker and filled with numbing care lifted high enough to shed a small golden glow. Takshin had already torn the bed apart and was going through a pile of rags near the door, searching for anything likely to hold a clue.

The cupboard held shaving implements, a small leather bag with alloy bits in its throat—and, tucked in the very back corner, in a nest of cobwebs and scrap paper, the other half of the copper ingot, as well as a smaller curved humpback of silver.

"Ah," he murmured. So Huo had meant to return to this lair and collect his fee, after taking care of his sister's hidden dowry. A woman with half an ingot could leave a husband if he proved unsatisfactory, though few did. Staying alive once one had left one's station and place was a difficult proposition at best.

Still, Huo Banh had been a good brother, and would disappear so no treason attached itself to his family or his poor, about-to-be wedded sister.

"Kai. Bring the lamp." Takshin crouched, easy and leonine, near the rag-pile. Water ran from his sleeves and hair, his topknot smashed almost flat. He was now deadly pale, and his eyes held a gleam Kai had not often seen.

"I found his payment." Kai carefully extricated the ingots. "He intended to return, then."

"He is dead, I care little." Takshin's leashed calm was more deadly than any irritation. "Bring the *lamp*."

"Yes, oh impatient one." Kai's own half-armor was soaked, and stray hairs pushed loose by the downpour fell into his eyes. He swiped at his forehead, irritated.

Takshin made a short frustrated sound. "There is a lady waiting upon us, Zakkar Kai, and I have no mind to tarry."

Kai knew it very well, indeed. He *also* knew more haste would not necessarily grant them a quicker finding. "What have you there?"

"I will not know until you bring the fucking lamp, now will I?" The last few words were uttered in a tone that suggested the Third Prince was losing his hold upon his temper.

Kai wisely chose not to answer, negotiated the few steps over uneven wooden boards, and lowered the guttering flame.

A scrap of rai-paper made soft stealthy sounds as Takshin spread it out and studied the markings. The lamp steadied, shedding its ration of light.

"Ah." Kai pointed. "The Great Market. There is the Ta Kau Theater. And there, at the edge, where the stone stalls for the metalsmiths... that must be the ambush, marked."

"What idiots, to leave a map behind." Takshin sniffed, but his gaze was avid, devouring all brushstroke details.

"Pawns, Taktak." And the thin, very cheap rai-paper would vanish once the damp touched it. "Upon a board too big for them."

"And we are chariots." With greater latitude to move came greater risk, though. "We should play again soon, Kai. It's been years."

"Certainly not." Kai studied the markings, fixing them in memory. "I am aware that you cheat."

Takshin's grim laugh was unamused, a fox's sharp bark. "And you do not?"

"Oh, only so much as necessary. Look." Hasty brushstrokes like eggbirds scrabbling in a courtyard, careful dots, and another location marked with a shaky character—*rest,* with its sinuous indication of tangled blankets, at the west end of the Great Market's uneven triangular protrusion, where the Great Fire of the Third Dynasty had scraped out the heart of the old city. The palace-liver, the seat of Zhaon's courage, had been left scarred but mostly intact, a tree standing after the scythe passed through fields all around it. "And there, and there."

Kai's damp fingers traced the markings. The third location was at the other edge of the Left Market, where the Spine Road poured from the South Gate and emptied into the Yuin like a river to a swamp—within the very same area that the imperfect trail left in the clothing of the latest assassin, the one Takyeo had slain in his own bedroom, had gone cold. "That is where they will meet their master," he said.

"So here is where they were to regroup, or pass the night?" Takshin's jaw was a piece of iron. "Amused with themselves, no doubt."

Or amusing themselves. Kai's hands ached for his swordhilt, and the rest of him was not far behind. *Yala. Simply stay alive, we shall handle the rest.* "Let us be on our way, then."

"Should we separate?" Takshin obviously did not think much of the idea, but he had to ask. "One to find Lady Yala, the other to find the author of this misery?"

No. Everything in him rebelled at the thought. Kai shook his head. "An attempt this well planned, with enough time and funds to seduce a Golden? I think it likely there are more blades waiting, and to split our forces would be folly."

"There speaks a strategist." Takshin smiled and refolded the map after a last long glance. He straightened, and the lampflame's dancing made shadows bend and waver as well. "You think we should find the head of this snake first, I presume?"

They should. Their duty to the Emperor and to Takyeo demanded it. Zakkar Kai struggled for a brief moment. "I think we should find Lady Yala. If she vanishes outright, there will be much gossip. *Then* we may cut the head from the snake. Besides, this artist is not likely to view what he has wrought until the appointed time."

The Third Prince looked up, studying Zakkar Kai in the uncertain lamplight for a few fractions of a moment too long. Kai's secret was no doubt blazoned upon his face, and there would be no end of teasing if Takshin caught it.

If he did, though, Kai would bear any jibe with good grace, for it would mean Yala was by some miracle whole and well—perhaps a little bruised, perhaps insulted, but not outraged.

And not dead.

Zakkar Kai was neither priest nor monk able to petition Heaven. His ancestors were silent, for their tablet held only a guess at their names. If there was a miracle of rescue to be wrought here, it rested upon him and Takshin alone.

"As you like." Takshin straightened, and that deep, chilling, familiar gleam intensified in his gaze. "Come, let us away to the Great Market, to see what we may find."

Pool of Deep Ink

Her teeth chattered unless she clenched them, and then her head ached so badly she imagined her *yue* had been forced through her skull. That was ridiculous, though, because it was in her hand, and she was propped against cold stone, her breath deep and slow despite the shivering that scraped her damp shoulders against the unforgiving wall.

They were asleep, or close to it. She had crept to the very end of the boxes and peered at them, three men huddled around a dying fire, the archer propped against a mound of rags with his mouth open, showing donjba-blackened teeth as his eyelids fluttered. The thick-legged man, his back to her, stretched out on a pallet that looked none too fresh, but her bones ached at the thought of rest, no matter how filthy and stinking the rough brownish pad might be.

She longed for a hot bath. Unscented, silky water cradling her, heat tingling fiercely in her numb fingertips.

The masked man had laid aside his cloth, revealing a round, pockmarked peasant face. He stared into the fire, poking at it idly when embers seemed in danger of dying. She had thought him asleep and gathered herself, but then he opened his eyes, shoveling more dung-pats onto the fire and adding a few sticks of scavenged wood. His eyes were puffy, and their dark irises gleamed.

Kaburei eyes, shifty and secretive. Not like a Khir noble's clear, light gaze.

Had her princess reached safety? Or was Yala still alive because nobody knew where Mahara was? The city would be a roiling hive if the Crown Princess was missing upon a royal banquet night, but Yala was a straw in a bale; who would think to look for her here?

She mattered little. If only she could be certain her princess was safe.

The leader's head nodded. He was on watch, but it had been an exacting day, and his chin dropped to his chest. Yala sought to peel herself from the wall's support and managed to rise, shakily, her legs protesting. Her market-shoes were wet clear through and faint threads of steam rose from her hands as she worked them to bring the warmth back, opening and closing, stretching her fingers, her eyes rolling and mouth opening a little as Ka-Ha-Nua, that vengeful fairy responsible for keeping the humors flowing in each limb, went about her work with ill grace.

She kept to the deep shadows, her *yue* held below her slipping sash, hidden in her torn skirt. The leader was across the fire; its glow would keep her hidden.

Or so she hoped.

She studied the three men, blinking furiously as her vision blurred. Her hair was heavy and still rain-wet, twisted low upon her nape and secured with Mahara's pin, its dangling glitter wrapped away so it would not betray her. She gauged the distance to the stairs, the depths of shadow outside uncertain rubescent glow. Her pupils expanded, and she carefully did not stare at the fire, turning her head slightly to preserve her night-eyes. The boxes were stacked perhaps to her shoulder, and she swam within a pool of deep ink.

She could, perhaps, move excruciatingly slowly over straw that might crackle or shift at the slightest provocation, and try to gain the stairs. If they lunged for her, then, they would be sleep-mazed, and the *yue* could bite them.

Yala braced herself. Once she reached the top of the stairs—oh, they looked very long, a sharp slope for a weary pair of legs—she would be faced with the problem of a city. An alley, perhaps, filthy and piled with refuse, or—

A soft, sliding sound struck her straining ears. Yala froze. The shivers made it difficult to think; she glared at the stairs and their promise of freedom, smoke drifting uneasily into a night probably much warmer than this dank hole. The weeping wall at her back was no friend, probably exhaling summerplague into her bones. Would she swell with the boils and cough up blood?

Worry about that later, Yala. It was enough that she was freed of her bonds and carrying her *yue*.

Another soft sound. Yala tilted her head. Was it the structure overhead speaking in its dreams like the thick-legged man, murmuring restlessly? Or something else, a product of her fevered imagination?

No, for it came again, and there was a flicker amid the smoke in the low stone doorway.

Yala inhaled sharply. The movement paused. Whoever it was wore black, a blot against the shadows, and her heart pounded so hard her hair threatened to shake itself free and go riding the night winds, a sucking ghost ready to strangle children.

Strange, how the tales told to frighten a small, helpless child returned. Yala's shoulder hit the wall as the figure slipped down the stairs, booted feet moving with soft assurance, not a sound from leather or fabric, its topknot in a dark, sober cage…

…and a gleam of gold at its left ear.

Behind Third Prince Takshin came another shadow, this one slightly taller, his dark-ringed eyes glittering almost as feverishly as Yala's own.

She sagged against the wall, her legs gone soft as hot-pounded rai with relief, and Third Prince Takshin took the last few stairs in a rush, gathering speed. His sword gleamed, its blade making a low sweet sound as it clove rising smoke, and the first blow splashed blood in a high rising arc.

The leader, free of his mask, died with a horrid gurgle.

Yala let out a soft, sipping breath. It all seemed very far away, shadow-figures moving upon a painted screen. The thick-legged man surged upright; Zakkar Kai cuffed him back onto his thin pallet. Takshin kicked the fire and coals sprayed over the archer, who had reached for his bow with the speed of a man accustomed to rough awakenings.

He did not have the chance to draw, for a solid silver semicircle cut seasoned, recurved wood and resin with a slight brittle sound of a bone snapping. The slightly curved Shan blade was quick, and shook the pockmarked leader's blood free of its shining as it clove hissing air.

"Don't kill him," Zakkar Kai called, the greenstone dragon on his swordhilt snarling atop his back. He kicked the thick-legged man, gauging the force merely to stun instead of truly damage. Yala's own cry was a wounded bird's; she slid down the wall and landed with a thump upon her sodden skirts. It was not that she minded the filthy peasant getting a boot to the belly. Rather, the tension of her achingly silent progress snapped, and the release forced a noise through her dry, cracking lips. "Yala, Lady Yala. It's Zakkar Kai and Prince Takshin, you are safe."

Nowhere is safe. She gathered her wits and coughed. Her *yue* slipped against slick palms, but Prince Takshin had the archer at swordpoint against the opposite wall, his back turned.

"And *stay* there, like a good cur." The Third Prince sounded soft, reflective. "Kai, is that indeed Lady Komor?"

"It appears to be," the general said, calmly enough. "*Don't* get up, fatherless dog." That last was directed at the thick-legged man, who curled about his violated belly, whimpering. "Lady Komor, simply stay where you are. All is well."

Her throat would not work. She simply sagged there, amid the dirty straw, and shut her eyes.

In short order the two traitors were trussed and their fire built into a respectable blaze licking broken wooden boxes, fresh smoke billowing for the stairs. Zakkar Kai drew Yala to warmth and light.

He examined her face while she blinked back swimming tears. "My princess," she whispered, and realized she had spoken in Khir. She found the words in Zhaon, with a harsh internal effort. "My princess, General? Tell me my princess is well."

He studied her wrists, stripped of the awful bindings. "Takshin? They tied her wrists; she's bleeding."

"Princess Mahara is well, and attending the banquet." Prince Takshin's lip curled, a silent snarl, the scar twitching madly. "Did they...?"

She realized what he was asking when Zakkar Kai's face changed. Yala shook her head.

"They did not... outrage me." Her mouth was dry as a just-fired bowl. "They thought I was Mahara. They were waiting to take me to another man. The Big Man, they called him." There was more to tell, but her head ached so dreadfully.

"A well-thrown lure." Prince Takshin settled his sheathed sword upon his back. The dragon-hilt over Zakkar Kai's shoulder watched them all, its cheeks bunched with a snarl very much like the Third Prince's. "How badly is she hurt?"

"My wrists..." Yala peered at them. She hadn't even noticed the cord wearing through her skin. No wonder her *yue* had been slippery. "I do not know."

Zakkar Kai moved each of her fingers in turn, his calluses rasping against her dirty, blood-slick skin. She flinched once or twice, more from a strange man's proximity than the pain of numbed appendages regaining vital fluid. Her *yue* was a reassuring weight against her right thigh again, and he had not remarked upon it. Perhaps he had not even noticed. "You shall play the sathron again, Lady Yala. Never fear."

I doubt my playing will be improved, however. It was a sane thought, an amusing one, and it bolstered her. "Yes, but shall I dance? They tied my ankles too."

"Are you—" He bent as if to look, his hand twitching at her skirt, but Yala backed away, two quick stumbling steps. Her hip hit a wooden crate, and she swayed. "Easy, my lady. All is well."

"I think I should return to the Jonwa." She sounded very young, as if she had been embarrassed at a feast or a gathering and wished to flee. "My princess..." They said she was well. Attending the banquet. Relief filled her much as her humors filled her tingling fingers, and her head grew light. Zakkar Kai caught her arm as she swayed again, his hand warm and oddly gentle.

"Take her back, General." Prince Takshin glanced at her, and his scarred cheek twitched once, twice. Or perhaps it was the leaping firelight. "She will not wish to see this."

The general braced her, an efficient, impersonal movement. "Perhaps we should bring one of these curs to the palace. Zan Fein will—"

"No, Kai. You've done your work, run along." Prince Takshin turned back to the archer, who lay on his side, gagged with a piece of cord. "Put the lady to bed, she is out well past the gong."

"I am not a child." Yala's voice was a husk. She had no wish to stay and see what transpired, but must he sound so...chiding, almost? As if she had *meant* to be carried away by a pair of filthy miscreants.

"You are not, Lady Komor. We are simply relieved at finding you unharmed." Zakkar Kai did not seem to take offense. "Takshin, are you certain you do not wish—"

"I know exactly what I wish," the Third Prince said coldly. "Take the little lure home and put her back in the cabinet, my friend; leave this to me. I will have answers, I care little how I extract them, and I would not have my lady see this."

With the matter put in such a fashion, Yala did not wish to remain. "Yes," she murmured. "Take me from here, Zakkar Kai."

"As you like, Taktak." The general's grasp softened further. He offered his arm, and she experimented with a few unsteady steps, clinging to him. Relief filled her head like stolen sips of sohju, and she swayed. "Slowly, slowly."

"Carry her up the stairs, grandson." It was a phrase from an old drinking song common in both lands, and Takshin's hand dropped to his belt. He drew free a Shan knife, curved like the crescent moon. A flawed ruby glittered in its hilt. "I shall visit you in a short while, Lady Yala." Faintly informal, his inflection was nevertheless sharp as her own *yue*. "Try not to be taken captive again in the meantime."

Irritation cleared her head and strengthened her knees. "I shall do my best, *Third Prince*."

"Come along." Zakkar Kai drew her up the stairs and out through a pall of smoke into a rain-freshened, steaming night.

Be Brief

The storm had sunk into dripping steam-heat, the Jonwa's heavy quiet enfolded both Crown Prince and Princess, Takyeo waved servants aside as they traversed the halls. He suspected Mahara's composure would not hold much longer, and when they gained his chambers he shut the door almost in the attendants' faces.

He slid his shoulders free of heavy, stiff-embroidered banquet-robe and sighed. His wife, her plump soft hands shaking, drew thick material away with admirable efficiency. The small shield covering her left smallest finger clicked against a button of gold-edged horn.

"You did well," Takyeo repeated, louder since there were no banqueters or servants to hear. "The servants may attend to me in a few moments, Mahara. I merely wished to give you a few moments to gather yourself."

"It is my honor." She set her chin, her large, pale eyes glimmering in lamplight. She had not broken, nor had she wept, but those eyes brimmed with salt water. "It is a beautiful robe, too. Do you think they will find her?"

"Takshin is...effective." And thank the gods Zakkar Kai had gone with him; the general was a moderating influence. Taktak might strike before wringing information from a traitor, but Kai was possessed of cooler humors. "If there is a sliver of hope, they will work a miracle."

His wife bit at her soft lower lip as she arranged his banquet-robe upon the gilded stand. The brazier underneath was dead and dark now, its purpose fulfilled until the next robe was readied. "I should not have let her take my cloak."

"You did what you must." He rubbed at his temples, massaging the persistent ache. "Let me loosen your robe, too."

A wan smile was his reward. She settled his robe more firmly, a coil of freshening incense ready in the brass bowl underneath. "I wish to retire, my husband. But first, let me—"

A soft knock at the dressing-room door brought her around in a tight circle, her robe's heavy scarlet-and-silver skirt flaring. "Enter," Takyeo said, and Steward Keh glided in catfoot. Takyeo had to stoop so the man could attempt whispering his news, and let out a long breath when Keh finished, steeling himself. *Ah.* "Take him to my study."

When the door closed, he faced Mahara, who clasped her soft, pretty hands. "Is it..." She swallowed, hard, and a tear tracked down her soft cheek.

She had borne herself with admirable grace, this warrior princess of Khir.

"Zakkar Kai has returned." Takyeo only hoped he had some measure of good news. "I will see him in my study, and—"

Mahara's ear-drops swung as she shook her head. Her elaborate braids were still in place, and though her eyes were ringed with weariness she was still wanly beautiful. "May I go with you? To hear what... if... if Yala..."

"Are you certain you wish to?" He should protect her, keep her from hoping for too much. "It is after the third watch; you must rest."

"I can have no rest until I know if she is well. Or dead." Her chin set, and a quite unwonted flicker was in her pale gaze. She was, after all, the same woman with the presence of mind to lunge for a paring-knife to face an assassin with. The Khir kept their women in bowers and kitchens, probably so they did not take matters into their own hands and rule.

She was a surprise, this woman. A rare, pleasant surprise, and

Takyeo's chest ached for what she would have to endure. Heaven was kind; if he was to take his father's burden, at least she would not be a Yulehi Gamwone, more dangerous as ally than enemy.

But Heaven's kindness did not extend very far; he had proof of that fact his entire life. He would have to do what he could to cover the celestial lack, and shield his wife from as much as he could.

"Very well," he said. "Come. We will be brief."

Loose Ends

The dawn watch was cried from the walls of Zhao-An; grey turned to stinging, throbbing red in the east and the night retreating into corners, drains, underhangs. Mist rose from wet stone and tiled roof.

The Shining Moon teahouse, its doors wide open but the criers squatting upon the step instead of hurrying patrons inside, was full of subtle noise. Merchants ready for the East Road stretched and yawned, drinking strong sweet hukai[53] to balance their humors for the day; mercenaries ready to accompany them and fight off bandits tossed dice without any real enthusiasm, probably still tasting sohju from the night before. Heavily veiled courtesans settled in a quiet corner behind a screen, steam rising through thin fine masking-fabric as they held their cups under its long flow, the gilt upon their hairpins glittering. A few rich men, soused from the Left Market's sinks or fending off hangovers, ordered pickled eggfruit and strong, unripe unlau, said to be a cure for the dragon of constipation nipping at an overindulger's temples and eyes.

Among them, a man in sober brown—neither merchant nor noble, but not a beggar either, safely anonymous—sipped bitter khiralau morning-tea. He was expecting a trio bearing a gift, since

---

53. Heavily sweetened laborer's tea with crushed rai stirred in, often taken with raw eggs.

the masked idiot had been under strict orders to relieve Huo Banh of the burden of breathing as soon as possible.

A man who had betrayed once would do so again, and it made sense to tidy up loose ends. The rest could be basket-woven in due time.

What the impresario did not expect, as he sat at the teahouse's balcony overlooking the crowded street, was a lean panther-stepping noble in Shan costume of unrelieved black, threading through the thin morning crowd and heading straight for the most flea-bitten of the East Road hostels at the edge of the Yuin's seethe.

The impresario noted the way the crowd parted for the walker, and also the wrapped swordhilt riding the walker's back. A gleam upon the left hand was perhaps a seal or signet; it would keep him from being accosted too directly.

The impresario tensed, watching as this strange visitor did not hesitate but plunged directly through the knot of gamblers in their preening finery clustered before a low black door. They did not challenge him, those loud, burly brawlers, but rather averted their gazes and laughed, uneasily.

Interesting.

Some time later, the man in Shan black left the nameless inn, his scarred jaw set and his eyes burning coals. By that time, the Shining Moon was full of morning custom and several merchants had already left with their retinues of bawling beast and heavy wagon, mercenaries upon apathetic nags or sturdy ponies riding to meet with the caravans in a wide pounded dusty fairground outside the East Gate, which cracked at dawn and not a moment before.

By then, though, the impresario had left alloy slivers to pay for his tea and vanished into Zhaon-An. He had another bow to retrieve, a Khir nobleman to visit with ill news, and other plans to attend to.

Much Disturbance

A bright clear morning stooped over the palace, the sun a swift circling thing searching for any weakness or movement below. "And you are quite certain?" Garan Tamuron said, shifting a little upon his dressing-stool's embroidered pillow. With only a thin silken robe covering his torso and lap, the heat was almost bearable. The itching and irritation was not very bad today, and his gaze was brighter. Perhaps soaks in tepid water full of gently stirred rai flour were working to soothe the angry skin, though they made the Emperor feel somewhat like a leftover dumpling.

"It was very clear." By the look of his topknot and the reddening of his eyelids, Third Prince Takshin had not yet slept. His boots held city-dust, and his glower was that of a caged beast through bars, exhausted but unwilling to surrender. "A man with a Wurei accent orchestrated this attempt."

Zakkar Kai, his arms folded, stared at a hanging scroll. The calligraphy upon it was an exhortation to magnanimity in victory and courage in defeat, and had hung in Tamuron's tent during every campaign since Shiera had presented it to him so many years ago. Now it was accorded pride of place in the Emperor's dressing-room, where he could view it every morning.

It was not a replacement. Nothing was. Still, the characters brushed by a dead woman were...comforting. There was little comfort to be found anywhere else. Zakkar Kai's countenance was one of deep thought, and the faint line between his eyebrows was not an encouraging sign.

When Kai looked this sullenly thoughtful, it was best to beware, for he had seen more problems looming than were immediately apparent. Garan Tamuron absorbed the news. "So, that is why you did not attend the banquet."

"I am hardly likely to be missed, and I needed Kai." *Push me further*, Takshin's shoulders said. *Go on. See what happens.* The mixture of arrogance and exhaustion was an explosive one; he had always been prickly, even as a child.

It was probably a mercy that Gamwone had not raised him. A Kurin with Takshin's temper would be almost unmanageable. On the other hand, the whispers of what the Third Prince had suffered from the Mad Queen were...disturbing, and Takshin's scars doubly so.

The boy did not answer when his father tried to indirectly inquire how he had received them, simply stared with that same mute, dull, furious resignation. By the time Tamuron had guessed where the damage lay it was too late to curb a restive youth's spirit. Takshin did not take to bit or bridle; spurs would only madden him, like the prong-headed beasts the god of mountain storms was said to ride.

"Quick thinking." Tamuron touched the heavy greenstone hurai upon his left first finger. The matching one on his right glinted, its edges cased with beaten silver. They did not leave his hands during sleeping, bathing, or squatting over a waste-catcher. "A palace guard suborned, arrows from the rooftop...why were those responsible not brought to the palace? Zan Fein will be sad to miss the chance to practice his art."

"Certainly I could have called the Market Guard or a brace of carters to haul the miscreants to the palace. I could have driven them right through the front gates with a whip, too. Which would have negated the benefit silence will gain us in this matter."

Takshin rolled his shoulders, only missing a dismissive shrug by a few fingerwidths.

Takyeo was a statue near the door, his arms folded like Zakkar Kai's and the echo of his mother in his features almost unbearable to gaze upon this morning. "Takshin," he murmured. "Enough."

Amazingly, the Third Prince subsided somewhat. "And yes, I am certain." His hands relaxed, his own hurai glinting. The characters of his name were spiked, too, despite their auspicious meaning. "A man with a thick Wurei accent; the landlady was quite clear upon that point."

"Those hired for dark deeds may come from any corner of Zhaon, and Wurei was lost long ago." Zakkar Kai's expression made sense, now. His head-meat, ever agile, did not like a cup it could not peer under, and the clan of his adoptive-mother was ash upon a cold wind. At least they could rule out any involvement of Kanbina's in this affair. "Without questioning this fellow, we cannot be sure. Would the Khir attempt a rescue from captivity, then?"

"Perhaps." Or a princess's outraged body would have been left in a public place to garner maximum effect and rid Khir of encumbrance. The first wains of tribute from the north were late, too. The country had been bled for the last five years, trade with every point south choked. Of course, they could—and did—trade with Ch'han, but bringing goods step by step through the northern wastes at the fringes of the Yaluin was difficult and dangerous. There were closer problems at hand than a missing wagon or two, though. "This Lady Komor. Are you certain of her innocence?"

"Yes," Takshin said, a little too quickly, and a little too loudly.

Tamuron studied his most difficult son, who returned his searching look with a lift of his stubborn chin and a banked fire in his dark eyes. Was he partial to this Khir girl? Wondrous times afoot, if he was.

He turned his gaze to Takyeo. "And you, my heir? She is of your household."

"Lady Komor is of the highest integrity." Takyeo's chin did not settle stubbornly to match his brother's, but it was close. He touched his hurai with a fingertip, to witness the truth of the statement. "She has been nothing but loyal to her princess's new household, and was cruelly treated for her bravery."

"Changing cloaks. It's like a novel." Which brought him to Sabwone. She had not even reached the Shan border yet, and was doing her best with daily letters to drive the court into a froth. If she was not sending thinly veiled hints of suicide to her uncle, she was bemoaning the barbarity of travel to her mother, and Heaven alone knew what she was sending to Jin, who stood behind Zakkar Kai as if seeking shelter from a cold wind. The boy's eyes were round, and his green morning-robe held Luswone's careful stitching at collar and cuffs.

Gamnae was old enough to be married, too. Negotiations with Khir upon that front were... unsatisfying. They had already given a princess; they did not wish to sacrifice a prince to matrimonial allegiance, even King Ashani Zlorih's byblow. A princess from Ch'han or even a high-ranking noble Shan girl sent to Khir was a thing to be avoided. Applying more pressure along the trade routes might work, or induce Khir to find other relief than sealing themselves to their richer southron neighbor.

Had they intended to bring their princess back, or simply to slide free of Zhaon's yoke? An outraged Khir princess was a powerful rallying point, and would give Kiron of Shan much leverage in negotiations too. Shan could very well refuse to accede to prohibitive trade measures against Khir in that eventuality, and Sabwone was not likely to be of any help.

It was a troubling development indeed. Tamuron sighed. It did not help that all was smoothed over, the Khir girlservant retrieved whole and presumably undamaged. "Keep the Khir lady out of sight for some little while."

"She is pleading an illness." Takyeo paused. "My wife is thankful for her safe return."

You must not trust a woman's gratitude, my son. "We should consider a second wife for you, Crown Prince."

"I am content, Father." Takyeo's cheeks did not pinken. Instead, his eldest regarded him narrowly. Almost—a ridiculous thought—as if insulted by the notion.

"As you like. Women are trouble, and a foreign one doubly so. Since you speak for this Komor girl, I shall not have her taken to Zan Fein to judge her involvement—"

"Father." Jin's eyes were round. "You wouldn't. They couldn't have planned to meet me in the Market, it isn't possible."

"*Possible* is one thing," Kai weighed in hurriedly. His hurai bore traces of mud from the night's searching, and his half-armor was still sodden. "Probable is another, yet just as unlikely."

"She finds many defenders, this foreign woman." Tamuron longed to scratch at his ribs, but such a gesture was unroyal. He sat, stiff-backed, and waved one hand. "Very well. That was deftly handled, Third Son. You have my gratitude."

"The Emperor is magnanimous." Takshin's tone could have been flat exhaustion or sharp sarcasm; it was difficult to tell. The leather wrapping of his Shan swordhilt was damp, too. His eyes half-lidded, his expression shutting like a heavy palace door. "If more surfaces in this matter, rest assured I will deal with it just as thoroughly."

"Mh." It disturbed Tamuron some little to think a son of his would share Zan Fein's... artistic tastes. All very well for a stoneless underling to take pleasure in his work, but a prince was another matter entirely.

They must do what was necessary, yes. But enjoying it was not to be encouraged.

"I think Takshin must rest." Takyeo, diplomatic as ever. At least he had gained some rest; the shadows under his eyes were not as dark. "And Zakkar Kai, too. No doubt Jin passed a restless night as well."

"I couldn't sleep for worrying." Jin's bottom lip pushed out slightly before he recollected himself. "I shouldn't have left her there. Is she really all right?"

"She was the last two times you asked," Takshin snapped.

"You did the right thing." Now it was Kai's turn to be diplomatic. "Lady Komor was right in telling you to guard the Crown Princess."

"It doesn't *feel* right," the boy grumbled.

So, Jin liked this foreign woman, she had Kai's approval, and she further had Takshin's protection. What witchery could a single foreign girl have, to accomplish such a thing? As usual, being silent taught Tamuron more about his sons than questioning. Keeping your beard-hole closed was a virtue much lauded in the Hundreds.

Unfortunately, like much else, it was only of limited use when your skin prickled with heat, irritation, and suppuration. It was not bad today, but he was already exhausted, and the morning's council meeting was likely to be interminable *and* useless. "Go and rest, Takshin. And you too, Jin. Do not speak upon this further, even among yourselves. There are ears everywhere in the palace."

"And scorpions too," Takshin muttered, but he bowed with admirable grace. "Come, Jin. Walk me to Takyeo's door."

"I'd be glad to." A hurried bow, and the pair left.

"I don't suppose I may be excused from council." Zakkar Kai stretched, a long lithe motion. Takyeo merely gazed at the floor, deep in thought.

"If I must suffer, so must you, my general. But you may have a hot bath first. In fact, I'd recommend it." Tamuron brooded for some short while. "Tell me truly, is there a chance this Lady Komor was part of the plot?"

Kai shook his head. "Neither possible nor probable."

Tamuron changed his direction. "What were they about in the market, anyway? Are there not baubles enough in the Artisans' Home?"

"Lady Komor was the Crown Princess's agent in commissioning a gift for her royal husband." Kai scratched at his cheek. "The Crown Princess decided that morning to view the progress upon that commission. The traitors were waiting for such an event."

"I thought Khir women did not leave the home." Tamuron sighed afresh. At least the Zhaon treated women with some respect. Gamwone could have used a dose of female Khir docility. "Something about this smells worse than the middens after battle."

"That it does." Takyeo folded his hands inside his sleeves. His air of almost-detachment was new, and his performance all through the banquet had been exemplary.

Disturbingly so. Even Tamuron had not guessed something was amiss, though he took pains not to bring attention to *that*.

"There is obviously a traitor in my household," his eldest son continued, musingly. "It is good Takshin is with us; he will be another pair of eyes to ferret that black spot out."

"Hrm." Beaten to the dice-throw, Tamuron tried not to feel even more irritated. His fingers longed to be moving, his ribs itched furiously, and he was already sweating. "Yes, indeed. Well played, the lot of you. Now leave me in peace, I would think upon this before Council."

Their bows were respectful, and once they were gone he could slip a hand inside his own morning-robe and rub at his ribs. Dho Anha trimmed his nails almost to the quick, gently scolding him for tearing at his own flesh, and it irked him.

Everything did. The Emperor of Zhaon sat, scratched like a common beggar, and brooded upon this latest indignity.

A Festival Dress

The rai-paper screen enfolding Lady Komor's bed was thin, but the princess obviously longed to push it wide.

"She must rest," Anh whispered, hoping she was not being too forward. "Her wrists are cut; they tied her like an eggfowl for travel."

"At least they did not hang her upside down." The Crown Princess's lovely round face was remote as the Moon Maiden's. Her hair and robe were very simple today; clearly, she did not plan upon leaving the Jonwa or even receiving visitors. "Or at least, I hope not."

"It does not seem so," Anh agreed, anxiously. Her entire body ached from the slipping, sliding, terrifying confusion yesterday, added to tossing and turning upon her mat before her lady was returned by Zakkar Kai. And in such awful condition—bedraggled, pale, with bleeding wrists. "Shall I look again, and—"

"Anh?" Yala's cracked, tiny whisper tiptoed from behind the partition. "Is that my princess?"

"'Tis indeed." The Crown Princess brushed past Anh, her fingers resting for a moment, a weightless touch upon the kaburei's shoulder. Anh tried not to lean into the motion—good luck flowed from those of higher rank—and peered around the edge of the screen.

Her mistress was a grand lady even though foreign, and Anh was all but bursting with the drama of events. The strict enjoinders to silence from the Crown Prince himself were barely enough to keep her contained, but she was able to hint darkly that Lady

Komor had suffered a severe shock and required much nursing. Running to and fro from the kitchens, bringing small things to tempt an invalid, carrying Lady Komor's pretty torn dress to the laundry and washing it herself despite the fact that she was of *much* higher quality than the water-rats kept her busy, in any case, and filled her with luminous sparkstick importance.

A great lady gave honor to those who served well.

The Crown Princess knelt at the edge of Princess Yala's bed. She said something soft and low in their funny, sharp-edged tongue, and Yala replied. The princess stroked her lady's forehead, softly, and held one of Yala's poor hands. Her wrists weren't cut as a suicide-ghoul's, but the skin had been worn bloody-raw by some cruel binding; Anh had solicitously dabbed herbal pastes Zakkar Kai himself had brought from his pet physician, the one with the shabby robes and sharp tongue, against the wounds. Lady Komor's ankles bore marks too, though not deep ones, and Anh had worked fine dry rai powder scented with sweetspice and berrypalm through her hair, combing the mixture free along with traces of mud and rainwater. It was not quite as good as a bath, but until her lady was ready for one, she would be as clean as possible.

The Crown Princess kept speaking, soft and fast. Was she weeping? It sounded like it. Anh kept peering into her lady's room, mirrorlight banished so a noblewoman could rest. A single small, exquisite clay lamp, heavily shielded, glittered upon the table where her lady wrote letter after letter, the slight sound of her brush loud in the silence.

Everyone had been so worried that the Khir would be barbarians, and cruel as well. Instead, the Crown Princess was a beautiful, amiable creature, and Lady Yala... well, she was quick and graceful, and even if she lacked beauty she had some other quality Anh could not quite name but which filled her kaburei close-servant with distinct pride.

"All is well." Lady Yala's queer grey gaze glittered as she spoke in Zhaon. She was not feverish, though she looked it, heavy-lidded with flushed cheeks. "I am relieved you are safe."

"We will not leave the palace." The Crown Princess's Zhaon was accented, but much better. Still, she used the informal inflection with Lady Yala. Perhaps childhood friends could speak so in Khir, even among royalty.

What was it like to be so far from your home, among strangers with mouths full of different words? No family, the Crown Prince was supposed to be Princess Mahara's family now, and whatever children she had would be Zhaon. And would Lady Yala return home to marry?

If she did, would Anh become the stranger in a different country? Or would Lady Yala give her to the Crown Princess? It made Anh's poor tired head spin to think of it. She hadn't dared dream of being a great lady's maid, but Lady Kue had called her quick and docile, and so Lady Yala had smiled and nodded, accepting her.

It was the first time Anh had been *chosen*, really, and her liver and heart both swelled again with the memory. She'd been afraid, when summoned to stand in a line that morning, that she would be sent to serve elsewhere. It would not be so bad to be a bath attendant, or to run and fetch for the artisans in the Home. It would be horrid to become a water-rat, or to be sent to the stinking hot hell of the kitchens, even though you could eat what you willed there.

The worst luck was to be sent to the Kaeje. Or more specifically, to the First Queen's household. The stories from *there* were enough to turn your liver sideways. Even if the First Queen wasn't cruel, her chief lady was, and had a taste for both the whip *and* the sudo.

Anh listened to their funny language, salted with a few Zhaon words here and there, and wondered what they were saying now. It was probably beyond her anyway, like brushstrokes upon paper. *This one is another way of spelling your name, Anh. It means "beautiful child."*

She heard her own name; the Crown Princess beckoned her. "Come in," she said, kindly enough, and Anh, her legs leaden, obeyed. She hadn't told anyone, yet, but still, the secret burned like one of Heaven's constant fireflowers and she wondered how long she could hold out. Maybe Tanh the head clothespress maid, or Dho Gani, Lady Kue's chief maid, might be able to keep it to themselves. But Anh couldn't lower herself to speak to a clothes-press girl, and Dho Gani carried a long thin flexible sudo to snap at any kaburei or porter who did not hurry enough to suit her.

Anh settled at a safe distance and bowed, her forehead touching her folded hands upon the floor.

"Oh, come closer, and sit up." The Crown Princess's remote beauty did not alter. She did not sound displeased, merely a trifle impatient. "You are very brave, and very clever. My Yala says you deserve a reward, and I agree."

"Your Highness... your... my lady..." For a moment, Anh could not remember how to address such august personages. "I ask nothing. It is my duty."

"There must be something you would like." Lady Yala, propped upon embroidered cushions solicitously fluffed every hour, smiled gently. There was a weary gleam to her too-thin face, that nameless quality that turned her almost-ugliness into something more. "A small stipend, perhaps? To save for a dowry?"

"My lady!" Slightly scandalized, Anh shook her head. A stipend for a kaburei was simply not done. Not until they were old, retreating to a farm or the Weavers' House. "No, no."

"What of your family, then?" Lady Yala persisted. "Your parents?"

"They are happy in the village." Anh scrubbed her hands together, fretful. Besides, they had sold her after a bad harvest. She had failed them by not being born a son who could sit for examinations or help with the fields; she would be ashamed to send them money. They would suspect she was earning it upon her back, instead of through hard work as a proper palace kaburei.

"There must be *something*," Lady Yala persisted. "Something small, perhaps?"

"Nothing. Only..." Anh hesitated.

"Tell us." The Crown Princess leaned forward, as if waiting upon the words of a simple kaburei.

Anh's cheeks were hot, deep embarrassment making her fidget. "It's very silly."

"Anh." Lady Yala closed her eyes, and the girl, wary of protesting too much or too little, hurried to explain.

"My festival dress is very old," she said, slowly. "I should like a new one."

"We will find beautiful cloth, and I will sew it myself," Lady Yala said. "As soon as I am rested."

A festival dress sewn by a great lady. Anh's throat was dry, and she stammered her thanks. She would not tell anyone, Anh decided as she bowed again, her forehead resting lightly upon her knuckles. She would *die* before she told anyone of these events, no matter how the secret burned.

And if Lady Yala was ever sent back to her cold, barbarous home, Anh would follow.

You Wish to Be Complimented

A feline scratch against the lintel, a low word at the door-guard, and Third Prince Takshin stalked, carefully placing his silk-soled slippers, into Princess Mahara's receiving-room. Gonwa Eulin's round, pretty face turned sour, her plump berry-stained mouth drawing down as if she tasted something bitter; Hansei Liyue looked up from her embroidery and just as swiftly back down again, straightening self-consciously. Su Junha, wrapping thread upon spools for Mahara's unfinished morning-robe, was listening to Huan Iyara's muttered asides and hid a smile behind her sleeve, her eyes sparkling, before she caught sight of the visitor and went pale, a spool of silken amber dropping into her lap.

Yala, aching and somewhat flushed, had just settled afresh upon her cushion to rework a dress-sleeve for Su Junha. It was an easy task, and restful, but she still had to pause every now and again to lay the fabric down and reach for a cup of cooling siao tea upon a small low table to her right, nestled next to a bed of multicolored floss ready to be pressed into service. She did not watch the Third Prince as he approached, seeming wholly occupied with her neat, even stitches.

"Hello, little lure." Freshly bathed, a little sweet oil in his top-knot, and with his scars drained pale, he halted before her cushion.

"Third Prince Takshin." Now she glanced up, the needle piercing thick orange silk. A bright, auspicious color, sunshine on a smoky afternoon. This robe, from the chests in the attic, was old, smelling of ceduan and nose-stinging mothbane, but after reworking and a long airing, it would do quite well for the Su girl. "We are honored by your visit. The Crown Princess is walking in the garden with Lady Kue, if you seek her."

He grimaced, a swift attempt at scowling vanishing as he studied her. "Now what would make you think I seek her? I came to see how you are faring."

"Well enough. I must wear my sleeves properly long for some while." She set the silk in her lap, carefully, and turned to the small basket at her side. Mirrorlight burnished her blue-black hair, glittered upon the small colorless crystals in her hairpin. They were not expensive, but they were bright, and cheered her this morning when she had to halt a few times during her own dressing, her ribs heaving and her hands trembling like wind-brushed leaves.

Even sleep and a good breakfast had not taken away the strange unsteadiness, though she told herself firmly that the adventure was over, had in fact ended quite well, and there was no need to be afraid.

Apparently her hands did not believe her. Her fingers trembled a little as she searched through the floss for the hank she wanted.

Third Prince Takshin examined her for a long moment before sinking down, arranging his knees upon the bare wooden floor. "It suits you. But truly, little lure, are you well?"

"You must not appear too interested," she replied, in an undertone. "It will cause gossip." Then, a little louder, "Will you not take a cushion, Third Prince? That cannot be comfortable."

His reply lacked volume and discretion both. "I am to care for gossip now, as well as the Crown Princess? And comfort too? You load me with cares, Lady Komor."

"Please." She lowered her lashes, occupying herself with measuring out a goodly portion of thread. "We must not let anyone guess what happened. It is dangerous."

He shook his dark head, disdaining a cushion and the danger at once. "Nobody will guess. They will think me enamored of you, that's all." His eyes glittered, pupil and iris blending into each other to give his gaze a directionless quality, difficult to meet.

Yala suppressed a shaky sigh, twisting the end of the thread. Slipping it through the needle's eye would be a chore if her hands would not steady. "And you should avoid that too, Third Prince."

"What if I do not wish to?" Amusement colored each word. Now he smiled, the unscarred half of his mouth curving higher than the other.

She still did not look at him. If he wished to settle upon bare floor like a peasant, well, there was little she could do. At least she had offered him proper seating, and no doubt Mahara's ladies, quiet now, were straining to catch every word. "Are you always this contrary?"

He made a slight motion, quite probably a shrug. The kyeogra glittered at his ear, and the greenstone hurai glinted against his left first finger. He wore no other ornament. "Strike where you are least anticipated."

"Cao Zhien." The rest of that passage was upon the joys of riding your enemies down in a bloody field, and it was not quite acceptable reading for a noblewoman, no matter if it was in the Hundreds.

His scarred lip now twitched with amusement. "They call you a scholar."

"Merely a poor reader of the Hundreds, Third Prince."

"Lady Yala?" Su Junha had risen and drifted closer upon slippered feet, bowing like a flower-stem in the Third Prince's general direction. She was still pale, and she knelt at a safe distance, tucking her skirt in the accustomed fashion and setting out a small square of silk the same color as Mahara's unfinished robe. "I beg leave to interrupt; do you think this thread will do for the sleeves, perhaps in twined *hau* characters?"

The spool was a deep plum color, and would *not* do at all, but the Third Prince might not know as much. A transparent ploy, but braving his temper in order to bolster Yala in her condition was a fine gesture upon Su Junha's part.

"Come, let me see." Yala indicated the cushion next to hers; thank Heaven the prince had not settled himself *there*. She watched as the girl spread silk and thread, and almost winced at the ugliness of the contrast. "Hm. It would be a strange choice, but perhaps effective."

Takshin made a dismissive noise. "Ugly, you mean."

Su Jinha cast her an agonized glance, but Yala had this well in hand. "And what would you know of a woman's sleeves, Third Prince Takshin?"

"Should not a woman who wishes to marry listen when a man tells her what is attractive, and what is not?" His crooked smile was genuine, and Yala realized he was truly amused, and playful. Just like Bai, sharp words and rough courtesy covering affection. He did not seem to have many friends in Zhaon; perhaps he was like the tufted-hair mountain pards who occasionally attached themselves to a monk or poor but honorable maiden, guarding their friend with ghostly ferocity. Their loyalty was absolute once given, the stories said, but very few humans were found worthy.

"That depends upon whether she finds the *man* attractive," Yala answered equably. "You are held to be somewhat ill-mannered, Your Highness."

Su Junha did not gasp at Yala's baiting, but it was close. She did lean toward Yala, holding the plum-thread spool, a slight nervous smile flickering upon her young lips. Bravery lurked in this girl, and Yala's heart warmed. She had, indeed, been a good choice.

"*Outright rude* is what you wish to say, Lady Yala." Third Prince Takshin laid quite unwonted stress upon her name, an incrementally more informal address than she would have preferred. "*Barbaric* is what this other court lady would no doubt add."

Su Junha made a small noise, and Yala subtracted the spool from her, deftly. "I shall thank you not to terrorize my princess's ladies,

Third Prince Takshin, or I will have you quit her receiving-room and ban you from the dinner table as well." Oh, yes, *now* she had his measure, and he was only as annoying as she would allow him to be. "Have you seen General Zakkar today?"

That brought a slight scowl to his thin lips, but Takshin's dark gaze gleamed. He *liked* being needled in return, just like Bai. "Oh, Kai's around. I'm sure he'll visit."

"That would be pleasant. The Head General is a fine conversationalist, and last time complimented Su Junha's hairpin." Yala found her fingers had steadied. She threaded the needle, blessing the bright mirrorlight, and knotted the end with a paired loop-twist. "I believe she blushed, did you not?"

"As a maiden should." Su Junha had recovered. She had most admirable grace, and took slight direction exceeding well. Her hands had softened still further, and though her pale peach morning-dress was worn, it was mended with exquisite care.

"So, it is compliments that make a fine conversationalist? I have no skill with those." Takshin did not quite sulk, but his expression had changed, and that gleam was gone. So mentioning Zakkar Kai took the bloom from his fretting.

Interesting. "You have other skills to recommend you." Abruptly, Yala tired of careful fencing. Soothing him was tiresome, even if she understood his prickling now.

"Such as?" He was not quite finished with her, it seemed. Why was he upon the floor instead of a proper cushion?

"Ah, so now *you* wish to be complimented." She allowed herself to consider the spool next to the orange sleeve, next. This was an ugly pairing too, but she would not let him remark upon it. "Very well. What can we say of the Third Prince, Su Junha?"

"He is very brave?" the girl offered, and shifted a bit closer to Yala's side, a chick seeking the eggfowl's protective bulk.

"Very," Yala agreed, gravely. A silver arc, the bright splatter of blood—she had not asked the fate of the two remaining kidnappers. It could not have been pleasant. *Take the lady home, she is out well past the gong.* "And I must tell you, Su Junha, the Third Prince is very kind."

"Kind?" Su Junha's eyebrows, naturally arched to the finest degree, shot upward. She almost lifted the back of her fingers to her mouth to cover a laugh, but hastily sobered and dropped her hand into her lap.

Takshin studied Yala narrowly. At his shoulder, the leather-wrapped hilt of his sword was a reminder; the curved Shan knife with its ruby was nowhere in evidence. "Careful, Lady Yala."

"Once it is known, you will get no peace." She smiled, and found she was quite enjoying herself. "But yes, Su Junha. Kind. Like a thornblossom, where the canes have claws to defend a tender flower. So it is with Prince Takshin. He does not wish anyone to know how kind he is, so he blusters and stamps and is rude. But he is here to help the Crown Prince with his many burdens, and does so quietly, not to be noticed or applauded. Therefore, he is also modest." She raised her lashes slightly, glanced at him. "Are compliments pleasant, Third Prince? You look rather stunned by their advent."

Was that a scowl darkening his complexion? The scar vanishing into his hair had flushed some little. "Mockery is never pleasant."

"Then it is as well I am not indulging in it." Yala settled her thimble more securely, set the plum thread aside, and pushed her needle through. "Su Junha, my dear, perhaps our visitor would like tea while he waits for the Crown Princess's return."

"Yes, Lady Yala." Worried but obedient, the girl rose and glided away. Sometimes she forgot herself, and hurried with straight steps like a farmgirl. No doubt she had been teased and snubbed for it, but at least here among so few court ladies and under Yala's watchful eye, the teasing was good-natured and minimal.

"She flees like a doe." Prince Takshin did not move. "Am I truly that unpleasant?"

"You do try to be." Yala watched her stitches, fine and even, take shape. "But I find myself glad to see you today, as well as... then."

"Unpleasantness is a habit, nothing more." He made a slight, restless movement, watching her hands. "Were you very glad then?"

She had just said as much, had she not? "Yes." *How could I not be?* The shaking threatened to return, and she paused, staring at her disobedient fingers. They settled only grudgingly.

Takshin's gaze was a heavy weight. "Do you know what happened to them?"

"I do not wish to." That was an unvarnished truth. Perhaps he would take it as such.

"I should tell you."

She settled the sleeve in her lap and regarded him. Her wrists ached under carefully wrapped bandages, and she had chosen this sky-blue dress because the sleeves were Khir-long. "Why?"

"So you know you are safe, Lady Komor Yala." Very softly, and he leaned forward, a subtle movement closing off the rest of the room. "The wolf cares for his own."

Of course, he could not have any scandal attaching to Mahara's husband. "The Crown Prince and his household are lucky to have your protection, Your Highness." Would that satisfy him?

"Oh, Takyeo's my Eldest Brother, and I like him, too." Takshin paused, still watching her hands. The impersonal glare, strangely enough, seemed to settle her fingers, and furthermore bolstered her liver. Perhaps she had used up much of her courage yesterday, and had to wait for the organ held to be the seat of that quality to refill. "That much is true."

Yala exhaled. Her shoulders loosened a trifle, then a little more. "I was very glad to see you," she said, finally. "I would ask how you found me, but..."

"Ask Kai. He loves to tell stories where I will not." Takshin settled his hands upon his thighs, the posture of a retainer waiting in a lord's hall, or a warrior careful of his weapons. She was, now that she had room to consider, thankful he had not seen her *yue*. "But now I *will* tell you something, little lure."

The nickname was not quite elegant, but she did not mind. It was even...well, somewhat comforting. There was a certain sense of relief in finding an edge that was not pointed at her, even if it somewhat halfheartedly menaced. He was difficult, this prince, but she sensed he might also be trustworthy.

After a fashion, and always upon his own terms. "Continue, Third Prince Takshin."

"You are never to risk yourself in that manner again." Delivered just as flatly as Baiyan's own pronouncements, when he stepped into his elder-brother stirrup and decided to ride over Yala's murmured objections. "Or I shall be angry."

To think she'd just been comforted by his presence. Or did he mean to scold her for not being a quick enough hare to distract *and* escape the hounds? Given his nature, it was most probably the latter. "We must all risk ourselves, in one way or another." Her head bent slightly, and she picked up her sewing. This sleeve would have a beautiful curve when she was done, suiting Su Junha's long arms. "My princess is more important—"

"No." He said it too loudly, drawing furtive glances from the gathered ladies. Thankfully, his tone dropped; he seemed to recognize little good would come of shouting at this turn in their conversation. "You are *never* to risk yourself like that again."

It was Yala's turn to cling to silence as she stitched. Perhaps he did think of himself as an elder brother, and that would account for his manner. How very like Bai, indeed. Her irritation had a familiar, and very welcome, edge.

"Do you hear me?" Prince Takshin leaned farther toward her, and his whisper was just as fierce as his expression. The scar upon his throat had flushed, and all trace of a smile, mocking or genuine, had fled. "Do you, Komor Yala?"

"I hear you, Third Prince Takshin." Certainly, she was possessed of ears and could hardly help it.

But Yala intended to do as she must, and if the next incident ended less happily than this one, it was the price of being Mahara's own *yue*. Not held in a hand, but a blade kept hidden, waiting in service.

And, if necessary, broken to allow the wielder to escape.

"Third Prince Takshin." Mahara was at the door, swaying gracefully in yellow-and-blue silk patterned with long stripes. "You honor us with a visit. Come, we must have tea."

The Third Prince was drawn away to make conversation with the Crown Princess, and such was Mahara's gratefulness to him that she kept him for a long while though he often glanced away, his look arresting before it could quite reach Komor Yala.

Yala kept at the seam, the needle tapping her thimble every so often, and said nothing else.

A Powerful Spark

The Old Tower was even more of a refuge today. Perhaps its sheath of blue tiles warded away some of the heat. "You are quite certain?" Mrong Banh clicked his tongue, his hands diving into his sleeves. There was a smear of green ink upon his cheek—he had been at his horoscopes again, and he looked almost as tired as Kai felt. "Quite, quite certain?"

Zakkar Kai stretched his aching hands. They longed to curl into fists, and his shoulders were tense as knotted silk between stretch-poles. No matter how often he reminded himself that she was safe, the battle-nerves would not loosen. At least he had been able to visit the baths. "Takshin is."

"And?" The astrologer's eyebrows, thick enough to qualify as a bush for tiny birds to nest in, rose to almost caricature height. He wiped his hands upon his robe-front, and one of them left a muddy fingerprint of green ink.

Kai had to suppress a weary laugh. "And that is good enough for me, Banh."

"Khir, using a Wurei catspaw, buying the services of thieves and kidnappers." Banh counted each item off on his fingers, an inn-boy reckoning the bill. "And the Crown Princess..."

"Can you think of a better way to light wet fuel?" Kai did not like how this chain was tending. Khir was bled white by years of southron trade choked as well as border skirmishes and the disaster at Three Rivers, true, but a princess dishonored by their conqueror was a powerful spark.

And giving Shan a reason to back away from Zhaon's trade hegemony would be disastrous. Unifying Zhaon and pacifying Khir was expensive business; recovery was fragile. The Mad Queen had been adamant in avoiding marriage negotiations for her son; with her gone and Khir no longer keeping Zhaon's armies busy in the North, they had been concluded with almost unseemly haste.

Banh frowned at his ink-stained fingertips. "Ashani Zlorih isn't a fool, and she is his daughter. Why would he—"

It was not like the astrologer to be so dense, but they had both passed a sleepless night. Kai settled in his usual chair with a not entirely untheatrical groan. "It could be a Khir noble, or a group of them."

"Yes, of course." Mrong Banh's eyebrows now came together, almost knotting in the middle. He turned halfway around, perhaps intending to make tea, then swung back, attacked by another notion. "How would they benefit, though? Paying tribute is cheaper than war, and the nobles were thoroughly winnowed."

That was what worried Kai, though he had not quite been able to articulate it. Of course Banh would strike upon the reed that needed to be heard. "Defeat is a stain upon a man's honor, there."

"Sometimes you must lose a battle to win a war." Banh came back to the table and picked up a round-bellied teapot of Anwei yellowglaze. He hunted for two clean cups and poured, but no steam rose from the liquid. It was no doubt cold tea, bitter with long steeping, but the man was distracted.

"I do not think many Khir noblemen believe they *lost*." Kai shook his head. "This goes no further, Banh."

He rolled his eyes like a much younger man. "Of course. I do not drop words in market wells, Kai."

"I know." Kai scrubbed at his face, stubble scratching. He wanted another bath, needed a shave, and could have put away a hearty dinner, too. And Tamuron wanted him in Great Council as well as the morning session. "I still must say it. This worries me."

"Which worries you more, the Khir or a certain lady?" Banh pushed the sloshing-full teacup toward him and cursed softly at the same moment, whisking rai-paper with arcane notations away from possible spillage.

Kai closed his eyes. "Don't."

"What was the other, that actress..." Banh's mouth twitched.

I was younger, and much more foolish then. Kai winced. Every part of him ached savagely. "Banh. Don't."

"You only like the unavailable. Is she married? Or betrothed?" It was small comfort that Banh had not guessed the identity of the lady Kai had been drinking to yet.

He could never again get drunk around the man, that much was certain. "For the last time. Don't."

"Mh." Banh sobered, his attempt at levity deflating like a festival bladder. He traced the rim of his cup with a green-dyed finger, frowning. "The Emperor knows?"

"Of the suspicions, yes. He no doubt has suspicions of his own." It wasn't like Tamuron to see lurkers where none existed, but current uncertainties and failing health made a man cautious.

"Poor Lady Komor." He shook his head, his loose topknot flopping. He must have scratched under it several times while watching the stars. "Is she... I mean, is she well?"

Kai regarded him narrowly, sniffing at the cup. Eong, heavy and smoky, bitter from oversteeping and stone-cold besides. At least it was tea, and did not have ink in it. "Why the interest, Banh?"

"She borrowed a book or two from me." Banh touched his own cup with a fingertip, snatching his hand away as if it were hot. He frowned, contemplating his hand, and made a face. "I'd like them back, that is all."

"You never let anyone borrow a book since Jin was caught with *The Pleasures of Lady Eight-Legs.*"

"He stole *that* one to look at the pictures, just as the rest of you did. He was more careless, though. Anyway." Banh clicked his tongue. "A Golden Guard, seduced. It hardly seems possible."

"Well, he paid for it with the final coin. Jin made sure of that." Kai stretched. If he was careful, Banh would not insist upon him drinking more than a single cup of the cold, quite nasty tea.

The astrologer lifted his cup, paused. "You look tired."

"Yes, well, the Emperor wanted me in morning council. I cannot tell why, his temper is too short for listening."

"He trusts you." Banh said it like a certainty. Dust danced in shafts of mirrorlight, a golden glow edging shelves of flatbooks, limning every item upon the cluttered tables. Cool air touched Kai's cheeks, a welcome caress.

Last night, Yala had clung to him as they mounted the stairs, her eyes all but closed. Trust. A dangerous thing. "Yes, well." *I owe Tamuron everything. And yet I do not care for his current temper.*

The Emperor was forgetting his sons were merely flesh, requiring more and more of Takyeo. You could not drive soldiers like beasts for too long, or they would break. Even oxen would drop in their tracks, if used mercilessly enough.

"It won't be long now," Banh said, quietly. Apparently his own thoughts were wending the way Kai's did. "Afterward, there is the Crown Prince's coronation."

"And keeping him alive for it." Their gazes met. Kai cleared his throat. "Banh, should untimely ill befall either of them..." Who else could he even broach the subject to?

"Let us not borrow trouble." The astrologer's tone was uncharacteristically grave. "Whatever happens, Kai, we are still friends."

"I should hope so." *After all, Banh, you are not a threat to any Garan who sits upon the Throne.* "I shall pass along your good wishes to Lady Komor."

Banh lifted his cup and took a deep draft. A curious look came over his round face, though he did not splutter.

Kai regarded him, levelly. Eong was hardly pleasant at the best of times, despite several sages chanting its praises.

Banh swallowed, his throat bobbing, and coughed, his cheeks and ears turning pink. “Ah. Well. Yes.” He grimaced, deeply, and coughed. “Please do.”

WELL IN HAND

There are the strangest rumors flying about." Kurin lounged elegantly enough upon a bolster, his robes quite unwontedly somber today. Even his forehead was troubled, and today he wore no zhu powder upon his gleaming face.

"Don't frown, it spoils your looks." Gamwone smoothed a scrap-square of silk upon her knee, considering its dye and grain. For once, she was not cold. The tapestries swathing the walls trapped summer's bountiful heat, and she could loosen the top of her dress for once, though not enough to show the claw marks of former pregnancies upon her breasts. "Rumors?"

"Nobody is looking at *my* face with yours about, mother dear." Kurin did not reach for a fan or his teacup. His daily visit to his beloved mother was not proceeding as usual. "Yes, there are rumors that one of the Crown Princess's ladies is ill."

"Is that so." Gamwone had to dispel her own frown. Her attempts to insert an eye or two into the foreign bitch's bower had not met with much success. That nose-in-the-air Shan whore Kue had an iron fist over the Jonwa, and the Crown Princess—oh, how annoying it was indeed, to name her thus—had a foreign lady who controlled her coterie much the same way. She'd even taken in that simpering Su girl, the one with the calluses and the clumsy feet.

She had a good bloodline; the Sus were an ancient family. But

Heaven had turned away from them, and they were threadbare now. Ill-luck rubbed off like cheap dye, and Gamwone wanted nothing to do with it.

Kurin studied a tapestry of Yu Hoan the Sage on his barrel, bare-legged and drifting down the Pai River. How many fingersore servants had filled in the blue waves? Gamwone reserved herself for the delicate work.

Finally, her most acceptable son half-lidded his eyes, and continued. "My little Shan brother is living in the Jonwa, too, and someone seems to have caught his eye." He was very thoughtful this morning, occupied with problems he did not wish to share.

"Oh?" Another disappointment. Takshin did not call at her palace; he seemed to have forgotten he had a mother. And that was a new development; he had made visits dictated by etiquette before, and sent brief uninformative letters she stopped replying to after his second year in Shan.

Her letters to him could have been opened, of course, and she would have had to be distressingly clear. He was not like Kurin, who understood from a look, or a gesture. It irked her that Kiron of Shan was still alive.

It should have been so easy, and Takshin was not one to cavil at drawing a blade. Why, the scars proved as much. He had no doubt left the Shan prince alive to pique his mother. The heavens knew nobody could be counted upon to make Gamwone's life *easier*.

"The Khir girl." Kurin's smile was pained. "Can you imagine?"

For a moment she thought he meant the Crown Princess, and a delicious heat curled through her. Then she realized what he meant. "You mean the foreigner's bigmaid?" An insulting term, but it applied. Gamwone wiggled her soft toes inside silken houseslippers embroidered with umu blossoms. It was a shame that sly head eunuch had made the scent of umu his signature; Gamwone would have liked to wear it more than once in a while.

"She is a noblewoman in her own country, Mother. A high-ranking one, too, enough to wear silk daily."

She picked up her own cup. The tea was cooling too quickly. Today was rapidly becoming unsatisfactory, and it was only morning. "A lady among horsefuckers is no lady."

"How very vulgar." Kurin straightened, pushing the bolster irritably aside. Against its red and blue, his burnt sienna silk was not pleasing at all.

Gamwone took a delicate sip. "I am an old woman, I may say what I please."

For once, Kurin did not immediately flatter her. Instead, he looked at a scroll upon a different wall, a delicately rendered and very expensive scene of a snowy mountain with a crane flying in the distance, signed by a master whose name escaped Gamwone at the moment. "It seems the lady snapped a golden leash upon our Taktak, and he is quite docile now."

Her interest piqued, the queen set down her inadequately warm tea and picked up an ivory fan with a rai-paper blade. It did not fold, but it moved the air in broad sweeps, and that was what she had wanted this morning. "Really."

"Yes. But that's just gossip." Kurin traced the characters upon his hurai with a fingertip, straightening instead of lounging. "It is not what worries me."

Ah, so now they came to it. "What worries you, my darling? Tell Mother."

"I have not heard from Sabwone."

Gamwone clicked her tongue, shaking her head. The affection between Kurin and the First Concubine's brat daughter had often seemed...well, not *concerning*, not *unnatural*, but...the word escaped her, at the moment, and that was another irritation. The day was turning out to be full of them, and her temper would fray as a result. Could not anyone think of her struggles, her delicate nerves? "She may be too busy for you, my dear. She is, after all, a queen by now. How proud that concubine must be." Distressingly proud. She would have to think of how to bring Luswone down a measure or two. Perhaps through her son...hm.

"She has not reached the Shan border yet, Mother."

Her interest sharpened, and so did the sense of danger. Gamwone brushed at her throat with her fingertips, a dragonwing's light footstep. "And how do you know that?"

Kurin made a slight restless movement, instantly controlled. Even his topknot-cage was unpleasantly dark today. "It pleases me to know, therefore, I do."

"Well, you'd do better to be pleased by whatever your father is hiding." Gamwone heard the sharp note of irritation in her words, and decided it was justified.

"Oh, that? He's caught some rash from the baths." Kurin waved the mystery aside with one hand, short and chopping instead of a languid movement. "The physician in favor now is a shabby little thing Zakkar Kai found, and the Emperor likes him."

A rash from the baths? Gamwone shuddered. Probably from the filthy, shrinking little mouse he kept there. Gamwone had plans for *that* courtesan, and all they required was some careful waiting. "Zakkar Kai." The very name itself was hateful.

"Quite a hero, our God of War. And Hailung Jedao needles him every chance he gets."

Well, such was to be expected from the Second Queen's uncle. Gamwone's own uncle Binei Jinwon, newly arrived at court for his traditional half-year of service, did not suffer fools or jumped-up peasants either. Gamwone sighed. "I should recommend civility to *my* uncle, but I am only his poor forgotten niece, slighted and despised." Uncle Jinwon had not hurried to visit her upon his arrival, and that was highly disappointing as well.

"Oh, Mother." Kurin's eyes did not roll, but he made a restless movement. "The Yulehi are thriving, don't worry about *them*. I take very good care of our clan."

So, Jinwon had visited Kurin instead. Of course, her darling was a man now, and the head of the clan would pay homage to its prince. "You are a joy to your poor mother." She paused, examining the fan. There were no holes in the paper blade, but she suddenly wished for one. Punishing a thoughtless maid for such a transgression would have been a welcome relief from the mounting pressure. "Has your father said anything about your sister?"

"He is worried for Sabwone, too. I gather she's writing to her own uncle."

Was he *deliberately* misunderstanding her? "I mean Gamnae, of course." Gamwone's daughter must be a queen, too, but not in Shan even if an accident could be arranged for Luswone's brat. That country had changed Takshin, who had been marred anyway but might have been useful if they had not done... well, whatever it was they had done to him. Ch'han was too far away, but they were mighty, and Anwei had no king, only a collection of princely houses fighting among each other for scraps.

There was a Crown Prince in Khir. Maybe that would do, except Khir was smaller than Shan.

Her son now examined his nails, frowning slightly as if he found something amiss upon their blunt, buffed surfaces. "Oh, he likes her singing."

"Kurin, do be serious." Gamwone's irritation mounted another small fraction. And the morning had started so well.

"I am." He had fine hands, her firstborn, and used one of them to accentuate his point, but it was another sharp, unlovely movement. He was *not himself*, and she wondered at it. "He thinks she has a lovely voice."

Well, if it pleased him to be opaque, she could play that game, as well. "Does he, now."

"In short, Mother, all is well in hand."

All desire to be hazy in her meanings, or to play, vanished in a hot flash of almost-anger, igniting deep in her belly and rising for her throat. "It cannot be well in hand. That brat, that *goatbird*,[54] is still Crown Prince."

---

54. A bird which places its eggs in other nests, to be raised by unsuspecting avians of higher class or worth.

A shadow of matching annoyance crossed Kurin's face, cheering her immensely. "You had best not say that where anyone unreliable can hear you, Mother. The Palace is strangely restive, of late."

Well, of course it was. The Emperor was no longer the dashing warlord of years ago, firm in the saddle and straight as a sword. His shoulders were stooping by fractions and his profligacy of wives was beginning to mark his face. Each time Gamwone saw him, at ritual intervals or in passing, she secretly stored up each of time's ravages upon his countenance. He had visibly deteriorated even since the Knee-High, and that sight was welcome indeed.

When he was gone, she would be free—oh, not completely, for a woman was subject to all manner of awful restriction.

But it would suit her very well to be a dowager. Very well indeed.

"Mother?" Kurin stretched and began to move, arranging his robe as if he intended to leave. "Do you hear me?"

"What?" Pulled from a brief dream of liberation, she regarded her eldest somewhat narrowly. Her fingers were not cold, and a prickle of sweat had begun along her lower back. She was always chilled, except for when she was too warm before the dry days, and today was turning out to be simply hideous even before lunch.

"Be careful what you say." He uncoiled from his cushions, and his expression had turned remote. "Especially now. I would not have you ruin things."

"Ruin what, my darling?"

But he only smiled, and gave her a very filial bow.

"Kurin, ruin what? Answer me."

But her first son, her joy, merely widened his smile, and left without asking her leave.

Gamwone's anger crested. A naughty little boy, but he was always this way when he was preparing a gift, was he not? Of course he was. She had raised him well, and he was cautious. Gamwone had only to wait.

Again. As she had all her life.

She clapped her hands for her maids, and looked about for

evidence of their carelessness. She would find some, she always did. They were lazy, none of them diligent, and she was cursed to suffer small insults all her life, too.

Her soft face set and her eyes flashing, the First Queen picked up her beautiful, fragile Shan bonefire teacup, and flung it across the room.

Metal of Necessity

How strange it was, the Great Rider of Khir thought. How strange.

A padded stone bench, its legs carved with ancient symbols whose meaning, if they had ever carried one, was long forgotten, a thin red velvet cushion. Behind it, the great wheel-carving of stone not native to Khir, the divisions of the calendar chiseled sharp and deep, immutable as the word *Khir* itself.

The name meant *people*, and *time*—the passage of seasons over the great grass sea the First People had ridden with the gods before settling among the sharpspine mountains and deep lush valleys. It meant *honor*, and *burden*, too.

But the word was not the thing, or so Ashani Zlorih often thought as he clasped his hands behind his back and regarded the cruelest master to set foot upon a royal kaburei's neck.

It did not look like much. Just a bench upon a dais, with the stone circle looming behind it. Sometimes he imagined the Great Calendar loosening from whatever ancient, rusting moorings held it fast to the palace wall, toppling forward with a great heaving groan, and smashing everything beneath. Including the frail sack of meat and humors who sat upon the bench and said, *This is what must be so.*

Overhead, standards taken in battle or sent from noble houses to indicate fealty rustled. A draft whistled through with the mirrorlight, both caught outside where they roamed freely and forced into servitude. The light would dissipate and the air, well, who could tell what happened to invisible things once they were used?

"Your Majesty seems troubled." Cat-faced, soberly robed Domari Ulo, clan-head and Grand Councilor, was well accustomed to the royal moods.

Perhaps too accustomed.

I miss my daughter. But such a thing could not be said. "These are troubling times, Ulo."

"Indeed. We are all called upon to sacrifice." Ulo's tone was placid, oiled, meant to spread calm upon a sharply troubled humor. He was ever urbane, ever soft-spoken, and ever full of intrigue for his own advantage. He was chief among those restive lords who would topple the house that ruled them if they could, and descend into a chaos of bloodletting until a new Great Rider rose from the wreckage of the Second Families. Those who could have proved a counterweight to Ulo were dead at Three Rivers or had retreated in grief, like Komori Dasho.

"Will there be anything left of Khir, after the immolation is finished?" Zlorih rubbed at his forehead. His fingers met warm metal—the simple circlet of beaten silver worn since the First Dynasty, a small smooth oval of greenstone resting above and between his eyes. The traditional silk padding to make it fit upon the wearer's head, wrapped securely with crimson thread, was not very thick.

The ruler conformed to the metal of necessity. Silk, and flesh itself, was more giving than governance.

"Is there anything left for Khir if honor is lost?" Ulo sounded certain. It was one of his nieces who would be married to Daoyan, if the boy could be found. Not a daughter—that would have been too much. But he no doubt had many ideas about arranging Khir to suit his mood, and as a loving uncle he no doubt would use access to the heir to do so.

"Still no news of him?" Zlorih's fingers tightened against each other. Daoyan had never been troublesome, not until acknowledged. In fact, had he not resembled Zlorih so closely, the Great Rider might have entertained certain . . . doubts.

A woman once honorless could be so again, though it pained him to think such a thing of her.

"None, Your Majesty." Ulo even sounded uneasy at the young heir's absence.

"Some excuse must be given."

"Yes, Your Majesty." The same conversation, repeated for weeks. The new prince had vanished, leaving only a cryptic letter for his royal father.

There is business to attend to, my lord. Please excuse me. Brushed in a steady hand—oh, Zlorih had made certain no education was lacking for the boy, and his mother Narikh Arasoe's tomb was swept regularly. Dying in childbirth was as honorable as any victorious battle, but she had succumbed to a fever and he would gladly trade *any* victory for a single afternoon with her again. A sathron ringing in her particular way, fingers plucking at strings and her profile serene with concentration.

Flesh, so much more giving, and perishable as well. A Great Rider must be as stone. Had not his own father repeated as much, over and over again? *Affairs of state*, the single word in Khir a piece of stubborn gravel trapped in a shoe during a long walk.

Zlorih closed his eyes. It was no use. He could still see the bench, the hovering calendar. Arasoe's face, round and calm, and her laughing, silvery eyes. If she agonized over her lost honor, she had made no sign, and the fire in Zlorih's blood had not cared. He could have married her, he supposed, if he had not been required to keep his councilors from committing mass mutiny. They had wanted him to marry some minor Ch'han princess, and while Ch'han was mighty, Zhaon was closer.

And far more dangerous.

"Your Majesty . . ." The words trailed away. "Sooner or later, our agents will succeed. It is the only way."

They all said as much, his crafty, conniving councilors. Zlorih pushed the metal band up, slipping fingertips underneath its circlet. What, really, would refusing or demanding a retraction of orders accomplish? Another set of buttocks upon the bench he now viewed, a more tractable Great Rider in the hands of counselors craving more blood, more agony. They were not satisfied with Khir's current ragged state, and doubly unsatisfied with a Great Rider whose last battle had not been completely won.

"Very well," Ashani Zlorih repeated, heavily. "But it must be quick. It must be painless."

"There are assurances given." Did Ulo feel the heaviness? No, all that noble vulture felt was the insult to his pride, and the lure of the profit he stood to gain when a royal pawn was sacrificed.

"Ah. One more thing, Ulo." Zlorih opened his eyes again. He had thought long and hard upon this move, and found he did not care if the consequences were unhappy. "Those who eventually perform the deed, and those who pay them, must be punished in the old way."

"Your Majesty... "

"What?" Zlorih's lips stretched, a predatory grin very much like his bastard son's. Only one son left, and he had vanished like the wind itself. All gone like an unwilling hawk—wife, sons, daughter, lover. Only metal and stone remained, and one last chance to strike back at the men who sought to hobble a Great Rider. "The punishment for killing one of the throne's saddle-bred is hot lead run into belly and head, and for the ears to be presented to the Great Rider." The oldest term for *king*, short and sharp. "Surely you do not intend the law to be cheated."

"No, Your Majesty." Ulo had gone pale; he only spoke so when he was choked by something unexpected.

Zlorih did not turn to witness, however satisfying the sight might be. *Oh, my daughter, my summer wind.*

Once it was done, he had a clear course to follow. He was trapped upon this wheel, bent upon the arc of the Great Calendar, and he would go to his end with the necessary tranquility.

But not, he thought, before a manner of revenge. Domari Ulo

would be the first to feel *that* sting. Ashani Zlorih's position was weakened, but he was still the Great Rider of the First People, chosen of the Great Mare, and he would wreak a few last stabs upon his foes.

Both inside Khir, and without.

"Leave me," the Great Rider said, softly. "I would think upon these things alone."

"Yes, Your Majesty." The Grand Councilor bowed and hurried away, his lacquer-soled court shoes clicking. He was no doubt feeling the first intimations of disquiet, and Ashani Zlorih was content to have it be so.

Let Domari Ulo wonder if his Great Rider was quite as weak as he appeared. Let them all wonder.

"Oh, my daughter," Zlorih said, softly. "It will be quick, at least."

Until They Have the Means

The Great Oval, once a shallow depression in bedrock but now a sunken amphitheater, was full of shoving both good-natured and ill-tempered. The crowd—kaburei filching time from their duties and betting alloy slivers, peasants from the provinces gawking, tradespeople and artisans betting with triangular alloy coins and sometimes square iron, nobles reclining under striped awnings—was the roar of surf upon a hungry shore, and at the bottom of the depression sand was being scraped for the second race of the day.

The best seats were cut out of the worn rock itself, and starred with bright-striped cotton awnings. Above, the stands turned to wood and masonry, crammed to groan-overflowing. Sometimes the danger of timber giving way and spilling the lower orders upon the heads of the higher even spurred repairs. The noise crested on the sixth race or later, betting reaching a frantic pace, but by then Makar customarily left his little brother to it and retreated to his study.

For the first few races, though, the Fourth Prince normally enjoyed himself roundly, though he rarely bet. Today, however, was different.

"Was it you?" Makar examined the crowd upon either side, idly waving a fan painted with a quotation from Xhiao the Younger. It was not quite fitting, but it was the one he had selected today, and there was no use in putting it away.

Sensheo poured them both a measure of jaelo tea. "What *are* you on about?" Come the fourth race, he would begin upon the sohju, and Makar would begin his preparations to retreat. Always leaving before the true fun started.

Makar frowned, turning his attention to the cheap, block-printed broadsheet with weights upon its corners, spread upon a low table before them. A flagrant waste of space, that table, but such was the manner of nobility. "Was. It. You?"

"Was what me?" Sensheo studied the broadsheet too.

"Come now, little brother." Makar's brows knitted as he brushed away a fly. Where there were races, there was dung; where there was dung, there were shiny carapaces and buzzing wings. Much as there were bright robes and buzzing at court, or under the awnings of the noble patrons of the Oval.

A great swell of crowd-noise drowned whatever Sensheo might have said, for the sand-scraping was finished and six light chariots had appeared, the drivers hung with floating ribbons and the archers bare-chested, slathered with sweetnut oil and gleaming just as the proud-stepping horses. Two from the Green faction, one from the Red, one from the Blue, and two unaffiliated—a purple-and-yellow-striped kaburei racing for his manumit, and a masked nobleman in a gilded chariot who set the audience packed in the high-tiered cheap seats abuzz.

Normally the game of deducing just who would be foolish enough to careen about in the bowl with commoners would have amused Makar. Today, however, he was after different prey, and it was proving more canny than usual.

Sensheo, stroking his archer's thumb-ring, settled against the cushions their kaburei had brought and lifted a flask to his carmined lips. He had taken to outlining his eyes, too, perhaps to make them appear less bloodshot.

Out late again last night, apparently. Had he been trawling the Yuin?

"Mother is concerned," Makar said, leaning over and cupping his hand near Sensheo's ear. The crowd bayed as each horse trotted demurely on a single circuit of the obstacle-free outside lane. Dust rose from pounded sand. This late in the season, the juicy green of spring growth at the sanded edges was yellowing, chunks of packed sand-sod replaced by the Oval's kaburei each evening. Last week's fourth-race had been during a sudden cloudburst, and highly unsatisfactory amid the gritty mud.

Sensheo had taken to spending nights away from the Kaeje and his own princely house; Makar's ears, sensitive to gossip, heard whispers of time spent in the sinks near the Left Market instead of the more respectable holes of the Theater District. And Sensheo's regular mistress, an actress much beloved at the Ta Kau Theater for her portrayal of thin, consumptive heroines, was now linked to another lord, one whose merchant pedigree was only whispered of—for though he was not quite *noble*, the man in question had touchy pride and enough money to make revenge a pleasant pastime.

Betting intensified, high and furious. Sensheo shook his head. "Care to wager, brother? I like the striped fellow, he's got a reason to win."

No. He likes his horse too much. Makar refused to be distracted. A hot breeze ruffled his robe and his topknot, but he could not retreat just yet. "You are causing gossip, little brother, and Mother is worried."

"Oh, Mother is always worried, it is what mothers *are*." Sensheo was not quite nettled yet, but he was well upon his way. "They should redraw the maternal characters in all the Hundreds to *pau-an*,[55] indeed."

The crowd-roar settled as the two-wheeled chariots took their ragged starting line, dokuei[56] with ivory batons darting back and forth to arrange them in a marginally fairer manner. Last-moment betting flickered fingers and beads upon counting-strings; fans

55. "Nagging."

56. Somewhat of a cross between a steward and an umpire.

appeared, children piped high, excited questions, dripping earthenware crocks dispensed tepid, foaming sweetwater for thirsty racegoers.

Makar was forced to think that Sensheo honestly had no idea what had occurred, for his little brother fixed him with a narrow glare. "Well, what is it this time? I've done nothing, but if you and Mother keep accusing me, I might as well take a few precautions."

"Oh, do not be a theater-maiden. Mother simply wishes you to be discreet, that is all."

"She wants me to swallow being fifth in line, and scrape and bow to that upstart general too." Sensheo did not bother to say it softly. No, he pitched the words to carry over the crowd-noise, and Makar's reflexive glance to see who was near to hear lit his brother's gaze with glee. "Even Sabwone could make him cry when he was a brat fresh from whatever midden Father found him rolling in."

Ah. Was Sensheo *still* full of hatred for Kai? Such an irrational distaste should have been set aside with childhood toys. "What irks you about being a prince who may not ever have to sit upon the throne, Sensheo? It is generally considered a pleasant life."

The green and orange starting-flag waved, and betting halted. The crowd bayed, then subsided to watch, tension building in every packed-tight body.

"Until one of your brothers ascends," Sensheo said, rather gently, "and decides to rid himself of impediments."

"Takyeo is not like that." More was the pity. Their eldest brother did not have the ruthlessness, Takshin did not have the restraint, and Zakkar Kai did not have the bloodline. If only the three of them could have been melded, like the old story of Ti Zhu's baby in the clay jar, parts shaken together and given the breath of life from a benevolent passing god—the result had been the great general Zao Zheon, who paved the way for the first Emperor of the Third Dynasty.

And married said emperor's daughter, placing himself at the summit of the world. He had died choking upon poison, an object lesson in reaching too high even for those blessed with heavenly pedigree.

"Oh, nobody is, until they have the means." Sensheo's own fan made an appearance, flicking at yet another lazy fly. The shade was welcome here, and a good breeze came from the distant river. Unfortunately, that wind carried dust upon its back, and fine particles would seep into every crack, be it in stone, wood, fabric, or flesh. The rasping was enough to drive even the most reasonable and restrained of men into an ill temper. "And how long do you think our dear Eldest Brother will last, Makar? Honestly. You are supposed to be the clever one."

"My concern is that you do not do something foolish and smirch our family." It sounded stiff and prim, but Makar was tired of his brother's antics. He would much prefer spending today in the Paper Alley, that long street of booksellers and lantern-makers, taking tea at the Brokentail Swallow among the chess-players and scholars. "I am your elder brother, and you are in my affections. Please, simply wait patiently for what may come."

"Mother always knows how to spoil my fun." Sensheo leaned back against his pillows, a languid hand summoning a sweating kaburei from the sun outside the awning to pour fresh tea. "Now be quiet, the race is afoot."

Makar snapped his fan shut and rose, smoothing his dark scholar's robe. "Enjoy it, little brother."

"You won't stay?"

The crowd began to mutter, then yell as the first slow circuit of the Oval was performed. Once the horses passed the starting line after that circuit, they would gallop. A strong restraining hand at the beginning turned aside trouble later.

It was a pity Sensheo could not see as much. Makar readied himself to take his leave. "There is no speaking to you, lately."

"No," Sensheo said, his gaze already fixed upon the chariots swinging into the second loop. Whips cracked, and the thunder began in earnest. The striped kaburei was in the lead, and the masked nobleman had locked wheels with the Blue. The archers, focusing on the targets atop pillars of varying heights, were now greased with sweat and powdered with flying dust. "There is not, Elder Brother. Sometimes I am even sorry for it."

Not sorry enough to halt your stupid, mannerless grasping. But Makar did not say it. There was no point.

The masked nobleman's archer was quite fine, arrow after arrow thudding home as the driver fought to keep his chariot steady. The Blue's chariot splintered, horses screaming in fear, rider and archer flung like dolls, pierced by sharp thin spars of lacquered wood. The masked noble pulled ahead, and the two Greens bracketed the striped kaburei, who cracked the whip over his team's back but did not let it bite their heaving flanks.

That was probably said kaburei's mistake, Makar thought, and turned away. Wood splintered afresh, and a hoarse yell rose from the stands, splashing down into the bowl.

Sometimes applying the whip more diligently sooner saved one trouble later. But if you had not, if you had chosen more subtle methods and the beast you wished to direct had grown into adult recalcitrance, one could do little but send it to the slaughteryard.

And try again, with another.

Character and Cleverness

Second Princess Gamnae was announced, and entered the Jonwa's smaller receiving-room with a light step and a sunny smile. Bedecked, beribboned, and in sheer pale peach, she looked like a stuffed pad for holding needles. Bracelets chimed upon her plump wrist, and her smile only widened when Mahara greeted her. It was a relief to see her instead of her mother, that much was certain.

"Are you very busy?" Gamnae inquired, once the pleasantries were done. "Mother is fretful and Kurin is gone somewhere; I thought to visit here for some peace."

"You are more than welcome. We are hard at work sewing." Mahara indicated bowed heads, servants and noble girls all bent to their tasks. "But I was just thinking a short turn in the shade would be welcome, before the afternoon turns sticky."

"May I accompany you, then?" A kittenish hopefulness shone from the Second Princess's features. She seemed to have little guile, and even Yala appeared to like her well enough. "Ah, and there is Lady Komor. May I inquire after her health? I heard she was ill."

"Certainly. It was merely a passing fever." Was she after gossip? Mahara beckoned and Yala rose swiftly, pulling her sleeves over her hands properly as she glided to her princess's side.

"Second Princess Gamnae." Yala's bow lacked nothing in grace or decorum, and in her lightly ornamented dark blue, she was quite the foil to Gamnae's florid furbelows. "You brighten our bower."

"Very poetic." Gamnae held out her hands, and after a brief moment, Yala clasped them. The contrast between dark blue and pale peach was piquant, but only for a short while. "I was a bit worried, and brought some small sweet pastries, to tempt your appetite. How are you?"

Mahara thought the girl looked very much like a pastry herself, dressed as she was. But at least she was polite, and a visit was one way to relieve boredom. Besides, she had pricked her fingers *again* just before Gamnae's advent, and had been struck with the altogether uncharacteristic desire to throw her work across the room and stamp upon it for good measure, like a boychild with a broken toy.

Yala appeared just the same as ever, though a bit wan. "Much better; I am honored by your concern. Pastries, how thoughtful. You are too kind to a mere lady-in-waiting, Second Princess."

"Nonsense." Gamnae squeezed Yala's hands, but gently, and that mark of high esteem was no doubt remarked by everyone in the receiving-room. "I have a selfish purpose in coming, you shall see. Shall we walk, Crown Princess, Lady Komor?"

Mahara assented with a nod, and kaburei scurried to fetch sunbells. None of the court ladies evinced a desire to come along—it was not quite sticky yet, but it would be, and the Jonwa's shade was not to be left lightly.

A short time later, Mahara and her guest ambled down a short colonnade near the Jonwa's second water-garden, pools rippling and high babu rustling, and Gamnae arrived quickly at her point. "You see, I am very selfish, imposing upon you. I thought I should learn more of Khir. Mother tells me I may be sent there."

Mahara's eyebrows rose. She studied a mass of blue and white flowers upon graceful stems, nodding over a slowly running streamlet. "Sent there?"

"The king of Khir has a remaining son, Mother says." Gamnae's round, pretty face flushed slightly, and she coughed into her sleeve to denote some embarrassment. Her ear-drops swayed, small rosy stone beads glowing to match her dress. "She says it's an insult to me but it can't be helped. Sabwone is gone to be a queen now, and I suppose I must too, if Mother says so. So I wished to ask you about Khir. And to see if the language is difficult to learn."

"They mean to marry you to Daoyan? But he's..." Mahara swallowed the words and glanced at Yala, who trailed them at a discreet distance. "I see."

"What? Is he ugly?" Now Gamnae looked concerned. She had hair enough for the brace of hairpins she wore, but both of them had such ornate heads they appeared to fight over her braids as two myonha over a ripe pearlfruit. "I...well, I suppose if one is a prince it does not matter, but..."

"Prince Daoyan is considered handsome," Yala said, smoothly, halting beside them. "My brother had the honor of his friendship; he was a frequent visitor to Hai Komori."

"Your brother? How is he, have you had news from home?" Gamnae's question was not an unkind one, that much was obvious from the tone. How had the First Queen given birth to such a sweet child? It strained belief.

Yala did not take offense. Her mouth did not even firm slightly. Instead, she glanced away, across a small pond ringed with flat green pads. "He rides the Great Fields."

"What does that mean?" Gamnae caught herself. "I am sorry, I am very stupid. I remember now, you said that before."

Who told her she was stupid? Mahara opened her mouth to protest, but Yala won the race. "It is not stupid to ask when you do not know, Second Princess. It is rather a mark of character and cleverness. My Elder Brother fell at the Battle of Three Rivers."

"That was where Zakkar Kai...I mean, oh. Oh." Gamnae's cheeks blanched and her eyes widened. "Forgive me, Lady Yala. I am very rude today."

"There is nothing to forgive, Second Princess." Kindly enough, though Yala's bright gaze was shadowed. Her hands, covered by her long Khir sleeves, might have been clasped a little tightly, but it was not visible. "When a Khir noble says someone rides the Great Fields, it means they have... passed. One does not say more, so as not to call them into returning."

A hot breeze mouthed all three women. Mahara studied the Second Princess and Yala, and twirled her sunbell's handle, idly.

"I see." Gamnae absorbed this. Perhaps she wore so much finery because she feared being ignored or forgotten. And yet, she seemed somewhat shy. "It is different in Zhaon. You must forgive me, Lady Komor, please."

Mahara let Yala take the conversation, thinking furiously. So, her father-in-law did not think her enough to cement the peace? Or perhaps there was some other consideration. Did they know Daoyan was, well, certainly *noble*, for his mother Lady Narikh Arasoe was of an old clan by both birth and her marriage into the Narikh. She had been widowed, too, instead of losing her honor while her husband still lived... and yet, the stain of illegitimacy hovered over her son. *Do not speak of him or* to *him*, Ashani Zlorih had told his daughter more than once, and she obeyed as always. Now she wondered if she should have.

A strange, altogether terrible idea struck her, and Mahara paused upon the garden path, her sunbell dipping.

She was the surety for peace between Zhaon and Khir, she knew that much. Were there those in her new country, among her husband's countrymen, who would welcome another war? Khir was weak, since the trade routes had been closed for so long and the flower of the warlike nobles lay dead at Three Rivers. A kidnapping could mean that she was to be taken back to her father like an escaped horse, lather-spattered at the end of a long twisted rope. It would be good to see Khir again. Except she was now a wife, and if she was taken from a husband, even a Zhaon, would she become honorless?

She was not supposed to speak upon politics, but Mahara thought perhaps she should. With Yala, certainly. Or perhaps with her husband, if he would countenance such talk from a woman.

Since she was already thinking about it, there was no harm in continuing while Yala kept Princess Gamnae occupied. Perhaps the kidnapping could mean something not nearly as... well, *nice* was not the proper word. If she was not to be *returned* to Khir, what was the other option?

Put that way, even a girl who was not supposed to think upon such things could hardly escape a certain conclusion. Perhaps Mahara *was* to be returned, but in a state that would leave her father no choice but to call for the nobles to raise banners again, and ride from the Great Keep.

She shuddered, and Yala's attention focused upon her. "My princess? Are you well?"

"It is very hot," Gamnae murmured. She looked truly chastened. "We should return, Crown Princess, if it pleases you. The servants will bring us something cool to taste, and more fans."

"That would be lovely." Mahara raised her chin. "I am sorry to be such a wilting reed, Second Princess. We are used to the North, Yala and I, and Zhaon's heat is sometimes oppressive."

"I was born here, yet I find it the same." The girl smiled, a wide, uncomplicated expression. How, under Heaven, had that nasty First Queen produced her? Would Mahara's own children be so different?

That was a question for another time. Mahara offered the Second Princess her arm and they set off, chatting amiably about Khir as Yala paused to allow them precedence. Mahara's head was abuzz with heat and the prickling, nagging feeling that she was missing something in her careful thoughts about peace, and war, and a princess's body caught between.

She had no leisure to indulge, either, for when they returned to her receiving-room, another guest had arrived. It was General Zakkar, who bore a letter to Komor Yala from the Second Concubine.

The Honor of Understanding

This shaded verandah looked out upon a familiar Jonwa dry-garden, succulents luxuriating in the heat, sand and stone rippling under sunshine. It was less humid than the water-gardens, and Lady Komor poured tea for both of them before breaking the seal upon Kanbina's letter and scanning the characters within. If it troubled her to be so near to the site of an assassin's death, she made no sign. Her kaburei maid, settled upon her knees inside the open partition-door to preserve the light fiction of chaperonage, was safely out of earshot if they were not overloud.

"She is somewhat worried for your health," Kai offered, somewhat awkwardly. He did not know what else Kanbina had written, and Yala's mouth turned up at the corners. That slight curve settled his liver, but it made his pulse do something strange. He could not decide whether his heart-gallop was too fast or too slow.

"It seems she is." Yala's smile broadened. Her ear-drops, small rounded slivers of dark blue glass, would glitter if sunlight reached them. "You are, no doubt, to return to her with a full report upon my condition."

"Of a certainty." As a matter of fact, that had been his adoptive-mother's last command. "I am glad she gave me a reason to visit, for I wished to inquire about your health as well."

"It seems a day for visits with secondary purposes. I am glad you came, General Zakkar; I wished to speak to you. It seems I am always thanking you."

That was pleasant, yet Kai wondered what Gamnae's purpose here was. The First Queen did not send her out to intrigue, perhaps knowing her daughter was less capable than most of such an operation. Still, even the most innocent of puddles could be seined for information.

Kai settled more firmly upon his cushion, glad he was not in half-armor today. All the same, his robe lacked the weight of leather and metal safety. The new hurai, a heavy satin weight, clasped his finger; he could not tell if it comforted him or not. "I told you I would be useful. And you have not thanked me yet, Lady Komor."

"Forgive me." She bowed slightly and refolded the letter with solicitous care. "I have been somewhat indisposed."

"Yes." And now he could have scolded himself with a practice-blade, for he had not meant to extract gratitude from her. "It was not my meaning to chide you, merely to remark thanks are unnecessary. And I wish to apologize."

Her hairpin beads stilled as she did, a watchful feline conserving energy. "For what?" She gazed at him, not upon the garden, and it was pleasant to have her attention.

Even if it did turn his pulse into a lesser battle-gallop, too fast for comfort but too slow for the shock of meeting an enemy. "For arriving so late to your rescue. Unpardonable in a general and even more so in a prince." If he kept a light tone, it could even be accounted a humorous sally. No matter that he meant it.

"So now you are a prince, as well as a general and a god of war." She listed them, holding up her slim left hand and counting off like a merchant with kombin. Her sleeve fell back, showing a well-bleached, well-wrapped bandage about her wrist.

He could not hide a smile, though his gut threatened to clench at the reminder. "Do you dislike all three, Lady Komor?"

"I am not given leave to dislike princes, generals I have little experience with, and a god of war seems above any feelings of mine." Her eyes all but sparkled, and she touched her teacup with a fingertip, gauging the heat. So the lady could enjoy herself, given the chance. "But it would be ill-mannered of me to dislike *you*, Zakkar Kai. Especially when you carried me from the wild boar's den with such care."

"Ah. Yes. Well." Did his cheeks redden? He could blame it upon the weather, perhaps. The afternoon was young, and a storm was lingering in the distance, perhaps to be driven off by the dry days arriving early. At least, there was room to hope the sky would not dump yet more water upon them. He was no farmer, to know or care if the field had enough rain. "Takshin and I were anxious to find you."

She raised a charcoal eyebrow, resettling her sleeve. The faint dewing of sweat upon the curve of her neck was a jeweled glitter. "To find me, and not the author of the plot?"

"It was very likely that one would lead to the other, Lady Komor. In any case, had we separated, we would have been less efficient at finding either." Somehow the "Big Man" the hapless kidnappers had referred to had sensed Takshin's arrival, or observed a prudent distance from the meeting place and been warned. There was no need to inform her more deeply, though.

A lady should not have to worry over such things. She had enough to worry her, as her next question proved. She leaned forward slightly, pale gaze fixed upon him. "And... you did not tell Prince Takshin of my *yue*."

"Of course not." He schooled himself to stillness, his gaze fixed upon her mouth. If he concentrated there, perhaps he would not stare at her neckline. Too high for a Zhaon dress, and yet lower than a Khir's, a fascinating slice of pale copper skin just showing the beginning of tender swellings that marked a woman. "That is how you freed yourself from the bindings."

"Yes." Her lips were slightly dry; they shaped the word with care. Now she glanced away at the dry-garden, and just as quickly settled her gaze upon Kanbina's letter, waiting patiently for a reply. "I was waiting for the masked... for the one Prince Takshin struck first to sleep a little more deeply before I attempted my escape."

"Hm." They had arrived in time, then. Just barely. "You did not trust that help would arrive?"

"It seemed a very slender chance. In any case, I could not risk staying in their clutches, for obvious reasons."

"Which were?" He could think of many, but he wished to hear her speak. If he knew where her concerns lay, he could soothe them; knowing how she thought and what she dreaded was the first step in his plan. If he did, indeed, have a plan, and not just a collection of half-formed wishes.

He was treating this as a battlefield, and could not shake the habit.

"Can you not guess?" She touched her cup again, perhaps impatient for her tea to cool. Her sleeve hid the bandage, but knowing it was there, that her blood had been loosed by harsh treatment, brought back the colorless sohju rage.

He throttled it. "Enlighten me." *Speak more, my lady, for I welcome it.* Zhe Har, again. The Archer had written much upon women.

Hopefully, he knew what he was about, and his guidance would not lead Kai astray.

"Well." Yala settled, tucking Kanbina's folded letter in her sleeve, and all her attention settled upon Kai, rain after a long thirst. "First, I had to move before I grew too weak to fight. And they were to take me to their Big Man, the author of the plot—"

"Or merely the middleman who paid them. He was wise to reserve some portion of the payment until your safe delivery." Perhaps he *should* tell her the man had escaped. This attempt had been expensive, though—who would waste another such investment? And why worry her, at all?

Yala made a brief restrained motion of agreement. "Well, yes, if one must plot, one must do so wisely. He could very well have discerned I was not my princess, and I had to act before that was a possibility. And I also did not think the three of them likely to keep any vows respecting their captive's condition before surrendered."

"Ah. Yes." Now he glanced away, embarrassed. "Had they outraged you, Lady Komor—"

Her back stiffened, and all trace of levity or enjoyment left her tone. "I would have cut my own throat with my *yue* before I allowed such a thing."

"I see." He had meant other injury, but she, of course, did not. She was determined, and spoke of opening her own throat as if it were an accepted risk of living.

Were all Khir women like her? Had they had been allowed to take the field, Three Rivers would have been a different battle indeed.

She finally turned away, ostensibly watching the heat-ripples, the dusty succulents glowing green. One or two had flowered, bright spikes of desert color atop swollen buttons and columns starred with spikes. Come winter, they would shrink and become dry sticks, waiting for more clement temperatures. But her attention was focused inward, and whatever she saw, it was not sand or greenery. "That is what the maiden's blade is for."

"You did not think rescue would come?" He was repeating himself but could not help it. Imagining how alone, how frightened even such a contained, pragmatic lady must have felt pained him, an oblique pang inside his higher ribs.

"I am not quite sure how you managed to find me." She examined her lap now, dark blue silk lying decorously heavy against fragile skin.

Now was the time to ease her anxieties, if he could. "Sheer dogged cunning, my lady. And Takshin is a good tracker."

"Is he." The mention of the Third Prince did not startle her.

Of course, Takshin lived in the Jonwa now. The Crown Prince was relying upon him to lend protection to Princess Mahara as well, which meant Taktak would pass words with Yala regularly. "One of the best." The Shan did not hunt with hawks, but read ground-signs of an animal's passage to find their prey. They also hunted bandits, and a Shan nobleman without a few marks of that nature upon his spear was accounted a sorry figure indeed.

She was not content to let the matter rest. "I suppose a city is a wilderness, but—"

"One day I shall tell you how we found you, but you are already pale. I should cease troubling you with this subject and return you to your princess; you are perhaps not recovered."

"It was a severe shock," she agreed. "But we have not yet finished our tea, and besides, I am made of strong silk, General Zakkar."

Oh, she was indeed. But even the strongest silk could be torn, or marred. Such fine material required care, and he would be the one to provide it. "It's Kai."

"And I am Yala," she said, softly. "It would be ill-mannered of me, also, to refuse you my name."

"You are gracious, my lady." He picked up his own cup. Its glow was different from the sun's heat, and it would cool him wonderfully once he drank enough to raise a sweat. "Yala."

"Hm?" She tested her tea with a decorous sip. Her shoulders had eased somewhat.

He risked a moment of absolute truthfulness. "You shall not ever be placed in that uncertainty again."

"I find it unlikely the attempts upon the Crown Prince's life, or upon my princess, will cease." She blew across the top of steaming liquid. "Even when the Emperor—long may he battle—is gone, they will not stop."

"I suppose not. But you are under the protection of a general now, Lady Yala. When you wish to leave the palace, I shall accompany you." There. His standards had risen; he was committed. Did she have the strategy to see as much?

She might not have, for she studied her teacup with an abstract, worried air. "I could not trouble you so. The Crown Princess already has guards—"

"Do me the honor, Lady Yala, of understanding me." Kai waited until her startled gaze returned to him. "The Crown Princess is in Takyeo's capable hands, and he is making arrangements. I am... concerned for you."

"Ah."

The silence was very long, and his heart thundered. How much plainer would he have to be? It was useless, of course, if she was already fond of Takshin, but...

"I think my father would like you, General Zakkar Kai." Her tone was not sharp, but instead, almost wondering. "He admires honorable men. I think his grief at Khir's defeat would be ameliorated somewhat, knowing you are such."

There were worse things to be called, and he had heard many of them applied to him. "A high compliment."

"One you are more than worthy of." Another gentle, altogether beautiful smile, lighting her pale eyes and changing her face from sharp-solemn to wistfully pretty. "You have kept my secrets admirably, and I shall strive to be worthy of your friendship."

Kai's chest eased. There was time, perhaps. At least he had chosen the ground for this campaign, and had room to maneuver. "Are we indeed friends?"

"I would like to be, if that is not irksome to you." She paused, weighing her response, and added more. A tinge of ruddiness had crept into her cheeks. "Perhaps you will accompany me, and linger while I write a reply to your mother?"

Hope bloomed sharp, bright, and vicious inside him, a weapon far sharper than any assassin's. "I wish for nothing else in this world, my lady. Allow me also, then, to accompany you should you need to visit the world outside the palace walls again. I shall make time for such sorties."

She gathered her skirts, preparing to rise, and he hurried to do so as well. "You think I will not be troubled by importunate kidnappers in your presence?" Again, her eyes sparkled, and her quiet amusement was more precious than silver ingots.

"Of course." He offered his hand. "And it will save me the trouble of coming to look for you."

"Ah." She laid her fingers in his, rising slowly, and the torch of her touch put the sun to shame. "This is to save yourself the labor. I see."

Kai's laugh surprised him. "Princes are lazy."

"Laziness does not suit you." She let her hands fall to her sides, arranged her skirts and sleeves, and darted him a mischievous glance. "Yes, Prince Kai. I will be honored to have your escort, at times convenient to you."

"Good." He restrained the urge to give a curt nod, as if she were a soldier accepting orders. "Now we shall repair inside. Mother is anxious to hear from you, but I am under strict orders not to bring you to her until you are quite recovered."

"Second Concubine Kanbina is very kind," she murmured, and waited, her eyebrows raised slightly.

Kai realized what she was waiting for, and offered his arm. She accepted it, sliding her small hand into the crook of his elbow, and another soft scalding went through him.

He set a slow pace, and waited while she bent over fine cloth-paper and brushwork at a study-desk in the receiving-hall. When he had the letter for Kanbina he took his leave. The heat did not bother him, and the palace was beautiful under its carapace of red tile and heavy golden sunshine.

He was late for the Great Council, but Zakkar Kai did not care.

Rare Birds

Late at night, with a single earthenware cup of cloudy rai brandy, Lord Komori Dasho gazed into a sullen ember-glowing fire. Two letters lay upon his knee, and he saw the characters they contained in the red of the coals, the black of charring, the edges of white ash.

One was from his daughter. *There have been some small incidents, but nothing of concern. Above all, I keep my honor unstained.* She had chosen a character with knifelike edges, his clever girl. If only she had been born a son... but that was useless.

He would have lost both his children at once, instead of slowly. The shock would not have killed him, but opening his veins afterward would. He would have made certain of it.

Do not be troubled for me. The court ladies here are kind enough, and I have built a small bulwark against ill-luck. My princess's husband has given her land, can you imagine, Father? An estate, with rai, mungh, flax, and kaburei. *I am reading agricultural treatises the court astrologer has collected, in order to know how the steward is managing. It is so busy I have little time for* sathron *playing, though there is a royal lady here who is quite the artist and I take lessons when I can.*

The minutiae of daily life, yet there were hints of unpleasantness scattered all through. Thank Heaven, the winds, and the gods he had insisted upon *yue* training; the maiden aunts had intimated once or twice that surely, a modern noblewoman should not bear any marks except inked hawk-kisses upon her flesh.

No, Hai Komori Dasho had answered once, his brow full of thunder, *the old ways endure in this clan, and in this house.*

They had not broached the subject again. Now he only hoped they had trained her thoroughly enough.

We play kaibok whenever we may, and there is a young prince who wishes to learn the game. He is a clumsy rider, but his spirit is generous. It was the term for a well-meaning bumbler, and the slight fillip at the end of her brushstrokes told him she was amused. Which prince? Was she an exotic figure at their court? Did the Zhaon men gather as he had kept the Khir noble boys from doing? It was a nest of snakes, that palace in the heart of the lazy, importunate South, and she had only her *yue* and tradition to sustain her.

Thank you for the silk; there was enough for two dresses and a few other items. The longer sleeves of Khir are too warm for the South, but I sew as modestly as possible. Some of the younger court ladies here expose their chests much as Su Ju-ong in the tale of the brazen arrows.

The servants or junior clan members would have been surprised to see the smile lingering upon Dasho's thin lips.

At the end, she scolded him gently as a daughter should. *Your health is important, Father. Remember the liniment upon your ribs, and have Auntie Muon prepare your bed with hot bricks. Remember not to eat pickled sahai during the month of thunder, as it will chill your liver. I shall send you some medicines with my next letter; the apothecaries here have much to recommend them.*

Her postscript, in different ink with a much smaller, finer brush, was hurried. *I spilled my tea today, and it made a flower upon the tablecloth. A small one, but I was still upset at my own clumsiness. At least I did not burn my hand.*

Komori Dasho's belly was cold, as if he had been stabbed. So. The characters were angular, but that was the nature of the message. Patiently, as she practiced her brushwork, he had told her the secret language of Komori, the way members of the clan hinted at things which could not be written and possibly read by spies or royal censors.

There had been an attempt upon the princess, a serious one, and it had been foiled. Which brought him to the other letter, its brushwork not nearly as flowing or decorative.

Dasho finally moved, massaging his left shoulder carefully. The pain was worse today, and he took a restorative sip of rai brandy once he had finished the ineffectual rubbing.

On the surface, the second letter was from a merchant inquiring after rare birds in the markets of Zhaon for a noble Khir client. A certain bird could not be procured, but a few more weeks should see a change in the weather, and the merchant promised a fine specimen would be brought to Hai Komori, not a feather of its plumage harmed during its travels, every measure taken to deliver it safely and above all, *intact.*

Slowly, Komori Dasho rose, shuffling to the fireplace. The second letter went into the embers, and he watched as it flared, a brief transitory light. His thumb sought the familiar weight of his signet, warm metal, and found nothing but the cold, dry, rasping underside of his own finger.

Ah, yes. A sign of age, forgetfulness. His signet was in other hands, working its way toward his little light. The head of Komori had retired from public life and the Great Rider did not ask his counsel. Ashani Zlorih was surrounded by others among the Second Families, those grasping at power or privilege a Komori would disdain.

Komori Dasho had made what arrangements he could. The clan would survive in a junior branch; all things, under the heavens, had their time. The last fading flower of Komori would hopefully fall upon a somewhat royal pillow, and take root.

His shoulder ached, ached. He tossed the last of the rai brandy far back and set the fused-glass cup upon the mantel. There was a rustling in the study's corners—perhaps the ancestors, gathering to scold him for betraying his Great Rider and a lifetime of honor for something so transitory, so worthless as a daughter.

Oh, but her laughter, heard far away in the nursery as he attended to clan business in this very study. Or her footsteps, first heavy with a child's heedlessness, then a girl's more decorous step, and finally a woman's gliding. His daughter on horseback, playing kaibok with his son and a bastard princeling, and her high hawk-cry of victory when a stick splintered and the ball rocketed past guard-posts into the nowhere-land. And what a rider she was, his little light. Melded to the rhythm, horse and girl one creature, her hairpin fallen free and a long sheaf of black unraveling upon a hot summer wind…

His left hand was a fist. It crumpled the first, more precious letter, and the rustling became a roar, a high-pitched whine.

A spear through his chest, high up on the left, and Hai Komori Dasho, veteran of many battles, finally fell.

How strange, was his last thought. *I thought I would see more of summer.*

Yala…

A Disagreeable Chore

The grand high-timbered receiving-hall of the Jonwa was second in size only to the Kaeje's, the Crown Prince rehearsing the look of rule as well as its practical aspects. Pearlfruit Month had arrived, the Blossom Festival hard approaching, and the traditional balancing of accounts meant three clerks were at the left side of the hall, busily chronicling the lines of soberly dressed artisans or stewards come to make their tribute to their lord. Along the right side, other clients cooled their heels or murmured, and two stewards shuttled between that well-mannered crowd and the dais at the far end, where Crown Prince Takyeo and his new wife sat in state under a satin-carved stone statue of paired snow-pards many armlengths high.

Yala stood behind her princess, the fan in her hands plumed with marsh-wailer feathers, and shifted from foot to foot. They both ached, but if she swayed a little, the discomfort from one made the other seem almost rested. Her thighs were unhappy too; the morning's kaibok had been a harsh game. Mahara was troubled about something, and hence a little harder to gracefully concede to.

So Yala had not tried, but she had exerted herself a bit too much. A long warm bath tonight was called for. At least her wrists were fully healed now, and the livid marks upon them fading quickly.

The stewards brought petitioners one by one—nobles seeking Takyeo's favor in some matter or another, merchants in need of a dispensation or license, farmers of the better sort seeking easement or a relief from the corvée, applicants for the Golden Guards seeking a patron's seal, sober brown-robed scholars seeking patronage as well. A few courtiers in their high, strange hats waited, too, either bearing messages or intent upon some profit or position. There was even a eunuch, sitting straight-backed upon a bench, his beardless, pale face a mask.

Yala studied the eunuch curiously as he rose, summoned by a harried steward's perfunctory bow. Mahara glanced back at her, and she hurried to produce a small flask of cold hanryeo tea. The princess took a decorous sip. "This is awful," she said, softly, dabbing at her mouth with the small cotton cloth Yala slipped from her sleeve.

"Courage, wife." Takyeo's smile was set, and he shifted slightly upon his bench-cushion. His own attendant, a sleepy-eyed Golden, unhelmeted and with a high but scanty topknot, blinked. "Only a few more candle-marks, and we shall be free to go riding."

"Will you come with, Yala?" Mahara's pleased smile was a reward all its own.

"Alas, I must write letters." It was not *quite* an untruth. But Yala's back was tight, her feet hurt, and her legs still felt the gallop-jolts. Tea and taking off her outer robe in the privacy of her shaded quarters was a much more attractive prospect than galloping in the heat.

"To your father?" Mahara gestured, and Yala capped the flask. "You write him every week, do you?"

"Of course. He asked me to." Even contemplating a bath did very little to relieve her present discomfort.

"Very filial." Takyeo's smile stretched, became natural. He gave her a very approving glance indeed. "He must miss you."

"I am not certain of that, Prince Takyeo. He may find the quiet of Hai Komori to his liking." Still, Yala returned his smile, refolding the cotton square. "Shall I fan you, my princess?"

"Yes, but not too much, I dislike the prickles."

It happened so quickly. The eunuch swayed to a halt at the foot of the dais, and Prince Takyeo's attention turned to this new petitioner. A slight frown bloomed upon the Crown Prince's face, the look of a man reaching to remember a name or a place and rising just a few fingerwidths short of the goal. Yala almost bent to retrieve the plumed fan, but her right hand plunged to her side, and warm metal filled her fingers.

Her body knew before the rest of her, and it was only later she realized the eunuch, though he swayed, had not made the distinctive tiptap noises of a Two-Face's high-blocked gait upon flagstones. His gaze rested upon Mahara instead of the Crown Prince, and his hands flickered, his own fan snapped shut, a wicked gleam springing from its long guard-edge.

"*For Zhaon!*" he yelled, in a voice oddly deep for one of his kind, and lunged up the steps.

Yala pitched forward, and silk tore. The *yue* swept up, its arc intercepting the fan-blade; she exhaled smoothly and turned her wrist, the strike jolting all the way down her arm. Her footing was not solid, her heel slipping upon the edge of Mahara's pooled robe, and her princess's high piercing shriek was a distraction so she closed it away.

The eunuch lunged again, seeking to stab past her, but Yala's hip dropped and the *yue* made a small circle called *threading-the-needle*, stinging his wrist. She was in Hawk Pose now, ready to fall upon this threat with claws and sharp beak, her princess safely behind her, rising shouts and screams as the crowd recognized danger in its midst.

Shimmerdrops of sweat stood upon the false eunuch's forehead. He jabbed again, and his other hand was full of a sharp gleam as well, a cruel curved blade. Yala's knees loosened, and she kicked Mahara's robe free of her heel with a quick dancer's flick.

Prince Takyeo cried out too, a wordless warning, but Yala had already seen the second blade. The *yue* dragged her hand aside and her right hip moved as she bent into a *hau* character, the curved blade whispering past her waist, its edge dragging through silken sash. It did not touch flesh only because she had bent to extremity, daily stretching returning its investment tenfold.

Oiled metal hissed free from a sheath behind her, but she could not worry for the Crown Prince. Her only worry was Mahara, who gasped and scrabbled backward, probably searching for a weapon too.

I really must visit the metalsmith soon, Yala thought, inconsequentially, and the *yue* slashed diagonally, tapping aside the eunuch's fan-blade. Cunning, to hide a weapon upon the edge of such a daily item. The *yue* halted, flashing back to the right to sting the eunuch's hand holding the curved knife, and the not-eunuch pitched forward, probably intending to rush her. She had the high ground, but if he was heavy enough he might be able to overwhelm—

Crunch.

The false eunuch halted, looking down at his chest, where a dripping spearpoint protruded. His dark robe swayed, and Yala saw he was indeed not wearing a eunuch's proper shoes but instead, sandals of twisted hempen twine.

How strange. Where had she seen similar ones? Upon the feet of those who had held her in a filthy basement while they fed a fire and spoke of the Big Man. The realization, useless at the moment, fled swiftly.

The Jonwa's great receiving-hall was full of golden-armored guards now, commoners fleeing or screaming and white-faced nobles in a tight knot, huddled like eggbirds seeking collective comfort.

A blood-bubble burst upon the eunuch's lips. Yala watched as he slumped, spilling to the side, and met the gaze of the pockmarked guard in glittering gold holding the spear. Dark, and flat, as if killing a man were simply a disagreeable chore, best done quickly. Behind him, other guards converged, shouting, and the chaos reached a fresh pitch.

Yala did not lower her blade. Instead, she watched the hall, and behind her, Mahara said her name over and over, a song of relief.

Komor Yala did not even mind when the guards surrounded her, the pockmarked one shouting something in Zhaon she again did not recognize until later, and she was borne away.

She has a blade! She has a blade within the Palace!

Follow Your Example

"Out of my way!" Takyeo shoved at the carved double doors, much harder than necessary. They flew wide, shivering against the walls on either side, and he strode into his father's vermilion-columned hall, his topknot slightly askew and his eyes blazing. "*Father!*"

The Emperor, in state upon his throne for his own Pearlfruit Month reckoning, glanced up, his eyebrows meeting. "Ah, the Crown Prince."

The lately arrived Binei Jinwon, Lord Yulehi, stared in unfeigned astonishment as Takyeo cut through knots of courtiers. Zan Fein, in his cloud of umu-blossom scent, frowned slightly, and Zakkar Kai, having just arrived from cavalry drill for afternoon Council through the smaller southron door, halted in amazement.

"Why?" Takyeo came to a halt at the foot of the throne-dais, his green-and-gold court robe swaying. He should have been in his own hall balancing accounts and dispensing patronage. Today was the day for such efforts. "By Heaven, *why*?"

"What—" Lord Yulehi began, but the Emperor lifted a hand.

"My son," he began, with deceptive calmness. "I am relieved to see you well."

"Do not hide behind etiquette, *Father.*" Takyeo drew himself up and glared at the man who had made him. "Why have you not released Lady Komor?"

Kai's feet turned to leaden tree roots. *What is he...*

"The Khir girl?" The Emperor affected astonishment. "She had an unsanctioned blade, my son. In the Palace, in the Jonwa itself."

"She *saved my wife's life.*" Takyeo's hands were fists.

Kai had often thought that someday, the Crown Prince's patience would come to an end. He had even, once or twice, thought such an event would be welcome. Now, though, it did not seem amusing, wise, or even particularly effective. This was a mistake, and he could not catch Takyeo's gaze to tell him as much.

"And she had a hidden weapon upon her person in the presence of a prince." Lord Yulehi's oiled, aristocratic tones rose, dulcet and stinging. "Perhaps more than once. Such things cannot be overlooked." Binei Jinwon smoothed his chin with one hand. The First Queen's uncle, recently arrived to take Hanweo Hailung Jedao's spot as prime councilor for the last half of the year, did not bother to hide his pleasure.

Of course. Takyeo was making a scene, and Kai could tell Tamuron was irritable today. It was a recipe for disaster. Had Yala somehow shown that stinging, deadly blade? She did not seem the type to drop it from a sheath while bowing; it could only mean there had been another attempt.

And he had been absent, and useless, during it.

"I did not ask your opinion, *Lord* Yulehi." Takyeo gazed steadily at the Emperor. "I was speaking to my father. Kindly keep your peace."

Oh, Takyeo. That's a bad move. Kai's mouth was salt-dry. Surely it was not Yala under suspicion of...and yet, she had that blade, and the will to use it. If a blade left the sheath in Mahara's presence, her lady-in-waiting would not think twice before moving to meet it.

"A prince does not punish a messenger for bad tidings, Takyeo." The Emperor lifted one royal hand, the silver upon his right hurai winking. He had been mostly silent during the arguments in morning council, and danger lurked in the set of his shoulders. "The Khir girl will be whipped for two hands instead of to death, for she is noble. Who can tell she was not part of the plot?"

Of course. At least one and possibly two of the recent assassins had been from the North, and the attempt upon Mahara would fuel Tamuron's suspicion.

"She was defending the Crown Princess," Takyeo insisted. "I was there, Father, and you were not; I saw what happened. It was an arm's length from me."

A suppressed gasp slithered through the Court.

Tamuron's cheeks turned the color of good-luck bricks. "Do you think me unaware of what happens in my own palace, my son?"

"I think it beneath you to order a noblewoman whipped for defending your daughter-in-law," Takyeo parried. Had he lost all his discretion at once? It was akin to seeing a patient beast that had given many years of service suddenly break a fence and lunge for freedom.

"The law is the law." Now Tamuron was well and truly irritated, and Kai knew that stubborn set to the older man's jaw. The Emperor could magnanimously blame his guards or allow Takyeo a shred of mercy for a single lady-in-waiting, certainly, but his current temper, ever more uncertain as illness frayed its bonds, might not grant such grace.

He racked his brains for something to say, anything. Yala, whipped?

I would open my own throat first.

Kai could very well say he had given her the blade, but then Tamuron would ask how she had learned to use it in such a short while, and—

"Do you wish the assassin had succeeded in killing my wife,

then? Do you, Father? Was this *your* doing?" Takyeo all but shook with rage. His cheeks were the same color as his father's, and they looked much alike in this moment.

The silence that fell upon the crimson-columned hall was even more marked than gasps of astonishment. The only person who was even remotely enjoying himself here was Binei Jinwon, and Kai could almost hear the First Queen laughing with glee over this affair. Any division between the Emperor and his eldest son was as food and tea to her.

"You are not Emperor yet," Garan Tamuron said, in a slow, even tone. "Remove yourself from our presence until you may act as befits your station."

Takyeo studied the older man for a long few moments, then clasped his hands. No—he reached for his left hand with his right, and worked his hurai from his left first finger. He lifted the heavy greenstone ring, glittering upon his palm.

"Crown Prince..." Zan Fein murmured, and tensed.

Kai's jaw felt suspiciously loose. Of all the things he suspected Tamuron's eldest son capable of, this was one of the last.

"If you are to be such an Emperor, Father, I shall be proud not to follow your example," the Crown Prince said, quietly, and turned his hand over. The hurai fell, bouncing upon stone with a small chiming sound, and he turned upon his heel, striding away. Courtiers parted like waves before a prow, eunuch, minister, and noble all bowing with the same air of shock-laced dismay.

"Takyeo." The Emperor raised his fist, pounded his royal knee. "*Takyeo!*"

The Crown Prince did not turn, halt, or even pause.

Zakkar Kai exhaled sharply. He strode for the throne, pushing aside two Golden Guards who stood slackjaw-witless. He bent to pick up the hurai, straightened, and glanced at the Emperor.

"Kai." Tamuron was scarlet now, bolt-upright, and shaking with rage as he had been only once or twice in Zakkar Kai's memory. "My faithful general."

Did the accent upon his faithfulness mean Tamuron was beyond sense, suspecting even the most loyal? It was a terrible thought.

"I shall return this to its owner," Kai said, numbly. Then, because he might as well, he finished Takyeo's work. "He is in the right, Emperor Garan Tamuron. Your eldest son is absolutely correct."

He turned, too, and hurried after the Crown Prince.

Time for Action

She had not asked for permission to leave the Jonwa, and some part of her quailed at the thought of her husband's displeasure. And yet here she stood, without even a veil to protect her honor but determined nonetheless. Mahara set her chin. "I am the Crown Princess of Zhaon," she repeated, "and I will see my lady-in-waiting, *now.*"

The full-cheeked Golden Guard in his glittering armor all but sneered. Behind him, a brick archway loomed, exhaling foul mouth-stench. Anh, cringing behind Mahara, clutched at a cotton-wrapped bundle and tried to make herself as small as possible.

"So sorry." The guard's tone suggested he was not sorry at all. "Upon the Emperor's orders, my lady. None may visit the Khir traitor."

Traitor? Mahara's entire body was cold, a flame so intense it was ice.

"Besides, no lady wants to be in the dungeons. Bad place for it." He grinned, wide and mocking. Even this *peasant* of a Zhaon did not quail before a princess of Khir, and the event turned Mahara into a statue for a moment, trembling with unseemly, highly unfeminine rage.

"Toh Dunh, is it?" A man's voice came from the hall behind Mahara; she whirled, her back alive with prickleflesh and her throat suddenly dry. "Yes, I thought I recognized you. How is your wife?"

"Better, Honorable Mrong Banh." The guard hurried to bow, as he had not for the Crown Princess. "Much better, since the physician's visit. She is thankful to you, and—"

"Good, good." The court astrologer, his brown robe hurriedly brushed clean and his topknot very tight as if he had just now rewrapped it, bustled to a stop next to Mahara and bowed deeply in her direction. "I am quite sorry I am late, Your Highness. Thank you for waiting for me. You are quite gracious."

Waiting for him? She caught the gleam in his shadowed eyes and hurried to nod. If he was offering aid, she would use it gratefully. Yala said he was a scholar, and furthermore, that he was kind. "I know you are very busy, Honorable Mrong." His name was funny, but she didn't do too badly pronouncing it. Or so she hoped. "I was simply passing the time with the… honorable… guard, here."

"Ah, yes." The astrologer's expression did not suggest he knew exactly how that had been faring, but she suspected all the same. "Toh Dunh's a good man. Well, we'll be on our way then."

"Well…" The guard shifted from foot to foot, rather like Yala during a long sleepy afternoon upon the dais but without her lady's grace. "The thing is, Honorable, well… orders, you know…"

"Pfft. Surely you don't believe the Crown Princess will be carrying tales to her husband, hmmm? Unless it is the tale of a guard who understands the sage's first duty of compassion." Mrong Banh swept forward and half-bowed, extending his arm. Mahara hurried to push forward as well, and in short order they were past the guard, who scratched under his helmet and looked much less terrifying.

And much less disdainful, too. Anh scurried in their wake, and Mahara let out a soft, tense breath.

"Regrettable lack of imagination, that blockhead." Mrong Banh shook his slicked-tight head and indicated a particular passage. "This way, I believe. Were you waiting long? I came as soon as Kai told me what was afoot."

Zakkar Kai? Of course, her husband held the general in high regard. He gave Mahara a shiver each time they met, though. The butcher of Three Rivers was not a friend to any Khir, even if his adoptive-mother was the best of the Emperor's wives. "They arrested Yala." Her lips were numb, and that circling, icy fury had retreated somewhat. "For having a... well, you must know."

"I know. Ease yourself, Crown Princess. We shall unknot this tangle."

There was a clanging, and barred doors rose on either side. Some of the cells had to be occupied, but Mahara did not look. She set her gaze straight ahead and followed Mrong Banh's long strides.

"I hope you are right," she muttered darkly.

These cells were larger, and Mrong Banh finally halted at one whose door was simply an iron grille. Torches smoked, and there was weak mirrorlight from an aperture overhead. And there, huddled in the far corner of the square room, on sour straw that had definitely *not* been changed for a good while, was a familiar form.

"Yala!" Mahara rushed to the grille. "Oh, Yala. I am so sorry."

Yala raised her head. Her hairpin was askew, and a few blue-black strands had come loose from her braids. For a moment, her eyes glittered, and she looked as if she did not recognize the woman at the cell entrance. Then, sense filtered back into her pale gaze and she unfolded, stiffly.

Mahara swallowed dryly. "Are you well? They did not... they did not harm you, did they?"

"No." Yala rose, approached the bars cautiously. "They were not overkind, but they were not cruel, either. They even accorded me the courtesy of asking if I carried other blades instead of pawing me. Are you well, my princess?"

How could she inquire of *Mahara's* health at a time like this? "Oh, Yala. It's all such a mess. Husband went to the Emperor and returned angry, the Jonwa is full of comings and goings, there is much gossip, and they are saying such horrible things."

"Of course." Yala peered past her. "It is Anh. Oh, and Mrong Banh. How pleasant to see you, Honorable."

"My lady." Banh's bow was just as deep as to Mahara, and that mark of respect suddenly raised him several ili in Mahara's water-clock. "You must be very brave, now."

"Why?" Yala indicated her surroundings with a single, graceful motion. "I am in the safest part of the palace. We should move everyone threatened by assassins here." A small smile lingered upon Yala's lips, but she was so pale. She hid her hands within her sleeves, too. Her shoulders trembled slightly, matching the quiver in Mahara's own.

"They say the Emperor intends to have you whipped," Anh whispered. "Oh, lady, my lady."

"I shall not suffer such a thing." Yala's chin lifted slightly. "But I do not have my *yue*. They took it, my princess. I am sorry."

"What under Heaven do *you* have to be sorry for?" Mahara slipped her hands into her sleeves, too, copying Yala's posture. It was unbecoming to show the shaking in her limbs. "You saved my life, again. The Emperor will not do this. Husband will not allow it."

Mrong Banh sounded doleful, and scratched at his hair, pulling his topknot a little off-center. "I'm not sure the Crown Prince has a choice, Your Highness. But we will find some way through the woods, I am certain."

"The Crown Prince will not let anything so awful happen." Mahara nodded firmly. "Listen, Anh brought some bedding, and food. I do not know what they will feed you."

"Gruel and water, as if in a novel." Yala set her chin, and looked steadily past Mahara. "Honorable Mrong, please tell me, what may I expect?"

Of course she would wish to know. Mahara should have taken steps to find out, but she had been consumed with the need to see her friend. Yala would have thought of it, had Mahara been the one imprisoned. Her nails dug into her palms, the sheath over the smallest on the left biting cruelly.

The discomfort was a tonic. It steadied her, but only for a short while.

"Much depends upon whether the Emperor can be conciliated." Mrong Banh's fuzzy eyebrows were well and truly knotted. "If not, they will fetch you during an afternoon, and—well."

Yala nodded. "You do not think conciliation likely."

"There are suspicions... the current attempt upon the Crown Princess, you understand. More to the point, the Crown Prince embarrassed him in front of the entire court. And the First Queen's uncle is firmly convinced you were part of the plot, or so he says. The guard who dispatched the assassin and called for your arrest has disappeared for a leave-day; when he is found, he will be questioned." Banh's mouth pulled down bitterly at the corners.

"You mean tortured," Yala murmured.

Mahara gaped. "But *why*? He saved me, too."

"It is not just that the First Queen wishes to inconvenience my princess, is it." Yala, thoughtful, accepted the bundle from Anh, whose cheeks gleamed suspiciously in the dimness.

"I cannot quite tell. But she will certainly do all she can to smirch the Crown Prince, and spread discord." Banh rubbed at his chin and clicked his tongue. "You are very calm, Lady Komor."

"What use would weeping do? Or screaming?" She was so pale, and her eyes glittered so feverishly. Her belt was slipping, too, and that was so unlike her calm, demure lady-in-waiting. "I am told the walls of any worthwhile dungeon are thick, and much happens in such places unseen by the sun or any living eyes."

"Tonh Duruoh." Mrong Banh shook his head. "The *Book of Seven Changes*."

"Applicable, don't you think?" Yala raised an eyebrow, but her sleeves trembled faintly.

Mahara sighed. "This is not the time for books, Yala, but for action."

"Certainly. I shall do all I can." Yala smiled, and set the bundle down. Then, carefully folding her sleeves away, she reached through the grillwork, two very small hands that had saved her princess's life.

Mahara clasped them. Strength flowed between them, a steady, quiet flame. "You are wonderful," she said, softly. "You must take care, and not catch an ill vapor here. I will straighten this tangle, and you will be home again before long."

"Home," Yala replied, just as softly. "It is a beautiful word." She leaned forward, and Mahara did as well. Their foreheads touched, and the princess breathed in jaelo, a hint of acrid sweat, and the familiar light-green, tealike tang of her friend. "You must take care while I am trapped here, my princess."

"I shall." She would take much care, and a novel idea occurred to her. She could even ask Third Prince Takshin to take her into the Yaol, to the metalsmith Yala had commissioned. He was frightening and rude, but nobody would dare jostle her in his company.

"Return directly to the Jonwa and stay with your husband, my princess." Yala straightened. "Honorable Mrong Banh, may I trouble you to carry a message for me?"

"Of course, my lady." He bowed again, just as deeply as he had the first time.

"Please ask Third Prince Takshin to take especial care of my princess, until I may return."

Mahara could not suppress a shudder. "He is fearsome indeed." Still, this sealed her intent. She would be as brave as her friend, and go directly to him. *I require your aid*, she would say. *It is for my Yala.* She squeezed Yala's hands, gently, her fingernail-sheath pricking just a little. "You are kind to think of me in your troubles."

"This is not trouble." Yala smiled, wearily. "Merely inconvenience. One way or another, I shall return to your side."

"Good." Mahara did not want to let go, but she had to. "I shall return to the Jonwa. Perhaps the guard will let Anh visit later, again, should you need anything."

"I shall see what I may arrange." Mrong Banh straightened from his bow. "I shall also accompany you now, Crown Princess, if you will have me."

"Of course." She decided at that moment that he was a friend, and she would do all she could for him.

"My lady," Anh whispered through the bars. "I will come back, I promise."

Yala nodded, and Mahara's last glimpse was of her standing, straight-backed and slim in a prison cell, watching her princess with shadowed eyes.

It Only Takes One

The Crown Prince's study was hushed and cool. Scroll-racks and bookcases, closed and secretive, watched three men, while a character-hanging upon the wooden wall—a rendering of the character for *calm thought*, traced by a much younger Takyeo—swayed slightly under an invisible draft.

Takshin folded his arms, leaning back in his eldest brother's chair again. He did not settle his boots upon the desk as he was wont to, though. There was a dangerous flush to Garan Takyeo's cheeks, and he was pacing his study in long swinging strides. One, two, three, four, five, six, seven to a bookshelf loaded with annals, a military turn, back the same way.

He was going to wear a rut in the floorboards. Besides, it wore upon Takshin's nerves. "Did you truly throw your hurai at him, Ah-Yeo?" He clicked his tongue like Mrong Banh. "Shocking, simply shocking."

"It is not wise to bait me at this moment, Taktak." About turn, pace some more. Takyeo halted, stared at the annals as if he were considering burning them wholesale. "He cannot seriously believe Lady Komor a traitor. He is simply determined, because he has been *challenged*."

"That was unwise of you." For once, Takshin was playing the part of the conscientious elder, and it might have amused him in another situation.

Now, it did not. At all.

Takyeo snorted. His hands were fists. Even his topknot was mussed, and his heavy account-day robe held dust at its hem. "What else can I do? He expects me to be a stuffed puppet until I gain the throne, and *then* become a man?"

"He is irritable, of late. You know as much." Takshin pressed his fingertips together. "He will calm himself; we must simply give him time."

"And meanwhile Lady Yala is in the dungeon."

Did Takyeo think he had forgotten? Takshin strangled a flare of irritation. "Banh says the guards will let her kaburei carry to her. I've already loaded the girl with comfortable things." The only reason he had not visited himself was . . . well, he was not certain he could keep his temper at the sight of her in a cell.

No doubt Kai and Banh would be surprised at his restraint. He had plenty, Takshin mused, he simply exercised it where most could not see.

A shadow near the door was Zakkar Kai, his mouth turned down at the corners and his arms crossed. He finally broke his long, dangerous silence with a simple observation. "Lord Yulehi is telling all who will listen that Lady Komor was part of the plot, since she reacted so swiftly. There is gossip that she was to strike Takyeo, and only the guards stopped her."

"Interesting." Takshin's hands ached. His palms itched for a hilt, but this was not a problem to be solved with an edge, no matter how much he longed to. "Perhaps I should speak to my great-uncle." He stretched, and turned the movement into standing, arching his back slightly to ease some small stiffness. Staying here to watch Takyeo pace would only fray his own nerves past bearing. "He seems very interested in these events."

"No doubt the First Queen is delighted to inconvenience the Crown Princess." Kai regarded Takshin. "I know that look. You are bent upon trouble, Taktak."

"Me?" Takshin's grin was broad, and he hoped it was unsettling. "A simple family visit."

"Takshin." Takyeo made his about-face, set off across the study again. "It will only cause more problems."

"I must do something. Lady Komor is part of your household, Eldest Brother. Don't you wish her returned to her quarters and those who speak against her given a sting to their fingers?" *And I shall be the one to return her, this time.* That much, Takshin was determined upon.

"What I wish most at this particular moment is to discern who sent a false eunuch to my receiving-hall to kill my wife." One, two, three, Takyeo continued, and it seemed only a matter of time before he stripped the heavy robe from his shoulders and called for half-armor.

"He cried, *For Zhaon*," Kai added, thoughtfully. "Interesting, no?"

"Indeed." Takyeo finished his trip across the room, halted, and swung about to face the general. "What do you think, Kai?"

Takshin halted too. His head cocked, and he settled upon his heels. *Ah.* "I had not heard this particular tale. Did he, now?" Perhaps his uncle could wait.

"Yes." Kai's eyelids dropped another fraction. It was the same face he wore when viewing a chessboard, or the terrain of a prospective battlefield.

"Loudly, too." Takyeo lifted his hands to his hair. His topknot, securely caged but somewhat worse for wear, twitched, and he pulled his fingers away, making fists again. "If harm befalls my wife, her country may decide even Three Rivers was not enough of a defeat to hold them quiescent. I cannot say I blame them, either."

"There is no peace if Zhaon kills an innocent princess." It made a certain amount of mad sense, and caught upon the battlefield like peasants in a strategic village were the princess—which Takshin did not mind so much, except for his Eldest Brother's comfort—and Komor Yala. Which Takshin *did* mind, and mightily so. "Are they truly so determined to go to war again?"

"Some of them might be." Takyeo had evidently thought the matter through. He was achieving some calm, as well, which was all to the good. "It only takes one, does it not?"

"There may be those in Zhaon who would profit from not just an armed peace, but deeper tribute from Khir's coffers. And there is the perennial matter of southron trade." Kai's stillness was that of a coiled spring. There was likely another piece or two to the puzzle, but if this was the general's reading of the fortune-teller's sticks, it deserved consideration. "And there *are* those who wish a Crown Prince embarrassed, and possibly removed from the line of succession."

"My mother." Takshin's lip lifted. "And Kurin."

"Not necessarily Kurin." Takyeo sighed, shaking the tension from his hands. At least he had stopped pacing, though that mercy might be of short duration. "If she were not whispering in his ear, perhaps he would see reason."

Oh, Takyeo. How little you know. Takshin did not give an inelegant snort of pained laughter, but it was close. "Unlikely, Eldest Brother. In any case, do not trouble yourself. This will be dealt with."

"And how exactly do you propose to do so, Takshin?" Kai's eyebrow rose a fraction. "By striding in, sword swinging?"

If it would have made a difference, he would already have done so. Takshin damped yet another surge of irritation. "I have subtlety to spare for this situation. What would you do, Head General?"

"I do not know yet." A knock at the door peeled Kai away from his station; it was Steward Keh, bowing deeply.

"The Crown Princess asks if you will come to dinner, Your Highness." His long nose twitched.

"Ah, women." Takshin attempted a smile. There was no use in airing his other suspicions. "Dinner must not be late. She is a winning one, your wife."

"I have found her so." Takyeo sounded very much like Tamuron, but nobody would tell him so at the moment. "We shall be along directly, Keh. Has dinner been taken to Lady Komor?"

The Steward nodded. His chain of office lay upon a round chest, but his legs were spindly from childhood malnutrition. "Her kaburei left a few moments ago; my lord the Third Prince was most explicit in his directions."

"Good." Takyeo glanced at Takshin. "She is running back and forth, this kaburei girl. Her feet will wear off."

Takshin shrugged. Let the girl limp, it was the price one paid for being born. "Lady Komor performed a rare service to the household. I would not see her suffer for it." And the kaburei girl now knew that she was being watched by no less than Takyeo's chained wolf. If she was tempted to skimp her duties or carry tales, the weight of his gaze would dissuade her upon both counts.

"Nor would I." Kai's expression darkened, which was thought-provoking. The man was too quiet for Takshin's liking; when Zakkar Kai had made his decisions he grew taciturn, and then he was truly dangerous.

"In that we are in agreement." The Crown Prince waved Keh Tanh away, and the man repeated his deep bow. "Come, dine with me. We shall soothe my wife's fears. Between the three of us, we will save Lady Komor from further distress."

Oh, that we will. But Takshin suspected neither of the others, used to the intrigue and subtlety of the palace, would do so directly.

That much was up to the wolf himself.

To Sharpen Its Flavor

A faded hanging-board painted with an approximation of a turtle had given this tavern its name, and creaked solemnly under flirting, uneasy breeze as a man with good boots, a better but extremely somber robe, and his head wrapped in muffling cloth paced underneath it. Two pot-boys scurried to greet the newcomer, but he made a short sharp gesture with one gloved hand and they retreated. Apparently the man had an appointment to keep, for he climbed the stairs at the back, followed the hallway around three sides of a square, and pushed aside the partition to a particular small room.

Inside, a tall man with pockmarked cheeks sat at a low table, a teapot and two cups set out with a bowl of pickled hanja. He did not rise when the muffle-swathed fellow entered, being entirely taken with staring morosely at the latticed wall, through which a murmur of conversation from the deep well of the tavern's common-room on the first floor bubbled.

The muffled man unwound some small portion of his head-covering and stripped his gloves free. A band of light flesh encircled his left first finger, showing where a nobleman's seal usually rested. Still, the pockmarked fellow did not rise from his seat.

The new arrival slid the partition shut with a decisive click. "That was quick thinking," he finally said, in a light Palace accent but without a lady's slight lisp.

"You never said anything about a girl with a knife." The pockmarked man scratched luxuriously at his neck, and when his tunic's neck was pushed aside a yellow scarf was visible. It marked him as a Golden, one of those fanatical palace guards given better pay and some education in return for their supposed loyalty.

Reward a man, and he might well consent to be loyal. In any case, the better pay lifted many a family from poverty into slim survival, and as long as a young man had some wit and the ability to swing a sword, he could apply for candidacy. All it took was a royal patron's seal.

That patron could, occasionally, reap a benefit or two of his own as well.

"Well, that was unfortunate. You did well to remove the other fellow, but why didn't you complete your half of the job?" The nobleman folded his arms, affecting to lean against the partition.

"What, and then have to fight my way out? I want silver, my lord, not a sword to the guts." The pockmarked man poured a single cup of tea and glared across the darkened room. Afternoon thunder rumbled in the distance, but the storms were arriving later and weaker every day.

The dry times were almost upon Zhaon-An. Preparations for the Blossom Festival had reached a fever pitch, and the great capital was restive with rumor and counter-gossip.

"And silver you shall have. When your work is done."

The pockmarked man shook his head. "*Ai*, my lord. The price has gone up, and I'll take half of it now. It's four ingots."

"A considerable sum." The nobleman paced to the table and lowered himself upon a thin, rancid cushion that had seen much better days. A faint moue of distaste said he would probably burn this robe after it had touched such a thing. "Convince me it will be worthwhile."

"I could go to the Emperor and tell him what I know. Or to the Head General." The pockmarked man's avid dark eyes gleamed.

Lattice-light fell across his face in dim diamond shapes. "Even a word to my square-leader would do."

"True." The nobleman laid his gloves in his lap, and the pockmarked man tensed.

"Bring your paws where I can see them, my lord."

"My what?" A slow, amused word, as if the rich man did not understand.

"I said, bring your hands up to the table, *my lord*." The Golden Guard did not reach for a hilt, but his right-hand fingers twitched. "I am a nervous man today."

"Are you." The nobleman placed his hands upon the table, with a token hesitation at the greasiness of the wood. "And what, precisely, would you tell the Emperor or your square-leader?"

"You think I don't know who you are?" The pockmarked guard scoffed, and took a deep draft of his tea, his gaze never leaving the nobleman's. "Money must soften your brain, my lord."

"Mh." The nobleman reached—slowly, slowly—to take the teapot, and poured himself a healthy dollop. He lifted the cup—hot, but not steaming—to his shrouded mouth, and sniffed, deeply. "Cheap tea."

"I don't have the coin to pay for better." The pockmarked guard grinned. "Yet."

"True." The corners of the nobleman's eyes crinkled. "Were you waiting long for my arrival?"

"It doesn't matter." He took another swallow, set his cup down with a grimace. "Four ingots, my fine lord. Two before I begin the work, the others to be left for me at a place I'll..." He paused, his nose wrinkling. "Ugh."

"This is a cheap place, indeed." The nobleman set his untasted cup down with a soft, decided noise. "Which means the servers are quite amenable to earning a few extra slivers by adding some little tincture to a tea, to sharpen its flavor." His eyes narrowed, their corners bunching as if he smiled, and the pockmarked man's broad, callused hands flew to his throat. "You arrived early, my friend, but others were earlier." Such were the words spoken by a villain in a play currently most popular in the smaller theaters instead of the more refined great high-roofed temples to educational entertainment.

When the pockmarked guard's choking ceased, the nobleman stood, brushing the rancid cushion's impress from the back of his robe with gloved hands. The sharp stink of death-loosened sphincters rose, and the nobleman's nose wrinkled. Still, he bent to his work, stripping the guard of identification and any loose coin, finally tugging a short curved knife from the guard's back-belt and sinking it into the corpse's throat.

It was always best to be sure, and anyone discovering this fellow would assume he had simply chosen the wrong drinking companion. The nobleman tugged at his gloves and left the knife standing in the guard's throat. None of the kitchen staff would breathe a word of poison; the consequences for killing one of the Emperor's Golden were severe.

He left a few slivers upon the table to pay for the mess, and left the room quietly as he had entered.

Practically Kisses

My lady?" A whisper at the bars. "My lady Yala?"

Ugh. Yala stretched, pushing at her hair. The quilted padding was better to sleep upon than filthy dungeon straw—she was seeing a depressing quantity of floor-scatterings, lately. She blinked, moving the thick blanket aside, and found Anh's face in the dimness, pale and strained. "Anh." She rubbed at her eyes. *What I would not give for a bath.*

While she was wishing, she might as well ask for a fast horse, a good hawk, and an endless flask, as the tale went.

"My lady." Anh clasped the bars, white-knuckled. Yet another bundle rested at her slippered feet. "'Tis morning."

Her dinner dishes were stacked neatly near the bars, too, though Yala had not had much appetite. And the girl's expression bode little good. Weak mirrorlight sifted down; this was a luxurious cell, to have such an amenity. "So it is. What ails you, Anh?"

"My lady...they...oh, the guard says they will come for you soon." Anh's eyes glittered, though whether with anger or salt water was difficult to tell. "It is very early, and they will not let me run to the Jonwa to tell the Crown Prince."

"Ah." Yala pushed the blanket even farther aside. Sleeping in her clothes, especially her ruined sash, was uncomfortable at best. At least Anh had been able to bring a comb, the bedding, and various small things, including a sealed jug of water. "Will they at least let you attend me before the festivities?"

"I can ask." She brightened at the thought of a task, this worthy girl.

You are a treasure, Anh. "Do so, then."

The girl vanished, her leather-wrapped braids bouncing. Yala extended her hands and watched them shake. So, the Emperor was determined to have her whipped for showing her *yue* in the palace. And, without it, she was helpless, and could not even open her own throat to avoid the dishonor.

Afterward, though, she could find a way…and there were stories of maidens who bit through their own tongues and bled to death, when robbed of their *yue*. Yala tested her teeth, lightly, against her tongue. Where did you bite? Perhaps she could do so before the whip touched her? Or would she need the pain of the first strike to give her the will?

Movement in the hallway. She stood, hurriedly, pushing her hair back and settling her clothes, lifting her chin.

The guard, a slab-faced peasant uncomfortable in his golden half-armor, shook his head as he rattled the keys. "I shouldn't be doing this," he said, darkly. "Orders, you know."

"But she has nobody to help her," Anh said, cajoling. "I must help my lady comb her hair."

"She has hands, don't she?" But he put the key in the lock and twisted it, and the door-bars in a heavy metal frame swung wide. "No tricks, now."

"Psh. Lock me in, if you must, silly man." Anh hurried to Yala's side. "My lady. Come, let us set you to rights. Where is the bedpan?"

She held the blanket so Yala could relieve herself without the guard's scrutiny and change her under-robe. Then Anh folded the bedding smartly, settling her lady upon it and beginning her work with comb, ribbon, and hairpin. In short order Yala's hair was dressed, her sliced sash folded and artfully arranged, her hands and feet chafed into suppleness, and her face brushed softly with a damp cloth. "I was coming to see what you wished for breakfast," Anh said in an undertone. "The Jonwa is full of lamentation. The Crown Princess is weeping in her room, the Crown Prince is full of thunder, Lady Kue is snappish, and the Third Prince did not sleep for pacing. General Zakkar spent the night in the Kaeje attempting to see the Emperor, and was closeted with the Crown Prince when I left. Normally, the...well, normally, this happens in the afternoon. The Emperor must be wroth."

"Or someone else must be." Yala closed her eyes. "No zhu powder, Anh. There is no use."

"But..." The kaburei changed to a softer, dry cloth. "Yes, my lady. You are so calm. It is simply awful, you should not be punished for what you did."

"Perhaps the Emperor has his reasons." Knowing them would not bring her any comfort at this point, but she still wondered. It had occurred to her, as she settled for last night's attempt at sleep, that it could very well be the Emperor himself who wished Mahara dishonored, to free his eldest son for marrying another princess. Such a thought made her head hurt. "I am surprised he is involved so deeply in my case."

"Well, it was an attack upon the Crown Prince." Anh's touch against her hair was familiar, and deeply comforting.

Was it? "I see." She did not at all, but her servant's next words dispelled much of the mystery.

"I hear it is the First Queen," Anh whispered. "Her uncle is a grand councilor now, and at the Emperor's ear saying that no matter what service you rendered, carrying a concealed weapon inside the palace deserves death. A whipping is a lesser punishment. Because you are a noblewoman."

"Is that so." Yala straightened her back, tested her teeth against her tongue again. How hard, exactly, did one have to bite? Did Zhaon noblewomen not feel the shame of being whipped like a traitor? This was a strange land, indeed.

More footsteps. Yala's eyes flew open; the color drained from Anh's face. The girl swallowed, hard, and if she started weeping now, Yala might find her own composure cracking. "Hush," she said, gently enough, and took Anh's hands in hers. "Help me rise, Anh. You are a treasure." She had not even finished the girl's festival dress yet; the cut pieces were waiting in the cloth-basket in her quarters.

"Oh... my lady..." Anh's chin trembled and her jaw worked. "Perhaps they will take me instead, and let me... I have asked the guard, but..."

"Certainly not." *A noblewoman could not allow such a thing.* Yala took stock. She could walk, she supposed. And keep her composure; she had a lifetime of practice, and now was when her true worth as a daughter of Komori would show itself. "Watch over my princess, Anh. I consign her to your care."

Anh clutched at her hands. "My lady..."

"My lady Komoroh?" The Zhaon could not say her name properly, at all. A Golden sergeant, his plumed helmet under one arm, halted at the open cell door. "Ah. I see you are awake, good. It is time. If you would come with us?"

How strange, he said it as if she had any choice. Yala lifted her chin and gently pushed Anh aside. The kaburei girl buried her face in her hands, and sank onto the straw.

It was a hot dry morning, and six Golden were far too many to shepherd one small Khir lady-in-waiting to a small stone semicircle, freshly swept and sprinkled. At least there was no filth here, and no windows pierced the bare frowning walls. Her shame would not be witnessed.

Yala's heart beat thinly in her throat. A lean man in a red cotton robe with the Emperor's seal upon its chest stood to one side, a long flexible leather coil clasped in his paired hands. He bowed as she passed, and she wondered if he liked his work. There was the post, clanking iron manacles depending from a length of chain, and that was Yala's only refusal.

"No," she said, quietly. "I will not be bound. I shall not seek to escape, but I will *not* be bound."

"My lady..." The sergeant had paled too. "It, er, may be necessary. If you faint."

"Then the whip may land as it pleases." *I am a noblewoman of Khir.* If she was to be treated thus, she would not accord them the luxury of thinking her resistant *or* afraid. "But I will not be bound like a common criminal, sergeant."

He glanced at the lean scarlet-clad man, who shrugged. "It is only two hands' worth. Practically kisses." Still, the whipmaster looked rather green.

Ten. Well, I shall endure. There was little in the Hundreds about the proper way to suffer such a thing; she was left to her own devices.

"Thank you, whipmaster." She could be as sarcastic as she wished, but Zhaon was not the language for it. "I shall forgive you, since you are merely performing your duty to your lord." Yala raised her chin again and glided forward. The guards tensed, but she simply walked to the post and studied it. A semicircle of iron sheathed its front, and she touched the warm metal, wincing slightly. When the sun cleared the lower walls of this place, it would be fierce, and perhaps a morning session was better than having to clasp a scorching post at the end of a long southron afternoon.

She turned her head slightly. "I am ready," she said. "Proceed." If she put her tongue to the right, and began to bite when the whip descended, perhaps the pain would give her strength?

The sergeant cleared his throat. "I should read the charges."

"If you like," the whipmaster weighed in. A slithering sound—the whip, uncoiled. "May be best to simply get this over with. Imagine, whipping a lady."

So the Zhaon did not whip noblewomen after all? Perhaps only foreign ones. They would dishonor what they could not break, if she let them.

But *only* if she let them.

"Mh." A restive motion, the sergeant's boots creaking. "Are you sure you don't want the post, my lady?"

Yala, her tongue held firmly between her molars—it made her

cheek bulge in a most unladylike fashion—shook her head. Perhaps her hairpin would fall out. That would be embarrassing.

The sergeant exhaled sharply. There was a crackle of rai-paper—the scroll detailing her offense, of course. He began to read, slowly.

More slithering, smacking sounds. She tried not to flinch, and shut her eyes. Was he testing the whip?

Crack.

She did not cower, though it was difficult to keep her shoulders straight and her knees locked. No pain—he had simply been assuring himself of a clear strike. The sergeant droned on.

Yala bit down, testing her tongue's resilience. Was it possible, or simply a story? She was about to find out. The world went away, blood pounding a gallop in her ears. She clasped her fingers against cool metal, waiting. The sergeant's drone halted, and a deep hush fell over the world.

Then came a rushing sound, like wind over water.

Crack.

It still did not hurt. A collective gasp echoed in the small stone enclosure. Her heart's hooves pounded so hard her head seemed to swell.

"Your Highness..." The sergeant, sounding as if he had been struck in the stomach.

"Hm." A familiar voice, amused and sharp, the scrape of a soldier's boot-heel against stone. "Rather early in the day for this, is it not?"

So. He had come to watch, or for some other reason?

"Your Highness." Again, the sergeant, with barely enough breath to form the words. "I must respectfully—"

"Shut your mouth. And you. Whipmaster. If you must, you may strike again."

"But... but you..." Slight, pale words. The whipmaster did not sound nearly so bored now.

"Indeed." The new arrival, grimly amused, moved with a rustle. "Refresh my memory. What is the penalty for attacking a prince?"

"Your Highness..." The sergeant could not find other words, apparently.

Yala could not help herself. She turned, slowly, every joint creaking as an old woman's. The slight brushing of her skirt must have told him she had moved, for he spoke again.

"This farce has gone far enough." Garan Takshin, Third Prince of Zhaon, stood with his back to her. His topknot was caged in gold today, and instead of his Shan costume he wore a noble's robe, gold embroidery chasing *hau* characters along his shoulders and the wide black silk cuffs. A ragged slice tore through the fabric over his broad back, a terrible diagonal slash from shoulder to hip. Silk moved, touched by a stray breeze, and blood crept out, freed into open air. "If my honored father wishes to have someone scourged, he may send his guards for me. I should warn you—and him—though, that I will not stay my hand. It is disgraceful for an Emperor to strike an innocent woman because a cockroach whistles in his ear."

Takshin turned upon his heel, and his lazy half-smile belied his glittering dark gaze. His scarred lip did not twitch, and high color stood in his cheeks. That terrible gaze lingered on her face, and Yala realized she was still biting her tongue. Her hands felt too large for her wrists, her feet were leaden, and a scalding flush had risen to her own face.

How had he moved so quickly? What manner of man would place himself *under* a whip-strike?

"It is a very good thing you were not harmed, Komor Yala." He offered his arm, as if he had not just been struck across the back. "Or I would cut off the hand that performed such a deed."

Dreaming-slow, she took a half-step forward. Her hand crept to the crook of his elbow. "Third Prince," she managed, through dry lips. "I am very happy to see you."

"I should hope so." He did not so much as glance at the sergeant, the half-dozen golden-gleaming guards, the scarlet-clad whipmaster whose leather snake lay discarded at his feet as he clasped both hands, wrapped with linen to wick away the sweat of hard work, to his mouth like a child. "Come, Yala. I shall take you home."

The Wrong Note to Strike

The deep, painful itching all over Garan Tamuron's torso, spreading down his legs, was not half as irritating as the feeling of being slightly outplayed. "He did *what*?"

Kai folded his arms. "Third Prince Takshin took Lady Komor from the whipping-post, my lord." He kept the words as neutral as possible. "He was struck, once, by the whipmaster."

"Clumsy of him." Whether the Emperor meant Takshin or the hapless whip-wielder was an open question, and he did not add more to dispel the mystery. By Heaven, he longed to slide his hands under his morning-robe and scratch at the suppurations. This morning he had snapped at Dho Anha again, too, whitening her face and causing her to withdraw as soon as possible. "So, he defied me."

Not that it was a surprise, but still... Takshin had been quicker off the mark than he anticipated. Tamuron had thought the boy would need prompting.

He could have hoped Kai would take *less* prompting at the moment, but the general forged ahead, an edge to each word. "And saved you from the shame of whipping an innocent woman."

I deserved that. His rage had cooled, and the consciousness of having committed a misstep irritated him, just as the itching did, and the tingling ache in fingers and toes, not to mention the creeping headache and the recurrent clumsiness. Physician Kihon was concerned about the royal urine taking on a purple tint, as well. The malady had raised its banners and was far past his border posts. "Shamed Gamwone and their clan in the bargain, too. And saved Takyeo from appearing weak, since most will suspect he sent Takshin to perform this deed."

"I take it your temper has abated somewhat." Kai arched an eyebrow. He did not move closer, staying at the distance etiquette required, and that was new.

"Hardly." *Come now, adoptive-son. Understand me.* "Now all the palace women will carry knives." It was disconcerting to piss in a different color, and it had occurred so suddenly. The body, like a horse run too hard in its youth, failed quickly once the course approached its end.

"It is a Khir custom, this *yue*." Kai said it as if Tamuron should have known. "They call it *maiden's blade*; it is meant to save them dishonor."

"Ah." Khir women were to be docile and discreet; hearing that a few of them bore such a sting was…well, not quite against nature and Heaven, but certainly disconcerting. Still, it would discourage rape if used with any facility; he wondered what the punishment for misuse was in the cold North.

Kai obviously expected more than a single syllable from his lord. "I am further told they do not speak of it outside noble houses."

"And yet you know." Now he longed to send his general away, and scratch. The skin had begun to separate; he had to be careful not to tear long strips. A stinging astringent salve was to be applied to the suppurations, reeking of acrid jellied jau. It burned like the God of Fire's own whips—an irony, indeed.

Now that he was not goaded past bearing, he could admit it was perhaps hasty to think the Khir lady-in-waiting was more than a decorous prop sent to protect a princess. Spies made themselves agreeable, certainly, but even the aristocracy of Khir would be mad to wish for more war.

"*Now* I know." Kai's fingers dug into leather, his half-armor creaking. *I could have told you, if you would have listened*, his tone and stance all but shouted.

"Does my daughter-in-law have one?" To think of Takyeo within striking distance of a foreign woman with a knife—it turned Tamuron's liver sideways within him.

"Ask her, my lord." Deliberately not *Your Majesty*, and Kai had not taken steps to find out something he suspected Tamuron would wish to know.

"Hrm." Tamuron eyed him narrowly. "What else could I do, Kai? Assassins from the North and an unsanctioned weapon in the palace, upon a foreign woman to boot. An example had to be made."

"Oh, it has been," the general said, darkly, and Tamuron leashed the growling irritation in his gut. Even plain rai tormented his innards, and his favorite pickled walanir spread sores upon the palace-roof of his mouth.

On his command Zhaon would trample any foe, and yet here he sat pissing strange colors, scratching like a monkey, and unable even to eat. Heaven had turned its face from its chosen one, or perhaps the Five Winds were consuming him from the inside now that he had served his purpose and unified Zhaon. "Are you taking me to task?"

His general did not shrug, though his shoulders tensed. "Would I dare?"

Tamuron shook his head. His neck ached. "You of all people, Kai."

"My lord, you are Emperor, and yet you shit in a pot like a common soldier." Kai did not move, and did not take the opportunity to soothe his lord. "The only difference is, a common soldier who whips a woman for performing her duty is punished by his square-leader, and an Emperor is not."

"You're angry." *Do I sound uncertain? Of him?* Times were dire indeed if even so steady and uncomplaining a tool as the Head General turned in Tamuron's hand.

"Perhaps. The Garan Tamuron I know would not have given such orders."

As if he had possessed a choice. Once a blade was drawn, the consequences followed even those with reason to strike. "To deal with someone who brought an unsanctioned weapon into the palace?"

Now a high flush was mounting Zakkar Kai's cheeks. Was he raising his own banners, readying for a charge? "To change the hour of a whipping so no clemency was possible."

"Change the hour?" Tamuron's expression darkened.

"Did you not know?" Kai's tone suggested he did not believe it. "She was taken from her cell just after the dawnwatch returned to their beds."

"Ah." So, Gamwone's uncle had arranged for a deeper embarrassment. And Takshin, perhaps anticipating as much, had moved to prevent it. "Lord Yulehi has been busy."

"His half of the year is arrived, after all." Kai dropped his arms and bent in a very correct bow. His own sword, carried by express permission, rode his back, and its dragon-snarling hilt glared over his shoulder. "I shall take my leave, my lord."

Tamuron could still remember gifting him that very blade after the Second Battle of Yulehi-Ahu. "Without *my* leave?"

"What else would you have of me?" The general did not raise his voice, but his tone held an unwonted edge.

"Hm." He studied Kai. "You are quite put out. I hear this Lady Komor visits the Second Concubine often, and so do you." *Help me, Kai. See my condition, and do not make it worse.*

"I am the Second Concubine's son now." Stiffly, each edge clipped. The general's face was blood-suffused granite, the expression he wore when some matter of deep indiscipline was brought to the head of Zhaon's armies.

"Take care, Kai." Perhaps a kind, fatherly injunction would help. "I mean for you to be a shield to Kanbina, not an additional grief."

As soon as he said it, Garan Tamuron knew it was the wrong note to strike no matter the instrument. The blood drained from Kai's cheeks. He watched his lord for several long moments, and finally swallowed visibly, the pad of chewed rai meant to keep a full-grown man from choking bobbing under shaven throat-skin.

The moment passed, and whatever Zakkar Kai would have said died unborn. His final bow was correct in every particular, and his deep-set eyes glittered. He turned, and left behind only the faint impression of a banked fire, ash and slow fierce heat.

Garan Tamuron sat in his small, windowless room, the scroll upon the wall with his first wife's careful brushwork glowering at him, and knew what Kai would have said.

I could not hope to grieve her more than her lordly husband. Oh, the general might sweeten the pill, or choose a more diplomatic way of expressing himself, for Zakkar Kai had grown into a man of restraint. Perhaps he had modeled such restraint upon Tamuron's own, and now he was disappointed.

For he was correct, of course. Tamuron's judgment had clouded itself in this particular instance. He could not admit as much now, even if he called Kai back. The child had worshipped him and the man fought for him, but the man also judged him. Time wore on, and a father's feet sank in liquid sand.

The Emperor of Zhaon coughed into a cupped hand. He had not told Kihon Jiao of the slick coppery heat coating the back of his throat when he did so.

His time was growing short, and he had indeed shamed himself. Dull fury circled in his belly, and he longed to return to bed, to lie there and watch the ceiling, a beast trapped in a tar-hole.

The empire he had built would not wait, and must be handed intact to his eldest son even if that son temporarily despised him.

Garan Tamuron cleared his throat and called for his dressing-servants.

A Distorted Mirror

The Jonwa was brim-full of hurrying feet and soft commotion. Lady Yala spoke quietly at the door of a small apothecary-chamber, and Steward Keh's reply was lost in a tide of whispers. Drawers and cabinets crowded the walls, and a table with the various implements of medicine-making scattered upon its back took up most of the available space. There was enough room for a three-legged stool, and Takshin, placed upon it, set his jaw as jellied jau stung his back with its bright, cold fire.

The whipmaster had not been cruel, but moving before Yala had placed Takshin closer to the whip, and thus, the fine gradations of an experienced wielder of the sorrowful snake were all but wasted. Fast-moving leather had cut deep, for Takshin disdained to wear padding or armor under his noble's robe even though he had suspected something of this nature might well occur.

After all, if he had simply countermanded the orders, they might have surged forward regardless. Better to simply take the blow and balance the threat of one punishment against the certainty of another, both equally unpalatable. This way, he could be blamed and there was nothing that could be taken from him.

Or so he thought. The danger of loss lay in another direction, now. He dispelled a wince, and Lady Kue made a soft sound of concentration. "The salve will come next," she murmured, and shifted slightly—perhaps looking over her shoulder.

"May I offer my aid?" Yala, quietly, Khir consonants rubbing through the Zhaon. Even her voice had a hidden edge, a claw under velvet.

She would no doubt see the other scars now, seamed and silvery or livid, striping his back. The Mad Queen's knotted cord was not a sorrow-snake, but it could still leave marks, especially upon a child's skin. They stretched as a man aged, too.

"Hand me that cloth." Lady Kue made a slight tongue-click, very much like Mrong Banh. "You should be resting."

"I find myself unable to settle." A slight note of amusement, though her voice shook somewhat. The tremor was restrained, of course. "It was a very dramatic morning. Does it sting overmuch, Third Prince?"

"Not enough." He turned his head slightly, enough to catch a shadow of her movement in his peripheral vision. She must be fresh from a bath; a sweetness of jaelo bloomed under the jau's acridity. "I should return for a few more, it would enliven my day."

"Hush, now." Lady Kue's Shan dialect was still lisp-soft, a reminder of his other country. "Do not pursue bad luck, it will come on its own."

He did not reply. Had the blood stopped flowing? Normally, it would irritate him to have a stranger see the torso-scars, but she did not remark upon them. Instead, Lady Yala set down whatever she was carrying. A whisper of silk and that ghost of jaelo, lingering as she did in his thoughts, a constant counterpoint. "Is that Shansian? It sounds gentle."

Takshin breathed in, deeply. If he concentrated upon her scent, the pain retreated. It was a new thing, to have such a refuge, and normally he would disdain to use it. But he faced a wall and a cabinet of apothecary drawers, with no one to see any weakness.

"It is a thorny pleasure to speak one's tongue in another country." Lady Kue sponged at his back again. "It will not require stitchery, Prince Takshin."

That was a relief. He disliked the needle, for he could not accept any numbing as it stitched flesh together. "Well enough."

"Now for the salve."

"Then be about it," he snapped.

A hand upon his left shoulder—cool soft skin, faintly damp. It had to be hers. "Easy, Third Prince."

He stilled. "When will you address me informally, Yala?"

"I shall begin today, Takshin." Her fingernails were crescent moons, and though her palm was soft he felt the slight thickening where the greenmetal blade's hatched hilt would rest. When did she find the time to practice its use? "I cannot even begin to think how to repay—"

"There is no need, little lure." His gaze unfocused, the world narrowing to her fingertips as Lady Kue began spreading the salve. It did sting, and plenty, but he decided not to move. "What is one more stripe to add to the collection? Do you wish to ask how I received them?"

"It may ease a warrior to speak of his wounds." An echo of their first meeting, a thornblossom pleasure. "Or not."

"Is there anything you take offense at, woman?" His traitorous eyes stung, full of salt water. He longed to rid himself of the useless reflex. Pain was not to be shown, no matter how sharp.

"Would you like me to?" Her gentle pressure upon his shoulder did not alter. "I can, should it please you. It is a small enough gift to give."

He could have laughed, but the sweat upon his neck and the salve's burning would have made the sound painfully bitter. So he did not, simply dropped his chin and closed his eyes. It was a familiar smell—Kiron's nurse had used something similar upon skinned knees and other wounds, creeping into his quarters at night to treat whatever mishap occurred during the day. *Let him take the rot*, the Mad Queen would hiss, or alternately coo over wounds she had just inflicted. *Oh, you poor little thing…*

Now he preferred those memories to ones of his actual mother. Strange how time became a distorted mirror, changing the shape of events. At least he had expected little good of Shan's queen, and was not disappointed.

The diagonal slash burned, scoring deeper, so he inhaled and spoke calmly enough. "I am glad to have arrived in time. It saves me the trouble of cutting a man's hands off." *And yes, had he marked you, I would have.*

Lady Kue's fingers paused. Was she exchanging a look with Yala? Two women, both far from their native lands, attending a man rejected by his. If he were a poet, he could have found something witty to mark the occasion.

"There," Lady Kue said. "Now, the wrapping. Lady Komor, if you would... yes, thank you."

Yala sank gracefully in front of him, averting her gaze from his bare chest as he opened his eyes halfway. The padding was pressed gently against the long slash upon his back, then the wrapping, shoulder to hip, passed between women's hands with soft murmurs. *There... yes, a little tighter, perhaps? Careful...*

He watched the head of her hairpin and the blue-black glimmer of her braids under soft mirrorlight. A Shan longshirt lay folded in his lap, and under it a slim weight. The bandaging finished, Yala sought to straighten and move away, but he shook his head and she halted, her strange, pale Khir gaze fixed upon him. If it pained her to be bent so, she made no sign.

"Here." He drew the blade from under his shirt. Wrapped in a rectangle of raw silk, its razor edge had almost worn through the threads. It lay balanced in his palms, and Yala's quick, embarrassed glance caught upon it. Her pale eyes widened, and she exhaled sharply, almost as if struck.

She accepted it with both hands, then stepped back, her skirt making a low sweet sound. She sank to her knees, slowly, then bent her forehead almost to the floor, the blade held carefully in both hands. Her hairpin glittered, a rough pebble wrapped in red silken thread dangling a few pale glimmering crystals.

One she wore often. Familiar, now.

"My lord Garan Takshin, Third Prince of Zhaon." Excruciatingly formal, the lowest Zhaon inflection addressing the mightiest. "Your handmaiden thanks thee."

The slice across his back twinged as he leaned forward, his clean longshirt almost slithering from his lap as he grasped her wrists, careful of the blade. "Don't."

"I have no other means of expressing my gratitude." She straightened, and he had to release her. At least she did not use that inflection again. It was unbearable to hear from her soft, pretty mouth. "This is my *yue*. My honor, returned unto me."

In Shan, peasant women carried a nail-paring knife to mark the face of a man who beat them too often. Takshin could not help but smile, and for once the movement of his face did not make him conscious of the scars. "Your honor never left you. I suspect it never will. Never do that again, Yala."

"Draw my *yue* in the palace?" Somber, she regarded him, her skirt tucked prettily under her, the picture of a lady-in-waiting attending a royal patron. "I cannot promise that."

"No. Never bow like that. To anyone." He unfolded his shirt, and Lady Kue's hands came to help it over his shoulders. He restrained the urge to slap them aside; she was seeking to aid him, and it was beneath him to strike a woman. At least he was better than his cursed father in *that* respect. "Now, both of you out. Leave me in peace, and go tell my eldest brother to give me a few moments before he comes to scold me."

He would have liked to invite Yala to stay, of course. But those shining eyes and her wondering expression made him wary. Better to ration anything sweet, lest he develop a taste. And who would wish to remain in such a dank small closet full of medicinal odors? Certainly not gentle creatures such as these.

"I doubt the Crown Prince wishes to scold." Lady Kue began gathering her implements. "Rather, I think he would congratulate you, for he knows how you hate to be thanked."

"Nevertheless." Yala rose, the blade—too long to be a proper knife, far too short to be a sword, and ideal for a woman's smaller hands and greater flexibility—balanced cherished-carefully upon her palms. "You have my thanks, Takshin. And, should you wish it, my friendship."

Not what I want. He occupied himself with his shirt-ties and a single, impolite grunt, waving her away. No, not what he wanted at all.

But it was a start.

Horsekillers

It was a beautiful morning, though too hot, as Zhaon was wont to be. The impresario in dun peasant's clothing, his shaven head wrapped as a tribesman's, yawned as he settled more deeply under leafy branches. Sleepless nights of watching and creeping, all wasted; a goodly portion of his funds wasted too.

If you wished for a silent, difficult task to be accomplished, it was wise to perform it yourself. A harsh lesson, applied over and over until a man took notice—or until he died of the recurring failure to heed Heaven's warnings.

He almost wished others attempting to snatch his prize had succeeded. If so, he could be on a horse for the border, leaving this sink of simmering sweat, strange spices that imparted no heat, and slithering incompetence well behind. He longed for a clear breeze across mountain meadows, and also, to be honest, for his promised ingots of sweet metal. He could travel northward and return through the last of summer, and if he was quick and luck was good, he would be in Shan before the winter rains, perhaps, and Anwei shortly thereafter.

It would not be healthy to remain in Khir after collecting the balance of his fee, after all. And the nobleman sent to hold his leash could make his own travel arrangements.

Periodically, the man checked his second bow, not the one he had used from the rooftops to make certain city-prey could be netted. This weapon was a long, heavy arc almost as tall as him, and its arrows heavy as well. They were inhuenyua, horsekillers; the bow was juenwa without the double curve of a horseback weapon, and instead of a thumb-ring the archer required a thin, three-finger glove. The single strip of wood, from the muscle and heart of the lyong[57] tree, was unwieldy and could not be carried upon the back of a fourfoot cousin—but it would send a barbed arrowhead through plenty of meat, and drop an ox if the archer was skilled and lucky enough. At the very northern fringes of Khir, such a bow was used to pick off lumbering shagbeasts from a herd, and also by peasants to fend off horseback bandits eking a living from violence and the Yaluin's harsh skirt-hems.

At least it would be a Khir weapon that struck this time, unless another of his kind was having better luck elsewhere. For a moment he almost felt sorry for the quarry, pursued by so many hunters.

This was the road they used most often for morning gallops. He had five horsekillers; it would have to be enough. Hunting required patience, and knowledge of the prey.

Sooner or later, his would appear.

57. The tree silkworms prefer to spin their cocoons upon.

An Offer, Interrupted

The Crown Princess's dressing-room was stifling, and alive with bright mirrorlight. Behind a carved wooden partition the bedroom had been put to rights; in the dressing-room proper two robe-holders stood silent sentinel waiting to be loaded for the day, and servants hurried in the hall past the antechamber.

"I long to go riding with you." There were shadows under Yala's eyes, perhaps mirrored by those under Mahara's own. They did not have to creep stealthily about for nightly stretching and practice now, Mahara handling Yala's wrapped *yue* and going through the basic forms and stances over and over, but neither of them were sleeping well in the now-dry heat. "But you hardly want me, with your husband along."

"I do not think it wise." Mahara, her veil held aside with a bent-pin, clasped Yala's hands in her own. "You should stay in the Jonwa, at least for some little while longer."

"At least I may go into the city to fetch your practice-blade?" Yala squeezed gently, searching Mahara's face. "Third Prince Takshin is visiting the astrologer, but Zakkar Kai will accompany me should I write him a letter."

Mahara bit her lip and shook her head. "No. Takyeo..." She colored a bit, saying his name so freely. "He thinks it best you stay out of sight. In a little while we shall have a proper kaibok game, once things are calmer." She loosened her grasp, reluctantly. "And once the weather is not quite so dismal."

"As my princess commands." Yala fussed at her princess's veil and sash, making certain Mahara's sleeves carried everything she might need. "When you return, we shall stretch again."

Mahara made a face. "Must we?"

Their shared laughter, birdlike, lightened the air, and Mahara swept away. Yala exhaled softly, then turned her attention to straightening the room and the antechamber. Royal dressing was a messy business, and her absence, however short, had created a truly amazing disorder.

She would much rather be riding, but at least when her princess returned it would be to neatness, cool crushed fruit to drink, and a light luncheon of her favorite things. Yala had already given the orders for the latter, and fell into her work with a smile. Some short while later there was a light step in the passageway.

"Oh, Lady Komor." It was Su Junha, returning from her morning errand. "You should rest. Where is Lady Eulin?"

"Visiting her esteemed aunt; I gave her leave and attended our princess's dressing myself." Yala arranged the bright green afternoon dress upon its babu rack, bending to taper-light the coil of freshening incense under its folds. "If I stay abed today I will fret myself into distemper."

"Tch." The slim girl sounded much older. Her dress, pale rosy silk edging upon peach cotton reworked from one of Lady Kue's festival gowns, suited her exactly, and Yala was looking forward to finishing sleeves for the orange one. Anh's festival gown was coming along nicely, too. "A stubborn lady you are, indeed. Have you had lunch, or tea?"

"Not yet, and I would not refuse another cup." Tired as she was, Yala could not help but smile as she snuffed the taper and returned it to its home in a bonefire holder. "How does anyone sleep during this heat? There must be some trick to it."

"Lady Komor?" Hansei Liyue appeared in the door. A book

lingered gracefully in her hand, her thumb holding her place, and she had the dreamy look of the interrupted reader. It did no good to scold her; the girl's head was firmly amid brushstrokes and paper. "We have a visitor; General Zakkar has arrived."

"I hear he went to the Emperor to plead for you." Su Junha grinned, a mischievous glint in her wide dark eyes. "You are lucky to have such a friend."

"It is far more likely he visited the Emperor upon other business; he is a counselor of much merit." Yala sought to sound somewhat severe. "Lady Liyue, have tea sent to the smaller receiving-room. Afterward, you may visit the weavers and inquire of the tasks I have set them. You will accompany me to the Second Concubine's house this afternoon. Lady Junha, when Lady Eulin returns, the two of you will set your chambers to rights and aid Lady Kue with her afternoon rounds."

They took their tasks with good grace, though Hansei Liyue would no doubt have liked to steal away and filch more reading-time. While Yala visited Kanbina, Liyue could read in the antechamber, and the girl's pleased expression showed she realized as much. The other two would learn much of domestic management from Lady Kue, and the Shan woman's stern glance would keep Eulin from shuffling too many of her tasks onto Junha's shoulders.

It took longer than Yala liked to finish setting the dressing-room to rights, even with their help. The household could easily hold another three ladies, but Yala was no closer to making a decision upon that matter just yet. There was time, and the court was in a ferment just now.

Those who did not turn away from the Crown Princess at such a moment, whether from kindness or ambition, deserved close inspection Yala did not quite have the endurance for.

The smaller receiving-room, dark wood opening onto a verandah skirting the main garden, was bright with mirrorlight. Zakkar Kai turned from the sliding doors, and his shoulders were tense under a sober black court robe. His belt was worked with orange, and likely the embroidery was Kanbina's, bearing delicacy and much thought.

"I hope you were not waiting long." Yala bowed, and realized she was smiling with relief. "Have you eaten?"

"Please do not trouble yourself, Lady Yala." He strode across the room. "I am relieved to see you unharmed; I regret I could not visit you earlier."

"I hear you hied yourself to the Emperor to plead for me, General." She halted, momentarily confused by his quick approach; he seized her hands.

"News flies like a hungry blur-wing, here in the Palace." His palms were rough and warm, fingers callused from swordhilt and other soldiery. "I am simply glad Takshin bethought to visit you in the morning instead of waiting for the traditional time. He is ever impatient."

"Is he?" She should, she supposed, free her hands, but her knees were not quite steady. A measure of strength flowed up her arms, strangely affecting her head. "And did you truly plead for me?"

"Of course. I wish I had been as impatient as the Third Prince, though. When I think of what could have happened..." A swift grimace crossed his face, surprising in one so carefully controlled.

"Let us be happy it did not." Strange. Why did she not wish to take her hands away? Why were her legs unsteady *now*? The danger was past, was it not?

Still... Zakkar Kai bent to study her face. This close, she saw the fine lines beginning at the corners of his deep-set eyes, and the tender border where his lips met the rest of his face, the weathering of his shaven cheeks. His topknot, pulled severely tight, was caged in leather with a sober wooden pin, and his house-slippers' wooden, leather-wrapped soles creaked slightly as he shifted, his gaze moving from her eyes to her chin, resting upon her mouth for a moment and sliding away. "I begin to think you need a close-guard to keep you from mischief, Lady Yala."

"It was not *mischief*, Zakkar Kai." She could not, it seemed, cease smiling. "Merely performing my duty."

"Yes, well." His hands tensed on hers. "I wish—"

Whatever he wished remained unsaid, for the tea was brought

and he dropped her hands as if they burned. Yala indicated a low table with a satin-smooth stone top and they settled upon cushions; she dismissed the servants and poured for them both. The door to the hall, wide open, meant that any who wished could glance in and see them at tea; there was no need for a chaperone.

Zakkar Kai's cheeks dark-flushed. He coughed, slightly, and accepted his cup. "So. Now you have seen the palace dungeons. Had I known you wished to view them I would have arranged a less exhausting tour."

Relief filled her again, hot and weightless. At least he was not treating her . . . well, *differently*. Perhaps they were more than friends after a fashion, and after all. "I did not know they were so interesting. The floors could stand a fresh measure of straw, though."

"Yes, well, the housekeeping there is not in a lady's capable hands." His mouth twisted wryly, and the greenstone ring upon his left first finger glinted. "I suppose that is why they wished you to remain."

"I was not of much use during my stay." She blew across steaming liquid, delicately. Lady Gonwa's heaven tea, heavy with jaelo, was most welcome. "And—forgive me for saying as much—I have no desire to return."

"They are not cheersome hosts, that is true." He shifted upon his cushion, as if it were not thick enough. "I wonder that Takyeo allowed your arrest at all."

It had all seemed rather out of the Crown Prince's hands. "He was attending to my princess's safety. By the time he thought to gainsay the guards, they had performed their function." Or the one with the pockmarked face had.

"Commendable zeal. The guard who struck down the false eunuch has not returned to the barracks."

"How strange." She met his gaze, and the troubled nature of his almost halted her. But she had to know. "I am told they were zealous in the matter of flogging, as well?" That was the question she had longed to ask, and his nod told her he took her meaning and could shed light upon the matter.

"Well." He looked into his tea, his brow wrinkling. Outside, an oven-hot wind sucked the moisture from the gardens and stole the shade of any coolness. "Did I tell you Lord Hanweo's half of the year is over? Lord Yulehi—the First Queen's uncle—has taken the Head Minister's position. Of course Lord Hanweo is still a minister, but it is Lord Yulehi who performs such duties as scheduling executions and other matters, now. His is the voice closest to the Throne for the last half of the year."

"I see." In other words, the First Queen had a hand in the matter. Given an opening, the woman wished to cause maximum discomfort to Mahara, and through her, to the Crown Prince. Not to mention tarnishing a foreign wife with the imputation of a treacherous servant brought from abroad. The opportunity had been too good to let pass. "I was unaware of this, but then, matters of government are above a simple court lady."

He nodded, perhaps relieved she had caught on so quickly. "There are perhaps other things you would wish to speak upon, Lady Yala. Forgive me, since such subjects are perhaps distressing to a noblewoman, but I shall answer all I can."

In other words, did she wish to know more? Yala hesitated, and perhaps he thought—or wished—her finished with the subject, for he forged ahead.

"There is something else I would speak upon, though."

"Ah." More trouble? She took a tiny sip, though the tea was still too hot. "Please do so, Zakkar Kai. I am attending closely."

His tone lowered. "It strikes me that you perhaps need protection inside the palace as well as outside."

"Recent events have been rather troubling." She regarded him closely. "It is my princess who requires protection, though. I am merely a shield."

"To her, perhaps." Zakkar Kai's throat moved as he swallowed. "Not . . . to me."

Yala allowed her eyelids to drift half-closed, as if she were enjoying the tea. Jaelo was a powerfully calming scent. Her pulse was behaving rather strangely, and a flush through her was no doubt the tea pouring warmth into a vessel already overflowing.

No doubt. It could not be otherwise, could it?

"To be plain..." Zakkar Kai swallowed again, the lump in his throat bobbing, and took a gulp of tea. It was far too hot for such cavalier treatment, and his expression suggested he had not foreseen as much. He set the cup down and grimaced, slightly. "To be very plain, Komor Yala, I would offer you more than my occasional small aid in minor matters."

"What else is there here, for me?" Her stomach made a restless motion inside her, and she hoped it would not gurgle with hunger. Such a thing would be embarrassing. What, precisely, was he proposing? "Your help is certainly not inconsiderable, General, but please be plainer."

A susurration in the hall caught her attention. Zakkar Kai cocked his head, listening, and his eyebrows drew together even more firmly. "I would like to be very plain," he said, softly. "Lady Komor... Yala, I wish to make you an offer."

Hurrying feet. Raised voices.

"An... offer?" Yala's heart began to thunder, and her fingers were cold. Her teacup shook slightly, the surface of the fragrant brew trembling. She wondered if her grasp of Zhaon was failing her. Was he sincerely—

Zakkar Kai opened his mouth.

The receiving-room door flew open. Lady Kue, pale, wringing her hands, burst through. "My prince," she gasped. A tendril of red-black hair had come free and fallen in her face; her hairpin was askew. "The Crown Princess... oh, Lady Yala... *oh*..."

A rushing filled Yala's ears. She set her cup down, careful of its brimming boil. Zakkar Kai leapt to his feet, the table shook, and she grasped its edge grimly, seeking to hear through the noise of the world turning off its axis and spinning into a hellish, howling darkness.

The Opposite of Luck

Only Kai's command and the presence of the Crown Prince's household guard, grim-faced and sweating in their snow-pard livery, kept back the crowd of servants, Golden, courtiers, and a sprinkling of eunuchs upon the dusty, sun-drenched steps of the Jonwa. The great double doors were slightly ajar, and in the dark stifling of the receiving-hall, the Emperor himself stood, attended by General Zakkar Kai. An inner hall resounded with activity, and from it issued forth a physician in a brown robe somewhat better than his normal, tattered everyday wear.

"He will survive," Kihon Jiao said, grimly, wiping his hands against each other in a brief scrubbing motion. "He may even use the leg again, with care."

Garan Tamuron's hands were fists inside his voluminous sleeves. He stared at the physician; a muscle in his cheek twitched. "Where were his guards?"

Kai glanced at him. "And the Crown Princess?"

"I cannot answer the first, I am not a guard." Jiao's mouth had turned to a thin line. "The princess... well, the arrow pinned her leg to the horse. She fell, the horse... there was little chance. They tell me she lasted some short while during the return to the palace, but not long."

The Emperor fixed Kai with a deadly glare. "Where were his guards? Where were my Golden, if not protecting my son?"

"I do not know either." Kai's jaw set itself, iron-hard. "I do not set the roster, my lord." *Ask Lord Yulehi.* He did not need to say it.

Did he?

Two spots of crimson burned high upon the Emperor's cheeks. He turned away and strode into the hall beyond. "*Takyeo*," he bellowed, and the chaos deeper in the Jonwa intensified further.

"He will do more harm than good," Kihon Jiao muttered. His longing to be gone, attending his patient, was palpable. He did not even have house-slippers, having stepped out of his sandals at the doorway and bolted inside to perform his duty. His strong bare feet were wide as a peasant's, and he was missing the smallest toe upon the left one. "Well, my lord?"

Kai shook his head. "He is a father concerned for his son."

"Mh." The physician's gaze darkened. He leaned forward, tense as a long-legged racing hound. "The arrows were barbed. There is much damage. I do not know if I can save the leg, even with good luck and much care."

"If anyone can, 'tis you." Kai clapped him upon the shoulder, but gently. The physician was a warrior in his own way, but he bruised like a peelfruit.

"I dislike the thought of the dungeons if I cannot."

Was that what worried Kihon Jiao enough to keep him here? Of course, he had witnessed the Emperor's temper firsthand, and plainly did not think much of it. A patron protected his own, and for better or worse, Kihon Jiao was Zakkar Kai's pet physician. "We will quietly arrange a journey for you, in that case. I hear the provinces are lovely in late summer." *In any direction.*

"The thought fills me with hope," Jiao said, somewhat sardonically, and, comforted upon his last worry, vanished into the dark hallway mouth again.

"Kai! *Kai!*" Sixth Prince Jin, his topknot knocked free and his cheeks almost rai-paper pale, had forced his way through the milling of guards and servants, and likewise through the Jonwa's great double doors. "Kai, it's me!"

Zakkar Kai set his shoulders and strode for the doors himself, filling his lungs for a battlefield shout.

It was time, he thought, to restore some order outside.

It took longer than he liked to bolster the household guard; scholar-robed Fourth Prince Makar arrived in short order, glancing briefly at Jin upon the sun-drenched steps. "How bad is it?" he murmured. His sleeves were not as precisely folded as usual; he had no doubt hurried through his afternoon dressing.

"I cannot tell yet." Kai beckoned a few Golden forward. "No more guests past this point except Third Prince Takshin, understood? You—" He pointed at another.

"My lord!" the young guard said, hopping forward with alacrity.

"Run to Guard Captain Hurao, tell him to send another dozen Golden with the same orders I have given these, and to double the patrols. Leave for any reason is canceled. *A white crushflower has bloomed*, tell him that. And also, have him send a relief for the guards here in four candle-marks. Go."

"My lord!" A deep bow, and the young man took off at a run, the crowd of onlookers parting like waves before a sharp prow.

"A relief. Yes. Quick thinking." Makar settled his hands in his sleeves. His topknot was not *quite* askew, but it was close, and sweat gleamed upon his forehead. "I take it you have a mission for me as well?"

"You are more in the nature of a reserve, Maki." The nickname slipped out, and could be explained by Kai's gratefulness for his calming presence. "Jin?"

"Right here." The youngest prince straightened self-consciously, attempting to smooth his own hair. "What shall I do?"

"Take charge of Crown Princess Mahara's body; it is under guard at the Star Garden. Have her moved to the House of Bees, and *set a guard*. Stay with her. Will you?"

"Princess...oh." He turned even paler, and almost swayed on his feet. "Kai..."

"Kai." Makar's tone wasn't unkind, but it was stern. His hurai glinted, and he wore the set expression of a man determined to finish any disagreeable task before it bloomed into something truly unpleasant. "Perhaps I should attend to that matter."

"No." Jin straightened. "No, I can do it. Everything will be done well for the Crown Princess, Kai." He turned and marched away, his bright green robe flapping slightly upon the hot breeze. The onlookers parted for him, slowly but thoroughly.

"Well done, lad," Kai murmured, before beckoning Makar into the Jonwa's shade and snapping again orders for the household guard to move farther up the stairs into the shade, and to bar all passage past this point to all but Takshin.

Lady Kue was just inside the door now, resettling her hairpin in a nest of braids and wide-eyed with shock. "My lord Head General, Fourth Prince." She hurried to bow, a short distracted motion. One of her sleeves was pushed high, and one of the buttons upon her Shan-style dress hung from a twist of thread. "The Emperor and Kihon Jiao are with my lord the Crown Prince."

"And Prince Takshin?" Makar accepted the bow with a nod. His gaze softened as it touched her face.

Lady Kue lowered her gaze. She stared at Kai's slipper-toes, and her voice was a monotone. "He went into the city early this morning, upon an errand for the Crown Prince."

"Lady Komor," Kai said, in an undertone. "How does she fare?"

Makar glanced at him, a quick sideways sipping motion, and settled his sleeves.

"She is... Lady Gonwa Eulin returned as soon as she heard, and has taken her to the Star Garden." Lady Kue's hands wrung at each other, nervous birds in a cage. "We could not stop her, she was... my lord general, I fear for her state of mind, and—"

"Send two of the household guard and her kaburei to attend her." Kai would have preferred for Yala to stay here, but... well.

Her face when the news arrived, all color draining away, her eyes gone cold and dark—it was a torment to remember, and he had other matters to attend to. He could have laughed, a soldier's bitter, unamused bark when the worst had happened and looked likely to continue.

The Crown Prince's bedroom was alive with mirrorlight. Kihon Jiao was at the bedside, his hands slippery with jau and smears of fresh blood, snapping orders at two under-physicians. Takyeo, his hair streaming across cushions and his face pale as polished rai, tipped his head back as his left leg streamed blood upon a pad of thick, absorbent cotton. The arrowhead worked free, heavy and barbarous, its triangular head a tearing snake-mouth. More blood welled.

Kihon Jiao made a short, irritated noise and his fingers flashed, applying pressure to the subtle body where it met the physical. The bleeding turned sluggish. "Start grinding the kohai root." One of the under-physicians hurried to obey, untangling a plump, maggot-pale herb from its wrapping and settling it in a mortar-cradle, pushing his sleeves up to reveal forearms no doubt much exercised by the making of pastes and tinctures.

"Kai," the Crown Prince said. His fever-glittering gaze lit upon Kai. "My wife. Tell me."

"Save your strength." The Emperor loomed behind the physicians, his gaze fixated upon his son's crushed thigh. "Bring him something for the pain, physician."

"Not yet," Kihon Jiao said immediately, and in tones that brooked no disagreement, royal or otherwise. "I need him alert for some short while."

It was too late. Takyeo read the truth upon Kai's face, and if he had not, it was plain enough upon Makar's. The Crown Prince sagged back onto hastily piled pillows, a short groan escaping his chapped lips.

"Hurry, the kohai," the physician said. "Move back... yes, there. More boiled cloths! You, fetch the Shan jau paste, we shall need its cooling." His sling-satchel lay open upon a swept-clear table at the bedside; small items lay scattered upon the floor. His fingers flashed again, and he was a general marshaling reserves, a lean hound upon the scent. Viewing a man working in the heat of the calling Heaven had decreed for him was normally a fine sight, one to be met with applause... but not now. "Ah, the bone is not crushed, *or* fractured. You are lucky beyond measure, Crown Prince."

"Lucky," Takyeo managed a faint, tight grin. "I would hate to see the opposite."

"Avert," Makar murmured, his left hand making a sign to push aside ill fortune. Uncharacteristic of him, and a sign this had rattled even *his* nerves.

Jiao's hand flashed again. He hit a pressure point, and Takyeo's body relaxed with a low grunt. "There. Not much longer, Crown Prince, then we will give you something for the pain."

"I can bear it for some while longer." Sweat oiled Takyeo's face. "Kai... Mahara... her... her body. Where?"

At least Kai could ease this concern. "Star Gardens. Jin is taking her to the House of Bees. Lady Komor is already with her, I should think."

The Emperor's face darkened at the mention of Yala, but he said nothing. His eyes were very dark, pupils swollen, and there was an uncertain glaze to them. "But you will live," he said. "Takyeo, my son, you will live."

"Oh, yes." A bitter laugh; Crown Prince Takyeo had no strength left to practice restraint. "No doubt. You will not have it otherwise, Father."

Whatever reply the Emperor might have made was lost, for Garan Tamuron, dry-lipped and far-eyed, swayed. Kai leapt, and was barely in time to keep the older man from collapsing onto Physician Kihon's back.

Sister's Prayer

The House of Bees held none of those docile, humming honey-makers. Instead, it was named for its shape, a dome with a round aperture through which the sun shone once a year at noon upon the summer solstice. It held no mirrorlight and its walls of porous stone were washed thrice yearly—once in the dead of winter by keening women, once at the height of summer by silent men, and third at the time of the rai harvest, when graves and tombs were also cleaned and families spent long twilight evenings singing and feasting amid their ancestors.

Inside, blocks of black stone stood rayed like the character for *fire*, and a crushed, limp form had been placed upon the largest, with its head pointing north.

Smashed-in ribs slumped, one leg did not match the other, and the bowl of the pelvis was shattered; a leg was longer because the horse had fallen and rolled to iron anything trapped beneath it flat, a fourfoot cousin maddened with pain and already dying as well.

Mahara's face was strangely untouched, her hair raveled out of the careful braiding and looping Yala had accomplished just that morning. Stiff with dried blood, the embroidery upon her torn riding habit glittered a little—the pale thread had set off dark brown silk, a cheerful contrast. The habit was of Zhaon cut; it was new.

Mahara would never wear it again. It would be burned, and the ashes buried with ritual curses.

Yala's throat burned. Her eyes, too. The fire was within her; its invisible smoke stung her nose and filled her head.

Springblades to cut dirty clothing loose, warm water full of bitter herbs to wash cooling, unresponsive flesh. *Scrub harder, Yala. I will never be free of dirt if you merely swipe with that cloth.*

Shall I scrub your skin right off, then?

Mahara's laughter, and the splashing when they were younger and at the bath together.

White linen arrived, strips and squares rolled or folded. Gonwa Eulin, pale and weaving, had to stop and rush outside, her throat full of bile. Su Junha, though, kept at the work, her face set and her tenderness speaking volumes.

She, like Yala, had performed this duty before, perhaps upon aunties taken by illness or old age.

Spiral grooves in the floor caught water poured jug by jug, carrying it toward the central drain. When Mahara was as clean as they could make her, every laceration pitilessly exposed, Yala leaned upon the stone and heard her own voice, reciting in Khir.

O She who rides endless,
Endless hear my plea;
Alone upon the wild wind
Upon the grassy sea...

It was the prayer for a sister dead in childbirth. Wrong, of course; she should be reciting the prayer for a princess, but *those* words would not come. Mahara had not died in the battle of bringing forth a son, but a death come while riding was a warrior's all the same.

And...well, in her own way, Mahara was braver than any Khir lord upon his horse. To go unarmed and almost alone to a foreign husband in a country brimful of assassins was a bravery overmatching any rider's, and though the Hundreds, the classics, the lords, and her own father might not agree, Komor Yala knew it was true.

Same-womb bore us,
Fire receive us,
Hoof-thunder consume us,
Ai, *sister, I shall follow thee.*

Clan Komori followed the old ways, and though Yala had no sister she had memorized the ancient prayers. It was the duty of a noble daughter to wash the body of a higher-ranked kinswoman and wrap it safely. There were no brothers to stand guard, but they would be watching, called by Yala's voice. Perhaps even Bai would be there, a shade among shades, watching as she fumbled this most important rite.

"O, Elder Brother," she whispered in Khir when the prayers failed her. "Help me. Please help me."

What would he say? He would shake his head slightly, not at her weakness but in resignation, and then his shoulders would rise, taking on a brother's burden. He would not have let her leave Khir, and Mahara would have gone alone. Mahara's brothers—Ashani Keiyan, Ashani Tlorih, dark and tall and pale-eyed, mild to their baby sister but fearsome to foes in battle—would no doubt tease Yala gently as they had in childhood when she forgot or fumbled a line of poetry. *Wrong words, Komor Yala. Recite again.*

So she did, but the proper prayer would not come. As she washed her princess's blood-caked hair until the water ran clear, as she gathered the linen, gently pushing aside well-meaning Zhaon hands, only the sister's prayer dripped from her lips. Perhaps the ancestors or Mahara's brothers were speaking it through her, she decided, and gave up resisting as she had given up withstanding the force of tradition, decorum, the weight of service to her clan.

To flow under the weight instead of shattering beneath it—but that was untrue. She had broken just as surely as Mahara's ribs, Mahara's poor left arm, Mahara's too-loose, almost certainly splintered neck.

Komor Yala, sent to be a *yue* and a shield, had failed in her duty.

That failure bore down mercilessly upon a living throat, upon shaking hands, upon a heart still traitorously beating instead of stopped with grief. Upon a voice singing an ancient prayer, over and over, weaving among notes that echoed drumming hooves, wind through grass, the cry of a hawk as it dove for prey.

She who rides endless,
She who begins,
She who gave us grass,
She who makes,
She who gave us honor,
She who gives,
O She has taken back.
She has gathered thee to Her,
She has given thee peace.
She who rides—

Mahara had passed the dark gates, ridden a spectral skeletal warhorse down the poured-ashen tide of the White Road to the end of all roads, and was now upon the Great Fields, where small white flowers were crushed by the hooves of the horse-goddess's tireless steeds. Ashan Mahara rode knee to knee with her vanished brothers and with Yala's own dead kin, and their song was glorious. Yala's own plaint would be lost in their joyous thrumming of hoof, hawk, and hunting-song.

Thou dost ride with Her now;
Thou who art endless
Thou who rideth, rideth eternal...
Same-womb bore us,
Fire receive us,
Hoof-thunder consume us,
Ai, *sister, I shall follow thee,*
I shall follow thee,
Ai, *sister,* ai, *my sister,*
I will follow thee.

Outside the House of Bees as a long hot still afternoon crumbled into slow slumbrous evening, the guards in snow-pard livery listened to the song, a foreign woman keening as their own grandmothers, mothers, aunties, sisters, or wives did when a family member was washed and wrapped, readied for the kiss of flame.

Strange, they thought, those men of Zhaon, as thunder muttered over the fields of rai and a summer storm lingered in the distance, held away by the dry days.

Strange, she sounds just like one of our girls.

Simple Mourning

In a Zhaon summer, the pyre must be quick.

It was built high and towering, and the linen-wrapped body, its shape the character for *corpse*, was laid upon and amid scented wood drenched with costly, fragrant oils. A great crimson and black headdress, gold thread glowing at its seams, crowned the many-wound layers of cloth; the great crimson wedding-robe was laced securely around the motionless Crown Princess. New slippers of red silk, their soles having never touched earth, were tied securely to the well-wrapped feet. Cushions of red-dyed cotton and plain red silk cradled her, and the stacked wood was built into a high prow on one end, a sharp stern at the other.

Crown Prince Takyeo, fever-cheeked but otherwise deadly pale, held a spitting everflame torch, drops of burning resin eating themselves into ash before they reached the ground. He leaned heavily upon Fourth Prince Makar, for his right leg was splinted and wrapped tightly in thick stiffened cloths impregnated with astringent oils and packed with pungent wound-healing herbs. Takyeo's plain bleached-silk robe bulged over the bulk, and Sixth Prince Jin carried a heavy ob-wood cane with a silver head for him.

Second Prince Kurin was in attendance, as was Fourth Prince Sensheo, the two standing shoulder to shoulder in their pale mourning-robes. Neither spoke, and neither smiled. Their ceremonial behavior was correct in every degree, and their funeral gifts piled amid the oiled wood lacked nothing in respect or costliness. It was generally agreed that the Second Prince had covered his mother's regrettable lack of etiquette in that direction upon this particular occasion. Second Princess Gamnae hovered behind her brother, her white gown entirely sober for once and her eyes wide like a frightened cat's.

Second Concubine Kanbina, heavily veiled, had left her seclusion for this event and stood with the Crown Prince's household. She held the arm of the foreign, grey-eyed court lady who stood straight as a young whitebark, her uncanny gaze fixed upon the lifeless crimson shell. The Khir woman's hair was unbound, a river of black, and her bleached-silk dress was torn. Her hands worked at its material, clutching and clawing, until the Second Concubine caught them in her own and held tightly.

Upon the foreign woman's other side, Lady Kue was rigid, her lips moving slightly as she repeated Shan prayers. Court Lady Gonwa was there too, veiled as the Second Concubine, her magisterial bulk leaning upon a cane with a fluted ivory curve near its top.

The ranks of the Crown Prince's personal guard were in full armor behind Head General Zakkar Kai, who—in deference to foreign feelings, no doubt—wore no armor himself, merely simple mourning. Third Prince Takshin, also robed in the pale colors of death, his arms folded, did not take his place with his brothers but lingered near the general, watching the pyre as if he expected the lifeless husk to perform some interesting feat.

Drums pounded a slow, heavy cadence. The Emperor was abed, having collapsed at his son's bedside. Consequently, the First and Second Queen were called to attend him, and First Concubine Luswone no doubt thought it best to refrain from making an appearance. It was taken as great delicacy upon her part; her son the Sixth Prince had brought her funeral gifts, nestled tastefully in their proper place.

Courtiers stood attentively, in order of precedence. Behind them, the eunuchs stood. Zan Fein had not brought his fan, and stood under the harsh morning sun with no sign of sweat or discomfort.

The astrologer Mrong Banh, in pale mourning as well, knee-bowed upon shimmer-hot stone. His had been the task of choosing the quickest, most auspicious date, and rumor had it his reddened eyes were not merely because of watching the stars but also with grief for the Crown Prince's loss.

The largest palace bell, in its squat five-sided casing upon the great Imperial Avenue leading to the Kaeje's largest door, vibrated. It was struck five times by a great timber as large as some battering rams, pulled back and released by those among the Golden chosen for this most momentous of tasks when the shadow under the bell filled the marker Mrong Banh had traced with red-dyed chalk upon the white stone floor of its house.

It was time. The astrologer knee-bowed thrice more and clasped his hands before his chest when he straightened the third time.

At that signal, the Crown Prince limped painfully forward, leaning upon the cane the Sixth Prince offered. In his other hand, the torch spat and crackled. He would not hear of staying abed to heal; he had felt much affection for the foreign wife foisted upon him to buy peace with the Khir horse-lords.

The pyre bloomed, flames thin under the assault of summer morn-sun. The Crown Prince retreated, step by step, a rushing crackle swallowing the tapping of the ob-wood cane. When he rejoined the Fourth and Sixth Princes, his face was pale as the sun-scorched stone beneath them, and sweat gleamed upon it.

A ripple ran through the onlookers.

The pale-eyed foreign court lady had rid herself of Second Concubine Kanbina's grasp—not harshly, but with the neutral irresistible force of a mother prying a child's fingers from her skirt for a moment. She stepped forward, and the court watched curiously—was this some Khir custom, like her unbound hair?

Neither fast nor slow, merely steadily as if in a procession, she walked toward the fire. She had almost reached it when several onlookers realized she did not mean to stop, but to mount the pyre like the wife of Emperor Tsan-li in the old stories. Would an orange-golden bird rise from the flames, tenderly encasing the ashes of a foreign princess and her faithful servant in an egg of mu-hir?[58]

Zakkar Kai stood frozen as Crown Prince Takyeo leaned upon his shoulder for support. It was Third Prince Takshin who sprinted for the Khir woman. She struggled in his grasp, making a small, lonely sound like a stilt-leg chick desperate for its mother. He dragged her away from roaring flame and billowing smoke. Sparks rose to Heaven with the greasy black pall of burning flesh.

His arms were iron bars and his scarred face was thoughtful, and when the Khir girl collapsed the Third Prince left the funeral to carry her through the somber hush of the palace complex to the Jonwa's gaping-wide doors.

58. A costly resin incense used for the burials of royalty, sweet and bitter-pungent at once.

In Different Coin

A ramshackle cottage upon the northern outskirts of Zhaon-An, half lost under roiling brambles, watched incuriously as a shaggy pony trotted along an overgrown path. Despite its disrepair, a smudge of smoke lifted from its hole-pierced chimney, and the pony's rider, a triangle of undyed cotton covering the lower half of his face and his shaven head bare and gleaming, squinted and let out a soft breath of relief.

Despite its abandonment the well was not dry, and the man let the pony drink his fill, watching the darkened cottage doorway. Of course his traveling companions would not come to greet him. They were probably sotted, and would moan, head-sore, tomorrow morning when they began the journey north.

Still, it would be pleasant to be among his two assistants again, for however short a time.

The impresario—his second bow was hidden in a midden-heap near Zhaon-An's Left Market, and would probably never be excavated—smiled at the thought, and hurried through the door.

Some small time passed.

Then the impresario retreated over the threshold, his throat jetting bright scarlet. Bright golden sunshine lay over the cottage-clearing, and the pony watched, tail flicking, as his erstwhile rider stumbled and fell.

A grey-eyed man clad in a merchant's sober brown robe but with very good foreign point-toe boots stepped into the sunshine as well, flicking crimson from his leather-hilted sword. A green gem flashed under its concealing wrapping, answering the spilled blood with an evil wink. Man and gem watched as the impresario kicked, the body not realizing its inhabitant had been pried loose.

When it was over, the grey-eyed nobleman sheathed his bright blade and searched the body, tucking a sheaf of letters into his own robe before bending to catch the impresario's ankles and dragging him into the dark mouth of the cottage. When he re-emerged, wiping his hands with a rag he tossed contemptuously over his shoulder, the man in brown crossed to the pony and examined it with a practiced eye before stripping the bridle and saddle, turning the beast loose to crop long unbruised grass.

"Poor fellows," the grey-eyed man said, softly. "They expected to be paid in different coin."

By the time he reached his own mount hidden in a small close-by copse, the cottage was well and truly afire. The bodies within might be found, or might not. Either way, they had been denuded of all that could identify them.

Ashani Daoyan, his face set like the granite of the mountains overlooking the Great Keep of Khir, had proof—written in Domari Ulo's own hand, among others—of the successful conspiracy to kill Ashan Mahara. Such proof would be useful later, when he returned to Khir with Komor Yala at his side.

Or, he thought, freeing his horse's reins, the last flower of Komori might not wish to return. Now that they had both seen Zhaon-An and found the world was much, much wider than their home country, it might be wise to travel a bit.

The heir to the throne of Khir smiled, mounted, and turned his horse toward the great city with a light heart.

A Prince of Shan

Three days after the funeral of Crown Princess Garan Ashan Mahara, Third Prince Garan Takshin visited his mother. Or, to be more precise, he stalked up the front steps of her part of the Kaeje, brushed aside two guards who sought to bar his passage, and broke like a peal of thunder into her receiving-hall, coming almost face-to-face with Lord Yulehi, round and placid in his bright orange court robe.

"Nephew." The head of Yulehi spread his arms, as if to welcome a prodigal returning. He had once been the head of a junior branch, but Garan Tamuron had raised him to primacy after wedding his niece. Perhaps he even felt grateful, in some measure. "What a singular pleasure."

Takshin, in severe Shan black, did not even waste a scowl upon the older man. "I doubt it. Where is my mother?"

"Why, her burial tablet is in Shan, of course." Lord Yulehi's smile widened. It would obviously please him to set a young prince in his place. "Oh, you mean the First Queen. Indisposed, I should think."

Takshin paced past, his shoulder hitting the older man, sending him staggering. The Third Prince moved unerringly past gasping, fishmouthed servants, through familiar halls, and a pair of double doors parted before him, banging upon stone walls upon either side and sending a very expensive character-hanging fluttering to the cushioned carpets. Not content with that, he ripped a partition aside, and looked upon his family.

First Queen Gamwone, her round face set, regarded him from a cushioned nest. Next to her, Kurin had settled, and Gamnae, her hand cupped over her mouth, stared at him with round eyes. The table before them was set for the day's first meal, and an elder's place at the head of it was left empty for a clan-head uncle.

"Taktak." Kurin recovered first and lifted his teacup, his gaze glittering with poisonous pleasure. "Come for breakfast?"

Gamwone made a hushing sound, laying one of her plump soft hands upon her eldest son's orange-silk arm. "You." Her eyes blazed, and she had gone deadly pale. "You were not invited."

"And yet, here I am." Takshin tossed the barbed, hideous head of a broken arrow that had nestled in Garan Takyeo's thigh. It clattered upon the table, and Gamnae let out a short, shocked cry. She looked very young again, the sister of the year he left, round-cheeked and cringing so helplessly you wished to pinch her viciously into weeping. "This is yours, no doubt." The other arrowhead, the one that had pinned a Khir princess's leg to a foundering horse, was safely wrapped and in Mrong Banh's possession.

But this one could be used.

"What? This?" The First Queen now flushed angrily, and the small still gleam of satisfaction in her gaze guttered for a few precious moments. "How ill-bred, even for you."

"It must be the influence of the merchant bitch who whelped me." Takshin's lip lifted, his scowl a blade sliding pitilessly home. "You have miscalculated, *Mother*. Again, and for the last time."

"I'm sure I don't know what you mean." Garan Gamwone's words shook, just a fraction. "Is this a threat?"

"Takshin—" Kurin, his mouth pulling down, tensed as if to rise.

His little brother ignored him. "You had best hope no further harm befalls my eldest brother Takyeo, *First Queen*. For if it does, I shall lay it at your door, no matter who is the true author of the misfortune. The Crown Prince and his household are my family now, and a prince of Shan looks after his own."

His little sister's other hand crept to her mouth as well, a scroll-illustration of deep shock. She stared at the arrowhead upon the table, then her gaze flickered to her mother and eldest brother, and a slow, horrifying idea began to bloom behind her wide dark eyes.

"Is that what you are now?" Gamwone hissed. "A prince of Shan?"

Garan Takshin's smile stretched, a bitter, wolfish baring of teeth. Each scar upon his face was livid. "This is your only warning, *First Queen*."

With that, he turned upon his soldier-booted heel and stalked away. Lord Yulehi, having followed to witness his nephew's actions, hurried to step aside, but not quickly enough, and Takshin's elbow hit his arm again, sending him staggering. A small vase tinkled into shards upon the high-polished wooden floor, and Gamnae let out another soft, shocked sound.

Kurin stared at the arrowhead next to a pot of fragrant om-diao tea, his eyebrows drawn together. Royal blood had dried upon its barbs and it sat amid expensive covered dishes; it would leave a mark upon the costly cloth protecting expensive lacquered wood beneath.

He was silent for a very long time, the Second Prince of Zhaon, as his mother succumbed to a fainting-fit, his sister sat rigid with blur-eyed shock, and his uncle snap-snarled at the creeping, cringing little spider-maids rushing to attend their mistress.

Finally, very slightly, the Second Prince smiled. He picked up the arrowhead with careful fingertips and pulled a square of cotton from his sleeve, wrapping it securely. Word of this act would spread like fire itself despite the First Queen's grasp upon her household staff, and suspicion—never far from his mother's door—would hold much more weight now that her own son had given it credence.

How theatrical of his little brother, indeed.

Lost Filly

The round-eyed envoy was shaggy, his face—the color of polished rai, as if he had not been cooked long enough in his mother's belly-oven—lost in a reddish cloud of frizzed hair tied with the bleached bones of small birds. His teeth were bad, his eyes had too much of their death-whites showing, he stank of sour sweat, and he loomed over the Great Steward of the Keep of Khir, who wrinkled his nose but kept a decorous pace through the halls. For all that, the Khir courtiers bowed as he passed, and did not whisper until long after his heavy barbarian step had faded. Even Domari Ulo, the Grand Councilor, did not seem to have anticipated this event, and that notable noble wore an expression of faint displeasure as he lingered outside the throne-room doors, uninvited and so, unable to pass through.

The great doors parted and the envoy was ushered into the presence of Ashani Zlorih, the Great Rider of Khir. The pale-eyed, long-nosed Great Rider sat upon his throne under the Great Calendar, clad in severe sober indigo. With one fist upon a knee, the other propped under his chin, he watched the lumbering stranger approach.

He did not even bring gifts, this envoy, and his Khir held an unpleasant buzz. Still, he bowed, folding his long self in half, and when he spoke, the burring of his accent was at least partly ameliorated by the trouble he had taken to learn proper address.

"Ashani Zlorih, Great Rider of the Khir, long may you gallop. My *hetman* Dha Ka Khubai, heir of Aro Ba Wistis, sends many greetings, and I, Nunik his stirrup-holder, salute you."

Ashani Zlorih nodded, kindly enough. "You have ridden far, and ridden fast. You are an honored guest in my humble home. Bring the *sohju*!" He did not raise his voice or clap, but a scurry of motion behind painted and carved screens said that servants had been ready for this command.

The envoy bowed again. His gaze—bleached, but not grey as the Khir but a pale blue like a clear winter sky—roved the surface of the hall, calculating. No doubt he would find much worth looting in this stone tent, and his greedy smile showed as much.

But the Great Rider dismounted from his throne and made a show of settling at a low table surrounded by rugs, servants bustling to pour sohju for the long pale man and his royal host. Courtiers whispered in the hall outside, and the guards at the door eyed the new arrival with some little trepidation.

Even one of the ghostly invaders was enough to make a man uneasy.

Nunik did not even wait for the end of the first bottle of sohju to begin his business. "My *hetman* was somewhat surprised to receive your message."

Ashani Zlorih merely smiled and filled his guest's cup again with clear fiery liquor. The dishes would arrive soon, and he would stuff this long white thing like a sausage. "We have little to lose by asking for aid, Honorable Nunik."

"Eh." Those avaricious eyes devoured everything upon the table, calculating worth like a merchant. "Was she a good breeder, this lost mare of yours?"

"Still a filly, but of high pedigree." Ashani Zlorih's smile did not falter, but his grey eyes were cold. "She was outraged and murdered by the Zhaon."

"Ah, well." *What can you do*, the man's spread hands said. He downed his sohju in one greedy gulp and held out the fine metalwork cup for more. "I traveled through their borders to reach yours.

Soft, very soft. A ripe underbelly." Nunik's laugh echoed in the high stone hall, bounced from the carven screens set to keep the character scrolls and portraits of Khir's royalty upon the walls from the pollution of a barbarian's gaze. "My *hetman* thinks they have grown proud, too proud indeed."

"Your *hetman* is wise." Ashani Zlorih poured yet another round of sohju, a high honor for this stinking guest. The appetizers arrived, great platters of them heaped high with somewhat coarse fare. "They are much richer than us, certainly."

"Mh." A noncommittal sound, but Nunik's ghost-blue gaze had sharpened. "If they give earth and salt, then perhaps my *hetman* will merely levy tribute from them to replace your lost filly. More, I cannot say."

"Ah, that would be more than I dared dream." Ashani Zlorih tipped his sohju cup and drank deep, perhaps to ameliorate the taste of this meeting. "But come, why should we discuss such things when there is drinking to be done and a guest to amuse? We are very humble, but we shall strive to show a stirrup-bearer to Dha Ka Khubai all the comfort we may."

The envoy of Tabrak's Pale Horde smiled. When he had left Zhaon's borders, having ridden across the northlands near the mountains, the Khir princess had still been alive.

To mention such a thing would have been unwise indeed, but it mattered little. His *hetman*'s plans were already laid, and this would merely smooth the way.

Burdened with Your Life

A darkened bedroom inside the Jonwa held its breath, hushed and dim. He wrung the wet cloth, folded it, and placed it upon her forehead. A glitter of grey eyes showed under heavy charcoal lashes.

"You may cease pretending," Takshin said, as gently as possible. "We must speak, you and I."

Yala's tongue crept out, touched her dry lips. "What is there to speak upon?" Hoarse and cracked, her voice was a shell of itself. She did not seem surprised to find him at her bedside.

Her faithful kaburei drowsed near the door, swaying every once in a while as sleep sought to claim her. She would almost crumple, the young Zhaon girl, and wake herself with a start, loath to leave her lady even for a moment.

"You are planning something honorable, are you not?" Takshin shook his head; his fingertips smoothed the damp cloth. The water was perfumed with araut, that pleasing herb said to ease grief, and the gold hoop at his ear glimmered in the dimness. "You must not."

Yala's throat worked as she swallowed. "Why did you stop me?"

"Ah." He nodded, as if she had said something profound. "There is a custom, in Zhaon."

"I care nothing for your barbarian customs." Her right hand, atop the thin summer coverlet, twitched. "My princess is dead."

"And you are still alive." There was no trace of sarcasm or sharpness in his tone. He sounded like a different man—older, perhaps, more thoughtful. Certainly gentler. None would have believed it, had they heard. "In any case, little lure, your life is not your own."

She moved again, restlessly, and her right hand became a fist. "Do you think I do not know as much?"

"Hush." He set the basin of cool, herb-scented water aside and took her hand, working his fingers between hers. When he had opened her palm, he placed it flat upon the covers, delicately, and tapped its back with his callused fingertips, twice. "In Zhaon, if you save a life, you become responsible for it."

Her eyelids drifted down. Rose, and she regarded him fully, a caged hawk eyeing its tormentors sidelong.

"Do you understand me, or must I be plainer?" Garan Takshin decided to leave no room for doubt. "You are indebted to me, Komor Yala. You may not climb upon a pyre or use that little claw-toy of yours to open your throat, for your life does not belong to your dead princess, may she ride eternal." The Khir phrase fit ill in his mouth, but at least he had taken the trouble to learn it. Perhaps it would even comfort her. "It belongs to me now, and you may not spend it uselessly."

A long silence enfolded them. Elsewhere in the Jonwa a physician shook his head, applying salve to a Crown Prince's leg, and the prince in question stared wordlessly over the heads of his attendants, his face set but not lifeless.

Garan Takyeo apparently considered words superfluous at this juncture, and his silence was dangerous. Takshin would solve that riddle when it presented itself more fully.

He was called to a more important matter, now.

"Why?" Tears gathered at the corners of Komor Yala's eyes, trickled down to vanish in the inkspill of her hair. "Why not let me go?"

"If I may not ride to meet my ancestors, you may not either."

He longed to be more gentle, but the sooner she understood, the better. "Not yet."

"I cannot return to Khir." She swallowed, and her mouth contorted. Unpretty grief upon a face too sharp for beauty, and yet he watched, fascinated. Each shadow across her face, clouds over a tormented sea, was another edged pleasure.

"Would you wish to?" He did not precisely wish her ill so he could comfort her, and yet, here he remained. "For if you did I would take you, my lady spyling, and any who lifted a hand to you in that land or any other would find himself upon my sword."

She made no answer. Her gaze turned away, lost in the shadows near the roof.

Takshin tried again. "Or I could take you to Shan. Kiron is a fine hunter, and his stables full of horses you may ride to exhaustion. Of course, Sabwone will be there, but I have dealt with her before."

Yala shook her head, her hair whispering against the pillow. "Why not simply leave me be?"

"I am burdened with your life, little lure." It was a weight he had taken willingly, though just when he could not say. Perhaps when she had given him the gift of a gaze unmarred by pity, or perhaps the first instant he saw her amid stone columns on an early spring morn, with his mother's poison still burning in his ears. "You may choose which country to spend it within, be it Ch'han to Anwei or Far Nihon, I will not complain. But you will not waste it in grieving. *That* I will not allow."

"Allow." Those trickling tears, each one a sharp glitter. Her voice was stronger now, no longer a cricket's dry threadiness. "You cannot stop me, Third Prince Takshin."

Could he not? She was determined, this lady-in-waiting, but he was willing to be ruthless. "Is that the proper way to thank the man who returned your *yue*? Or the man who took a whip-mark in your stead?"

The trapped bird in her gaze mantled, and a sharp beak flashed. "You are a merchant, to account a debt thus."

The insult cheered him tremendously. Anger, no matter how

reined, was always better than numb passivity. "Call me what you like, it does not change the debt itself. Now rest, little lure. I will be watching."

She turned away, presenting her back to him, and the damp cloth fell from her forehead. Silently, she sobbed, curled around a square unta[59]-stuffed pillow, and Takshin sat straight and motionless, his hands aching to touch, to soothe. In the end, though, it was probably best that he did not.

He was no use at comfort. On the table next to the bed, the greenmetal blade in its cunningly sewn sheath, stripped efficiently as he laid her upon the bed after her pyre-walk, witnessed both tears and immobility. Takshin thought it very likely the blade would not comfort her, either.

But when she was ready, she would find the Third Prince of Zhaon waiting.

---

59. A sweet grass. When dried, it is said to promote fair dreams.

So Much Consideration

Tap. Tap. Sunlight and shade in alternating stripes lay across the long Kaeje verandah. *Tap. Tap.* A silvershod cane marked off time, step by step.

"You should not." Kihon Jiao did not look up. He paced at the Crown Prince's side, shortening his usual brisk stride without appearing to. "You will lame yourself, do you continue thus. The bone was not broken, but is badly bruised and may twist."

"He is my father." Takyeo kept his gaze upon the ground as well, and cursed the deep drilling pain each movement of his crushed leg sent up to detonate in his head. "And, if you are correct . . ."

The physician did not quite bristle, but he did take some manner of umbrage despite his lowly rank. "Do you think I would lie to you, Crown Prince?"

"No, Honorable Kihon." Takyeo longed to grit his teeth, but he needed his mouth for speaking. "I merely mean to account for the possibility that he may prove more stubborn than this malady. Whatever it is."

The physician puffed out his cheeks but did not quite sigh. They were fast approaching a door into the Kaeje, and past that point he clearly did not think it wise to accompany the Crown Prince. "He is certainly stubborn. In that, you are quite alike."

"Thank you, Honorable Kihon Jiao." Takyeo's forehead gleamed with sweat, but he did not slow. He still wore mourning, a robe of pale death that flapped when his bulky injured leg moved.

"I shall visit your palace this afternoon, as usual." Was that uncertainty in the physician's tone? The man halted, but only for a breath, for Takyeo did not.

"Good." The Crown Prince did not even appear to notice his companion's hesitation. "Takshin is quite eager for Lady Komor to regain her strength."

"I have a crowd of royal clients," Kihon Jiao muttered, but not ill-naturedly. He walked about hatless, and the sun brought out the reddish undertones in his topknot handsomely. "Lady Komor is the least of my worries."

"She is the least of many worries for everyone, I suspect." Crown Prince Takyeo said no more, but lengthened his painful stride, and the physician let himself be outpaced.

It never did to press a prince's uncertain temper.

The Emperor's bedchamber, full of mirrorlight and the healing fumes of kuluri incense, pulsed with activity. The shell of Garan Tamuron, propped upon stiff, round pillows, waved away his ministers at Takyeo's limping approach. "You should be abed," he said, without preamble.

He was thin-cheeked now, and though the physician's attentions abated his discomfort somewhat, the nameless malady was ransacking the walled city of the imperial body. The suppurating sores widened, and his hair had become thin. Seeing the Emperor after a short absence, many a minister dropped his gaze, unable to look upon the ruin.

Takyeo essayed a reasonable approximation of a bow. "They will not carry my bed to yours, Father. Therefore, I must walk."

The Emperor's cheekbones stood out, and fingers of virulent purplish rash crept up his neck. His left hand lay curled as an archer's claw after a heavy battle, and his thinning hair was loose upon his shoulders. "At least tell me you availed yourself of a palanquin."

"I am not a woman." A thin ghost of a smile touched Takyeo's lips, submerged into his usual somberness. "In any case, should I lie?"

"Sit, sit." The Emperor indicated a gilt-figured chair by the bedside. "Draw away, all of you. Leave me some space, and open the verandah door. I wish for air."

Takyeo could not stifle a small groan as he sank down, stretching out his left leg. The chamber did not quite empty—a knot of dark-robed eunuchs lingered inside the heavy sliding door, and most of the courtiers flowed outside to the scant shade of the verandah, overlooking the Kaeje's greatest jewel-garden.

"Well." Tamuron eyed his pale-robed son. "You are still mourning."

"My wife is dead, Father." Under his robe, a small bag of crimson silk held a lock of blue-black hair tied with red silken thread by a grieving Khir lady-in-waiting. His close-servant did not remark upon it, but pinned it even inside his lord's sleeping-robe. Chill and somewhat remote, the Crown Prince continued. "Choking upon her own blood, a goodly portion of her bones crushed."

"Kai is investigating." Tamuron coughed, a deep racking noise, and grimaced, swallowing whatever had dredged from his lungs. "There are larger problems."

Takyeo's eyelids lowered a fraction. That was all. It was a very hot morning, thunder in the distance but no rain touching thirsty earth.

The murmuring eunuchs watched; ministers and courtiers peered through the verandah's other sliding doors as well. The weight of eyes, familiar after so many years, pressed hard upon them both.

"We will be receiving an envoy," Tamuron said, finally. "No doubt you have heard."

The Crown Prince nodded. "Zan Fein gave me to understand there was another, visiting our neighbors to the north." His expression, set and grim, did not alter. "Perhaps Shan has had to endure a pale barbarian guest, too, while they prepare for Sabwone's advent."

"Shan is Takshin's matter, not ours. He will do his duty there, if you insist." Tamuron lifted his knotted left hand, let it drop. "You will receive the Tabrak in the Great Hall. No doubt he will ask for earth and salt to carry back to his lord, and a fat tribute, too. You must awe him, Takyeo, but not too much, and—"

"Perhaps it will be best to let the barbarian cool his heels, like any other petitioner." Takyeo gazed at the table nearest the bedside, scattered with the effluvia of the medical trade. Mortar-cradles, pestles both circular and pillar, two scales, jars of herbs, a block of heavy white clay from a river where a goddess was said to have cried during the morning of the world, imparting healing onto sodden ground along with her grief.

Garan Tamuron was silent for a long moment. "I am dying," he said, finally. "You will be Emperor, my son."

Takyeo nodded, a trifle distractedly, a man listening to an inner song instead of a merchant's sell-chant. "Are you so certain?"

"I have ordered the line of succession, and the ministers—"

"They will be loyal, do you think?" Takyeo's expression turned thoughtful, deceptively mild. He studied the phoenix embroidered upon the hanging at the bed's head, its wings spread and its own gaze disturbingly direct. "Really?"

"Kai is loyal." Tamuron gazed upon his eldest son, his wasted face flushed and pale in turn. "You must send Takshin to Shan."

"Do you think he will go?" Another mild inquiry, only half interested. Takyeo's long fingers played with the silver cane-head, plucking notes from invisible strings.

"Do you hear me?" The Emperor of Zhaon, peerless under Heaven, mastered himself. His right hand patted at his chest, scratching lightly at his bed-robe and the bandages underneath. "I am *dying*, Ah-Yeo my first son, and you will have the throne. You must keep it."

"You haven't called me that in years." Takyeo's hand firmed, gripping the cane's glittering head. "I hear the nobles of Zhaon will not follow a cripple."

His father made an irritated noise, also familiar. There was a time it would have struck dread into an eldest prince's very core. "Then you must rest, and recover, and ride as soon as you are able."

"Father." Takyeo's gaze sharpened, finally. "My wife is *dead*."

They stared at each other. "You will take another very soon," Tamuron said, finally, consigning the death of a brave, gentle, beautiful girl to a royal cabinet with other irrelevancies. "We must consider the prospects."

"Her name was Mahara," Takyeo replied. "It meant *summer wind*. She was fond of spicy food and northern bean-curd, and she liked jaelo tea."

"So did your mother." Tamuron's left hand curled against itself even more tightly, a battle-worn fist finally frail and shaking. The malady, a greedy conflagration, feasted upon his wasted strength. "We cannot waste time, Takyeo. There is Zhaon to consider."

"Indeed." Crown Prince Takyeo gathered himself. The floor squeaked as he rose, leaning heavily upon the cane. "There is no shortage of those considering Zhaon, my father. They crowd this room, they jostle in every palace corridor, they whisper, and they hand silver ingots to assassins." He took a deep breath. Thick kuluri smoke coated his throat and threatened to choke him. "Zhaon has had so much consideration, in fact, that I find myself wondering if he needs mine."

"Ah-Yeo—"

"Your ministers are anxious, my lord." Takyeo shook his head. "No doubt they will help you with many plans and schemes. I wish you a pleasant morning." With that, the Crown Prince of Zhaon turned, and his cane landed heavily as he left the sickroom at the heart of the Land of Five Winds.

A father's cry pursued him; robbed of vigor, the shout fell short of its goal. "Ah-Yeo! *Takyeo!*"

Even a beast so thoroughly caged as a Crown Prince could break a bar or two when spurred enough.

Received the News

Again!" Kai roared, and the guards replied, a massive yell rising from many heaving chests. Sweat flew, weighted blades glinted, and the drillyard echoed.

At least while he was practicing he did not think of her. Or at least, not much.

Morning drill was coming to an end. The guards were no doubt looking forward to the baths and relief from the glaring eye of the sun, but Kai kept them to it for another form, the blades sweeping laterally, the overhand cut, the thrust, the din of sparring along the sides of the stone-floored yard enough to fill a skull with nothing but cut, cut, move, *hua*, one, two, jab, *hua*!

"*Lively*, my sons!" the general-father cried, and they replied, full-throat.

Finally, though, he had to let them go. The ceremony of dismissal, accepting the bows of the square-leaders and column captains, the stacking of practice arms and the good-natured grumbling—oh, he longed for the army, and the familiar rounds of watches set, scout reports to ponder, and other generals to outwit, outlast, outflank.

It was cleaner work than palace life.

Wiping his forehead with an already sweat-sodden cloth, he squinted at the angle of the shadows. What was she doing now?

Sewing listlessly, or staring at one of the Jonwa's smaller, exquisite gardens? Yala did not speak even for politeness, nor did Takyeo while in the Jonwa's hush. The Crown Prince seemed to find some solace in her company, but who knew whether she found solace in anything?

My princess is dead, was all she had said to Kai, and turned her attention away. And that sharp blade, perhaps somewhere in her clothing. All it would take was a steady hand to drive it home.

The image stayed with him during the long walk to his own quarters, through Steward Anlon's fussing and his close-servant's fumbling of sun-hot half-armor peeled away from a general's body, through a tepid plunge and the dressing in a fresh robe. It hung before him while he sorted correspondence in his bare, dark-walled study—the eastron and southron armies were in good hands, and his estates were thriving.

Tamuron had been good to him. Now the Emperor was abed, an unknown malady progressing at a gallop through his once vigorous frame, and if Komor Yala decided to press the sharp tip of that maiden's blade against her pulse, a single drop of scarlet rising through soft skin...

Kai did his duty, wrote his replies, and boiled inwardly. At least once he finished this he could present himself at the Jonwa and perhaps sit with her in a darkened room, watching her attempt to sew, the needle pausing in her hands and the material sliding free as her head drooped—

"My lord?" Steward Anlon was at the door. "A dispatch, from the Northern Army."

Kai suppressed a curse. He beckoned the man forward and frowned thunderously as he snapped the seal with an unsatisfying crunch, the breaking of a small bone between sharp teeth. Anlon retreated hastily.

For a few moments the brushwork made no sense. Kai stared, his brow furrowed and his back and arms reminding him that he had punished himself just as mercilessly as the rows of Golden and princely guards in the drillyard this morning. His head throbbed, an ache from sun, noise, and tension threatening to blind him.

Then his hands turned cold, and he straightened. "Anlon!"

His steward reappeared, his dry dark eyes blinking like a confused night-hunter's. "My lord?"

"Send a messenger to Mrong Banh. Tell him it is urgent, and to meet me at the Kaeje at once." Takyeo could not walk, so he could wait to hear the ill news. "Send a messenger to Zan Fein, telling him the same, and one to my adoptive—no, to my *mother*, telling her I have been called away and will not attend dinner, but not to fret."

"My lord." But Anlon hesitated, knowing his master might have something to add, as he frequently did.

It was, Kai thought, occasionally useful to be anticipated. His pulse throbbed high and frantic, but he took a deep calming breath. "Send another messenger to the Jonwa. Tell Takyeo I shall be visiting perhaps very late tonight; tell Lady Komor I have been called away upon urgent business, but will visit her as soon as I may."

"Yes, my lord." Anlon whirled and vanished, surprisingly light upon his feet for such an old soldier.

Kai studied the missive again. His head began to pound afresh, and the copper laid against the back of his palate was an old friend.

The message was ludicrously simple. Smoke rose from northern border posts vacated after Three Rivers. Patrols upon horseback were now visible, riding the marches. The bridges over the foaming Lu Au and the deep, silent Ka Au were reoccupied. Banners had been raised at the customs houses along the great artery of the Ch'han Trade Road.

Khir had received the news of their princess's fate.

The tenuous peace was over.

To Be Continued...

The story continues in…

BOOK TWO OF THE HOSTAGE OF EMPIRE

Keep reading for a sneak peek!

Acknowledgments

Writing a book is a lonely process; bringing it to publication requires a village. Thanks are due to Miriam Kriss and Sarah Guan for seeing me through and to my family for putting up with me during the whole thing. Thanks are also due to the many historians and linguists whose passion and detailed work provided a foundation for this fictional world, as well as the many actors, directors, and film/television crews who brought several aspects to vivid imaginary life. Any errors, of course, are mine alone.

extras

meet the author

S. C. Emmett is a pseudonym for bestselling author Lilith Saintcrow. She lives in Vancouver, WA.

if you enjoyed
THE THRONE OF THE FIVE WINDS
look out for
HOSTAGE OF EMPIRE: BOOK TWO
by
S. C. EMMETT

A STRANGE PAIR

Outside the westron walls of bustling Zhaon-An, a foreign princess was the second to be laid in the newly built, bone-white tombs.

The ancient, crumbling mausoleum of petty historical princes and ambitious, likewise-historical warlords was to the north of the city's seethe, but the Emperor had decreed a new, more auspicious site for the Garan dynasty just outside the westron walls. His first wife's urn was sealed in a restrained, costly wall there, and any in Zhaon could have reasonably expected that another wife or concubine would follow—or, in the worst case, the Emperor himself.

Instead, it was Garan Ashan Mahara, daughter of the Great Rider of Khir, whose restrained and beautifully carved egg-stone urn was immured next to the Emperor's sword-wife, and the interment had proceeded with almost unseemly haste.

Thunder lingered over distant hills as a slight woman in bright pale mourning robes put her palms together and bowed thrice. A small broom to sweep the tomb's narrow, sealed entrance was set neatly aside, and the carved stone denoting the name and titles of a new ancestor's shade was marked first in Zhaon characters, then in Khir. Each symbol had the painfully sharp edges of fresh, grieving chisel marks.

The mourner's black hair held blue highlights and a single hairpin thrust into carefully coiled braids, the stick crowned with an irregular pebble wrapped with red silken thread. Neither ribbon nor string dangled small semiprecious beads or any other tiny bright adornment fetchingly from that pebble, for mourning did not admit any excess.

At least, not in that particular direction.

Komor Yala's chin dropped over her folded hands. The hem of her unbleached dress fluttered, fingered by a hot, unsteady breeze. It was almost the long dry time of summer, but still, in the afternoons, the storms menaced. The lightning was more often than not dry, leaping from cloud to cloud instead of deigning to strike burgeoning earth. At least the harvest would be fine, or so the peasants cautiously hoped.

A bareheaded man in very fine leather half-armor waited at a respectful distance, his helm under his left arm, while the dragon carved upon his swordhilt peered balefully over his shoulder. He stayed motionless and patient, yet leashed tension vibrated in his broad shoulders and occasionally creaked in his boots when he shifted his weight.

For all that, Zakkar Kai did not speak, and if it irked him to wait on a woman's prayers, he made no sign. The head general of Zhaon's mighty armies had arrived straight from morning drill to accompany Crown Princess Mahara's lone lady-in-waiting outside the city walls, and his red-black topknot was slightly disarranged from both helm and exertion.

Finally, it could be put off no longer. Komor Yala, her lips moving slightly, finished her prayers, and she brushed at her damp cheeks. She had swept the dimensions of a Khir pailai clean in front of Mahara's wall, and took up the small broom again after another trio of bows. Her clear grey eyes, glittering feverishly, held sleepless smudges underneath, and her cheekbones stood out in stark curves.

She backed from the tomb's august presence, pausing to bow again; when she turned, she found Zakkar Kai regarding her thoughtfully, his deep-set eyes gleaming and mouth relaxed. He offered his armored arm, still silent.

The absence of platitudes was one more thing to admire in such a man. Her brother would have liked him very much. A slow smolder and a hidden fire, that had been Komori Baiyan, but he had been struck down at Three Rivers, and Yala could not decide if he had likely faced Zakkar Kai upon that bloody field, or not.

She also could not decide how to feel about either prospect. It was not likely Kai would speak of such an event, even if he had noticed a particular Khir rider during the screaming morass of battle.

Yala placed her fingers in the crook of his right elbow, and the general matched his steps to hers. Finally, he spoke, but only the same mannerly phrase he used every other time he accompanied her upon this errand. "Shall we halt for tea upon our return voyage, Lady Yala?"

"I am hardly dressed for it," she murmured, as she did every time. Near the entrance to this white stone courtyard, in the shade of a long-armed fringeleaf tree, her kaburei, Anh, leaned against the wall like a sleeping horse, leather-wrapped braids dangling past her round shoulders. "And your duties must be calling you, General."

"They may call." He never left his helm with his horse, as if he expected ambush even here. Or perhaps it was a soldier's habit. "I am the one who decides the answer, though."

A man could afford as much, of course. Yala's temples ached. She made this trip daily; it was not yet a full moon-cycle since her princess's last ride. Yala herself had attended her princess's dressing upon that last day, grateful to be free of the dungeons.

Had she still been imprisoned, or had she not avoided a whipping, would Mahara still be alive?

"I am not dressed for it either," Kai continued, levelly. "We make a strange pair." He halted inside the fringeleaf's shade as Anh yawned into alertness.

"Very." Yala's throat ached. The tears came at inopportune moments, and she wondered why she had not wept for Bai so. The grief of her brother's passage to the Great Fields was still a steady ache, but Mahara... Oh, the sharp, piercing agony was approaching again, a silent house-cat stalking small vermin. Yala forced herself to breathe slowly, to keep her pace to a decorous glide.

"There is a cold-flask tied to my saddle," Kai said, almost sharply, his intonation proper for commanding a kaburei. "Our lady grows pale."

"I am well enough," Yala began, but Anh bowed and hurried off down the long colonnade. It would take her time to reach the horses, but her mistress and the general would still be in sight.

Zakkar Kai was careful of Yala's reputation, though it mattered little now. Nothing truly mattered, with her princess turned into ash and fragments of bone.

The general fixed his gaze forward as if upon parade. They walked through bars of sunlight and shade in silence, and Yala kept herself occupied in counting the columns, the numbers pushing away the black cloud seeking to fill her skull. When he halted between one step and the next, half turning to face her with a sharp military click of his boots, she did not look at him, studying instead the closest carven pillar.

So much room; Zhaon was a country of wastage and luxury, even with their dead.

Kai's gaze was a weight upon her profile. "Yala."

"Kai." Her hand dropped to her side, hung uselessly. *What now?* Was he about to observe that he could not, after all, accompany her here every morning? He had been silent well past the point of politeness, today.

"I must eventually ride north." His jaw tightened, and the breeze played with his topknot, teasing at strands. "The Emperor..."

No more needed to be said. "Of course," she replied, colorlessly. Khir, hearing the news of the princess's death, had reoccupied the border crossings and bridges. The entire court of Zhaon was alive with rumor, from the lowest kaburei to the princes themselves; no doubt even the Emperor heard the mutters upon his padded bench-throne high above the common streets. "He is your lord."

"He is also my friend, and he is dying." Kai did not glance over his shoulder to gauge who might be in earshot, but here among empty apartments eventually to be filled with only shades and incense, who would gossip?

"Yes." The rai gave up its fruit for eating and next year's crop, children died before their naming-days, men rode to war and women retreated to childbed, and every street was paved with thousands of smaller deaths—insects, birds, beasts of burden and cherished or useful pets.

Death had its bony fists wrapped about the world's throat, and its grasp was final.

"I may speak to him before I leave, should I find opportunity." Kai's gaze was unwontedly heavy. "But not unless you tell me plainly whether or not I may hope."

What was there to hope for, with Mahara gone? Yala blinked, and his features came into focus, swimming through the heavy water in her eyes. A single traitorous drop slipped free, tracing a cool phantom finger down her cheek.

She studied him afresh—long nose; deep eyes; the usual hint of a sardonic smile absent from full, almost cruel lips; mussed topknot. The heat-haze of a male used to healthy exertion tinged with a breath of leather enfolded her, without touching the chill streamlets coursing through her bones. "Should I ask you to be plainer in turn?"

"I've been *exceedingly* plain." A faint ghost of a smile touched one corner of his mouth, but he continued. "I can offer you protection. I have estates; they are modest, but I could well acquire more." The wad of pounded rai in his throat, meant to keep a man from choking on what he must do, bobbed as he swallowed. "And . . . there is much affection, Yala. Even if I am loathsome to a Khir lady."

Was that what had held him back? She could not ask. "*Loathsome* is not the word I would use, General Zakkar. Even if my Zhaon is somewhat halting."

"Your Zhaon is very musical, my lady." The compliment was accompanied by a slight grimace, as if he expected her to bridle at it. "Dare I ask what word you *would* use?"

"Kind." She thought for a moment. "And deadly, when you see the need."

"Another strange pairing. Yala, will you marry me?"

Finally, he had said it directly. She could now answer *I am still in mourning* and be done. She could turn her shoulder and deliver the cut with the calm chill of a noblewoman well used to clothing a sharp edge in pretty syllables.

Instead, she watched his eyes, muddy like a half-Khir's. His face was not sharp enough; he did not have mountain bones. Gossip spoke of some barbarian in his vanished bloodline, of a foundling taken up by a warlord who became Emperor.

His careful generalship—standing fast to bleed his enemy, breaking away to replenish his army and make his foe tire by chasing—had broken the back of Khir's resistance, and the victory at Three Rivers had brought her princess to wasteful, perfumed Zhaon as a sacrifice. That Crown Prince Garan Takyeo had been kind to his foreign bride was beside the point. This terrible country had swallowed Mahara and her lady-in-waiting whole, and now Yala, bereft, was a pebble in the conqueror's guts.

Another traitorous tear struggled free and followed its sister down her cheek.

Leather made a soft noise as Kai's callused fingertips brushed the tear away. It was the first time a man other than her own brother had touched her thus, and Komor Yala almost swayed.

His was the hand that had wielded that dragon-hilted sword, cutting down many of Khir's finest sons. It was the same hand that had sent the sword-point through an assassin in a darkened dry-garden upon a wedding night, defending Yala. That he had thought her the Crown Princess was beside the point as well; it was also Zakkar Kai who had brought her back to the palace after tracking her captors, who had *definitely* mistaken Yala for her princess.

How could she possibly put each event onto scales and find their measure? She was no merchant daughter, used to weighing.

"If I were free to answer," she said slowly, "I would marry you, Zakkar Kai." There was little point in dissembling. He was, she supposed, not the worst fate for a Khir noblewoman trapped in a southron court, and she—oh, it was useless to deny it, she rather... liked him.

The more he showed of the man behind his sword, the more she found him interesting and honorable, until she could not be sure her estimation of his actions was from their merit or her own feelings.

A high flush stood along his cheekbones, perhaps from morning drill or the heat. "But you are not?"

"I must write to my father."

He nodded. "Of course. I will not speak to the Emperor until you have word." His throat worked again, and he did not take his rough fingertips from her face. A strange heat, not at all like Zhaon's sticky, hideously close summer, spilled from that touch down her aching neck, and somehow eased the terrible hole in her chest. "*I will wait as long as I must.*"

It was the warrior's reply to the Moon Maiden. A smile crept to her lips, horrifying her. How could she, in the house of the dead, feel even the palest desire to laugh or seek comfort? "You are quite partial to Zhe Har, scholar-general."

"Only some few of his works." Kai still did not move, leaning over her in welcome shade, the rest of the world made hazy and insignificant by the mere fact of his presence.

Why had he not been born a Khir? Of course, he would have been dead at Three Rivers, or Komori Dasho—as he had told his daughter once—might have refused any suit for her hand. It did no good to wish, or to ask uncaring Heaven for any comfort. A single noblewoman's grieving was less than a speck of dust under the grinding of great cart wheels as the world went upon its way.

He leaned forward still farther, and Yala felt a faint, dozing alarm.

But Zakkar Kai the terror of Zhaon's enemies, stern in war and moderate in counsel, merely pressed his lips to her damp forehead before straightening and stepping back, leaving her oddly bereft. "Come." He offered his arm again. "We must see you home, my lady."

Home. If her father sent word quickly enough, she could plead filial duty and no doubt Crown Prince Takyeo would provide an escort to at least the border. She could be in Hai Komori's dark, severe, familiar halls by the middle harvest, facing her father's disappointment.

Yala bowed her head and once more took Zakkar Kai's arm. Her head was full of a rushing, whirling noise, but she held grimly to her task, placing one foot before the other on bruising, sun-scorched stone.

After all, she had been sent to protect her princess, and had failed.

if you enjoyed
THE THRONE OF THE FIVE WINDS
look out for
THE RAGE OF DRAGONS
The Burning: Book One
by
Evan Winter

The Omehi people have been fighting an unwinnable fight for almost two hundred years. Their society has been built around war and only war. The lucky ones are born gifted. One in every two thousand women has the power to call down dragons. One in every hundred men is able to magically transform himself into a bigger, stronger, faster killing machine.

Everyone else is fodder, destined to fight and die in the endless war.

Young, giftless Tau knows all this, but he has a plan of escape. He's going to get himself injured, get out early, and settle down to marriage, children, and land. Only, he doesn't get the chance.

Those closest to him are brutally murdered, and his grief swiftly turns to anger. Fixated on revenge, Tau dedicates himself to an unthinkable path. He'll become the greatest swordsman to ever live, a man willing to die a hundred thousand times for the chance to kill the three who betrayed him.

PROLOGUE

LANDFALL

Queen Taifa stood at the bow of *Targon*, her beached warship, and looked out at the massacre on the sands. Her other ships were empty. The fighting men and women of the Chosen were already onshore, were already killing and dying. Their screams, not so different from the cries of those they fought, washed over her in waves.

She looked to the sun. It burned high overhead and the killing would not stop until well past nightfall, which meant too many more would die. She heard footsteps on the deck behind her and tried to take comfort in the sounds of Tsiory's gait.

"My queen," he said.

Taifa nodded, permitting him to speak, but did not turn away from the slaughter on the shore. If this was to be the end of her people, she would bear witness. She could do that much.

"We cannot hold the beach," he told her. "We have to retreat to the ships. We have to relaunch them."

"No, I won't go back on the water. The rest of the fleet will be here soon."

"Families, children, the old and infirm. Not fighters. Not Gifted."

Taifa hadn't turned. She couldn't face him, not yet. "It's beautiful here," she told him. "Hotter than Osonte, but beautiful. Look." She pointed to the mountains in the distance. "We landed on a peninsula bordered and bisected by mountains. It's defensible, arable. We could make a home here. Couldn't we? A home for my people."

She faced him. His presence comforted her. Champion Tsiory, so strong and loyal. He made her feel safe, loved. She wished she could do the same for him.

His brows were knitted and sweat beaded on his shaved head. He had been near the front lines, fighting. She hated that, but he was her champion and she could not ask him to stay with her on a beached ship while her people, his soldiers, died.

He shifted and made to speak. She didn't want to hear it. No more reports, no more talk of the strange gifts these savages wielded against her kind.

"The *Malawa* arrived a few sun spans ago," she told him. "My old nursemaid was on board. She went to the Goddess before it made ground."

"Sanura's gone? My queen... I'm so—"

"Do you remember how she'd tell the story of the dog that bit me when I was a child?"

"I remember hearing you bit it back and wouldn't let go. Sanura had to call the Queen's Guard to pull you off the poor thing."

Taifa turned back to the beach, filled with the dead and dying in their thousands. "Sanura went to the Goddess on that ship, never knowing we found land, never knowing we escaped the Cull. They couldn't even burn her properly." The battle seemed louder. "I won't go back on the water."

"Then we die on this beach."

The moment had arrived. She wished she had the courage to face him for it. "The Gifted, the ones with the forward scouts, sent word. They found the rage." Taifa pointed to the horizon, past the slaughter, steeling herself. "They're nested in the Central Mountains, the ones dividing the peninsula, and one of the dragons has just given birth. There is a youngling and I will form a coterie."

"No," he said. "Not this. Taifa..."

She could hear his desperation. She would not let it sway her.

"The savages, how can we make peace if we do this to them?" Tsiory said, but the argument wasn't enough to change her mind, and he must have sensed that. "We were only to follow them," he said. "If we use the dragons, we'll destroy this land. If we use the dragons, the Cull will find us."

That sent a chill through her. Taifa was desperate to forget what they'd run from and aware that, could she live a thousand cycles, she never would. "Can you hold this land for me, my champion?" she asked, hating herself for making this seem his fault, his shortcoming.

"I cannot."

"Then," she said, turning to him, "the dragons will."

Tsiory wouldn't meet her eyes. That was how much she'd hurt him, how much she'd disappointed him. "Only for a little while," she said, trying to bring him back to her. "Too little for the Cull to notice and just long enough to survive."

"Taifa—"

"A short while." She reached up and touched his face. "I swear it on my love for you." She needed him and felt fragile enough to break, but she was determined to see her people safe first. "Can you give us enough time for the coterie to do their work?"

Tsiory took her hand and raised it to his lips. "You know I will."

CHAMPION TSIORY

Tsiory stared at the incomplete maps laid out on the command tent's only table. He tried to stand tall, wanting to project an image of strength for the military leaders with him, but he swayed slightly, a blade of grass in an imperceptible breeze. He needed rest and was unlikely to get it.

It'd been three days since he'd last gone to the ships to see Taifa. He didn't want to think he was punishing her. He told himself he had to be here, where the fighting was thickest. She wanted him to hold the beach and push into the territory beyond it, and that was what he was doing.

The last of the twenty-five hundred ships had arrived, and every woman, man, and child who was left of the Chosen was now on this hostile land. Most of the ships had been scavenged for resources, broken to pieces, so the Omehi could survive. There would be no retreat. Losing against the savages would mean the end of his people, and that Tsiory could not permit.

The last few days had been filled with fighting, but his soldiers had beaten back the natives. More than that, Tsiory had taken the beach, pushed into the tree line, and marched the bulk of his army deeper into the peninsula. He couldn't hold the ground he'd taken, but he'd given her time. He'd done as his queen had asked.

Still, he couldn't pretend he wasn't angry with her. He loved Taifa, the Goddess knew he did, but she was playing a suicidal game. Capturing the peninsula with dragons wouldn't mean much if they brought the Cull down on themselves.

"Champion!" An Indlovu soldier entered the command tent, taking Tsiory from his thoughts. "Major Ojore is being overrun. He's asking for reinforcements."

"Tell him to hold." Tsiory knew the young soldier wanted to say more. He didn't give him the chance. "Tell Major Ojore to hold."

"Yes, Champion!"

Harun spat some of the calla leaf he was always chewing. "He can't hold," the colonel told Tsiory and the rest of the assembled Guardian Council. The men were huddled in their makeshift tent beyond the beach. They were off the hot sands and sheltered by the desiccated trees that bordered them. "He's out of arrows. It's all that kept the savages off him, and Goddess knows, the wood in this forsaken land is too brittle to make more."

Tsiory looked over his shoulder at the barrel-chested colonel. Harun was standing close enough for him to smell the man's sour breath. Returning his attention to the hand-drawn maps their scouts had made of the peninsula, Tsiory shook his head. "There are no reinforcements."

"You're condemning Ojore and his fighters to death."

Tsiory waited, and, as expected, Colonel Dayo Okello chimed in. "Harun is right. Ojore will fall and our flank will collapse. You need to speak with the queen. Make her see sense. We're outnumbered and the savages have gifts we've never encountered before. We can't win."

"We don't need to," Tsiory said. "We just need to give her time."

"How long? How long until we have the dragons?" Tahir asked, pacing. He didn't look like the man Tsiory remembered from home. Tahir Oni came from one of the Chosen's wealthiest families and was renowned for his intelligence and precision. He was a man who took intense pride in his appearance.

Back on Osonte, every time Tsiory had seen Tahir, the man's head was freshly shaved, his dark skin oiled to a sheen, and his colonel's uniform sculpted to his muscular frame. The man before him now was a stranger to that memory.

Tahir's head was stubbly, his skin dry, and his uniform hung off a wasted body. Worse, it was difficult for Tsiory to keep his eyes from the stump of Tahir's right arm, which was bleeding through its bandages.

Tsiory needed to calm these men. He was their leader, their inkokeli, and they needed to believe in their mission and queen. He caught Tahir's attention, tried to hold it and speak confidently, but the soldier's eyes twitched like a prey animal's.

"The savages won't last against dragons," Tsiory said. "We'll break them. Once we have firm footing, we can defend the whole of the valley and peninsula indefinitely."

"Your lips to the Goddess's ears, Tsiory," Tahir muttered, without using either of his honorifics.

"Escaping the Cull," Dayo said, echoing Tsiory's unvoiced thoughts, "won't mean anything if we all die here. I say we go back to the ships and find somewhere a little less... occupied."

"What ships, Dayo? There aren't enough for all of us, and we don't have the resources to travel farther. We're lucky the dragons led us here," Tsiory said. "It was a gamble, hoping they'd find land before we starved. Even if we could take to the water again, without them leading us, we'd have no hope."

Harun waved his arms at their surroundings. "Does this look like hope to you, Tsiory?"

"You'd rather die on the water?"

"I'd rather not die at all."

Tsiory knew where the conversation would head next, and it would be close to treason. These were hard men, good men, but the voyage had made them as brittle as this strange land's wood. He tried to find the words to calm them, when the shouting outside their tent began.

"What in the Goddess's name—" said Harun, opening the tent's flap and looking out. He couldn't have seen the hatchet that took his life. It happened too fast.

Tahir cursed, scrambling back as Harun's severed head fell to the ground at his feet.

"Swords out!" Tsiory said, drawing his weapon and slicing a cut through the rear of the tent to avoid the brunt of whatever was out front.

Tsiory was first through the new exit, blinking under the sun's blinding light, and all around him was chaos. Somehow, impossibly, a massive force of savages had made their way past the distant front lines, and his lightly defended command camp was under assault.

He had just enough time to absorb this when a savage, spear in hand, leapt for him. Tsiory, inkokeli of the Omehi military and champion to Queen Taifa, slipped to the side of the man's downward thrust and swung hard for his neck. His blade bit deep and the man fell, his life's blood spilling onto the white sands.

He turned to his colonels. "Back to the ships!"

It was the only choice. The majority of their soldiers were on the front lines, far beyond the trees, but the enemy was between Tsiory and his army. Back on the beach, camped in the shadows of their scavenged ships, there were fighters and Gifted, held in reserve to protect the Omehi people. Tsiory, the colonels, the men assigned to the command camp, they had to get back there if they hoped to survive and repel the ambush.

Tsiory cursed himself for a fool. His colonels had wanted the command tent pitched inside the tree line, to shelter the leadership from the punishing sun, and though it didn't feel right, he'd been unable to make any arguments against the decision. The tree line ended well back from the front lines, and he'd believed they had enough soldiers to ensure they were protected. He was wrong.

"Run!" Tsiory shouted, pulling Tahir along.

They made it three steps before their escape was blocked by another savage. Tahir fumbled for his sword, forgetting for a moment that he'd lost his fighting hand. He called out for help and reached for his blade with his left. His fingers hadn't even touched the sword's hilt when the savage cut him down.

Tsiory lunged at the half-naked aggressor, blade out in front, skewering the tattooed man who'd killed Tahir. He stepped back from the impaled savage, seeking to shake him off the sword, but the heathen, blood bubbling in his mouth, tried to stab him with a dagger made of bone.

Tsiory's bronze-plated leathers turned the blow and he grabbed the man's wrist, breaking it across his knee. The dagger fell to the sand and Tsiory crashed his forehead into his opponent's nose, snapping the man's head back. With his enemy stunned, Tsiory shoved all his weight forward, forcing the rest of his sword into the man's guts, drawing an open-mouthed howl from him that spattered Tsiory with blood and phlegm.

He yanked his weapon away, pulling it clear of the dying native, and swung round to rally his men. He saw Dayo fighting off five savages with the help of a soldier and ran toward them as more of the enemy emerged from the trees.

They were outnumbered, badly, and they'd all die if they didn't disengage. He kept running but couldn't get to his colonel before Dayo took the point of a long-hafted spear to the side and went down. The closest soldier killed the native who had dealt the blow, and Tsiory, running full tilt, slammed into two others, sending them to the ground.

On top of them, he pulled his dagger from his belt and rammed it into the closest man's eye. The other one, struggling beneath him, reached for a trapped weapon, but Tsiory shoved his sword hilt against the man's throat, using his weight to press it down. He heard the bones in the man's neck crack, and the savage went still.

Tsiory got to his feet and grabbed Dayo, "Go!"

Dayo, bleeding everywhere, went.

"Back to the beach!" Tsiory ordered the soldiers near him. "Back to the ships!"

Tsiory ran with his men, looking back to see how they'd been undone. The savages were using gifts to mask themselves in broad daylight. As he ran, he saw more and more of them stepping out of what his eyes told him were empty spaces among the trees. The trick had allowed them to move an attacking force past the front lines and right up to Tsiory's command tent.

Tsiory forced himself to move faster. He had to get to the reserves and order a defensive posture. His heart hammered in his chest and it wasn't from running. If the savages had a large enough force, this surprise attack could kill everyone. They'd still have the front-line army, but the women, men, and children they were meant to protect would be dead.

Tsiory heard galloping. It was an Ingonyama, riding double with his Gifted, on one of the few horses put on the ships when they fled Osonte. The Ingonyama spotted Tsiory and rode for him.

"Champion," the man said, dismounting with his Gifted. "Take the horse. I will allow the others to escape."

Tsiory mounted, saluted before galloping away, and looked back. The Gifted, a young woman, little more than a girl, closed her eyes and focused, and the Ingonyama began to change, slowly at first, but with increasing speed.

The warrior grew taller. His skin, deep black, darkened further, and, moving like a million worms writhing beneath his flesh, the man's muscles re-formed thicker and stronger. The soldier, a Greater Noble of the Omehi, was already powerful and deadly, but now that his Gifted's powers flowed through him, he was a colossus.

The Ingonyama let out a spine-chilling howl and launched himself at his enemies. The savages tried to hold, but there was little any man, no matter how skilled, could do against an Enraged Ingonyama.

The Ingonyama shattered a man's skull with his sword pommel, and in the same swing, he split another from collarbone to waist. Grabbing a third heathen by the arm, he threw him ten strides.

Strain evident on her face, the Gifted did all she could to maintain her Ingonyama's transformation. "The champion has called a retreat," she shouted to the Omehi soldiers within earshot. "Get back to the ships!"

The girl—she was too young for Tsiory to think of her as much else—gritted her teeth, pouring energy into the enraged warrior, struggling as six more savages descended on him.

The first of the savages staggered back, his chest collapsed inward by the Ingonyama's fist. The second, third, and fourth leapt on him together, stabbing at him in concert. Tsiory could see the Gifted staggering with each blow her Ingonyama took. She held on, though, brave thing, as the target of her powers fought and killed.

It's enough, thought Tsiory, leave. It's enough.

The Ingonyama didn't. They almost never did. The colossus was surrounded, swarmed, mobbed, and the savages did so much damage to him that he had to end his connection to the Gifted or kill her too.

The severing was visible as two flashes of light emanating from the bodies of both the Ingonyama and the Gifted. It was difficult to watch what happened next. Unpowered, the Ingonyama's body shrank and his strength faded. The next blow cut into his flesh and, given time, would have killed him.

The savages gave it no time. They tore him to pieces and ran for the Gifted. She pulled a knife from her tunic and slit her own throat before they could get to her. That didn't dissuade them. They fell on her and stabbed her repeatedly, hooting as they did.

Tsiory, having seen enough, looked away from the butchery, urging the horse to run faster. He'd make it to the ships and the reserves of the Chosen army. The Ingonyama and Gifted had given him that with their lives. It was hard to think it mattered.

Too many savages had poured out from the tree line. They'd come in force and the Chosen could not hold. The upcoming battle would be his last.

orbit